The White Prophet

[Page 190.]

" 'Oh, children of Allah, . . . let us be men !' "

The White Prophet

A NOVEL

BY
HALL CAINE

AUTHOR OF
THE MANXMAN, THE DEEMSTER, THE CHRISTIAN,
THE ETERNAL CITY, THE PRODIGAL SON, ETC.

*" I know that my Redeemer liveth and that He
shall stand at the latter day upon the earth."*

ILLUSTRATIONS BY
R. CATON WOODVILLE

Fredonia Books
Amsterdam, The Netherlands

The White Prophet:
A Novel

by
Hall Caine

ISBN: 1-4101-0402-8

Reprinted from the 1909 edition

Fredonia Books
Amsterdam, The Netherlands
http://www.fredoniabooks.com

In order to make original editions of historical works available to scholars at an economical price, this facsimile of the original edition of 1909 is reproduced from the best available copy and has been digitally enhanced to improve legibility, but the text remains unaltered to retain historical authenticity.

AUTHOR'S NOTE

Many erroneous statements made in the press during the serial publication of this story, coupling its characters and incidents with distinguished living persons and recent public events, make it necessary to say that "The White Prophet" is intended to be read as a work of fiction only.

H. C.

GREBA CASTLE, ISLE OF MAN, 1909.

CHIEF PERSONS OF THE STORY

LORD NUNEHAM . . . . British Agent, Consul-General, and Minister Plenipotentiary in Egypt

LADY NUNEHAM . . . . Born in Massachusetts, U. S. A.

COLONEL GORDON LORD, A.A.G. . Son of Lord and Lady Nuneham, born and brought up in Egypt

MAJOR-GENERAL GRAVES . . . . Commanding the British Army of Occupation in Egypt

HELENA GRAVES . . . . Daughter of General Graves, born in India

SIR REGINALD MANNERING . . . Pasha, Sirdar of the Egyptian Army, and Governor-General of the Soudan

PRINCESS NAZIMAH . . . . . . Member of the Khedivial family

THE CHANCELLOR OF THE ARABIC UNIVERSITY OF EL AZHAR, CAIRO

THE GRAND CADI . . . . . . From Constantinople

ISHMAEL AMEER, commonly called "THE WHITE PROPHET" . . . Born on the Libyan desert, brought up in Khartoum

FIRST BOOK

THE CRESCENT AND THE CROSS

I

IT was perhaps the first act of open hostility, and there was really nothing in the scene or circumstance to provoke an unfriendly demonstration.

On the broad racing-ground of the Khedivial Club a number of the officers and men of the British Army quartered in Cairo, assisted by a detachment of the soldiers of the army of Egypt, had been giving a sham fight in imitation of the Battle of Omdurman, which is understood to have been the death-struggle and the end of Mahdism.

The Khedive himself had not been there—he was away at Constantinople—and his box had stood empty the whole afternoon; but a kinsman of the Khedive's, with a company of friends, had occupied the box adjoining, and Lord Nuneham, the British Consul-General, had sat in the centre of the grand pavilion, surrounded by all the great ones of the earth, in a sea of muslin, flowers, and feathers. There had been European ladies in bright spring costumes, Sheikhs in flowing robes of flowered silk, Egyptian Ministers of State in Western dress and British Advisers and Under-Secretaries in Eastern tarbooshes, officers in gold-braided uniforms, foreign Ambassadors, and an infinite number of pashas, beys, and effendis.

Besides these, too, there had been a great crowd of what is called the common people, chiefly Cairenes—the volatile, pleasure-loving people of Cairo, who care for nothing so little as the atmosphere of political trouble. They had stood in a thick line around the arena, all capped in crimson, thus giving to the vast ellipse the effect of an immense picture framed in red.

There had been nothing in the day, either, to stimulate the spirit of insurrection. It had been a lazy day, growing hot in the afternoon, so that the white city of domes and minarets, as far up as to the Mokattam hills and the self-conscious Citadel, had seemed to palpitate in a glistening haze, while the steely ribbon of the Nile that ran between was reddening in the rays of the sunset.

General Graves, an elderly man with martial bearing, commanding the army in Egypt, had taken his place as umpire in the judge's box in front of the pavilion; four squadrons of British and Egyptian cavalry, a force of infantry, and a grunting and ruckling camel corps, had marched and pranced and bumped out of a paddock to the left, and then young Colonel Gordon Lord, Assistant Adjutant-General, who was to play the part of commandant in the sham fight, had come trotting into the field.

Down to that moment there had been nothing but gaiety and the spirit of fun among the spectators, who with ripples of merry laughter had whispered "Lyttelton's," "Wauchope's," "Macdonald's," and "Maxwell's," as the white-faced and yellow-faced squadrons had taken their places. Then the General had rung the big bell that was to be the signal for the beginning of the battle, a bugle had been sounded, and the people had pretended to shiver as they smiled.

But all at once the atmosphere had changed. From somewhere on the right had come the *tum*, *tum*, *tum* of war-drums of the enemy, followed by the *boom, boom, boom* of their war-horns, a melancholy note, half bellow and half wail. Then everybody in the pavilion had stood up, everybody's glass had been out, and a moment afterwards a line of strange white things had been seen fluttering in the far distance.

Were they banners? No! They were men, they were the dervishes, and they were coming down in a deep white line, like sheeted ghosts in battle array.

"They're here!" said the spectators, in a hushed whisper, and from that moment onward to the end there had been no more laughter either in the pavilion or in the dense line around the field.

The dervishes had come galloping on, a huge, disorderly horde in flying white garments, some of them black as ink, some brown as bronze, brandishing their glistening spears, their swords, and their flint-locks, beating their war-drums, blowing their war-horns, and shouting in high-pitched, rasping, raucous voices their war-cry and their prayer, "Allah! Allah! Allah!"

On and on they had come, like champing surf rolling in on a reef-bound coast; on and on, faster and faster, louder and louder, on and on until they had all but hurled themselves into the British lines, and then—*crash!* A sheet of blinding flashes, a roll of stifling smoke, and, when the air cleared, a long empty space in the front line of the dervishes, and the ground strewn as with the drapery of two hundred dead men.

In an instant the gap had been filled and the mighty horde had come on again, but again and again, and yet again they had been swept down before the solid rock of the British forces like the spent waves of an angry sea.

At one moment a flag, silver white and glistening in the sun, had been seen coming up behind. It had seemed to float here, there, and everywhere, like a disembodied spirit, through the churning breakers of the enemy; and while the swarthy Arab who carried it had cried out over the thunder of battle that it was the angel of death leading them to victory or Paradise, the dervishes had screamed "Allah! Allah!" and poured themselves afresh on to the British lines.

But *crash, crash, crash!* the British rifles had spoken, and the dervishes had fallen in long swathes like grass before the scythe, until the broad field had been white with its harvest of the dead.

The sham fight had lasted a full hour, and until it was over the vast multitude of spectators had been as one immense creature that trembled without drawing breath. But then the umpire's big bell had been rung again, the dead men had leaped briskly to their feet and scampered back to paddock, and a rustling breeze of laughter, half merriment and half surprise, had swept over the pavilion and the field.

This was the moment at which the atmosphere had

2

seemed to change. Some one at the foot of the pavilion
had said:

"Whew! What a battle it must have been!"

And some one else had said:

"Don't call it a battle, sir; call it an execution."

And then a third, an Englishman in the uniform of an
Egyptian Commandant of Police, had cried:

"If it had gone the other way, though—if the Mah-
dists had beaten us that day at Omdurman, what would
have happened to Egypt then?"

"Happened?" the first speaker had answered—he was
the English Adviser to one of the Egyptian Ministers.
"What would have happened to Egypt, you say? Why,
there wouldn't have been a dog to howl for a lost master by
this time."

Lord Nuneham had heard the luckless words, and his
square-hewn jaw had grown harder and more grim. Unfortunately, the Egyptian Ministers, the Sheikhs, the pashas,
the beys, and effendis had heard them also, and, by the
mysterious law of Nature that sends messages over a trackless desert, the last biting phrase had seemed to go like an
electric whisper through the thick line of the red-capped
Cairenes around the arena.

In the native mind it altered everything in an instant;
transformed the sham battle into a serious incident; made
it an insult, an outrage, a prearranged political innuendo,
something got up by the British Army of Occupation, or
perhaps by the Consul-General himself, to rebuke the Egyptians for the fires of disaffection that had smouldered in
their midst for years, and to say as by visible historiog-
raphy:

"See, that's what England saved Egypt from—that
horde of Allah-intoxicated fanatics who would have cut off
the heads of your Khedives, tortured and pillaged your
pashas, flogged your effendis, made slaves of your fellaheen,
or swept your whole nation into the Nile."

Every soldier on the field had distinguished himself that
day, the British by his bull-dog courage, the Soudanese by
fighting as dervishes like demons, the Egyptian by standing

his ground like a man; but not even when young Colonel Lord, the most popular Englishman in Egypt, the one officer of English blood who was beloved by the Egyptians, not even when he had come riding back to paddock after a masterly handling of his men, sweating but smiling, his horse blowing and spent, the people on the pavilion receiving him with shouts and cheers, the clapping of hands, and the fluttering of handkerchiefs—not even then had the Cairenes at the edge of the arena made the faintest demonstration. Their opportunity came a few minutes later, and, sullen and grim under the gall of their unfounded suspicion, they seized it in fierce and rather ugly fashion.

Hardly had the last man left the field when a company of mounted police came riding down the fringe of it, followed by a carriage drawn by two high-stepping horses, between a bodyguard of Egyptian soldiers. They drew up in front of the box occupied by the kinsman of the Khedive, and instantly the Cairenes made a rush for it, besieging the barrier on either side, and even clambering on each other's shoulders as human scaffolding, from which to witness the departure of the Prince.

Then the Prince came out, a rather slack, feeble, ineffectual-looking man, and there were the ordinary salutations prescribed by custom. First the cry from the police in Turkish and in unison, "Long live our Master!" being cheers for the Khedive whose representative the Prince was, and then a cry in Arabic for the Prince himself. The Prince touched his forehead, stepped into his carriage, and was about to drive off when, without sign or premeditation —by one of those mischievous impulses which the devil himself inspires—there came a third cry, never heard on that ground before. In a lusty, guttural voice, a young man standing on the shoulders of another man—both, apparently, students of law or medicine—shouted over the heads of the people, "Long live Egypt!" and in an instant the cry was repeated in a deafening roar from every side.

The Prince signalled to his bodyguard and his carriage started, but all the way down the line of the enclosure,

where the red-hatted Egyptians were still standing in solid
masses, the words cracked along like fireworks set alight.

The people on the great pavilion watched and listened,
and to the larger part of them, who were British subjects,
and to the officers, Advisers, and Under-Secretaries, who
were British officials, the cry was like a challenge which
seemed to say, "Go home to England; we are a nation of
ourselves and can do without you." For a moment the air
tingled with expectancy, and everybody knew that something else was going to happen. It happened instantly,
with that promptness which the devil alone contrives.

Almost as soon as the Prince's company had cleared
away, a second carriage, that of the British Consul-General,
came down the line to the pavilion, with a posse of native
police on either side and a sais running in front. Then
from his seat in the centre Lord Nuneham rose and stepped
down to the arena, shaking hands with people as he passed,
gallant to the ladies as befits an English gentleman, but
bearing himself with a certain brusque condescension toward the men, all trying to attract his attention—a medium-
sized yet massive person, with a stern jaw and steady gray
eyes, behind which the cool brain was plainly packed in ice,
a man of iron who had clearly passed through the pathway
of life with a firm high step.

The posse of native police cleared a way for him, and,
under the orders of an officer, rendered military honours,
but that was not enough for the British contingent in the
fever of their present excitement. They called for three
cheers for the King, whose representative the Consul-General was in Egypt, and then three more for Lord Nuneham,
giving, not three, but six, with a fierceness that grew more
frantic at every shout, and seemed to say, as plainly as
words could speak, "Here we are and here we stay."

The Egyptians listened in silence, some of them spitting as a sign of contempt, until the last cheer was dying
down, and then the lusty, guttural voice cried again,
"Long live Egypt!" and once more the words rang like a
rip-rap down the line.

It was noticed that the stern expression of Lord Nune-

ham's face assumed a death-like rigidity, that he took out
a pocket-book, wrote some words, tore away a leaf, handed
it to a native servant, and then, with an icy smile, stepped
into his carriage. Meantime the British contingent were
cheering again with yet more deafening clamour, and the
rolling sound followed the Consul-General as he drove away.
But the shout of the Egyptians followed him, too; and when
he reached the high road the one was like muffled drums
at a funeral far behind, while the other was like the sharp
crack of Maxim guns that were always firing by his side.

The sea of muslin, ribbons, flowers, and feathers in the
pavilion had broken up by this time; the light was striking
level in people's eyes, the west was crimsoning with sunset
tints, the city was red on the tips of its minarets and ablaze
on the bare face of its insurgent hills, and the Nile itself,
taking the colouring of the sky, was lying like an old serpent of immense size which had stretched itself along the
sand to sleep.

II

GENERAL GRAVES'S daughter had been at the sports that
day, sitting in the chair immediately behind Lord Nuneham's. Her name was Helena, and she was a fine, handsome girl in the early twenties, with coal-black hair, very
dark eyes, a speaking face, and a smile like eternal sunshine,
well grown, splendidly developed, and carrying herself in
perfect equipoise with natural grace and a certain swing
when she walked.

Helena Graves was to marry Lord Nuneham's son, Colonel Gordon Lord, and during the progress of the sham
fight she had had eyes for nobody else. She had watched
him when he had entered the field, sitting solid on his Irish
horse, which was stepping high and snorting audibly; when
at the "Fire!" he had stood behind the firing line, and at
the "Cease fire!" galloped in front; when he had threaded
his forces round and round, north, south, and west, in and
out as in a dance, so that they faced the enemy on every

side; when somebody had blundered and his cavalry had
been caught in a trap, and he had had to ride without sword
or revolver through a cloud of dark heads that had sprung
up as if out of the ground; and, above all, when his horse
had stumbled and he had fallen, and the dervishes, forgetting that the battle was not a real one, had hurled their
spears like shafts of forked lightning over his head. At
that moment she had forgotten all about the high society
gathered in a brilliant throng around her, and had clutched
the Consul-General's chair convulsively, breathing so audibly that he had heard her, and, lowering the glasses through
which he had watched the distant scene, had patted her
arm and said:

"He's safe—don't be afraid, my child!"

When the fight was over her eyes were radiant, her
cheeks were like a conflagration, and, notwithstanding the
ugly incident attending the departure of the Prince and
Lord Nuneham, her face was full of a triumphant joy as
she stepped down to the green, where Colonel Lord, who
was waiting for her, put on her motor cloak—she had come
in her automobile—and helped her to fix the light veil,
which in her excitement had fallen back from her hat and
showed that she was still blushing up to the roots of her
black hair.

Splendid creature as she was, Colonel Lord was a match
for her. He was one of the youngest colonels in the British
Army, being four-and-thirty, of more than medium height,
with crisp brown hair, and eyes of the flickering, steel-like
blue that is common among enthusiastic natures, especially
when they are soldiers—a man of unmistakable masculinity,
yet with that vague suggestion of the woman about him
which, sometimes seen in a manly face, makes one say, without knowing any of the circumstances, "That man is like
his mother, and whatever her ruling passion is, his own
will be, only stronger, more daring, and perhaps more
dangerous."

"They're a lovely pair," the women were saying of them
as they stood together; and soon they were surrounded by
a group of people, some complimenting Helena, others

congratulating Gordon, all condemning the demonstration which had cast a certain gloom over the concluding scene.

"It was too exciting, too fascinating, but how shameful that conduct of the natives! It was just like a premeditated insult," said a fashionable lady, a visitor to Cairo; and then an Englishman—it was the Adviser who had spoken the first unlucky words—said, promptly:

"So it was—it must have been. Didn't you see how it was all done at a preconcerted signal?"

"I'm not surprised. I've always said we English in Egypt are living on the top of a volcano," said a small, slack, gray-headed man, a judge in the native courts; and then the Commandant of Police, a somewhat pompous person, said, bitterly:

"We saved their country from bankruptcy, their backs from the lash, and their stomachs from starvation, and now listen: 'Long live Egypt!'"

At that moment a rather effusive American lady came up to Helena and said:

"Don't you ever recognise your friends, dear? I tried to catch your eye during the fight, but a certain officer had fallen, and, of course, nobody else existed in the world."

"Let us make up our minds to it—we are not *liked*," the judge was saying. "Naturally we were popular as long as we were plastering the wounds made by tyrannical masters; but the masters are dead and the patient is better, so the doctor is found to be a bore."

At that moment an Egyptian Princess, famous for her wit and daring, came down the pavilion steps. She was one of the few Egyptian women who frequented mixed society and went about with uncovered face—a large person, with plump, pallid cheeks, very voluble, outspoken, and quick-tempered, a friend and admirer of the Consul-General's, and a champion of the English rule. Making straight for Helena, she said:

"Goodness, child, is it your face I see or the light of the moon? The battle? Oh, yes, it was beautiful, but it was terrible, and thank the Lord, it is over. But tell me about yourself, dear. You are desperately in love, they say, and no wonder. I'm in love with him myself, I really am, and if . . . Oh, you're there, are you? Well, I'm telling Helena I'm in love with you. Such strength, such courage —*pluck* you call it, don't you?"

Helena had turned to answer the American lady, and Gordon, whose eyes had been on her as if waiting for her to speak, whispered to the Princess:

"Isn't she looking lovely to-day, Princess?"

"Then why don't you tell her so?" said the Princess.

"Hush!" said Gordon, whereupon the Princess said:

"My goodness, what ridiculous creatures men are! What cowards, too! As brave as lions before a horde of savages, but before a woman—*mon Dieu!*"

"Yes," said the judge, in his slow, shrill voice, "they are fond of talking of the old book of Egypt, yet the valley of the Nile is strewn with the tombs of Egyptians who have perished under their hard task-masters, from the Pharaohs to the pashas. Can't they hear the murmur of the past about them? Have they no memory if they have no gratitude?"

At the last words General Graves came up to the group, looking hot and excited, and he said:

"Memory? Gratitude? They're a nation of ingrates and fools."

"What's that?" said the Princess.

"Pardon me, Princess. I say the demonstration of your countrymen to-day is an example of the grossest ingratitude."

"You're quite right, General. But *ma'aleysh!* (no matter). The barking of dogs doesn't hurt the clouds."

"And who are the dogs in this instance, Princess?" said a thin-faced Turco-Egyptian with a heavy moustache, who had been congratulating Colonel Lord.

"Your Turco-Egyptian beauties, who would set the country ablaze to light their cigarettes," said the Princess. "Children I call them. Children, and they deserve the rod. Yes, the rod, and serve them right. Excuse the word. I know! I tell you plainly, pasha."

"And the clouds are the Consul-General, I suppose?"

"Certainly; and he's so much above them that they can't even see he's the sun in their sky, the stupids."

Whereupon the pasha, who was the Egyptian Prime Minister under a British Adviser, said, with a shrug and a dubious smile:

"Your sentiments are beautiful, but your similes are a little broken, Princess."

"Not half so much broken as your Treasury would have been if the English hadn't helped it," said the Princess; and when the pasha had gone off with a rather halting laugh, she said:

"*Ma'aleysh!* When angels come the devils take their leave. I don't care. I say what I think. I tell the Egyptians the English are the best friends Egypt ever had, and Nuneham is their greatest ruler since the days of Joseph. But Adam himself wasn't satisfied with Paradise, and it's no use talking. 'Don't throw stones into the well you drink from,' I say. But serve you right, you English. You shouldn't have come. He who builds on another's land brings up another's child. Everybody is excited about this sedition, and even the harem are asking what the Government is going to do. Nuneham knows best, though. Leave him alone. He'll deal with these half-educated upstarts. Upstarts—that's what I call them. Oh, I know! I speak plainly!"

"I agree with the Princess," chimed the judge. "What is this unrest among the Egyptians due to? The education we ourselves have given them."

"Yes; teach your dog to snap, and he'll soon bite you."

"These are the tares in the harvest we are reaping, and perhaps our Western grain doesn't suit this Eastern desert."

"Should think it doesn't, indeed. 'Liberty,' 'Equality,' 'Fraternity,' 'Representative Institutions'! If you English come talking this nonsense to the Egyptians what can you expect? Socialism, is it? Well, if I am to be Prince and you are to be Prince, who is to drive the donkey? Excuse the word! I know! I tell you plainly. Good-bye, my dear! You are looking perfect to-day. But then you are so happy. I can see when young people are in love by their

3

eyes, and yours are shining like moons. After all, your Western ways are best. We choose the husbands for our girls, thinking the silly things don't know what is good for them, and the chicken isn't wiser than the hen; but it's the young people, not the old ones, who have to live together, so why shouldn't they choose for themselves?"

At that instant there passed from some remote corner of the grounds a brougham containing two shrouded figures in close white veils, and the Princess said:

"Look at that, now—that relic of barbarism! Shutting our women up like canaries in a cage, while their men are enjoying the sunshine. Life is a dancing girl—let her dance a little for all of us."

The Princess was about to go, when General Graves appealed to her. The judge had been saying:

"I should call it a religious rather than a political unrest. You may do what you will for the Moslem; but he never forgets that the hand which bestows his benefits is that of an infidel."

"Yes, we're aliens here, there's no getting over it," said the Adviser.

And the General said: "Especially when professional fanatics are always reminding the Egyptians that we are not Mohammedans. By the way, Princess, have you heard of the new preacher, the new prophet, the new Mahdi, as they say?"

"Prophet! Mahdi! Another of them?"

"Yes, the comet that has just appeared in the firmament of Alexandria."

"Some holy man, I suppose. Oh, I know! Holy man, indeed! Shake hands with him and count your rings, General! Another impostor riding on the people's backs—and they can't see it, the stupids! But the camel never *can* see his hump—not he! Good-bye, girl. Get married soon, and keep together as long as you can. Stretch your legs to the length of your bed, my dear; why shouldn't you? Say good-bye to Gordon? Certainly; where is he?"

At that moment Gordon was listening, with head down, to something the General was saying with intense feeling.

"The only way to deal with religious impostors who sow disaffection among the people is to suppress them with a strong hand. Why not? Fear of their followers? They're fit for nothing but to pray in their mosques, 'Away with the English, O Lord, but give us water in due measure!' Fight? Not for an instant. There isn't an ounce of courage in a hundred of them, and a score of good soldiers would sweep all the native Egyptians of Alexandria into the sea."

Then Gordon, who had not yet spoken, lifted his head and answered, in a rather nervous voice:

"No, no, no, sir! Ill usage may have made these people cowards in the old days, but proper treatment since has made them men, and there wasn't an Egyptian fellah on the field to-day who wouldn't have followed me into the jaws of death if I had told him to. As for our being aliens in religion"—the nervous voice became louder, and at the same time more tremulous—"that isn't everything. We're aliens in sympathy and brotherhood, and even in common courtesy as well. What is the honest truth about us? Here we are to help the Egyptians to regenerate their country, yet we neither eat nor drink nor associate with them. How can we hope to win their hearts while we hold them at arm's length? We've given them water—yes, water in abundance, but have we given them—love?"

The woman in Gordon had leaped out before he knew it, and he had swung a little aside as if ashamed, while the men cleared their throats, and the Princess, notwithstanding that she had been abusing her own people, suddenly melted in the eyes, muttered to herself, "Oh, our God!" and then, reaching over to kiss Helena, whispered in her ear:

"You've got the best of the bunch, my dear, and if England would only send us a few more of his sort we should hear less of 'Long live Egypt!' Now, General, you can see me to my carriage if you would like to. By-bye, young people!"

At that moment the native servant to whom the Consul-General had given the note came up and gave it to Gordon, who read it and then handed it to Helena. It ran:

"Come to me immediately. Have something to say to you.—N."

"We'll drive you to the Agency in the car," said Helena, and they moved away together.

In a crowded lane at the back of the pavilion people were clamouring for their carriages, and complaining of the idleness and even rudeness of the Arab runners, but Helena's automobile was brought up instantly, and when it was moving off with the General inside, Helena at the wheel and Gordon by her side, the natives touched their foreheads to the colonel and said, "*Bismillah!*"

As soon as the car was clear away and Gordon was alone with Helena for the first time, there was one of those privateering passages of love between them which lovers know how to smuggle through, even in public and the eye of day.

"Well!"

"Well!"

"Everybody has been saying the sweetest things to me and you've never yet uttered a word."

"Did you really expect me to speak—there—before all those people? But it was splendid—glorious—magnificent!"

And then, the steering-wheel notwithstanding, her gauntleted left hand went down to where his right hand was waiting for it.

Crossing the iron bridge over the river, they drew up at the British Agency, a large, ponderous, uninspired edifice, with its ambuscaded back to the city and its defiant front to the Nile, and there, as Gordon got down, the General, who still looked hot and excited, said:

"You'll dine with us to-night, my boy—usual hour, you know."

"With pleasure, sir," said Gordon, and then Helena leaned over and whispered:

"May I guess what your father is going to talk about?"

"The demonstration?"

"Oh, no!"

"What, then?"

"The new prophet at Alexandria."

"I wonder," said Gordon, and with a wave of the hand

he disappeared behind a screen of purple blossoms as Helena and the General faced home.

Their way lay up through the old city, where groups of aggressive young students, at sight of the General's gold-laced cap, started afresh the Kentish fire of their "Long live Egypt!" Up and up until they reached the threatening old fortress on the spur of the Mokattam hills, and then through the iron-clamped gates to the wide courtyard where the mosque of Mohammed Ali, with its spiky minarets, stands on the edge of the ramparts like a cock getting ready to crow, and drew up at the gate of a heavy-lidded house which looks sleepily down on the city, the sinuous Nile, the sweeping desert, the preponderating pyramids, and the last saluting of the sun. Then, as Helena rose from her seat, she saw that the General's head had fallen back and his face was scarlet.

"Father, you are ill."

"Only a little faint—I'll be better presently."

But he stumbled in stepping out of the car, and Helena said:

"You *are* ill and you must go to bed immediately, and let me put Gordon off until to-morrow."

"No; let him come. I want to hear what the Consul-General had to say to him."

In spite of himself he had to go to bed, though, and half an hour later, having given him a sedative, Helena was saying:

"You've over-excited yourself again, father. You were anxious about Gordon when his horse fell and those abominable spears were flying about."

"Not a bit of it. I knew he would come out all right. The fighting devil isn't civilised out of the British blood yet, thank God! But those Egyptians at the end—the ingrates! the dastards!"

"Father!"

"Oh, I am calm enough now—don't be afraid, girl. I was sorry to hear Gordon standing up for them, though. A soldier every inch of him, but how unlike his father! Never saw father and son so different. Yet so much alike.

too! Fighting men, both of them. Hope to goodness they'll never come to grips. Heavens! that would be a bad day for all of us."

And then, drowsily, under the influence of the medicine:

"I wonder what Nuneham wanted with Gordon? Something about those graceless tarbooshes, I suppose. He'll make them smart for what they've done to-day. Wonderful man, Nuneham! Wonderful!"

III

JOHN NUNEHAM was the elder son of a financier of whose earlier life little or nothing was ever learned. What was known of his later life was that he had amassed a fortune by Colonial speculation, bought a London newspaper, and been made a baronet for services to his political party. Having no inclination toward journalism, the son became a soldier, rose quickly to the rank of brevet-major, served several years with his regiment abroad, and at six-and-twenty went to India as private secretary to the Viceroy, who, quickly recognising his natural tendency, transferred him to the administrative side and put him on the financial staff. There he spent five years with conspicuous success, obtaining rapid promotion and being frequently mentioned in the Viceroy's reports to the Foreign Minister.

Then his father died, without leaving a will, as the cable of the solicitors informed him, and he returned to England to administer the estate. Here a thunderbolt fell on him, for he found a younger brother, with whom he had nothing in common and had never lived at peace, preparing to dispute his right to his father's title and fortune on the assumption that he was illegitimate—that is to say, was born before the date of the marriage of his parents.

The allegation proved to be only too well founded, and as soon as the elder brother had recovered from the shock of the truth he appealed to the younger one to leave things as they found them.

"After all, a man's eldest son is his eldest son; let matters rest," he urged, but his brother was obdurate.

"Nobody knows what the circumstances may have been. Is there no ground of agreement?" But his brother could see none.

"You can take the inheritance, if that's what you want; but let me find a way to keep the title, so as to save the family and avoid scandal." But his brother was unyielding.

"For our father's sake. It is not for a man's sons to rake up the dead past of his forgotten life." But the younger brother could not be stirred.

"For our mother's sake. Nobody wants his mother's good name to be smirched—least of all when she's in her grave." But the younger brother remained unmoved.

"I promise never to marry. The title shall end with me. It shall return to you or to your children." But the younger brother would not listen.

"England is the only Christian country in the world in which a man's son is not always his son. For God's sake, let me keep my father's name!"

"It is mine, and mine alone," said the younger brother, and then a heavy and solitary tear, the last he was to shed for forty years, dropped slowly down John Nuneham's hard-drawn face, for at that instant the well of his heart ran dry.

"As you will," he said. "But if it is your pride that is doing this I shall humble it, and if it is your greed I shall live long enough to make it ashamed."

From that day forward he dedicated his life to one object only, the founding of a family that should far eclipse the family of his brother, and his first step toward that end was to drop his father's surname in the register of his regiment and assume his mother's name of Lord.

At that moment England, with two other European Powers, had, like Shadrach, Meshach, and Abednego, entered the fiery furnace of Egyptian affairs, though not so much to withstand as to protect the worship of the golden image. A line of Khedives, each seeking his own advantage, had culminated in one more unscrupulous and tyrannical than the rest, who had seized the lands of the people, borrowed money upon them in Europe, wasted it in wicked personal extravagance, as well as in reckless imperial expenditure that had not yet had time to yield a return, and thus brought the country to the brink of ruin, with the result that England was left alone at last to occupy Egypt, much as Rome occupied Palestine, and to find a man to administer her affairs in a position analogous to that of Pontius Pilate. It found him in John Lord, the young financial secretary who had distinguished himself in India.

His task was one of immense difficulty, for, though nominally no more than the British Consul-General, he was really the ruler of the country, being representative of the sovereign whose soldiers held Egypt in their grip. Realising at once that he was the official receiver to a bankrupt nation, he saw that his first duty was to make it solvent. He did make it solvent. In less than five years Egypt was able to pay her debt to Europe. Therefore Europe was satisfied, England was pleased, and John Lord was made Knight of the Order of St. Michael and St. George.

Then he married a New England girl whom he had met in Cairo, daughter of a Federal General in the Civil War, a gentle creature, rather delicate, a little sentimental, and very religious.

During the first years their marriage was childless, and the wife, seeing with a woman's sure eyes that her husband's hope had been for a child, began to live within herself and to weep when no one could see. But at last a child came and it was a son, and she was overjoyed and the Consul-General was content. He allowed her to christen the child by what name she pleased, so she gave him the name of her great Christian hero, Charles George Gordon. They called the boy Gordon, and the little mother was very happy.

But her health became still more delicate, so a nurse had to be looked for, and they found one in an Egyptian woman —with a child of her own—who, by power of a pernicious law of Mohammedan countries, had been divorced through no fault of hers, at the whim of a husband who wished to marry another wife. Thus Hagar, with her little Ishmael, became foster-mother to the Consul-General's son, and the two children were suckled together and slept in the same cot.

Years passed, during which the boy grew up like a little Arab in the Englishman's house, while his mother devoted herself more and more to the exercises of her religion, and his father, without failing in affectionate attention to either of them, seemed to bury his love for both too deep in his heart and to seal it with a seal, although the Egyptian nurse was sometimes startled late at night by seeing the Consul-General coming noiselessly into her room before going to his own, to see if it was well with his child.

Meantime, as ruler of Egypt, the Consul-General was going from strength to strength, and, seeing that the Nile is the most wonderful river in the world and the father of the country through which it flows, he determined that it should do more than moisten the lips of the Egyptian desert while the vast body lay parched with thirst. Therefore he took engineers up to the fork of the stream where the clear and crystal Blue Nile of Khartoum, tumbling down in mighty torrents from the volcanic gorges of the Abyssinian hills, crosses the slow and sluggish White Nile of Omdurman, and told them to build dams, so that the water should not be wasted into the sea, but spread over the arid land, leaving the glorious sun of Egypt to do the rest.

The effect was miraculous. Nature, the great wonder-worker, had come to his aid, and never since the Spirit of God first moved upon the face of the waters had anything so marvellous been seen. The barren earth brought forth grass and the desert blossomed like a rose. Land values increased; revenues were enlarged; poor men became rich; rich men became millionaires; Egypt became a part of Europe; Cairo became a European city; the record of the progress of the country began to sound like a story from "The Arabian Nights," and the Consul-General's annual reports read like fresh chapters out of the Book of Genesis, telling of the creation of a new heaven and a new earth. The remaking of Egypt was the wonder of the world; the faces of the Egyptians were whitened; England was happy, and Sir John Lord was made a baronet. His son had gone to school in England by this time, and from Eton he was to go on to Sandhurst and to take up the career of a soldier.

Then, thinking the Englishman's mission on foreign soil was something more than to make money, the Consul-General attempted to regenerate the country. He had been sent out to re-establish the authority of the Khedive, yet he proceeded to curtail it; to suppress the insurrection of the people, yet he proceeded to enlarge their liberties. Setting up a high standard of morals, both in public and private life, he tolerated no trickery. Finding himself in a cockpit of corruption, he put down bribery, slavery, perjury, and a hundred kinds of venality and intrigue. Having views about individual justice and equal rights before the Law, he cleansed the Law Courts, established a Christian code of morals between man and man, and let the light of Western civilisation into the mud-hut of the Egyptian fellah.

Mentally, morally, and physically his massive personality became the visible soul of Egypt. If a poor man was wronged in the remotest village, he said, "I'll write to Lord," and the threat was enough. He became the visible conscience of Egypt, too, and if a rich man was tempted to do a doubtful deed he thought of "the Englishman," and the doubtful deed was not done.

The people at the top of the ladder trusted him, and the people at the bottom, a simple, credulous, kindly race, who were such as sixty centuries of misgovernment had made them, touched their breasts, their lips, and their foreheads at the mention of his name, and called him "The Father of Egypt." England was proud, and Sir John Lord was made a peer.

When the King's letter reached him he took it to his wife, who now lay for long hours every day on the couch in the drawing-room, and then wrote to his son, who had left Sandhurst and was serving with his regiment in the Soudan, but he said nothing to anybody else, and left even his secretary to learn the great news through the newspapers.

He was less reserved when he came to select his title.

and, remembering his brother, he found a fierce joy in calling himself by his father's name, thinking he had earned the right to it. Twenty-five years had passed since he had dedicated his life to the founding of a family that should eclipse, and even humiliate, the family of his brother, and now his secret aim was realised. He saw a long line succeeding him—his son, and his son's son, and his son's son's son, all peers of the realm, and all Nunehams. His revenge was sweet; he was very happy.

IV

IF Lord Nuneham had died then, or if he had passed away from Egypt, he would have left an enduring fame as one of the great Englishmen who twice or thrice in a hundred years carve their names on the granite page of the world's history; but he went on and on, until it sometimes looked as if in the end it might be said of him, in the phrase of the Arab proverb, that he had written his name in water.

Having achieved one object of ambition, he set himself another, and having tasted power he became possessed by the lust of it. Great men had been in England when he first came to Egypt, and he had submitted to their instructions without demur, but now, wincing under the orders of inferior successors, he told himself, not idly boasting, that nobody in London knew his work as well as he did, and he must be liberated from the domination of Downing Street. The work of emancipation was delicate but not difficult. There was one power stronger than any Government whereby public opinion might be guided and controlled—the Press.

The British Consul-General in Cairo was in a position of peculiar advantage for guiding and controlling the Press. He did guide and control it. What he thought it well that Europe should know about Egypt, that it knew, and that only. The generally ill-informed public opinion in England was corrected; the faulty praise and blame of the

British Press was set right; within five years London had ceased to send instructions to Cairo; and when a diplomatic question created a fuss in Parliament the Consul-General was heard to say:

"I don't care a rush what the Government think, and I don't care a straw what the Foreign Minister says; I have a power stronger than either at my back—the public."

It was true, but it was also the beginning of the end. Having attained to absolute power, he began to break up from the seeds of dissolution which always hide in the heart of it. Hitherto he had governed Egypt by guiding a group of gifted Englishmen who, as secretaries and advisers, had governed the Egyptian governors; but now he desired to govern everything for himself. As a consequence the gifted men had to go, and their places were taken by subordinates whose best qualification was their subservience to his strong and masterful spirit.

Even that did not matter as long as his own strength served him. He knew and determined everything, from the terms of treaties with foreign Powers to the wages of the Khedive's English coachman. With five thousand British bayonets to enforce his will, he said to a man, "Do that," and the man did it or left Egypt without delay. No Emperor or Czar or King was ever more powerful, no Pope more infallible; but if his rule was hard it was also just, and for some years yet Egypt was well governed.

"When a fish goes bad," the Arabs say, "is it first at the head or at the tail?" As Lord Nuneham grew old his health began to fail, and he had to fall back on the weaklings who were only fit to carry out his will. Then an undertone of murmuring was heard in Egypt. The Government was the same, yet it was altogether different. The hand was Esau's, but the voice was Jacob's. "The millstones are grinding," said the Egyptians, "but we see no flour."

The glowing fire of the great Englishman's fame began to turn to ashes, and a cloud no bigger than a man's hand appeared in the sky. His Advisers complained to him of friction with their Ministers; his inspectors, returning from tours in the country, gave him reports of scant courtesy at the hands of natives, and to account for their failures they worked up in his mind the idea of a vast racial and religious conspiracy. The East was the East, the West was the West, Moslem was Moslem, Christian was Christian; Egyptians cared more about Islam than they did about good government, and Europeans in the Valley of the Nile, especially British soldiers and officials, were living on the top of a volcano.

The Consul-General listened to them with a sour smile, but he believed them and blundered. He was a sick man now, and he was not really living in Egypt any longer; he was only sleeping at the Agency, and he thought he saw the work of his lifetime in danger of being undone. So, thinking to end fanaticism by one crushing example, he gave his subordinates an order like that which the ancient King of Egypt gave to the midwives, with the result that five men were hanged and a score were flogged before their screaming wives and children for an offence that had not a particle of religious or political significance.

A cry of horror went up through Egypt. The Consul-General had lost it; his thirty years of great labour had been undone in a day.

As every knife is out when the bull is down, so the place-hunting pashas, the greedy Sheikhs, and the cruel governors whose corruptions he had suppressed found instruments to stab him, and the people who had kissed the hand they dared not bite thought it safe to bite the hand they need not kiss. He had opened the mouths of his enemies, and, in Eastern manner, they assailed him first by parable. Once there had been a great English eagle; its eyes were clear and piercing; its talons were firm and relentless in their grip; yet it was a proud and noble bird; it held its own against East and West, and protected all who took refuge under its wing. But now the eagle had grown old and weak; other birds, smaller and meaner, had deprived it of its feathers and picked out its eyes, and it had become blind and cruel and cowardly and sly. Would nobody shoot it or shut it up in a cage?

Rightly or wrongly, the Consul-General became convinced that the Khedive was intriguing against him, and one day he drove to the Royal palace and demanded an audience. The interview that followed was not the first of many stormy scenes between the real governor of Egypt and its nominal ruler, and when Lord Nuneham strode out with his face aflame, through the line of the quaking bodyguard, he left the Khedive protesting plaintively to the people of his Court that he would sell up all and leave the country. At that the officials put their heads together in private, concluded that the present condition could not last, and asked themselves how, since it was useless to expect England to withdraw the Consul-General, it was possible for Egypt to get rid of him.

By this time Lord Nuneham, in the manner of all strong men growing weak, had begun to employ spies, and one day a Syrian Christian told him a secret story. He was to be assassinated. The crime was to be committed in the Opera-house, under the cover of a general riot, on the night of the Khedive's State visit, when the Consul-General was always present. As usual, the Khedive was to rise at the end of the first act and retire to the saloon overlooking the square; as usual, he was to send for Lord Nuneham to follow him, and the moment of the Khedive's return to his box was to be the signal for a rival demonstration of English and Egyptians that was to end in the Consul-General's death. There was no reason to believe the Khedive himself was party to the plot, or that he knew anything about it, yet none the less it was necessary to stay away, to find an excuse—illness at the last moment, anything.

Lord Nuneham was not afraid, but he sent up to the Citadel for General Graves, and arranged that a battalion of infantry and a battery of artillery were to be marched down to the Opera Square at a message over the telephone from him.

"If anything happens you know what to do," he said, and the General knew perfectly.

Then the night came, and the moment the Khedive left his palace the Consul-General heard of it. A moment later

a message was received at the Citadel, and a quarter of an
hour afterward Lord Nuneham was taking his place at
the Opera. The air of the house tingled with excitement,
and everything seemed to justify the Syrian's story.

Sure enough, at the end of the first act the Khedive
rose and retired to the saloon, and sure enough at the next
moment the Consul-General was summoned to follow him.
His Highness was very gracious, very agreeable, all trace
of their last stormy interview being gone, and gradually
Lord Nuneham drew him up to the windows overlooking
the public square.

There, under the sparkling light of a dozen electric
lamps, in a solid line surrounding the Opera-house, stood a
battalion of infantry with the guns of the artillery facing
outward at every corner, and at sight of them the Khedive
caught his breath and said:

"What is the meaning of this, my lord?"

"Only a little attention to your Highness," said the
Consul-General, in a voice that was intended to be heard
all over the room.

At that instant somebody came up hurriedly and whispered to the Khedive, who turned ashen white, ordered his
carriage, and went home immediately.

Next morning at eleven Lord Nuneham, with the same
force drawn up in front of Abdeen Palace, went in to
see the Khedive again.

"There's a train for Alexandria at twelve," he said,
"and a steamer for Constantinople at five—your Highness
will feel better for a little holiday in Europe"; and half an
hour afterward the Khedive, accompanied by several of his
Court officials, was on his way to the railway-station with
the escort, in addition to his own bodyguard, of a British
regiment whose band was playing the Khedivial Hymn.

He had got rid of the Khedive at a critical juncture,
but he had still to deal with a sovereign that would not
easily be chloroformed into silence. The Arabic Press, to
which he had been the first to give liberty, began to attack
him openly, to vilify him, and systematically to misrepre-
sent his actions, so that he who had been the great torch-

bearer of light in a dark country saw himself called the Great Adventurer, the Tyrant, the Assassin, the worst Pharaoh Egypt had ever known—a Pharaoh surrounded by a kindergarten of false prophets, obsessed by preposterous fears of assassination and deluded by phantoms of fanaticism.

His subordinates told him that these hysterical tirades were inflaming the whole of Egypt; that their influence was in proportion to their violence; that the huge untaught mass of the Egyptian people were listening to them; that there was not an ignorant fellah possessed of one ragged garment who did not go to the coffee-house at night to hear them read; that the lives of British officials were in peril; and that the promulgation of sedition must be stopped or the British governance of the country could not go on.

A sombre fire shone in the Consul-General's eyes while he heard their prophecy, but he believed it all the same; and when he spoke contemptuously of incendiary articles as froth, and they answered that froth could be stained with blood, he told himself that if fools and ingrates, spouting nonsense in Arabic, could destroy whatever germs of civilisation he had implanted in Egypt, the doctrine of the liberty of the Press was all moonshine.

And so, after sinister efforts to punish the whole people for the excesses of their journalists by enlarging the British Army and making the country pay the expense, he found a means to pass a new Press law, to promulgate it by help of the Prime Minister—now Regent in the Khedive's place—and to suppress every native newspaper in Egypt in one day. By that blow the Egyptians were staggered into silence, the British officials went about with stand-off manners and airs of conscious triumph, and Lord Nuneham himself, mistaking violence for power, thought he was master of Egypt once more.

But low, very low on the horizon a new planet now rose in the firmament. It was not the star of a Khedive jealous of Nuneham's power, or of an Egyptian Minister girding under the orders of his Under-Secretary, or yet of a journalist vilifying England and flirting with France, but that of a simple Arab in a turban and caftan, a swarthy son of the desert whose name no man had heard before, and it was rising over the dome over the mosque, within whose sacred precincts neither the Consul-General nor his officials could intrude, and where the march of British soldiers could not be made. There a reverberation was being heard, a new voice was going forth, and it was echoing and re-echoing through the hushed chambers that were the heart of Islam.

When Lord Nuneham first asked about the Arab he was told that the man was one Ishmael Ameer, out of the Libyan desert, a carpenter's son and a fanatical, backward, unenlightened person of no consequence whatever; but with his sure eye for the political heavens the Consul-General perceived that a planet of no common magnitude had appeared in the Egyptian sky, and that it would avail him nothing to have suppressed the open sedition of the newspapers if he had only driven it underground into the mosques, where it would be a hundredfold more dangerous.

If a political agitation was not to be turned into religious unrest, if fanaticism was not to conquer civilisation and a holy war to carry the country back to its old rotten condition of bankruptcy and barbarity, that man out of the Libyan desert must be put down. But how and by whom? He himself was old—more than seventy years old; his best days were behind him, the road in front of him must be all downhill now, and when he looked around among the sycophants who said, "Yes, my lord!" "Excellent, my lord!" "The very thing, my lord!" for some one to fight the powers of darkness that were arrayed against him, he saw none.

It was in this mood that he had gone to the sham fight, merely because he had to show himself in public, and there, sitting immediately in front of the fine girl who was to be his daughter soon, and feeling at one moment her quick breathing on his neck, he had been suddenly caught up by the spirit of her enthusiasm and had seen his son as he had never seen him before. Putting his glasses to his eyes, he had watched him—he and, as it seemed, the girl together. Such courage, such fire, such resource, such insight, such foresight! It must be the finest brain and firmest character in Egypt, and it was his own flesh and blood—his own son Gordon!

Hitherto his attitude toward Gordon had been one of placid affection, compounded partly of selfishness, being proud that he was no fool and could forge along in his profession, and pleased to think of him as the next link in the chain of the family he was founding; but now everything was changed. The right man to put down sedition was the man at his right hand. He would save England against Egyptian aggression; he would save his father, too, who was old and whose strength was spent; and perhaps—why not?—he would succeed him some day and carry on the traditions of his work in the conquest of civilisation and its triumph in the dark countries of the world.

For the first time for forty years a heavy and solitary tear dropped slowly down the Consul-General's cheek, now deeply scored with lines, but no one saw it, because few dared look into his face. The man who had never unburdened himself to a living soul wished to unburden himself at last, so he scribbled his note to Gordon and then stepped into the carriage that was to take him home.

Meantime he was aware that some fool had provoked a demonstration, but that troubled him hardly at all, and while the crackling cries of "Long live Egypt!" were following him down the arena he was being borne along as by invisible wings.

Thus the two aims in the great Proconsul's life had become one aim, and that one aim centred in his son.

V

As Gordon went into the British Agency a small, wizened man with a pock-marked face, wearing Oriental dress, came out. He was the Grand Cadi (Chief Judge) of the Mohammedan Courts and representative of the Sultan of Turkey in Egypt, one who had secretly hated the Consul-

General and raved against the English rule for years; and as he saluted obsequiously with his honeyed voice and smiled with his crafty eyes it flashed upon Gordon—he did not know why—that just so must Caiaphas, the high priest, have looked when he came out of Pilate's judgment hall after saying, "If thou let this man go thou art not Cæsar's friend."

Gordon leaped up the steps and into the house as one who was at home, and, going first into the shaded drawing-room, he found his mother on the couch looking to the sunset and the Nile—a sweet old lady in the twilight of life, with white hair, a thin face almost as white, and the pale smile of a patient soul who had suffered pain. With her, attending upon her, and at that moment handing a cup of chicken broth to her, was a stout Egyptian woman with a good homely countenance—Gordon's old nurse, Fatimah.

His mother turned at the sound of his voice, roused herself on the couch, and with that startled cry of joy which has only one note in all Nature, that of a mother meeting her beloved son, she cried, "Gordon! Gordon!" and clasped her delicate hands about his neck. Before he could prevent it, his foster-mother, too, muttering in Eastern manner, "Oh, my eye! oh, my soul!" had snatched one of his hands and was smothering it with kisses.

"And how is Helena?" his mother asked, in her low, sweet voice.

"Beautiful," said Gordon.

"She couldn't help being that. But why doesn't she come to see me?"

"I think she is anxious about her father's health and is afraid to leave him," said Gordon; and then Fatimah, with blushes showing through her Arab skin, said:

"Take care. A house may hold a hundred men, but the heart of a woman has only room for one of them."

"Ah, but Helena's heart is as wide as a well, mammy," said Gordon, whereupon Fatimah said:

"That's the way, you see! When a young man is in love there are only two sorts of girls in the world—ordinary girls and his girl."

At that moment, while the women laughed, Gordon heard his father's deep voice in the hall saying, " Bid good-bye to my wife before you go, Reg," and then the Consul-General, with "Here's Gordon, also," came into the draw-ing-room, followed by Sir Reginald Mannering, Sirdar of the Egyptian Army, and Governor of the Soudan, who said:

"Splendid, my boy! Not forgotten your first fight, I see! Heavens, I felt as if I was back at Omdurman and wanted to get at the demons again."

"Gordon," said the Consul-General, "see His Excellency to the door and come to me in the library," and when the Sirdar was going out at the porch he whispered:

"Go easy with the Governor, my boy. Don't let any-thing cross him. Wonderful man, but I see a difference since I was down last year. By-bye!"

Gordon found his father writing a letter, with his valet, Ibrahim, in green caftan and red waistband, waiting by the side of the desk, in a plain room, formal as an office, being walled with bookcases full of blue books and relieved by two pictures only, a portrait of his mother when she was younger than he could remember to have seen her, and of himself when he was a child and wore an Arab fez and slippers.

"The General—the Citadel," said the Consul-General, giving his letter to Ibrahim, and as soon as the valet was gone he wheeled his chair round to Gordon and began.

"I've been writing to your General for his formal con-sent, having something I wish you to do for me."

"With pleasure, sir," said Gordon.

"You know all about the riots at Alexandria?"

"Only what I've learned from the London papers, sir."

"Well, for some time past the people there have been showing signs of effervescence. First, strikes of cabmen, carters, Gods knows what—all concealing political issues. Then open disorder. Europeans bustled and spat upon in the streets. A Sheikh crying aloud in the public thorough-fares, 'Oh, Moslems, come and help me to drive out the Christians!' Then a Greek merchant warned to take care, as the Arabs were going to kill the Christians that day or the day following. Then low-class Moslems shouting in the

square of Mohammed Ali, 'The last day of the Christians
is drawing nigh.' As a consequence, there have been conflicts. The first of them was trivial and the police scattered the rioters with a water-hose. The second was more
serious and some Europeans were wounded. The third was
alarming and several natives had to be arrested. Well,
when I look for the cause, I find the usual one."

"What is it, sir?" asked Gordon.

"Egypt has at all times been subject to local insurrec-
tions. They are generally of a religious character, and are
set on foot by mad men who give themselves out as divinely
inspired leaders. But shall I tell you what it all means?"

"Tell me, sir," said Gordon.

The Consul-General rose from his chair and began to
walk up and down the room with long strides and heavy
tread.

"It means," he said, "that the Egyptians, like all other
Mohammedans, are cut off by their religion from the spirit
and energy of the great civilised nations; that, swathed in
the bands of the Koran, the Moslem faith is like a mummy,
dead to all uses of the modern world."

The Consul-General drew up sharply, and continued:
"Perhaps all dogmatic religions are more or less like that,
but the Christian religion has accommodated itself to the
spirit of the ages, whereas Islam remains fixed, the religion
of the seventh century, born in a desert and suckled in a
society that was hardly better than barbarism."

He began to walk again and to talk with great animation.

"What does Islam mean? It means slavery, seclusion
of women, indiscriminate divorce, unlimited polygamy, the
breakdown of the family, and the destruction of the nation.
Well, what happens? Civilisation comes along, and it is
death to all such dark ways. What next? The scheming
Sheikhs, the corrupt pashas, the tyrranical caliphs, all the
rascals and rogues who batten on corruption, the fanatics
who are opponents of the light, cry out against it. Either
they must lose their interests or civilisation must go. What
then? Civilisation means the West; the West means

Christianity. So, 'Down with the Christians! Oh, Moslems, help us to kill them!'"

The Consul-General stopped by Gordon's chair, put his hand on his son's shoulder, and said:—

"There comes a time in the history of all our Mohammedan dependencies—India, Egypt, every one of them—when England has to confront a condition like that."

"And what has she to do, sir?"

The Consul-General lifted his right fist and brought it down on his left palm, and said:

"To come down with a heavy hand on the lying agitators and intriguers who are leading away the ignorant populace."

"I agree, sir. It is the agitators who should be punished, not the poor, emotional, credulous Egyptian people."

"The Egyptian people, my boy, are graceless ingrates who, under the influence of momentary passion, would brain their best friend with their nabouts, and go like camels before the camel-driver."

Gordon winced visibly, but only said, "Who is the camel-driver in this instance, sir?"

"A certain Ishmael Ameer, preaching in the great mosque at Alexandria, the cradle of all disaffection."

"An alim?"

"A teacher of some sort, saying England is the deadly foe of Islam, and must therefore be driven out."

"Then he is worse than the journalists?"

"Yes; we thought of the viper, forgetting the scorpion."

"But is it certain he is so dangerous?"

"One of the leaders of his own people has just been here to say that if we let that man go on it will be death to the rule of England in Egypt."

"The Grand Cadi?"

The Consul-General nodded and then said: "The cunning rogue has a grievance of his own, I find, but what's that to me? The first duty of a Government is to keep order."

"I agree," said Gordon.

"There may be picric acid in prayers as well as in bombs."

" There may."

" We have to make these fanatical preachers realise that, even if the onward march of progress is but faintly heard in the sealed vaults of their mosque, civilisation is standing outside the walls with its laws and, if need be, its soldiers."

" You are satisfied, sir, that this man is likely to lead the poor, foolish people into rapine and slaughter? "

" I recognise a bird by its flight. This is another Mahdi —I see it—I feel it," said the Consul-General, and his eyes flashed and his voice echoed like a horn.

" You want me to *smash* the Mahdi? "

" Exactly. Your namesake wanted to smash his predecessor—romantic person, too fond of guiding his conduct by reference to the prophet Isaiah—but he was right in that and the Government was wrong, and the consequence was the massacre you represented to-day."

" I have to arrest Ishmael Ameer? "

" That's so. In open riot, if possible, and if not, by means of testimony derived from his sermons in the mosques."

" Hadn't we better begin there, sir?—make sure that he is inciting the people to violence? "

" As you please."

" You don't forget that the mosques are closed to me as a Christian? "

The Consul-General reflected for a moment and then said, " Where's Fatimah's son, Hafiz? "

" With his regiment at Abbassiah."

" Take him with you. Take two other Moslem witnesses as well."

" I'm to bring this new prophet back to Cairo? "

" That's it; bring him here. We'll do all the rest."

" What if there should be trouble with the people? "

" There's a battalion of British soldiers in Alexandria. Keep a force in readiness—under arms night and day."

" But if it should spread beyond Alexandria? "

" So much the better for you. I mean," said the Consul-General, hesitating for the first time, " we don't want bloodshed, but if it must come to that it must, and the eyes of

England will be on you. What more can a young man want?
Think of yourself "—he put his hand on his son's shoulder
again—" think of yourself as on the eve of crushing England's enemies and rendering a signal service to Gordon
Lord as well. And now go—go up to your General and get
his formal consent. My love to Helena! Fine girl, very!
She's the sort of woman who might . . . yes, women are
the springs that move everything in this world. Bid good-
bye to your mother and get away. Lose no time. Write to
me as soon as you have anything to say. That's enough for
the present. I'm busy. Good day! "

Almost before Gordon had left the library the Consul-
General was back at his desk—the stern, saturnine man once
more, with a face that seemed to express a mind inaccessible
to human emotions of any sort.

" As bright as a light—sees things before one says them,"
he said to himself, as Gordon closed the door on going out.
" Why have I wasted myself with weaklings so long? "

Gordon kissed his pale-faced mother in the drawing-room
and his swarthy foster-mother in the porch, and went back
to his quarters in barracks—a rather bare room with bed,
desk, and bookcase, many riding boots on a shelf, several
weapons of savage warfare on the walls, a dervish's suit of
chain armour with a bullet-hole where the heart of the man
had been, a picture of Eton, his old school, and above all,
as became the home of a soldier, many photographs of his
womankind—his mother with her plaintive smile, Fatimah
with her humorous look, and, of course, Helena with her
glorious eyes, Helena, Helena, everywhere Helena.

There, taking down the receiver of a telephone, he called
up the headquarters of the Egyptian Army and spoke to
Hafiz, his foster-brother, now a captain in the native
cavalry.

" Is that you, Hafiz? . . . Well, look here, I want to
know if you can arrange to go with me to Alexandria for a
day or two? . . . You can? Good! I wish you to help me
to deal with that new preacher, prophet, Mahdi. What's
his name, now? . . . That's it—Ishmael Ameer. He has
been setting Moslem against Christian, and we've got to

lay the gentleman by the heels before he gets the poor, credulous people into further trouble. . . . What do you say? . . . Not that kind of man, you think? . . . No? . . . You surprise me. . . . Do you really mean to say? . . . Certainly; that's only fair. . . . Yes, I ought to know all about him. . . . Your uncle? . . . Chancellor of the University? . . . I know—El Azhar. . . . When could I see him? . . . What day do we go to Alexandria? To-morrow, if possible. . . . To-night the only convenient time, you think? Well, I promised to dine at the Citadel; but I suppose I must write to Helena. . . . Oh, needs must when the devil drives, old fellow. . . . To-night, then? . . . You'll come down for me immediately? Good! By-bye!"

With that he rang off and sat down to write a letter.

VI

GORDON LORD loved the Egyptians. Nursed on the knee of an Egyptian woman, speaking Arabic as his mother-tongue, lisping the songs of Arabia before he knew a word of English, Egypt was under his very skin, and the spirit of the Nile and of the desert was in his blood.

Only once a day in his childhood was there a break in his Arab life. That was in the evening about sunset, when Fatimah took him into his father's library, and the great man with his stern face, who assumed toward him a singularly cold manner, put him through a catechism which was always the same: "Tutor been here to-day, boy?" "Yes, sir." "Done your lessons?" "Yes, sir." "English—French—everything?" "Yes, sir." "Say good night to your mother and go to bed."

Then for a few moments more he was taken into his mother's boudoir, the cool room with the blinds down to keep out the sun, where the lady with the beautiful, pale face embraced and kissed him, and made him kneel by her side while they said the Lord's Prayer together in a rustling whisper, like a breeze in the garden. But, after that, off to

4

bed with Hafiz—who, in his Arab caftan and fez, had been looking furtively in at the half-open door—up two steps at a time, shouting and singing in Arabic, while Fatimah, in fear of the Consul-General, cried, "Hush! Be good, now, my sweet eyes!"

In his boyhood, too, he had been half a Mohammedan, going every afternoon to fetch Hafiz home from the kuttab, the school of the mosque, and romping round the sacred place like a little king in stocking feet, until the Sheikh in charge, who pretended as long as possible not to see him, came with a long cane to whip him out, always saying he should never come there again—until to-morrow.

While at school in England he had felt like a foreigner, wearing his silk hat on the back of his head as if it had been a tarboosh, and while at Sandhurst, where he got through his three years more easily—in spite of a certain restiveness under discipline—he had always been looking forward to his Christmas visits home—that is to say, to Cairo.

But at last he came back to Egypt on a great errand, with the expedition that was intended to revenge the death of his heroic namesake, having got his commission by that time, and being asked for by his father's old friend, Reginald Mannering, who was a colonel in the Egyptian Army. His joy was wild, his excitement delirious; and even the desert marches under the blazing sun and the sky of brass, killing to some of his British comrades, was a long delight to the Arab soul in him.

The first fighting he did, too, was done with an Egyptian by his side. His great chum was a young lieutenant named Ali Awad, the son of a pasha, a bright, intelligent, affectionate young fellow who was intensely sensitive to the contempt of British officers for the quality of the courage of their Egyptian colleagues. During the hurly-burly of the Battle of Omdurman both Gordon and Ali had been eager to get at the enemy, but their Colonel had held them back, saying, "What will your fathers say to me if I allow you to go into a hell like that?" When the dervish lines had been utterly broken, though, and one coffee-coloured demon in chain armour was stealing off with his black banner, the Colonel said, "Now's your time, boys; show what stuff you are made of; bring me back that flag," and before the words were out of his mouth the young soldiers were gone.

Other things happened immediately, and the Colonel had forgotten his order when, the battle being over, and the British and Egyptian Army about to enter the dirty and disgusting city of the Caliph, he became aware that Gordon Lord was riding beside him with a black banner in one hand and some broken pieces of horse's reins in the other.

"Bravo! You've got it, then?" said the Colonel.

"Yes, sir," said Gordon, very sadly, and the Colonel saw that there were tears in the boy's eyes.

"What's amiss?" he said, and, looking round, "Where's Ali?"

Then Gordon told him what had happened. They had captured the dervish and compelled him to give up his spear and rifle, but just as Ali was leading the man into the English lines the demon had drawn a knife and treacherously stabbed him in the back. The boy choked with sobs while he delivered his comrade's last message: "Say good-bye to the Colonel, and tell him Ali Awad was not a coward. I didn't let go the Baggara's horse until he stuck me, and then he had to cut the reins to get away. Show the bits of the bridle to my Colonel and tell him I died faithful. Say my salaams to him, Charlie. I knew Charlie Gordon Lord would stay with me to the end."

The Colonel was quite broken down, but he only said, "This is no time for crying, my boy," and a moment afterward, "What became of the dervish?" Then, for the first time, the fighting devil flashed out of Gordon's eyes, and he answered:

"I killed him like a dog, sir."

It was the black flag of the Caliph himself which Gordon had taken, and when the Commander-in-Chief sent home his despatch he mentioned the name of the young soldier who had captured it.

From that day onward for fifteen years honours fell thick on Gordon Lord. Being continually on active service, and generally in staff appointments, promotions came quick, so that when he went to South Africa, the graveyard of so many military reputations, in those first dark days of the nation's deep humiliation, when the very foundations of her army's renown seemed to be giving way, he was one of the young officers whose gallantry won back England's fame. Though hot-tempered, impetuous, and liable to frightful errors, he had the imagination of a soldier as well as the bravery that goes to the heart of a nation, so that when in due course, being now full colonel, he was appointed, though so young, Second-in-Command of the Army of Occupation in Cairo, no one was surprised.

All the same, he knew he owed his appointment to his father's influence, and he wrote to thank him and to say he was delighted to return to Cairo. Only at intervals had he heard from the Consul-General, and, though his admiration of his father knew no limit, and he thought him the greatest man in the world, he always felt there was a mist between them. Once, for a moment, had that mist seemed to be dispelled, when, on his coming of age, his father wrote a letter in which he said:

"You are twenty-one years of age, Gordon, and your mother and I have been recalling the incidents of the day on which you were born. I want to tell you that from this day forward I am no longer your father; I am your friend; perhaps the best friend you will ever have. Let nothing and no one come between us."

Gordon's joy on returning to Egypt was not greater than that of the Egyptians on receiving him. They were waiting in a crowd when he arrived at the railway station, a red sea of tarbooshes, over faces he remembered as the faces of boys, with the face of Hafiz, now a soldier like himself, beaming by his carriage window.

It was not good form for a British officer to fraternize with the Egyptians, but Gordon shook hands with everybody and walked down the platform with his arm round Hafiz's shoulders, while the others who had come toward him cried, "*Salaam*, brother!" and laughed like children.

By his own choice, and contrary to custom, quarters had

been found for him in the barracks on the bank of the Nile, and the old familiar scene from there made his heart leap and tremble. It was evening when at last he was left alone, and throwing the window wide he looked out on the river, which flowed like liquid gold in the sunset, with its silent boats, that looked like birds with outstretched wings, floating down without a ripple, and the violet blossom of the island on the other side spreading odours in the warm spring air.

He was watching the traffic on the bridge—the camels, the cameleers, the donkeys, the blue-shirted fellaheen, the women with tattooed chins and children astraddle on their shoulders, the water-carriers with their bodies twisted by their burdens, the Bedouins with their lean, lithe, swarthy forms and the rope round the head-shawls which descended to their shoulders—when he heard the toot of a motor-car and saw a white automobile threading its way through the crowd. The driver was a girl, and a scarf of white chiffon which she had bound about her head instead of a hat was flying back in the light breeze, leaving her face framed within, with big black eyes and a firm but lovely mouth.

An officer in general's uniform was sitting at the back of the car, but Gordon was conscious of the man's presence without actually seeing him, so much was he struck by the spirit of the girl, which suggested a proud strength and self-reliance, coupled with a certain high gaiety, full of energy and grace.

Gordon leaned out of his window to get a better look at her, and, quick as the glance was, he thought she looked up at him as the motor glided by. At the next instant she had gone, and it seemed to him that in one second, at one stride, the sun had gone, too.

That night he dined at the British Agency, but he did not stay late, thinking his father, who looked much older, seemed preoccupied, and his mother, who appeared to be more delicate than ever, was over-exciting herself; but early next morning he rode up to the Citadel to pay his respects to his General in command, and there a surprise awaited him. General Graves was ill and unable to see him, but his

daughter came to offer his apologies—and she was the driver
of the automobile.

The impression of strength and energy which the girl
had made on him the evening before was deepened by this
nearer view. She was fairly tall, and as she swung into
the room her graceful, round form seemed to be poised from
the hips. This particularly struck him, as he told himself
at that first moment that here was a girl who might be a
soldier, with the passionate daring and chivalry of women
like Joan of Arc and the Rani of Jhansi.

At the next moment he had forgotten all about that, and
under the caressing smile which broke from her face and
fascinated him, he was feeling as if for the first time in his
life he was alone with a young and beautiful woman. They
talked a long time, and he was startled by an unexpected
depth in her voice, while his own voice seemed to him to
have suddenly disappeared.

"You like the Egyptians, yes?" she asked.

"I love them," said Gordon. "And coming back here is
like coming home. In fact, it is coming home. I've never
been at home in England, and I love the desert, I love the
Nile, I love everything and everybody."

She laughed—a fresh, ringing laugh, that was one of
her great charms—and told him about herself and her female
friends—the Khediviah, who was so sweet, and the Princess
Nazimah, who was so amusing, and finally about the Sheikh
who for two years had been teaching her Arabic.

"I should have known you by your resemblance to your
mother," she said. "But you are like your father, too; and
then I saw you yesterday—passing the barracks, you remember."

"So you really did . . . I thought our eyes——"

His ridiculous voice was getting out of all control, so he
cleared his throat and got up to go, but the half smile that
parted her lips and brightened her beautiful eyes seemed to
say as plainly as words could speak, "Why leave so soon?"

He lingered as long as he dared, and when he took up
his cap and riding-whip she threw the same chiffon scarf
over her head and walked with him through the garden to

the gate. There they parted, and when, a little ashamed of himself, he held her soft, white hand somewhat too long and pressed it slightly he thought an answering pressure came back from her.

In three weeks they were engaged.

The General trembled when he heard what had happened, protested he was losing the only one he had in the world, asked what was to become of him when Helena had to go away with her husband, as a soldier's wife should, but finally concluded to go on half-pay and follow her, and then said to Gordon: "Speak to your father. If he is satisfied, so am I."

The Consul-General listened passively, standing with his back to the fireplace, and after a moment of silence he said:

"I've never believed in a man marrying for rank or wealth. If he has any real stuff in him he can do better than that. I didn't do it myself and I don't expect my son to do it. As for the girl, if she can do as well for her husband as she has done for her father, she'll be worth more to you than any title or any fortune. But see what your mother says. I'm busy. Good day!"

His mother said very little; she cried all the time he was telling her, but at last she told him there was not anybody else in the world she would give him up to except Helena, because Helena was gold—pure, pure gold.

Gordon was writing to Helena now:

"DEAREST HELENA: Dreadfully disappointed I cannot dine with you to-night, having to go to Alexandria to-morrow and finding it necessary to begin preparations immediately.

"You must really be a witch—your prediction proved to be exactly right—it *was* about the new Mahdi, the new prophet, my father wished to speak with me.

"The Governor thinks the man is making mischief, inciting the people to rebellion by preaching sedition; so, with the General's consent, I am to smash him without delay.

"Hafiz is to go with me to Alexandria, and, strangely enough, he tells me over the telephone that the new prophet, as far as he can learn, is not a firebrand at all; but I am just off to see his uncle, the Chancellor of the University, and he is to tell me everything about him.

"Therefore, think of me to-night as penned up in the thick atmosphere of El Azhar, *tête-à-tête* with some sallow-faced fossil with pock-marked cheeks perhaps, when I hoped to be in the fragrant freshness of the Citadel, looking into somebody's big, black eyes, you know.

"But really, my dear Nell, the way you know things without learning them is wonderful, and seems to indicate an error of Nature in not making you a diplomatist, which would have given you plenty of scope for your uncanny gift of second sight.

"On second thought, though, I prefer you as you are, and am not exactly dying to see you turned into a man.

"*Maa-es-Salamah!* I kiss your hand!

"GORDON.

"P.S.—Your father would get a letter from the Consul-General suggesting my task, but, of course, I must go up for his formal order, and you might tell him I expect to be at the Citadel about tea-time to-morrow, which will enable me to kill two birds with one stone, you know, and catch the evening train as well.

"Strange if it should turn out that this new Mahdi is a wholesome influence after all, and not a person one can conscientiously put down! I have always suspected that the old Mahdi was a good man at the beginning, an enemy created by our own errors and excesses. Is history repeating itself? I wonder! And, if so, what will the Consul-General say? I wonder! I wonder!"

Gordon was sealing and addressing his letter when his soldier servant brought in Hafiz, a bright young Egyptian officer, whose plump face seemed to be all smiles.

"Halloa! Here you are!" cried Gordon; and then, giving his letter to his servant, he said: "Citadel—General's house, you know. . . . And now, Hafiz, my boy, let's be off."

VII

El Azhar is a vast edifice that stands in the midst of the Arab quarter of Cairo like a fortress on an island rock, being surrounded by a tangled maze of narrow, dirty, unpaved streets, with a swarming population of Mohammedans of every race; and the Christian who crosses its rather forbidding portals feels that he has passed in an instant out of the twentieth century and a city of civilisation into scenes of Bible lands and the earliest years of recorded time.

It is a thousand years old and the central seat of Moslem learning, not for Egypt only, but for the whole of the kingdoms and principalities of the Mohammedan world, sending out from there the water of spiritual life that has kept the Moslem soul alive through centuries of persecution and pain.

As you approach its threshold a monotonous cadence comes out to you, the murmur of the mass of humanity within, and you feel like one who stands at the mouth of some great subterranean river whose waters have flowed with just that sound on just that spot since the old world itself was young.

It was not yet full sunset when the two young soldiers reached El Azhar, and after yellow slippers had been tied over their boots at the outer gate they entered the dim, bewildering place of vast courts and long corridors with low roofs supported by a forest of columns, and floors covered by a vast multitude of men and boys, who were squatting on the ground in knots and circles, all talking together, teachers and pupils, and many of them swaying rhythmically to and fro to a monotonous chanting of the Koran, whose verses they were learning by heart.

Picking their way through the classes on the floor, the young soldiers crossed an open quadrangle and ascended many flights of stairs until they reached the Chancellor's room in the highest roof, where the droning murmur in the courts below could be only faintly heard, and the clear voice of the muezzin struck level with their faces when he came out of a minaret near by and sent into the upper air, north, south, east, and west, his call to evening prayers.

They had hardly entered this silent room, with its thick carpets on which their slippered feet made no noise, when the Chancellor came to welcome them. He was a striking figure, type of the grave and dignified Oriental such as might have walked out of the days of the Prophet Samuel, with his venerable face, long white beard, high forehead, refined features, graceful robes, and very soft voice.

"Peace be on you!" they said.

"And on you, too! Welcome!" he said, and motioned them to sit on the divans that ran round the walls.

Then Hafiz explained the object of their visit—how Gordon was ordered to Alexandria to suppress the riots there, and if need be to arrest the preacher who was supposed to have provoked them.

"I have already told him," said Hafiz, "that so far as I know Ishmael Ameer is no firebrand, but hearing through the mouth of one of our own people that he is another Mahdi, threatening the rule of England in Egypt——"

"Oh, peace, my son," said the Chancellor, "Ishmael Ameer is no Mahdi. He claims no divinity."

"Then tell me, O Sheikh," said Gordon, "tell me what Ishmael Ameer is, that I may know what to do when it becomes my duty to deal with him."

Leisurely the Chancellor took snuff, leisurely he opened a folded handkerchief, dusted his nostrils, and then, in his soft voice, said:

"Ishmael Ameer is a Koranist—that is to say, one who takes the Koran as the basis of belief and keeps an open mind about tradition."

"I know," said Gordon. "We have people like that among Christians—people who take the Bible as the basis of faith and turn their backs on dogma."

"Ishmael Ameer reads the Koran by the spirit, not the letter."

"We have people like that, too—the letter killeth, you know, the spirit maketh alive."

"Ishmael Ameer thinks Islam should advance with advancing progress."

"There again we are with you, O Sheikh. We have people of the same kind in Christianity."

"Ishmael Ameer thinks slavery, the seclusion of women, divorce, and polygamy are as much opposed to the teaching of Mohammed as to the progress of society."

"Excellent! My father says the same thing. *Wallahi!* (I assure you.) Or rather, he holds that Islam can never take its place as the religion of great progressive nations until it rids itself of these evils."

"Ishmael Ameer thinks the corruptions of Islam are the work of the partisans of the old barbaric ideas who are associating the cause of religion with their own interests and passions."

"Splendid! Do you know the Consul-General is always saying that, sir?"

"Ishmael Ameer believes that, if God wills it—praise be to be Him, the Exalted One!—the day is not distant when an appeal to the Prophet's own words will regenerate Islam, and banish the caliphs and sultans whose selfishness and sensuality keep it in bondage to the powers of darkness."

"Really," said Gordon, rising impetuously to his feet, "if Ishmael Ameer says this, he is the man Egypt, India— the whole Mohammedan world—is waiting for. No wonder men like the Cadi are trying to destroy him, though that's only an instinct of self-preservation—but my father, the Consul-General . . . What is there in all this to create . . . Why should such teaching set Moslem against Christian?"

"Ishmael Ameer, oh, my brother," the Chancellor continued, with the same soft voice, "thinks Islam is not the only faith that has departed from the spirit of its founder."

"True!"

"If Islam for its handmaidens has divorce and polygamy, Christianity has drunkenness and prostitution."

"No doubt; certainly."

"Coming out of the East, out of the desert, Ishmael Ameer sees in the Christianity of the West a contradiction

of every principle for which your great Master fought and
suffered."

Gordon sat down again.

"His was a religion of peace, but while your Christian
Church prays for unity and concord among the nations,
your Christian States are daily increasing the instruments
of destruction. His was a religion of poverty, but while
your Christian priests are saying, 'Blessed are the meek,'
your Christian communities are struggling for wealth and
trampling upon the poor in their efforts to gain it. Ishmael Ameer believes that if your great Master came back
now he would not recognise in the civilisation known by
his name the true posterity of the little, faithful church
he founded on the shores of the Lake of Galilee."

"All this is true—too true," said Gordon; "yet under
all that . . . doesn't Ishmael Ameer see that under all
that . . ."

"Ishmael Ameer sees," said the Chancellor, "that the
thing known to the world as Christian civilisation is little
better than an organised hypocrisy, a lust of empire in nations, and a greed of gold in men, destroying liberty, morality, and truth. Therefore he warns his followers against
a civilisation which comes to the East with religion in one
hand and violence and avarice in the other."

"But surely he sees," said Gordon, "what Christian
civilisation has done for the world, what science has done
for progress, what England, for example, has done for
Egypt?"

"Ishmael Ameer thinks," replied the Chancellor in the
same slow, soft voice, "that the essential qualities of national greatness are moral, not material; that man does not
live by bread alone; that it is of little value to Egypt if her
barns are full, if the hearts of her children are empty; that
Egypt can afford to be patient, for she is old and eternal;
that many are the events which have passed before the eyes
of the crouching Sphinx; that the life of man is three score
and ten years, but when Egypt reviews her past she looks
back on three score and ten centuries."

There was silence for a moment, during which the muezzin's voice was heard again, calling the first hour of night, and then Gordon, visibly agitated, said:

"You think Ishmael Ameer a regenerator, a reformer, a redeemer of Islam; and if his preaching prevailed it would send the Grand Cadi back to his Sultan—isn't that so?" But the Chancellor made no reply.

"It would also send England out of Egypt—wouldn't it?" said Gordon, but still the Chancellor gave no sign.

"It would go farther than that, perhaps; it would drive Western civilisation out of the East—wouldn't that be the end of it?" said Gordon, and then the Chancellor replied:

"It would drive a corrupt and ungodly civilisation out of the world, my son."

"I see," said Gordon. "You think the mission of Ishmael Ameer transcends Egypt, transcends even Europe, and says to humanity in general, 'What you call civilisation is killing religion, because the nations—Christian and Moslem alike—have sold themselves to the lust of empire and the greed of gold.' Isn't that what you mean?"

The Chancellor bowed his gray head and, in a scarcely audible voice, said, "Yes."

"You think, too," said Gordon, whose breathing was now quick and loud, "that Ishmael Ameer is an apostle of the soul of Islam—perhaps of the soul of religion itself, without respect of creed; one of the great men who come once in a hundred years to call the world back from a squalid and sordid materialism, and are ready to live—aye, and to die, for their faith—the Savonarolas, the Luthers, the Gamal-ed-Deens—perhaps the Mohammeds, and "—dropping his voice —"in a sense, the Christs?"

But the Egyptian soul, like the mirage of the Egyptian desert, recedes as it is approached, and again the Chancellor made no reply.

"Tell me, O Sheikh," said Gordon, rising to go, "if Ishmael Ameer came to Cairo, would you permit him to preach in El Azhar?"

"He is an alim (a doctor of the Koran); I could not prevent him."

"But would you lodge him in your own house?"

" Yes."

" That is enough for me. Now I must go to Alexandria
and see him for myself."

" May God guide you, oh, my son," said the Chancellor,
and a moment afterward his soft voice was saying farewell
to the two young soldiers at the door.

" Let us walk back to barracks, Hafiz," said Gordon.
" My head aches a little, somehow."

VIII

IT was night by this time, the courts and corridors of
El Azhar were empty, and even the tangled streets outside were less loud than before with the guttural cries of a
swarming population; but a rumbling murmur came from
the mosque of the University, and the young soldiers stood
a moment at the door to look in. There, under a multitude of tiny lanterns, stood long rows of men in stocking
feet and Eastern costume, rising and kneeling in unison,
at one moment erect and at the next with foreheads to the
floor, while the voice of the Iman echoed in the arches of
the mosque and the voices of the people answered him.

Then, through narrow alleys full of life, lit only by
the faint gleam of uncovered candles, with native women,
black-robed and veiled, passing like shadows through a
moving crowd of men, the young soldiers came to the quarter of Cairo that is nicknamed the " Fish Market," where
the streets are brilliantly lighted up, where the names over
the shops are English and French, Greek and Italian, and
where girls with painted faces lean out of the windows of
upper stories and smile down at men who sit at tables in
front of the *cafés* opposite, drinking wine, smoking cigarettes, and playing dominoes. The sound of music and
dancing came from the open windows behind the girls, who
glittered with gold brocade and diamonds, and among the
men were young Egyptians in the tarboosh and British soldiers in khaki, who looked up at the women in the flare of
the coarse light and laughed.

At the gate of the Kasr el Nil barracks the young men parted.

"Tell me, Hafiz," said Gordon, "if a soldier is ordered to act in a way he believes to be wrong, what is he to do?"

"His duty, I suppose," said Hafiz.

"His duty to what—his commander or his conscience?"

"If a soldier is under orders I suppose he has no conscience."

"I wonder!" said Gordon, and, promising to write to Hafiz in the morning, he went up to his quarters.

The room was in darkness, save for the moonlight with its gleam of mellow gold, which seemed to vibrate from the river outside, and Gordon stood by the window with a dull sense of headache, looking at the old Nile, that had seen so many acts in the drama of humanity and still flowed so silently, until he became conscious of a perfume he knew, and then, switching on the light, he found a letter in a scented envelope lying on his desk. It was from Helena, and it was written in her bold, upright hand, with the gay raillery, the passionate tenderness, and the fierce earnestness which he recognised as her chief characteristics:

"MISTER, most glorious and respected, the illustrious Colonel Lord, owner of Serenity and Virtue, otherwise my dear old Gordon:

"It was wrong of you not to come to dinner, for though father over-excited himself at Ghezirah to-day and I have had to pack him off to bed, I made every preparation to receive you, and here I am in my best bib and tucker, wearing the crown of pink blossom which my own particular Sultan says suits my gipsy hair, and nobody to admire it but my poor little black boy, Mosie—who is falling in love with me, I may tell you, and is looking at me now with his scrubby face all blubbered up like a sentimental hippopotamus.

"I am not surprised that the Consul-General talked about the new 'holy man,' and I do not wonder that he ordered you to arrest him, but I am at a loss to know why you should take counsel with that old fossil at El Azhar, and you can tell Master Hafiz I mean to dust his jacket for suggesting it, knowing your silly old heart is like wax and they have only to recite something out of the 'noble Koran,' and you'll be as weak as—well, as a woman.

"As for holy men generally, I agree with the Princess that they are holy humbugs, which is the title I would give to a good many of the *genus* at home as well as here. So I say with your namesake of glorious memory (who wasn't an ogre, goodness knows), *Smash the Mahdi!*

"A thousand to one he is some ugly, cross-eyed old fanatic who would destroy every germ of civilisation in Egypt and carry the country back to barbarity and ruin, so I say again, *Smash the Mahdi!*

"As for your 'conscience,' I cry, marry-come-up, by what right does it push its nose where it isn't wanted, seeing it is the conscience of the Consul-General that will be damned if the work is wrong and wicked, and there won't be so much as a plum of Paradise for yours if it is right and good, so once again I say, *Smash the Mahdi!*

"Moreover, and furthermore, and by these presents, I rede ye beware of resisting the will of your father; for if you do, as sure as I'm a 'witch,' and 'know things without learning them,' I have a 'mystic sense' there will be trouble; and nobody can say where it will end, or how many of us may be involved in it. So again, and yet again, I say, *Smash the Mahdi!*

"The Consul-General's letter has come, but I shall not read it to father until morning; and meantime, if I ever pass through your imagination, think of me as poor Ruth sitting on the threshing-floor with Boaz and dreaming of Zion—that is to say, of stuffy old El Azhar, where somebody who ought to know better is now talking to an old frump in petticoats instead of to me.

"*Inshallah!* The slave of your Virtues.

"HELENA.

"P.S.—Dying for to-morrow afternoon, dear.
"P.P.S.—IMPORTANT—*Smash the Mahdi!*"

IX

HELENA GRAVES was everything to her father, for the General's marriage had been unhappy and it had come to a tragic end. His wife, the daughter of a Jewish merchant in Madras, had been a woman of strong character and great beauty but of little principle, and they had been married while he was serving as senior major with a battalion of his regiment in India, and there Helena, their only child, had been born.

Things had gone tolerably between them until the major returned to England as lieutenant-colonel commanding the battalion of his regiment at home, and then, in their little military town, they had met and become intimate with the Lord-Lieutenant of the county, a nobleman, a bachelor, a sportsman, a breeder of race-horses, and a member of the Government.

The end of that intimacy had been a violent scene, in which the husband, in his ungovernable rage, had flung the nobleman on the ground and trampled on him, torn the jewels out of his wife's breast and crushed them under his heel, and then, realising the bankruptcy his life had come to, had gone home and had brain-fever.

Helena, like her father, was passionate and impetuous, and her mother had neglected and never really loved her. With the keen eyes of a child who is supposed to see nothing, she had seen from the first what was going on at home, and all her soul had risen against her mother and her mother's lover with a hatred which no presents could appease. Being now a girl of eighteen, well grown and developed, and seeing with what treachery and cruelty her father had been stricken down, her heart went out to him, and she became a woman in one day.

When the brain-fever was gone the General, weak both in body and mind, was ordered rest and change. Somebody suggested the Lake country, as his native air, so Helena, who did everything for him, took him to a furnished cottage in Grasmere, a sweet place bowered in roses, with its face to the sedgy lake, and with the beautiful river, the Rotha, laughing and babbling by the garden at the back.

There he recovered bodily strength, but it was long before his mind returned to him, and meantime he had strange delusions. Something, perhaps, in the place of their retreat brought ghosts of the past out of a world of shadows, for he thought he was a boy again and Helena was his mother, who was thirty years dead and buried in the little churchyard lower down the stream, where the Rotha was deep and flowed with a solemn hush.

Helena played up to his pathetic delusion, took the tender endearments that were meant for the grandmother she had never known, and as his young days came to the surface with the beautiful persistence of old memories in the human mind she fell in with them as if they had been her own. Thus on Sunday morning, when the bells rang, she would walk with him to church, holding his hand in her hand as if she were the mother and he the child.

It was very sweet to look upon, for in the sleep of the General's brain he was very happy, and only to those who saw that the brave girl, with her eyes of light and her lips of dew, was giving away her youth to her old father, was it charged with feeling too deep for tears.

But at length the stricken man came out of the twilight land and his dream faded away. Helena had to play their little American organ every evening that he might sing a hymn to it, for that was what his mother had always done when she was putting her boy to bed and thinking, like a soldier's wife, of his father who was away at the wars. It was always the same hymn, and one breathless evening, when the sun had gone down and the vale was still, they had come to:

"Hide me, O my Saviour, hide,
    Till the storms of life be past—"

and then his voice stopped suddenly, and he shaded his eyes as if something were blinding them.

At that moment the past which had been dead so long

seemed to rise from its grave with all its mournful incidents—his wife and his shattered home—and Helena was
not his mother but his daughter, and he was not a happy
boy but an old soldier with a broken life behind him.

Seeing by the look in his eyes that he was coming to
himself, Helena tried to comfort him, and when he gasped,
"Who is it?" she answered, in a voice she tried to render
cheerful. "It is I; it is Helena. Don't you know me,
father?" And then the years rolled back upon him like a
flood and he sobbed on her shoulder.

The awakening had been painful, but it was not all
pain. If he had lost a wife he had gained a daughter, and
she was the strongest, stanchest creature in the world. For
her sake he must begin again. Having had so much shadow
in her young life she must now have sunshine. Thus Helena became her father's idol, the one thing on earth to
him, and he was more to her than a father usually is to a
daughter, because she had seen him in his weakness and
mothered him back to strength.

Two years after the breakdown they were in London,
and there Helena met Lord Nuneham on one of his few
visits to England. The great Proconsul, who had heard what
she had done, was most favourably impressed by her, and as
she talked to him he said to himself, "This girl has the
blood of the great women of the Bible, the Deborahs who
were mothers in Israel, aye, and the Jaels who revenged
her." At that time the post of Major-General to the British Army in Egypt was shortly to become vacant, and by
Lord Nuneham's influence it was offered to Graves. Six
months later father and daughter arrived in Cairo.

It had been an exciting time, but Helena had managed
everything, and the General had borne up manfully until
they took possession of the house assigned to them, a reno-
vated old palace on the edge of the Citadel. Then in a
moment he had collapsed and fallen from his chair to the
floor. Helena had lifted him in her strong arms, laid him
on the couch, and sent his aide-de-camp for the medical
officer in charge.

Consciousness came back quickly, and Helena laughed

through the tears that had gathered in her great eyes, but the Surgeon continued to look grave.

"Has the General ever had attacks like this before?" he asked.

"Never that I know of," said Helena.

"He must be kept quiet. I'll see him in the morning."

Next day the medical officer had no doubts of his diagnosis—heart disease, quite unmistakably. The news had to be broken to the General, and he bore it bravely, but, thinking of Helena, he made one request—that nothing should be said on the subject. If the fact were known at the War Office he might be retired, and there could be no necessity for that until the Army was put on active service.

"But isn't the Army always on active service in Egypt, sir?" said the Surgeon.

"Technically, perhaps—not really," said the General. "In any case, I'm not afraid, and I ask you to keep the matter quiet."

"As you please, sir."

"You and I and Helena must be the only ones to know anything about it."

"Very well, but you must promise to take care. Any undue excitement, any over-exertion, any outburst of anger even——"

"It shall not occur; I give you my word for it," said the General.

But it had occurred, not once but frequently, during the twelve months following. It occurred after Gordon asked for Helena, and again last night, the moment the General reached his bedroom on his return from the Khedivial Club.

He was better next morning, and then Helena took up the letter from Lord Nuneham. "Read it," said the General, and Helena read:

"DEAR GENERAL: Gordon is here, and I will send him up to tell you what I think it necessary tb do in order to put an end to the riots at Alexandria and make an example of the ringleaders.

"The chief of them is the Arab preacher, Ishmael Ameer, and I propose that we bring him up to Cairo immediately, try him by special tribunal, and despatch him without delay to our new penal settlement in the Soudan.

"For that purpose (as the local police are chiefly nåtive, and therefore scarcely reliable, and your colonel on the spot might hesitate to act on his own initiative in the possible event of a rising of the man's Moslem followers) I propose that you send some one from Cairo to take command, and therefore suggest Gordon, your first staff officer, and the most proper person (always excepting yourself) to deal with a situation of such gravity.

"Yours in haste,

"NUNEHAM."

While Helena was reading the letter the General could hardly restrain his excitement.

"Just as I thought!" he said. "I knew the Consul-General would put down that new Mahdi. Wonderful man, Nuneham! And what a chance for Gordon! By Gad, he'll have all Europe talking about him. He deserves it, though. Ask the staff. Ask the officers. Ask the men. I see what Nuneham's aiming at—making Gordon his successor! Well why not? Why not Gordon Lord, the Consul-General? I ask, why not? Good for Egypt and good for England, too. Am I wrong?"

Then, remembering to whom he was addressing these imperative challenges, he laughed and said: "Ah, of course! I congratulate you, my child! I'll live to see you proud and happy yet, Helena. Now go—I'm going to get up."

And when Helena warned him that he was over-exciting himself again, he said: "Not a bit of it. I'm all right now; but I must write to Alexandria immediately and see Gordon at once. Coming up this afternoon, you say? That will do. Splendid fellow! Fine as his father! Father and son—both splendid!"

X

WHEN Gordon reached the General's house at five o'clock that day there was for a while a clash of opposing wills. Thinking of Helena's peremptory advice, *Smash the Mahdi!* he was determined to tell her what the Chancellor of El Azhar had said of Ishmael Ameer, and she was resolved that he should say nothing about him. So, while Gordon stood by the shaded window, looking down on the city below, which still lay hot under the sun's fierce eye, Helena talked of his mother, her father, and of the Princess Nazimah, who had invited her, in a funny letter, to join the ladies' council for the emancipation of Egyptian women and the abolition of polygamy, saying, among other things, "The needle carries but one thread, my dear, and the heart cannot carry two." But at length she said:

"When do you leave for Alexandria?"

"To-night at half-past six. My servant is to take my bag to the railway station, and Hafiz and two other Moslems are to meet me there."

"Good gracious! No time to lose, then. Mosie!" she cried, and a small black boy with large, limpid eyes, wearing a scarlet caftan and blue waistband, came into the room.

"Tea, Mosie, quick! Tell the cook the Colonel has to catch a train."

The black boy kissed her hand and went bounding out, whereupon she talked again to prevent Gordon from talking.

"Didn't I tell you that boy was falling in love with me? I found him fighting in the market-place. That was a week ago, since when he has adopted me, and now he is always kissing my hand or the hem of my gown, as who would say—'I have none but her, and I love her like my eyes.' A most dear little human dog, and I do believe—yes, I really do believe—if I wished it he would go to his death for me."

Gordon, who was gloomy and dejected, and had been

drumming on the window-pane without listening, then said:

"Helena, can you imagine what it is to a soldier to feel that he is on the wrong side in battle? If he is to fight well he ought to feel that he is fighting for his country, his flag, and—justice. But when the position is the reverse of that; when, for example——"

But at that moment the General came into the room and welcomed Gordon with a shout.

"Just been writing to Alexandria telling Jenkinson to keep a force in readiness for you night and day," he said. "Only way, my boy! Force is the one thing the Easterns understand. Of course, we don't want bloodshed, but if these rascals are telling the people that the power is not in our hands, or that England will not allow us to use it, we must let them see—we can't help it. Glorious commission, Gordon! I congratulate you! My job, though, and there's only one man I could give it up to—only one man in the world."

And then Gordon, who had been biting his underlip, said, "I almost wish you could do it yourself, General."

"Why, what the deuce——"

"Gordon has been taking counsel with the Chancellor of El Azhar," said Helena, "and the old silly seems to have given him 'the eye,' or talked nonsense out of the noble Koran."

"Not nonsense, Helena, and not out of the Koran, but out of the book of life itself," said Gordon, and after the black boy had brought in the tea he told them what the Chancellor had said.

"So you see," he said, "the preaching of this new prophet has nothing to do with England in Egypt—nothing more, at least, than with England in India, or South Africa, or even Canada itself. It transcends all that, and is teaching for the world, for humanity. Isn't it true, too? Take what he says about the lust of empire, and look at the conduct of the Christian countries. They are praying in their churches 'that it may please Thee to give to all nations unity, peace, and concord,' yet they are increasing

their armaments every day, what for—defence? Certainly!
But what does that mean?—fear of aggression. So while in
our Kings' speeches and our Presidents' messages, in our
newspapers and even in our pulpits we keep up the pretence
that we are at peace with the world, we are always, according
to the devil's code of honour, preparing for the time when
two high-spirited nations may find it convenient to fly at
each other's throats. Peace with the world! Lies, sir; all
lies, and barefaced hypocrisy! The nations never are at
peace with the world, never have been, never want to be."

The General tried to protest, but Gordon, who was now
excited, said:

"Oh, I know—I'm a soldier, too, sir, and I don't want to
see my country walked upon. It may be all right, all necessary to the game of empire, but, for Heaven's sake, let
us call it by its proper name—Conquest, not Christianity
—and put away the cant and quackery of being Christian
countries."

Again the General tried to protest, but Gordon did not
hear.

"Think of it! Kaisers and Kings and Presidents asking
God's blessing on their Ministers of War! Bishops and
Archbishops praying for more battleships! Christians?
Followers of Christ? Why, in the name of God, do they not
tear the scales from their eyes and stand revealed to them-
selves as good, upright, honest, honourable Pagans, bent on
the re-paganisation of the world and the destruction of
Christian civilisation? I'm a soldier, yes, but I hope to
Heaven I'm not a hypocrite, and show me the soldier worth
his salt who is not at heart a man of peace."

The General's face was growing scarlet, but Gordon saw
nothing of that.

"Then take what this new preacher says about the greed
of wealth—isn't that true, too? We pretend to believe that
'it is easier for a camel to go through the eye of a needle
than for a rich man to enter into the Kingdom of God,' yet
we are nearly all trying, struggling, fighting, scrambling to
be rich."

He laughed out loud and then said:

"Look at America—I'm half an American myself, sir, so I've a right to say it—where a man may become a millionaire by crushing out everybody else and appropriating the gifts of nature which God meant for humanity. But America is a Christian country, too, and its richest men build, of their abundance, churches in which to glorify the widow's mite! Is the man to be silenced who warns the world that such sordid and squalid materialism is swallowing up religion, morality, and truth? Such a man may be the very soul of a country, yet what do we do with him? We hang him, or stone him, or crucify him—that's what we do with him, sir."

Gordon, who had been walking up and down the room and talking in an intense and poignant voice, stopped suddenly and said:

"General, did you ever reflect upon the way in which Jesus Christ was brought to his death?"

"Good gracious, man, what has that subject to do with this?" said the General.

"A good deal, I think, sir. Did you ever ask yourself who it was that betrayed Jesus?"

"Judas Iscariot, I suppose."

"No, sir; Judas was only the cat's-paw, scorned through all the ages and burnt in a million effigies, but nearly as innocent of the death of his Master as you or I. The real betrayer was the high priest of the Jews. He was the head of the bad system which Christ came to wipe out, and he saw that if he did not destroy Jesus, Jesus would destroy him. What did he do? He went to the Governor, the Consul-General of the Roman Occupation, and said: 'This man is setting himself up against Cæsar. If you let him go you are not Cæsar's friend.'"

"Well?"

"That's what the High Priest of Islam is doing in Egypt now. As I was going into the Agency yesterday I met the Grand Cadi coming out. You know what he is, sir—the most fanatical supporter of the old dark ways—slavery, divorce, polygamy, all the refuse of bad Mohammedanism?"

"Well, well?"

"Well, my father told me the Grand Cadi had said, 'If you let Ishmael Ameer go on it will be death to the rule of England in Egypt.'"

"And what does it all come to?"

"It comes to this, sir—that if the Chancellor of El Azhar has told me the truth—*if*, I say, *if*—when we take Ishmael Ameer, and shut him up in prison for life with nothing but a desert around him, we shall be doing something that bears an ugly resemblance to what the Romans did in Palestine."

Then the General, who had not once taken his eyes off Gordon, rose in visible agitation and said:

"Gordon Lord, you astonish me! If what you say means anything, it means that this man Ishmael is not only preaching sedition, but is justified in doing so. That's what you mean? Am I wrong?"

In his excitement he spoke so rapidly that he stammered, and Helena cried, "Father!"

"Leave me alone, Helena. I'm calm; but when a man talks of . . . When you talk of conquest you mean England in Egypt—yes, you do—and you refuse to see that we have to hold high the honour of our country, and to protect our dominions in the East."

His voice sounded choked, but he went on:

"More than that, when you compare our Lord's trial and death with that of this—this half-educated Arab out of the desert—this religious Don Quixote who is a menace, not only to government but to the very structure of civilised society—it's shocking, it's blasphemous, and I will not listen to it."

The General was going out in white anger when he stopped at the door and said:

"Gordon Lord, I take leave to think this man an impostor—a scheming impostor, and if you want my view of how to deal with him, and with the credulous simpletons who are turning sedition into crime and crime into bloody anarchy, I give it to you—martial law, sir, and no damned nonsense!"

Save for one word, Helena had not yet spoken, but now with tightly compressed lips, and such an expression on her face as Gordon had never before seen there, she said:

"I hate that man! I hate him! I hate him!"

Her eyes blazed and she looked straight into Gordon's face, as she said: "I hate him because you are allowing yourself to be influenced in his favour against your own father and your own country. An Englishman's duty is to stand by England, whatever she is and whatever she does. And the duty of an English soldier is to fight for her and ask no questions. She is his mother, and to inquire of himself whether she is right or wrong, when her enemies are upon her, is not worthy of a son."

The colour rushed to Gordon's face and he dropped his head.

"As for this man's teaching, it may transcend Egypt, but it includes it, and these people will take out of it only what they want, and what they want is an excuse to resist authority and turn their best friends out of the country. As for you," she said, with new force, "your duty is to go to Alexandria and bring this man back to Cairo. It begins and ends there, and has nothing to do with anything else."

Then Gordon raised his head and answered: "You are right, Helena. You are always right. A son is not the judge of his father. And where would England be to-day if her soldiers had always asked themselves whether she was in the right or the wrong? I thought England would be sinning against the light if she sent Ishmael Ameer to the Soudan and so stifled a voice that might be the soul of the East; but I know nothing about him except what his friends have told me. . . . After all, grapes don't grow on pine trees, and the only fruit we see is . . . I'll see the man for myself, Helena, and if I find he is encouraging the rioters . . . if even in his sermons in the mosques . . . Hafiz and the Moslems are to tell me what he says in them. . . . They must tell me the truth, though . . . Whatever the consequences . . . they must tell me the truth. They shall—my God, they *must!*"

XI

THE clock struck six, and Gordon rose to go. Helena
helped him to belt up the sword he had taken off and to
put on his military great-coat. Then she threw a lace
scarf over her head and went out with him into the garden,
that they might bid good-bye at the gate.

The sun was going down by this time, the odourless air
of the desert was cooler and fresher than before, and all
Nature was full of a soothing and blissful peace.

"Don't go yet; you have a few minutes to spare still.
Come," said Helena, and taking his hand she drew him to a
blossom-thatched arbour which stood on the edge of the
ramparts.

There, with the red glow on their faces as on the face
of the great mosque which stood in conscious grandeur by
their side, they looked out in silence for some moments on
the glittering city, the gleaming Nile, the yellow desert, and
all the glory of the sky.

It was just that mysterious moment between day and
night when the earth seems to sing a silent song which
only the human heart can hear, and, stirred by an emotion
she could scarcely understand, Helena, who had been so
brave until now, began to tremble and break down, and the
woman in her to appear.

"Don't think me foolish," she said, "but I feel—I feel
as if—as if this were the last time you and I were to be
together."

"Don't unman me, Helena," said Gordon. "The work
I have to do in Alexandria may be dangerous, but don't
tell me you are afraid——"

"It isn't that. I shouldn't be fit to be a soldier's daughter or to become—to become a soldier's wife if I were afraid
of that. No, I'm not afraid of that, Gordon. I shall never
allow myself to be afraid of that, but——"

"But what, Helena?"

"I feel as if something has broken between you and me,
and we shall never be the same to each other after to-night.

It frightens me. You are so near, yet you seem so far away. Coming out of the house a moment ago I felt as if I had to take farewell of you, here and now."

Without more ado Gordon took her firmly in his arms, and with one hand on her forehead that he might look full in her face, he said:

"You are not angry with me, Helena, for what I said to your father just now?"

"No, oh, no. You were speaking out of your heart, and perhaps it was partly that——"

"You didn't agree with me, I know that quite well, but you love me still, Helena?"

"Don't ask me that, dear."

"I must; I am going away, so speak out, I entreat you. You love me still, Helena?"

"I am here. Isn't that enough?" she said, putting her arms about his neck and laying her head on his breast.

He kissed her, and there was silence for some moments more. Then in a sharp, agitated whisper she said:

"Gordon, that man is coming between us."

"Ishmael Ameer?"

"Yes."

"What utter absurdity, Helena!"

"No, I'm telling you the truth. That man is coming between us. I know it—I feel it—something is speaking to me—warning me. Listen! Last night I saw it in a dream. I cannot remember what happened, but he was there, and you and I, and your father and mine, and then——"

"My dear Nell, how foolish! But I see what has happened. When did you receive the Princess Nazimah's letter?"

"Last night—just before going to bed."

"Exactly! And you were brooding over what she said of the needle carrying only one thread?"

"I was thinking of it—yes."

"You were also thinking of what you had said yourself in your letter to me—that if I resisted my father's will the results might be serious for all of us?"

"That, too, perhaps."

"There you are, then—there's the stuff of your dream, dear. But don't you see that whatever a man's opinions and sympathies may be, his affections are a different matter altogether—that love is above everything else in a man's life—yes, everything—and that even if this Ishmael Ameer were to divide me from my father or from your father— which God forbid!—he could not possibly separate me from you?"

She looked up into his eyes and said—there was a smile on her lips now—"Could nothing separate you and me?"

"Nothing in this world," he answered.

Her trembling lips fluttered up to his, and again there was a moment of silence. The sun had gone down, the stars had begun to appear, and under the mellow gold of mingled night and day the city below, lying in the midst of the desert, looked like a great jewel on the soft bosom of the world.

"You must go now, dear," she whispered.

"And you will promise me never to think these ugly thoughts again?"

"'Love is above everything.' I shall only think of that. Good-bye!"

"Good-bye!" he said, and he embraced her passionately. At the next moment he was gone.

Shadows from the wing of night had gathered over the city by this time, and there came up from the heart of it a surge of indistinguishable voices, some faint and far away, some near and loud, the voices of the muezzins calling from a thousand minarets to evening prayers—and then came another voice from the glistening crest of the great mosque on the ramparts, clear as a clarion and winging its way through the upper air over the darkening mass below:

"God is Most Great! God is Most Great!"

AL - LA - HU AK - BAR.   AL - LA . . HU AK - BAR.

XII

AT half-past six Gordon was at the railway-station. He found his soldier-servant halfway down the platform, on which blue-shirted porters bustled to and fro, holding open the door of a compartment labelled " Reserved." He found Hafiz, also, and with him were two pale-faced Egyptians, in the dress of Sheikhs, who touched their foreheads as Gordon approached.

"These are the men you asked for," said Hafiz.

Gordon shook hands with the Egyptians, and then, standing between them, with one firm hand on the shoulder of each and the light of an electric arc lamp in their faces, he said:

"You know what you've got to do, brothers?"

"We know," the men answered.

"The future of Egypt, perhaps of the East, may depend upon what you tell me—you will tell me the truth?"

"We will tell you the truth, Colonel."

"If the man we are going to see should be condemned on your report and on my denunciation, you may suffer at the hands of his followers. Protect you as I please, you may be discovered, followed, tracked down—you have no fear of the consequences?"

"We have no fear, sir."

"You are prepared to follow me into any danger?"

"Into any danger."

"To death, if need be?"

"To death, if need be, brother."

"Step in, then," said Gordon.

At the next moment there was the whistle of the locomotive, and then, slowly, rhythmically, with its heavy, volcanic throb shaking the platform and rumbling in the glass roof, the train moved out of the station on its way to Alexandria.

XIII

ISHMAEL AMEER was the son of a Libyan carpenter and boat builder, who, shortly before the days of the Mahdi, had removed with his family to Khartoum. His earliest memory was of the solitary figure of the great white pasha on the roof of the palace, looking up the Nile for the relief army that never arrived, and of the same white-headed Englishman, with the pale face, who, walking to and fro on the sands outside the palace garden, patted his head and smiled.

His next memory was of the morning after the fall of the desert city, when, awakened by the melancholy moan of the great onbeya, the elephant's horn that was the trumpet of death, he heard the hellish shrieks of the massacre that was going on in the streets, and saw his mother lying dead in front of the door of the inner closet in which she had hidden her child, and found his father's body on the outer threshold.

He was seven years of age at this time, and being adopted by an uncle, a merchant in the town, who had been rich enough to buy his own life, he was sent in due course first to the little school of the mosque in Khartoum, and afterward, at eighteen, to El Azhar, in Cairo, where, with other poor students, he slept in the stifling rooms under the flat roof, and lived on the hard bread and the jars of cheese and butter which were sent to him from home.

Within four years he had passed the highest examination at the Arabic University, taking the rank of alim (doctor of Koranic divinity), which entitled him to teach and preach in any quarter of the Mohammedan world, and then, equally by reason of his rich voice and his devout mind, he was made Reader in the mosque of El Azhar.

Morality was low among the governing classes at that period, and when it occurred that the Grand Cadi, who was a compound of the Eastern voluptuary and the libertine of the Parisian boulevards, marrying for the fourth time, made a feast that went on for a week, in which the days were spent in eating and drinking and the nights in carousing of an unsaintly character, the orgy so shocked the young alim from the desert that he went down to the great man's house to protest.

"How is this, your Eminence?" he said, stoutly. "The Koran teaches temperance, chastity, and contempt of the things of the world—yet you, who are a tower and a light in Islam, have darkened our faces before the infidel."

So daring an outrage on the authority of the Cadi had never been committed before, and Ishmael was promptly flung into the streets; but the matter made some noise and led, in the end, to the expulsion of all the governors (the Ulema) of the University except the one man who, being the first cause of the scandal, was also the representative of the Sultan, and therefore could not be charged.

Meantime Ishmael, returning no more to El Azhar, had settled himself on an island far up the river, and there, practising extreme austerities, he gathered a great reputation for holiness, and attracted attention throughout the valley of the Nile by breathing out threatenings and slaughter—not so much against the leaders of his own people, who were degrading Islam, as against the Christians under whose hated bondage, as he believed, the whole Mohammedan world was going mad.

So wide was the appeal of Ishmael's impeachment, and so vast became his following, that the government (now Anglo-Egyptian), always sure that after sand-storms and sand-flies holy men of all sorts were the most pernicious products of the Soudan, thought it necessary to put him down, and for this purpose they sent two companies of Arab camel police, promising a reward to the one that should capture the new prophet.

The two camel corps set out on different tracks, but each resolving to take Ishmael by night, they entered his village at the same time by opposite ends, met in the darkness, and fought and destroyed one another, so that when morning dawned they saw their leaders on both sides lying dead in the crimsoning light.

The gruesome incident had the effect of the supernatural on the Arab intellect, and when Ishmael and his followers,

6

with nothing but a stick in one hand and the Koran in the other, came down with a roar of voices and the sand whirling in the wind, the native remnant turned tail and fled before the young prophet's face.

Then the Governor-General, an agnostic with a contempt for " mystic senses " of all kinds, sent a ruckling, swearing, unbelieving company of British infantry, and they took Ishmael without further trouble, brought him up to Khartoum, put him on trial for plotting against the Christian Governor of his province, and imprisoned him in a compound outside the town.

But soon the Government began to see that, though they had crushed Ishmael, they could not crush Ishmaelism, and they lent an ear to certain of the leaders of his own faith, judges of the Mohammedan law courts, who, having put their heads together, had devised a scheme to wean him from his asceticism, and so destroy the movement by destroying the man. The scheme was an old one, the wiles of a woman, and they knew the very woman for the purpose.

This was a girl named Adila, a Copt, only twenty years of age, and by no means a voluptuous creature, but a little, winsome thing, very sweet and feminine, always freshly clad and walking barefoot on the hot sand with an erect confidence that was beautiful to see.

Adila had been the daughter of a Christian merchant at Assouan, and there, six years before, she had been kidnapped by a Bisharin tribe, who, answering her tears with rough comfort, promised to make her a queen.

In their own way they did so, for, those being the dark days of Mahdism, they brought her to Omdurman and put her up to auction in the open slave-market, where the black eunuch of the Caliph, after thrusting his yellow fingers into her mouth to examine her teeth, bought her, among other girls, for his master's harem.

There, with forty women of varying ages, gathered by concupiscence from all quarters of the Soudan, she was mewed up in the close atmosphere of two sealed chambers in the Caliph's crudely gorgeous palace, seeing no more of her owner than his coffee-coloured countenance as he passed once a day through the curtained rooms, and signalled to one or other of their bedecked and beringleted occupants to follow him down a hidden stairway to his private quarters. At such moments of inspection Adila would sit trembling and breathless, in dread of being seen, and she found her companions only too happy to help her to hide herself from the attentions they were seeking for themselves.

This lasted nearly a year, and then came a day when the howling in the streets outside, the wailing of shells overhead, and the crashing of cannon-ball in the dome of the Mahdi's tomb, told the imprisoned women, who were creeping together in corners and clinging to each other in terror, that the English had come at last, and the Caliph had fallen and fled.

When Adila was set at liberty by the English Sirdar, she learned that, in grief at the loss of their daughter, her parents had died, and so, ashamed to return to Assouan, after being a slave-girl in Omdurman, she took service with a Greek widow who kept a bakery in Khartoum. It was there the Sheikhs of the law courts found her, and they proceeded to coax and flatter her, telling her she had been a good girl who had seen much sorrow, and therefore ought to know some happiness now, to which end they had found a husband to marry her, and he was a fine, handsome man, young and learned and rich.

At this, Adila, remembering the Caliph, and thinking that such a person as they pictured could only want her as the slave of his bed, turned sharply upon them and said, "When did I ask you to find me a man?" and the Sheikhs had to go back discomfited.

Meantime Ishmael, raving against the Christians, who were corrupting Mohammedans while he was lying helpless in his prison, fell into a fever, and the Greek mistress of Adila, hearing who had been meant for her handmaiden, and fearing the girl might think too much of herself, began to taunt and mock her.

"They told you he was rich, didn't they?" said the widow. "Well, he has no bread but what the Government gives him, and he is in chains and he is dying, and you would only have had to nurse him and bury him. That's all the husband you would have got, my girl, so perhaps you are better off where you are."

But the widow's taunting went wide, for as soon as Adila had heard her out she went across to the Mohammedan court-house and said:

"Why didn't you tell me it was Ishmael Ameer you meant?"

The Sheikhs answered with a show of shame that they had intended to do so eventually, and if they had not done so at first it was only out of fear of frightening her.

"He's sick and in chains, isn't he?" said Adila.

They admitted that it was true.

"He may never come out of prison alive—isn't that so?"

They could not deny it.

"Then I want to marry him," said Adila.

"What a strange girl you are!" said the Sheikhs, but without more ado the contract was made while Ishmael was so sick that he knew little about it, the marriage document was drawn up in Ishmael's name, Adila signed it, half her dowry was paid to her, and she promptly gave the money to the poor.

Next day Ishmael was tossing on his angerib in the mud-hut which served for his cell when he saw his Soudan-ese guard come in, followed by four women, and the first of them was Adila, carrying a basketful of cakes, such as are made in that country for a marriage festival. One moment she stood over him as he lay on his bed with what seemed to be the dews of death on his forehead, and then, putting her basket on the ground, she slipped to her knees by his side and said:

"I am Adila. I belong to you now and have come to take care of you."

"Why do you come to me?" he answered. "Go away. I don't want you."

"But we are married and I am your wife, and I am here to nurse you until you are well," she said.

"I shall never be well," he replied. "I am dying and will soon be dead. Why should you waste your life on me, my girl? Go away and God bless you! Praise to His name!"

With that she kissed his hand and her tears fell over it, but after a moment she wiped her eyes, rose to her feet, and, turning briskly to the other women, she said:

"Take your cakes and be off with you—I'm going to stay."

XIV

THREE weeks longer Ishmael lay in the grip of his fever, and day and night Adila tended him, moistening his parched lips and cooling his hot forehead, while he raged against his enemies in his strong delirium, crying, "Down with the Christians! Drive them away! Kill them!" Then the thunging and roaring in his poor brain ceased, and his body was like a boat that had slid in an instant out of a stormy sea into a quiet harbour. Opening his eyes, with his face to the red wall, in the cool light of a breathless morning, he heard behind him the soft and mellow voice of a woman who seemed to be whispering to herself or to Heaven, and she was saying:

"Forgive us our trespasses as we forgive them that trespass against us, and lead us not into temptation but deliver us from evil, for Thine is the kingdom, the power, and the glory. Amen."

"What is that?" he asked, closing his eyes again; and at the next moment the mellow voice came from somewhere above his face:

"So you are better? Oh, how good that is! I am Adila. Don't you remember me?"

"What was that you were saying, my girl?"

"That? Oh, that was the prayer of the Lord Isa (Jesus)."

"The Lord Isa?"

"Don't you know? Long ago my father told me about Him, and I've not forgotten it even yet. He was only a poor man, a poor Jewish man, a carpenter, but He was so good that He loved all the world, especially sinful women when they were sorry, and little, helpless children. He never did harm to his enemies either, but people were cruel and they crucified Him. And now He is in heaven, sitting at God's right hand, with Mary, His mother, beside Him."

There was silence for a moment, and then:

" Say His prayer again, Adila."

So Adila, with more constraint than before, but still softly and sweetly, began afresh:

" Our Father Who art in heaven, hallowed be Thy name; Thy kingdom come; Thy will be done on earth as it is in heaven; give us this day our daily bread, and forgive us our trespasses, as we forgive them that trespass against us; and lead us not into temptation but deliver us from evil; for Thine is the kingdom, the power, and the glory. Amen."

Thus the little Coptic woman, in her soft and mellow voice, said her Lord's Prayer in that mud-hut on the edge of the desert, with only the sick man to hear her, and he was a prisoner and in chains; but long before she had finished Ishmael's face was hidden in his bedclothes and he was crying like a child.

There were three weeks more of a painless and dreamy convalescence, in which Adila repeated other stories her father had told her, and Ishmael saw Christianity for the first time as it used to be, and wondered to find it a faith so sweet and so true, and, above all, save for the character of Jesus, so like his own.

Then a new set of emotions took possession of him, and with returning strength he began to see Adila with fresh eyes. He loved to look at her soft, round form, and he found the air of his gloomy prison full of perfume and light when she walked with her beautiful erect bearing and smiling blue eyes about his bed. Hitherto she had slept on a mattress which she had laid out on the ground by the side of his angerib, but now he wished to change places, and when nothing would avail with her to do so he would stretch out his arm at night until their hands met and clasped, and thus linked together they would fall asleep.

At length he would awake in the darkness, not being able to sleep for thinking of her, and finding one night that she was awake, too, he said in a tremulous voice:

" Will you not come on to the angerib, Adila? "

" Should I? " she whispered, and she did.

Next day the black Soudanese guard that had been set to watch him reported to the Mohammedan Sheikhs that the devotee had been swallowed up in the man, whereupon the Sheikhs, with a chuckle, reported the same to the Government, and then Ishmael with certain formalities was set free.

At the expense of his uncle a house was found for him outside the town, for, in contempt of his weakness in being tricked, as his people believed, by a Coptic slave-girl, his following had gone and he and Adila were to be left alone. Little they recked of that, though, for in the first sweet joys of husband and wife they were very happy, talking in delicious whispers and with the frank candour of the East of the child that was to come. He was sure it would be a girl, so they agreed to call it Ayesha (Mary), she for the sake of the sinful soul who had washed her Master's feet with her tears and wiped them with the hair of her head, and he in memory of the poor Jewish woman, the mother of Isa, whose heart had been torn with grief for the sorrows of her son.

But when at length came their day of days, at the height of their happiness a bolt fell out of a cloudless sky, for though God gave them a child, and it was a girl, He took the mother in place of it.

She made a brave end, the sweet Coptic woman, only thinking of Ishmael and holding his hand to cheer him. It was noon, the sun was hot outside, and in the cool shade of the courtyard three Moslems chanted the Islamee la Il-laha, for so much they could do even for the infidel, while Ishmael sat within on one side of his wife's angerib, with his uncle, seventy years of age now, on the other. She was too weak to speak to her husband, but she held up her mouth to him like a child to be kissed. A moment later the old man closed her eyes, and said:

"Be comforted, my son—death is a black camel that kneels at the gate of all."

There were no women to wail outside the house that night, and next day, when Adila had to be buried, it was neither in the Mohammedan cemetery with those who had "received direction," nor in the Christian one with English soldiers who had fallen in fight, that the slave-wife of a prisoner could be laid, but out in the open desert where there was nothing save the sand and the sky.

They laid her with her face to Jerusalem, wrapped in a cocoa-nut mat, and put a few thorns over her to keep off the eagles, and when this was done they would have left her, saying she would sleep cool in her soft bed, for a warm wind was blowing and the sun was beginning to set, but Ishmael would not go.

In his sorrow and misery, his doubt and darkness, he was asking himself whether, if his poor Coptic wife was doomed to hell as an unbeliever, he could ever be happy in heaven. The moon had risen when at length they drew him away, and even then in the stillness of the lonely desert he looked back again and again at the dark patch on the white waste of the wilderness in which he was leaving her behind him.

Next morning he took the child from the midwife's arms, and, carrying it across to his uncle, he asked him to take care of it and bring it up, for he was leaving Khartoum and did not know how long he might be away. Where was he going to? He could not say. Had he any money? None, but God would provide for him.

"Better stay in the Soudan and marry another woman, a believer," said his uncle, and then Ishmael answered, in a quivering voice:

"No, no, by Allah! One wife I had, and if she was a Christian and was once a slave, I loved her, and never— never—shall another woman take her place."

He was ten years away, and only at long intervals did anybody hear of him, and it was sometimes from Mecca, sometimes from Jerusalem, sometimes from Rome, and finally from the depths of the Libyan desert. Then he reappeared at Alexandria, and, entering a little mosque, he exercised his right as alim and went up into the pulpit to preach.

His teaching was like fire, and men were like fuel before it. Day by day the crowds increased that came to hear him, until Alexandria seemed to be aflame, and he had to remove to the large mosque of Abou Abbas in the square of the same name.

Such was the man whom Gordon Lord was sent to arrest.

XV

"HEADQUARTERS, CARACOL ATTARIN, ALEXANDRIA.

"MY DEAREST HELENA: I have seen my man and it is all a mistake! I can have no hesitation in saying so—a mistake! *Wallahi!* Ishmael Ameer is not the cause of the riots which are taking place here—never has been, never can be. And if his preaching should ever lead by any indirect means to sporadic outbursts of fanaticism the fault will be ours—ours, and nobody else's.

"Colonel Jenkinson and the Commandant of Police met me on my arrival. It seems my coming had somehow got wind, but the only effect of the rumour had been to increase the panic, for even the conservative elements among the Europeans had made a run on the gunsmiths' shops for firearms and—could you believe it?—on the chemists' for prussic acid, to be used by their women in case of the worst.

"Next morning I saw my man for the first time. It was outside Abou Abbas, on the toe of the East port, where the native population, with quiet Eastern greeting, of hands to the lips and forehead, were following him from his lodging to the mosque.

"My dear girl, he is not a bit like the man you imagined. Young—as young as I am, at all events—tall, very tall (his head showing above others in a crowd), with clean-cut face, brown complexion, skin soft and clear, hands like a woman's, and large, beaming black eyes as frank as a

7

child's. His dress is purely Oriental, being white throughout, save for the red slippers under the caftan and the tip of the tarboosh above the turban. No mealy-mouthed person, though, but a spontaneous, passionate man, careless alike of the frowns of men and the smiles of women, a real type of the Arab out of the desert, uncorrupted by the cities, a man of peace, perhaps, but full of deadly fire and dauntless energy.

"My dear Helena, I liked my first sight of Ishmael Ameer, and thinking I saw in him some of the barbarous virtues we have civilised away, some of the fine old stuff of the Arab nobleman who would light his beacon to guide you to his tent even if you were his worst enemy, I could not help but say to myself, 'By ——, here's a man I want to fight!'

"As soon as he had gone into the mosque I sent Hafiz and the two Egyptians after him by different doors, with strict injunctions against collusion of any kind, and then went off to the police headquarters in the Governorat to await their report. Hafiz himself was the first to come to me, and he brought a circumstantial story. Not a word of sedition, not a syllable about the Christians, good, bad, or indifferent! Did the man flatter the Moslems? Exactly the reverse! Never had Hafiz heard such a rating of a congregation even from a Mohammedan preacher.

"The sermon had been on the degradation of woman in the East, which the preacher had denounced as a disgrace to their humanity. Christians believed it to be due to their faith, but what had degraded woman in Mohammedan countries was not the Mohammedan religion but the people's own degradation.

"'I dreamt last night,' he said, 'that in punishment of your offences against woman God lifted the passion of love out of the heart of man. What a chaos! A cockpit of selfishness and sin! Woman is meant to sweeten life, to bind its parts together—will you continue to degrade her? Fools, are you wiser than God, trying to undo what He has done?'

"Such was Ishmael's sermon, as Hafiz reported it, and

when the Egyptians came their account was essentially the same; but just at the moment when I was asking myself what there could be in teaching like this to set Moslem against Christian, tinkle-tinkle went the bell of the telephone, and the Commandant of Police, who had been listening with a supercilious smile, seemed to take a certain joy in telling me that his inspector in the quarter of Abou Abbas was calling for reinforcements because a fresh disturbance had broken out there.

"In three minutes I was on the spot, and the first thing I saw was the white figure of Ishmael Ameer lashing his way through a turbulent crowd, whereupon the Commandant, who was riding by my side, said, 'See that? Are you satisfied now, sir?' to which I answered, 'Don't be a fool,' with a stronger word to drive it home, and then made for the middle of the throng.

"It was all over before I got there, for Christians and Moslems alike were flying before Ishmael's face, and, without waiting for a word of thanks, he was gone, too, and in another moment the square was clear, save for a dozen men, native and European, whom the police had put under arrest.

"With these rascals I returned to the Governorat and investigated the riot, which turned out to be a very petty affair, originating in an effort on the part of a couple of low-class Greeks to attend to the Scriptural injunction to spoil the Egyptians by robbing a shop (covered only by a net) while its native owner was in the mosque.

"Next morning came a letter from Ishmael Ameer, beginning, 'In the name of God, the Compassionate, the Merciful,' but otherwise written without preamble or circumlocution, saying he was aware that certain incidents in connection with his services had assumed an anti-Christian aspect, and begging to be permitted, in the interests of peace and in order to give a feeling of security to Europeans, to preach openly at noon the next day in the square of Mohammed Ali.

"I need not tell you, my dear Helena, that everybody at the Governorat thought the letter a piece of appalling effrontery, and, of course, the Commandant—who is one of the good Christians, with a rooted contempt for anything in a turban (forgetting that Jesus Christ probably wore one)—made himself big with phrases out of Blue Books about the only way to suppress disorder being to refuse to let sedition show its head. But I have never been afraid of a mob, and, thinking the situation justified the experiment, I advised the Governor to let the man come.

"One thing I did, though, my dear Helena, and that was to dictate a pretty stiff reply, saying I should be present myself with a battalion of soldiers, and if, instead of pacifying the people, he aggravated their hostility, I should make it my personal business to see that he would be the first to suffer.

"That night all the world and his wife declared that I was fishing in troubled waters, and I hear that some brave souls fled panic-stricken by the last train to Cairo, where they are now, I presume, preferring their petitions at the Agency; but next morning (that is to say, this morning) the air was calmer, and the great square, when I reached it, was as quiet as an inland sea.

"It was a wonderful sight, however, with the First Suffolk lining the east walls, and the Second Berkshire lining the west; and the overflowing Egyptian and European populace between, standing together yet apart, like the hosts of Pharaoh and of Israel with the Red Sea dividing them.

"I rode up with Jenkinson a little before twelve, and I think the people saw that, though we had permitted this unusual experiment in the interests of peace, we meant business. A space had been kept clear for Ishmael at the foot of the statue of the great Khedive, and hardly had the last notes of the midday call to prayers died away when our man arrived. He was afoot, quite unattended, walking with an active step and that assured nobility of bearing which belongs to the Arab blood alone. He bowed to me, with a simple dignity that had not a particle either of fear or defiance, and again, Heaven knows why, I said to myself, 'By ——, I want to fight that man!'

"Then he stepped on to the angerib that had been placed

for him as a platform and began to speak. His first words
were a surprise, being in English, and faultlessly spoken:

"'The earth and the sky are full of trouble. God has
afflicted us; praise to His name,' he began, and then, pointing to the warships that were just visible in the bay, he
cried:

"'Men who are watching the heavens and who speak
with authority tell us that great conflicts are coming among
the nations of the world. Why is it so? What is dividing
us? Is it race? We are the sons of one Father. Is it
faith? It is the work of religion not only to set men free,
but to bind them together. Our Prophet says: "Thou shalt
love thy brother as thyself, and never act toward him but
as thou wouldst that he should act toward thee." The Gospel of Jesus Christ and the Law of Moses say the same.
The true Christian is the true Moslem—the true Moslem
is the true Jew. All that is right in religion includes itself
in one commandment—love one another! Then, why warfare between brethren so near akin?'

"His voice, my dear Helena, was such as I had never
in my life heard before. It throbbed with the throb that
is peculiar to the voice of the Arab singer and seems to go
through you like an electric current. His sermon, too,
which was sometimes in English, sometimes in Arabic, the
two languages so intermingled that the whole vast congregation of the cosmopolitan seaport seemed to follow him
at once, was not like preaching at all, but vehement, enthusiastic, extempore prayer.

"I have sent a long account of it to the Consul-General,
so I dare say you will see what it contained. It was the
only preaching I have ever heard that seemed to me to deserve the name of inspiration. Sedition? In one passage
alone did it so much as skirt the problem of England in
Egypt, and then there was a spirit in the man's fiery words
that was above the finest patriotism. Speaking of the universal hope of all religions, the hope of a time to come
when the Almighty will make all the faiths of the world
one faith, and all the peoples of the world one people, he
said:

"'In visions of the night I see that promised day, and what is our Egypt then? She, the oldest of the nations, who has seen so many centuries of persecution and shame, trodden under the heel of hard taskmasters, and buried in the sands of her deserts, what is she? She is the meeting-place of nations, the hand-clasp of two worlds, the interpreter and the peacemaker between East and West. We can never be a great nation—let us be a good one. Is it not enough? Look around! We stand amid ruins half as old as the earth itself—is it not worth waiting for?'

"Then in his last word, speaking first in Arabic and afterward in English, he cried:

"'O men of many races, be brothers one to another! God is Most Great! God is Most Great! Take hands, O sons of one Father, believers in one God! Pray to Him who changes all things but Himself changeth not! God is Most Great! God is Most Great! Let Allahu-Akbar sound for ever through your souls!'

"The effect was overwhelming. Even some of the low-class Greeks and Italians were sobbing aloud, and our poor Egyptian children were like people possessed. Hungry, out of work, many of them wearing a single garment, and that a ragged one—yet a new magnificence seemed to be given to their lives. Something radiant and glorious seemed to glimmer in the distance, making their present sufferings look small and mean.

"And I? I don't know, my dear Helena, how I can better tell you what I felt than by telling you what I did. I was looking down from the saddle at my First Suffolk and my Second Berkshire, standing in line with their poor little rifles, when something gripped me by the throat, and I signed to the officers, shouted 'Back to your quarters!' and rode off, without waiting to see what would happen, because I *knew*.

"I have written both to the General and to my father, telling them I have not arrested Ishmael Ameer and don't intend to do so. If this is quackery and spiritual leger-demain to cover sedition and conspiracy, I throw up the sponge and count myself among the fools. But Ishmael

Ameer is one of the flame-bearers of the world. Let who will put him down—I will *not.*

"My dearest Helena, I've written all this about the new prophet and not a word about yourself, though I've been feeling the quivering grip of your hand in mine every moment of the time. The memory of that delicious quarter of an hour in the garden has sweetened the sulphurous air of Alexandria for me, and I'm in a fever to get back. 'Smash the Mahdi!' you said, thinking if I didn't obey my father and yours I should offend both and so lead to trouble between you and me. But the Consul-General is a just man, if he is a hard one, and I should not deserve to be his son if I did not dare to warn him when he was going to do wrong. Neither should I deserve to be loved by the bravest girl alive if I hadn't the pluck to stand up for the right.

"Good night, sweetheart! It's two in the morning, the town is as quiet as a desert village, and I am going to turn in.   GORDON.

"P. S.—Forgot to say Ishmael Ameer is to go up to Cairo shortly, so you'll soon see him for yourself. But Heaven help me, what is to become of Gordon Lord when you've once looked on this son of the wilderness?

"P. P. S.—Not an arrest since yesterday!"

XVI

"GENERAL'S HOUSE, CITADEL, CAIRO.

"MY DEAR GORDON: You're in for it! In that whispering gallery which people call the East, where everything is known before it happens to happen, rumours without end were coming to Cairo of what you were doing in Alexandria, but nobody in authority believed the half of it until your letters arrived at noon to-day, and now—heigho, for the wind and the rain!

"My dear dad is going about like an old Tom with his tail up, and as for the Consul-General—whew! (a whistle, your Excellency).

"Let me take things in their order, though, so that you may see what has come to pass. I was reading your letter for the third (or was it the thirtieth?) time this afternoon, when who should come in but the Princess Nazimah, so I couldn't resist an impulse to tell her what your son of Hagar had to say on the position of Eastern women, thinking it would gratify her and she would agree. But no, not a bit of it; off she went on the other side, with talk straight out of the harem, showing that the woman of the East isn't worthy of emancipation and shouldn't get it—*yet*.

"It seems that if the men of the East are 'beasts,' the women are 'creatures.' Love? They never heard of such a thing. Husband? The word doesn't exist for them. Not *my* master, even! Just master! Living together like school-girls and loving each other like sisters—think of that, my dear!

"And when I urged that we were all taught to love one another—all Christians, at all events—she cried: 'What! And share one man between four of you?' In short, the condition was only possible to cocks and hens, and that Eastern women could put up with it showed they were crea-tures—simple creatures, content and happy if their hus-bands (beg pardon, their masters) gave them equal presents of dresses and jewels and Turkish delight. No, let the woman of the East keep a little longer to her harem win-dow, her closed carriage, and her wisp of mousseline de soie she calls her veil, or she'll misuse her liberty. 'Oh, I know. I say what I think. I don't care.'

"As for your Ishmael, the Princess wouldn't have him at any price. He's just another Mahdi, and if he's cham-pioning the cause of women the son of a duck knows how to swim. His predecessor began by denouncing slavery and ended by being the biggest slave-dealer in the Soudan. Ergo, your Ishmael, who cares neither for 'the frowns of man nor the smiles of woman,' is going to finish up like Solomon or Samson, either as the tyrant of a hundred women or the victim of one of them whose heart is snares and nets. 'Oh, I know. Every man is a sultan to himself, and the tail of a dog is never straight.'

"But as for you, it seems you are 'a brother of girls,' which being interpreted means you are a man to whom God has given a clean heart to love all women as his sisters, and courage and strength to fight for their protection. 'Didn't I tell you that you had the best of the bunch, my child?' (She did, Serenity.) 'But though he is a soldier and as brave as a lion, he has too much of the woman in him.' In this respect you resemble, it seems, one of the Princess's own husbands, but having had a variety of them, both right and left-handed, she found a difficulty in fixing your prototype. 'My first husband was like that—or no, it was my second—or perhaps it was one of the other ones.'

"But this being so, O virtuous one, it became my duty to get you back from Alexandria as speedily as possible. 'Love, like the sparrows, comes and goes. Oh, I know. I've seen it myself, my child.'

"'And listen, my moon. Don't allow your Gordon' (she calls you Gourdan) 'to go against his father. Nuneham is the greatest man in the world, but let anybody cross him— mon Dieu! If you go out as the wind you meet the whirlwind, and serve you right, too.'

"In complete agreement on this point, the Princess and I were parting in much kindness when father came dashing into my drawing-room like a gust of the Khamseen, having just had a telephone message from the Consul-General requiring him to go down to the Agency without delay. Whereupon, with a word or two of apology to the Princess and a rumbling subterranean growl of 'Don't know what the d—— that young man . . .' he picked up your letter to himself and was gone in a moment.

"It is now 10 P.M. and he hasn't come back yet. Another telephone message told me he wouldn't be home to dinner, so I dined alone, with only Mosie Gobs for company, but he waits on me like my shadow, and gives me good advice on all occasions.

"It seems his heart is still on fire with love for me, and, having caught him examining his face in my toilet-glass this morning, I was amused, and a little touched, when he asked me to-night if the Army Surgeon had any medicine to make people white.

"Apparently, his former love was a small black maiden who works in the laundry, and he shares your view (as revealed in happier hours, your Highness) that there's nothing in the world so nice as a little girl except a big one. But I find he hasn't the best opinion of you, for when I was trying to while away an hour after dinner by playing the piano I overheard the monkey telling the cook that to see her hands (i. e., mine) run over the teeth of the music-box amazes the mind—therefore, why should her husband (*id est*, you) spend so much time in the coffee-shop?

"Since then I've been out in the arbour trying to live over again the delicious quarter of an hour you speak of, but though the wing of night is over the city and the air is as soft as somebody's kiss is (except sometimes), it was a dreadful failure, for when I closed my eyes, thinking hearts see each other, I could feel nothing but the sting of a mosquito, and could only hear the watchman crying 'Wahhed!' and what that was like you've only to open your mouth wide and then say it, and you'll know.

"So here I am at my desk talking against time until father comes, and there's something to say. And if you would know how I am myself, I would tell you, most glorious and respected, that I'm as tranquil as can be expected considering what a fever you've put me in, for, falling on my knees before your unsullied hands, O Serenity, it seems to me you're a dunce after all, and have gone and done exactly what your great namesake did before you, in spite of his tragic fate to warn you.

"The trouble in Gordon major's case was that the Government gave him a discretionary power and he used it, and it seems as if something similar has happened to Gordon minor, with the same results. I hope to goodness they may send you a definite order as the consequence of their colloguing to-night, and then you can have no choice, and there will be no further trouble.

"That is not to say that I think you are wrong in your view of this new Mahdi, but merely that I don't want to know anything about him. His protests against the spirit of the world may be good and beneficial, but peace and quiet are better. His predictions about the millennium may be right, too, and if he likes to live on that dinner of herbs let him. Can't you leave such people to boil their own pot without you providing them with sticks? I'm a woman, of course, and my Moslem sisters may be suffering this, that, or the other injustice, but when it comes to letting these things get in between your happiness and mine, what the dickens, and the deuce, and the divil do I care?—which is proof of what Mosie said to the cook about the sweetness of my tongue.

"As for your 'Arab nobleman' taking me by storm, no, thank you! I dare say he has red finger-nails, and if one touched the tip of his nose it would be as soft as Mosie's. I hate him anyway, and if you are ever again tempted to fight him, take my advice and *fall!* But look here, Mr. Charlie Gordon Lord! If you're so very keen for a fight come here and fight *me*—I'm game for you!

"Soberly, my dear—dear, don't think I'm not proud of you that you are the only man in all Egypt, aye, or the world, who dares stand up to your father. When God made you he made you without fear—I know that. He made you with a heart that would die rather than do a wrong—I know that, too. I don't believe you are taking advantage of your position as a son, either; and when people blame your parents for bringing you up as an Arab I know it all comes from deeper down than that. I suppose it is the Plymouth Rock in you, the soul and blood of the men of the *Mayflower.* You cannot help it, and you would fight your own father for what you believed to be the right.

"But, oh, dear, that's just what makes me tremble. Your father and you on opposite sides is a thing too terrible to think about. English gentlemen? Yes, I'm not saying anything to the contrary, but British bulldogs, too, and, as if that were not enough, *you've* got the American eagle in you as well. You'll destroy each other—that will be the end of it. And if you ask me what reason I have for saying so, I answer—simply a woman's, I *know!* I *know!*

"Father just back—dreadfully excited and exhausted—had to get him off to bed. Something fresh brewing—cannot tell what.

"I gather that your friend, the Grand Cadi, was at the Agency to-night—but I'll hear more in the morning.

"It's very late and the city seems to be tossing in its sleep—a kind of somnambulant moan coming up from it. They say the Nile is beginning to rise, and by the light of the moon (it has just risen) I can faintly see a streak of red water down the middle of the river. Ugh! It's like blood and makes me shiver, so I must go to bed.

"Father much better this morning. But, oh! oh! oh! . . . It seems you are to be telegraphed for to return immediately. Something you have to do in Cairo—I don't know what. I'm glad you are to come back, though, for I hate to think of you in the same city as that man Ishmael. Let me hear from you the minute you arrive, for I may have something to say by that time, and meantime I send this letter by hand to your quarters at Kasr el Nil.

"That red streak in the Nile is plain enough this morning. I suppose it's only the first water that comes pouring down from the clay soil of Abyssinia, but I hate to look at it.

"Take care of yourself, Gordon, dear—I'm really a shocking coward, you know.   HELENA.

"P. S.—Another dream last night! Same as before exactly—that man coming between you and me."

XVII

RETURNING to Cairo by the first train the following morning, Gordon received Helena's letter and replied to it:

"Just arrived in obedience to their telegram. But don't be afraid, dearest. Nothing can happen that will injure either of us. My father cannot have wished me to arrest an innocent man. Therefore set your mind at ease and be happy. Going over to the Agency now, but hope to see you

in the course of the day.   Greetings to the General and all
my love to his daughter.   GORDON."

But in spite of the brave tone of this letter, he was not
without a certain uneasiness as he rode across to his father's
house.   "I couldn't have acted otherwise," he thought.
And then, recalling Helena's hint of something else which
it was intended he should do, he told himself that his father
was being deceived and did not know what he was doing.
"First of all I must tell him the truth—at all costs, the
truth," he thought.

This firm resolution was a little shaken the moment he
entered the garden and the home atmosphere began to creep
upon him.   And when Ibrahim, his father's Egyptian servant, told him that his mother, who had been less well since
he went away, was keeping her bed that morning, the shadow
of domestic trouble seemed to banish his stalwart purpose.

Bounding upstairs three steps at a time, he called in a
cheery voice at his mother's door, but almost before the
faint, half-frightened answer came back to him he was in
the room, and the pale-faced old lady in her nightdress was
in his arms.

"I knew it was you," she said, and then, with her thin,
moist hands clasped about his neck, and her head against
his breast, she began in a plaintive, hesitating voice, as if
she were afraid of her own son, to warn and reprove him.

"I do not understand what is happening, dear, but you
must never let anybody poison your mind against your
father.   He may be a little hard sometimes—I'm not deny-
ing that—but then he is not to be judged like other men—
he is really not, you know.   He would cut off his right hand
if he thought it had done him a wrong, but he is very tender
to those he loves, and he loves you, dear, and wants to do
so much for you.   It was pitiful to hear him last night, Gordon.   'I feel as if my enemy has stolen my own son,' he
said.   'My own son, my own son,' he kept saying, until I
could have cried, and I couldn't sleep for thinking of it.
You won't let anybody poison your mind against your father
—promise me you won't, dear."

Gordon comforted and kissed her, and rallied her and laughed, but he felt for a moment as if he had come back as a traitor to destroy the happiness of home.

Fatimah followed him out of the room, and, winking to keep back her tears, she whispered some disconnected story of what had happened on the day on which his father received his letter.

"Oh, my eye, my soul, it was sad! We could hear his footsteps in his bedroom all night long. Sometimes he was speaking to himself. 'The scoundrels!' 'They don't know what shame is!' 'Haven't I had enough? And now he, too! My son, my son!'"

Gordon went downstairs with a slow and heavy step. He felt as if everything were conspiring to make him abandon his purpose. "Why can't I leave things alone?" he thought. But just as he reached the hall the Egyptian Prime Minister, who was going out of the house, passed in front of him without seeing him, and a certain sinister look in the man's sallow face wiped out in an instant all the softening effect of the scenes upstairs. "Take care!" he thought. "Tell him the truth, whatever happens."

When he entered the library he expected his father to fly out at him, but the old man was very quiet.

"Sit down—I shall be ready in a moment," he said, and he continued to write without raising his eyes.

Gordon saw that his father's face was more than usually furrowed and severe, and a voice seemed to say to him, "Don't be afraid!" So he walked over to the window and tried to look at the glistening waters of the Nile and the red wedges of Pyramids across the river.

"Well, I received your letter," said the old man, after a moment. "But what was the nonsensical reason you gave me for not doing your duty?"

It was the brusque tone he had always taken with his secretaries when they were in the wrong, but it was a blunder to adopt it with Gordon, who flushed up to the forehead, wheeled round from the window, walked up to the desk, and said, beginning a little hesitatingly, but gathering strength as he went on:

"My reason, father . . . for not doing my . . . what I was sent to do . . . was merely that I found I could not do it without being either a rascal or a fool."

The old man flinched and his glasses fell. "Explain yourself," he said.

"I came to the conclusion, sir, that you were mistaken in this matter."

"Really!"

"Possibly misinformed——"

"Indeed!"

"By British officials who don't know what they are talking about, or by native scoundrels who do."

Not for forty years had anybody in Egypt spoken to the Consul-General like that, but he only said:

"Don't stand there like a parson in a pulpit. Sit down and tell me all about it." Whereupon Gordon took a seat by the desk.

"The only riot I witnessed in Alexandria, sir, was due simply to the bad feeling which always exists between the lowest elements of the European and Egyptian inhabitants. Ishmael Ameer had nothing to do with it. On the contrary, he helped to put it down."

"You heard what he had said in the mosques?"

"I had one of his sermons reported to me, sir, and it was teaching such as would have had your own sympathy, being in line with what you have always said yourself about the corruptions of Islam and the necessity of uplifting the Egyptian woman as a means of raising the Egyptian man."

"So you decided, it seems——"

"I decided, father, that to arrest Ishmael Ameer as one who was promulgating sedition and inciting the people to rebellion would be an act of injustice which you could not wish me to perpetrate in your name."

The Consul-General put up his glasses, looked for a letter which lay on the desk, glanced at it, and said:

"I see you say that before you arrived in Alexandria it was known that you were to come."

"That is so, sir."

"And that after the riot you counselled the Governor

to consent to the man's request that he should preach in public."

"I did, sir. I thought it would be a good experiment to try the effect of a little moral influence."

"Of course, the experiment was justified?"

"Perfectly justified—the people dispersed quietly and there has not been a single arrest since."

"But you had a battalion of soldiers on the spot?"

"I had—it was only right to be ready for emergencies."

The old man laughed bitterly. "I'm surprised at you. Don't you see how you've been hoodwinked? The man was warned of your coming—warned from Cairo, from El Azhar, which I find you were so foolish as to visit before you left for Alexandria. Everything was prepared for you. A trick, an Eastern trick, and you were so simple as to be taken in. I'm ashamed of you—ashamed of you before my servants, my secretaries."

Gordon coloured up to his flickering steel-blue eyes and said:

"Father, I must ask you to begin by remembering that I am no longer a child and not quite a simpleton. I *know* the Egyptians. I know them better than all your people put together."

"Better than your father himself, perhaps?"

"Yes, sir, better than my father himself, because—because I love them, whereas you—you have hated them from the first. They've never deceived me yet, sir, and, with your permission, I'm not going to deceive them."

The passionate words were hotly, almost aggressively spoken, but in some unfathomable depth of the father's heart the old man was proud of his son at that moment—strong, fearless, and right.

"And the sermon in public—was that also on the corruption of Islam?"

"No, sir, it was about the spirit of the world—the greed of wealth which is making people forget in these days that the true welfare of a nation is moral, not material."

"Anything else?"

"Yes—the hope of a time when the world will have so

far progressed toward peace that arms will be laid down and a Redeemer will come to proclaim a universal brotherhood."

"That didn't strike you as ridiculous—to see one unlettered man trying to efface the laws of civilised society—asking sensible people to turn their backs on the facts of life in order to live in a spiritual hot-house of dreams?"

"No, father, that did not strike me as ridiculous, because——"

"Because what—what, now?"

"Because John the Baptist and Jesus Christ did precisely the same thing."

There was silence for a moment, and then the old man said:

"In this golden age that is to come, he predicts, I am told, a peculiar place for Egypt—is that so?"

"Yes, sir. He holds that in the commonwealth of the world Egypt, by reason of her geographical position, will become the interpreter and peacemaker between the East and the West—that that's what she has lived so long for."

"Yet it didn't occur to you that this was sedition in its most seductive form, and that the man who promulgated it was probably the most dangerous of the demagogues—the worst of the Egyptians who prate about the natives governing themselves and the English being usurping foreigners."

"No, sir, that didn't occur to me at all, because I felt that a Moslem people had a right to their own ideals, and also because I thought——"

"Well? Well?"

"That the man who imagines that the soul of a nation can be governed by the sword—whoever he is, King, Kaiser, or—or Czar—is the worst of tyrants."

The old autocrat flinched visibly. The scene was becoming tragic to him. For forty years he had been fighting his enemies, and he had beaten them, and now suddenly his own son was standing up as his foe. After a moment of silence he rose and said, with stony gravity:

"Very well! Having heard your views on Ishmael Ameer, and incidentally on myself, and all I have hitherto attempted to do in Egypt, it only remains to me to tell you what I intend to do now. You know that this man is coming on to Cairo?"

Gordon bowed.

"You are probably aware that it is intended that he shall preach at El Azhar?"

"I didn't know that, sir, but I'm not surprised to hear it."

"Well, El Azhar has to be closed before he arrives."

"Closed?"

"That is what I said—closed, shut up, and its students and professors turned into the streets."

"But there are sixteen thousand of them—from all parts of the Mohammedan world, sir."

"That's why! The Press as a medium of disaffection was bad enough, but El Azhar is worse. It is a hotbed of rebellion, and a word spoken there goes, as by wireless telegraphy, all over Egypt. It is a secret society, and as such it must be stopped."

"But have you reflected——"

"Do I do anything without reflection?"

"Closed, you say? The University? The mosque of mosques? It is impossible! You are trifling with me."

"Have you taken leave of your senses, sir?"

"I beg your pardon, father. I only wish to prevent you from doing something you will never cease to regret. It's dangerous work to touch the religious beliefs of an Eastern people—you know that, sir, better than I do. And if you shut up their University, their holy of holies, you shake the foundations of their society. It's like shutting up St. Peter's in Rome, or St. Paul's in London."

"Both events have happened," said the old man, resuming his seat.

"Father, I beg of you to beware. Trust me, I know these people. No Christian nation nowadays believes in Christianity as these Moslems believe in Islam. We don't care enough for our faith to fight for it. But these dusky millions will die for their religion. And then there's Ishmael Ameer—you must see for yourself what manner of man he is—careless alike of comfort or fame, a fanatic, if you like, but he has only to call to the people and they'll follow him. All the wealth and well-being you have bestowed on them will go to the winds and they'll follow him to a man."

The Consul-General's lip curled again, and he said, quietly, "You ask me to believe that at the word of this man without a penny and with his head full of worthless noise, the blue-shirted fellaheen will leave their comfortable homes and their lands——"

"Aye, and their wives and children, too—everything they have or ever hope to have! And if he promises them nothing but danger and death, all the more they'll go to him."

"Then we must deal with him also."

"You can't—you can't do anything with a man like that —a man who wants nothing and is afraid of nothing—except kill him, and you can't do that either."

The Consul-General did not reply immediately, and, coming closer, Gordon began to plead with him.

"Father, believe me, I know what I am saying. Don't be blind to the storm that is brewing, and so undo all the good you have ever done. For Egypt's sake, England's, your own, don't let damnable scoundrels like the Grand Cadi and the Prime Minister play on you like a pipe."

It was Gordon who had blundered now, and the consequences were cruel. The ruthless, saturnine old man rose again, and on his square-hewn face there was an icy smile.

"That brings me," he said, speaking very slowly, "from what *I* have done to what *you* must do. The Ulema of El Azhar have received an order to close the University. It went to them this morning through the President of the Council, who is acting as Regent in the absence of the Khedive. If they refuse to go, it will be your duty to turn them out."

"Mine?"

"Yours! The Governor of the city and the Commandant of Police will go with you, but, where sixteen thousand students and a disaffected population have to be dealt with, the military will be required. If you had brought Ishmael Ameer back from Alexandria this step might have been unnecessary, but now instead of one man you may have to arrest hundreds."

" But if they resist—and they will—I know they will——"

" In that case they will come under a special tribunal as persons assaulting the members of the British Army of Occupation, and be despatched without delay to the Soudan."

" But surely——"

" The Ulema are required to signify their assent by to-morrow morning, and we are to meet at the Citadel at four in the afternoon. You will probably be required to be there."

" But, father——"

" We left something to your discretion before, hoping to give you an opportunity of distinguishing yourself in the eyes of England, but in this case your orders will be definite, and your only duty will be to obey."

" But will you not permit me to——"

" That will do for the present. I'm busy. Good day! "

Gordon went out dazed and dumbfounded. He saw nothing of Ibrahim, who handed him his linen-covered cap in the hall, or of the page-boy at the porch who gave him his reins and held down his stirrup. When he came back to consciousness he was riding by the side of the Nile, where the bridge was open, and a number of boats with white sails, like a flight of great sea-gulls, were sweeping through.

At the next moment he was at the entrance to his own quarters, and found a white motor-car standing there. It was Helena's car, and, leaping from the saddle, he went bounding up the stairs.

XVIII

HELENA was at his door, with an anxious and perplexed face, talking to his soldier servant. At the next instant they were in each other's arms, and their troubles were gone. Her smile seemed to light up his room more than all its wealth of sunlight, and nothing else was of the smallest consequence. But after a moment she drew out a letter and said:

"I told father you were back, and he dictated a message to you. He was going to send it by his A.D.C., but I asked to be allowed to bring it myself and he consented. Here it is, dear."

Gordon opened and read the General's letter. It was a formal request that he should be in attendance at the Citadel at four the following day to receive urgent and important instructions.

"You know what it refers to, Helena?"

"Yes, I know," she answered.

The look of perplexity had returned to her face, and for some minutes they stood arm in arm by the open window, looking down at the Nile in a dazed and dreamy way.

"What are you going to do, Gordon?"

"I don't know—yet."

"It will be an order now, and as an officer you can do nothing but obey."

"I suppose not, dear."

"There are so many things calling for your obedience, too —honour, ambition, everything a soldier can want, you know."

"I know! I know!"

She crept closer and said, "Then there's something else, dear."

"What else, Helena?"

"Haven't I always told you that sooner or later that man would come between us?"

"Ishmael?"

"Yes. Last night my father said . . . but I hate to mention it."

"Tell me, dear, tell me."

"He said: 'You couldn't marry a man who had disobeyed and been degraded?'"

"Meaning that if I refused to obey orders, you and I perhaps . . . by arrangement between your father and mine, maybe——"

"That is what I understood him to mean, dear, and therefore I came to see you."

He flushed crimson for a moment and then began to laugh.

"No, no! I'll never believe that of them. It would be monstrous—impossible!"

But the questioning look in Helena's eyes remained and he tried to reassure her. So many things might happen to remove the difficulty altogether. The Ulema might take the order of the Government as a protest against the visit of Ishmael Ameer, and send him instructions not to come to Cairo.

"He's here already, dear," said Helena.

As she drove down from the Citadel she had crossed a crowd of natives coming from the direction of the railway station, and some one had said it was a procession in honour of the new prophet, who had just arrived from Alexandria.

"Then you've seen him yourself, Helena?"

"I saw a man in a white dress on a white camel, but I didn't look—I had somebody else to think about."

He was carried away by the singleness of her love, and with a score of passionate expressions he kissed her beautiful white hands and did his best to comfort her.

"Never mind, dear! Don't be afraid! The Governors of El Azhar may agree to close their doors—temporarily, at all events. Anyhow, we'll muddle through somehow."

She made him promise not to go near the "new Mahdi," and then began to draw on her long, yellow driving gloves.

"I suppose the gossips of Cairo would be shocked if they knew I had come to see you," she said.

"It's not the first time you've been here, though. You're here always—see!" he said, and with his arm about her waist he took her round his room to look at her portraits that hung on the walls. It was Helena here, Helena there, Helena everywhere, but since that was the first time the real Helena had visited his quarters, she must drink his health in them.

She would only drink it in water, and when she had done so she had to slip off her glove again and dip her finger into the same glass that he might drink her own health as well. In spite of the shadow of trouble which hung over them they were very happy. A world of warm impulses coursed through their veins, and they could hardly permit themselves to part. It was sweet to stand by the window again and look down at the dazzling Nile. For them the old river flowed, for them it sang its sleepy song. They looked into each other's eyes and smiled without speaking. It was just as if their hearts saw each other and were satisfied.

At length she clasped her arms about his neck, and he felt the warm glow of her body.

" You think that still, Gordon ? "

" What, dearest ? "

" That love is above everything ? "

" Everything in the world," he whispered, and then she kissed him of herself, and nothing else mattered—nothing on earth or in heaven.

XIX

WHEN Helena had gone the air of his room seemed to be more dumb and empty than it had ever been before; but the bell of the telephone rang immediately, and Hafiz spoke to him.

Hafiz had just heard from his uncle that the Ulema were to meet at eight o'clock to consider what course they ought to adopt. The Chancellor was in favour of submission to superior force, but some of his colleagues of the reactionary party—the old stick-in-the-muds made in Mecca —not being able to believe the Government could be in earnest, were advocating revolt, even resistance.

" Hadn't you better go up to El Azhar to-night, Gordon, and tell them the Government means business ? They'll believe *you*, you know, and it may save riot, perhaps bloodshed."

" I hadn't intended to go there again, Hafiz, but if you think I can do any good——"

" You can—I'm sure you can. Let me call for you at eight, and we'll go up together."

" Can't see why we shouldn't. . . . But wait! Ishmael Ameer is in Cairo. Will he be there, think you ? "

"Don't know—should think it very likely."

"Well, it can't be helped. Eight o'clock, then! By-
bye!" said Gordon, and with that he rang off and wrote
to Helena, telling her what he was going to do. He was
going to break his word to her again, but it was only in
the interests of peace and with the hope of preventing
trouble.

"Don't suppose these people can influence me a hair's
breadth, dearest," he wrote, " and, above all, don't be angry."

At eight o'clock Hafiz came for him, and, dressed in
mufti, they walked up to the University. With more than
usual ceremony they were taken to the Chancellor's room
in the roof, and there, in a tense, electrical atmosphere, the
Ulema were already assembled—a group of eight or nine
rugged and unkempt creatures in their farageeyah (a loose
gray robe, like that of a monk), squatting on the divans
about the walls. All the members of the Board of El Azhar
were present, and the only stranger there, except themselves,
was Ishmael Ameer, who sat, in his spotless white dress and
with his solemn face, on a chair beside the door.

In silence, and with many sweeping salaams from floor
to forehead, Gordon was received by the company, and at
the request of the Chancellor he explained the object of
his visit. It was not official, and it was scarcely proper,
but it was intended to do good. There were moments when,
passion being excited, there was a serious risk of collision
between governors and governed. This was one of them.
Rightly or wrongly, the Consul-General was convinced that
the University of Cairo was likely to become a centre of
sedition. Could they not agree to close it for a time, at all
events?

At that the electrical atmosphere of the room broke into
rumblings of thunder. The order of the Government was
an outrage on the Mohammedan religion, which England
had pledged herself to respect. El Azhar was one of the
three holy places of the Islamic world, and to close it was
to take the bread of life from the Moslems. "The Government might as well cut our throats at once and have done
with it." said some one.

From denouncing the order of the Government, the Ulema went on to denounce the Government itself. It was eating the people! It was like wolves trying to devour them! "Are we to be body and soul under the heel of the infidel?" they asked themselves.

After that they denounced Lord Nuneham. He was the slave of power! He was drunk with the strong drink of authority! The University was their voice—he had deprived them of every other—and now he was trying to strike them dumb! When somebody, remembering that they were speaking before the Consul-General's son, suggested that if he was doing a bad act it might be with a good conscience, an alim with an injured eye and a malignant face cried: "No, by Allah! The man who usurps the place of God becomes a devil, and that's what Nuneham is and long has been."

Listening to their violence Gordon had found himself taking his father's part, and at this moment his anger had risen so high that he was struggling against an impulse to take the unkempt creature by the throat and fling him out of the room, when the soft voice of the Chancellor began to plead for peace.

"Mohammed—to him be prayer and peace—always yielded to superior force; and who are we that we should be too proud to follow his example?"

But at that the reactionary party became louder and fiercer than before. "Our Prophet," cried one, "has commanded us not to seek war and not to begin it. But he has also told us that if war is waged against Islam we are to resist it under penalty of being ourselves as unbelievers, and to follow up those who assail us without pity and without remorse. Therefore, if the English close our holy El Azhar they will be waging war on our religion, and, by the Most High God, we will fight them to the last man, woman, and child."

At that instant Hafiz, who had been trembling in an obscure seat by the door, rose to his feet and said, in a nervous voice, addressing his uncle:

"Eminence, may I say something?"

8

"Speak, son of my sister," said the Chancellor.

"It is about Colonel Lord," said Hafiz. "If you refuse to close El Azhar, an order to force you to do so will be issued to the military and Colonel Lord will be required to carry it into effect."

"Well?"

"He is the friend of the Muslemeen, your Eminence, but if you resist him he will be compelled to kill you."

"Wouldn't it be well to say 'With God's permission?'" said the man with the injured eye, whereupon Hafiz wheeled round on him and answered, hotly:

"He has the bayonets and he has the courage, and if you fight him there won't be so much as a rat among you that will be left alive."

There was a moment of tense and breathless silence, and then Hafiz, now as nervous as before, said quietly: "On the other hand, if he refuses to obey his orders he will lose his place and rank as a soldier. Which of these do you wish to see, your Eminence?"

There was another moment of breathless silence, and then Ishmael Ameer, who had not spoken before, said in his quivering voice:

"Let us call on God to guide us, my brothers—in tears and in fervent prayer, all night long in the mosque, until His light shines on us and a door of hope has opened."

XX

As Gordon returned to barracks the air of the native section of the city seemed to tingle with excitement. The dirty, unpaved streets with their overhanging tenements were thronged. Framed portraits of Ishmael Ameer, with candles burning in front of them, were standing on the counters of nearly all the *cafés* and the men squatting on the benches about were chanting the Koran. One man, generally a blind man, with his right hand before his ear, would be reciting the text, and at the close of every Surah the others would be crying "Allah! Allah!"

In the densest quarter, where the streets were narrowest and most full of ruts, the houses most wretched and the windows most covered with cobwebs, a company of dervishes were walking in procession, bearing their ragged banners and singing their weird Arab music to the accompaniment of pipes and drums, while boys parading beside them were carrying tin lamps and open flares. Before certain of the houses they stopped, and for some minutes they swayed their bodies to an increasing chorus of "Allah! Allah! Allah!"

Gordon saw what had happened. With the coming of the new teacher a wave of religious feeling had swept over the city. Dam it up suddenly, and what scenes of fanatical frenzy might not occur.

Back in his room, with the window down to shut out the noises of the river and the bridge, he tried to come to a conclusion as to what he ought to do the following day if the Ulema decided to resist. They *would* resist; he had no doubt about that, for where men were under the influence of gusts of religious passion they might call on God, but God's answer was always the same.

If the Ulema were to decide not to close their sacred place they would intend to die in defence of it, and, seeing the issue from the Moslem point of view, that El Azhar was the centre of their spiritual life, Gordon concluded that they would be justified in resisting. If they were justified the order to evict them would be wicked, and the act of eviction would be a crime. "I can't do it!" he told himself. "I can't and I won't!"

This firm resolve relieved him for a moment, and then he began to ask himself what would happen if he refused to obey. The bad work would be done all the same, for somebody else would do it. "What then will be the result?" he thought.

The first result would be that he himself would suffer. He would be tried for insubordination, and, of course, degraded and punished. As a man he might be in the right, but as a soldier he would be in the wrong. He thought of his hard-fought fights and of the honours he had won, and his head went round in a whirl.

The next result would be that he would bring disgrace
on his father as well. His refusal to obey orders would
become known, and if the consequences he expected should
come to pass he would seem to stand up as the first of his
father's accusers. He, his father's only son, would be the
means of condemning him in the eyes of England, of
Europe, of the world! In his old age, too, and after all he
had done for Egypt!

Then, above all, there was Helena! The General would
side with the Consul-General, and Helena would be required
to cast in her lot with her father or with him. If she sided
with him she would have to break with her father; if she
sided with her father she would have to part from him.
In either case the happiness of her life would be wasted—
he would have wasted it, and he would have wasted his own
happiness as well.

This thought seemed to take him by the throat and stifle
him. He leaped from the bed on which he had been lying
in restless pain and threw open the window. The river and
the bridge were quiet by that time, but through the breathless night air there came the music of a waltz. It was the
last dance of the visiting season at an hotel near by—a
number of British officers were dancing on the edge of the
volcano.

Gordon shut the window and again threw himself on
the bed. At length the problem that tormented him seemed
to resolve itself into one issue. His father did not realise
that the Moslems would die rather than give up possession
of their holy place, and that in order to turn them out of
it he would have to destroy them—slaughter them. A man
could not outrage the most sacred of human feelings without being morally blind to what he was doing. His father
was a great man—a thousand times greater than he himself
could ever hope to be—but in this case he was blind and
somebody had to open his eyes.

"I'll go and bring him to reason," he thought. "He
may insult me if he likes, but no matter!"

The last cab had rattled home and the streets were silent
when Gordon reached the entrance to the Agency. Then he

saw that it was late, for the house was in darkness, and not even the window of the library showed a light. The moon was full, and he looked at his watch. Good heavens! It was two o'clock!

The house dog heard his footsteps on the gravel path, and barked and bounded toward him; then, recognising him, it began to snuffle and to lick his hands. At the same moment a light appeared in an upper window. It was the window of his mother's room, and at sight of it his resolution began to ebb away, and he was once more seized with uncertainty.

Strife between himself and his father would extinguish the last rays of his mother's flickering life. He could see her looking at him with her pleading and frightened eyes.

"Am I really going to kill my mother—that, too?" he thought.

He was as far as ever from knowing what course he ought to take to-morrow, but the light in his mother's window, filtering through the lace curtains that were drawn across it, was like a tear-dimmed, accusing eye, and with a new emotion he was compelled to turn away.

XXI

As two o'clock struck on the soft cathedral bell of a little clock by the side of her bed, Fatimah rose with a yawn, switched on the electric light, and filled a small glass from a bottle on the mantelpiece.

"Time to take your medicine, my lady," she said, in a sleepy voice.

Her mistress did not reply immediately, and she asked: "Are you asleep?"

But her lady, who was wide awake, whispered: "Hush! Do you hear Rover? Isn't that somebody on the path?"

Fatimah listened as well as she could through the drums of sleep that were beating in her ears, and then she answered:

"No; I hear nothing."

"I thought it was Gordon's footstep," said the old lady, raising herself in bed to take the medicine that Fatimah was holding out to her.

"It's strange! Gordon's step is exactly like his grandfather's."

"Don't spill it, my lady," said Fatimah, and with a trembling hand the old lady drank off her dose.

"He's like his grandfather in other things, too. I remember when I was a girl there was a story of how he struck one of his soldiers in the Civil War, thinking the man was guilty of some offence. But afterward he found the poor fellow was innocent and had taken the blow for his brother without saying a word. Father never forgave himself for that—never!"

"Shall I put on the eiderdown? The nights are cold if the days are hot, you know."

"Yes—no—just as you think best, nurse. . . . I'm sure Gordon will do what is right, whatever happens. I'm sorry for his father, though. Did you hear what he said when he came to bid me good night: 'They think they've caught me now that they've caught my son, but let them wait—we'll see.' "

"Hush!" said Fatimah, and she pointed to the wall of the adjoining room. From the other side of it came the faint sound of measured footsteps.

"He's walking again—can't sleep, I suppose," said Fatimah, in a drowsy whisper.

"Ah, well!" said the old lady, after listening for a moment; and then Fatimah put out the light and went back to her bed.

"God bless my boy!" said a tremulous voice in the darkness.

After that there was a sigh, and then silence—save for the hollow thud of footsteps in the adjoining room.

XXII

BEFORE Gordon was out of bed next morning Hafiz rang him up on the telephone. He had just heard from his uncle, the Chancellor, that as a result of their night-long deliberation and prayer the Ulema had decided to ask the Consul-General to receive Ishmael Ameer and listen to a suggestion.

" What will it be? " asked Gordon.

" That the Government should leave El Azhar alone on condition that the Ulema consent to open it, and all the mosques connected with it, to public and police inspection, so as to dissipate the suspicion that they are centres of sedition."

" Splendid! To make the mosques as free as Christian churches is a splendid thought—an inspiration. But if the Government will not agree, what then? "

" Then the order to close El Azhar will be resisted. ' Only over our dead bodies,' they say, ' shall the soldiers enter it.' "

Gordon went about his work that morning like a man dazed and dumb, but after lunch he dressed himself carefully in his full staff uniform, with his aiguilettes hanging from his left shoulder, his gold and crimson sash, his sword and his white be-spiked helmet. He put on all his medals and decorations, too—his Distinguished Service Order; his King's and South African War Medal with four clasps; his British Soudan Medal; his Medjidieh, and his Khedive's Medal with four clasps. It was not for nothing that he did this, nor merely because he was going to an official conference, but with a certain pride as of a man who had won the right to consideration.

Taking a cab by the gate of the barracks, he drove through the native quarters of the city and saw crowds surging through the streets in the direction of El Azhar. The atmosphere seemed to tingle with the spirit of revolution, and seeing the sublime instinct of humanity which leads people in defence of their faith to the place where danger is greatest, he felt glad and proud that what was best in him was about to conquer.

Arriving at the Citadel he found Helena's black boy waiting for him at the door of the General's house with a message from his mistress, saying the gentlemen had not arrived and she wished to see him. The city below lay bright under the warm *soolham* of the afternoon sun, and the swallows were swirling past the windows of Helena's sitting-room, but Helena herself was under a cloud.

" I see what it is—you are angry with me for going to El Azhar last night," said Gordon.

" No, it isn't that, though I think you might have kept faith with me," she answered. " But we have no time to lose, and I have something to say to you. In the first place, I want you to know that Colonel Macdonald, your Deputy Assistant Adjutant, has been ordered to stand by. He will be only too happy to take your place if necessary."

" He's welcome! " said Gordon.

Her brows were contracted, her lips set. She fastened her eyes on him and said:

" Then there is something else I wish to tell you."

" What is it, Helena ? "

" When my father asked me if I could marry a man who had disobeyed and been degraded, I said . . . But it doesn't matter what I said. My father has hardly ever spoken to me since. It has been the first cloud that has come between us—the very first. But when I answered him as I did there was something I had forgotten."

" What was it, dearest ? "

" I cannot tell you what it was—I can only tell you what it comes to."

" What does it come to, Helena ? "

" That whatever happens to-day I can never leave my father—never as long as he lives."

" God forbid that you should be tempted to do so—but why ? "

" That is what I cannot tell you. It is a secret."

" I can think of no secret that I could not share with you, Helena."

"Nor I with you—if it were my own—but this isn't."

"I cannot understand you, dear."

"Say it is somebody's else's secret, and that his life, his career, depends upon it. Say it couldn't be told to you without putting you in a false position, involving you in responsibilities which you have no right to bear."

"You puzzle me, bewilder me, Helena."

"Then trust me, dear; trust me for the present, at all events, and some day you shall know everything," she said, whereupon Gordon, who had not taken his eyes off her, said:

"So what it really comes to is this—that whatever course your father takes to-day I must take it also, under pain of a violent separation from you! Isn't that it, Helena? Isn't it? And, if so, isn't it like sending a man into battle with his hands tied and his eyes blindfolded?"

She dropped her head, but made no reply.

"That is not what I expected of you, Helena. The Helena who has been living in my mind is a girl who would say to me at a moment like this, 'Do what you believe to be right, Gordon, and whether you are degraded to the lowest rank or raised to the highest honour, I will be with you—I will stand by your side!'"

Her eyes flashed and she drew herself up.

"So you think I couldn't say that—that I didn't say anything like it when my father spoke to me? But if you have been thinking of me as a girl like that, I have been thinking of you as a man who would say, 'I love you, and do you know what my love means? It means that my love for you is above everything and everybody in the world.'"

"And it is, Helena, it is."

"Then why," she said, with her eyes fixed on his, "why do you let this Egyptian and his interests come between us? If you take his part after what I have just told you, will it not be the same thing in the end as choosing him against me?"

"Don't vex me, Helena. I've told you before that your jealousy of this man is nonsense."

The word cut her to the quick and she drew herself up again.

9

"Very well," she said, with a new force, "if it's jealousy and if it's nonsense you must make your account with it. I said I *couldn't* tell you why I cannot leave my father—now I *won't*. You must choose between us. It is either that man or me."

"You mean that if the General decides against Ishmael Ameer you will follow your father, and that I—whatever my conscience may say—I must follow you?"

Her eyes blazed and she answered, "Yes."

"Good God, Helena! What is it you want me to be? Is it a man or a manikin?"

At that moment the young lieutenant who was the General's aide-de-camp came in to say that the Consul-General and the Prime Minister had arrived, and required Colonel Lord's attendance.

"Presently," said Gordon, and as soon as the lieutenant had gone he turned to Helena again.

"Helena," he said, "there is not a moment to lose. Remember, this is the last time I can see you before I am required to act one way or the other. God knows what may happen before I come out of that room. Will you send me into it without any choice?"

She was breathing hard and biting her under lip.

"Your happiness is dearer to me than anything else in life, dear; but I am a man, not a child, and if I am to follow your father in order not to lose you, I must know why. Will you tell me?"

Without raising her eyes, Helena answered, "No!"

"Very well!" he said. "In that case it must be as the fates determine." And, straightening his sword-belt, he stepped to the door.

Helena looked up at him and in a fluttering voice called, "Gordon!"

He turned, with his hand on the handle. "What is it?"

For one instant she had an impulse to break her promise and tell him of her father's infirmity, but at the next moment she thought of the Egyptian and her pride and jealousy conquered.

"What is it, Helena?"

"Nothing," she said, and fled into her bedroom.

Gordon looked after her until she had disappeared, and then—hot, angry, nervous, less able than before to meet the ordeal before him—he turned the handle of the door and entered the General's office.

XXIII

THE Consul-General, the General, and the Egyptian pasha in his tarboosh were sitting in a half-circle. The General's Military Secretary, Captain Graham, was writing at the desk, and his aide-de-camp, Lieutenant Robson, was standing beside it. Nobody was speaking as Gordon entered, and the air of the room had the dumb emptiness which goes before a storm. The General signalled to Gordon to sit, requested his aide-de-camp to step out but wait in his own office, and then said, speaking in a jerky, nervous way:

"Gordon, I have an order of the utmost importance to give you, but before I do so your father has something to say."

With that he took a seat by the side of the desk, while the Consul-General, without changing the direction of his eyes, said, slowly and deliberately:

"I need hardly tell you, Gordon, that the explanation I am about to make would be quite unnecessary in the case of an ordinary officer receiving an ordinary command, but I have decided to make it to you out of regard to the fact of who you are and what your relation to the General is to be."

Gordon bowed without speaking. He was struggling to compose himself, and something was whispering to him, "Above all things, be calm!"

"I regret to say the Ulema have ignored the order which His Excellency sent to them," said the Consul-General, indicating the pasha.

"Ignored?"

"That's what it comes to, though it's true they asked me to receive the man Ishmael Ameer and to consider a suggestion."

"You did, sir?"

"I did. The man came, I saw him, and heard what he had to say—and now I am more than ever convinced that he is a public peril."

"A peril?"

"First, because he advises officers and men to abstain from military service on the ground that war is incompatible with religion. That is opposed to the existing order of society, and therefore harmful to good government."

"I agree," said the General, swinging restlessly in his revolving chair.

"Next, because he tells the Egyptian people that where the authority of the law is opposed to what he is pleased to consider the commandments of God, they are to obey God and not the Government. That is to make every man a law to himself and to cause the rule of the Government to be defied."

The pasha smiled and bowed his thin face over his hands, which were clasped at his breast.

"Finally, because he says openly that in the time to come Egypt will be a separate State with a peculiar mission, and that means Nationalism and the end of the rule of England in the Valley of the Nile."

Gordon made an effort to speak, but his father waved him aside.

"I am not here to argue with you about the man's teaching, but merely to define it. He is one of the mischievous people who, taking no account of the religious principles which lie at the root of civilisation, would use religion to turn the world back to barbarism. What is true in his doctrines is not new, and what is new is not true. As for his reforms of polygamy, divorce, seclusion of women, and so forth, I have no use for the people who, in Cairo or in London, are for ever correcting the proof-sheets of the Almighty by reading their holy book as they please, whether it is the Koran or the Bible. And as for his prophecies, there are such things as mental strong drinks, and a man like this is providing them."

"You spoke of a suggestion, sir," said Gordon, who was still struggling to keep calm.

"His suggestion," said the Consul-General, with icy composure—"his suggestion was an aggravation of his offence. He proposed that we should leave El Azhar unmolested on condition that the Ulema opened it to the public. That meant that the Government must either countenance his sedition or suppress it by the stupid means of discussing his principles in courts of law."

The pasha smiled and the General laughed, and then in a last word the Consul-General said, quietly:

"General Graves will now tell you what we require you to do."

The General, still jerky and nervous, then said:

"All the necessary preparations have been made, Gordon. The—the Governor of the city will call you up at your quarters, and on—on receiving his message you will take a regiment of cavalry, which is ready here in the Citadel, and one battalion of infantry, which is under arms at Kasr el Nil, and accompany him to El Azhar. There—as—as commander of the troops, you—at the request of the Governor —you will take such military steps as in your opinion will be required to enter the University—and—and clear out its students and professors. You will cause ten rounds of ammunition to be issued to the men, and you will have absolute discretion as to the way you go to work, and as to the amount of force necessary to be used, but you—of course, you will be responsible for everything that is done— or not done—in carrying out your order. I—I ask you to attend to this matter at once, and to report to me to-night if possible."

When the General's flurried words were spoken there was silence for a moment, and then Gordon, trying in vain to control his voice, said, haltingly:

"You know I don't want to do this work, General, and if it *must* be done I beg of you to order some one else to do it."

"That is impossible," replied the General. "You are the proper person for this duty, and to give it to another officer would be to—to strengthen the party of rebellion by saying in so many words that there is disaffection in our own ranks."

"Then permit me to resign my appointment on your staff, sir. I don't want to do so—God knows I don't. My rank as a soldier is the one thing in the world I'm proudest of, but I would rather resign it——"

"Resign it if you please—if you are so foolish. Send in your papers; but until they are accepted you are my officer, and I must ask you to obey my order."

Gordon struggled hard with himself, and then said, boldly:

"General, you must pardon me if I tell you that you don't know what you are asking me to do."

The three old men looked sharply round at him, but he was now keyed up and did not care.

"No, sir—none of you! You think you are merely asking me to drive out of El Azhar a number of rebellious students and their teachers. But you are really asking me to kill hundreds, perhaps thousands, of them."

"Fudge! Fiddlesticks!" cried the General, and then, forgetting the presence of the pasha, he said: "These people are Egyptians—miserable, pigeon-livered Egyptians! Before you fire a shot they'll fly away to a man. But even if they stay, the responsibility will be their own—so what the dev——"

"That's just where we join issue, General," said Gordon. "There isn't a worm that hasn't a right to resent a wrong, and this will be a wrong, and the people will be justified in resenting it."

The General, who was breathing hard, turned to the Consul-General and said, "I'm sorry, my lord, very sorry, but you see——"

There was a short silence, and then the Consul-General, still calm on the outside as a frozen lake, said, "Gordon, I presume you know what you will be doing if you refuse to obey your General's order?"

Gordon did not answer, and his father, in a biting note, continued:

"I dare say you suppose you are following the dictates of conscience, and I don't question your sincerity. I'm beginning to see that this Empire of ours is destined to be destroyed in the end by its humanitarians, its philanthropists, its foolish people who are bewitched by good intentions."

The sarcasm was cutting Gordon to the bone, but he did not reply, and presently the old man's voice softened.

"I presume you know that if you refuse to obey your General's order you will be dealing a blow at your father—dishonouring him, accusing him. Your refusal will go far. There will be no hushing it up. England as well as Egypt will hear of it."

A deep flush overspread the Proconsul's face.

"For forty years I've been doing the work of civilisation in this country. I think progress has received a certain impetus. And now, when I am old and my strength is not what it was once, my son—my only son—is pulling the lever that is to bring my house down over my head."

The old man's voice trembled and almost broke.

"You've not thought of that, I suppose?"

Gordon's emotions almost mastered him. "Yes, sir," he said, "I have thought of it, and it's a great grief to me to oppose you. But it would be a still greater grief to help you—to help you to undo all the great work you have ever done in Egypt. Father, believe me, I know what I'm saying. There will be bloodshed, and as sure as that happens there will be an outcry all over the Mohammedan world. The prestige of England will suffer—in India—in Europe—America—everywhere. And you, father, you alone will be blamed."

At that the General rose in great wrath, but the Consul-General interposed.

"One moment, please! I am anxious to make allowances for fanaticism, and at a moment of tension I could wish to avoid any act that might create a conflagration. Therefore," he said, turning to Gordon, "if you are so sure that there will be bloodshed, I am willing to hold my hand, on one condition—that the man Ishmael, the mouthpiece of the sedition we wish to suppress, should leave Egypt without delay."

Gordon did not reply immediately, and his father continued: "Why not? It is surely better that one man should go than that the whole nation should suffer. Send him out, drive him out, walk him over the frontier, and for the present I am satisfied."

"Father," said Gordon, "what you ask me to do is impossible. The Egyptians believe Ishmael to be one of the prophets who are sent into the world to keep the souls of men alive. He is like the Mahdi to them, and—who knows? —they may come to think of him as the Redeemer, the Christ, who is to pacify the world. Right or wrong, they think of him already as a living protest against that part of Western civilisation which is the result of force and fraud. Therefore, to drive him out of the country would be the same thing to them as to drive out religion. In their view it would be a sin against humanity—a sin against God."

But the General could bear no more. Rising from the desk, he said, contemptuously:

"All that's very fine, very exalted, I dare say, but we are plain soldiers, you and I, and we cannot follow the flights of great minds like these Mohammedan Sheikhs. So without further argument I ask you if you are willing to carry out the order I have given you."

"It would be a crime, sir."

"Crime or no crime, it would be no concern of yours. Do you refuse to obey my order?"

"Recall your order, sir, and I shall have no reason to refuse to obey it."

"Do you refuse to obey my order?"

"It would be against my conscience, General."

"Your conscience is not in question. Your only duty is to carry out the will of your superior."

"When I accepted my commission in the army did I lose my rights as a human being, sir?"

"Don't talk to me about losing your rights. In the face of duty an officer loses father and mother, wife and child.

According to the King's regulations, you are an officer first, remember."

"No, sir; according to the King's regulations I am first of all a man."

The General bridled his gathering anger and answered: "Of course, you can ask for a written order—if you wish to avoid the danger of blame."

"I wish to avoid the danger of doing wrong, sir," said Gordon, and then, glancing toward his father, he added: "Let me feel that I'm fighting for the right. An English soldier cannot fight without that."

"Then I ask you as an English soldier if you refuse to obey my order?" repeated the General. But Gordon, still with his face toward his father, said:

"Wherever the English flag flies men say, 'Here is justice.' That's something to be proud of. Don't let us lose it, sir."

"I ask you again," said the General, "if you refuse to obey my order?"

"I have done wrong things without knowing them," said Gordon, "but when you ask me to——"

"England asks you to obey your General—will you do it?" said General Graves; and then Gordon faced back to him, and in a voice that rang through the room he said:

"No; not for England will I do what I *know* to be wrong."

At that the Consul-General waved his hand and said, "Let us have done"; whereupon General Graves, who was now violently agitated, touched a hand-bell on the desk, and when his servant appeared he said:

"Tell my daughter to come to me."

Not a word more was spoken until light footsteps were heard approaching, and Helena came into the room with a handkerchief in her hand, pale as if she had been crying, and breathless as if she had been running hard. The three old gentlemen rose and bowed to her as she entered, but Gordon, whose face had frowned when he heard the General's command, rose and sat down again without turning in her direction.

"Sit down, Helena," said the General; and Helena sat.

"Helena, you will remember that I asked you if you could marry an officer who, for disobedience to his General —and that General your father—had been court-martialled and perhaps degraded?"

In a scarcely audible voice Helena answered, "Yes."

"Then tell Colonel Lord what course you will take if, by his own deliberate act, that misfortune should befall him."

A hot blush mounted to Helena's cheeks, and, looking at the hem of her handkerchief, she said:

"Gordon knows already what I would say, father. There is no need to tell him."

Then the General turned back to Gordon. "You hear?" he said. "I presume you understand Helena's answer. For the sake of our mutual peace and happiness I wished to give you one more chance. The issue is now plain. Either you obey your General's order or you renounce all hope of his daughter—which is it to be?"

The young man swallowed his anger, and answered: "Is it fair, sir—fair to Helena, I mean—to put her to a test like that—either violent separation from her father or from me? But as you have spoken to Helena, I ask you to allow me to do so also."

"No; I forbid it," said the General.

"Don't be afraid, sir. I'm not going to appeal over your head to any love for me in Helena's heart. That must speak for itself now—if it's to speak at all. But "—his voice was so soft and low that it could hardly be heard—" I wish to ask her a question. Helena——"

"I forbid it, I tell you," said the General, hotly.

There was a moment of tense silence, and then Gordon, who had suddenly become hoarse, said: "You spoke about a written order, General. Give it to me."

"With pleasure!" said the General, and, turning to his Military Secretary at the desk, he requested him to make out an order in the Order Book according to the terms of his verbal command.

Nothing was heard in the silence of the next moment but

the spasmodic scratching of Captain Graham's quill pen. The Consul-General sat motionless, and the pasha merely smoothed one white hand over the other. Gordon tried to glance into Helena's face, but she looked fixedly before her out of her large, wide-open, swollen eyes.

Only one idea shaped itself clearly through the storm that raged in Gordon's brain: to secure his happiness with Helena he must make himself unhappy in every other relation in life—to save himself from degradation as a soldier he must degrade himself as a man.

Presently, through the whirling mist of his half-consciousness, he was aware that the Military Secretary had ceased writing and that the General was offering him a paper.

"Here it is," the General was saying, with a certain bitterness. "Now you may set your mind at ease. If there are any bad consequences you can preserve your reputation as an officer. And if there are any complaints from the War Office, or anywhere else, you can lay the blame on me. You can go on with your duty without fear for your honour, and when——"

But Gordon, whose gorge had risen at every word, suddenly lost control of himself, and, getting up with the paper in his hand, he said:

"No, I will not go on. Do you suppose I have been thinking of myself? Take back your order. There is no obedience due to a sinful command, and this command is sinful. It is wicked, it is mad, it is abominable. You are asking me to commit murder—that's it—murder—and I will not commit it. There's your order—take it back, and damn it!"

So saying, he crushed the paper in his hands and flung it on the desk.

At the next instant everybody in the room had risen. There was consternation on every face, and the General, who was choking with anger, was saying, in a half-stifled voice:

"You are no fool—you know what you have done now. You have not only refused to obey orders—you have insulted your General and been guilty of deliberate insubordination.

Therefore you are unworthy of bearing arms. Give me your
sword."

Gordon hesitated for a moment, and the General said:
" Give it me—give it me! "

Then with a rapid gesture Gordon unbuckled his sword
from the belt and handed it to the General.

The General held it in both his hands, which were vibrating like the parts of an engine from the moving power
within, while he said, in the same half-stifled voice as before:

" You have had the greatest opportunity that ever came
to an English soldier and—thrown it away. You have humiliated your father, outraged the love of your intended
wife, and insulted England. Therefore you are a traitor! "

Gordon quivered visibly at that word, and, seeing this,
the General hurled it at him again.

" A traitor, I say. A traitor who has consorted with the
enemies of his country." With that he drew the sword from
its scabbard, broke it across his knee, and flung the fragments at Gordon's feet.

Helena turned and fled from the room in agony at the
harrowing scene, and the Consul-General, unable to bear the
sight of it, rose and walked to the window, his face broken
up with pain as no one had ever seen it before.

Then the General, who had been worked up to a towering
rage by his own words and acts, lost himself utterly, and
saying: " You are unfit to wear the decorations of an
English soldier. Take them off—take them off! " he laid
hold of Gordon's medals—the Distinguished Service Order,
the South African Medal with its four clasps, the British
Soudan Medal, the Medjidieh, and the Khedive's star—and
tore them from his tunic, ripping pieces of the cloth away
with them, and threw them on the ground.

Then, in a voice like the scream of a wild bird, he cried:
" Now go! Go back to your quarters and consider yourself
under arrest. Or take my advice and be off altogether. Quit
the army you have dishonoured and the friends you have
disgraced, and hide your infamous conduct in some foreign
land. Leave the room at once! "

Gordon had stood through this gross indignity bolt upright, and without speaking. His face had become deathly white and his colourless lower lip had trembled. At the end, while the old General was taking gusts of breath, he tried to say something, but his tongue refused to speak. At length he staggered rather than walked to the door, and, with his hand on the handle, he turned, and said, quietly, but in a voice which his father never afterward forgot:

"General, the time may come when it will be even more painful to you to remember all this than it has been to me to bear it."

Then he stumbled out of the room.

XXIV

OUT in the hall he had an impulse to turn toward Helena's room on the right; but through his half-blind eyes he saw Helena herself on the left, standing by the open entrance to the garden, with her handkerchief at her mouth.

"Helena!"

She made a little nervous cry, but stifling it in her throat she turned hotly round on him.

"You told me that love was above everything," she said, "and this is how you love me!"

Torn as he was to his heart's core, outraged as he believed himself to be, he made a feeble effort to excuse himself.

"I couldn't help it, Helena—it was impossible for me to act otherwise."

"Oh, I know! I know!" she said. "You were doing what you thought to be right. But I am no match for you. You have duties that are higher than your duty to me."

Her tone cut him to the quick, and he tried to speak, but could not. Like a drowning man he stretched out his hand to her, but she made no response.

"It was not to be, I see that now," she said, while her eyes filled and her bosom heaved. "I am not worthy of you. But I loved you and I thought you loved me, and I believed you when you told me that nothing could come between us."

Again he tried to speak, to explain, to protest, but his tongue would not utter a sound.

"If you had really loved me you would have been ready to . . . even to . . . But I was mistaken and I am punished, and this is how it is to end!"

"Helena, for God's sake—" he began, but he could bear no more. He did not see that the girl's love was fighting with her pride. The hideous injustice of it all was working like madness in his brain, and after a moment he turned to go.

As he walked across the garden the ground under his feet sounded hollow in his ears, like the ground above a new-covered grave. When he reached the gate he thought he heard Helena calling in a pleading, sobbing voice:

"Gordon!"

But when he turned to look back she had disappeared.

Then, bareheaded, without helmet or sword, with every badge of rank and honour gone, he pulled the gate open and staggered into the square.

XXV

HELENA returned to her father's room and found the two old men getting ready to go. In the pasha's face there were traces of that impulse to smile which comes to shallow natures in the presence of another person's troubles. But the face of the Consul-General was a tragic sight. The square-set jaw hung low, and the eyes were heavy as with unshed tears. It was easy to see that the iron man was deeply moved—that the depths of his ice-bound soul were utterly broken up.

Only in short, disjointed sentences did he speak at all. It was about his enemies—the corrupt, cruel, and hypocritical upholders of the old, dark ways. They had bided their time; they had taken their revenge; they had hit him at last where he could least bear a blow; they had struck him in the face with the hand of his only son.

"There is no shame left in them," he said, and then he turned to Helena as if intending to say some word of sympathy. He wanted to tell her that he had hoped for other things, and would have been happy if they had come to pass. But when he saw the girl standing before him with her red eyes and pale cheeks he hesitated, grasped her hand, held it for a moment, and then walked away without a word.

The Military Secretary accompanied the Consul-General and the pasha to their carriages, and so father and daughter were left together. The General, labouring under the most painful of all senses, the sense of having done an unworthy thing, walked for some minutes about the room and talked excitedly, while Helena sat on the sofa in silence, and, resting her chin on her hand, looked fixedly before her.

"Well, well, it's all over, thank God! It couldn't be helped, either. It had to be. Better as it is, too, than if it had come later on. . . . How hot I am! My throat is like fire. Get me a drink of water, girl."

"Let me give you your medicine, father. It's here on the desk," said Helena.

"No, no! Water, girl, water! That's right. There! . . . He has gone, I suppose? Has he gone? Yes? Good thing, too. Hope I'll never see him again. I never will—never! . . . How my head aches! No wonder, either."

"You're ill, father; let me run for the doctor."

"Certainly not. I'm all right. Sit down, girl—sit down and don't worry. . . . You mustn't mind me. I'm a bit put out—naturally. It's hard for you, I know, but don't cry, Helena."

"I'm not crying, father—you see I'm not."

"That's right! That's right, dear! It's hard for you, I say, but then it isn't easy for me, either. I liked him; I did—I confess it. I really liked him, and to . . . to do that was like cutting off one's own son. But . . . give me another drink of water, Helena . . . or, perhaps, if you think you ought to run . . . no, give me the medicine, and I'll be better presently."

She poured out a dose and he drank it off.

"Now I'll lie down and close my eyes. I soon get better

when I lie down and close my eyes, you know. And don't fret, dear. Think what an escape you've had! Merciful heavens! A traitor! Think if you had married a traitor! A man who had sold himself to the enemies of England! I was proud of you when you showed him that, come what would, you must stand by your country. Splendid! Just what I expected of you, Helena. Splendid!"

After a while his excited speech and gusty breathing softened down to silence and to something like sleep, and then Helena sat on a stool beside the sofa and covered her face with her hands. A hot flush mounted to her pale cheeks when she remembered that it had not been for England that she had acted as she had, but first for her father and next for herself.

Perhaps she ought to have told Gordon why she could not leave her father. If she had done so he might have acted otherwise. But the real author of the whole trouble had been the Egyptian. How she hated that man! With all the bitterness of her tortured heart she hated him.

As for Gordon, traitor or no traitor, he had been above them all! Far, far above everybody! Even the Consul-General, now she came to think of it, had been a little man compared with his son.

With her face buried in both hands and the tears at last trickling through her fingers, she saw everything over again, and one thing above all—Gordon standing in silence while her father insulted and degraded him.

The General opened his eyes, and seeing Helena at his feet he tried to comfort her, but every word he spoke went like iron into her soul.

"I'm sorry for you, Helena—very sorry! We must bear this trouble together, dear. Only ourselves again now, you know, just as it was five years ago at home. Your dark hour this time, darling; but I'll make it up to you. Come, kiss me, Helena," and, drying her weary eyes, she kissed him.

The afternoon sun was then reddening the alabaster walls of the mosque outside, and they heard a surging sound as of a crowd approaching. A moment later little black Mosie ran in to say that the new Mahdi was coming, and almost before the General and Helena could rise to their feet a tall man in white Oriental costume entered the room. He came in slowly, solemnly, and with head bent, saying:

"Excuse me, sir, if I come without ceremony——"

"Ishmael Ameer?" asked the General.

"My name is Ishmael—you are the Commander of the British forces. May I speak with you alone?"

The General stood still for a moment, measuring his man from head to foot, and then said:

"Leave us, Helena."

Helena hesitated, and the General said, "I'm better now —leave us."

With that she went out reluctantly, turning at the door to look at her enemy, who stood in his great height in the middle of the floor and never so much as glanced in her direction.

XXVI

BOTH men continued to stand during the interview that followed—the one in his white robes, by the end of the sofa, resting two tapering fingers upon it, the other in his General's uniform by the side of the desk, except when, in the heat of his anger, he strode with heavy step and the jingling of spurs across the space between.

"Now, sir, now," said the General. "I have urgent work to do, and not much time to give you. What is it?"

"I come," said Ishmael, who was outwardly very calm, though his large black eyes were full of fire and light, "I come to speak to you about the order to close El Azhar."

"Then you come to the wrong place," said the General, sharply. "You should go to the Agency—the British Agency."

"I have seen the English lord already. He refuses to withdraw his order. Therefore I am here to ask you—forgive me—I am here to ask you not to obey it."

The General tried to laugh. "Wonderful!" he said. "Your Eastern ideas of discipline are wonderful! Please understand, sir, *I* am here as the instrument of authority—that, and that only."

"An instrument has its responsibility," said Ishmael. "If there were no instruments to do evil deeds, would evil deeds be done? It is not your fault, sir, that the order has been issued, but it *will* be your fault if it is carried into effect."

"Really!" said the General, again trying to laugh. "Permit me to tell you, sir, that in this case there will be no fault in question, either of mine or anybody else's. El Azhar is a hotbed of sedition, and it is high time the Government cleared it out."

"El Azhar," said Ishmael, "is the heart of the Moslem faith. Take their religion away from them and the Moslems have nothing left. You are a Christian, and when your great Master was on earth He fed the souls of the people first."

"Yes, and he whipped the rascals out of the temple, and that's what the Government is going to do now—to drive out the pretentious impostors who are putting a lying spirit into the mouth of the people and making it impossible to govern them."

The Egyptian showed no anger. "I am here only to plead for the people, sir. Do not harden your heart against them. Do not send armed men among an unarmed populace. It will be slaughter."

"Tell them to submit to the Government, and there will be no harm done to anyone. It's their duty, isn't it? Whatever the Government may be, isn't it their duty to submit to it?"

"Yes," said Ishmael. "We who are Moslems are taught by the Prophet—blessed be his name—that even if a negro slave is appointed to rule over us we ought to obey him."

"Deuce take it, sir, what do you mean by that?" said the General.

"But government is a trust from God," said the Egyptian, "and at the day of Resurrection the Most High will ask you what you have done to His children."

"Damn it, sir, have you come here to preach me a sermon?"

"I have come to plead with you for justice—the justice you look for from your Saviour. Be merciful to the weak, He taught, and it is for the weak I appeal to you. He was meek and lowly—will you forget His precepts? 'Love one another'—will you make strife between man and man? He is dead—shall it be said that His spirit has died out among those who call Him their Redeemer?"

The General brought his fist heavily down on the desk as if to command silence.

"Listen here, sir," he said. "If you imagine for one moment that this tall talk will have any effect upon me, let me advise you to drop it. Being a plain soldier who has received a plain command, I shall take whatever military steps are necessary to see it faithfully carried out, and if the precious leaders of the people, playing on their credulity and fanaticism, should instigate rebellion, I shall have the honour—understand me plainly—I shall have the honour to lodge them in safe quarters, whosoever they are and whatsoever their pretensions may be."

The Egyptian's eyes showed at that moment that he was a man capable of wild frenzy, but he controlled himself and answered:

"I am not here to defend myself, sir. You can take me now if you choose to do so. But if I cannot plead with you for the people, let me plead with you for yourself—your family."

The General, who had turned away from Ishmael, swung round on him.

"My family?"

"'He that troubleth his own house,' saith the Koran, 'shall inherit the wind.' Will you, my brother, allow your daughter to be separated from the brave man who loves her? A woman is tender and sweet; all she wants is love; and love is a sacred thing, sir. Your daughter is your flesh and blood—will you make her unhappy? I see a day when you are dead—will it comfort you in the grave that two who should be together are apart?"

"They're apart already, so that's over and done with," said the General. "But listen to me again, sir. My girl needs none of your pity. She has done her duty as a soldier's daughter, and cut off the traitor whom you, and men like you, appear to have corrupted. Look here—and here," he cried, pointing to the broken sword and the medals, which were still lying where he had flung them on the floor. "The man has gone—gone in disgrace and shame. That's what you've done for him, if it's any satisfaction to you to know it. As for my daughter," he said, raising his voice in his gathering wrath and striding up to Ishmael with heavy steps and the jingling of his spurs—"as for my daughter, Helena —I will ask you to be so good as to keep her name out of it. Do you hear? Keep her name out of it, or else——"

At that moment the men heard the door open and a woman's light footsteps behind them. It was Helena coming into the room.

"Did you call me, father?" she asked.

"No. Go back immediately."

She looked doubtfully at the two men, who were now face to face as if in the act of personal quarrel, hesitated, seemed about to speak, and then went out slowly.

There was silence for a moment after she was gone, and then Ishmael said:

"Do I understand you to say, sir, that Colonel Lord has gone in disgrace?"

"Yes; for consorting with the enemies of his country and refusing to obey the order of his General."

"Lost his place and rank as a soldier?"

"Soon will, and then he will be alone and have you to thank for it."

The Egyptian drew himself up to his full height and answered: "You are wrong, sir. He who has no one has God, and if that brave man has suffered rather than do an evil act, will God forget him? No!"

"God will do as He thinks best without considering either you or me, sir," said the General. "But I have something to do, and I will ask you to leave me. . . . Or wait one moment! Lest you should carry away the impression

[Page 128.]

" ' The man has gone—gone in disgrace and shame.' "

that because Colonel Lord has refused to obey his General's order the order will not be obeyed, wait and see."

He touched the bell, and called for his aide-de-camp.

"Tell Colonel Macdonald to come to me immediately," said the General, and when the aide-de-camp had gone he turned to his desk for papers.

The Egyptian, who had never moved from his place by the sofa, now took one step forward and said in a low, quivering voice, "General, I have appealed to you on behalf of my people and on your own behalf, but there is one thing more."

"What is it?"

"Your country."

The General made an impatient gesture, and the Egyptian said, "Hear me, I beg, I pray! Real as life, real as death, real as wells of water in a desert place, is their religion to the Muslemeen, and if you lay so much as your finger upon it your Government will die."

He raised his hand and with one trembling finger pointed upward. "Do you think your swords will govern them? What can your swords do to their souls? By the Most High God, I swear to you that I have only to speak the word, and the rule of England in Egypt will end."

At that moment Colonel Macdonald, a large man in khaki, a Highlander, with a ruddy face and a glass in his left eye, opened the door and stood by it, while the General, whose own face was scarlet with anger, said:

"So! So that's how you talked to Colonel Lord, I presume—how you darkened the poor devil's understanding! Now see—see what effect your threats have upon me. Step forward, Colonel Macdonald."

The Colonel saluted and stepped up to the General, who repeated to him word for word the order he had given to Gordon, and then said:

"You will arrest all who resist you, and if any resist with violence you will *compel* obedience—you understand?"

"Perfectly," said the Colonel, and saluting again he left the room.

"Now, sir, you can go," said the General to Ishmael,

whereupon the Egyptian, whose face had taken on an extreme pallor, replied:

"Very well. I have warned you and you will not hear me. But I tell you that at this moment Israfil has the trumpet to his mouth, and is only waiting for God's order to blow it! I tell you, too, that I see you—you—on the Day of Judgment, and there are black marks on your face."

"Silence, sir!" said the General, bringing his clenched fist heavily down on the desk. Then he struck the bell and in a choking voice called first for his servant and afterward for his aide-de-camp. "Robson! See this man out of the Citadel! This damnable, presumptuous braggart! Robson! Where are you?" But the servant did not appear and the aide-de-camp did not answer.

"No matter," said the Egyptian. "I will go of myself. I will try to forget the hard words you have said of me. I will not retort them upon you. You are a Christian, and it was a Christian who said, 'Resist not evil.' That is a commandment as binding upon us as upon you. God's will be done!"

With that Ishmael went out as he had entered, slowly, solemnly, with head bent and eyes on the ground.

XXVII

The General was now utterly exhausted. Being left alone he leaned against the desk, intending to wait until his breathing had become more regular and he could reach the sofa. Standing there he heard the surging noise of the crowd that had been waiting outside for their Arab prophet, and were now going away with him. He wanted to call Helena, but restrained himself, remembering how often she had warned him.

"Robson!" he called again, but again the aide-de-camp did not answer—he must have gone off on some errand for Colonel Macdonald.

The General took up his medicine and gulped down a

large dose, drinking from the neck of the bottle, and then sank on to the sofa.

Some minutes passed, and he began to feel better. The sunset was deflected into his face from the alabaster walls of the mosque outside, but he could not get up to pull down the blind of his window. So he closed his eyes and thought of what had happened.

It seemed to him that Gordon had been to blame for everything. But for Gordon's monstrous conduct they would have been spared this trouble—Lord Nuneham's crushing blow, his own humiliating action, so wickedly forced upon him, and, above all, Helena's sorrow.

In the delirium of his anger against Gordon he felt as if he would choke. Thinking of Helena and her ruined happiness, he wondered why he had let Gordon off so lightly, and he wanted to follow and punish him.

Then he heard the door open, and, thinking Helena was coming into the room, he rose to his feet and faced around, when before him, with a haggard face, stood Gordon himself.

XXVIII

WHEN Gordon Lord, after parting with Helena, had left the Citadel, his mental anguish had been so intense as to deaden all his faculties. His reason was clogged, his ideas were obscure, he could not see or hear properly. Passing the sentry in his lodge by the gate, he did not notice the man's bewildered stare or acknowledge his abbreviated salute. The whole event of the last hour had overwhelmed him as with a terrible darkness, and in this darkness he plodded on until he came into the streets, dense with people and clamorous with all the noises of an Eastern city—the clapping of water-carriers, the crying of lemonade-sellers, the braying of donkeys, and the ruckling of camels.

"Where am I going?" he asked himself at one moment, and when he remembered that he was going back to his quarters, for that was what he had been ordered to do, that

he might be under arrest and in due course tried by court-
martial, he told himself that he had been tried and condemned and punished already. At that thought, though
clouded and obscure, he bit his lip until it bled, and thought,
" No, I cannot go back to quarters—I will not!"

At the next moment a certain helplessness came over him,
and up from the deep place where the strongest man is as
a child, by the pathetic instinct that keeps the boy alive in
him to the last dark day of his life and in the hour of death,
came a desire to go home—to his mother. But when he
thought of his mother's pleading voice as she begged him to
keep peace with his father, and then, by some juggling twist
of torturing memory, of the first evening after his return to
Egypt, when he wore his medals and she fingered them on
his breast with a pride that no queen ever had in the jewels
in her crown, he said to himself, " No, I can never go home
again."

His mind was oscillating among these agonising thoughts
when he became aware that he was walking in the Esbekiah
district, the European quarter of Cairo, where the ooze of
the gutter of the city is flung up under the public eye; and
there under the open piazza, containing a line of drinking-
places, in an atmosphere that was thick with tobacco smoke,
the reek of alcohol, the babel of many tongues, the striking
of matches, and the popping of corks, he sat down at a table
and called for a glass of brandy.

The brandy seemed to clear his faculties for a moment,
and his aimless and wandering thoughts began to concen-
trate themselves. Then the scene in the General's office came
back to him—the drawing of his sword from its scabbard,
the breaking of it across the knee, the throwing of the
wretched fragments at his feet, the ripping away of his medals, and the trampling of them underfoot. The hideous memory of it all, so illegal, so un-English, made his blood boil,
and when his beaten brain swung back to the scenes in which
he won his honours at the risk of his life—Omdurman,
Ladysmith, Pretoria—the rank injustice he had suffered almost stifled him with rage, and he swore and struck the
table.

All his anger was against the General, not against his father, of whom he had hardly thought at all; but the cruellest agony he passed through came at the moment when his wrath rose against Helena. As he thought of her he became dizzy; his brain reeled with a dance of ideas in which no picture lasted longer than an instant, and no emotion would stay. At one moment he was seeing her as he saw her first, with her big eyes, black as a sloe, the joyous smile that was one of her greatest charms, the arched brow, the silken lashes, the gleam of celestial fire, the "Don't go yet" that came in her look, and then the quickening pulse, the thrill that passed through him, and the mysterious voice that whispered, "It is She!"

Without knowing it he groaned aloud as he thought of the ruin all this had come to; and at the next moment he was in the midst of another memory—a memory of the future as he had imagined it would be. They were to be married soon, and then, realising one of the dreams of his life, they were to visit America, for his mother's blood called to him to go there, to see the great new world—yes, but above all to stand, with Helena's quivering hand in his, on that rock at Plymouth where a handful of fearless men and women had landed on a bleak and hungry coast, afraid of no fate, for God was with them, and in two short centuries had peopled a vast continent and created one of the mightiest empires of the earth. Remembering this as a vanished dream, his wretched soul was on the edge of a vortex of madness, and he laughed outright with a laugh that shivered the air around him.

Then he was conscious that somebody was speaking to him. It was a young girl in a gaudy silk dress, with a pasty face, lips painted very red, eyebrows darkened, a flower in her full bosom, which was covered with transparent lace, and a little satchel swinging on her wrist.

"Overdoing it a bit, haven't you, dear?" she said in French, and she smiled at him, a poor sidelong smile, out of her crushed and crumpled soul.

At the same moment he became aware that three men at a table behind him were winking at the girl and joking at

10

his expense. One of them, a little, fat American Jew with puffy cheeks, chewing the end of a cigar, was saying:

"Guess a man don't have no use for a hat in a climate like this—sun so soft, and only ninety-nine in the shade."

Whereupon an Englishman, with a ripped and ragged mouth and a miscellaneous nose, half pug and half Roman, answered:

"Been hanging himself up on a nail by the breast of his coat, too, you bet."

Putting his hand to his hair and looking down at the torn cloth of his tunic, Gordon realised for the first time that he was bareheaded, having left his helmet at the Citadel, and that to the unclean consciousness of the people about him he was drunk.

At that moment he started up suddenly, and coming into collision with the American, who was swinging on the back legs of his chair, he sent him sprawling on the ground, where he yelled:

"Here, I say, you blazing——"

But the third man at the table, a dragoman in a fez, whispered:

"Hush! I know that gentlemans. Leave him alone, sirs, please. Let him go."

With heart and soul aflame, Gordon walked away, intending to take the first cab that came along and then forgetting to do so. One wild thought now took possession of him and expelled all other thoughts. He must go back to the Citadel and accuse the General of his gross injustice. He must say what he meant to say when he stood by the door as he was going out. The General should hear it—he should, and, by ——, he must!

The brandy was working in his brain by this time, and in the blind leading of passion everything that happened on the way seemed to fortify his resolve. The streets of the native city were now surging with people, as a submerged mine surges with the water that runs through it. He knew where they were going—they were going to El Azhar—and when he came near to the great mosque he had to fight his way through a crowd that was coming from the opposite direction, with the turbaned head of a very tall man in the midst of the multitude, who were chanting verses from the Koran and crying in chorus, " La ilaha illa-llah!"

At sight of this procession, knowing what it meant, that the Moslems were going to the doomed place to defend it or die, a thousand confused forms danced before Gordon's eyes. His impatience to reach the Citadel became feverish and he began to run, but again he was kept back. This time it was a troop of cavalry, who were trotting hard toward El Azhar. He saw his deputy, Macdonald, with his blotchy face and his monocle, but he was himself seen by no one, and in the crush he was almost ridden down.

The Citadel, when he reached it, seemed to be deserted, even the sentry standing with his back to him in the sentry-box as he hurried through. There was nobody in the square of the mosque or yet at the gate to the General's garden, which was open, and the door of the house, when he came to it, was open, too. With the hot blood in his head, his teeth compressed and his nostrils quivering, he burst into the General's office and came face to face with the old soldier as he was rising from the sofa. Thus in the blind swirl of circumstance the two men met at the moment when the heart of each was full of hatred for the other.

They were brave men both of them, and never for one instant had either of them known what it was to feel afraid. They were not afraid now, but they had loved each other once, and up from what deep place in their souls God alone can say there came a wave of feeling that fought with their hate. The General no longer wanted to punish Gordon, but only that Gordon should go away, while Gordon's rage, which was to have thundered at the General, broke into an agonising cry.

"What are you doing here? Didn't I order you to your quarters? Do you wish me to put you under close arrest? Get off!"

"Not yet. You and I have to settle accounts first. You have behaved like a tyrant. A tyrant—that's the only word for it! If I was guilty of insubordination, you were guilty of outrage. You had a right to arrest me and to order that

I should be court-martialled. But what right had you to condemn me before I was tried, and punish me before I was sentenced? Before or after, what right had you to break my sword and tear off my medals? Degradation is obsolete in the British Army. What right had you to degrade me? Before my father, too, and before Helena! What *right* had you?"

"Leave my house instantly! Leave it! Leave it!" said the General, his voice coming thick and hoarse.

"Not till you hear what I've come to tell you," said Gordon, and then—who knows on what inherited cell of his brain imprinted?—he repeated the threat his father had made forty years before:

"I've come to tell you that I'll go back to my quarters and you shall court-martial me to-morrow *if you dare*. Before that England may know, by what is done to-night, that I refused to obey your order because I'm a soldier—not a murderer. But if she never knows," he cried, in his broken voice, "and you try me and condemn me and degrade me even to the ranks, I'll get up again—do you hear me?—I'll get up again and win back all I've lost and more—until I'm your own master and you'll have to obey *me!*"

The General's face became scarlet, and, lifting his hand as if to strike Gordon, he cried, in a choking voice:

"Go, before I do something . . ."

But Gordon, in the delirium of his rage, heard nothing except the sound of his own quivering voice.

"More than that," he said, "I'll win back Helena. She was mine, and you have separated her from me, and broken her heart as well as my own. Was that the act of a father, or of a robber and a tyrant? But she will come back to me, and when you are dead and in your grave we shall be together, because . . . Stop that! Stop it, I say!"

The General, unable to command himself any longer, had snatched up the broken sword from the floor, and was making for Gordon as if to smite him.

"Stand away! You are an old man and I am not a coward. Drop that, or, by God, you——"

But the General, losing himself utterly, flung himself on

Gordon with the broken sword, his voice gone in a husky growl and his breath coming in hoarse gusts.

The struggle was short but terrible. Gordon, in the strength of his young manhood, first laid hold of the General by the upper part of the breast to keep him off, and then, feeling that his hand was wounded, he gripped at the old man's throat with fingers that clung like claws. At the next moment he snatched the sword from the General, and at the same instant, with a delirious laugh, he flung the man himself away.

The General fell heavily with a deep groan and a gurgling cry. Gordon, with a contemptuous gesture, threw the broken sword on to the floor, and then, with the growl of a wild creature, he turned to go.

"Fight me—would you, eh? Kill me, perhaps! We've settled accounts at last—haven't we?"

But hearing no answer he turned at the door to look back and saw the General lying where he had fallen, outstretched and still. At that sight the breath seemed to go out of his body at one gasp. His head turned giddy, and the red gleams of the sunset, which were deflected into the room, appeared to his half-blind eyes to cover everything with blood.

XXIX

Gordon stood with his mouth open, the brute sense struck out of him by the dead silence. Then he said, " Get up! Why don't you get up?" hardly knowing what he was saying.

He got no answer, and a horrible idea began to take shape in his mind. Though so hot a moment ago, he shivered and his teeth began to chatter. He looked around him for a moment in the dazed way of a man awakening from a nightmare, and then stepped up on tiptoe to where the General lay.

Raising his head, he looked at him and found it hard to believe that what he vaguely feared had happened. There was no sign of injury anywhere. The eyes were open, and they looked fixedly at him with so fierce a stare that they seemed to jump out of their sockets.

"Stunned—that's all—stunned by the fall," he thought, and, seeing a bottle of brandy on the shelf of the desk, he got up and poured a little into the medicine glass, and then, kneeling and lifting the General's head again, he forced the liquor through the tightly compressed lips.

It ran out as it went in, and then, with gathering fear and fumbling fingers, Gordon unbuttoned the General's frock-coat and laid a trembling hand over his heart. At one moment he thought he felt a beat, but at the next he knew it was only the throb of his own pulse.

At that the world seemed for a moment to be blotted out, and when he came to himself again he was holding the General in his arms and calling to him.

"General! General! Speak to me! For God's sake, speak to me!"

In the torrent of his remorse he was kissing the General's forehead and crying over his face, but there was no response.

Then a great trembling shook his whole body, and dropping the head gently back to the floor he rose to his feet. The General was dead, and he knew it.

He had seen death a hundred times before, but only on the battle-field, amid the boom of cannon, the wail of shell, the snap of rifles, and the oaths of men, but now it filled him with terror.

The silence was awful. A minute ago the General had been a living man, face to face with him, and the room had been ringing with the clashing of their voices; but now this breathless hush, this paralysing stillness, in which the very air seemed to be dead, for something was gone as by the stroke of an almighty hand, and there was nothing left but the motionless figure at his feet.

"What have I done?" he asked, and when he told himself that in his headstrong wrath he had killed a man, his head spun round and round. He who had refused to obey orders because he would not commit murder was guilty of murder himself! What devil out of hell had ordered things so that, as the very consequence of refusing to commit a crime, he had become a criminal?

"God have pity upon me and tell me it is not true," he thought.

But he knew it was true, and when he told himself that the man he had killed was his General, his pain increased tenfold. The General had loved him and favoured him, been proud of him and upheld him, and never, down to the coming of this trouble, had their friendship been darkened by a cloud.

"Oh, forgive me! God forgive me!" he thought.

In his blind misery, which hardly saw itself yet for what it was, the impulse came to him to carry the burden of his sin, too heavy for himself, to Helena, that she might help him to bear it; and he had taken some steps toward the door leading to her room when it struck him as a blow on the brain that she was the daughter of the dead man, and he was going to her for comfort after killing her father.

At that thought he stopped and laid hold of the desk for support, being so weak that he could scarcely keep on his legs. He remembered Helena's love for the General, how much of her young life she had given to him, and how the quarrel that had divided himself from her had come of her determination not to leave her father as long as he lived. And now he had killed him—he! he! he!

Beads of sweat started from his forehead, but after a moment he told himself that, if he could not expect comfort from Helena, it was his duty to comfort her—to break the news to her. He saw himself doing so. "Helena, listen, dear; be brave." "What is it?" "Your father—is—is dead." "Dead?" "Worse—a thousandfold worse—he is murdered." "Murdered?" "It was all in the heat of blood —the man didn't know what he was doing." "Who was it? Who was it?" "Don't you see, Helena? It was I."

He had turned again to the door leading to Helena's room when another blow from an invisible hand seemed to fall upon him. He saw Helena's eyes fixed on his face in the intensity of her hate, and he heard her voice driving him away. "Go; let me never see you again." That was more than he could bear, and staggering to the sofa he sat down.

Some minutes passed. The red glow in the room deepened to a dull brown, and at one moment there was a groan in the gathering gloom. He heard it and looked up, but there was nobody there, and then he realised that it was he who had groaned. At another moment his mind occupied itself with lesser things. He saw that one finger of his left hand was badly wounded, and he bound it up in his handkerchief. Then he looked at himself in a mirror that hung on the wall in front of the sofa, but he could not see his face distinctly—eyes, nose, and mouth being blurred. He did not attempt to escape. Never for an instant did it occur to him to run away.

The sun went down behind the black pyramids across the Nile, and after a while the dead silence of the evening of the Eastern day was broken by the multitudinous cries of the muezzin, which came up from the city below like a deep ground swell on a rugged coast.

After that Gordon knelt again by the General's body, trying to believe he was not dead. The eyes were still open, but all the light was gone out of them, and seeing their stony stare the thought came to him that the General's soul was with him in the room. The stupor of his senses had suddenly given way to a supernatural acuteness, and at one moment he imagined he felt the touch of a hand on his shoulder.

At the next instant he was plainly conscious of a door opening and closing in the inner part of the house, and of light and rapid footsteps approaching. He knew what had occurred—Helena had been out on the terrace or in the parade ground and had just come back.

She was now in the next room, breathing hard as if she had been running. He could hear the rustling of her skirt and her soft step as she walked toward the door of the General's office.

At the next moment there came a knock, but Gordon held his breath and made no answer.

Then "Father!" in a tremulous voice, full of fear, as if Helena knew what had happened.

Still Gordon made no reply, and the frightened voice came again.

"Are you alone now? May I come in?"

Then Gordon felt an impulse to throw the door open and confess everything, saying: "I did it, Helena, but I didn't intend to do it. He threw himself upon me, and I flung him off and he fell, and that is the truth, as God is my witness."

But he could not do this, because he was afraid. He who had never before known fear, he who had stood in the firing line when hordes of savage men had galloped down with fanatical cries—he was trembling now at the thought of meeting a woman's face.

So, treading softly, he stole out of the room by the outer door, the door leading to the gate, and as he closed it behind him he felt that the door of hope, also, was now for ever closed between Helena and him.

But going through the garden he had to pass the arbour, and at sight of that a wave of tender memories swept over him, and in pity of Helena's position he wanted to return. She would be in her father's room by this time, standing over his dead body, and alone in her great grief.

"I will go back," he thought. "She has no one else. She may curse me, but I cannot leave her alone. I will go back —I will—I must!"

That was what his soul was saying to itself, but at the same time his body was carrying him away—through the open gate and across the deserted square, swiftly, stealthily, like a criminal leaving the scene of his crime.

The day was now gone, the twilight was deep, and as he passed under the outer port of the Citadel in the dead silence of the unquickened air, a voice like that of an accusing angel, telling of judgment to come, fell upon his ear. It was the voice of the last of the muezzin on the minaret of the Mohammedan mosque calling to evening prayer:

"God is Most Great! God is Most Great!"

AL-LA-HU AK-BAR.   AL-LA - - HU AK-BAR.

SECOND BOOK

THE SHADOW OF THE SWORD

WHEN Helena had left the General and Ishmael Ameer together, the signs she knew so well of illness in her father's face suggested that she should run at once for the medical officer. One moment she stood in the room adjoining the General's office, listening to the muffled rumble that came from the other side of the wall, the short snap of her father's impatient voice and the deep boom of the Egyptian's, and then she hurried into the outer passage to pin on her hat. There she met the General's aide-de-camp who, seeing her excitement, asked if there was anything he could do for her, but she answered " No," and then,

" Yes, I think you might go over to the Colonel " (meaning the Colonel commanding the Citadel) " and tell him this man is here with a crowd of his followers."

" He must know it already, but I'll go with pleasure," said the young Lieutenant; at the next moment there were three hasty beats on the General's bell followed by a summons from the General's servant, but the aide-de-camp had disappeared.

Helena went out by the back of the house, and seeing her cook and the black boy as she passed the kitchen quarters, an impulse came to her to send somebody else on her errand, lest anything should happen in her absence; but telling herself that nobody but herself and the doctor must know the secret of her father's condition, she hurried along.

Her way was through the unoccupied courts of the old palace, down a flight of long steps, through an old gateway whereof the iron-clamped door always stood open, across a disused drawbridge, and so on to the open parade ground. The Army Surgeon's quarters were on the farther side of it and never before had it seemed so broad.

When she reached her destination the Surgeon was out on his evening round of the hospital, so she wrote a hur-

ried note asking him to come to the General's house immediately, sent his assistant in search of him, and then turned
back.

Returning hurriedly by the "married quarters," she was
detained for some moments by a soldier's wife, a young
thing, almost a child, who stood at the door of her house
with a red woollen shawl about her shoulders, a baby in
long clothes in her arms, and a look of radiant happiness
in her round face.

"Ye've not seen 'im yet, have ye, Miss?" said the little
mother, and then, holding out her baby to be admired, "Only
six weeks old and 'e weighs ten pounds. Colonel says as
'ow e's a credit to the reg'ment and I'm agoin' to shorten
'im soon. To-morrow I'm 'avin' 'im photoed to send to
mother. She lives in Clerkenwell, Miss, and she ain't likely
to show 'is photo to nobody in our court. Oh, no!"

Helena did her best to play up to the pride of the little
Cockney mother, and was turning to go when the girl said:

"But my Harry tells me as 'ow you're to be married
yourself soon, so I wish ye joy, and many of 'em."

"Good-bye, Mrs. Dimmock," said Helena, but the young
thing was not done yet. With a look of wondrous wisdom
she said:

"They're a deal of trouble, Miss, but there ain't no love
in the house without 'em. As mother says, they keeps the
pot a-boilin'," and she was ducking down her head to kiss
the child as Helena hurried away.

In the bright light of the young mother's life and the
breadth of shadow that lay upon her own, Helena thought
of Gordon and her anger rose against him again; but at
the next moment she saw him in her mind's eye as she had
seen him last, going out of the garden, a broken, bankrupt
man, and then her eyes filled and it was as much as she
could do to see her way.

In the quickening flow of her emotion this riot in her
heart between anger with Gordon and with herself only led
to deeper hatred of the Egyptian, and even the memory
of his dignity and largeness in the single moment in which
she had looked upon him made her wrath the more intense.

A vague fear, an indefinite forewarning, hardly able yet to assume a shape, was beginning to take possession of her. She recalled the scene she had left behind her in the General's office, the two men face to face, as if in the act of personal quarrel, and told herself that if anything happened to her father as the result of the excitement caused by the meeting, the Egyptian would be the cause of it.

In her impatience to be back she began to run. How broad the parade ground was! The air, too, was so close and lifeless. The sun had nearly set, the arms of night were closing round the day, but still the sky was a hot dark red like the inside of a transparent shell that had a smouldering fire outside of it.

At one moment she heard harsh and jarring voices that seemed to come from the square of the mosque in front of the house. Perhaps the Egyptian and his people were going off with their usual monotonous chanting of " Allah! " " Allah! " She was glad to reach the cool shade and silence of the empty courts of the old palace, but coming to the gateway she found it closed.

A footstep was dying away within, so she knocked and called, and after a moment an old soldier, a kind of caretaker of the Citadel, opened the gate to her.

" Beg pardon, Miss! Lieutenant Robson told me to shut up everything immediately," he said, but Helena did not wait for further explanation.

There was nobody in sight when she passed the kitchen quarters, and when she entered the house a chill silence seemed to strike to the very centre of her life.

Then followed one of those mystic impulses of the human heart which nobody can understand. In her creeping fear of what might have happened during her absence she was at first afraid to go into her father's room. If she had done so, there and then, and without an instant's hesitation, she must have found Gordon kneeling over her father's body. But in dread of learning the truth she tried to keep back the moment of certainty, and in a blind agony of doubt she stood still and tried to think.

The voices of the men were no longer to be heard

through the wall and the deep rumble of the crowd outside
had died away, therefore the Egyptian must have gone.
Had her father gone, too? She remembered that he was in
uniform and took a step back into the hall to see if his cap
hung on the hat-rail. The cap was there. Had he gone
into his bedroom? She crossed to the door. The door was
open and the room was empty.

Hardly able to analyse her unlinked ideas, but with a
gathering dread of the unknown, she found herself stepping
on tiptoe toward the General's office. Then she thought
she heard a faint cry within, a feeble, interrupted moan,
and in an unsteady voice she called.

There was no answer. She called again, and still there
was no reply. Then girding up her heart to conquer her
vague fear, which hardly knew itself yet for what it was,
she opened the door.

The room was almost dark. She took one step into the
gloom, breathing rapid breath, then stopped and said:

"Father! Are you here, Father?"

There was no sound, so she took another step into the
room, thinking to switch on the light over the desk and at
the same time to reach the sofa. As she did so she
stumbled against something, and her breath was struck out
of her in an instant.

She stooped in the darkness to see what it was that lay
at her feet, and at the next moment she needed no light
to tell her.

"Father! Father!" she cried, and in the dead silence
that followed the voice of the muezzin came from without.

She was lying prostrate over her father's body when the
door was burst open as by a gust of wind and the Army
Surgeon came into the room. Without a word he knelt and
laid his hand over the heart of the fallen man, while Helena,
who rose at the same instant, watched him in the awful
thraldom of fear.

Then young Lieutenant Robson came in hurriedly,
switching on the light and saying something, but the Surgeon silenced him with the lifting of his left hand. There

was one of those blank moments in which time itself seems to stand still, while the Surgeon was on his knees and Helena stood aside with whitening lips and with eyes that had a wild stare in them. Then, lifting his face that was stamped with the heaviness of horror, and told before he spoke what he was going to say, the Surgeon rose and, turning to Helena, said in a nervous voice:

"I regret, I deeply regret to tell you——"

"Gone?" asked Helena, and the Surgeon bowed his head.

She did not cry or utter a sound. Only the trembling of her white lips showed what she felt, but all the cheer of life had died out of her face, and in a moment it had become hard and stony.

There was an instant of silence and then the Surgeon and the young Lieutenant, casting sidelong looks at Helena, began to whisper together. At sight of her tearless eyes a certain fear had fallen on them which the presence of death could not create.

"Take her away," whispered the Surgeon, and then the Lieutenant, whose throat was hard and whose eyes were dim, approached her and said with the sadness of sympathy:

"May I help you to your room, please?"

Helena shook her head and stood immovable a moment longer, and then with a firm step she walked away.

II

ALL the moral cowardice that had paralysed Gordon Lord was gone the moment he left the Citadel, and as soon as he reached the streets of the city the power of life came back to him. There in tumultuous swarms the native people were swinging along in one direction, uttering the monotonous cries of the Moslems when they are deeply moved. Into this maelstrom of emotion Gordon was swept before he knew it, and hardly conscious of where he was going, he followed where he was led.

He felt—without knowing why—the lust of violence which comes to the soldier in battle who wants to run away until the moment when the first shot has been fired, and then— all fear and moral conscience gone in an instant—forges his path with shouts and oaths to where danger is greatest and death most sure.

In the thickening darkness he saw a great glow coming from a spot in front of him, as of many lanterns and torches burning together. Toward this spot he pushed his way, calling to the people in their own tongue to let him pass or sweeping them aside and ploughing through. In his delirious excitement his strength seemed to be supernatural and men were flung away as if they had been children.

At length he reached a place where a narrow lane, opening on to a square, was blocked by a line of soldiers, who were coming and going with the glare of the torchlight on their faces. Here the monotonous noises of the crowd behind him were pierced by sharp cries, mingled with screams. Perspiration was pouring down Gordon's neck by this time and he stopped to see where he was. He was at the big gate of El Azhar.

On leaving the Citadel, Colonel Macdonald had taken two squadrons with him, telling the Lieutenant-Colonel commanding the regiment to follow with the rest.

"Half of these will be enough for this job and we'll clear the rascals out like rats," he said.

The Governor of the city, a small man in European dress, acting on the order of the Minister of the Interior as Regent in the absence of the Khedive, had met him at the University. They found the gate shut and barred against them, and when the Governor called for it to be opened there was no reply. Then the Colonel said:

"Omar Bey, have I your permission to force an entrance?"

Whereupon the Governor, in whom the wine of life was chiefly vinegar, answered promptly:

"Colonel, I request you to do so."

A few minutes afterward a stout wooden beam was brought up from somewhere and six or eight of the soldiers laid hold of it and began to use it on the closed gate as a battering ram. The gate was a strong one, clamped with iron, but it was being crunched by the blows that fell on it when some of the students within clambered on to the top of the walls and hurled down stones on the heads of the soldiers.

One of them was a young boy of not more than fourteen years, and while others protected themselves by hiding behind the coping stones, he exposed his whole body to the troops by standing on the very crest of the parapet. The windows of the houses around were full of faces and from one that was nearly opposite to the gate came the shrill cry of a woman, calling to the boy to go back. But in the clamour of the noises he heard nothing or in the fire of his spirit he did not heed, for he continued to hurl down everything that came to his hand, until Colonel Macdonald commanded the troops to dismount with rifles, and said:

"Stop that young devil up there!"

At the next moment there was the crack of a dozen rifles, and then the boy on the parapet swayed aside, lurched forward, and fell into the street. The Colonel was giving orders that he should be taken up and carried away when the woman's cry was heard again, this time in a frenzied shriek, and at the next instant the soldiers had to make way for the mightiest thing on earth, an outraged mother in the presence of her dead.

The woman, who had torn the black veil from her face, lifted the boy's head on to her breast and cried: "My God! My good God! My boy! Ali! Ali!" But just then the gate gave way with a crash and the Colonel ordered one of the squadrons to ride into the courtyard of the mosque, where five thousand of the students and their professors could be seen squirming in dense masses like ants on an upturned ant-hill.

The soldiers were forcing their horses through the crowds and beating with the flat of their swords when two or three shots were fired within, and it became certain that some of the students were using firearms. At that the bull-dog in the British Colonel got the better of the man and he wanted to shout a command to his men to use the edge of their weapons and clear the place at any cost, but the shrill cry of the mother over her dead boy drowned his thick voice.

"He is dead! They have killed him! My only child! His father died last week. God took him, and now I have nobody. Ali, come back to me! Ali! Ali!"

"Take that yelping b—— away," shouted the Colonel, ripping out an oath of impatience, and that was the moment when Gordon came up.

What he did then he could never afterward remember, but what others saw was that with the spring of a tiger he leaped up to Macdonald, laid hold of him by the collar of his khaki jacket, dragged him from the saddle, flung him headlong on to the ground and stamped on him as if he had been a poisonous snake.

In another moment there would have been no more Macdonald, but just then, while the soldiers, recognising their first staff officer, stood dismayed, not knowing what it was their duty to do, there came over the sibilant hiss of the crowd the loud clangour of the hoofs of galloping horses, and the native people laid hold of Gordon and carried him away.

His great strength was now gone, and he felt himself being dragged out of the hard glare of the light into the shadow of a side street where he was thrust into a carriage, and held down in it by somebody who was saying:

"Lie still, my brother! Lie still! Lie still!"

For one instant longer he heard deafening shouts through the carriage glass, over the rumble of the moving wheels, and then a blank darkness fell on him for a time and he knew no more.

When he recovered consciousness his mind had swung back, with no memory of anything between, to the moment when he was leaving the General's house, and he was saying to himself again: "I must go back. She may curse me, but I cannot leave her alone. I cannot—I will not."

Then he was aware of a voice—it was the quavering

voice of an old man and seemed to come out of a toothless mouth—saying:

"Be careful, Michael! His poor hand is injured. We must send for the Surgeon."

He opened his eyes and saw that he was being carried through a quiet courtyard where he could hear the footsteps of the men who bore him and see by the light of a smoking lantern the façade of a church. Then he heard the same quavering voice say:

"Take him up to the salamlik, my brother," and then there was a jerk and a jolt and he lost consciousness again.

He was lying on a bed in a dimly lighted room when memory returned and the events of the day unrolled themselves before him. He made an effort to raise himself on his elbows, but in his weakness he fell back, and after a while he dropped into a delirious sleep. In this sleep he saw first his mother and then Helena, and then Helena and again his mother—everything and everybody else being quite blotted out.

III

Soon after sunset Lady Nuneham had taken her last dose of medicine, and had got into bed, when the Consul-General came into her room. He had the worn and jaded look by which she knew that the day had gone heavily with him, and she waited for him to tell her how and why. With a face full of the majesty of suffering he told her what had happened, describing the scene in the General's office and all the circumstances whereby matters had been brought to such a tragic pass.

"It was pitiful," he said. "The General went too far—much too far—and the sight of Gordon's white face and trembling lips was more than I could bear."

His voice thickened as he spoke, and it seemed to the mother at that moment as if the pride of the father in his son, which he had hidden so many years in the sealed cham-

ber of his iron soul, had only come up at length that she
might see it die.

"It's all over now, I suppose, and we must make the
best of it. He promised so well, though! Always did—ever
since he was a boy. If one's children could only remain
children! The pity of it! Good-night! Good-night,
Janet!"

She had listened to him without speaking and without
a tear coming into her eyes, and she answered his good-
night in a low but steady voice. Soon afterward the gong
sounded in the hall, and as she lay in her bed she knew that
he would be dining alone—one of the great men of the
world and one of the loneliest.

Meantime Fatimah, tidying up the room for the night
and sniffling audibly, was talking as much to herself as to
her mistress. At one moment she was excusing the Consul-
General, at the next she was excusing Gordon. Lady Nuneham let her talk on and gave no sign until darkness fell
and the moment came for the Egyptian woman also to get
into her bed. Then the old lady said:

"Open the door of this room, Fatimah," pointing to a
room on her right.

Fatimah did so, without saying a word, and then she
lay down, blowing her nose demonstratively as if trying to
drown other noises.

From her place on her pillow the old lady could now see
into the adjoining chamber and through its two windows
on to the Nile. A bright moon had risen, and she lay a
long time looking into the silvery night.

Somewhere in the dead waste of the early morning the
Egyptian woman thought she heard somebody calling her,
and rising in alarm she found that her mistress had left
her bed and was speaking in a toneless voice in the next
room.

"Fatimah! Are you awake? Isn't the boy very restless
to-night? He throws his arms out in his sleep and uncov-
ers little Hafiz, too."

She was standing in her night dress and lace night-cap
with the moon shining in her face by the side of one of the

two beds the room contained, tugging at its eiderdown coverlet. Her eyes had the look of eyes that did not see, but she stood up firmly and seemed to have become younger and stronger—so swiftly had her spirit carried her back in sleep to the woman she used to be.

"Oh, my heart, no," said Fatimah. "Gordon hasn't slept in this room for nearly twenty years—nor Hafiz neither."

At the sound of Fatimah's husky voice and the touch of her moist fingers the old lady awoke.

"Oh, yes, of course," she said, and after a moment, in a sadder tone, "Yes, yes."

"Come, my heart, come," said Fatimah, and taking her cold and nerveless hand, she led her, now a weak old woman once more, back to her bed, for the years had rolled up like a tidal wave and the spell of her sweet dream was broken.

On a little table by the side of her bed stood a portrait of Helena in a silver frame, and she took it up and looked at it for a moment, and then the light which Fatimah had switched on was put out again. After a little while there was a sigh in the darkness, and after a little while longer a soft, tremulous:

"Ah, well!"

IV

HELENA was still in her room when the Consul-General, who had been telephoned for, held an inquiry into the circumstances of the General's death. She was sitting with her hands clasped in her lap and her eyes looking fixedly before her, hardly listening, hardly hearing, while the black boy darted in and out with broken and breathless messages which contained the substance of what was said.

The household servants could say nothing except that, following in the wake of the new prophet when he left the Citadel, they had left the house by the side gate of the garden without being aware of anything that had happened in the General's office. The Surgeon testified to the finding of the General's body and the aide-de-camp explained that the last time he saw his chief alive was when he was ordered to call Colonel Macdonald.

"Who was with him at that moment?" asked the Consul-General.

"The Egyptian, Ishmael Ameer."

"Was there anything noticeable in their appearance and demeanour?"

"The General looked hot and indignant."

"Did you think there had been angry words between them?"

"I certainly thought so, my lord."

Other witnesses there were, such as the soldier servant at the door, who made a lame excuse for leaving his post for a few minutes while the Egyptian was in the General's office, and the sentry at the gate of the Citadel, who said no one had come in after Colonel Macdonald and the cavalry had passed out. Then some question of calling Helena herself was promptly quashed by the Consul-General, and the inquiry closed.

Hardly had the black boy delivered the last of his messages when there was a timid knock at Helena's door, and the Army Surgeon came into the room. He was a small man with an uneasy manner, married, and having a family of grown-up girls who were understood to be a cause of anxiety to him.

"I regret—I deeply regret to tell you, Miss Graves, that your father's death has been due to heart-failure, the result of undue excitement. You will do me the justice—I am sure you will do me the justice to remember that I repeatedly warned the General of the danger of over-exciting himself, but unfortunately his temperament was such——"

The Consul-General's deep voice in the adjoining room seemed to interrupt the Surgeon, and making a visible call on his resolution he came closer to Helena and said:

"I have not mentioned my previous knowledge of organic trouble. Lord Nuneham asked some searching questions, but the promise I made to your father——"

Again the Consul-General's voice interrupted him, and with a flicker of fear on his face he said:

"Now that things have turned out so unhappily it might perhaps be awkward for me if— In short, my dear Miss Graves, I think I may rely on you not to— Thank you, thank you!" he said, as Helena, understanding his anxiety, shook her head.

"I thought it would relieve you to receive my assurance that death was due to natural causes only—purely natural. It's true I thought for a moment that perhaps there had also been violence——"

"Violence?" said Helena.

"Don't let me alarm you. It was only a passing impression and I should be sorry, very sorry——"

But just at that moment, when a new thought was passing through the stormy night of Helena's mind like a shaft of deadly lightning, the Chaplain of the Forces came into the room and the Surgeon left it.

The Chaplain was a well-nurtured person who talked comfort out of a full stomach with the expansiveness which sometimes comes to clergy who live long amongst soldiers.

"I have come to say, my dear young lady, that I place myself entirely at your service. With your permission I will charge myself with all the sad and necessary duties. So sudden! So unexpected! How true that in the midst of life we are in death!"

There was more coin from the same mint, and then the shaft of deadly lightning as before.

"It is perhaps the saddest fact of death in this Eastern climate that burial follows so closely after it. As there seems to be no sufficient reason to believe that the General's death has been due to any but natural causes, it will probably be to-morrow. I say it will probably——"

"Sufficient?" said Helena, and with a new poison at her heart she hurried away to her father's room.

She found the General where they had placed him, on his own bed and in his uniform. His eyes were now closed, his features were composed, and everything about him was suggestive of a peaceful end.

While she was standing by the bed in the gloomy, echoless chamber, the Consul-General came in and stood beside her. Though he faintly simulated his natural composure he was deeply shaken. For a moment he looked down at his dead friend in silence, while his eyelids blinked and his lips trembled. Then he took Helena's hand, and drawing her aside he said:

"This is a blow to all of us, my child, but to you it is a great and terrible one."

She did not reply, but stood with her dry eyes looking straight before her.

"I have made strict inquiry and I am satisfied—entirely satisfied—that your father died by the visitation of God."

Still she did not speak and after a moment he spoke again.

"It is true that the man Ishmael Ameer was the last to be with him, but what happened at their interview it would be useless to ask—dangerous, perhaps, in the present state of public feeling."

She listened with complete self-possession and strong hold of her feelings, though her bosom heaved and her breathing was audible.

"So let us put away painful thoughts, Helena. After all, your father's end was an enviable one, and harder for us than for him, you know."

He looked steadily for a moment at her averted face and then said, in a husky voice:

"I'm sorry Lady Nuneham is so much of an invalid that she cannot come to see you. This is the moment when a mother——"

He stopped without finishing what he had intended to say, and then he said:

"I'm still more sorry that one who——"

Again he stopped, and then in a low, smothered, scarcely audible voice, he said, hurriedly:

"But that is all over now. Good-night, my child! God help you!"

Helena was standing where the Consul-General had left her, fighting hard against a fearful thought which had only vaguely taken shape in her mind, when the black boy came back with his mouth full of news.

The bell of the telephone had rung furiously for the English lord and he had gone away hurriedly, his horses galloping through the gate; there had been a riot at El Azhar; a boy had been shot; a hundred students had been killed with swords; the cavalry were clearing the streets, and the people were trooping in thousands into the great mosque of the Sultan Hâkim, where the new prophet was preaching to them.

Helena listened to the terrible story as to some far-off event which in the tempest of her own trouble did not concern her, and then she sent the boy away. Gordon had been right—plainly right—from the first, but what did it matter now?

Some hours passed, and again and again the black boy came back to the room with fresh news and messages, first to say that her supper was served, next that her bedroom was ready, and finally, with shamefaced looks and a face blubbered over with tears, to explain the cause of his absence from the house when the tragic incident happened. He had followed the crowd out of the Citadel, and only when he found himself at the foot of the hill had he thought, "Who is to take care of lady while Mosie is away?" Then he had run back fast, very fast, but he was too late—it was all over.

"Will lady ever forgive Mosie? Will lady like Mosie any more?"

Helena comforted the little twisted and tortured soul with some words of cheer and then sent him to bed. But with a sad longing in his big eyes and the look of a dumb creature that wanted to lick her hand, he came back to say he could not sleep in his own room because death was in the house, and might he sit on the floor where lady was and keep her company?

Touched by the tender bit of human nature that was tearing the big little soul of the black boy who worshipped her, Helena went back to her own bedroom, and then a grin of delight passed over Mosie's ugly face, and he said:

"Never mind! It's nothing! Lady will forget all about it to-morrow. Now lady will lie down and sleep."

Helena put out the light in her room, and sitting by the open window she looked long into the moonlight that lay over the city. At one moment she heard the clatter of horses' hoofs—Macdonald's cavalry were returning to the Citadel after their efforts in the interests of peace and order. At intervals she heard the ghafirs (watchmen) who cried "Wahhed!" (God is One) in the silent streets below. Constantly she looked across to the barracks that stood at the edge of the glistening Nile, and at every moment the cruel core in her heart grew yet more hard.

Why had not Gordon come to her? He must know of her father's death by this time—why was he not there? Why had he not written to her at all events? It was true they had parted in anger, but what of that? He had never loved her or he would be with her now. She had done well to drive him away from her, and thank God she would never see him again!

The moon died out, a cold breath passed through the air, the city seemed to yawn in its sleep, the dawn came with its pale pink streamers and with its joyous birds—the happy, heart-breaking children of the air—twittering in the eaves, and then the pride and hatred of her wounded heart broke down utterly.

She wanted Gordon now as she had never wanted him before. She wanted the sound of his voice, she wanted the touch of his hand, she wanted to lay her head on his breast like a child and hear him tell her that it would all be well.

She found a hundred excuses for him in as many minutes. He was a prisoner—how could he leave his quarters? They might be keeping him under close arrest—how could he get away? Perhaps they had never even told him of her father's death—how could he write to her about it?

In the fever of her fresh thought she decided that she herself would tell him, and in the tumult of her confused brain she never doubted that he would come to her. Regulations? They would count for nothing. He was brave, he was fearless, he would find a way. Already she could see him flinging open the door of her room, and she could feel herself flying into his arms.

Thus with a yearning and choking heart, in the vacant stillness of the early dawn, she sat down to write to Gordon. This is what she wrote:

> "*Six o'clock, Sunday morning.*

"DEAREST: The greatest sorrow I have ever known—God, our good God, has taken my beloved father.

"He loved you and was always so proud of you. He thought there was nobody like you. I try to think how it all happened at the end, and I cannot.

"Forgive me for what I said yesterday. It seems you were right about everything, and everybody else was wrong. But that doesn't matter now—nothing matters.

"I want you. I have nobody else. I am quite alone. God help me! Come to me soon——"

Unconsciously she was speaking the words aloud as she wrote them, and sobbing as she wrote. Suddenly she became aware of another voice in the adjoining room. She thought it might be Gordon's voice, and catching her breath she rose to listen. Then in a muffled, broken, tear-laden tone, these words came to her through the wall:

"O Allah, most High, most Merciful, make lady sleep. Make lady sleep, O Allah, most High, most Merciful!"

Her black boy had been lying all night like a dog on the mat behind her door.

V

BEFORE Gordon opened his eyes that morning he heard the tinkling of cymbals and the sweet sound of the voices of boys singing in a choir, and he felt for a moment as if he were carried back to his school at Eton, where the morning dawned on green fields to the joyous carolling of birds.

Then he looked and saw that he was lying in a little yellow-curtained room which was full of the gentle rays of the early sun, and opened on a garden in a quiet courtyard, with one date tree in the middle and the façade of a Christian Church at the opposite side. In the disarray of his senses he could not at first remember what had happened to him and he said aloud:

"Where am I?"

Then a cheery voice by his side said: "Ah, you are awake?" and an elderly man with a good, simple, homely face looked down at him and smiled.

"What place is this?" asked Gordon.

"This?" said the good man. "This is the house of the Coptic Patriarch. And I am Michael, the Patriarch's servant. He brought you home in his carriage last night. Out of the riots in the streets, you know. But I must tell him you are awake. 'Tell me the moment he opens his eyes, Michael,' he said. No time to lose, though. Listen! They're at matins. He'll be going into church soon. Lie still! I'll be back presently."

Then Gordon remembered everything. The events of the night before rose before him in a moment and he drank of memory's very dregs. He had closed his eyes again with a groan when he heard shuffling footsteps coming into the room, and a husky, kindly voice, interrupted by gusty breathing, saying cheerfully:

"God be praised! Michael tells me you are awake and well."

The Coptic Patriarch was a little man in a black turban and a kind of black cassock, very old, nearly ninety years of age, and with a saintly face in which the fires of life had kindled no evil passions.

"Don't speak yet, my son. Don't exhaust yourself. The Surgeon said you were to have rest—rest and sleep above all things. He came last night to dress your poor hand. It was wounded in the cruel fight at El Azhar. I was passing at the moment and the people put you into my carriage. 'Save him, for the love of God,' they said. 'He is our brother and he will be taken.' So I brought you home, seeing you were hurt and not knowing what else to do with you. But now I am glad and thankful, having read the newspapers this morning and learned that you were in great peril—No, no, my son—lie still."

Gordon made an effort to raise himself on his elbow, but

resting his weight on his left hand and finding it was closely bandaged and gave him pain, he was easily pushed back to his pillow.

"Lie still until the Surgeon comes. Michael has gone for him. He will be here immediately. A good man—make yourself sure about that. He will be secret. He will say nothing."

Then there came through the open window the sound of footsteps on the gravel path of the garden, and the old Patriarch, leaning over Gordon, said in the same husky, kindly whisper:

"They are coming, and I must go into church. But don't be afraid. You did bravely and nobly, and no harm shall come to you while you are here."

Hardly knowing what to understand, but choking with confusion and shame, Gordon heard the old man's shuffling step going out of the room, and, a moment afterward, the firm tread of the Surgeon coming into it.

The Surgeon, who was a middle-aged man, a Copt, with a bright face and a hearty manner, took Gordon's right arm to feel his pulse, and said:

"Better! Much better! Last night the condition was so serious that I found it necessary to inject morphia. There was the hand, too, you know. The third finger had been badly hurt, and I was compelled to take the injured part away. This morning, however——"

But Gordon's impatience could restrain itself no longer. "Doctor," he said, clutching at the Surgeon's sleeve, "close the door and tell me what has happened."

The Surgeon repeated the reports which appeared in the English newspapers—about the clearing out of El Azhar, the shooting of the boy, the killing of a hundred students by the sword and the imprisonment of nearly four hundred others. And then, thinking that the drug he had administered was still beclouding his patient's brain, he spoke of Gordon's own share in the bad work of the night before— how he had refused to obey instructions and been ordered under open arrest to return to his own quarters; how he had defied authority, and, making his way to the University, had perpetrated a violent personal attack on the officer commanding the troops there.

"I know nothing about it, you know, but what Colonel Macdonald has communicated to the press—contrary, I should think, to Army regulations and all sense of honour and decency—but he says you have been guilty of a three-fold offence, first mutiny, next desertion, and finally gross assault on an officer while in the execution of his duty."

Gordon had hardly listened to this part of the Surgeon's story, but his face betrayed a feverish eagerness when the Surgeon said:

"There is something else, but I hardly know whether I ought to tell you."

"What is it?" asked Gordon, though he knew full well what the Surgeon was about to say.

"It occurred last night, too, but the Consul-General has managed to keep it out of the morning newspapers. I feel I ought to tell you, though, and if I could be sure you would take it calmly——"

"Tell me."

"General Graves is dead. He was found dead on the floor of his office. His daughter found him."

Gordon covered his face and asked, in a voice which he tried in vain to render natural, "What do they say he died of?"

"God!" said the Surgeon. "That's what the Mohammedans call it, and I don't know that science can find a better name."

Suffocating with the sickness of fear, Gordon said: "What about his daughter?"

"Bearing herself with a strange stoicism, they say. Not a tear on her face, they tell me. But if I know anything of human nature she is suffering all the more for that, poor girl!"

Gordon threw off the counterpane and rose in bed. "I'm better now," he said. "Let me get up. I must go out."

"Impossible!" said the Surgeon. "You are far too weak to go into the streets. Besides, you would never reach

your destination.   Macdonald would take care of that.
Haven't I told you?   He has given it out that the penalty
of military law for the least of your offences is—well,
death!"

Gordon dropped back in bed and the Surgeon continued:
"But if you have a message to send to any one, why not
write it?   Michael will see that it reaches safe hands.   I'll
send him in.   He's cooking some food for you and I'll tell
him to bring paper and pens."

With that the Surgeon left him, and a moment later the
serving-man's cheery face came into the room behind a
smoking basin of savoury broth.

"Here it is!   You're to drink it at once," he said, and
then, taking a writing pad from under his arm-pit, he laid
it with pens and ink on a table by the bed, saying the Doctor
had told him he was to deliver a letter.

Gordon replied that he would ring when he was ready,
whereupon Michael said: "Good!   You'll take your broth
first.   It will put some strength into you," and he smiled and
nodded his simple face out of the room.

In vain Gordon tried to write to Helena.   His first impulse was to tell her all, to make a clean breast of everything: "Dearest Helena: I am in the deepest sorrow and
shame, but I cannot live another hour without letting you
know that your dear father——"

But that was impossible.   At a moment when one great
blow had fallen on her it was impossible to inflict another.
If she suffered now when she thought her father had died
by the hand of God, how much more would she suffer if
she heard that his death had been due to violence, to foul
play, to the hand of the man who said he loved her?

Destroying his first attempt, Gordon began again: "My
poor, dear Helena: I am inexpressibly shocked and grieved
by the news of——"

But that was impossible also.   Its hypocrisy of conceal-
ment seemed to blister his very soul.   He tried again and
yet again, but not a word would come that was not cruel or
false.   Then a great trembling came over him as he realised
that being what he was to Helena, and she being what she
12

was to her father, he was struck dumb before her as by the hand of heaven.

Hours passed, and, though the day was bright, a deep, impenetrable darkness seemed to close around him. At certain moments he was vaguely conscious of noises in the streets outside, a great scuttling and scurrying of feet, a loud clamour of tongues chopping and ripping the air, the barking and bleating of a mob in full flight, and then the clattering of horses' hoofs and the whistling and shouting of soldiers.

Michael came back of himself at last, having waited in vain to be summoned, and he was full of news. All business in Cairo had been suspended, the Notables had met in the Opera Square to condemn the action of the British Army, a vast multitude of Egyptians had joined them, and they had gone up to the house of the Grand Cadi to ask him to call on the Sultan to protest to England.

"Well, well?" said Gordon.

"The Cadi was afraid, and hearing the crowd were coming, he barricaded his doors and windows."

"And then?"

"They wrecked his house, shouting: 'Down with the Turks!' 'Long live Egypt!' But the Cadi himself was inside, sir, speaking on the telephone to the officer commanding on the Citadel, and they came galloping up and took a hundred and fifty prisoners."

In spite of his better feelings Gordon felt a certain joy in the bad news Michael brought him. He had been right! Everybody would see that he had been right! What, then, was his duty? His duty was to deliver himself up and say: "Here I am! Court-martial me now if you will—if you dare!"

Plain, practical sense seemed to tell him that he ought to go to the Agency, where his father (the highest British authority in Egypt, even though a civil one), seeing the turn events had taken, the chaos into which affairs had fallen, and the ruin which Macdonald's brutality threatened, and having witnessed the utterly illegal circumstances which had attended his arrest, would place him in command, pending instructions from the War Office, and trust to his influence with the populace to restore peace. He could do it, too. Why not?

But the General? A sickening pang of hope shot through him as he told himself that no one knew he had killed the General, that even if he had done so it had only been in self-defence, that the veriest poltroon would have done what he did, and that the mind that counted such an act as crime was morbid and diseased.

Helena? She thought her father had died by the visitation of God—why could he not leave her at that? She was suffering, though, and it was for him to comfort her. He would fly to her side. All their differences would be over now. She, too, would see that he had been right and that her jealousy had been mistaken and then death with its mighty wing would sweep away everything else.

Thus in the blind labouring of hope he threw off the counterpane again and got out of bed, whereupon Michael, whose garrulous tongue had been going ever since he came into the room, first asking for the letter which the Surgeon had told him to deliver, then protesting in plaintive tones that the broth was untouched and now it was cold, laid hold of him and said:

"No, brother, no! You cannot get up to-day. Doctor says you must not, and if you attempt to do so I am to tell the Patriarch."

But Michael's voice only whistled by Gordon's ear like the wind in a desert sand-storm, and seeing that Gordon was determined to dress, the good fellow fled off to fetch his master.

Hardly had Michael gone when the barrenness of his hope was borne down on Gordon's mind, and he was asking himself by what title he could go out as a champion of the right, being so deeply in the wrong. Even if everything happened as he expected, if his threefold offence against the letter of military law were overlooked in the light of his obedience to its spirit, if the Consul-General were able to place him in command, pending instructions from the War

Office, and if he were capable of restoring order in Cairo by virtue of his influence with the inhabitants—what then?

What of his conscience, which had clamoured so loud, in relation to his own conduct? Could he continue to plead extenuation of his own offence on the ground of the General's unjustifiable and unsoldierly conduct? Or to tell himself that what he had done in the General's house had been in self-defence? Had it been in self-defence that he had returned to the Citadel after he was ordered to his own quarters? Or that he had hurled hot and insulting words at the General, such as no man could listen to without loss of pride or even self-respect?

" No, no, by God, no," he thought.

And then Helena? With what conscience could he comfort her in her sufferings, being himself the cause of them? With what sincerity could his tongue speak if his pen refused to write? And if he juggled himself into deceiving her, could he go on, as his affections would tempt him to do—now more than ever since her father was gone and she was quite alone—to carry out the plans he had made for them before these fearful events befell?

" Impossible! utterly impossible! " he told himself.

A grim vision rose before him of a shameful life, corrupted by hypocrisy and damned by deceit, in which he was married to Helena, having succeeded to her father's rank and occupying his house, his room, his office, with one sight standing before his eyes always—the sight of the General's body lying on the floor where he had flung it.

" O God, save me from that," he thought.

Gordon dropped back to the bed and sat on the edge of it, doubled up, and with his hands covering his face. How long he sat there he never knew, for his mind was deadened to all sense of time, and only at intervals of lucidity was he partly conscious of what was going on outside the little pulseless place in which he was hidden away while the world went on without him.

At one moment he heard the bells of the Coptic Cathedral ringing for evensong; then the light pattering as of rain when the people passed over the pavement into the church; and then suddenly there came a sound that seemed to beat on his very soul.

It was the firing of the guns at the Citadel, and as a soldier he knew what they were—they were the minute-guns for the General's funeral. *Boom—boom!* He could see what was taking place as plainly as if his eyes beheld it, the square of the mosque lined up with troops—two battalions of Infantry, one regiment of Cavalry and two batteries of Artillery. *Boom—boom!* The coffin on the gun-carriage covered with the silken Union Jack and with the General's sword and his plumed white helmet on the top of all. *Boom—boom!* The General's charger immediately behind the body, with his spurred boots in the stirrups reversed. *Boom—boom—boom!* The officers of the Army of Occupation drawn up by the door of the General's house, every one of them that could be spared from duty except himself, who ought, above all others, to be there. Then the carriages of the Consul-General and of the Egyptian Prime Minister, and then *Boom—boom—boom—boom!* as the cortège moved away, to the slow skirling of the funeral march, through the square of the mosque and under the gate of the old fortress.

The firing ceased, and in the dumb emptiness of the air Gordon saw another sight that tore at his heart still more terribly. It was a room in the General's house, dark and blind with curtains drawn, and Helena sitting there, alone for the first time, and no one to comfort her. Seeing this, and thinking of the barrier that was between them, of the blood that was dividing them, and that they could never again come together, all his manhood went down at last and he burst into tears like a boy.

"Forgive me, Helena! I am alone, too! Forgive me, forgive me!"

Then over the sound of his own voice he heard the innocent voices of the choir boys singing their evening hymn: "Remove my sin from before Thy sight, O God!" and at the next moment he was conscious of an old and wrinkled hand being laid on his bare arm and of somebody by his side who was saying huskily:

"Peace, my son! God is merciful!"

Then the sharp rattle of three volleys of musketry coming from far away.

The body of the General had been committed to the grave.

VI

HELENA had been in the act of sending out her letter when the General's aide-de-camp came in with news of the doings of the night before—the riot at El Azhar, Gordon's assault on Colonel Macdonald, and then his disappearance, before the troops could recover from their surprise, as suddenly and unaccountably as if he had been swallowed up by the earth.

"Of course Macdonald acted like a brute," said the young Lieutenant, "and the Colonel did exactly what might have been expected of him under the circumstances. He would have done the same if the offender had been the Commander-in-Chief himself. But now he has to pay the penalty and it cannot be a light one. Macdonald is scouring the city to find him—every nook and corner of the Mohammedan quarter. He has two motives for doing so, too—ambition and revenge."

As Helena tore up her letter and dropped it bit by bit into the waste-paper basket, she felt as if the last of her hopes dropped with it. But they rose again with the thought that though Gordon might be in danger he could not be afraid, and that his love for her was so great, so unconquerable, that it would bring him back to her now, in her time of trouble, in the teeth of death itself.

"He'll come—I'm sure he'll come," she thought.

In this confidence she sat in the semi-darkness of her room during the preparations for the military funeral, hearing all that was being done outside with that supernatural acuteness which comes to the bereaved—the marching of troops, the rolling of the gun-carriage, and the arrival of friends, as well as the soul-crushing booming of the minute-gun. She was waiting to be told that Gordon was there, and was listening for his name as her black boy darted in and out with whispered news of Egyptian Ministers, English Advisers, inspectors and judges, and finally the Consul-General himself.

When the last moment came, and the band of the Guards had begun to play " Toll for the Brave," and it was certain that Gordon had not come, her heart sank low; but then she told herself that if he ran the risk of arrest, that was reason enough why he should not show himself at the fortress.

"He will be at the chapel instead," she thought, and though she had not intended to be present at the funeral she now determined that she would do so.

She was put into a carriage with the Consul-General, and sat by his side without speaking, merely looking through the windows at the crowds that stood in the streets, quietly, silently, but without much grief on their faces, and listening to the slow squirling of the " Dead March " and the roll of the muffled drums over the dull rumbling of the closed coach.

When they reached the cemetery in the desolate quarter of old Cairo, and the band stopped and the drumming ceased, and she stepped out of the carriage, and the breathing silence of the open air was broken by the tremendous words, " I am the Resurrection and the Life," she was sure, as she took the arm of the Consul-General and walked with him over the crackling gravel to the door of the chapel, that the moment she crossed its threshold the first person she would see would be Gordon.

Her heart sank lower than ever when she realised that he was not there, and after she had taken her seat and the chill chapel had filled up behind her and the service began, she tried in vain, save at moments of poignant memory, to fix her mind on the awful errand that had brought her.

"He will be at the graveside," she thought. No one would arrest him at a place like that. English soldiers were English gentlemen, and if the Arab nobleman in the desert could allow the enemy who had stumbled into his tent at night to get clear away in the morning, Gordon would be allowed to stand by the grave of his friend and General and no one would know he was there.

When the short service was over and the Consul-General drew her hand through his arm again, and they walked together over the gravel and through the grass to the open grave behind the rosebushes that grew near to the wall, she thought she knew she had only to raise her eyes from the ground and she would see Gordon standing there, shaken with sobs.

She knew, too, that the moment she saw him she would break down altogether, so she kept her head low as long as she could. But when the troops had formed in a rectangle, and the Chaplain had taken his place and the last words had been spoken, and through a deeper hush the bugle had led the voices of the soldiers with:

> "Father, in thy sacred keeping
> Leave me now thy servant sleeping,"

and she looked up at last and saw that Gordon had not come at all, she felt as if something that was soft and tender within her had broken and something that was hard and bitter had taken its place.

While the volleys were being fired over the grave the officers of the army came up to her one by one—brave men all of them, but many of them hardly able at that moment to speak or see. Still she did not weep, and when the Consul-General with twitching lips said, "Let us go," she gave him her hand again, though it was limp and nerveless now, and, under her long black glove, as cold as snow.

The blinds were drawn up in her room when she returned to the Citadel, and with eyes that did not see she was staring out on its far view of the city, the Nile, the pyramids and the rolling waves of the desert beyond, when a knock came to the door and the Consul-General entered. He was clearly much affected. His firm mouth, which often looked as if it had been cast in bronze, seemed now to be blown in foam.

"Helena," he said, "the time has come to speak plainly. I am sorry. It is quite unavoidable."

After the first salutation she continued to stand by a chair and to stare out of the window.

"Gordon has gone. I can no longer have any doubt about that. Others, with other motives, have been trying to find him and have failed. I have been trying, with better purposes perhaps, but no better results."

His voice was hoarse; he was struggling to control it.

"I am now satisfied that when he left this house after the scene—the painful, perhaps unsoldierly scene of his—his degradation, he took the advice your father gave him —to fly from Egypt and hide his shame in some other country."

He paused for a moment and then said:

"It was scarcely proper advice, perhaps; but who can be hot and cold, wise and angry in a moment? Whatever the merits of your father's counsel, I think Gordon made up his mind to follow it. Only as the conduct of a despairing man who knew that all was over can I explain his last appearance at El Azhar."

Again he paused for a moment, and then, after clearing his throat, he said:

"I do not think we shall see him again. I do not think I wish to see him. A military court would probably hold him responsible for the blood that has been shed during the past twenty-four hours, thinking the encouragement he gave the populace had led them to rebel. Therefore its judgment upon his offences as a soldier could hardly be less than— than the most severe."

His voice was scarcely audible as he added:

"That would be harder for me to bear than to think of him as dead. Therefore, whatever others may be doing— his mother or—or yourself, I am cherishing no illusions. My son is gone. His career is at an end. Let us—please let us say no more on the subject."

Helena did not reply. Her bosom was stirred by her rapid breathing, but she continued to stare out of the window. After a moment the Consul-General said more calmly:

13

"Have you any plans for the future?"

Helena shook her head.

"No desire to remain in Egypt?"

"No."

"Any relatives or friends in England?"

"None."

"Hm! All the same, I think it will be best for you to return home."

Helena bowed without speaking.

"The sooner the better, perhaps."

"Very well."

"This is Sunday. There is a steamship from Alexandria on Saturday—will it suit you to sail by that?"

"Yes."

"One of my secretaries shall make arrangements and see you safely aboard. Meantime, have no anxieties. England will take care of your father's daughter."

Then he rose, and taking her ice-cold hand, he said:

"I think that is all. I'll come up on Saturday morning to see you off. Good-bye for the present." And then, in the same hoarse voice as before, looking steadfastly into her face for a moment, "God bless you, my girl!"

For some minutes Helena did not move from the spot on which Lord Nuneham left her. A sense of double bereavement had fallen on her for the first time with a crushing blow. That some day she would lose her father was an idea to which her mind had long been accustomed, but never for one moment until then—not even in the bitter hour in which they had parted at the door—had she allowed herself to believe that a time would come when she would have to live on without Gordon. It was here now. The past and the future alike were closed to her. A black curtain had fallen about her life. If Gordon could not return without the risk of arrest what right had she to expect him to come back to her at all? He was gone. He was lost to her. She was alone.

The city, which had been lying hot in the quivering sun, began to grow red and hazy, and in the gathering twilight Helena became conscious of criers in the streets below.

The black boy, who was always bustling about her, interpreted their cries. They were crying the funeral of the students who had fallen at El Azhar. It was to take place that night. Ishmael Ameer called on the people to gather in the great market-place of Mohammed Ali and walk up by torchlight to the Arab cemetery outside the town.

"Would lady like Mosie go and see? Then Mosie come back and tell lady everything," said the black boy, and in the hope of being alone Helena allowed him to go.

But hardly had the boy gone when a timid knock came to her door and the Army Surgeon entered the room. The man's thin lips were twitching and he was clearly ill at ease.

"Excuse me," he said, "but hearing you were soon to leave for home—I thought it only fair to myself— In fact, I have come to make an explanation."

"What is it?" asked Helena, without a trace of interest in her tone.

The Surgeon gnawed the ends of his moustache for an instant, and then, looking uneasily at Helena, he said:

"When you come to turn things over in your mind you may perhaps think I was to blame in keeping your dear father's secret. His condition, however, was not so serious but that under ordinary circumstances—I say *ordinary* circumstances—he might have lived five years, ten years, even fifteen. The truth is, though——"

"Well?"

"I want to prove the sincerity of my friendship, Miss Graves. I am sure you prefer that I should speak plainly."

"The truth is—what?" asked Helena, who was now listening with strained attention.

"That—that your dear father's death—I am now fully convinced of it—was due—partly due at all events—to circumstances that—that were *not* ordinary."

Helena's pale face turned white, but she made no answer, and after a moment the Surgeon said:

"It would have been cruel to tell you this last night, immediately after the shock of your bereavement, but—

but now that you are going away— Besides, I spoke to Lord Nuneham. I mentioned my surmises. But you know what he is—a great man, undoubtedly a great man, but incapable of taking counsel. Always has been, always will be; we all of us find it so."

Helena, seized with an undefinable fear, was speechless, but the Surgeon's blundering tongue went on:

"'Better not speak of it,' said Lord Nuneham. 'Drop it! Don't let us weaken our case against the man and rouse popular fury by an accusation we cannot possibly bring home. Wait! We'll get hold of him to better purpose by and by.'"

Helena's heart was beating violently, but she only said, with laboured breathing:

"Can't we dispense with all this? You have come to tell me that my father did not die from natural causes—isn't that it?"

"Yes—that is to say—pardon me—we are alone?"

Helena bowed impatiently.

"Then, to tell you the truth—I am satisfied that violence—as a contributing cause at all events—I looked at him again this morning when—at the last moment in fact—and the marks were even plainer than before."

"Marks?"

"Marks of a man's hand about the throat."

"A man's hand?" said Helena, with her lips rather than with her voice.

"I thought at first it might have been the General's own hand, but there was one peculiarity which forbade that inference."

"Tell me."

"It was the left hand, and while the thumb and the first, second, and fourth fingers were plainly indicated, there was no impression made by the third."

"So?"

"So I concluded that the marks about the throat must have been made by somebody who had lost the third finger of his left hand."

Helena gazed a long time blankly into the Surgeon's

face, until at length, frozen by fear, having said all, he tried to convey the impression that he had said nothing.

"Miss Graves, I have given you pain. I feel I have. And mind, I do not say certainly that the hand at your father's throat was the cause of his death. It may have been used merely to push him off. But if the person seen last in the General's company was apparently quarrelling with him — please understand, I make no accusations. I have never met Ishmael Ameer. And even if it should be found that he had this peculiarity—of the third finger, I mean— In any case, the Consul-General will not hear of an indictment, so I'm sure—I'm sure I can rely on your discretion. But hearing you were going home, I felt I could not allow you to think that I had permitted your dear father——"

The Surgeon went stammering on for some time longer, but Helena did not listen, and when at last the man backed himself out of her room, hugging his shallow soul with the flattering thought that in following his selfish impulse he had done well, she did not hear him go.

She was now sure of a fact which she had hitherto only half suspected. The Egyptian had killed her father! Killed him, there was no other word for it, not merely by the excitement his presence engendered, but by actual violence. The authorities knew it, too, they knew it perfectly, but they were afraid—afraid in the absence of conclusive evidence to risk the breakdown of a charge against one whom the people in their blindness worshipped.

The sky had grown blue and luminous by this time, the stars had come out in the distant depths of the heavens, and from the market-place below the ramparts of the Citadel there came up into the clear air the thick murmuring of the vast multitude that had gathered there, with ten thousand smoking torches, to follow the new prophet to the Arab cemetery beyond the town.

When Helena thought of the Egyptian again it was with an intensity of hatred she had never felt before. He had not only killed her father but he had been the first cause of the devilish entanglement which had led to Gordon's disgrace. Yet he was to escape punishment for these offences, he was to go on until some sin against the State had brought him into the meshes of its Ministers, while her father was in his grave and Gordon was in banishment and she—she was sent home in her womanish helplessness and shame!

"O God! is there no one to punish this man?" she thought, in the dark searching of her soul, while her finger-nails were digging trenches in her palms and from the hard clenching of her teeth her lips were bleeding.

Then suddenly, in the delirium of her hatred of the Egyptian and the tragic tangle of her error, while she was standing alone in her desolate room, with the "Allah!" "Allah!" of Ishmael's followers surging up from below, a new feeling—a feeling she had never felt before—stirred in the depths of her abased and outraged soul.

"Shall I go back to England?" she asked herself. "Shall I?"

VII

As soon as Lord Nuneham reached the Agency, he went up to his wife's room. The sweet old lady was sitting in her dressing-gown with her face to the windows on the west, while the Egyptian woman was combing out her thin white hair and binding it up for the night. The sun was gone, but the river and the sky were shining like molten gold, and a faint reflected glow shone on her soft, pale cheeks.

"Ah, is it you, John?" she said in a nervous voice, and while he was taking a seat she looked at him with her deep, slow, weary eyes as if waiting for an answer to a question she was afraid to ask.

"Helena is going home, Janet," said the old man after a moment.

"Poor girl!"

"There is a steamship on Saturday. I thought it better she should sail by that."

"Poor thing! Poor darling!"

"Her will seems to be quite gone—she agrees to everything."

"Poor Helena!"

"I don't think she has shed a tear since her father died. It is extraordinary. She startles me, almost frightens me. Either she is a girl of astonishing character or else——"

"She has had a great shock, poor child! Only yesterday at this time her father was with her, and now——"

"True—quite true!"

A hush fell upon all. Even Fatimah's comb was quiet. It was almost as if a spirit were passing through the room. At length the old lady said:

"Any news of——"

"None."

"Would you tell me if there were?"

"If you asked me—yes."

"My poor boy!"

"Hafiz has inquired everywhere. Nobody knows anything about him."

"He will come back, though, I am sure he will," said Lady Nuneham with a nervous trill, and then a strange contraction passed over the Consul-General's face, and he rose to go.

"We'll not speak about that again, Janet," he said, but full of the sweetest and bitterest emotion that comes to the human heart—the emotion of a mother when she thinks of the son that is lost to her—the old lady did not hear.

"I remember that his grandfather—it was in the early days of the civil war, I think—— He had done something against his General, I suppose——"

She had been speaking for some moments when Fatimah, who was standing behind, reached round to her ear and said:

"His lordship has gone, my lady," and then there was a sudden and deep silence.

The molten gold died out of the river and the sky, and in the luminous blue twilight the old lady got into bed.

"Fatimah," she said, "do you think Doctor would allow me to go up to the Citadel one day this week?"

"Why not, if the carriage were closed and the blinds down?"

"And, Fatimah?"

"What is it, oh, my heart?"

"What do you think the Consul-General meant when he said Helena frightened him?"

"I think he meant that she's one of the girls who do things when they're in trouble—drown themselves, take poison or something."

"My poor Helena! My poor Gordon!"

There was the rustling whisper of a prayer at the pillow, and then, for the weary and careworn old lady, another day slid into another night.

VIII

MEANTIME Gordon, with a heart filled with darkness, sat huddled up on his bed in the little guest-room of the Coptic Cathedral. On a table at his left a small green-shaded lamp was burning, and on a chair at his right sat the saintly old Patriarch, gently patting his bare arm and trying in vain to comfort him.

"Yes, God is merciful, my son, and it is just because we are such guilty creatures that our Lord came to deliver us."

"But you don't know, father, you don't know," said Gordon.

"Know what, my son?"

"You don't know what reason I have to reproach myself," said Gordon; and then, catching by the sure instinct of a pure heart some vague sense of Gordon's position, the old man began to talk of confession, wherein the soul of man lays down its sins before God and begins to feel as if it had wings.

"On receiving the penitent's confession," he said, "it is the duty of the Coptic priest to take his sin upon himself just as if it were his own, and if I, my son——"

"But you can't! It's impossible! God forbid it," said Gordon, and then the saintly old soul, allowing that there were sacred places in the heart of man which only God's eye should see, spoke of atonement, whereby he that is guilty of any sin may begin his journey toward repentance, and be numbered at last, if his penitence be true, among the living who live in God's peace.

"Why should any of us, my son, no matter how foul the stain of sin we have contracted, live in the dread of miscarrying for ever while we have energy to atone?" said the good old man in his worn and husky voice, and then the tides of Gordon's troubled mind, which had ebbed and flowed like the sea on a desolate shore under the blank darkness of a starless night, seemed to be suddenly brightened by a light from the morning.

"Father," he said, "could you send for somebody?"

"Indeed I could—who is it?" asked the Patriarch.

"Captain Hafiz Ali of the Egyptian Army. He can be found at headquarters. Say that some one he knows well wishes to see him at once."

"I'll tell Michael to take the message immediately," said the Patriarch, and his shuffling old feet went off on his errand.

The new light that had dawned on Gordon's mind was the same as he had seen before and yet it was now quite different. He would deliver himself up, as he had first intended to do, but in humility, not in pride, in submission to the will of God, not defiance of the power of man. A reclaiming voice seemed to say to him: "Atone for your crime! Confess everything! Die—on the gallows if need be! Better suffer the pains of death than the furies of remorse! Give your own life for the life you have taken, no matter by what impulse of self-defence or devilish accident of fate!"

Hafiz would carry his message to headquarters, or perhaps help him to go there, and the good old Patriarch would explain why he had not gone before.

"It is the only way now, the only hope," he thought.

Within half an hour Hafiz arrived hot and breathless, as

if he had been running. One moment he stood near the door, while his lip lagged low and his cheerful face darkened at sight of Gordon's white cheeks, and then he gushed out into words which tried their best to be brave but were tragic with tears.

"I knew it," he said, "I've said so all day long. 'He's lying ill somewhere or he would show up now whatever the consequences.' You're wounded, aren't you? Let me see."

"It's nothing," said Gordon. "Nothing at all. Sit down, old fellow."

And then Hafiz sat on the right of the bed, holding Gordon's hand in his hand, and told him what had happened during the day—how Macdonald and his bloodhounds had been out in pursuit of him, expecting to arrest and court-martial him, and how he also had been searching for him since yesterday, but with the hope of helping him to escape.

"High and low we've looked everywhere—everywhere except here—and who would have thought of a place like this?" said Hafiz. "So much the better, though! You'll stay here until you are well and I can get you safely away. I will, too! You'll see I will!"

It was hard to listen to the good fellow's schemes for his escape and tell him at once of his intention to give himself up, so Gordon asked one by one the questions that were uppermost in his mind, little thinking that Hafiz's answers would break up his purpose and stifle for ever the cry of the voice of his tortured heart.

"The General is buried, isn't he?" he said, turning his face away as he spoke, and when Hafiz answered "Yes," that he had died by the hand of God and been buried that afternoon, and that everybody was saying that he had been a good man and a great soldier and Egypt would never again see his equal, Gordon asked himself what after all would be the worth of an atonement which offered as an equivalent for a life like the General's a life such as his own, which was no longer of any use to him or to any one.

And again, when he asked, in a voice that was breathless with fear, how his father was, and Hafiz answered that the iron man whose name had been a terror in Egypt for so many years, though calm on the outside still, was breaking up like a frozen lake from below; that he had been calling him over the telephone all day long, and entreating him to find his son that he might tell him to deliver himself up immediately, in spite of everything, lest he should be charged with desertion and be liable to death, Gordon sickened with a sense of the shame into which he was about to plunge his father in his last days by the confession he intended to make and the fate he meant to meet.

And again, when with deepening emotion he asked about his mother—was she worse for the disgrace that had overtaken himself?—and Hafiz told him " No," that though sitting in a sort of bewilderment, waiting for God's light in the darkness that had fallen on her life, she was yet living in a beautiful, blind hope that he would come back to justify himself, and meantime sending messages to him saying, " Tell him his mother is sure he only did what he believed to be right, because her boy could not do what was wrong," Gordon's heart knocked hard at his breast with the thought that the brave atonement to which he had set his face would surely kill his mother before it had time to kill him.

And when, last of all, in the sore pain of a wounded tenderness, he asked about Helena—was she well and was she asking after him?—and Hafiz again answered " No," but, that he had seen her at the General's funeral (where he could not trust himself to speak to her for pity of the dumb trouble in her pale face), and that, leaning on the arm of the Consul-General, she had lifted her tearless eyes as if looking for somebody she could not see, and that she was to go back to England soon, very soon, on Saturday, without any one for company, being alone in the world now, then Gordon broke down altogether, for he saw himself following her on her lonely journey home with a cruel and needless blow that would ruin the little that was left of her peace.

" On Saturday, you say? "

" Yes, by the English steamer from Alexandria," said Hafiz, and then, eagerly, as if by a sudden thought, " Gordon? "

"Well?"

"Why shouldn't you go with her?"

Gordon shook his head.

"But why? You'll be better by that time, and even if you're not— You can't stay here for ever, and if you should fall into Macdonald's hands— Besides, it's better in any case to let the War Office deal with you. They'll know everything before you reach London and they'll see you've been in the right. You'll get justice there, Gordon, whereas here— Then there's Helena, too—she's expecting you to join her—I'm sure she is—why shouldn't she, being friendless in Egypt now and without any one to go to even at home? And if the worst comes to the worst, and you have to leave the Army, which God forbid, you'll be together at all events—she'll be with you, anyway——"

"No, no, my boy, no," cried Gordon, but Hafiz, full of his new hope, was not to be denied.

"You think it's impossible, but it isn't. *Wallahi!* Leave it to me. I'll arrange everything. Trust me," he said, and in the warmth of his new resolve and the urgency of another errand, he got up to go.

The hundred and fifty Notables who had been arrested that morning before the Grand Cadi's house had been tried in the afternoon by a Special Tribunal, and despatched in the evening as dangerous rebels to the penal settlement in the Soudan. In protest against this injustice as well as in lamentation for the loss of the students who had fallen at El Azhar, Ishmael Ameer had called upon the people of Cairo to follow him in procession to the Arabic cemetery outside the city, that there, without violence or offence, they might appeal from the barbarity of man to the judgment seat of God.

"They've gone with him, too," said Hafiz, "tens of thousands of them, so that the streets are deserted and half the shops shut up. Oh, they've not done with Ishmael yet —you'll see they have not! I must find out what he's doing, though, and come back and tell you what's going on. Meantime I'll say nothing about you—about knowing where you are, I mean—nothing to the Consul-General, nothing to my mother, nothing to anybody. Good-bye, old fellow! Leave yourself to me. I'll see you through."

When Hafiz went off with a rush of spirits, Gordon, being left alone, sank to a still deeper depression than before. He felt as if he were thrown back again on that desolate shore where the tides of his mind ebbed and flowed under the blank darkness of a starless sky.

The proud atonement whereby he had expected to wipe out his crime had fallen utterly to ashes. It looked like nothing better now than a selfish impulse to escape from a life that had become a burden to him by killing his father's honour, his mother's trust, and the last hope of Helena's happiness.

"No, I cannot deliver myself up. It is impossible," he thought.

But if death itself was denied to him what was there left to him in life? His career as a soldier was clearly at an end, his father's house was for ever closed to him, and his days with Helena were over. Without work, without home, without love, what could he do, where could he go?

"Then, what can I do? Where can I go?" he asked himself.

Suddenly he remembered what the General had said in that delirious moment when with bitter taunts he had told him to fly to some foreign country where men would know nothing of his disgrace. Cruel and unjust as that sentence had seemed to him then, it appeared to be all that was left to him now, when work and home and love alike were gone from him.

"Yes, I'll go away," he thought, with a choking sob. "I'll bury myself as far from humanity as possible."

Yet at the next moment the hand of iron was on his heart again, and he told himself that though he might fly from the sight of man he could not escape from the eye of God, and to be alone with that was more than a guilty man could bear and live.

"But why can't I go to America?" he asked himself.

It was his mother's home and a country to which something in his blood had always been calling him. But no!

That refuge also was denied to him, for though he might hide in New York or Boston or Philadelphia or Chicago or San Francisco, better than in the trackless desert itself, yet in the very pulse of life he would still be alone, with a mind that must always be rambling through the ways of the past, seeing nothing in the happiness of other men but cruel visions of what might have come to him also, but for one blind moment of headstrong passion.

"Is life, then, to be utterly closed to me?" he thought.

Was he neither to die for his crime nor live for his repentance? Had God Almighty set His face against both?

He thought of Helena as she would be in England, alone like himself, cut off for the rest of her life from every happiness except the bitter one of her memory of their few short days together, thinking ill of him as she needs must for leaving her in her sore need, while all the time his heart was yearning for love of her, and he would have given his soul to be by her side, but for the barrier of blood which seemed to separate them for ever now.

And then in the bitterness of his remorse and the depths of his abased penitence, thinking the Almighty Himself must be against him, he began to pray—never having prayed since the days when his mother held him at her knee.

"O God, have pity upon me!" he cried, as he sat huddled up on his bed. "I only intended to do what was right, yet I have plunged everybody I love into trouble. What can I do? Where can I go? Let it be anything and anywhere! O Lord, speak to me, lead me, deliver me, tell me what I ought to do, tell me, tell me!"

The green-shaded lamp on the table had gone out by this time, the darkness of the night had gone and a dim gleam of saffron-tinted light from the dawn had begun to filter through the yellow window curtains of the room.

Then suddenly the silence of the little pulseless place was broken by the sound of eager footsteps running over the gravel path of the courtyard and leaping up the stone staircase of the house.

It was Hafiz returning from the cemetery.

IX

THE Mohammedan cemetery of Cairo lies to the north-east of the city, outside the Bab en-Nasr (the Gate of Victory), on the fringe of the desert and down a dusty road that leads to a group of tomb-mosques of the Caliphs, now old and falling into decay.

No more forlorn and desolate spot ever lay under the zealous blue of the sky. Not a tree, not a blade of grass, not a rill of water, not a bird singing in the empty air. Only an arid waste, dotted over by an irregular encampment of the narrow mansions of the dead, the round hummocks of blistered clay, each with its upright stone, its shahed capped with turban or tarboosh. The barren nakedness and savage aridity of the place make it a melancholy spectacle by day, but in the silence of night, under the moon's quiet eye, or with the darkness flushed by the white light of the stars, the wild desolation of the city of the dead is an awesome sight to see. Such was the spot in which the people of Cairo had concluded to pass their Night of Lamentation—such was their Gethsemane.

When tidings of their intention passed through the town there were rumblings of thunder in the ever-lowering diplomatic atmosphere. The Consul-General heard it and sent for the Commandant of Police.

" This gathering of great numbers of natives outside the walls," he said, " looks like a ruse for an organised attack on the European inhabitants. Therefore let your plans for their protection be put into operation without delay. As the ostensible object of the demonstration is a funeral, you cannot stop it, but see that a sufficient body of police goes with it and that your entire force is in readiness."

After that he called up the officer who was now in command of the Army of Occupation, and advised that troops at Kasr el Nil, at the Citadel, and particularly at the barracks of Abbassiah should be strictly confined and kept in readiness for all emergencies.

" If all goes well to-night," he said, " give your men an

airing in the streets in the morning. Let their bands go
with them, so that when the turbulent gentlemen who are
organising all this hubbub take their walks abroad they
may meet one of your companies coming along. If they
turn aside to avoid it let them meet another and another.
—And wait!" said the old man, while his brow contracted and his lip stiffened. "The man Ishmael Ameer
has escaped us thus far. He has been lying low and allowing others to get into trouble. But he seems to be putting
his head into the noose this time. Follow him, watch him;
don't be afraid."

The bodies of the students who were to be buried that
night had been lying in the mosque of the Sultan Hasan
at the foot of the Citadel, and as soon as word came that
the Imams had recited the prayer for the dead, asking,
"Give your testimony respecting them—were they faithful?" and being answered, "Aye, faithful unto death," the
cortège started.

First a group of blind men at slow pace chanting the
first Surah of the Koran; then the biers, a melancholy line of
them, covered with red and green cloths and borne head
foremost; then schoolboys singing, in shrill voices, passages
from a poem describing the last judgment; then companies
of Fikees, reciting the profession of faith; then the female
relatives of the dead, shrouded black forms with dishevelled
hair, sitting in carriages or squatting on carts, wailing in
their woe, and finally, Ishmael Ameer himself and his vast
and various following.

Never had any one seen so great a concourse, not even
on the day when the sacred carpet came from Mecca. There
were men and women, rich and poor, great and small, religious fraternities with half-furled banners and dervishes
with wrapped-up flags, Sheikhs in robes and beggars in rags.
Boys carried lamps, women carried candles, and young men
carried torches and open flares which sent coils of smoke
into the windless air.

Their way lay down the broad boulevard of Mohammed
Ali, across the wide square of the Bab-el-Khalk, past the
Governorat and the Police Headquarters. As they walked

at slow pace they chanted the Surah which says: "O Allah! There is no strength nor power but in God! To God we belong and to him we must return!" The shops were shut, and the muezzin called from the minarets as the procession went by the mosques.

Thus like a long sinuous stream, sometimes flowing deep and still, sometimes rumbling in low tones, sometimes breaking into sharp sounds, they passed through the narrow streets of the city and out by the Bab en-Nasr to the Mohammedan cemetery beyond the walls.

As Hafiz approached this place the deep multitudinous hum of many tongues that came up from it was like the loud sighing of the wind. Calm as the night was it was the same as if a storm had broken over that spot, while the desert around lay sleeping under the unclouded moon. Through a thick haze that floated over the ground there were bubbles and flashes of light, the red and white flames of the lamps and torches spurting and steaming like electrical apparitions from a cauldron.

A cordon of mounted police surrounded the cemetery, and a few were riding inside of it. The funerals were over, and the people were squatting in groups on the bare sand. Hafiz could hear the solemn chanting of the Fikees as they passed their beads through their fingers and recited to the spirits of the dead. Some of the dervishes were dancing and some of the women were swaying their bodies to a slow, monotonous, hypnotic movement that seemed to act on them like a drug.

A number of the Ulema, professors of El Azhar and teachers of the Koran, were passing from group to group, comforting and counselling the people. Behind each of them was a little crowd of followers, and where the crowd of such followers was greatest there always was the erect white figure and pale face of Ishmael Ameer. He stood in his great stature above the heads of the tallest of the men about him, and as he passed from company to company he left hope and inspiration behind him, for his lips seemed to be touched with fire.

"Night has fallen on us, oh, my brothers!" he said in

[Page 189.]

" ' To God we belong and to Him we must return ! ' "

his throbbing voice. " Our path is desolate, we are encompassed by sorrows, we envy the dead who are in their graves. Oh, ye people of the tombs, you have passed on before us. Peace be to you! Peace be to us also! A woman is here who has lost her husband—the camel of her house is gone! A mother is here who has lost her son—the eye of her heart is blind! Oh, Thou most merciful of those that show mercy, comfort and keep them and send them safely to thy Paradise! Sleep, oh, servants of God, in the arms of the Mighty and Compassionate!"

" Poor me, poor my children, poor all the people! " cried the women who crouched at his feet.

" Oppressors have risen against us, O God! but let us not cry to Thee for vengeance against them. They are Christians and it was a Christian who said: ' Father, forgive them, for they know not what they do.'"

" La ilaha illa-llah! " cried the men, but their faces were dark and stern.

" Oh, sons of Adam," cried Ishmael, " shall the children of one Father fight before His face? To-night the lamps are lit to the Lord on the rock at Mecca. To-night, too, the lamps are burning to God on the Calvary at Jerusalem. So it has been for a thousand years. So it will be for a thousand more. Father, forgive them for they know not what they do."

At that a great shout went up from the clamorous billow of human beings about him, and " Oh, children of Allah," he cried, " religion is the bread of our souls, and the strangers who have come to us from the West are trying to take it away. Let us fight to preserve it! Let us draw the sword of our spirit against a black devouring world! By the life of our God, let us be men! By the tombs of our fathers, let us be living souls! By the beard of the Prophet—praise to his name!—let us no longer be mere machines for the making of gold for Europe! Better the mud hut of the fellah with the spirit of God within than the palace of the rich man with the devil's arms on the doorpost. If we cannot be free in the city, let us go out to the desert—out from the empire of man to the empire of Allah! And if we must leave behind our gorgeous mosques, built on the bones of slaves and cemented with the blood of conquest, we shall worship in a vaster and more magnificent temple, the dome whereof is the sky."

By this time the excitement of the people amounted to frenzy. "Allah!" "Allah!" they shouted as they followed Ishmael from group to group in an ever-increasing crowd that was like a boiling, surging, rushing river, flashing in fierce brilliance under the light of the lamps and torches.

"Brothers," said Ishmael again, "your homes are here, and your wives and children. I am going out into the desert and you cannot all follow me. But give me one hundred men and your enemies will afflict you no more. One hundred men to carry into every town and village the word of the message of God, and the reign of Mammon will be at an end. Our Prophet—praise to his name!—was driven out of Mecca as a slave, but he returned to it as a conqueror. We are driven out of Cairo in disgrace, but we shall come back in glory. So the years pass and repeat themselves," he cried, and then, in triumphant tone, "Yes, by Allah!"

The emotional Egyptian people were now like children possessed, and the fever in Ishmael's own face seemed to have consumed the natural man.

"I ask for martyrs, not for soldiers," he cried. "Shall not the reward of him who suffers daily for his brethren's sake be equal to that of the man who dies in battle? I ask for the young man and the strong, not the weak and the old. Difficulty is before us, and danger, and perhaps death. I ask for sinners, not saints. Though you are as pure as the sands of the seashore, like the sands of the shore you may be fruitless. But are you sin-laden and suffering? Do the ways of life seem to be closed to you? Does the sweet light of morning bring you no joy? Are you praying for the darkness of death to cover you? Is your repentance deep? In the bitterness of your soul are you calling upon God for a way of redemption? Then come to me, my brothers! Your purification is here! A pilgrimage is before you that will cleanse you of all sin."

"Allah!" "Allah!" "Allah!" cried the people with one

voice, and the cry of their thousand throats in that desolate place was like the quake of breakers on cavernous rocks.

It was one of those moments of life when by a spontaneous impulse humanity shows how divine is the heart of man. In an instant more than five hundred men, some of them looked upon as low and base, leaped out in answer to Ishmael's call and were struggling, quarrelling, almost fighting to go with him.

For two hours thereafter the professors and teachers were busy selecting one hundred from the five, telling them what they had to do and where they had to go, each man to his allotted place, while the mounted police rode round and through them in a vain effort to find out what was being said.

The night was now near to morning, the lamps and torches were dying out, and a dun streak, like an arrow's barb, was shooting up into the darkness of the sky. In this vague fore-dawn the hundred chosen men were drawn up before the tomb of a sheikh, and Ishmael, standing on the dome of it, with his tall figure against the uncertain light, spoke to them and to the vast company of the people that had gathered about.

"Brothers," he said, "you offer yourselves as messengers of the Compassionate to carry His word to the uttermost ends of this country and as far as the tongue you speak is spoken. You have been told what to say and you will say it without fear. You are no rebels against the State, but if the commandments of the Government are against the commandments of God, you are to tell the people to obey God and not the Government."

At that word the sea of faces seemed to flash white under the heaviness of the sky, but Ishmael only looked down at the hundred men who stood below and said calmly:

"You are soldiers of God, therefore you will carry no weapons of the devil with you on your journey. Do you expect to conquer by the sword? Stand back, this pilgrimage is not yours! Do you wish to drive the English out of Egypt, to establish Khedive or Sultan, to found Kingdom or Empire? Go home! This work is not for you! Only one enemy will you drive out and that is the devil! Only one Sultan will you establish and that is God!"

The mass of moving heads seemed to sway for a moment, and then amid the deep breathing of the people Ishmael said:

"You will take nothing with you on your way, neither purse nor scrip nor second coat. In the city or the village or the desert the Merciful will make your beds, the Compassionate will provide for you. Where the Muslemeeh is, there is your brother—greet him, he will welcome you. Where his house is there is your home—enter it, it will shelter you. But you are slaves of God, therefore look for no ease and comfort. Burning heat by day, weary marches by night, hunger and thirst, and toil and pain—these only are the allurements God offers to his servants—these and glory!"

At that last word a loud shout broke from the people, but when Ishmael spoke again the burden of a great awe seemed to fall upon them.

"Say farewell to one another and to your wives and children. If God wills it you will come back. If He does not will it you will go on, never more to look in each other's faces."

Then in a louder, shriller voice than before, he cried:

"But fear nothing! The battle is not yours but God's! You will be purified by your pilgrimage, your sins will be forgiven you, and when death comes that stands at the foot of life's account, Paradise will wait for you and the arms of the Merciful be open! In the name of the Compassionate, Peace!"

"Peace! Peace!" cried the vast mass in a voice that seemed to ring through the empty dome of the sky.

The men who had been standing before Ishmael now prostrated themselves with their faces to the east, and then rising to their feet they embraced each other. A subdued murmur passed through the people, and at the next moment the crowd parted in many places, leaving long, wide ways that went out from the foot of the tomb. Down these paths the men passed in twos and threes as if going in different directions, some north, some south, some east, some west.

Thus the hundred messengers set out on their pilgrimage, each his own way and none knowing if they should ever meet again. Though the eager, emotional Egyptian people were ready to sob at sight of them, yet they kept back their cries. Some of the women held out their children to be kissed by their husbands as they passed, but they dried their own eyes lest the men should see them weep.

The dawn was coming up by this time in a thin streak of pink across the eastern sky, and the people watched the men as they passed away—beyond the ruined tombs of the Caliphs, toward the barracks of the soldiers at Abbassiah and over the reddening crest of the Mokattam hills—until they could be seen no more.

Then slowly as the great mass of the crowd had opened, it closed again, and while women sobbed and men broke down in tears, the tall figure of Ishmael, forgotten for a moment, was seen standing in the mystic light of the dawn above the multitude of moving heads, and his throbbing voice was heard pealing over them.

"Oh, children of God," he cried, "be comforted! Go back to your homes and wait! Be patient! Is not that what Islam means? Shed no tears for those who have gone away from you. As sure as the sun will rise your brethren will return. Look! Already it is gilding the fringes of the clouds; it is sending away the spirits of darkness; it is approaching the gates of morning! Even so in life or in death, in the spirit or in the flesh those who have left you will return, and when they come back our Egypt will be God's."

With that, amid an answering cry from the people, he stepped down from the tomb. Then the crowd parted as before and he passed through them toward the town in the direction of the Bab en-Nasr, the Gate of Victory. There was no shouting or waving of banners as he went away, but only the silent, Eastern greeting of hands to the lips and forehead, with hardly a noise as loud as the sound of human breath.

The sun was now rising above the yellow Mokattam hills, the day was reddening over the desert, the gleaming streak of the Nile was shooting out of the mist, and in the radiance of morning the crowd began to break up and return to the city. Their eyes were shining with a new light, a new joy, a new hope. They had come out to mourn and they were going back rejoicing.

Hafiz was among the first to go. With a mouth full of a fresh message he was flying back to Gordon. As he passed through the echoing streets he met the band of one of the British battalions and it was playing a march from the latest opera.

X

Gordon, lying in his bed, heard the voice of Hafiz in the hall.

"Only me, Michael! All right! Don't get up yet."

At the next moment Hafiz himself, puffing and blowing, and with the cool air of morning in his clothes, came dashing into the room.

"Halloa! Thought I was never coming back, I suppose! Couldn't tear myself away—had to see it through—only just over. Tell you what, though—I do believe—yes, I do really believe that brute of a Macdonald has set the trackers on to you! Coming down by El Azhar, behold two damned blacks—Soudanese, I mean—poking their noses into the soft ground as if looking for footsteps. But no matter! We'll dish the devil yet!"

Thus the good fellow, after the night-long flight of his spirit among sacred things, was giving way to the natural man, with chuckles and crows and shouts of joy and even harmless oaths that had no bitterness behind them.

"Lord God, you should have seen it, Gordon. Just like one of the 'Nights of the Prophet,' only bigger—yes, by my soul, bigger!"

Then, sitting on the side of the bed, he described the doings of the night—how Ishmael had passed from group to group, comforting the mourners and laying a soothing hand on every mother's sorrow, every father's grief.

"Can't tell what the deuce it is in the man—whether it's the prophet or the poet or the diviner—but he doesn't need that anybody should tell him anything, because he *knows*."

It was not at first that Gordon, coming out of the long night of his sufferings, caught the contagion of Hafiz's good spirits, but his weary, bloodshot eyes began to shine when Hafiz described Ishmael's appeal to the people to leave everything behind them and go with him into the desert— out of the empire of man into the empire of Allah.

"It was thrilling! *Wallahi!* You had to hear it, though. It was not so much what he said as something in the man himself that set all your nerves tingling."

And when Hafiz went on to tell of Ishmael's appeal for help, not to the saints, the men whom God had cleansed from all sin, the souls that were as pure as the sands of the seashore and as fruitless, but to the sinners, the sin-laden and sin-stained, to whom the peace of life and the repose of death were both denied, he felt Gordon's hand clutching at his own and his whole body quivering.

"Sinners, not saints—did he say that, Hafiz?"

"Yes! 'Come to me, my brothers,' he said. 'Your purification is here. A pilgrimage is before you that will cleanse you from all sin.' They took him at his word, too. Good Lord! You never saw such scrambling! Such a crew! Sinners, by Jove! Some of them the most notorious scoundrels in Cairo—rich rascals who have been living for themselves all their lives and beggaring everybody about them. Assassins, too, or men who have been suspected of being so. Yet there they were, fighting for a chance of going out to starvation and danger and death."

Gordon's eyes were running over by this time, but they were glistening, too, like the sun when it shines through a cloud of rain.

"Open the curtains, Hafiz," he said, and when Hafiz had done so it was almost as if an angel of hope had parted them and come sweeping with a stream of sunlight into the room.

Then Hafiz told of the going away of the hundred messengers, of Ishmael's triumphant prediction that they would come back, and finally of the return of the people to their homes with the flow as of a great tide, filled with a new spirit, comforted, changed, transformed, transfigured.

" And Ishmael himself ? " asked Gordon.

" He has gone also," said Hafiz.

" Where has he gone ? "

" That was kept quiet, but the Chancellor was there, and I got it out of him—he has gone to Khartoum."

" Khartoum ? "

" That's where he comes from—where he lived in his youth at all events. He has to take the early train for Upper Egypt, so he'll be on his way already. Oh, something is going to happen! Wait—you'll see! Couldn't find out exactly what the men were told to do, but Government has its work cut out for it."

" There was to be no resistance to the rule of England —do you say he said that, Hafiz ? "

" That's true. ' Do you wish to drive England out of Egypt? Go home,' he said; ' this pilgrimage is not yours. Do you expect to conquer by the sword? Stand back! This work is not for you.' All the same there'll be a mighty stir at the Ministry of the Interior. Omdehs and Moudirs and all the miscellaneous blackguards will be watching Ishmael and his men. So much the better for us, my boy. Now's your time! Now's your opportunity! "

While Gordon listened a great burden seemed to fall from him. A sort of electric revelation appeared to suffuse the path that had been so obscure a few moments before. His prayers seemed to be answered; the bright glory of a new hope seemed to be born within him and he thought he saw his way at last.

Though his career as a soldier was at an end; though his father, his mother and Helena were gone from him; though he had lost everything he had loved and been proud of; though the ways of life seemed to be for ever closed to

14

him and the world had no use for him any longer, and he
was beaten and broken and alone, there was One who was
with him still—there was God!

"With our God is forgiveness," and in the immensity
and majesty of His compassion the Almighty had willed it
that he, even he, might yet do something.

He would join the forces of the new prophet!

Why not? Their cause was a good one. It was not
a crusade of Egypt against England, but of right against
wrong, of justice against injustice, of belief against unbelief, of God against the world.

Hold! A traitor to his church and country?

No, for this was the great universal war—the war of an
empire that had no boundaries, the holy war that had been
waged all the earth over and all the ages through—the war
of religion and truth against the powers of darkness and
death.

So thinking God's hand was leading him, he saw himself
—white man, and Christian, and British soldier though he
was—following Ishmael Ameer into the desert, working by
his side, and then coming back at last when his sin had been
forgiven and his redemption won.

"Yet wait! What about my father?" he thought, but
could not think of his father at the same time that he
thought of his return. He remembered his mother, though,
and saw himself taking her in his arms and saying: "Mother,
I've come back to you, as you always said I would. I only
meant to do what was right and if I did what was wrong
God has pardoned me."

And then far off, very far, hardly daring to see itself
yet, in his awakened soul there was a hope of Helena.
Somehow and somewhere he would meet her again—he
knew not how or where or when, but Heaven knew everything and the end would be with God.

Thus with a labouring and quivering heart, and with
bleared eyes that were running over, he sat on his bed, looking into the stream of sunlight that was pouring into the
room, and feeling with an immense joy that God had mani-
fested His will at last. Meantime Hafiz, still tuning his

speech to the spirit of the natural man, was chuckling and crowing over his new chance of getting Gordon out of the country.

"Damn it all, man, we'll beat them yet, if you'll only leave yourself to me. And you will, I know you will!"

"Hafiz," said Gordon, "you thought last night you could help me to get away from here—do you still think you could?"

"Certainly! Isn't that what I'm saying?"

"Do you think you could do it now?"

"Why not—that is to say, if you are well enough—it's your hand, isn't it?"

"That's nothing—only a sore finger, you know."

"God! A sore finger, and old Michael says it's gone—half of it anyway! But if it had been half your arm it wouldn't have stopped you—I know that quite well. So if you're game I'm ready. The sooner the better, too! The dear old Patriarch will close his eyes, and as for Michael——"

"What day is this, Hafiz?" said Gordon—he had lost count of them.

"Monday—that's the worst of it. The steamer doesn't sail until Saturday, and you'll have to stay in Alexandria until—Or wait! Why not take a foreign boat? The French one to Marseilles, or—let me think—the Italian boat to Messina. The very thing! She sails on Wednesday. You can join the English at Naples. Splendid! Better than joining her at Alexandria. There's Helena, you know."

"Helena?"

"A woman's a woman after all, my boy. Mind, I don't say Helena would give you away, but she might—not having seen you since her father's death and then coming so unexpectedly upon you at Alexandria—at the ship's side perhaps. Better not risk it. Get out of the country before you meet her—away from that brute of a Macdonald and all the tags and bobs of the Intelligence Department."

"I'll want a disguise of some sort, Hafiz."

"Good idea!" said Hafiz, slapping his knee. "You can't set foot in the streets of Cairo without being recognised. Then if I'm right about the trackers—but we'll not talk about that. Something Eastern, eh? What do you say to a Coptic priest? Old Michael could lend us a black gown and a black turban. Or no, a Bedouin going to Naples for ammunition! Why, it happens every day! Splendid costume! Covers your head and nearly all your face, you know —Oh, we'll lick him, the big, bloated, blithering—Ha, ha! Effendi thinks he holds the field, and he is walking about the city like a leopard among dogs. But wait! We'll see!"

Then getting up from the side of the bed and walking to and fro in the room, Hafiz laughed out loud in his savage joy at the thought of defeating Macdonald, until Gordon said:

"I shall want a man to go with me. Can you find me a man, Hafiz?" and at that the good fellow's spirits dropped suddenly and his laughing mouth began to lag.

"A man? To go with you? Well, I—I thought of doing that myself, Gordon—as far as the boat, I mean—just to see the last of you—not knowing when I may—But perhaps you're right. I might cause you to be suspected and then— Yes, I must give that up, I suppose."

"That's all right, Hafiz—we'll meet again somewhere," said Gordon, and when Hafiz's face had brightened afresh he added:

"I'll want camels, Hafiz—two good strong camels."

"Camels? Why, what the deuce—Ah, of course! What a fool I am! Every station watched! Wonder I never thought of that before! The jackals are all along the line, and if you had gone by train, damn it, man, where should we have been? In Macdonald's mouse traps in no time! Oh, yes, camels, of course. I'll get you camels. Good ones, too. Bedouins always have good camels. Ha, ha! Effendi will go to the place he is fit for, and God increase the might of Islam!"

"I'll want money, too, Hafiz."

"Don't trouble about that. I've got a little myself—all you'll want to get away."

"I'll want a good deal, Hafiz. There's a bundle of bank notes in the top drawer of my desk at the barracks. You'll find the key in my trousers' pocket, and if you can only contrive——"

"Of course I can. Your soldier boy has been asking after you ever since you went away. He'll manage it. Macdonald's bloodhounds are beating about the barracks of course, but Tommy—trust Tommy to get the money for you—In your trousers' pocket, you say?—All right! Here's the key!—Let me see now—you'll want your berth booked— to Messina, I mean. I'll do that myself and give you whatever's left—I must keep out of people's way until after Wednesday, though. No calling at the Agency—not if I know it! My mother must be told I've been sent off somewhere, and as for the Consul-General and the telephone— I'll break the blessed receiver, that's what I'll do!—Never mind about my not seeing you off. Lord alive, that's nothing! Hope to get leave before long and then I'll slip over to England. So I'll not be saying good-bye to you when you go away, Gordon—not altogether, you know—not for good, I mean. And if all goes well with you and Helena——"

But the chuckling and the crowing and the laughing out loud in savage exultation at the thought of beating Macdonald were beginning to break down, and then Gordon, unable to keep back the truth any longer, said in a voice that chilled the ear of Hafiz:

"Hafiz, old fellow!"

"Well?"

"I don't intend to go back to England."

"You don't intend to go back——"

"No."

"Then where the—where are you going to, Charlie?"

"I'm going to Khartoum."

XI

DURING the earlier hours of the Night of Lamentation Helena sat in her room looking over bundles of old letters and tying them up with ribbon. The letters were nearly all from Gordon, but being written under different conditions and meant to be read in happier hours, every playful passage in them stung and every word of affection scorched.

She was waiting for the black boy to come back from the demonstration and thinking out a course of conduct. Instead of returning to England she was to remain in Cairo, and by help of the new evidence she was to compel the law to arrest and convict the guilty man. It was her right to do so, and since the authorities, thinking of other things, were shirking their responsibility, it was her duty, her solemn and sacred duty.

What did State considerations matter to her? Nothing! She remembered the predicament of the Army Surgeon without compunction, and even when she thought of the position of the Consul-General she did not care. Her father was dead, Gordon was lost to her, she was a woman and she was alone, and nothing else was of the smallest consequence. Thus seeing to the bottom of her own misery, she had now no pity for anybody else.

At midnight the black boy had not returned, and being worn out with sleeplessness, and assured by her other servants that Mosie was well able to take care of himself, she went to bed. But the moonlight filtered through the white window blind and she lay for some time with wide-open eyes thinking what she would do next day. She would go down to the Ministry of the Interior and set the law in motion. There would be no time to lose, for if Ishmael escaped the consequences of to-night's proceedings he might leave Cairo without delay.

She slept a few hours only and when she awoke the sun was flecking with fiery bars a window that faced to the east. While she lay on her back with her arm under her head, looking at the ceiling, and working herself up into a still greater hatred of Ishmael, there came a timid knock at the door and the black boy entered the room. He was breathless and dishevelled and full of apologies.

"Lady angry with Mosie? Mosie stop all night to tell lady everything," he said, and then he told her what had happened in the Mohammedan cemetery—a wild, disordered, delirious story of the departure of the hundred men.

"But the prophet himself—what has become of him?" asked Helena, raising her head from her pillow.

"White Prophet gone," said Mosie.

"Gone?"

"Mosie follow him to station. White Prophet go by train, lady."

"By train?"

"Yes, lady. White Prophet go by train to Upper Egypt," said Mosie, and then Helena heard no more.

Her head fell back to her pillow and she covered her eyes with her hands. The guilty man was gone, the authorities had allowed him to go, and if the evil-doer was to be punished there was nothing left but personal vengeance.

In the delirium of her hatred of the Egyptian and the tragic tangle of her awful error, every tender impulse of her heart was now dead. Overwhelmed as by a new burden and haunted by a dark responsibility—that of seeing God's vengeance brought down upon her father's murderer—she saw herself at one moment prompting Gordon to kill Ishmael. Why not? There was no other way. Gordon should kill Ishmael Ameer because Ishmael Ameer had killed her father!

At the next moment the recollection that Gordon had gone took her back once more to the bitterest part of her suffering. She had always thought that when God made Gordon He had made him without fear, yet he had run away from the consequences of being court-martialled. It was intensely painful to her to despise Gordon, but do what she would she could not help feeling a growing contempt for him. If he had only stood up to his punishment she would have been proud of him, and even if he had been drummed out of the Army, or any fate had befallen him less terrible than death, he would have found her standing by his side.

But he had fled, he had left her, and being useless to all purposes of righteous vengeance, a woman without a man behind her, she could do nothing now but go back to England.

During the next three days she was kept busy by the mechanical preparations for her departure. There was not much she had to do, for the contents of the General House belonged to the Army, and beyond her own and her father's personal possessions there was little to pack up, yet the black boy was always beside her, with a helping hand but a lagging lip and many plaintive lamentations.

"Lady not want Mosie any more now—no?"

On the Thursday he came running into Helena's room to say that Lady Nuneham, with her Egyptian maid, had come to call on her.

Helena met Gordon's mother at the door, the sweet old soul with her pale, spiritual face, suffering visibly but bearing herself bravely as she stepped out of her closely curtained carriage and crossed the garden path, under the white heat of the noonday sun, with one arm through Fatimah's, and the other trembling hand on the ebony handle of a walking stick.

As soon as she reached the hall the old lady lifted her veil and stretched out her arms to Helena and kissed her, and then patted her shoulder with her mittened hand as if Helena had been a child and she had come to comfort her.

"My poor Helena! It's hard for you, I know, but if God sends the cross He sends the strength to carry it. I've always found it so, my dear," she said, and when she was seated on the sofa with Helena beside her, she began to talk of her own father, how they had been everything to each other, and when he had died she had thought she could not live without him, but God had been good—He had sent her her husband and then——"

But that was a blind alley down which she could walk no farther, for there was one name that was trembling on the lips of both women and neither of them could yet bring herself to speak it.

"When my mother died, too—I was married then and living here in Cairo, but mother couldn't leave the old home in Massachusetts where I was brought up as a child —poor mother, she used to play blind-man's-buff in the hall with me, I remember, for we were far away from other peo-

ple and I had no little playmates—when she died I thought
I should have died, too, but God was good to me again—
He sent me my own child, my boy, my——"

It was just as if all roads converged to one centre, and
to escape from it the old lady began to talk of little things,
asking simple questions and giving motherly advice, while
Helena held down her head and drew the hem of her handkerchief through her fingers.

"You are sailing on Saturday, are you not?"

"Yes, on Saturday."

"You must take good care of yourself, dearest. It is
hot in Cairo, but it may be cool in Alexandria and even
cold on the sea. Put some warm clothing on, dear, some
nice warm underclothing, you know."

She was sure to meet pleasant people on the steamer and
they would see her safely into the train at Marseilles. It
would be such an agreeable break to travel overland through
Paris, and when she reached London——"

"Have you anybody to meet you in London, Helena?"

Still drawing the hem of her handkerchief through her
fingers, Helena shook her head.

"I'm sorry for that, dear, very sorry."

Landing in London was so trying, so bewildering, especially if you were a woman. Such crowds, such confusion! It always made her feel so helpless. And then she
had the Consul-General to look after her, and once Gordon
had come to meet her, too. He was at the Staff College at
that time, and before she alighted from the carriage she had
seen him forging his way down the platform, and he kissed
his hand to her.

But the sweet old thing could bear up no longer, and
while Helena pressed her handkerchief to her lips, she said:

"Oh, Helena, how happy we might have been! It's
wrong of me, I know it's wrong, but I can't reconcile myself
to it even yet. 'Why is my life prolonged?' I have often
thought, and then I have told myself it was because God
intended that I should live to see my dear children happy.
Ah, my darling, it would have been so beautiful! My children and perhaps my children's children. If I could only

15

have seen them all together once! It would have been so easy to go then. But now my son is gone—I don't know what has become of him—and my daughter—my sweet daughter that was to be——"

Helena sank to her knees. "Mother!" she said, and burying her face in Lady Nuneham's shoulder, she felt, for the first time in her life, that a mother's heart was beating against her own.

After a while the old lady, whose arms had been about Helena's neck, began to stroke her forehead and the top of her head, and to say in a calmer voice:

"It was wrong of me to repine, dear. Happiness does not depend on us. It depends on God, and we should leave everything to Him. He will do what is best. I'm sure He will."

Then in a nervous way she attempted to defend Gordon. They were not to be too hard on him. No doubt he thought he was doing what was right.

"And he was, too, wasn't he? In a sense at least. Don't you think so, Helena?"

Helena could not answer, but she made a helpless motion with her head.

They were not to suppose he meant to forsake them either, and if he had fled away he was not thinking of himself only—they might be sure of that. He never did—never had done—never once since he was a child.

"You couldn't give him a handful of sweets when he was a boy but he asked for another for Hafiz."

Perhaps he was thinking of his father—that if he gave himself up and there was an inquiry, a court-martial, the Consul-General would suffer in his influence in Egypt and his esteem in England. Perhaps he was thinking of Helena herself—that it might seem as if her father's death had been hastened by the painful scene with himself. And perhaps he was thinking a little of his mother, too—of the pain she would suffer at sight of her husband and her son at war before the world.

However this might be he would come back. She knew he would. Oh, yes, she knew quite well he would come back.

For four days she had asked God, and He had answered her at last.

" 'Help me, O God, for Christ's sake!' I said. 'Will my dear son come back to me? Shall I see him again? O God, give me a sign?' And He did, my dear. Yes, it was just before dawn this morning. 'Janet!' said a voice, and I was not afraid. 'Be patient, Janet! All will be well!'"

Helena dared not look up, being afraid to penetrate by so much as a glance the sanctity of the sweet old lady's soul.

"So you see it's wrong to repine, dear. Everything will work out for the best. You are going to England, but that doesn't matter in the least. We'll all come together again yet. And when my dear ones are united, my sweet daughter and my boy—my brave, brave boy——"

The old lady's voice was quivering with the excitement of her joy, when Fatimah, who had stood aside in silence, stepped forward and said:

"Better go home now, my lady. His lordship will be waiting for his lunch."

Lady Nuneham took Helena's head between her hands and kissed her on the forehead, then dropped her veil and rose to her feet by help of Fatimah's arm on the one side and her stick on the other.

"Good-bye for the present, Helena! Be sure you write as soon as you get to England. Take good care of yourself on the voyage, dear. And don't forget to put on some nice warm underclothing, you know. Good-bye!"

Helena saw her back to the door, the sweet, helpless old child, living by the life of her beautiful love. As she passed down the path she waved her delicate hand in its silken mitten, and Helena said farewell to her with her eyes, knowing she would see her no more.

XII

AFTER a while Helena began to think tenderly of Gordon and to conjure up the beautiful moments of their love—the moment in the harbour before he set off for Alexandria, the moment in his quarters when she had to slip off her glove and dip her finger in the glass from which he drank her health, and above all the moment of their first meeting, when he said he loved Egypt and the Egyptians and everything and everybody, and they laughed and looked into each other's eyes, and smiled without speaking, and he took her hand and kept on holding it, and a world of warm impulses coursed through her veins, and something whispered to her, " It is he! "

But thinking like this about Gordon only made her remember with even more bitterness than before the man who had taken him away from her. Presently she saw that there was a kind of dishonour to Gordon in hating the Egyptian for that, and though she tried to justify herself by thinking of Gordon's mother, and of the beautiful blind faith that was doomed to death, she was compelled to go back at length to the one sure ground on which she could continue to hate Ishmael and keep a good conscience—that the man had killed her father.

So intensely did she work up her feelings on this subject that, awaking in the middle of the night after Lady Nuneham's visit, she held out her hands in bed and prayed to God to let his vengeance fall on the Egyptian.

"Punish him, O God, punish him, punish him! My father is dead! My dear father is dead! He was so weak, so ill, so old! O God, let Thy vengeance fall on the coward who killed him! Let thy hand be on him as long as he lives! Follow him wherever he goes! Destroy him whatever he does! Let him never know another happy hour! Let him be an exile and an outcast to the last hour of his life! O God, hear me, hear me!"

Next morning she felt ashamed of this outburst, but less because of its bitterness than its futility, and then with a sense of utter helplessness she began to feel the misery of being a woman. It was a part of the cruel scheme of nature that however injured and outraged, a woman could do nothing. In the East, above all, she was useless—useless to all purposes of justice or vengeance or revenge.

On the Friday afternoon, having made the last preparations for her departure, she was sitting at her desk, writing labels for her trunks and portmanteaus, when Mosie dashed in upon her to say that the Princess Nazimah, with outriders and footmen and eunuchs, was driving up to the door. A moment later the Princess entered the room. Her plump person, redolent of perfume, was clad in a tussore silk gown, and under the latest of Paris hats her powdered face was plainly visible through the thinnest of chiffon veils.

"I hear you are leaving Egypt, so I've come to bid good-bye to you," she said, and then taking Helena by the shoulders and looking into her face she cried:

"Merciful powers, what has become of your eyes, my beauty? What have you been doing to yourself, my moon?"

"Nothing," said Helena.

"Nothing? Don't tell me. You are not sleeping, no, nor eating neither. Come, sit down and tell me all about it," and sitting heavily on the sofa, with Helena beside her, she proceeded to do the talking herself.

"But my dear creature, my good girl, this is nonsense. Excuse the word—nonsense! Good God! Is a girl to kill herself because her father dies before her? Fathers do, and why shouldn't they? Mine did. He was a beast. Excuse the word—a beast. Forty wives—or was it fifty—but he died, nevertheless."

With that she lifted her veil, used a smelling bottle, and then began again:

"I see what it is, though—your ways are not our ways, and all this comes of your religion. It makes you think about death and the grave, whereas ours tells us to think about life. Your Christianity is a funeral mute, my dear, while Islam is a dancing girl, God bless her! You groan and weep when your kindred die. We laugh and are happy, or if we are not we ought to be. I'm sure I was when my first husband died. 'Thank the Lord he's gone,' I said. It's true I hadn't lived on the best of terms with him, but then——"

"It's not my father's death only," began Helena haltingly, whereupon the Princess said:

"Yes, of course! I've heard all about it. He's gone, and I suppose you know no more than anybody else what has become of him. No?"

"No!"

"Ah, my dear, my moon, my beauty, all this wouldn't have happened if you had taken my advice. When your Gordon began to oppose his father you should have stopped him. Yes, *you* could have done it. Of course you could."

"I couldn't, Princess," said Helena.

"What? You mean to say you tried to and you couldn't? You couldn't get him to give up that ridiculous holy man for a girl like— Then God have mercy upon us, what are you moaning about? Who ever heard of such a thing? A young woman like you eating her heart out for the loss of a man who prefers—well, upon my word!"

The Princess put her smelling bottle to both nostrils in quick succession and then said:

"It's true I thought him the best of the bunch. In fact I simply lost my heart to him. But if he had been the only man in the world—oh, I know! You think he *is* the only one. I thought that myself when my first husband left me. It wasn't a Mahdi in his case. Only a milliner, and I was ready to die of shame. But I didn't. I just put some kohl on my eyes and looked round for another. It's true my second wasn't much of a man, but a donkey of your own is better than a horse of somebody else's."

Again the smelling bottle, and then:

"Listen to me, my dear. I'm a woman of experience at all events. Have a good cry and get him out of your head. Why not? He's gone, isn't he? He can never come back to the Army, and his career as a soldier is at an end. The felled tree doesn't bear any more dates, so what's the good of him anyway? Oh, *I* know! You needn't tell *me!* Love is sweet in the suckling and bitter in the weaning, and you think you can't do it, but you can. You are going back to England, I hear. So much the better! Far from the eyes, far from the heart, and quite right, too. Get married as soon as possible and have some big bouncing babies. I haven't had any myself certainly, but that's different—I thought I wouldn't repeat the crime of my mother, God forgive her!"

Helena's head was down—she was hardly listening.

"Lose no time either, my sweet. Time is money, they say, and perhaps it is, though it has different prices on the bourse, I notice. I've known days that would have been dear at two piastres and a few quarters of an hour that I wouldn't have parted with for millions of money. Perhaps you've felt like that, my beauty. But perhaps you haven't. You're only a child yet, my chicken."

"The man Ishmael has gone, hasn't he?" asked Helena.

"Yes, they've let him go, the stupids! Back to the Soudan—to Khartoum they tell me."

"Khartoum?"

"Just like you English! Dunces! Excuse the word. I say what I think. You judge of the East by the West, and can't see that force is the only thing these people understand. I stood it for five days, boiling all over inside, and then I went down to the Agency. 'Good gracious,' I said, 'why has the Government allowed these men to slip through their fingers?' And when Nuneham said he had laid a hundred and fifty of them by the heels, I said 'Tut!' Taking water by drops will never fill the water-skin. You should have laid hold of a hundred and fifty thousand and that man Ishmael above all. But you've let him go—him and his hundred messengers—and now you'll have to take the consequences. Serve you right, too! What was the use of putting down the Arabic press if you let the Arabic preachers go unmolested?'"

"What did he say to that, Princess?"

"He said he had scotched the snake but he was not forgetting the scorpion. It's no use talking, though. Nuneham is a great man, but he has lost his nerve and is always asking himself what they are saying about him in England. Boobies in Parliament, I suppose, and he wants to be ready to reply to them. But goodness me, if you throw a missile at every dog that barks at you the stones in your street will be as precious as jewels soon. Oh, I know! I'm a woman of experience."

Helena was staring straight before her.

"I see what is going to happen," said the Princess. "This man will sow sedition all over the country and meantime preach peace in Khartoum and throw dust in the eyes of Europe."

"He is a scoundrel, a hypocrite——"

"Of course he is, my dear, but when people are bad they always pretend that they want to make other people better."

"Can the Government do nothing to stop him, to destroy him——?"

"No, my dear. There is only one thing that can do that now."

"What?"

"A woman!"

"A woman?"

"Why not? Follow the holy man no farther than his threshold, they say. But some woman always does so. Always!"

Helena's staring eyes with their far-away look had come back to the Princess's face. The Princess was beating her hand and laughing.

"You English think woman has no power in the East. Rubbish! She is more powerful here than anywhere else. Even polygamy gives her power—for a time at all events. While she is first favourite she rules everything, and when she ceases to be that—" The Princess laughed again, closed her eyes, and said: "She who doesn't take her revenge has an ass for uncle."

Helena's heart began to beat so violently that she could scarcely speak, but she said:

"You mean that some woman will betray this man——"

"What is more likely? They all fall that way sooner or later, my beauty. This one has taken a kind of vow of celibacy, they say, but what matter? When I was as young as you are there was nothing I loved so much as to meet with a man of that sort. It was child's play, my darling."

All the blood in Helena's body was now boiling under the poison of a new thought.

"I hear he says he will come back in glory and then

Egypt will be at his feet. *Bismillah!*" said the Princess, raising her eyes in mock reverence, and then laughing gaily she added:

"Perhaps—who knows?—before that time comes some woman of the harem may find her opportunity. Jealousy—envy—revenge—one may see how the world goes without eyes, my beauty!"

Helena sat motionless; she was scarcely able to breathe.

"Good luck to her, I say!" said the Princess. "She'll do more for Egypt than all the Nunehams and Sirdars put together."

Then she looked round at Helena and said:

"I've shocked you, haven't I, my dear? Women in the West don't do these things, do they? No, they are civilised, and when they have been wronged by men they take them into the courts and make them pay. Faugh! There can be no red blood in women's veins in your countries."

The Princess rummaged in her bag for her powder puff, used it vigorously, put away her smelling bottle, and then rose to go, saying:

"I don't mean you, my sweet. Your mother was Jewish —wasn't she?—and it was a Jewish woman who destroyed the captain of the Assyrians and smote off his head with her own falchion. Women can't fight their battles with swords, though. But," laughing and patting Helena's hand again, "what has Allah given them such big black eyes for? Adieu, my dear! Adieu!"

Helena stood in the middle of the floor where the Princess had left her and slowly looked around. For a long time she remained there thinking. Was woman so utterly helpless as she had supposed? And when she was deeply wronged, when her dear ones were torn from her, when she was a victim of cruel violence and heartless hypocrisy, and the law failed her, and the State, having its own ends to serve, tried to shuffle her off, was she not justified in using against her enemy the only weapons which God had given her?

At that she grew hot and then cold, and then a sense of shame came over her and she covered her face with her

hands. "What am I thinking of?" she asked herself, and
the floor seemed to slide from under her feet. The thought
which the Princess had put into her mind was treason to
her love for Gordon. That love was a sacred thing to her,
and it would always remain so, even though she might never
see Gordon again. Love itself was sacred, and she who gave
it away for any gain of vengeance or revenge was a bad
woman.

Helena sat down with her elbows on the desk and her
chin resting on her hands and stared out of the window.
After a while a kind of relief came to her. She began to
recall some of the Princess's parting words. "She will do
more for Egypt than all the Nunehams and Sirdars put
together." That seemed to justify the thought that had
taken possession of her. She began to feel herself the champion of justice and to find the good conscience for which
she sought.

This man Ishmael, who had killed her father, and by
hypocritical pretences had deceived Gordon and caused him
to be carried away from her, was an impostor who would
turn England out of Egypt by playing on the fanaticism
of an ignorant populace. He was another Mahdi who, with
words of peace in his mouth, would devastate the country
and sow the very sands of its deserts with blood. When law
failed to defeat an enemy like that, and the machinery of
civilised government proved to be impotent against him,
were there any means, any arts, which it was not proper
to use?

Love? It was quite unnecessary to think about that.
This man pretended to be an emancipator of the Eastern
woman. Therefore a woman might go to him and offer to
help him, and while helping him she might possess herself
of all his secrets. "Follow the holy man no farther than
his threshold," said the Arabs. She would do it nevertheless,
and in doing it she would be serving England and Egypt
and even the world.

Thus she fought with herself in a fierce effort to hold
on to her good conscience. But, staring out of the window,
she felt as if something from the river were stretching out

its evil hands to her. The red streak in the rising Nile was now wider than before, and it looked more than ever like blood.

Ishmael Ameer would not know her. During the single moment in which she had stood in the same room with him he had never so much as looked in her direction. The Sirdar and the British officers of the Soudan had not yet seen her. If there were any danger of their asking questions the Consul-General could set them at rest. "I can do it," she thought. "I can and I will."

The black boy, who had been creeping in and out of her room, looking more and more miserable as he found her always in the same position, now approached her and said, pointing to the labels under her elbows:

"Mosie tie them onto boxes, lady?"

She looked round at him and the utter slavishness in his little soul touched her pity. It also stirred her caution for she told herself that she might need the boy's help and that he would die for her if need be.

"Mosie," she said, "would you like to go away with me?"

Mosie, in his delirious joy, could hardly believe his ears.

"Lady take Mosie to England with her?"

"No, to your own country, to the Soudan."

Mosie first leaped off the floor as if he wanted to fly up to the ceiling, and then began to make himself big, saying Mosie was a good boy, he was lady's own boy from one hand to the other, and what would have become of lady if she had gone away without him?

"Then bring up two cabs immediately, one for the luggage and the other for ourselves, and don't say a word to anybody," said Helena, who had risen to consult a railway time-table and was now tearing up her labels.

Hugging himself with delight, the black boy shot away instantly. Helena heard his joyous laughter as it rippled like a river along the garden path, and then she sat down at the desk to write to the Consul-General.

XIII

GORDON, in the meantime, living on the heights of his new resolve, had been waiting impatiently for the opportunity of departure. No prisoner looking forward to the hour of his escape ever suffered more from the slow passage of time. He lost all appetite for food, sleep deserted him, and as the week went on he was in an increasing fever of excitement. On Tuesday he received through Michael a letter from Hafiz saying:

"We must be careful. I'll tell you why. I was right about the trackers. That beast Macdonald, having sworn that he would find you if you were above ground, and being sure that you were still in Cairo and that the people were concealing you, employed the services of a couple of serpents from the Soudan. These human reptiles, with green eyes like the eyes of boa-constrictors, had no difficulty in tracing your footsteps to a side street in the neighbourhood of El Azhar, but there your footsteps failed them as absolutely as if you had sunk into the earth.

"Perplexed and baffled, they were on the point of giving up the search when in the soft mud of the disgusting thoroughfare they found the marks of horses' hoofs and of the hoops of wheels, and from these they concluded that you had been carried off in a conveyance of some sort. But track of the carriage was lost the moment they reached the paved way which passes through the Muski, and now they are again bewildered.

"In this extremity, however, they have thought of another device for your discovery, which is—what do you think?—to watch *me!* Under the impression that I know where you are, they are dogging my footsteps every moment I am off duty. No matter! I'll beat the beasts! As a bloodhound is nothing but a nose, so a tracker is nothing but an eye, and he has hardly as much brain as you could push into a mushroom. Therefore wait! Trust yourself to Hafiz! Why not? You cannot depend on a better man."

Next day, Wednesday, the doctor, with his bright face and cheery voice, came again to dress the wounded finger.

"Wonderful!" he cried. "Almost healed already! That's what youth and decent living does for a man."

"I have no money at present, doctor," said Gordon, "but I expect to receive some very soon, and before I go your fee will be paid."

"Of course it will—when I ask for it. But 'go'? Not yet, I think."

The streets were like a sackful of eyes and every eye seemed to be looking for Gordon—either to attack or to protect him.

"But wait! Things don't seem to be going too smoothly for the Government."

Cables at the clubs made it clear that England was not very pleased with the turn events had taken in Cairo. There had been questions in Parliament and the Foreign Minister at his wits' end to defend the Consul-General. Mentions of Gordon himself, too, and some of the Liberal Opposition up in arms for him.

"So wait, I say! Who knows? You may walk out without danger by and by."

Thursday passed heavily with Gordon, who was alone all day long save for the visits of old Michael when bringing the food, which went away untouched, but toward midnight Hafiz arrived, with his eyes full of mischief and his fat cheeks wreathed in smiles.

"Look!" he said, "that's the way to beat the brutes," and holding up one foot he pointed to a native yellow slipper which he wore over his military boots. He had made a circuit of six miles to get there, though—it was like taking a country walk in order to cross the street.

"But no matter! Trust yourself to Hafiz."

He carried a small bundle under his arm, and throwing it on a chair, he said:

"Your Bedouin clothes, my boy—you'll find them all right, I think."

Gordon caught the flame of his eagerness and was asking a dozen questions at once, when Hafiz said:

"A moment, old chap! Let us speak of everything in its place. First," taking a roll of bank notes out of his pocket, "here's your money—short of what I've spent for you. Tommy got it. Couldn't get anything else, though."

Thinking civilian clothes might be useful, Hafiz had told Gordon's soldier servant to smuggle a suit out, also, but it had been found impossible to do so.

"That comes of taking up your quarters in a barracks instead of at the club or at a private house, as staff officers always do," said Hafiz, and when Gordon gave some hint of explanation he added: "Oh, I know! You wanted to make common cause with the men, but now you have to pay the price of it."

"What about the man to go with me?" asked Gordon.

"I've got him. You remember the two Sheikhs who went with us to Alexandria? It's one of them."

His name was Osman. He had been tutor to the Khedive's children, but he wished to become a teacher of Mohammedan law in the college at Khartoum, so the journey suited his book exactly.

"And the camels?"

"I've got them also. Young ones, too, with ripping big humps! They'll want their humps before they've crossed that desert."

"Where and when am I to meet them, Hafiz?"

"At the first village beyond the fort on the Gebel Mokattam at eleven o'clock to-morrow night. But I'll come for you at ten and see you safely started."

Gordon looked up in alarm.

"Don't be afraid for me. Leave everything to Hafiz. You can't depend on a better man."

"I'm sure I can't," said Gordon, and then in a lower tone, "But, Hafiz?"

"Well?"

"What about Helena?"

"Packed up and ready to go. The Consul-General's Secretary booked her berth to-day, and she sails, as I said she would, on Saturday."

Next day, Friday, the hours went by with feet of lead,

but Gordon's impatience to get away from Cairo had now begun to abate. More easily could he have reconciled himself to go if Helena had gone before him, but to leave her behind, if only for a few hours, was like cowardice. Little by little his spirit fell from the elevation on which it had lived for the better part of a week, and in the face of his flight he felt ashamed.

Toward nightfall, nevertheless, he began to make preparations for his departure, and, opening the bundle of clothes which Hafiz had left for him, he found that they consisted of a Bedouin's outer garments only, caftan, skull-cap, kufiah (head-shawl), and head-rope, but no underclothing and no slippers. This seemed for a moment like an insurmountable difficulty, but at the next instant, with the sense of a higher power ruling everything, he saw the finger of God in it, compelling him to wear his soldier's clothes and military boots beneath his Bedouin costume, lest leaving them behind him might lead to trouble for the good people who had befriended him.

By ten o'clock he had finished his dressing and then the door of his room was opened by a man in the flowing silk garments of a Sheikh, with the light of a smile on his chubby face and a cautionary finger to his lip.

"Here I am—are you ready?"

It was Hafiz, tingling with excitement but chuckling with joy, and having looked at Gordon in his head-shawl descending to his shoulders, with the head-rope coiled about it, he said:

"Marvellous! Your own father wouldn't know you."

The disguise was none too good, though, for the trackers were keenly on the trail that night, having got it into their heads that Gordon would try to leave Egypt with Helena in the morning.

"So the sooner we are on the safe side of the Gebel Mokattam the better, my boy—one moment, though."

"What is it?"

"Remember—your name is Omar—Omar Benani."

"Omar Benani."

The last moment having come, Gordon, who seemed now

to catch at every straw that would delay his departure, was unwilling to leave the house that had been his refuge without bidding farewell to the Patriarch. Hafiz tried to dissuade him from doing so, saying that the Patriarch, who knew all, wished to be blind to what was going on. But Gordon was not to be gainsaid, and after a while Michael was called and he led the way to the Patriarch's room.

The old man had just finished his frugal supper of spinach and egg, and was lifting his horn-rimmed spectacles from his nose to wipe his rheumy eyes with his red-print handkerchief when Michael opened the door.

" A poor traveller asks your blessing, Patriarch," said Michael, and then Gordon, in his Bedouin costume, stepped forward and knelt at the old priest's feet.

The Patriarch rose and stood for a moment with a look of perplexity on his wrinkled face. Then, lending himself to the transparent deception, the saintly old man laid his bony hand, trembling visibly, on Gordon's head, and speaking in a faltering voice, with breath that came quickly through his toothless jaws, he said:

" God bless you, my son, and send you safely to your journey's end and to your own place and people."

But seeing at the next instant how pathetic was the error which in his momentary confusion he had unwittingly made, he corrected himself and added:

" Fear not, my son, neither in the days of thy life, nor in the hour of death, for God will go with thee and *He will bring thee back*."

A moment later Gordon, with Hafiz by his side, had passed out of the echoing harbour of the little cathedral close into the running tides of the streets without.

XIV

THE Coptic Cathedral stands in the midst of the most ancient part of Cairo and it is coiled about by a cobweb of close and narrow thoroughfares. Through these thoroughfares, which are lit by tin lanterns and open candles only, and dense with a various throng of native people—hawkers, pedlars, water-carriers, fruit-sellers, the shrouded black forms of women gliding noiselessly along, and the blue figures of men lounging at coffee-stalls or squatting at the open mouths of shops—Gordon in his Bedouin costume walked with a long, slow step and the indifference to danger which he had learned in war, while Hafiz, who was now quivering with impatience and trembling with the dread of detection, slackened his speed to keep pace with him.

"Can't we go faster?" whispered Hafiz, but Gordon did not seem to hear. Slowly, steadily, with a rhythmic stride that might have come out of the desert itself, he pushed his way through the throng of town-dwellers, always answering the pious ejaculations of the passers-by and returning their Eastern greetings.

Before Hafiz was aware of the direction they were taking they had passed out of the dim-lit native streets, where people moved like shadows in a mist, into the coarse flare of the Esbekiah (the European) quarter, where multitudes of men in Western dress sat drinking at tables on the pavement, while girls in gold brocade and with painted faces smiled down at them from upper windows.

"Why should we go this way?" said Hafiz in Arabic, but still Gordon made no reply.

Two mounted police who were standing at guard by the entrance to a dark alley craned forward to peer into their faces, and a group of young British officers, smoking cigarettes on the balcony of a hotel, watched them while they passed and broke into a subdued trill of laughter when they were gone.

"Are we not exposing ourselves unnecessarily?" whispered Hafiz; but Gordon only gripped the hand that hung by his side and went on without speaking.

Presently they crossed the Opera Square and turned down an avenue that led to the Nile, and then Hafiz's impatience could contain itself no longer.

"We are going in the wrong direction," he whispered. "It's nearly eleven o'clock and Osman is waiting for us."

"Come on," said Gordon, and he continued to walk steadily forward.

At length it dawned on Hafiz that, in spite of all possible consequences, Gordon intended to go to the Agency before he left Cairo, and having assured himself that this was so, he began to pour out a running whisper of passionate entreaties.

"But, Gordon! My dear Gordon! This is madness. It cannot be done," he said.

"It must!" said Gordon.

"The trackers will be there if they are anywhere."

"Hush!"

"It is the one place they'll keep watch upon to-night."

"I can't help that," said Gordon without stopping, and Hafiz had no choice but to follow on.

A few minutes later the good fellow, whose heart was now panting in his throat, walked close to Gordon's side and whispered in a breaking voice:

"If you have any message to send to your mother I'll take it—I'll take it after you are gone."

"I must see her myself," said Gordon, and then Hafiz could say no more.

They passed through populous places into thoroughfares that were less and less crowded, and came out at last by the barracks on the banks of the Nile. There the broad street was empty and silent, and the white moonlight lay over the river, which flowed like liquid steel. Under the dark window of his own quarters Gordon paused for a moment, for it was the spot on which he had first seen Helena. He could see it still as he saw it then, with its tide of clamorous traffic from the bridge—the camels, the cameleers, the blue-shirted fellaheen, the women with tattooed chins and children astride on their shoulders, and then the girl driving the automobile, with the veil of white chiffon about her head and the ruddy glow of the sunset kissing her upturned face as she lifted her eyes to look at him.

Hafiz was choking with emotion by this time, but his sense of Gordon's danger came uppermost again when they turned into the road that led to the Consul-General's house and caught sight of a group of men who were standing at the gate.

"There they are," he whispered. "What did I tell you? Let us go back. Gordon, I implore you! I entreat you! By all you love and who love you——"

"Come on," said Gordon again, and, though quaking with fear, Hafiz continued to walk by his side.

There were only three men at the gate of the Agency and two of them were the native porters of the house, but the third was a lean and lank Soudanese, who carried by a cord about his neck a small round lantern whereof the light was turned against his breast. A cold glitter in the black man's eyes was like the gleam of a dagger to Hafiz, but Gordon paid no heed to it. He saluted the porters, saying he had come to see Ibrahim, the Consul-General's servant, and then without waiting for permission, he walked through.

Hafiz followed him into the garden, where the moonlight lay over the silent trees and made blotches of shadow on the path.

"Stay here," he said, and leaving Hafiz in the darkness he stepped up to the door.

Ibrahim himself opened it, and the moment he had done so, Gordon entered the outer hall.

"Tell Fatimah I come from her son and wish to see her at once," he said.

Ibrahim looked searchingly at the stranger and a shade of doubt and anger crossed his face.

"I can't do that, my man," he answered.

"Why can't you?" asked Gordon.

"I won't," said Ibrahim.

There was a little lodge at the right of the hall where visitors to the Consul-General wrote their names in a book. Into this lodge Gordon drew Ibrahim by the arm and whispered a few hasty words in his ear. The man's lips whitened and quivered in an instant and he began to stutter and stammer in his fright.

"Are you, then—can it be—is it really——"

"Hush! Yes. Ibrahim," said Gordon. "I wish to see my mother."

Ibrahim began to wring his hands. It was impossible. Yes, impossible. Quite impossible. Her ladyship was ill.

"Ill?"

"She went up to the Citadel yesterday, sir, and came home utterly exhausted."

"Do you mean that my mother is very ill—dangerously ill, Ibrahim?"

"I don't know, sir. I can't say, sir. I fear she is, sir."

"Then all the more I wish to see her," said Gordon.

But again Ibrahim wrung his hands. The doctor had been there four times that day and ordered absolute rest and quiet. Only Fatimah was permitted to enter the patient's room—except the Consul-General and he went up to it every hour.

"It would be a shock to her, sir. It might kill her, sir. *Wallahi!* I beg of you not to attempt it, sir."

Ibrahim was right, plainly right, but never until that moment had Gordon known the full bitterness of the cup he had to drink from. Because his mother was ill, dangerously ill, dying perhaps, therefore he must not see her—he of all others! He was going far and might never see her again. Was another blank wall to be built about his life? It was monstrous, it was impossible, it should not be!

In the agony of his revolt a wild thought came to him —he would see his father! Why not? Back to his memory across the bridge of so many years came the words which his father had written to him when he came of age: "You are twenty-one years of age, Gordon, and your mother and I have beeen recalling the incidents of the day on which you were born— From this day forward I am no longer your father; I am your friend; perhaps the best friend you will ever have; let nothing and no one come between us." Then why not? What was there to be afraid of?

"Ibrahim," said Gordon, "where is the Consul-General now?"

"In the library with his secretary, sir," replied Ibrahim.

"Then tell him—" began Gordon, but just at that moment there was a flat and deadened step on the soft carpet of the landing above, and then a cold voice that chilled his ear came from the upper hall.

"Ibrahim!"

It was the Consul-General himself with a letter in his hand.

"Hush!" said Ibrahim, and, leaving the lodge, he walked up the three or four steps to meet his master.

"Take this to the office of the Commandant of Police— take it yourself and see it safely delivered."

"Yes, my lord."

"If the Commandant has gone home for the night you will ask for his Deputy and say my answer is: 'Yes, I let nothing come between me and the law. If you suspect that the person you refer to is still in Cairo, you will deal with him as you would deal with anybody else.' You understand me?"

"Yes, my lord," said Ibrahim, but he was staring stupidly at the letter as if he had lost his wits.

"Who is that in the lodge with you?" asked the Consul-General, and then Ibrahim, fumbling the letter until it almost fell out of his fingers, seemed unable to reply.

The wild thought had gone from Gordon by this time and he said in a voice which he did not recognise as his own, "Tell Fatimah that her brother will come again to see her," and then, feeling ashamed of his sorry masquerade, and less than a servant in his father's house, he stumbled out into the garden.

Hafiz was waiting for him there and he was in a state of still greater terror than before. The moment Gordon had gone a light footstep, trying to make itself noiseless, had come crackling over the gravel from the direction of the gate. It was that of the Soudanese and he had crept along the path like a serpent, half doubled up and with his eyes and his lantern to the ground. After a while he had returned to where he came from, and Hafiz had followed him, walking stealthily in the shadow of the trees, in order to hear what he had to say. "Your Bedouin is a child of Cairo and his boots were made in England," he had said, and then chuckling to himself he had hurried away.

"Are you wearing your military boots, Gordon? Did you forget the slippers? Or was it Osman who forgot them? It can't be helped, though. The man was a tracker —I told you so—and now he has gone for the others and we shall be followed by the whole troop of them. Let us be off."

But still Gordon was in no hurry to go. The sense of stealing like a stranger from a spot that was dear to him by a thousand memories seemed to be more than he could bear. Leaving Hafiz on the path, he went round the house until he reached a place from which he could see the light in his mother's window. His mother, his sweet and sainted mother, innocent of everything, yet the victim of all! God forgive him! Was it worth while to go away at all? A gentle breeze had risen by this time and Hafiz was starting at every leaf that rustled over his head.

When at length they had left the Agency they were going in the right direction, but Gordon was once more choosing the lighter and more crowded thoroughfares. Again the hawkers, the pedlars, the water-carriers, the shrouded black forms of women and the blue figures of men. Again the salutations, the pious ejaculations, the silent Eastern greetings. It was almost as if Gordon were tempting Providence, as if he were trying to leave time for the trackers to overtake him.

"Every moment we lose fills me with fear. Can't we go faster now?" whispered Hafiz in English, but Gordon continued to walk with the same even step.

"I know it might look like fright and arouse suspicion, but still——"

As often as he dared to do so Hafiz looked back to see if they were pursued.

"Nothing in sight yet—God has delivered us thus far —but must we walk so slow?"

In the agony of his impatience every noise in the streets was like the sound of a pursuer. If a boy shouted to his playmate he shuddered; if a hawker yelled over his tray he trembled. When they had passed out of the busy thoroughfares into the darker streets, where watchmen call to each other through the hours of the night, the cry of a ghafir far ahead ("Wahhed!") seemed to Hafiz like the bay of a blood-hound, and the answer of another close behind was like the shrill voice of some one who was pouncing upon his shoulders.

"It would be a pity to be taken now—at the last moment, too," he whispered, and he strained his ear to catch the faintest sound of footsteps behind them.

After that no more was said until they came to the open space under the heights of the Citadel where one path goes up to the Mokattam hills and another crosses the arid land that lies on the east bank of the Nile. Then suddenly Hafiz, who had been panting and gasping, began to laugh and crow.

"I know what we've got to do," he said. "Good Lord alive, why didn't I think of it before?"

With that he stooped and whipped off the slippers he wore over his boots and called on Gordon to hold up his foot.

"What for?" asked Gordon.

"I have a reason—a good one. Hold up! The other one! Quick!"

In a moment the slippers he had taken off his own boots had been pulled over Gordon's.

"Right! And now, my dear Gordon, you and I are going to part company."

"Here?" said Gordon.

"Yes, here," said Hafiz, and then, pointing with one hand to the hill and with the other to the waste, he said: "You are going that way—I am going this."

"Why so?"

"Why? Do you ask me why? Because the trackers are after us—because they may be here at any moment—because they know there are two of us, but when they find we have separated they'll follow up the man who wears the military boots."

"Hafiz!"

"Well, I wear them, don't I?"

"Do you mean it, Hafiz—that you are going to turn the trackers onto yourself?"

"Why shouldn't I? Lord God, what can they do to me? If they catch me I'll only laugh in their dirty black faces. I'll give them a run before that, though. Bedrashen, Sakkara, Mena, Gizeh—a man wants some fun after a night like this, you know."

He was laughing as if he were beside himself with excitement.

"By that time you'll be far away from here, please God! Six hours at least—I'll see it's six, Gordon—six hours' start on good camels—across the desert, too—and not a black devil of them all to know what the dickens has become of you."

His fear was as great as ever, but it had suddenly become heroic.

"Hafiz!" said Gordon. His voice was faltering and he was holding out both hands, but Hafiz, unable to trust himself, was pretending not to hear or see.

"No time to lose, though! Time is life, brother, and you mustn't stay here a moment longer. Over the hill— first village beyond the fort—Osman will be waiting for you."

"Hafiz!"

"Can't wait for farewells, Gordon. Besides, you're not going for good, you know. Lord no, not a bit of it! You'll come back some day—Ishmael too—and then there'll be the deuce to pay by some of them."

He was running a few paces away, then stepping back again.

"Why don't you go? I'm going, anyway! It's a race for life or death to-night, my boy! Such fun! I'll beat the brutes! Didn't I tell you to leave everything to Hafiz? I said you couldn't depend on a better man."

"Hafiz!"

"Good-night, old chap! Good-night, Charlie! Charlie Gordon Lord has been a good old chum to me, but damn it all, I'm going to be quits with him!"

With that he went bounding away, laughing and crying

and swearing and sobbing at the same time, and in a moment he had disappeared in the darkness.

XV

BEING left alone, Gordon looked up at the Citadel and saw that a light was burning in the window of Helena's sitting room. That sight brought back the choking sense of shame which he had felt some days before at the thought of leaving Helena behind him.

"I cannot go without seeing her," he thought. "It is impossible—utterly impossible."

Then back to his mind, as by flashes of mental lightning, came one by one the reasons which he had forged for not seeing Helena, but they were all of no avail. In vain did he ask himself what he was to say to her, how he was to account for his past silence, and what explanation he was to give of his present flight. There was no answer to these questions, yet all the same an irresistible impulse seemed to draw him up to Helena's side. He must see her again, no matter at what risk. He must take her in his arms once more, no matter at what cost.

"I must, I must," he continued to say to himself, while the same animal instinct which had carried him away from the Citadel on the night of the crime was now carrying him back to it.

Almost before his mind had time to tell him where he was going he found himself ascending the hill that leads up to the Bab-el-Gedid. The sight of the gate of the Citadel suggested fresh considerations that might have acted as warnings, but he paid no heed to them. It was nothing to him in his present mood that he was like a man who was putting his head into a noose, walking deliberately into a trap, marching straight into the camp of the enemy whose first interest it was to destroy him. The image of Helena and the sense of her presence so near to him left little else to think about.

The gate was still open, for it was not yet twelve o'clock,
16

and in deference to the ritual of the Moslem faith, the muezzin, who lived outside the walls, was permitted to pass through that he might chant the midnight call to prayers from the minaret of the mosque inside the fortress.

"Goin' to sing 'is bloomin' song, I suppose," thought the sentry, a private of a Middlesex regiment, when Gordon, as one having authority, walked boldly through the gateway.

Being now within the Citadel, Gordon began to be besieged by thoughts of the trackers who would surely keep watch upon the General's house also, if, as Hafiz had said, there was a suspicion that Helena and he intended to go away together. But again the vision of Helena rose before him and all other considerations were swept away.

"To leave Cairo while Helena remains in it would be cowardly," he told himself, and emboldened by this thought he walked fearlessly across the square of the mosque and round the old arsenal to the gate of the General's house without caring whom he met there.

He met no one. The gate was standing wide and the door of the house itself, when he came to it, was open also and there was nobody anywhere about. With a gathering sense of shame such as he had never felt before he stood there for a moment, wondering what course he ought to take, whether to ring for a servant or to walk through as he had been wont to do before the dread events befell. Suddenly the walls of the house within resounded to a peal of raucous laughter, followed by a burst of noisy voices in coarse and clamorous talk.

Utterly bewildered, he stepped forward in the direction of Helena's boudoir and then he realised that that was the room the voices came from. After a moment of uncertainty he knocked, whereupon somebody shouted to him in Arabic to enter, and then he opened the door.

Helena's servants, being paid off, and required to leave the house in the morning, had invited certain of their friends and made a feast for them. Squatting on the floor, around a huge brass tray, which contained a lamb roasted whole and various smaller dishes, they were now regaling themselves after the manner of their kind with the last contents of the General's larder, washed down by many pious speeches and by stories less devotional.

"A little more, oh, my brother?"

"No; thanks be to God, I have eaten well."

"Then by the beard of the Prophet—on whom prayer and praise—coffee and cigarettes and the tale of the little dancing girl."

At the height of their deafening merriment the door of the room opened and a man in Bedouin dress stood upon the threshold, and then there was silence.

Gordon stood for a moment in amazement at sight of this coarse scene on a spot associated with so many delicate memories. Then he said:

"You don't happen to know if—if the boy Mosie is about?"

"Gone!" shouted several voices at once.

"Gone?"

"Yes, gone, O Sheikh," said one of the men—he was the cook—pausing to speak with a piece of meat between his finger and thumb, halfway to his mouth. "Mosie has gone to England with the lady Helena. They left here at six o'clock to catch the night train to Alexandria, so as to be in good time for to-morrow's steamer."

Gordon stood a moment longer, looking down at the grinning faces about the tray, and then, with various apologies and after many answering salaams, he closed the door behind him, whereupon he heard the buzz of renewed conversation within the room, followed by another but more subdued burst of laughter.

Alone in the corridor, he asked himself why, since Helena was gone, he had been brought back to this place. Was it for punishment, for penance? It must have been so. "All that had to be expiated," he told himself, and then he turned to go.

But walking through the outer hall he had to pass the door of the General's office, and thinking it would be a sort of penance to enter the room itself, he persuaded himself to do so.

The room seemed naked and dead now, being denuded of the little personal things that had made it live. It was dark, too, save for a ray of light that came from a lamp outside, but the first thing that met Gordon's eyes was the spot on which the General fell. He forced himself to look at that spot; for some moments he compelled himself to stand by it, though his hair rose from his crown and beads of perspiration broke from his forehead.

"All that had to be expiated," he told himself again, and again he turned to go.

But back in the hall he was on the spot where he had last parted from Helena and there a new penance awaited him. He remembered that in the hideous moment when he had tried in vain to reply to her reproaches he had been telling himself that if she loved him as he loved her she would be trying to see things with his eyes. That thought had helped him to leave her then, but it brought him no comfort now. Why had he not seen that the girl's love was fighting with her pride? Why had he not followed her into the house when in her pleading, sobbing voice she had called after him?

"Yes, everything had to be expiated," he told himself, and once more he turned to go.

But passing through the garden he caught sight of the arbour on the edge of the ramparts, and it seemed to him that the deepest penance of all would be to stand for an instant on that loved spot. Giving himself no quarter, abating nothing of the bitterness of his expiation, drinking to the dregs the cup that fate had forced to his lips, he entered the arbour and there the image of the girl he had loved, the girl he still loved, rose most vividly of all before him.

He could almost feel her bodily presence by his side— the gleam of her eyes, the odour of her hair, the heaving of her bosom. He could see the caressing smile that broke from her face, he could hear the freshness of her ringing laugh. Her proud strength and self-reliance; her energy and grace; her passionate daring and chivalry and the gay raillery that was her greatest charm—everything that was Helena appeared to be about him now.

"Love is above everything—I shall only think of that,"
she had said.

The moon was shining, the leaves were rustling, the
silvery haze of night-dew was in the near air, while the
lights of the city were blinking below and the river was
flowing silently beyond. How often on such a night had
he walked on the ramparts with Helena leaning closely on
his arm and springing lightly by his side! It almost
seemed as if he had only to turn his head and he would see
her there, with her light scarf over her head and crossed
under her chin and thrown over her shoulders.

"Could nothing separate you and me?" she had asked,
and he had answered, "Nothing in this world."

His grief was crushing. It was of that kind, unequalled
for bitterness and sweetness combined, which comes to the
strong man who has been robbed of the woman he loves by
a fate more cruel than death. Helena was not dead, and
when he thought of her on her way to England while he
was a homeless wanderer in the desert, shut out from love
and friendship, the practice of his profession, and the progress of the world, the pain of his position was almost more
than he could bear.

After a while he was brought back to himself by another
burst of raucous laughter—the laughter of the servants inside the house—and at the next moment he saw a light
running along the ground in the dark market-place below
—the light of the trackers who were going off on the wrong
scent with a company of mounted police in the direction
taken by Hafiz.

XVI

GORDON left the Citadel unchallenged and unobserved
and in less than half an hour he was climbing the yellow
road—white now in the moonlight—that goes up to the
Mokattam hills. By this time he was beginning to see the
meaning of that night's experience. Unconsciously he had
been putting Providence to the proof. Unwittingly he had

been asking the fates to say if the path he had marked out for himself had been the right one when he had decided to follow Ishmael Ameer to Khartoum, to work by his side, and to come back at last when his sin had been forgiven and his redemption won.

Providence had decided in his favour. If destiny had determined that he should not leave Cairo he might have been taken a hundred times. Because he had not been taken it was clear to him that it was intended that he should go.

He had tried to see his mother, and if he could have done so he must have stayed with her at all hazards, since she was so ill and perhaps so near to death. He had tried to see Helena, also, and if she had not gone to England already he must have clung to her at all costs and in spite of all consequences. On the other hand he had seen his father and heard from his very lips that nothing—not even the liberty or yet the life of his own son—could stand between him and his duty to the law.

What did it mean that he should be so cut off, so stripped naked, so deprived of his place as son and lover and soldier and man that all that had hitherto stood to him as himself, as Gordon Lord, was gone? It meant that another existence was before him; another work, another mission. Destiny was carrying him away from his former life and he had only to go forward without fear.

Thus once again on the heights of his great resolve he pushed on with a quick step, not daring to look back lest the sense of seeing things for the last time should be more than he could bear, lest the thought of leaving the city he loved, the people who loved him, his men and his brother officers, his mother and the memory of his happiness with Helena, his father and the consciousness of having wrecked the hopes of a lifetime, should drag him back at the last moment.

In the midst of these emotions he was startled by a loud sharp voice that was without and not within him.

"Enta min?" (Who are you?)

Then he realised that he had reached the fort on the

top of the hill, and that the Egyptian sentry at the gate was challenging him. For a moment he stood speechless, trying in vain to remember the name by which he was henceforward to be known.

"Who are you?" cried the sentry again, and then Gordon answered:

"Omar."

"Omar—what?" cried the sentry.

Again Gordon was speechless for a moment.

"Answer," cried the sentry, and he raised his rifle to his shoulder.

"Omar Benani the Bedouin," said Gordon at last, and then the sentry lowered his gun.

"Pass, Omar Benani. All's well!"

But Gordon had a still greater surprise in store for him. As he was going on he became aware that the Egyptian soldier was walking by his side and speaking in a low tone.

"Have they taken him?" he was saying.

"Taken whom?" asked Gordon.

"Our English brother—the Colonel—Colonel Lord. Have they arrested him?"

It was not at first that Gordon could command his voice to reply, but at length he said:

"Not yet—not when I came out of Cairo."

"El Hamdullillah (Praise be to God)!" said the sentry, and then in a louder voice he cried:

"Peace to you, O brother!" whereupon Gordon answered as well as he could for the thickening of his throat which seemed to stifle him.

"And to you!"

More sure than ever now that God's hand was leading him, he walked on with a quicker step than before, and presently he saw in the distance a dark group which he recognised as Osman and the camels.

"Allah be praised, you've come at last," whispered Osman.

He was a bright and intelligent young Egyptian and for the last hour he had lived in a fever of alarm, thinking Gordon must have fallen into the hands of the police.

"They got wind that you were hiding at the Coptic Patriarch's house," he said, "and were only waiting for the permission of the Agency to raid it at eleven o'clock."

"I left it at ten," said Gordon.

"Thank God for that, sir," said Osman. "The Prophet must have taken a love for you to carry you off so soon. We must start away now, though," he whispered. "It's past twelve and the village is fast asleep!"

"Is everything ready?" asked Gordon.

"Everything—water, biscuits, dates, durah, rifles——"

"Rifles?"

"Why not, sir? Two good Bedouin flintlocks. Even if we never have occasion to use them they'll help us to divert suspicion."

"Let us be off, then," said Gordon.

"Good," said Osman. "If we can only get away quietly our journey will be as white as milk."

In the shadow of a high wall the camels sat munching their food under their saddles covered with green cloth and decorated with fringes of cowries, and with their sahharahs (square boxes for provisions) hanging on either side. They were restive when they had to rise and it was as much as Osman could do to keep them from grunting, being so fresh and so full of corn. But he held their mouths closed until they were on their feet and then mounted his own camel by climbing on its neck. A moment afterward the good creatures were gliding swiftly away into the obscurity of the night, with their upturned steadfast faces, their noiseless tread and swinging motion.

Both men were accustomed to camel riding and both knew the track before them, therefore they lost no time in getting under way. The first village was soon left behind, and as they came near to other hamlets the howling of dogs warned them of their danger and they skirted round and quickened their pace.

A little beyond Helwan they came upon a Bedouin camp with its long irregular dark tents and an open fire around which a company of men sat talking, but Gordon pushed forward with his flintlock swung across his saddle-bow, while Osman, thinking to avoid suspicion, hung back for a moment to exchange news and greetings.

Then on and on they went, up and down the yellow hills, across sandy plains that were still warm with the heat of the day, and over rocky gorges that seemed to echo a hundred times to the softest footfall.

In less than three hours they were out on the open desert, lonely and grand, without a soul or yet a sound, save the faint thud of the camel's tread on the sand and the dice-like rattle of the cowries that hung from the saddles.

"*Allah khalasna!* God has delivered us," said Osman at last, as he wiped the cold sweat of fear from his forehead.

But never for a moment had Gordon felt afraid. No more now than before did he know what fate was before him, but if a pillar of fire had appeared in the dark blue sky he could not have been more sure that—sinful man as he was—God's light was leading him.

He had fallen in the dark, but he was about to rise again. God's wrath had burned against him, but he was soon to be forgiven. After the emotions and experiences of that night he knew of a certainty that the path he had chosen was the path which it was intended that he should take. Somewhere—he knew not where—and somehow—he knew not how—Heaven had uses for him still.

As he rode over the sandy waste it became fixed in his mind that being rejected by all the world now, and stripped of everything that man holds dear, it was meant by God that he should offer his life in some great cause. That thought did not terrify him at all. It delighted and inspired him, and stirred every passion of the soldier in his soul.

To be, perhaps, a link between East and West, to carry the white man's burden into the black man's country for higher ends than greed of wealth or lust of empire, he would die, if need be, a thousand deaths.

How did he come to think of this as the fate before him? Who can know? Who can say? There are moments when man feels the influence of invisible powers which it is equally impossible to explain and to control. Such a

17

moment was this to Gordon. He was flying away as a homeless fugitive, yet he was going with a full heart and a high resolve. Somewhere his great hour waited for him —somewhere and somehow—he could only follow and obey.

But meanwhile there was nothing before him except the rolling waves of the desert, nothing about him except the silence of immensity, and nothing above him but the unclouded glory of the moon.

XVII

As midnight had struck on the soft cathedral bell of the clock in Lady Nuneham's room the old lady had raised herself in bed and looked round with bright and joyful eyes.

"Fatimah?"

"Yes, my heart," said Fatimah, rising hurriedly from the chair in which she had been knitting and stepping up to the bedside.

"Has he gone, Fatimah?"

"Has who gone, oh, my lady?"

The bright eyes looked at the Egyptian woman with a reproving smile.

"Why, you know quite well, Fatimah. You saw him yourself, didn't you?"

"You mean his lordship?"

"No, no, but——"

The old lady paused, looked round again and said:

"Can it be possible that you didn't see him, Fatimah?"

"See whom, my lady?"

"Why, Gordon!"

Fatimah made an upward gesture with her hand.

"When, my heart?"

"Just now—not a moment ago."

Fatimah raised both hands and seemed for a moment unable to speak.

"He knocked at the door—I knew his knock immediately. Then he said outside, 'Don't be afraid'—I knew his voice, too. And then he opened the door and came in, and I thought at first it was a Bedouin, for he wore Eastern clothes, but he whispered, 'Mother,' and it was Gordon himself."

"Oh, my dear eyes, you have been dreaming," said Fatimah, whereupon the old lady looked reproachfully at her and said:

"How can you say that, Fatimah? I clasped my arms around his neck, and he put his arms about me and kissed me, and then——"

"Well?"

The old lady thought for a moment. "I think I must have fainted," she said. "I cannot remember what happened then."

"Oh, my lady, oh, my heart, you have been sleeping for nearly an hour," said Fatimah.

"Sleeping?"

"Yes, but a little after eleven o'clock you were resting and threw out your arms, and I covered them up again."

The joyful gleam had now gone from the old lady's eyes, and a troubled look had taken the place of it.

"Do you say that Gordon has not been here, Fatimah?"

"Alas! no, my lady."

"Has nobody been?"

"Nobody at all, my lady, since his lordship was up last."

"But I could have been sure that——"

She stopped; a smile crossed her bewildered face and she said in a soft, indulgent voice:

"My poor Fatimah! I wear you out. I wear out everybody. You must have dozed off at that moment and so——"

"Oh, no, my lady, no! *Wallahi!* I've not closed my eyes since yesterday."

"How strange!"

"But Ibrahim ought to know if anybody has come upstairs. Should I call him, my lady?"

"Yes—no—that is to say—wait!"

There was silence for a moment, and then, all the sweet illusion being gone, the old lady said in a sadder tone:

"Perhaps you are right, Fatimah. But it was so dear to think that—Hush!"

She had heard her husband's footsteps on the stairs, and she began to straighten her lace cap with her delicate white fingers.

The Consul-General had gone through a heavy and trying day. In the morning he had received from the Secretary of State for Foreign Affairs a despatch which was couched in terms more caustic than had been addressed to him from London at any time during his forty years in Egypt. He had spent the night in dictating an answer to this despatch, and his reply, though framed in diplomatic form, had been no less biting and severe.

Having finished his work in some warmth, he was now on his way to bed, and thinking of the humiliation to which he had been exposed in England by the late disturbance in Cairo he was blaming his son for the worst of it. Every step of his heavy foot as he went upstairs was like a word or a blow against Gordon. It was Gordon who had encouraged the people to rebel; it was Gordon's name that was being used (because it was his own name also) by pestilent prattlers in Parliament to support the accusation that he had outraged (contrary to the best traditions of British rule) the religious instincts of an Eastern people; therefore it was Gordon who had poisoned the source of his authority in Egypt and the fount of his influence at home.

In this mood he entered his wife's room, and there Fatimah, who had been frightened for all her brave show of unbelief, fell at once to telling him of her mistress's delusion.

"But this is wrong of you, Janet, very, very wrong," said the Consul-General with a frown. "These visions and dreams are doing more than anything else to destroy your health, and they will kill you if you continue to encourage them. Gordon is gone. You must make up your mind to it."

"Is it quite certain that he is gone, dear?" said the old

lady, who was now nervously plucking at the counterpane. "For instance, Fatimah told me to-day that there was a story in town——"

"Fatimah has no business to repeat such idle rumours," said the Consul-General sharply. He was walking to and fro in the room with a face that was hard and furrowed.

"As for the story you speak of, they sent it up to me as late as ten o'clock to-night, saying Gordon was being sheltered in a certain place and asking what steps they were to take with respect to him."

The old lady fixed her frightened eyes on her husband's face and began to ask in a whisper:

"And what did you——"

"The rumour was groundless," said the Consul-General. "I've just heard so from the Commandant of Police. Gordon was not there. There was no sign that he ever had been."

The old lady wept silently, and the Consul-General continued to walk to and fro at the foot of her bed as if he were trying to avoid her face.

"You still think he left Cairo on the night of the riot, dear?"

"I trust he did. I trust, too, that he is far from here by this time—on his way to America, India, Australia, anywhere. And as he has broken the law and his career is at an end, I think the kindest thing we can do is to hope that he may never come back again."

The old lady tried to speak, but her voice failed her.

"More than that," continued the Consul-General, "as he deliberately took sides against us, I also think it is our duty—our strict and bounden duty—to dismiss all further thought of him."

Saying this with heat and emphasis, he caught sight of his wife's wet eyes and his conscience began to accuse him.

"I don't say it is easy to do," he said, taking a chair by the side of the bed. "Perhaps it is the reverse of easy —especially for you—for his mother."

At that the sweet old woman wished to take the part of her absent son—to say that if he had taken the wrong course and allowed himself to be led away by some one, he could not have counted on any gain in doing so and must have been moved by the most unselfish motives—but her tears prevented her and still she could not speak.

"Why should we continue to think of *him* if he never thinks of *us*—of either of us?" asked the Consul-General.

He was calmer now and was speaking with less anger.

"Was he thinking of you when he took the step which broke up your health like this? Was he thinking of me when he took the side of my enemies—of one of my enemies at all events—perhaps the worst of them—and left me to the mercy of—in my old age, too—a childless man?"

There was a moment in which nothing was spoken, and then in a voice that quivered perceptibly the Consul-General said:

"Let us trifle with ourselves no longer, Janet. Our son has gone. He has abandoned us. We have to think no more about him."

After that there was a long silence, during which the Consul-General sat with his head down and his eyes tightly closed. Then a voice came softly from the bed:

"John!"

"Well?"

"It is harder for you, dear."

The old man turned his head aside.

"You wanted a son so much, you know."

Fatimah, who had been sitting out of sight, now stepped into the boys' room and closed the door noiselessly behind her, leaving the two old people alone together, with the sanctities of their married life on which no other eye should look.

"I thought at first that God was not going to give me any children, but when my child came, and it was a boy, how happy we both were!"

The old man closed his eyes still more tightly and stiffened his iron lip.

"Foolish people used to think in those days that you didn't love our little one because you couldn't pay much heed to him. But Fatimah was telling me only to-night that you never went to bed without going into her room to see if it was well with our child."

The tears were now forcing themselves through the old man's eyelids.

"And when our dear boy had the fever, and he was so ill that we had to shave his little head, you never went to bed at all—not until the crisis came, and then—don't you remember?—just when we thought the wings of death were over us, he opened his beautiful blue eyes and smiled. I think that was the happiest moment of all our lives, dear."

She was on her husband's side at last—thinking for him—seeing everything from his point of view.

"Then all the years afterward you worked so hard, and won such high honours and such a great name, only to leave them behind to our son, and now—now——"

The Consul-General laid one of his wrinkled hands on the counterpane, and in a moment the old lady had put her delicate white hand on top of it.

"Yes, it's harder for you, dear."

"No, Janet, no!—But it's hard for both of us."

There was another moment of silence, and then, pressing the hand that lay under her hand, the old lady said:

"I think I know now what people feel when they are old and their children die before them. They feel that they ought to be more to each other than they have ever been before, and keep together as long as they can."

The Consul-General drew his hand away and covered his face with it. He was asking himself why, through so many years, he had buried his love for his wife so deep in his heart and sealed it as with a seal. Presently a more cheerful voice came from the bed:

"John!"

"Yes?"

"I'm going to get up to-morrow."

"No, no!"

"But I must! Mohammed" (the cook) "is so forgetful when there's no mistress about—I must see that he gives you good food, you know. Besides, it must be lonely to eat your meals by yourself—I must make it a rule to go down to lunch at all events."

"That is nothing, Janet. You are weak and ill—the doctor will not permit you to disturb yourself."

At that there was a sigh, and then in a faltering voice the old lady said:

"You must forgive me, dear—I've not been what I ought to have been to you."

"No, Janet, no, it is I——"

He could not utter another word, but he rose to his feet, and, clasping his wife in his arms, he kissed her on her wrinkled forehead and her whitened hair more fervently than he had ever done in their youth.

At the next moment the old lady was speaking about Helena. The Consul-General would see her off in the morning and he was to give all her motherly love to her. He was also to warn her to take good care of herself on the voyage and not to be anxious or to repine.

"Tell her to remember what I said, dear. She is going back to England, but that doesn't matter in the least. God keeps all His promises, and he will keep His promise in this case, too—I'm sure he will. Tell her that, dear."

The Consul-General answered "Yes" and "Yes" to all her messages, but he did not hear them. Bent almost double, with the light of his wearied eyes almost extinct, he stumbled out of the room. He was no longer angry with Gordon, but he was choking with hatred and scorn and, above all, with jealousy of the man who had robbed him of his son, the man who had robbed his wife of her only pride and joy and left them hopeless and old and lone.

At the door of his bedroom one of his secretaries was waiting for him with a paper in his hand.

"Well, well, what is it now?" he asked.

"An important telegram from the Soudan, sir," said the Secretary. "Ishmael Ameer has turned up in Khartoum."

Then the austere calm of the stern old man deserted him for a moment, and the pent-up agony of the broken and bankrupt hopes of a lifetime broke into a shout:

"Damn him! Damn him! Tell the Sirdar to kill him like a dog," he cried, and his Secretary fled in a fright.

XVIII

HOURS passed before the Consul-General slept. He was telling himself that there were now two reasons why he should suppress and destroy the man Ishmael Ameer.

First because "this madman, this fanatic, this false prophet," under the cloak of religion and the mantle of prophecy, was a cover for the corruption and the self-seeking which in the name and the guise of Nationalism were trying to drive England out of the valley of the Nile; because he was the rallying point of the retrograde forces which were doing their best to destroy whatever seeds of civilisation had been implanted in the country during forty sleepless years; because he was trying to turn prosperity back to bankruptcy, order back to anarchy, and the helpless millions of the unmoving and the uncomplaining peasantry back to slavery and barbarity; because, in a word, he was the head centre of the schools and nurseries of sedition which were undoing the hard labour of his lifetime and striving to wipe his name out of Egypt as utterly as if he had never been.

This was the first of the Consul-General's two reasons why he should suppress and destroy Ishmael Ameer, and the second was still more personal and more intimate.

His second reason was because "this madman, this fanatic, this false prophet" had stepped in between him and the one hope of his life—the hope of founding a family. That hope had been a secret which he believed he had never betrayed to any one, not even to his wife, but all the more on that account it had been sweet and sacred. Born in a moment of fierce anger and in a spirit of revenge, it had grown to be his master passion. It had cheered his darkest hours, brightened his heaviest labour, exalted his drudgery into duty, given joy to his success and wings to his patriotism itself.

That, at the end of his life of hard work, and as the reward and the crown of it, he should see the name he had made for himself among the great names of the British nation, and that his son should succeed to it, and his son's son, and his son's son's son, being all peers of the realm and all Nunehams—this had been the cherished aspiration of his soul.

But now his high-built hope was in the dust. By robbing him of his son—his only son—"this madman, this fanatic, this false prophet" had turned his one aim to ashes. When he was old, too, and his best powers were spent, and his life was behind him, and there was nothing before him but a few short years of failing strength and then—the end.

"Damn him! Damn him!" he cried again in the darkness as he rolled about in his bed.

But when he tried to think out some means, some swift and silent tribunal, perhaps, by which he could destroy and suppress the man Ishmael, who had laid waste his own life and was joining with the worst elements in Egypt to make the government of the country impossible, he had to tell himself how powerless after all was the machinery of Western civilisation against the hypocritical machinations of Eastern fanaticism.

On the one side the clogs and impediments of representative government, and on the other the subtlety, secrecy, duplicity and deceit of men like Ishmael Ameer. If he could only scotch these troubles once for all by a short and sharp military struggle—how different the results would be!

But with every act of his life watched from Whitehall and with operations of frightful urgency kept back by cable; dogged by foreign diplomats who, professing to be England's friends, were yet waiting to find their opportunity in the hour of England's need; vilified by boobies in Parliament who did not know the difference between the East and the West, between the Muski and the Mile End Road, and were constantly sending the echo of their parrot-like prattle down the Mediterranean to add to the difficulties of his position in Cairo; scolded by Secretaries of State who were appointed to their places for no better reason than their power to command votes; jibed at by journalists at home who could not see that a free press and a foreign occupation were things that could never exist together, and preached at by religious milksops in the pulpit who were so simple as to suppose that the black man and the white man were one flesh, that all men were born free and equal and that it was possible to govern great nations according to the precepts of the Sermon on the Mount—what could he do against the religious delirium of an ignorant Eastern populace who were capable of mistaking a manifest impostor, practising his spiritual legerdemain, for a Prophet, a Redeemer, a Mahdi, a Messiah, a Christ? Nothing!

He had found that out to his bitter disappointment during the past few days when working with Western machinery he had tried in vain to catch the man Ishmael in some seditious expression that would enable the Government to lay him openly by the heels.

"Fools! Fools! Fools!"

Why could not people see that all this vapouring unrest in Eastern dominions was a religious question from first to last, that it was Islamism against Christianity, slavery against liberty, corruption against purity, the backwash of retrogression against the flowing tide of progress, and that to fight the secret methods of the mosque and the insidious crimes of a vicious superstition with any weapons less swift and sure than the rifle and the rope was to be weak and wicked?

"If I could only permit myself to meet Eastern needs by Eastern means," he thought, "subtlety by subtlety, secrecy by secrecy, duplicity by duplicity, treachery by treachery, deceit by deceit!"

"And why not?" he asked himself suddenly. "In a desperate case like this, why not? In the face of anarchical conspiracy and menace to public safety, why not? Before the catastrophe comes, why not?" he asked himself again and again during the long hours in which he lay awake.

"It is a case of civilisation on the one side and a return to barbarism on the other. Why not? Why not?"

And that, with the cruel memory of his wasted hopes, was the last thought present to his mind before he slept.

It was late when he awoke in the morning, and then, remembering that he had promised to call on Helena before her departure, he rang the bell that he might order his carriage to take him up to the Citadel. Ibrahim answered it, and brought him a number of letters. The first of them to come to hand was a letter from Helena herself. It was written with many signs of haste, and some of emotion, and it ran:

"DEAR LORD NUNEHAM: Do not come up to see me off tomorrow morning, and please forgive me for all the unnecessary trouble I have given you. I cannot go back to England —I really cannot—it is impossible. There is nothing for me there but a useless and lonely life— Oh, how lonely and how full of bitter and cruel memories!

"On the other hand, there seems to be something I can do in Egypt, and though it is not the kind of work a woman could choose for herself, I cannot and I will not shrink from it.

"To tell you the truth at once I am on the point of taking the night train *en route* for Khartoum, but that is a secret which I am revealing to nobody else, so I beseech you to say nothing about it. I also beseech you not to follow me or to send after me or to inquire about me in any way, and lest the Sirdar and his officers should recognise me on my arrival in the Soudan (though I shall try to make it difficult for them to do so), I beg of you to ask them to forget that they have ever seen me before and to leave me entirely alone."

The Consul-General dropped the hand that held the letter and thought, "What on earth does the girl intend to do, I wonder?"

"You may ask me why I am going to Khartoum, and I find it hard to answer you, but you will remember that another person is reported to have gone there already, and perhaps you will put the two facts together. That person is neither your friend nor mine. He has wrecked my life and darkened your happiness. He has also been an evil influence in the country, and, thus far, you have tried in vain to punish him. Let me help you to do so. I can—I am sure I can —and before I have finished with the man who has injured both of us I shall have done some service to England and to Egypt as well.

"Don't think I am mad or that I am idly boasting, and please don't despise my help because I am only a woman. In the history of the world women have saved nations even when kings and armies have failed. And if that has happened in the past may it not happen in the future also? It can, and it shall."

Again the Consul-General dropped the hand that held the letter and he looked fixedly before him for a moment.

"Dear Lord Nuneham, I know what you are thinking. You are thinking that if I am not mad, and if I am not boasting, I am cruel and revengeful and vindictive. I am sorry if you are thinking that, sir, but if so I cannot help it. I have lost my father and I have lost Gordon, and I am alone and my heart is torn. Oh, if you knew how much this means to me you would not judge me too harshly. When I think of my father in his grave and of Gordon in disgrace —at the ends of the earth perhaps—never to be seen or heard of any more—I feel that anything is justified—anything— that will punish the man who has brought things to this pass."

The Consul-General removed his spectacles, wiped away the moisture that had gathered on them, put them back and resumed the reading of the letter.

"Sometimes I tell myself I might have saved Gordon if I had been less proud and hard—if I had told him more and allowed him to feel that I could see things from his side also. But it is too late to think of that. I can think of nothing now but how to degrade and destroy the man who deceived and misled him, and is deceiving and misleading these poor Egyptian people also, and will end, as such men always end, in sowing the sand of their deserts with blood.

"But don't be afraid that I shall permit myself to do anything unwomanly, or that I shall ever be false for a moment to the love—the wronged and outraged love—which prompts me. Gordon is gone, I have lost him, but I can never do that—never!

"I know exactly how far I intend to go and I shall go no farther. I also know exactly what I intend to do, and I shall do it without fear or remorse.

"Good-bye, or rather *au revoir!* You will hear from me, or perhaps see me again before long, I think, and then—then your enemy and mine and Gordon's, as well as England's and Egypt's, will be in your hands.

"HELENA GRAVES.

"P.S.—Please don't speak about this to Lady Nuneham. Give her my fondest, truest love and let her believe that I have gone home to England. It would only make her unhappy to be told what I intend to do, and she might even think me a wicked woman. *You* will not do that, I hope —will you?"

The letter dropped on to the counterpane out of the Consul-General's hand and again he looked fixedly before him. After a moment his wearied old eyes began to gleam with light and fire.

"What did I say when I saw her first?" he thought. "This girl has the blood of the great women of the Bible— the Deborahs who were mothers in Israel, aye, and the Jaels who revenged her."

THIRD BOOK

THE LIGHT OF THE WORLD

I

A MIXED Eastern and Western city lying in the midst of a wide waste of grim desert, with a fierce sun blazing down on it by day and a rain of stars over it by night; a strip of verdure with slender palms and red and yellow blossoms, stretching for some three miles along the banks of the Nile, where the great river is cleft in twain as by the sweep of a giant's hand, and one arm goes up through the brown and yellow wilderness to the Abyssinian hills and the other to the lakes of the Equator—such is Khartoum.

The city had changed since Ishmael Ameer spent his youth there. Lifeless and vacant then, it had risen out of the dust of its own decay. On the river's front a line of western buildings, a college, a barrack and a palace over which the white Crescent and the Union Jack crackled in the breeze together; at the back of these a great open market, with rows of booths and shanties, a native quarter with lines of mud-brick houses, and a handsome mosque; and behind all this an encampment of the tribes in tents, fronting a horizon of sand, empty and silent as the sea.

When Ishmael returned to the city of his boyhood British officials of the Anglo-Egyptian Government, wearing the Crescent on their pith helmets, were walking in the wide streets with Soudanese blacksmiths, Arab carpenters, and women of many races, some veiled in white, others in black, and yet others nearly naked of body as well as face. Two battalions of British soldiers, a British Sirdar, a British Inspector-General, and British Governors of provinces were there as signs and symbols of the change that had been wrought since Khartoum was shrivelled up in a blast of fire.

Ishmael's fame had gone before him, from Alexandria and from Cairo, and both the British and the native population

of Khartoum looked for his coming with a keen curiosity.
The British saw a man taller and more powerful than the
common, with the fiery, flashing black eyes that they associated with their fears of the fanatic; but the natives, to their
disappointment, recognised a face they knew, and they said
among themselves: " Isn't this Ishmael Ameer, the nephew
of old Mahmud and the son of the boat-builder ? " And that
was a discovery which for a while dispelled some of the
marvel as well as the mystery which had hitherto surrounded
the new prophet's identity.

Ishmael made his home in his uncle's house on the fringe
of the native quarter, a large Arab dwelling with one face
to the desert and another to the white river and the forts
of Omdurman. Besides the old uncle himself, now more
than fourscore, a God-fearing man devoted to his nephew,
the household consisted of Ishmael's little daughter, Ayesha,
a sweet child of ten, who sang quaint little Soudanese songs
all day long, and had the animal grace of the gazelle; an
Arab woman, Ayesha's nurse, Zenoba, a voluptuous person,
with cheeks marked by three tribal slits, wearing massive
gold ear-rings and hair twisted into innumerable thin ring-
lets; and Abdullah, a Soudanese servant, formerly a slave.

Before Ishmael had been long in Khartoum most of the
British officials had made up their minds about his personal character. He was one of those complex beings whom
they recognised as essentially Eastern—that mixture of
hypocrisy and spirituality, of sincerity and quackery, which
they believed to be most dangerous of all in its effects upon
a fanatical populace. The natives, on the other hand, began
to see that, though a spontaneous and passionate man, outspoken and vehement in his dealings with the strong and
the rich, he was very tender to the old and to the erring,
that he was beloved of children, and trusted by the outcast
and the poor.

Before many days had passed the Moslems of Khartoum
asked him to lecture to them, and in the evenings he would
sit on an angerib which Abdullah brought out of the house,
with a palm net spread over it, and speak to the people who
squatted on the ground about him. Clad in his white caftan

and Mecca skull-cap, with its white muslin turban bound round it, the British Inspectors would see him there on the edge of the desert surrounded by a multitude of Arabs, olive and walnut, and of Soudanese, brown and black, holding his hearers by the breathless intensity with which he uttered himself.

Yet he did not flatter them. On the contrary, no man had ever so condemned the evils which they had come to regard as part and parcel of their faith. All the Arab soul and blood of the man seemed to be afire and his wonderful voice, throbbing over their heads, far away to the silent desert beyond, carried such denunciations of the corruptions of Islam as the people had never heard before.

"Beware of slavery," he said. "What says the Koran? 'Righteousness is to him who freeth the slave.' Beware of sorcery, of spells, of magic, of divinations—they are of the devil."

Teaching like this might drive away the dominant races, but it brought the subject ones, and among others that attached themselves to Ishmael was a half-witted Nubian (an Ethiopian of the Bible), known as Black Zogal, who from that time forward followed him about by day and lay like a dog at the door of his house by night, crying the confession of faith at the end of every hour.

After condemning slavery and sorcery Ishmael came to closer quarters—he denounced polygamy and divorce.

"Beware of polygamy," he said. "It pulls down the pillars of the house. No man would permit another man to join with him in love for his wife. Why, therefore, ask a woman to allow another woman to join with her in love for her husband?

"Beware of divorce, for it brings sorrow and shame. What says the Prophet, to whom be prayer and peace? 'Of all lawful things hated of God, divorce is the most hateful.'

"Brothers," he cried, "I see a house that is full of light. There is a new wife there. She is very happy. But in the upper rooms I hear children weeping. They are weeping for their mother who has been put away. She has done no wrong, she has committed no crime, but while the guests feast and the new wife counts her jewels, the mother's heart is bleeding for the children she may see no more."

"O men," he cried again in his throbbing voice, "night is for sleep, and your children slumber, but in their dreams their mother comes to them. She embraces them and they dry their tears. But they awake in the morning and she is gone. Where is your father's heart, O ye men of righteousness? Has all justice died out of you? Shame on you! May heaven punish you as you deserve! Divorce shakes the throne of Islam! Wipe it out that your faces may be whitened before the world!"

After condemning polygamy and divorce Ishmael came to closer quarters still—he denounced the seclusion and the degradation of women.

"Remove the veil from your women," he said. "At the beginning it was the badge of shame. What says the Koran? 'O Prophet! speak to thy wives and thy daughters that they let their wrappers fall so that they may not be affronted.'

"Dismiss the madness of a bygone age that woman is inferior to man. We are all children of one Mother. What says the Prophet? 'Paradise lies under the feet of mothers.' The proverb of our people says, 'The threshold weeps for forty days when a girl is born,' but I tell you the stars sing for joy and the dry wells of the desert spring afresh. Man's dominion over woman is the product of darkness—put it away. Oh, my brothers, woman's suffering in the world is so great that if she does not cry aloud the mountains themselves will groan."

If Ishmael's teaching offended certain of the men, it attracted great multitudes of the women, many of whom laid aside their veils to come to him, and among others that came were a number of black girls from Omdurman who were known to have been the paramours of British and Egyptian soldiers at Khartoum. His bearing toward these girls had that shy tenderness which is peculiar to the pure-minded man in his dealings with erring women, and when some of his followers grumbled at his intercourse with such notorious sinners he told them a story of the Lord Isa (Jesus).

It was the story of His visit to the rich man's house and of the sinful woman who did not cease to wash His feet with her tears and to dry them with the hair of her head.

"Shall I be less charitable than the Lord of the Christians?" he asked, and the choking pathos of his story silenced everybody.

In his preaching he turned for ever to the prophets—the prophet Abraham, the prophet Moses, the prophet Mohammed, and above all, the prophet Isa. He called Jesus the divine teacher of Judæa, one of the great brother souls.

"Only a poor Jewish man," he said, with a memory of his own that none might share, "only a poor carpenter, but perhaps the greatest and noblest spirit save one that ever lived in the world."

Thus evening after evening when the blazing sun had gone down, Ishmael sat on the angerib in front of his uncle's house and taught the ever-increasing crowds that squatted before him on the brown and yellow sand. The heat and flame of his teaching burned itself into the wild Arab souls of the great body of his hearers, but there were some among his own people who asked:

"Isn't this the Ishmael Ameer who denounced the Christians as the corrupters of our faith?"

And there were others who answered:

"Yes, the same Ishmael Ameer that married the Coptic woman who lies buried on the edge of the desert."

And meantime the British Inspectors, suspecting some hidden quackery and fatuity, some fanatical intrigue masquerading as religious liberalism, were whispering among themselves:

"This is a new kind of religious game—what the deuce does it mean, I wonder?"

II

WITHIN a month an immense concourse of people had gathered about Ishmael at Khartoum. They came first from Omdurman and the little shipbuilding village of Khogali,

on the other side of the Blue Nile, which sent daily through
the desert air a ceaseless noise of the hammering of rivets;
then they came from Kordofan and still farther south, and
from Berber and yet farther north.

A few who had means lodged in the houses of the native
quarter, but the larger number encamped in tents on the
desert side of old Mahmud's house. Men, women, and children, they flocked in thousands to see the holy man of Khartoum and to drink of the river of his words. They began to
see in him a man sent from God, to call him "Master," and
to speak of him as the "White Prophet."

At that the Governor of the city, a British Colonel, began to be alarmed, and with certain of his Inspectors he
went over to see Ishmael.

"What can these people want here?" he asked. "What
bread is there for them in this wilderness?"

"The bread of life," Ishmael answered, and the Christian
Governor went away silenced, though unsatisfied.

During Ishmael's first weeks in Khartoum his house was
open, and anybody might come and go in it; but somewhat
later it was observed that he was daily receiving messengers,
agents, emissaries, and missionaries of some sort in secret.
They came and went by camel, by boat and by train, and
rumour had it that they communicated with every quarter
of Egypt and the Soudan. Ishmael appeared to spend the
morning of every day in his house receiving and despatching these people. What did it mean? The British Inspectors suspected the existence of a vast network of fanatical
conspiracy, but only the members of Ishmael's own household knew what was going on.

Meantime at noon every day Ishmael, exercising his
right as an alim, lectured in the mosque. What he said in
that sealed chamber no Christian might know, and never an
echo of his message there was permitted to escape from its
hushed and guarded vaults. But still after sunset he sat on
the angerib in front of his uncle's house and taught the excited crowds that were eager to catch a word of his inspired
doctrine.

His lectures took a new subject. They denounced the

spirit of the age. It was irreligious, for it put a premium on selfishness. It was idolatrous, for it provoked to the worship of wealth.

"Oh, my brothers," cried Ishmael, "when Mohammed, —to him be prayer and peace!—arose in Mecca, men worshipped the black wooden idols of the Koreish. To his earnest soul this was a darkness, a mockery, an abomination. There was only one god, and that was God. God was great, and there was nothing else great. Therefore he went out from Mecca that he might gather strength to assail the black wooden idols of the Koreish, and when he returned he broke them in pieces.

"That was thirteen centuries ago, oh, my brothers, and behold! darkness covers the earth again. Men are now worshipping the yellow idols of a corrupt civilisation. Moslems and Christians alike are bending the knee to the golden calf. It is idolatry as rank as the Prophet destroyed, and tenfold more damnable because it is done in the name of God."

With that he called on his people to renounce the things of this world. Its prizes were not the prizes that could enrich them. Time and its shows rested on Eternity. The things of the other world were the only true realities. Why struggle for the semblance and form of things and neglect the substance and essence? This poor earth of ours was the threshold of heaven—let them forget the affairs of this life and fix their minds on the life to come.

The people listened to Ishmael with bated breath. Ignorant, unlettered, wild creatures as they were, sons and daughters of the desert, they knew what application of his words they were intended to make.

But the authorities were perplexed. Just as sure as before of the presence of a far-reaching fanatical conspiracy, and that Ishmael's teaching meant opposition to the Government, some of them said:

"This is the doctrine of the Mahdi, and it will end as it ended before, in destruction and desolation—let us put it down before the storm breaks."

But others said:

"It is the Gospel of Christ—what the dickens are we to do with it?"

Meantime Ishmael's own people had begun to see him not as a poet, a dreamer, but as a prophet with a mighty mission. In moments of rapture he told them of a new order that was coming, a great day when all the religions of the world would be united, when all faiths would be one faith, all races one race, all nations one nation, when East and West would be one world, and there would be only one God in it, one King and one Law.

They saw him with tears in his eyes looking over the desert as he foretold the conquest of the world for God, and listening eagerly to his predictions of a better and happier day, they began to see something Godlike in himself, to regard him as a God-inspired man, a man sent down from the skies with a message.

"Our souls lie beneath his sheepskin," they would say, and then they would tell each other stories of supernatural appearances that surrounded the new prophet—how while he preached, celestial lights floated about his head, and when he rode on his milk-white camel into the desert of an afternoon, as it was his habit to do, flights of angels were seen to descend and attend him.

The creation of this kind of myth led to trouble, for among Ishmael's secret enemies were certain of the Ulema of Khartoum, who, jealous of his great influence with the people and suspecting him of an attempt to change the immutable law of Islam, conceived the trick of getting him to avow himself as a re-incarnation of the Mahdi in order that they might betray him to the Government. So three of the meanest of them came one morning to old Mahmud's house, and sitting in the guest-room, under its thatch of cornstalks, began to flatter Ishmael and say:

"From the moment I beheld you I knew that you were the messenger of God—the Expected One."

"Yes, indeed, Mohammed Ahmed is dead, but Ishmael Ameer is alive!"

Ishmael listened to them for a moment in silence, and

then with a flash of fire out of his big black eyes he clapped his hands and cried:

"Zogal! Abdullah! Turn these men out of the house," and in another moment his two black giants had swept out the spies like rats.

But the crowds continued to come to Khartoum from north, south, east, and west, and at length, in fear that many might die of want, the Governor of the city went up to Ishmael again and said:

"Send these people back to their homes, or they'll die of starvation."

Whereupon Ishmael looked at him and answered:

"Colonel, you are a Christian, and when your divine Master was on earth a great multitude came to him in a desert place, and his disciples said, 'Send these people away that they may return to their villages and buy themselves food.' And then your Master answered them, 'They need not depart; *give ye them to eat.*'"

Thus Ishmael was irresistible. There was nothing and nobody that seemed to have the power to touch him.

III

"To every sun its moon; to every man a woman."

Wise and powerful as Ishmael was, people began to whisper that there was a woman who ruled him. He submitted everything to her judgment, and was guided and even governed by her counsel.

Who was this woman? A Soudanese? No! An Egyptian? No! Rumour had it that she was a stranger, totally unknown to Ishmael down to the moment of his coming back to the Soudan—a Muslemah (Mohammedan lady) from India, the sister of a reigning prince of the Punjab, who, having been educated under British rule, and therefore Western influences, had revolted against the captivity of the zenana, and broken away from her own people.

Attracted by the face of the new prophet as an eman-

18

cipator of women and a reformer of bad Mohammedan customs, this woman had, according to report, followed him
from Alexandria and Cairo to Khartoum, where she had
settled herself with a black boy as her servant at the house
of the Greek widow—the same that had formerly been the
mistress of Ishmael's first wife, Adila.

The black boy called his mistress "The Lady," and most
of the people about her knew her by the same name, but
some called her the Sit, the Khatoun (the White Lady), and
others the Emireh, and the Rani (the Queen, the Princess),
in recognition of what they believed to be her rank and
wealth.

It was in the early days of Ishmael's return to Khartoum, when women of all classes were coming to him un-
veiled, that he met with the "Princess" first. Sitting alone
in the late afternoon on the bank of a broad stretch of land
which was flooded by the high Nile, and looking across its
glistening waters to where the sky was red behind the shattered dome of the Mahdi's tomb in Omdurman, he saw a
young and beautiful woman approaching him.

She seemed to him to be a splendid creature under those
southern skies—tall, well-developed, with shining coal-black
hair, long black lashes and brilliant eyes, and a mouth that
was full of fire and movement. Her dress was such as is
worn by Parsee ladies both in the East and in the West,
having nothing more noticeably Oriental than a silken scarf
which was bound about her head as a turban, and a light,
silver-edged muslin veil that fell back on her shoulders.

She came up to him with a certain air of timidity, as
of one who might be afraid to be thought immodest, or, perhaps, of being recognised, yet with the proud bearing of a
woman who had passed through life with a high step and
would not shrink from any consequences.

He rose to receive her, and she looked at him for a
moment without speaking—almost as if she had for an instant lost the power of speech, being at last face to face with
a man whom she had long thought of and long sought.

On his side, too, there was a momentary silence and a
look of enthusiastic admiration which he tried in vain to

control. The lady seemed to see this in an instant, and an expression of joy which she could not restrain shone in her face.

Then, gathering confidence, she began to tell him the object of her visit to Khartoum—how, hearing so much about him, she had wished to see him for herself, and now begged to be allowed to serve him in any way whatever that lay within her power.

He listened to her with the same expression of enthusiastic admiration in his face, and it would have been obvious to an observer that the lady was congratulating herself upon the power of the impression she had made. But at the next moment he set her a very humble task, namely, that of seeing to the welfare of the women who were employed at sixpence a day by the Government to draw and carry water for the public streets.

The lady looked surprised and a little chagrined, but finding it impossible to recede from the unconditional offer she had made she went away to the work that had been given to her.

It was ugly and thankless work enough, for the water-women of Khartoum were among the coarsest and most degraded of their sex, being chiefly of the black tribes from south of Kordofan, going about bare from the waist upward and herding like animals in the brown huts that were beyond the barracks outside the town.

After a little while the " Princess " came to Ishmael again, and this time he was sitting with old Mahmud, his uncle, in the guest-room which divided the women's side from the men's side in their house.

She was dressed still more attractively than before, in a gold-embroidered bodice and a clinging diaphanous gown, and was attended by her black boy. Ishmael salaamed and the old man struggled to his feet as, with a certain air of embarrassment, she stepped forward and begged to be pardoned if what she came to ask should displease the Master.

Ishmael looked at her with the same expression of enthusiastic ecstasy which she had observed before, and said:

"No, no, my sister cannot displease me. What is the request she wishes to make?"

Then she told him that the work he had given her was good and necessary, but was there nothing she could do for himself? She had been educated in India by English governesses and could read English, French, and German—could she act as his translator or interpreter? Having lived so long among Arabs of the higher classes, she had also taught herself to write as well as speak Arabic—could she not serve him as his secretary?

Ishmael remembered his busy mornings with the messengers, agents, emissaries, and missionaries who came to him from all corners of Egypt and the Soudan, bringing many letters and foreign newspapers; and before he had time to reflect on what he was doing he had answered:

"Yes, such help is exactly what I need."

If any eyes less dim than old Mahmud's had been there at that moment they would have seen a look of triumph in the lady's face which she vainly struggled to conceal. But at the next moment it was full of humility and gratitude as she bowed herself out and promised to come again the following day.

Hardly had the lady gone when Ishmael's simple nature began to recover itself from the spell of her sex and beauty, but the old uncle's admiration was quite ungovernable, and he began to hint at the possibility of yet more intimate relations between his nephew and the devoted young Muslemah.

"I have always told you that you ought to marry again—a good woman and a believer," he said, whereupon Ishmael, with the ecstasy created by the "Princess's" loveliness still shining in his eyes, answered:

"No! I have always said, 'No, no, by Allah! One wife I had, and, though she was a Christian and had been a slave, I loved her, and never, never shall another woman take her place!'"

"Ah, well, God knows best what to do with us," said the old man. "But life is a passing shadow and youth a departing guest."

Next morning the white lady came according to appointment and Ishmael set her to read some European newspapers containing accounts of recent doings in Cairo.

She was translating these newspapers aloud when Ishmael's little daughter Ayesha came bounding into the house, followed by her nurse, the Arab woman, Zenoba—the child barefoot as her mother used to be, and with her mother's beautiful erect confidence as she moved about, lightly clad, with her middle small-girt by a scarlet sash over her pure white shirt—the woman in her blue habareh and with a silver ring in her nose.

Ishmael presented both of them to the lady, whereupon the child by an instinctive impulse ran over to her and kissed her hand and held it, but the Arab woman only bowed with a look of mistrust, and, as long as she remained in the guest-room, continued to watch her furtively out of the sidelong slits of her eyes.

The Arab woman's obvious mistrust made more impression upon Ishmael than his daughter's spontaneous liking, for as soon as he was alone with the lady again, he began to talk to her of the gravity of the task he had undertaken and of the need for caution and even secrecy with respect to all his doings.

The lady's brilliant eyes glistened under their long black lashes as she listened to him, and she answered his warnings with assuring words, until, coming to closer quarters, he proposed that for his people's sake rather than his own she should take an oath of fidelity to him and to his cause.

At that she looked startled, and could with difficulty conceal her agitation. And when he went on to recite the terms of the oath to her—solemn terms, taking God and his prophet to witness that she would never reveal anything which came to her knowledge within the walls of that house —she seemed to be stifling with a sense of fear and shame.

Not as such, however, did Ishmael's unsuspecting nature recognise the lady's embarrassment, but setting it down to the heat of the day, for the khamseen, the hot wind, was blowing, he clapped his hands for water.

The Arab woman brought it in, although it was Abdullah's task to do so, and she lingered long in the room and looked searchingly at the lady while Ishmael again recited his oath.

The lady did not at first respond, but continued to look out at the open door on to the slow waters of the White Nile, and there was silence in the air both within and without, save for the far-off hammering from the dockyards across the river.

At length she asked in a tremulous voice:

"Master, is this necessary?"

Ishmael reflected for a moment, and then said:

"No, it is not necessary, and we shall do without it. What says the Lord of the Christians? 'Swear not at all, neither by heaven, for it is God's throne; nor by the earth, for it is his footstool.'"

With that the lady drew a long breath of relief and went on with her foreign newspapers.

IV

HARDLY had the "Princess" gone for the day when the Arab woman, Zenoba, with all her dusky face contracted into lines of jealousy, came to Ishmael to warn him.

"Forgive me, O Master!" she said, "if the thing I say displeases you."

"What is it, O Zenoba?" asked Ishmael.

"Is it well to trust the secrets of God and of His people to two tongues and four eyes?"

Ishmael's face darkened visibly, but he held himself in check, and answered with dignity:

"Zenoba, ask pardon of God for a suspicious mind. The least of all noble traits is to keep a secret, the greatest is to forget that you have confided it."

The Arab woman was stung by the rebuke, but assuming the meekest expression of face she changed her course entirely.

"Master, I beg of you to listen to me until I have done,"

she said, and then she began to talk of the visits of the white lady.

The lady was young and beautiful. Evil minds were many. If she was to come to Ishmael's house every day and to be closeted alone with him, what would people say?

"Forgive me, O Master! it is nothing to me, and I have no right to speak," said the Arab woman, with the agony of a jealous spirit imprinted on every feature of her face. "I only wish to put you on your guard against the slanderous tongues that would love to injure you."

Ishmael listened to her with the look of a man who had never once reflected on the interpretation that might be put upon his conduct, and then he said:

"You are right, O Zenoba! and I thank you for reminding me of something I had permitted myself to forget."

When the white lady came next day Ishmael began to speak to her about her position in his house.

"My sister," he said, "I have been thinking this is not good. The thoughts of the world are evil, and if you continue to come here according to the agreement we made together your pure name will be tarnished."

The lady's brows contracted slightly, for it flashed upon her that Ishmael was about to send her away. But that was not his intention, and in the winding way of Eastern explanations he proceeded to propound his plan.

"When the Prophet—to him be prayer and peace!—lost his first wife, Khadija, the mother of Islam, and took a second wife it was a widow, well stricken in years, and without wealth or beauty. Why did the Prophet marry her? That he might care for her and protect her and shield her from every ill."

The lady looked on the ground and listened. A strange sensation of joy mingled with fear took possession of her, for she saw what Ishmael was going to say.

"If the Prophet did this for her who was so far removed from the slanders of evil tongues, shall not his servant do as much for one who is young and beautiful?"

The lady's head began to swim, and the ground to sway under her feet as if she were on a rolling ship at sea, but

Ishmael saw nothing in her agitation but modesty, and he
went on in a soft voice to tell her what he wished to do.

He wished to marry her, that is to say, to *betroth* himself to her, to make her his wife, his spiritual wife, his wife
in name only—never to be claimed of him as a husband, for,
besides his consecration to the great task he had undertaken
for God, there was a vow he had made to the memory of
one who was dead, and both forbade him ever to think again
of the joys of the life of a man.

The lady was now totally unable to conceal her agitation,
and taking out her handkerchief she kept running her
trembling fingers along the hem. She was asking herself
what she could do, how she could reply, for she could plainly
see that the Oriental in Ishmael had never for one instant
allowed him to think that if he were willing to give her
the protection of his name she could have any possible objection.

It was the still hour of noon, and pale with fear she sat
silent for a moment looking into the palpitating air that
floated over the glistening waters of the Nile. Then assuming, as well as she could, an expression of humility and confusion, she said, while her heart was beating violently:

"Master, it is too much honour—I can hardly think
of it."

He could see by her face how hard she fought with herself, but still taking her agitation for maidenly modesty he
dropped his voice and whispered:

"Do not decide at once. Wait a little. Go away now,
and think of what I have said."

He held out his hand to help her to her feet, and she
went off with an unsteady step, first stopping, then going
quickly, as if she had an impulse to speak again and could
not do so, because of the feeling, akin to terror, which
seemed to stifle her.

If any one, following the white lady to her lodging in
the Greek widow's house, had been able to look into the
depths of her soul, he would have found a tragic struggle
going on there. A score of conflicting voices were clamouring to be heard at once. "What am I doing?" "Where am

I?" "Am I myself, or some one else?" "Don't take on this fearful responsibility to such a man." "But I must do so, or I can do nothing." "I must go on or else go back." "But isn't this going too far?" "Nonsense, this is no marriage: it is merely a nominal union—a betrothal. I shall only be his wife *pro formâ*. According to an alien faith, too, a faith that does not bind my conscience." "It must be done—it shall!"

When the white lady returned to Ishmael's house on the following day it was with a firm, decided step, as if she were lifted up and sustained by some invisible power. With a strange light in her eyes and an expression in her face that he had never seen there before, she told him that she agreed to his proposal.

He received her consent with a glad cry, and clapping his hands to summon his household he announced the good news to them with a bright look and a happy voice.

The old uncle was overjoyed, and little Ayesha leaped into the lady's arms and kissed her, but Zenoba, with a face full of confusion, drew Ishmael aside and began to stammer out objections and difficulties. The house was small, there was no separate room for the white lady. Then her black boy—there was not even a corner that could be occupied by him.

"Put the Rani in the room with the child, and let the boy sleep on the mat at her door," said Ishmael, and without more ado he went on to make arrangements for the wedding.

The arrangements were few, for Ishmael determined that the marriage should be concluded immediately and conducted without any kind of pomp.

But in order that all his world might know what he was doing he invited the Cadi of Khartoum to make the contract, and then, having sent the lady to her lodging, he set out to fetch her back on the milk-white camel he usually rode himself.

It was Sunday, and the sun had gone down in a blaze of red as he walked by the camel's side through the native quarter of the town with the white lady—the Rani, the Princess—wearing a gold-edged muslin shawl over her head

19

and descending to her shoulders, riding on the crimson saddle fringed with cowries.

By the time they reached old Mahmud's house it was full of guests in wedding garments, gorgeous in crimson curtains hanging over all the walls, and illuminated by countless lamps both large and small.

But the ceremony was of the simplest.

First, the Fatihah (the first chapter of the Koran), recited by the whole company standing, and then the bride and bridegroom on the ground, face to face, grasping each other's hands.

Down to this moment the white lady had been sustained by the same invisible power, as if clad in an impenetrable armour of defiance which no other emotion could pierce; but when the Cadi stepped forward and placed a handkerchief over the clasped hands and began to say some words of prayer, she felt faint, and could scarcely breathe.

With a struggle, nevertheless, she recovered herself when the Cadi, leaning over her, told her in a low voice to repeat after him the words that he should speak:

"I betroth myself to thee—to serve thee and to submit to thee——"

"I betroth myself to thee—to serve—to serve thee—and to—to submit to thee——"

With an effort she got the words spoken, feeling numb at her heart and with a sense of darkness coming over her, but being spurred at last by sight of the Arab woman's glittering eyes watching her intently.

But when the Cadi turned from her to Ishmael, and the bridegroom, in his throbbing voice, said loudly:

"And I accept thy betrothal and take thee under my care, and bind myself to afford thee my protection, as ye who are here bear witness," she felt as if the tempest of darkness had overwhelmed her and she were falling, falling, falling into a bottomless abyss.

When the lady came to herself again the Arab woman was holding a dish of water to her mouth, and her own black boy, with big tears like beads dropping out of his eyes, was fanning her with a fan of ostrich feathers.

But now the people, who had been saying among themselves, in astonishment at such maimed rites, "Is this a widow or a divorced woman?" being determined not to be done out of such marriage fêtes as they considered only decent, had begun to gather in front of the house, the men in their brown skull caps and blue galabiahs, the married women in their black silk habarahs with silver rings in their noses, and the unmarried girls in their white scarves with coins in their hair and with big silver anklets.

And while the Sheikhs and Notables within, sitting on the dikkahs around the guest-room, listened to a blind man's chanting of the Koran, the peasant people, squatting on the sand under the stars, employed themselves after their own fashion with the beating of drums, big and little, the playing of pipes, and the singing of love songs. And through and among them as they huddled together, with their faces to the illuminated house of joy, and both the bride and the bridegroom before them, a water-carrier, a Sakka, went about with his water-skin and a brass cup, distributing drinks of water; a girl, with jingling jewels, squirted scent; and Abdullah and Black Zogal, showing their shining white teeth in their happiness and pride, handed round sweetmeats and cups of thick coffee.

Meantime the white lady sat, with her flushed face uncovered and her gold-edged veil thrown back, where Ishmael had placed her, near to the threshold, in order that, contrary to bad custom, the people might see her; and the child, with its sweet olive-brown face, sat by her side, almost on her lap, amusing herself by holding her hand and drawing off and putting on a beautiful diamond ring which she wore on the third finger of her left hand.

That innocent action of the sweet child seemed to torture the lady at certain moments, and never more than when one of the male singers, sitting close beneath her, sang a camel-boy's song of love. He was far away on the desert, but the soft eyes of the gazelle recalled the timid looks of his beloved. And when he reached the oasis in the midst of the wilderness, the song of the bird in the date tree brought back the voice of his darling.

As soon as the singer finished, the women on the ground made their shrill quavering cry of joy, the zaghareet, and then the white lady drew her hand away from the child with an abrupt and almost angry gesture.

After that she sat for a long hour without stirring, merely gazing out on the people in front of the house as if she saw and comprehended nothing. A taste of bitterness was in her mouth, and as often as she was recalled to herself by some question addressed to her she looked as if she wished to disappear from sight altogether.

At length she thought her torture was at an end, for the Cadi rose and said in a loud voice:

"If your friend is sweet do not eat him up," whereupon the tom-toms were silenced and with a laugh everybody rose, and then, all standing, the whole company chanted the Fatihah:

"Praise be to God, the Lord of all creatures, the most merciful, the King of the Day of Judgment. Thee do we worship and of Thee do we beg assistance. Direct us in the right way, in the way of those to whom Thou hast been gracious; not of those against whom Thou art incensed, nor of those who go astray."

The solemn words died away like a receding wave on the outskirts of the crowd, and then the people broke up and went back to their houses and tents, leaving Ishmael and his household together. A little later the household also separated for the night, the child, now very sleepy, being carried to bed by her nurse, and old Mahmud shuffling off to his room after saying to the white lady:

"An old man's blessing can do you no harm, my daughter; therefore God bless you and bring you joyful increase."

The white lady was now alone with Ishmael, and her agitation increased tenfold.

"Let us sit again for a while," he said in a soft voice, and leading her to one of the wooden benches, covered with carpet, which faced the open front of the house, he placed himself beside her.

There the moon was on their faces, and from time to

time there was a silvery rain of southern stars. They sat
for a while in silence, she with a sense of shame, he with a
momentary thrill of passion that came up from the place
where he was no longer a prophet but a man.

She felt that he was trying to look into her face with his
lustrous black eyes, and she wished to turn away from him.
This brought the colour of hot blood into her cheeks and
only made her the more beautiful.

A sense of physical fear began to take possession of her,
and a storm of thoughts and memories came in rapid succession. She could not express even to her own mind
the intricacies of her emotions. This man was an Oriental, and she believed him to be capable of treachery and
guilty of violence. Yet she was his wife, according to
his own view, and what at this moment, when they were
alone, was the worth of the pledge whereby she (for her
own purposes) had consented to be his wife in name only,
his betrothed!

Her nervousness increased every moment. When he
touched her arm, she recoiled slightly and felt her skin
creep. He seemed to be conscious of this, for he sat by her
side a little longer without speaking.

The silence of night was on the desert and along the
moon track across the river as far as to the ruined dome of
the Mahdi's tomb, which seemed so threatening and so near.

At length, in a soft voice, he said, "Come," and held
out his hand to help her to rise.

She rose, trembling all over with fright and a sort of
physical humiliation—she who had always been so proud,
so strong, so brave.

He led her to the women's side of the house, without
speaking a word until they got there, and then, almost in a
whisper, he said:

"You sleep here with little Ayesha. May your night be
happy and your morning good!"

She looked up at him as he recommended her to God,
and was amazed at the calm, luminous face that now met
her own. At the next moment he was gone.

It was an immense relief to find herself in her bedroom.

where a little open lamp was burning, and there was no sound but the soft and measured breathing of the child, who was asleep in bed.

At the first moment the sleeping child was like a great protector, but when she became calmer and began to think of this she felt the more ashamed.

"What impossible, terrible thing has happened?" she thought, and then she asked herself again, "Am I really myself, or some one else?"

"Oh, what have I done?" she thought, and a sense of sin took possession of her, which was almost like that which a good woman feels when she has committed adultery.

"It is terrible, but it is inevitable," she thought, and then she fought against the sentiment of shame which oppressed her by telling herself that Ishmael was a crafty hypocrite, whose soft words were a sham, whose religion was a lie, whose wicked deeds deserved punishment at any price whatever.

"But no, I cannot think of that now," she thought, and after a while she turned the light bedclothes aside, and, putting out the lamp, got into bed by the side of the child, who was smelling sweet with the soft odours of sleep.

She lay a long time motionless, with her eyes open, and still the horror of what she had done weighed on her like a nightmare. Then she covered her eyes with her hands, and the image of another filled her with emotions that were at once sweet and bitter. With a woman's sense of injustice she was blaming the absent one for the position of shame in which she found herself.

"Why did he choose this man instead of me?" she thought, and then, at last, in the fiercest fire of jealousy and hatred, weeping bitter tears in the darkness, she reconciled her tormented conscience to everything she had done, everything she intended to do, by saying to herself with quivering lips:

"*He killed my father!*"

At that moment she was startled by a voice outside that broke sharp and harsh upon the silence of the night:

"There is no god but God! There is no god but God!"

It was Black Zogal, the half-witted Nubian, crying the confession of faith at the door of Ishmael's house.

The Lady, the White Lady, the Rani, the Princess, was Helena Graves.

V

WHILE Ishmael's followers had been squatting on the sands to celebrate his betrothal the Sirdar had been having a dinner-party in the palace, composed of the chief officers of his military government and the cream of the British society at Khartoum.

Toward ten o'clock the large after-dinner group of ladies in low-cut corsage, showing white arms and shoulders, and officers in full-dress uniform, had come out on to the terrace with its open arches and its handsome steps sweeping down to the silent garden.

Below were the broad lawns, the mimosa trees filling the night air with perfume, the trembling sycamores and the tall dates, sleeping under the great deep heaven with its stars. Behind was the lamp-lit palace from which native servants in gold-embroidered crimson were carrying silver trays laden with decanters and glasses and small cups and saucers.

It was almost the spot on which "the martyr of the Soudan" fell under the lances of the dervishes, yet one of the Sirdar's servants, Abdullahi, with three cross-cuts on his cheeks, his tribal mark as a son of the bloodthirsty Baggara, and with the pleasantest of smiles on his walnut-coloured face, was drawing corks, pouring out whisky and soda-water, and striking matches to light the men's cigarettes.

The company was full of the gaiety and animation which comes after a pleasant dinner, with a little of the excitement which follows when people have partaken of wine. The eyes of the ladies sparkled and the faces of the men smiled, and both talked freely and laughed a good deal.

The conversation was made up of trifles until one of the

ladies—it was the wife of the Governor of the city, clad in
the lightest of lace chiffon gowns and shod in yellow satin
slippers—inquired the meaning of the sounds of rejoicing,
the blowing of pipes and the beating of tom-toms, which had
come through the wide-open windows of the palace from the
direction of the native quarter.

To this question the Inspector-General of the Soudan—
an English Pasha, whose gold-laced tunic was half covered
with medals—replied that the new prophet, who had lately
arrived in Khartoum, had that day taken to himself a wife.

"How *interesting!*" cried the ladies in chorus, with a
note of laughter that was intended to belie the word, and
then the lady in the yellow slippers turned to the Inspector-
General and said:

"Of course he has as many as the Mahdi already—but
who is the new one, I wonder?"

"No, he has only one wife at present—runs 'em tandem,
I hear—and the new bride is the beautiful person in Parsee
costume who arrived here about the same time as himself."

"The Mohammedan Rani, you mean? My husband tells
me she is perfectly lovely. But they say she will never let
a European get a glimpse of her face—puts down her Parsee
veil, I suppose—so goodness knows how *he* knows, you
know."

"Perhaps your husband is a privileged person, my dear!"
said one of the other ladies, whereupon there was a trill of
laughter and the little feet in satin slippers were beaten
upon the floor.

"But a Rani! Think of that! Who can she be, I wonder?" said another of the ladies, and then the mistress of
the palace, Lady Mannering, hinted that she believed the
Sirdar knew something about her.

"Oh, tell us! Tell us!" cried a dozen female voices at
once; but the Sirdar, a shrewd and kindly autocrat who had
been smoking a cigarette in silence, merely answered:

"Time will tell you, perhaps." Then turning to the Inspector-General he said:

"She has *married* the man, you say?"

"That's so, your Excellency."

[Page 276.]

"'How *interesting*!' cried the ladies in chorus."

"There must be some mistake about that, surely."

The company broke up late, and the ladies went off in light wraps and the men bare-headed through the soft, reverberant air of the southern night. But the Sirdar had asked certain of his officers to remain for a few moments, and among them were the Inspector-General, the Financial Secretary, and the Governor of the town. To the latter came his Zabit, a police officer, whose duty it was to report to his chief early and late, and as soon as the men had seated themselves the Sirdar said:

"Any further news about this man Ishmael Ameer?"

"None, your Excellency," said the Governor.

"You've discovered nothing about his object in coming here?"

"Nothing at all."

"He is not sowing dissension between Moslems and Christians?"

"No! On the contrary he professes to be opposed to all that, sir."

"Then you see no reason to think that he is likely to be a danger to the public peace?"

"Unfortunately no, sir, no!"

The Sirdar laughed. "He hasn't yet given 'divine' sanction for your removal, Colonel?"

"Not that I know of at all events."

"Then you and your wife may sleep in peace for the present, I suppose."

There was a little general laughter, and then the Inspector-General, a sceptic with a contempt for holy men of all kinds, said:

"All the same, your Excellency, I should make short work of this pseudo-Messiah."

"Without plain cause we cannot," said the Sirdar, who was the friend of all faiths and the enemy of none. "Indeed, a broad-minded Mohammedan such as this man is said to be might possibly be of service in directing the religion of the Soudan."

"Yes, sir, but too many of these religious celebrities are contaminated by Mahdism."

"Surely Mahdism is dead, my dear fellow."

"Not yet, sir! Only yesterday I saw a man kneeling by the Mahdi's tomb—so hard do religions die! As for this man Ishmael, he may be preaching peace while he is gathering his followers, but wait till they're numerous enough to fight, and you'll see what he will do. Besides, isn't there evidence enough already that the tranquillity of the Soudan has been disturbed?"

"What evidence do you mean?"

"I mean—my informers all over the country tell me the people are no longer pleading poverty as an excuse for remission of taxation—they are boldly *refusing* to pay."

The Financial Secretary corroborated this statement, saying that the taxes due on the land and the date trees had not yet been collected, and that he had heard from Cairo that the same difficulty was being met with in Egypt in respect of the taxes on berseem and wheat.

"You mean," said the Sirdar, "that a conspiracy of passive resistance to the Government has been set afoot?"

"It looks like it, sir," said the Inspector-General. "A pretty insidious kind of conspiracy it is, too, and I think all the signs are that Ishmael Ameer is at the head of it."

There was silence for some minutes, during which the Sirdar was telling himself that if this was so the rule of England in Egypt was face to face with a most subtle enemy—subtler far than the Mahdi and immeasurably more dangerous.

"Well, the first thing we've got to do is to find out the truth," he said, and with that he gave the Zabit an order to summon the Ulema of Khartoum, the Cadi, the Notables and Sheikhs to a meeting in the palace.

"Let it be soon," he said.

"Yes, sir."

"And secret."

"Certainly, your Excellency."

The Governor and the Financial Secretary went off with the police officer, but for some minutes longer the Inspector-General remained with the Sirdar.

"If the man were likely to cause a disturbance," said

the Sirdar, "it would be easy to deal with him, but he's not. Public security is in no present danger. On the contrary, everything I hear of the man's teaching is calculated to promote peace."

"As to that, sir, if you believe all he *says*, he is the prince of peace himself, and his Islam isn't Islam at all as we know it, but something quite different."

"If he were claiming 'divine' authority and telling people to resist the Government——"

"Oh, he is far too clever for that, sir, and his conspiracy is the deep-laid plan of a subtle impostor, not the unpremeditated action of a lunatic."

"All I hear about his personal character is good," said the Sirdar. "He is tender to children, charitable to the poor, and weeps like a woman at a story of distress."

The Inspector-General laughed.

"Pepper in his finger-nails—the hoary old trick, sir! Good-night, Sirdar!"

"Good-night, Colonel!" And the Inspector-General descended the steps.

Being left alone, the Sirdar walked for a long hour to and fro on the terrace, trying to see what course he ought to take in dealing with a religious leader who differed so dangerously from the holy men that were more troublesome but hardly more deadly than the sand-flies of the desert.

At midnight he found himself standing on the very spot on which General Gordon met his death, and in an instant, as by a flash of mental lightning, he saw the scene that had been enacted there only a few years before—the gray dawn, the mad rush of the howling dervishes in their lust of blood, up from the dim garden to the top of these steps, on which stood, calmly waiting for them, the fearless soul who had waited for his own countrymen in vain. "Where is your Master, the Mahdi?" he cried. Then a barbarous shriek, the flash of a score of lances, and the martyr of the Soudan fell.

Was this to be another such revolt, more subtle if not more bloody, turning England out of the Valley of the Nile by making it impossible for her to meet the expense of governing the country, and thereby uprooting the seeds of civilisation that had been sown in the Soudan through so many toilsome years?

On the other hand, was it the beginning of a great spiritual revolution that was intended by God to pass over the whole face of the world? It might even be that, though the Soudan was only a brown and barren wilderness, for had not all great faiths and all great prophets sprung out of the desert—Moses, Mohammed, Christ!

This brought the Sirdar back to a memory that had troubled him deeply for many weeks—the memory of the disgrace that had fallen in Cairo on his comrade of long ago the son of his old friend Nuneham, young Gordon Lord.

Then it dawned upon him for the first time that, however serious his offence as a soldier, the son of his friend had done no more and no less than his great namesake did before him when he resisted authority *because authority was in the wrong!*

Good God! could it be possible that young Gordon was in the right after all, and that this movement of the man Ishmael was the beginning of a world-wide revolt against the materialism, the selfishness, the venality, and the oppression of a corrupt civilisation that mocked religion by taking the name of Him who came to earth to destroy such evils?

If that was so, could any Christian country in these days dare to repeat the appalling error of the Roman Empire in Palestine two thousand years ago—the error of trying to put down moral forces by physical ones?

The Sirdar laughed when he thought of that, so grotesque seemed the mysterious law of the mind by which he had coupled an olive-faced Arab like Ishmael Ameer with Christ!

The southern night was silent. Not a sound came up from the moonlit garden except the croaking of frogs in the pond. Presently a voice that was like a wave of wind came sweeping through the breathless air:

"There is no god but God! There is no god but God!"

The Sirdar shuddered. and turned into the house.

VI

BEING betrothed to Ishmael, and therefore in effect his wife, Helena had now no difficulty in reading the secret he had so carefully hidden from British eyes. Every morning she sat with him in the guest-room while he received his messengers and agents, and if they demurred at her presence, being distrustful of her because she was a woman, he would say:

"Have no fear. My wife is myself. Think of her as you think of me."

Thus little by little she realised what the plan of his opposition to the Government had been, when, in Cairo, after the closing of El Azhar, he had sent out his hundred emissaries. It was to tell the people in every village of Egypt and the Soudan to pay no taxes until their faith was free and the Government took its hand off the central seat of their religion.

She also realised that the people had obeyed Ishmael and had suffered as the consequence. Agents were coming every day with secret letters and messages concealed in their turbans, telling of the pains and penalties already endured by those who had boldly refused to pay the taxes due at that season of the year.

At first these lamentations were couched after Eastern manner in the language of metaphor. Pharaoh was laying intolerable burdens upon the people—what were they to do? God had once sent Moses, a man of prayer, to plead with Pharaoh to loosen his hand—would He not do so again?

But as the people's sufferings increased, the metaphors were dropped and the injustices they laboured under were stated in plain terms. Hitherto, when a summons had been taken out against a man for the nonpayment of his taxes, the magistrate might remit or cancel or postpone, but now there was nothing but summary execution everywhere, with the result that stock and crops were being sold up by the police, and neither the Mudirs (the Governors) nor their sarrafs (cashiers) cared what price was realised so long as the amount of the taxes was met.

"Is there no redress, no remedy, no appeal? What are we to do?" asked the people in the messages that came in the turbans.

"Be patient!" replied Ishmael. "It is written, 'God is with the patient.'"

A hundred times Helena wrote this answer, at Ishmael's dictation, on pieces of paper hardly bigger than a large postage stamp, and it was hidden away in some secret place in the messenger's clothes.

As time went on the messages became more urgent and painful. The law said that at times of distraint the clothes of the debtor, his implements of cultivation, and the cattle he employed in agriculture were to be exempt from seizure, but the district officers were seizing everything by which the people worked, and yet requiring them to pay taxes just the same.

"What are we to say?" asked the messengers.

"Say nothing," answered Ishmael. "Suffer and be strong. Not for the first time on the banks of the Nile have people been required to make bricks without straw. But God will avenge you. Wait!"

This message, also, Helena wrote a hundred times, wishing it had been more explicit, but Ishmael committed his signature to no compromising statement, no evidence of conspiracy, and that deepened Helena's conviction of his cunning and duplicity.

The intensity of her feeling against Ishmael did not abate by coming to close quarters. Day by day, as she sat in the guest-room, she poisoned her mind and hardened her heart against him. She even found herself taking the side of his people in the sufferings he continued to impose upon them. She was sure, too, that in addition to his plan of passive resistance he had some active scheme of vengeance against the Government. What was it? She must wait and see.

After a while letters began to arrive from Cairo. They were from the Chancellor of El Azhar and contained the messages of the Ulema.

The Ulema had appealed to the representatives of the Powers, who had answered them that they could do nothing unless it became clear to all the world that the action of England was imperilling the peace of Egypt, and thereby the lives of the Europeans. What were they to say?

"Fools!" cried Ishmael. "Don't you see that they *want* you to rebel? Grasp every hand that is held out to you in good-will, but fly from the finger that would point you into the fire."

Helena thought she saw light at last. Having expelled England from Egypt by making it impossible for her to govern the country, Ishmael intended to establish, like the Mahdi, an entirely worldly and temporal power, with himself at the head of it.

The second letter from the Ulema at Cairo contained a still more serious message. Having met and concluded that the action of the Government justified the proclamation of a Jehad, a holy war, on the just ground that the unbelievers were trying to expel them from their country, they had solemnly sworn on the Koran to turn England out of Egypt or die in the attempt.

To this letter Ishmael sent an instant answer, saying:

"No! What will it profit you to turn England out of Egypt while she holds the Soudan and the sources of the Nile? Oh, blind and weak! If you have forgotten your souls, have you no thoughts for your stomachs?"

Then came further letters from the Chancellor of El Azhar, saying that the fellaheen were being evicted from their houses and lands, and that their sufferings were now so dire that no counsels could keep them from revolt. Even the young women were calling upon the young men to fight, saying they were not half the men their fathers had been, or they would conquer or die for the homes that were being taken from them and for the religion of God and his prophet.

To this message also Ishmael returned a determined answer.

"War is mutual deceit," he said. "Avoid it! Fly from it! I will countenance no warfare! That is my unalterable mind! Hear it, for God's sake!"

But hardly had Ishmael's answer gone from Khartoum when messengers began to arrive from all parts of Egypt, saying that the fellaheen had already risen in various places and that battalions of the British Army had been sent out to suppress them; that the people had been put down with loss of life and suffering, and that many were now trooping into the cities, homeless and hopeless, and crying in their despair, "How long, O Lord, how long?"

It was a black day in Khartoum when this news came, for among Ishmael's immediate following there were not a few who had lost members of their own families. Some of these, that night when all was still, went out into the desert, far away from the tents, and sang a solemn dirge for the dead. It was a melancholy sight in that lonesome place, for they were chiefly women, and their voices under the deep-blue sky with its stars made a most touching lamentation, like that of the sobbing of the sea.

Helena heard it, and, with her heart still poisoned against Ishmael, it made her yet more bitter against him, as against one who for his own ends was holding the poor, weak people under their cruel fate by the spell of superstitious hopes and fears.

Knowing the Moslem ethics of warfare, that it is only wicked when it is likely to fail, she convinced herself that Ishmael was merely biding his time for the execution of some violent scheme, and remembering his own secret (the secret of the crime he thought he had hidden from everybody), the idea took possession of her that he was laying some personal plot against the Consul-General.

One day a lanky fellow, with a short-cut Moslem beard, arrived by train, and, after the usual Arabic salutations, produced a letter. It ran:

"The bearer of this is Abdel Kader, and he is our envoy to you with a solemn message which is too secret to commit to paper. Trust him. He is honest and his word is true. Your friends, who wait for you in Cairo with outstretched arms——"

And then followed the names not only of many of the Ulema of Cairo, but of most of the Notables as well.

Abdel Kader proved to be a sort of Arab Don Quixote, full of fine language and grand sentiments. Much of this he expended upon Ishmael in the secrecy of the carefully guarded guest-room before he came to the substance of his message, which was to say that as a great doctor of Moslem law, Gamal-ed-Deen, had upheld assassination itself as a last means of righting the wrongs of the people, the leaders had reluctantly concluded that the English lord (Lord Nuneham) must be removed in order that his heavy foot might be lifted from the necks of the oppressed. To this end they had decided that he should be assassinated some day as he passed in his carriage on his afternoon drive over the Kasr el Nil bridge, but lacking a person capable of taking the lead in such an affair, they appealed to Ishmael to return to Cairo for this purpose.

Having discharged himself of the burden of his message, the Arab Don Quixote was proceeding with many large words that were intended to show how safely this act of righteous vengeance might be executed by one whom the law dare not touch for fear of the people, when Ishmael, who had listened breathlessly, burst out on him and cried:

"No, no, I tell you, no! Return to them that sent you, and say, 'Ishmael Ameer is no murderer.' Say, too, that the world has no use for patriots who would right the people by putting them in the wrong. Away with you! Away!"

At that he rose up and went out of the guest-room with a flaming face, leaving the envoy to strike his forehead and to curse the day that had brought him.

Helena, who alone, save old Mahmud, had been present at this interview, found herself utterly shaken at the end of it by a storm of conflicting feelings, and from that time forward her heart was constantly being surprised by emotions which she had hitherto struggled to suppress.

Day by day, as messengers came thronging into Khartoum with sadder and yet sadder stories of the people's sufferings—how, living under the shadow of the sword, impoverished by the law and by the cruel injustice of the native officers, the Omdehs and the sarrafs, sold up and evicted from their homes, they were tramping the deserts, men,

women, and children, hungry and naked and with nothing
of their own except the sand and the sky—Helena saw that
Ishmael's face grew paler and paler, as if his sleep had left
him, and under the burden of his responsibility for what
had befallen the country as the consequence of its obedience
to his will, his heart was bleeding and his life ebbing away.

"Master, is there no help for us?" the messengers would
ask, with tears in their half-witted eyes. "You are our
father, we are your children—what are we to do? We are
sheep without a shepherd—will you not lead us?"

To all such pleading Ishmael would show a brave face
and say:

"Not yet! Wait! The clouds that darken your sky
will lift. Be patient! The arm of our God is long! Never
despair! Allah feeds the worm that lies between the stones.
Will He not feed you also? Yet better your bodies should
starve than your souls should perish! Hold fast to the
faith! Your children and your children's children will bless
you!"

But sometimes in the midst of his comforting his voice
would fail, and, like Joseph, whose bowels yearned over his
brethren, he would stop suddenly and hasten away to his
room, lest he should break down altogether.

Helena saw all this, and it was as much as she could do
to withstand it, when one night she was awakened in the
small hours by Mosie, who was whispering through the door
of her bedroom:

"Lady, lady, Master sick; come to him."

Then she walked across to the men's side of the house
and heard Ishmael, in his own room, calling God to forgive
him, and crying like a child.

At that moment, in spite of herself, Helena felt a wave
of pity take possession of her, but at the next, being back in
her bedroom, she remembered her own secret, and asked herself again:

"What pity had he for me *when he killed my father?*"

VII

Down to this time Ishmael's conduct had been marked by the most determined common sense; but now came an incident that seemed to change the trend of his mind and character.

One day a man of the Jaalin tribe arrived with a letter in the sole of his sandal.

"God give you greeting, Master," he said in his West-country dialect and a tone that seemed to foretell trouble.

With trembling fingers Ishmael tore open the letter and read that to drown the cries of distress and to throw dust in the eyes of Europe (for so the Ulema understood the otherwise mysterious object, the Consul-General was organising a general festival of rejoicing to celebrate the ——th anniversary of the British occupation of Egypt.

At this news Ishmael was overwhelmed. Helena saw his lips quiver and his cheeks grow pale as he held the crinkling paper in his trembling hands. In the absence of other explanation the cold-blooded cruelty of the scheme seemed to be almost devilish.

That day he disappeared, escaping from the importunities of his people into the desert. He did not return at night, and at sunrise next morning Black Zogal went in search of him. But the Nubian returned without him, telling some wild supernatural tale of having come upon the master in the midst of an angelic company. His face was shining with a celestial radiance, so that at first he could not look upon him. And when at length he was able to lift his eyes, the master, who was alone, sent him back, saying he was to tell no man what he had seen.

Four days afterward Ishmael returned to Khartoum, and there was enough in his face to explain Black Zogal's story. His eyes, which seemed to stare, had a look of unearthly joy. This was like flame to the fuel of his people's delirium, for they did not see that, under the torment of his private sufferings, the dauntless courage and hope of the man had begun to turn toward madness.

He began to preach in the mosque a wild, new message. The time of the end had come! Famine and pestilence, poverty and godless luxury, war and misery—were not these the signs foretold of the coming of the latter day?

Lo, the cup of the people's sufferings was full! Behold, while the children of Allah wept, men feasted and women danced! Never since the black night when the first-born of Egypt were slain had Egypt been so mocked! Egypt, the great, the ancient, the cradle of humanity—what was she now but a playground for the idle wealthy of the world?

"But, no matter!" he cried. "The world travaileth and groaneth like a woman in labour; but as a woman forgets her pains when the hope of her heart is born, so shall the children of God forget Pharaoh and his feastings when the Expected One is come. He is coming now, the Living, the Deliverer, the Redeemer! Wait! Watch! The time is near!"

The new message flashed like fire through Ishmael's followers. Every eventide for thirteen centuries the prayer had gone up to heaven in Islam for the advent of the divinely appointed guide who was to redeem the world from sorrow and sin, to deliver believers from the hated bondage of the foreigner, and to re-establish the universal Caliphate; and now, in the utmost depths of their oppression and suffering, when hope had all but died out of their hearts, the true Mahdi, the Messiah, the Christ was about to come!

The people were beside themselves with joy. They were like children of the desert who, after a long drought in which their wells have been dried up, run about in glee when the first drops of rain begin to fall. They were ready for any task, any enterprise, and Ishmael, who began to make plans for going back to Cairo (for it was there, according to his view, that the Expected One was to appear), sent them with letters to all corners of the country, telling his messengers to return home.

Helena wrote these letters with a trembling hand. In spite of her secret errand she was surprised by a certain sympathy. The great hope, the great dream touched her pity and gave her at the beginning some moments of compunction. But after a while she began to see it as a wicked madness, and that enabled her to steel her heart against Ishmael again.

The man who held out such crazy hopes to a credulous people might be harmless in England, but in Egypt he was a peril. Once let an ignorant and superstitious populace believe that the end of the world was coming, that a Messiah was about to appear, and human government was a dead letter. What then? Revolution and bloodshed, for the first duty of a government was to preserve law and order!

Helena asked herself if the time had not come at last to write to the Consul-General, or perhaps to steal away from Khartoum and return to Cairo that she might report what she had seen and learned.

After reflection she concluded that the only result of doing so would be that of punishing yet further the poor, misguided people who had been punished enough already. It was Ishmael alone who ought to suffer, whether for his offences against his followers, his conspiracy against the Government, or his crime against herself, and in order to punish him apart she would have to separate him from his people.

How was she to do this? It seemed impossible; but fate itself assisted her.

A few days after Abdel Kader had gone off in his humiliation the shadow of his lanky body appeared across the threshold of the guest-room, where Ishmael was sitting with no other company than old Mahmud and Helena, who was writing the usual letters while little Mosie fanned her to drive off the flies.

" The peace of God be with you, Master," he said in a low and humble voice, and then, with a shy look of triumph, he produced a letter which had been given to him at Halfa.

The letter was from the Chancellor of El Azhar, and it told Ishmael, after the usual Arabic salutations, that the festival of which he had already been informed was to take place on the Ghezirah (the island in front of Cairo); that the rejoicings were to begin on the anniversary of the birthday of the English King, something more than a month hence; that the British soldiers would still be in the provinces at that time, quelling disturbances and helping the district officers to enforce the payment of taxes, and that, as a consequence, the Egyptian Army alone would be left in charge of the city.

"The Egyptian soldiers are Moslems, oh, my brother—the brothers and sons of our poor afflicted children of Allah. It needs only the right word from the right man, and they will throw down their arms at the city gates and the army of God may enter."

Ishmael read the letter aloud in his throbbing voice, and his face began to shine with ecstasy. In an instant a wild scheme took shape in his mind.

He would announce a pilgrimage! With ten thousand, twenty thousand, fifty thousand of his followers he would return to Cairo to meet and greet the Expected One! The native army would not resist their co-religionists, and once within the city, the struggle would be at an end! In a single hour his fifty thousand would be five hundred thousand! The Government would not turn them out; it dare not make war upon them; the whole world would cry out against a general massacre, and God Himself would not permit it to occur.

But somebody must go into Cairo in advance to prepare the way—to make sure there should be no bloodshed. Some trusty messenger, some servant of the Most High, who could kindle the souls of the Egyptian soldiers to such a blazing flame of love that not all the perils of death could make them take up arms against the children of God when they came to their gates!

While Ishmael propounded this scheme, with gathering excitement and a look of frenzy, Helena sat trembling from head to foot and clutching with nervous fingers the reed pen she held in her hand, for she knew that her hour had struck at last—the hour she had waited and watched for, the hour she had come to Khartoum to meet. She held her breath and gazed intently into Ishmael's quivering face as long as he continued to speak, and then, in a voice which she could scarcely recognise as her own, she said:

"But the messenger who goes in advance into Cairo—

he must be one whose wisdom as well as courage you can trust."

"True, true, most true," said Ishmael, speaking eagerly and rapidly.

"Some one whose word will carry influence with the Egyptian army."

"Please God, it shall be so," said Ishmael.

"If the soldiers are native and Moslem, the officers are British and Christian, therefore the risks they run are great."

"Great, very great; but God will protect them."

"To disobey may be to suffer imprisonment, perhaps discharge, possibly death."

"I know! I know! But God will bring them to a happy end."

"Therefore," said Helena, whose nervousness was gathering feverish strength, "the messenger who goes into Cairo in advance must be one who can make them forget the dangers of death itself."

Ishmael reflected for a moment, and then, in a burst of eagerness, he said:

"The counsel is good. *I will go myself!*"

Helena's flushed face looked triumphant. "The man of all men," she said. "What messenger from Ishmael could be so sure as Ishmael himself?"

"Yes, please God, I will go myself," said Ishmael in a louder voice, and he began to laugh—it was the first laugh that had broken from his lips since Helena came to Khartoum. Then he paused and said:

"But the people?"

"Anybody can follow with them," said Helena. "Their loyalty is certain; they need no persuading."

"I'll go," said Ishmael, "for above all there must be no bloodshed."

Then old Mahmud, who alone of the persons present in the guest-room seemed to be untouched by the excitement of the moment, turned to Helena and said:

"But is Ishmael the only one for this enterprise, my daughter?"

"He knows every one and every one knows him," said Helena.

"But he who knows everybody, everybody knows," the old man answered; "not the soldiers merely, but their masters also."

At that Helena's nervousness gathered itself up into a trill of unnatural laughter, and she said: "Nonsense! He can be disguised. The kufiah" (head-dress) "of a Bedouin, covering his head and nearly all his face—what more is wanted?"

"So you are not afraid for him, my daughter?"

"Afraid? I will make the kufiah myself, and with my own hands I will put it on."

"Brave heart of woman!" cried Ishmael. "Stronger than the soul of man! It is *my* duty and I will do it!"

With that he turned to Abdel Kader, who had looked on with his staring eyes, and said:

"Go back to Cairo by the first train, and say, 'It is well—God willing, he will come.'" And then, in the fever of his new purpose, he went off to the mosque.

There he first called upon the people to repeat the Shehada, the Moslem creed, and after that he administered an oath to them—never, by the grace of God and His Prophet, to reveal what he was going to say except to true believers, and only to them on their taking a like oath of secrecy and fidelity.

The people repeated in chorus the words he spoke in a loud voice, and concluded—each man with his right hand on the Koran and his left upraised to heaven—with a solemn "Amen!"

Then Ishmael told them everything—how the time had come for their deliverance from bondage and corruption to the glorious liberty of the children of God; how, as the people of the Prophet had returned from Medina to Mecca, so they were to go up from Khartoum to Cairo; how he was to go before them, and they, under another leader, were to follow him, and God would give them a great reward.

At this news the poor, unlettered people grew delirious in their excitement, each man interpreting Ishmael's message according to his own vision of the millennium. Some saw themselves turning the hated foreigner out of Egypt; others were already in imagination taking possession of Cairo and all the rich lands of the valley of the Nile; while a few, like Ishmael himself, were happy enough in the expectation of prostrating themselves at the feet of the divinely appointed guide who was to redeem the world from sorrow and sin.

As soon as prayers were over Black Zogal ran back to old Mahmud's house with a wild story of flashes of light which he saw darting from Ishmael's head while he spoke from the pulpit.

Helena heard him. She was sitting alone in the guest-room, tortured by conflicting thoughts. "Am I a wicked woman?" she asked herself, remembering how easily she had taken advantage of Ishmael's fanatical ecstasy. But then she hardened her heart against Ishmael again, telling herself that his simplicity was cunning and that he was an impostor who had gone so far with his imposture that he could even impose upon himself.

How could one who had committed a crime, a cruel and cowardly crime, be anything but a villain? A madman, perhaps, but all the same a villain!

And then other thoughts thronged upon her, sweet and bitter thoughts, with memories of Gordon, of her father, of the early days in Grasmere, of the short morning of happiness in Cairo, and of the brief lift in the clouds of her life that was now plunged in perpetual night.

Thus she stifled every qualm of conscience by going back and back to the same plea, the same support:

"*After all, he killed my father!*"

VIII

In a village outside blind-walled, dead Metimmeh, with its blank and empty hovels, emblems of Mahdist massacres, two travellers were encamped. One of them was what the quick-eyed natives called a "white Egyptian," but he was

20

dressed as a Bedouin Sheikh; the other was his servant. They were travelling south, and having been long on their journey, their camels had begun to fail them. A she camel, ridden by the Bedouin, was suffering in one of its feet, and the men were resting while a doctor dressed it.

Meantime the villages were feeding them with the best of their native bread and making a fantasia for their entertainment. The night was a little cold, and the people had built a fire, before which the travellers were sitting with the Sheikh of the village by their side.

In a broad half-circle on the other side of the fire a group of blue-shirted Arabs were squatting on the sand. A singer was warbling love-songs in a throbbing voice, a number of his comrades were beating time on the ground with sticks, and a swaggering girl, who glittered with gold coins in her hair and on her hips, was dancing in the space between. On their nut-brown faces was the flickering red light of the fire and over their heads was the great, wide, tranquil whiteness of the moon.

In the midst of their fantasia they heard the hollow thud of a camel's tread, and presently a stranger arrived, a lanky fellow, with wild eyes and a North-country accent. The Sheikh saluted him, and he made his camel kneel and got down to rest and to eat.

"The peace of God be with you!"

"And with you! What is your name?" asked the Sheikh.

"They call me Abdel Kader, and I am riding all night to catch the train from Atbara in the morning."

"It must be great news you carry in such haste, O brother!"

"The greatest! When the sun rises above the horizon we see no more the stars."

It was obvious enough, through all his fine language, that the stranger was eager to tell his story, and after calling for an oath of secrecy and fidelity he told it to the Sheikh and the Bedouin in bated breath.

The time of the end had come! A pilgrimage had been proclaimed! Ishmael Ameer was to go up to Cairo secretly, and his people were to follow him; the Egyptian Army were to help them to enter the city, the hated foreigner was to be flung out of the country, and Egypt was to be God's!

The Sheikh of the village was completely carried away by the stranger's news, but the Bedouin listened to it with unconcealed alarm.

"Is this the plan of Ishmael Ameer?" he asked.

"It is," said the stranger; "and God bring it to a happy end."

"Did anybody put it into his head?" asked the Bedouin.

"Yes, a woman, his wife, and God bless and reward her!"

"His wife, you say?"

"Wallahi!" said the stranger; and then, with many fine sentiments and much flowery speech, he told of the lady, the White Lady, the Rani, the Princess, who had lately been married to Ishmael Ameer and had now so much power over him.

"What says the old saw?" said the stranger. "'He who eats honey risks the sting of bees,' but no danger in this case."

And then followed more fine sentiments on the sweetness and wisdom of woman in general and of the Rani in particular.

"Well, he who lives long sees much," said the Bedouin, with increasing uneasiness; and turning to the Sheikh, he asked if he might have the loan of a fresh camel in the place of the one that was disabled.

"Certainly; but my brother is not leaving me to-night?" asked the Sheikh.

"I must," said the Bedouin.

"But the night is with us," said the Sheikh.

"And so is the moon, and the tracks are clear," said the Bedouin. "But one thing you can do for me, O Sheikh— send a letter into Khartoum by the train that goes up from Metimmeh in the morning."

That was agreed to, and then, by the light of a large tin lamp which his servant held before him as he sat on the sand, the Bedouin wrote a hurried message to Ishmael

Ameer, saying who he was and why he was making his journey, and asking that nothing should be done until they came together.

By this time the fantasia was over, the fire had died down, the camels had been brought up, the flowery stranger had started afresh on his northward way, and the Sheikh and his people were standing ready to say farewell to the two travellers, who were facing south.

"God take you safely to your journey's end, O brother!" said the Sheikh. Then with a grunt the camels knelt and rose, and at the next moment, amid a chorus of pious ejaculations, into the glistening moon track across the sand the Bedouin and his man disappeared.

The Bedouin was Gordon. He was thinner and more bronzed, yet not less well than when he left Cairo, for he had the strength of a soldier inured to hardship. But Osman, his servant and guide, having lived all his life in the schoolroom and the library, had dwindled away like their camels, which were utterly debilitated and had lost their humps.

Their journey had been long, for they had missed their way, being sometimes carried off by mirages and sometimes impeded by mountain ranges that rose sheer and sharp across their course. And often in the face of such obstacles, with his companion and his camels failing before his eyes, Gordon's own spirit had also failed, and he had asked himself why, since he knew of no use that heaven could have for him there, he continued to trudge along through this bare and barren wilderness.

But doubt and uncertainty were now gone. He was in a fever of impatience to reach Khartoum that he might put an end to Ishmael's scheme. That scheme was madness, and it could only end in disaster. Carried into execution it would be another Arab insurrection, and would lead to like failure and as much bloodshed.

The Englishman and the British soldier in Gordon, no less than the friend of the Egyptian people, rebelled against Ishmael's plot. It was political mutiny against England, which Ishmael in Cairo had protested was no part of his spiritual plan. What influence had since played upon him to make him change the object of his mission? Who was this white woman, this Rani, this princess who had put an evil motive into his mind? Was she acting in the folly of good faith, or was she deceiving and betraying him? His wife, too! What could it mean?

In Gordon's impatience only one thing was clear to him —that for England's sake, and for Egypt's also, he must reach Khartoum without delay. He must show Ishmael how impossible was his scheme, how dangerous, how deadly, how certain to lead to his own detection and perhaps death.

"We are thirty hours from Omdurman—can we do it in a day and a night, Osman?" he said, as soon as the camels swung away.

"God willing, we will," said Osman, in a voice that betrayed at once his weakness and his devotion.

They rode all night, first in the breathless moonlight with its silvery shimmering haze, then in a strong wind that made the clouds sail before the stars and the camels beneath them feel like ships that were riding through a running sea, and last of all in the black hour before the dawn, when it was difficult to see the tracks and the beasts stumbled in the darkness.

The morning grew gray, and they were still riding. But Osman's strength was failing rapidly, and when, half an hour afterward, the sun in its rising brightness began to flush with pink the stony heights of distant hills, they drew rein, made their camels kneel, and dismounted.

They were then near to a well, from which a group of laughing girls, with bare bronzed arms and shoulders, were drawing water in pitchers and carrying it away on their heads. While Osman loosened the saddles of the camels and fed the tired creatures with durah, Gordon asked one of the girls for a drink, and she held her pitcher to his lips, saying, with a smile, "May it give thee health and prosperity!"

After half an hour's rest, having filled their water-skins and being refreshed with biscuits and dates, they readjusted the saddles of the camels, mounted and rose, and started again, making their salaams to the young daughters of the desert who stood grouped together in the morning sunshine and looked after them with laughing eyes.

The clear, vivifying, elastic desert air breathed upon their faces, and their camels, strengthened by rest and food, swung away with better speed. All day long they continued to ride without stopping. Gordon's impatience increased every hour as he reflected upon the probable consequence of the scheme with which the unknown woman had inspired Ishmael, and Osman, being told of the danger, forgot his weakness in the fervour of his devotion.

The shadows lengthened along the sea-flat sand while they passed over wastes without a bush or a scrub or a sign of life, but just as the sun was setting they entered the crater-like valley of Kerreri, with its clumps of mimosa and its far view of the innumerable islands of the Nile.

This was the scene of Gordon's first battle, the battle of Omdurman, and a score of tender and thrilling memories came crowding upon him from the past. Yonder was the thicket in which he had taken the Caliph's flag, the spot where he had left Ali: "Show the bits of the bridle to my Colonel and tell him I died faithful. Say my salaams to him, Charlie. I knew Charlie Gordon Lord would stay with me to the end."

How different the old battlefield was to-day! Instead of the deafening roar of cannon, the wail of shell, the frenzied shouts of the dervishes, and the swathes of sheeted dead, there was only the grim solitude of stony hills and yellow sand, with here and there some white and glistening bones over which the vultures circled in the silent air.

Night had fallen when they entered Omdurman, and the change in the town, too, struck a chill into Gordon's heated spirit. No longer the dirty, disgusting Mahdist's capital, it was deodorised, swept, and sweet. Could it be possible that he was opposing the forces which had brought this civilising change?

When the travellers reached the ferry the last boat for Khartoum had gone, and, the Nile being high, they had no choice but to remain in Omdurman until morning.

"*Ma 'aleysh!* All happens as God ordains," said Osman. But Gordon's impatience could scarcely contain itself, so eager was he to undo the work of the woman who had done so much ill.

They lodged in a kahn of the old slave market, which was now full of peaceful people sitting about coffee-stalls lit by lanterns and candles, where formerly the air was tense with the frenzied gallopings of the wild Baggarah and the melancholy boom of the great ombeya, the fearful trumpet of death.

Before going to bed Gordon wrote another letter to Ishmael, saying he had got so far and expected to meet him in the morning. Then, being unable as yet to sleep under a roof, after sleeping so long on the desert, he dragged his angerib into the open and stretched himself under the stars.

There, gazing up into the great vault of heaven, a memory came back to him which had never once failed to come when he lay down to sleep—the memory of Helena. Every night on his long desert journey, whatever the discomfort of his bed, if it was only the hole between two stones which the Arab shepherds build to protect themselves from the wind, his last thought had been of her.

She was gone, she was lost to him, she would be in England by this time, and he was exiled from home for ever; but in the twilight moments of the heart and mind that go between the waking sense and sleep she was with him still.

And now, lying on his angerib in Omdurman, he could see her radiant eyes and hear her deep, melodious voice, and catch the note of the gay raillery that was perhaps her greatest charm. Though he had done this ever since he left Cairo, he felt to-night as if the sweet agony of it all would break his heart.

He looked up at the stars and found pleasure in thinking that the same sky was over Helena in England. Then he looked across at Khartoum and saw that all the windows of the Palace were lit up, as for a dance.

A mystic sense of some impending event came over him. What could it be? he wondered. Then he remembered the word of Osman, who was now breathing heavily at his side.

"*Ma 'aleysh!* All happens as God ordains," he thought. And then, sending a last greeting to Helena in England, he turned over and fell asleep.

IX

EARLY that morning Abdullah had entered Ishmael's room while the Master was still sleeping, for a messenger from Metimmeh, coming by train, had brought an urgent letter.

Ishmael read the letter and rose immediately, and when Helena met him in the guest-room half an hour afterward she saw that he was excited and disturbed.

"Rani," he said, "I have been thinking about our plan, and have certain doubts about it. Better let it rest for a few days, at all events."

Helena asked why, and she was told that a stranger was coming whose counsel might be wise, for he knew Cairo, the Government, and the Egyptian Army, and he had asked Ishmael to wait until he arrived before committing himself to any course.

"Who is he?" she asked.

"One who loves the people and has suffered sorely for his love of them."

"What is his name?"

"They call him Sheikh Omar Benani."

At that moment she learned no more than that the stranger was a Bedouin chief of great fame and influence, that he had rested at Metimmeh the night before, but was now coming on to Khartoum as fast as a camel could carry him.

"He may be here to-night—to-morrow at latest," said Ishmael; "so let us leave things where they are until our brother arrives."

This news threw Helena into a fever of excitement. She saw the possibility of her scheme coming to naught. The Bedouin who was now on his way might destroy it.

She was afraid of this Bedouin. If he knew Cairo, the Government, and the Egyptian Army, he must also know that the plan which Ishmael had proposed to himself was impossible. That being so, he would advise Ishmael against it. His influence with Ishmael would be greater than her own, and as a consequence her plan would fail. Then all she had hoped for, all she had come for, all she had sacrificed so much for, would be lost and wasted.

What was she to do? There was only one thing possible —to cause Ishmael to commit himself to her plan before the Bedouin arrived in Khartoum.

Again fate assisted her. The same train that brought the Bedouin's letter brought another messenger from Cairo. He was an immensely tall Dinka, who had been employed to avert suspicion. As soon as he was alone with Ishmael and his household he slipped off his sandal and, tearing open the undersole, produced a very small letter.

It was from the Ulema of El Azhar, and gave further particulars of the forthcoming festivities, with one hint of amazing advice that certainly could not have come from men of the world.

The Consul-General had decided to give his annual dinner in honour of the King's birthday not as usual at the British Agency, but in the Pavilion of the Ghezirah Palace, on the island in front of the city. All the authorities would be there that night, housed under one roof. The British Army would still be in the provinces, and the Egyptian Army alone would be left in defence of the town. Therefore, to prevent the possibility of bloodshed, there was only one thing to do—turn the key on the Pavilion, in order to imprison the persons in command, and then open the bridge that crossed the Nile, that Ishmael's following, with the consent of the native soldiers, might enter Cairo unopposed!

It was a plot whereof the counterpart could only have been found in the history of Abu Moslim and "Al Mansour," and perhaps for that reason alone it took Ishmael's heart by storm. But it required immediate confirmation, for if the secret scheme was to be carried out the arrangements were matters of urgency and the reply must be received at once.

There were some moments of tense silence after Ishmael

21

had read the letter, for already he had begun to hesitate, to talk again of waiting for the Bedouin, who knew Egypt better than any one in the Soudan and was wise and brave and learned in war. But Helena, seeing her advantage, began to speak, with a flushed face and a trembling tongue, of the train that was to leave Khartoum for Cairo that morning and of the interval of four days before the departure of another one.

"There can be no time to lose," she said, with a stifling sense of duplicity, "especially if the Ulema are to arrange for your own arrival as well."

At length Ishmael, no longer the man he used to be, strong above all in common sense, but an enthusiast living in a world of dream, was swept away by the Ulema's scheme. Seeing only one sure way to avoid bloodshed—that of shutting up the British officials in the midst of their festivities, while the bridge that crossed the Nile was opened and his followers took peaceful possession of the city—he called on Helena to write his reply. It ran:

"To his Serenity the Chancellor of El Azhar from the slave of God, Ishmael Ameer: Good news! In the interests of peace I agree, though liking not for other reasons your plan of imprisoning Pharaoh and his people in their Pavilion, lest it should be said of us, 'Behold the true believer resorts to the tricks of the infidels, who trust not in the good arm of God, praise be to Him, the Exalted One!'"

"Nevertheless, I send you this word of greeting, giving my consent and saying, 'Shortly I go down to Cairo myself to call upon our brothers under arms to our very great Lord, the Khedive, to refuse, when the day of our deliverance comes, to shed the blood of the children of the Most High.'"

Having dictated this letter, and added the usual Arabic salutations, he signed it, and then, full of a fresh enthusiasm, he went off to midday prayers in the mosque, where with greater fervour than before he delivered his new message about the coming of the end.

Helena was now alone, for the Dinka had gone in with Abdullah to eat and to rest. The signed letter lay before her, and she knew that her time had come. In great haste she made a copy of the letter, and without waiting to think what she was doing she added Ishmael's name to it. Then, hiding the original in her bosom, she called for the Dinka, gave him the copy, and hurried him off to the train, which was leaving immediately. After that, with a sense of mingled shame and triumph, she wrote to the Consul-General. Her excitement was so great that she could hardly hold the pen or frame coherent sentences. This was what she wrote:

"DEAR LORD NUNEHAM: You will remember that in the letter I wrote to you before I left Cairo I told you that I should write again, and that when I wrote, your enemy and mine and Gordon's, as well as England's and Egypt's, would be in your hands.

"I am now fulfilling my promise, and you shall judge for yourself whether I am justifying my word. Ishmael Ameer, at the instigation of the Ulema, is about to return to Cairo. His object is to organise a meeting among the soldiers of the Egyptian Army, so that a vast multitude of his followers, coming behind him, may take possession of the city.

"This is to be done during the forthcoming festivities, and it is to reach its climax on the night of the King's Birthday. Proof enclosed. It is the original of a letter to the Chancellor of El Azhar, a copy having been sent instead.

"Ishmael will travel by train—probably within a week— and he will wear the disguise of a Bedouin Sheikh. I leave you to wait and watch for him.

"Did I not say I was not idly boasting? In haste,
                                        "HELENA GRAVES.

"P.S.—I send this by my boy, Mosie. Please keep him in Cairo until you hear from me again."

When she had finished her letter she paused for a moment and looked fixedly before her. Although she said nothing her lips moved as if she were interrogating the empty air. She was asking herself again, "Am I cruel and revengeful and vindictive?" And she was replying to herself as she had replied before: "If so, I cannot help it. I have lost my father and I have lost Gordon, and I am alone and my heart is torn."

Strengthened by this thought she took Ishmael's letter from her bosom and folded it inside her own. But while she was in the act of putting both into an envelope she paused again, for a new and more startling memory had flashed upon her. It was the memory of the marks upon her father's throat and of the missing finger print which had somehow formed so fatal an evidence of Ishmael's guilt.

How had it happened that she had forgotten this fact until now—that during all the time she had been in Khartoum she had never once remembered to verify it—that even at the moment she could not say whether the third finger of Ishmael's left hand was intact or not?

But no matter! It was not a fact of the greatest consequence, and in any case she was too far gone to think of it now.

She sealed her envelope and addressed it and then called for Mosie. The black boy came running at the sound of her agitated voice.

"Mosie," she said in a breathless whisper, "you have always said that you loved me so much that you would lay down your life for me." The black boy showed his shining white teeth as if from ear to ear. "Do you think you could find your way back to Cairo alone and deliver a letter to the English lord?"

"Let lady try me," said Mosie, who was ablaze with excitement in an instant.

Then she told him how he was to go—by train to Halfa, by Government boat to Shellal, by train again from Assouan to his journey's end, travelling always in compartments occupied by natives. She also gave him strict injunctions against speaking to any one, either in Khartoum or on the way, or in Cairo until he came to the British Agency. There he was to ask for the Consul-General and give into his hands—his only—her private letter.

"The train leaves in half an hour, Mosie, so you'll have to be quick," she whispered.

"Yes, lady, yes, yes," said Mosie at every word, and in

his eagerness to be gone he almost snatched the letter out of her hand.

"No; give me one of your sandals," she said; and when he had whipped it off, she took her scissors and lifting the inner sole she hid her letter underneath.

Then she hurried into her room, and returning with a small canvas bag, which contained nearly all the money she had left in the world, she gave it to the black boy and sent him off.

X

AFTER that she sat down, for her heart was beating violently and she could scarcely breathe. At the same moment she caught sight of her face in a hand glass that stood on the table at which she wrote, and the features looked so strange that they scarcely seemed to be her own.

If anybody with the eye of the spirit could have gazed at that moment into the deepest recesses of her soul— harder to look into than the obscurity of the sea—he would have seen a battlefield of contending passions. She was reflecting for the first time on the whole meaning of what she had done. She had condemned Ishmael Ameer to death! Or at least, at the very least, to lifelong imprisonment in Damietta or Torah!

When she put it so the furnace of her conscience seemed to consume her, and in order to live with herself she had to oppose that thought with thoughts of Gordon—Gordon gone, she knew not where, an exile, an outcast, his brilliant young life wasted, never to be seen again.

This relieved the riot in her brain, and to ease her heart still further she made herself believe that what she had done had not been to revenge herself, but to avenge Gordon, whom Ishmael's evil influence had destroyed.

"Serves him right," she thought. "Let him go to Damietta! What better does he deserve?"

At that moment Ayesha, Ishmael's little daughter, came running with bare feet into the house, and seeing Helena

she leaped into her arms and kissed her. The kiss of th
child seemed like a blow—it made her dizzy.

At the next moment, while Ayesha was mumbling affec
tionate play-words which Helena did not hear, and Zenoba
the Arab nurse, stood beating her impatient foot upon th
floor, there came from outside the murmur of a crowd. I
was the crowd of Ishmael's followers bringing him home
from the mosque.

They were calling upon God and His Prophet to bles
him, touching his white caftan as if it were divine and
virtue were coming out of him.

He dismissed them with words of rebuke—gentler and
more indulgent than before, perhaps—and entering the house
he called for food.

A few minutes afterward Ishmael and Helena and old
Mahmud were sitting in the guest-room together, drinking
new milk and eating soft bread.

"But where is your boy, O Rani?" asked Ishmael, who
missed the great fan of ostrich feathers.

Helena made a halting excuse. Mosie had been troublesome—she had sent him back to where he came from—Cairo.

"Cairo?" asked the Arab woman, with a glance of suspicion.

Helena looked confused, but Ishmael saw nothing. He
was more than usually excited, enthusiastic, and full of
great hopes. After a while he talked of the Bedouin who
was coming.

"Our brother is not, in fact, a Bedouin," he said.

"Not a Bedouin?"

"Neither is he a Moslem. He is a Christian, and indeed
an Englishman."

"An Englishman?"

"Ah, yes; but he is one who loves the Moslems and has
gone through shame and degradation rather than do them
a wrong."

Helena was afraid to ask further questions. She could
only listen, terrified by a vague apprehension.

"Truly, O lady, he who loveth all the children of God,
him God loveth," said Ishmael. "This brave man was a

soldier, and if he has suffered rather than do an evil act, will God forget him? No!"

Helena shuddered. The idea that was taking shape in her mind seemed incredible. Ishmael was speaking in the softest tones, yet his voice seemed like the subterranean sounds that precede great shocks of earthquake.

"He is coming. Be good to him, my Rani. If we could take his heart out and weigh it we should find it gold."

Helena was struck with a sort of stupor. "Am I dreaming?" she asked herself. "What am I thinking about?" It was one of those mysterious moments on the eve of the great events of life when murmurs come from we know not where.

The long hours of that day passed in a sort of dark confusion. At last the sun set, and the moon rose over the desert, the golden southern moon, in the purple of the Eastern sky, and lit up the wilderness of sand as with a softer sun.

It grew late and Helena rose to go to her room. As she did so she almost fell from dizziness, and Ishmael helped her to the door of the women's quarters. She had seen his lustrous eyes upon her with the expression that had made her tremble on the night of the betrothal; but again, in the same scarcely audible voice, he said:

"God give you a good morning!" and putting, for the first time, his lips to her hand, he went away.

When she was alone a long hour passed in silence. The bedroom was in a state of perfect calm, yet a frightful tumult was going on in her brain. Could it be possible that he who was coming was——

No! The wild irony of that thought was too terrible.

That at the very moment when she thought she was avenging Gordon for the injury he had suffered at the hands of Ishmael—that at that moment, by some sinister eccentricity of destiny, he—he himself——

In the midst of her hideous pain a sweet and joyous sound fell upon her ear. It was the voice of the child, who had awakened for a moment from her peaceful sleep:

"Will you not come into bed, Rani?"

"Yes, yes, dear, presently," she answered, and at the next moment the child's equal and tranquil breathing, so gentle, so calm, fell on her ear again.

Innocence is the most formidable of all spectacles that can confront an uneasy conscience, and when at length Helena got into bed, and the child, in the blind mists of sleep, put her arms about her neck, she had to justify herself by thinking that in everything she had done, everything she had tried to do, she had been moved by the incidents of the most irresistible provocation.

"After all, *he killed my father!*" she thought.

But nevertheless she felt again, as she was dropping off to sleep, that she was falling, falling, falling over the edge of a yawning precipice.

XI

WHEN Helena awoke next morning she was immediately conscious of a great commotion both within and without the house. After a moment Zenoba came into the bedroom and began to tell her what had happened.

"Have you not heard, O Rani?" said the Arab woman in her oily voice. "No? You sleep so late, do you? When everybody is up and doing, too! Well, the Master has news that the great Bedouin is at Omdurman, and he is sending the people down to the river to bring him up. The stranger is to be received in the mosque, I may tell you. Yes, indeed, in the mosque, although he is English and a Christian."

Then Ayesha came skipping into the room in wild excitement.

"Rani! Rani!" she cried. "Get up and come with us. We are going now—this minute—everybody!"

Helena excused herself—she felt unwell and would stay in bed that day; so the child and the nurse went off without her.

Yet left alone she could not rest. The feverish uncertainty of the night before returned with redoubled force, and after a while she felt compelled to rise.

Going into the guest-room she found the house empty
and the camp in front of it deserted. She was standing by
the door, hardly knowing what to do, when the strange sound
which she had heard on the night of the betrothal came from
a distance:

"Lu-lu-lu-u-u!"

It was the zaghareet, the women's cry of joy, and it
was mingled with the louder shouts of men. The stranger
was coming, the people were bringing him on. Who would
he be? Helena's anxiety was almost more than her brain
and nerves could bear. She strained her eyes in the direction of the jetty, past the Abbas Barracks and the Mongers
Fort.

The moments passed like hours, but at length the crowd
appeared. At first sight it looked like a forest of small
trees approaching. The forest seemed to sway and to send
out monotonous sounds, as if moved by a moaning wind.
But looking again, Helena saw what was happening—the
people were carrying green palm branches and strewing them
on the yellow sand in front of the great stranger.

He was riding on a white camel, Ishmael's camel, and
Ishmael was riding beside him. Long before he came near
to her Helena saw him, straining her sight to do so. He
was wearing the ample robes of a Bedouin and his face was
almost hidden by the sweeping shawl (the kufiah) which covered his head and neck.

But it was *he!* It was Gordon! Helena could not mistake him. One glance was enough. Without looking a
second time she ran back to her bedroom and covered her
eyes and ears.

For a time the voices of the people followed her through
the deadening walls.

"Lu-lu-u-u!" cried the women.

"La ilaha illa-llah! La ilaha illa-llah!" shouted the
men.

But after a while the muffled sounds died away, and
Helena knew that the great company had passed on to the
mosque. It was like a dream, a mirage of the mind. It
had come, and it was gone, and in the dazed condition of

her senses she could almost persuade herself that she had imagined everything.

Her impatience would not permit her to remain in the house. She, too, must go to the mosque, although she had never been there before. So, putting on her Indian veil, she set out hurriedly. When she came to herself again she was in the gallery, people were making way for her, and she was dropping into a place. Then she realised that she was sitting between Zenoba and little Ayesha.

The mosque was a large, four-square edifice, full of col, umns and arches, and with a kind of inner court that was open to the sky and had minarets at every corner. The gallery looked down on this court, and Helena saw below her, half in shadow, half in sunshine, the heads of a great concourse of men in turbans, tarbooshes, and brown felt skull-caps, all kneeling in rows on bright red carpets. In the front row, with his face toward the Kibleh (the niche toward Mecca), Ishmael knelt in his white caftan, and by his side, with all eyes upon him, as if every interest centred on that spot, knelt the stranger in Bedouin dress.

It was Friday and prayers were proceeding, now surging like the sea, now silent like the desert, sometimes started, as it seemed, by the voice of the unseen muezzin on the minarets above, then echoed by the men on the carpets below, but Helena hardly heard them. Of one thing only was she conscious—that by the tragic play of destiny *he* was there while *she* was here.

After a while she became aware that Ishmael had risen and was beginning to speak, and she tried to regain composure enough to listen to what he said.

"My brothers," he said, "it is according to the precepts of the Prophet—peace to his name!—to receive the Christian in our temples if he comes with the good-will of good Moslems and with a heart that is true to them. You know, oh, my brothers, whether I am a Moslem or not, and I pray to the Most Merciful to bless all such Christians as the one who is here to-day."

More of the same kind Ishmael said, but Helena found it hard, in the tumult of her brain, to follow him. She

saw that both the women about her and the men below were
seized with that religious fervour which comes to the human soul when it feels that something grand is being done.
It was as though the memory of a thousand years of hatred
between Moslem and Christian, with all its legacy of cruelty
and barbarity, had been wiped out of their hearts by the
stranger on whom their eyes were fixed—as though by some
great act of self-sacrifice and brotherhood he had united
East and West—and this fact of his presence at their
prayers was the sign and symbol of an eternal truce.

The sublime spectacle seemed to capture all their souls,
and when Ishmael turned toward the stranger at last and
laid his hand on his head and said, "May God and His
prophet bless you for what you have done for us and ours,"
the emotions of the people were raised to the highest pitch,
and they rose to their feet as one man, and holding up their
hands they cried, the whole congregation together, in a
voice that was like the breaking of a great wave:

"You are now one of us, and we are of you, and we
are brothers!"

By this time the women in the gallery were weeping
audibly, and Helena, from quite other causes, was scarcely
able to control her feelings. "Why did I come here?" she
asked herself, and then, seeing that the Arab woman was
watching her through the slits of her jealous eyes, she got
up and pushed her way out of the mosque.

Back in her room, lying face down upon the bed, she
sought in vain to collect her faculties sufficiently to follow
and comprehend the course of events. Yes, it was Gordon.
He had come to join Ishmael. Why had she never thought
of that as a probable sequel to what had occurred in Cairo?
Had he not been turned out by his own?—in effect, cashiered
from the Army? Forbidden his father's house? And had
she not herself driven him away from her? What sequel was
more natural? More plainly inevitable?

Then she grew hot and cold at a new and still more
terrifying thought—Gordon would come *there!* How could
she meet him? How look into his face? A momentary
impulse to deny her own identity was put aside immedi-

ately. Impossible! Useless! Then how could she account to Gordon for her presence in that house? Ishmael's wife! According to Mohammedan law and custom not only betrothed but married to him!

When she put her position to herself so, the thread of her thoughts seemed to snap in her brain. She could not disentangle the knot of them. A sense of infidelity to Gordon, to the very spirit of love itself, brought her for a moment the self-reproach and the despair of a woman who has sinned.

In the midst of her pain she heard the light voices of people returning to the house, and at the next moment Ayesha and Zenoba came into her room. The child was skipping about, full of high spirits, and the Arab woman was almost bitterly merry.

"Rani will be happy to hear that the Master is bringing the stranger home," said Zenoba.

Helena turned and gazed at the woman with a stupefied expression. What she had foreseen as a terrifying possibility was about to come to pass! She opened her mouth as if to speak, but said nothing.

Meantime the Arab woman, in a significant tone that was meant to cut to the quick, went on to say that this was the highest honour the Moslem could show the unbeliever, as well as the greatest trust he could repose in him.

"Have you never heard of that in your country, O Rani? No? It is true, though. Quite true!"

People supposed that every Moslem guarded his house so jealously that no strange man might look upon his wife, but among the Arabs of the desert, when a traveller, tired and weary, sought food and rest, the Sheikh would sometimes send him into his harem and leave him there for three days, with full permission to do as he thought well.

"But he must never wrong that harem, O lady! If he does the Arab husband *will kill him!* Yes, and *the faithless wife as well!*"

So violent was the conflict going on within her that Helena hardly heard the woman's words, though the jealous spirit behind them was piercing her heart like needles. She became conscious of the great crowd returning, and it was making the same ululation as before, mingled with the same shouts. At the next moment there came a knock at the bed-room door, and Abdullah's voice, crying:

"Lady! Lady!"

Helena reeled a little in rising to reply, and it was with difficulty that she reached the door.

"Master has brought Sheikh Omar Benani back and is calling for the lady. What shall I say?"

Helena fumbled the hem of her handkerchief in her fingers as she was wont to do in moments of great agitation. She was asking herself what would happen if she obeyed Ishmael's summons. Would Gordon see through her motive in being there? If so, would he betray her to Ishmael?

Already she could hear a confused murmur in the guest-room, and out of that murmur her memory seemed to grasp back, as from a vanishing dream, the sound of a voice that had been lost to her.

She felt as if she were suffocating. Her breathing was coming rapidly from the depth of her throat. Yet the Arab woman was watching her, and while a whirlwind was going on within she had to preserve a complete tranquillity without.

"Say I am coming," she said.

The supreme moment had arrived. With a great effort she gathered up all her strength, drew her Indian shawl over her head in such a way that it partly concealed her face, and then, pallid, trembling, and with downcast eyes, she walked out of the room.

XII

GORDON had that day experienced emotions only less poignant than those of Helena. In the early morning, after parting with Osman, the devoted comrade of his desert journey, he had encountered the British Sub-Governor of Omdurman, a young captain of cavalry who had once served under himself, and now spoke to him, in his assumed character as a Bedouin, with a certain air of command.

This brought him some twinges of wounded pride, which were complicated by qualms of conscience, as he rode through the streets, past the silversmiths' shops, where grave-looking Arabs sold bracelets and necklets; past the weaving quarter, where men and boys were industriously driving the shuttle through the strings of their flimsy looms; past the potter's bazaar and the grain market, all so sweet and so free from their former smell of sun-dried filth and warm humanity packed close together.

"Am I coming here to oppose the power that in so few years has turned order into chaos?" he asked himself; but more personal emotions came later.

They came in full flood when the ferry steamer by which he crossed the river approached the bank on the other side, and he saw standing there, near to the spot on which the dervishes landed on the black night of the fall of Khartoum, a vast crowd of their sons and their sons' sons who were waiting to receive him.

Again came qualms of conscience, when out of this crowd stepped Ishmael Ameer, who kissed him on both cheeks and led him forward to his own camel amid the people's shouts of welcome. Was he, as a British soldier, throwing in his lot with the enemies of his country? As an Englishman and a Christian, was he siding with the adversaries of religion and civilisation?

The journey through the town to the mosque, with the lu-luing and the throwing of palm branches before his camel's feet, was less of a triumphant progress than an abject penance. He could hardly hold up his head. The sight of the bronze and black faces about him, shouting for him—for him of another race and creed—making that act his glory which had led to his crime—this was almost more than he could bear.

But when he reached the mosque; when he found himself, unbeliever though he was, kneeling in front of the Kibleh; when Ishmael laid his hand on his head and called on God to bless him, and the people cried with one voice,

"You are one of us and we are brothers," the sense of human sympathy swept down every other emotion and he felt as if at any moment he might burst into tears.

And then, when prayers were over and Ishmael brought up his uncle, and the patriarchal old man, with a beard like a flowing fleece, said he was to lodge at his house, and finally, when Ishmael led him home and took him to his own chamber and called to Abdullah to set up another angerib, saying they were to sleep in the same room, Gordon's twinges of pride and qualms of conscience were swallowed up in one great wave of human brotherhood.

But both came back with a sudden bound when Ishmael began to talk of his wife, and to send the servant to fetch her. They were sitting in the guest-room by this time, waiting for the lady to come to them, and Gordon felt himself moved by the inexplicable impulse of anxiety he had felt before. Who was this Mohammedan woman who had prompted Ishmael to a scheme that must so surely lead to disaster? Did she know what she was doing? Was she betraying him?

Then a door on the women's side of the house opened slowly and he saw a woman enter the room. He did not look into her face. His distrust of her, whereof he was now half ashamed, made him keep his head down while he bowed low during the little formal ceremony of Ishmael's presentation. But instantly a certain indefinite memory of height and step and general bearing made his blood flow fast, and he felt the perspiration breaking out on his forehead.

A moment afterward he raised his eyes, and then he felt as if his hair rose upright. He was like a man who has been made colour-blind by some bright light. He could not at first believe the evidence of his senses—that she who appeared to be there was actually before him.

He did not speak or utter a sound, but his embarrassment was not observed by Ishmael, who was clapping his hands to call for food. During the next few minutes there was a little confusion in the room—Black Zogal and Abdullah were laying a big brass tray on trestles and covering it with dishes. Then came the ablutions and the sitting down to eat—Gordon at the head of the table, with Ishmael on his right and old Mahmud on his left, and Helena next to Ishmael.

The meal began with the beautiful Eastern custom of the host handing the first mouthful of food to his guest as a pledge of peace and brotherhood, faith and trust. This kept Gordon occupied for the moment, but Helena had time for observation. In the midst of her agitation she could not help seeing that Gordon had grown thinner, that his eyes were bloodshot and his nostrils pinched as if by physical or moral suffering. After a while she saw that he was looking across at her with increasing eagerness, and under his glances she became nervous and almost hysterical.

Gordon on his part had now not the shadow of a doubt of Helena's identity, but still he did not speak. He, too, noticed a change—Helena's profile had grown more severe, and there were dark rims under her large eyes. He could not help seeing these signs of the pain she had gone through, though his mind was going like a windmill under constantly changing winds. Why was she there? Could it be that the great sorrow which fell upon her at the death of her father had made her fly to the consolation of religion?

He dismissed that thought the instant it came to him, for behind it, close behind it, came the recollection of Helena's hatred of Ishmael Ameer and of the jealousy which had been the first cause of the separation between themselves. "Smash the Mahdi!" she had said, not altogether in play. Then why was she there? Great God, could it be possible—that after the death of the General—she had——

Gordon felt at that moment as if the world were reeling round him.

Helena, glancing furtively across the table, was sure she could read Gordon's thoughts. With the certainty that he knew what had brought her to Khartoum, she felt at first a crushing sense of shame. What a fatality! If anybody had told her that she would be overwhelmed with confusion by the very person she had been trying to avenge, she would have thought him mad, yet that was precisely what Providence had permitted to come to pass.

The sense of her blindness and helplessness in the hands of destiny was so painful as to reach the point of tears. When Gordon spoke in reply to Ishmael's or old Mahmud's questions the very sound of his voice brought back memories of their happy days together, and, looking back on the past of their lives and thinking where they were now, she wanted to run away and cry.

All this time Ishmael saw nothing, for he was talking rapturously of the great hope, the great expectation, the near approach of the time when the people's sufferings would end. A sort of radiance was about him, and his face shone with the joy and the majesty of the dreamer in the full flood of his dream.

When the meal was over, the old man, who had been too busy with his food to see anything else, went off to his siesta, and then, the dishes being removed and the servants gone, Ishmael talked in lower tones of the details of his scheme—how he was to go into Cairo in advance, in the habit of a Bedouin such as Gordon wore, in order to win the confidence of the Egyptian Army, so that they should throw down the arms which no man ought to bear, and thus permit the people of the pilgrimage, coming behind, to take possession of the city, the citadel, the arsenal, and the engines of war, in the name of God and His Expected One.

All this he poured out in the rapturous language of one who saw no impediments, no dangers, no perils from chance or treachery, and then, turning to where Helena sat with her face aflame and her eyes cast down, he gave her the credit of everything that had been thought of, everything that was to be done.

"Yes, it was the Rani who suggested it," he said; "and when the triumph of peace is won, God will write it on her forehead."

The afternoon had passed by this time, and the sun, which had gone far round to the west, was glistening like hammered gold along the river, in the line of the forts of Omdurman. It was near to the hour for evening prayers, and Helena was now trembling under a new thought—the thought that Ishmael would soon be called out to speak to the people who gathered in the evening in front of the house, and then she and Gordon would be left alone.

When she thought of that she felt a desire which she had never felt before and never expected to feel—a desire that Ishmael might remain to protect her from the shock of the first word that would be spoken when he was gone

Gordon on his part, too, was feeling a thrill of the heart from his fear of the truth that must fall on him the moment he and Helena were left together.

But Black Zogal came to the open door of the guest-room, and Ishmael, who was still on the heights of his fanatical rapture, rose to go.

"Talk to him, Rani! Tell him everything! About the kufiah you intend to make, and all the good plan you propose to prevent bloodshed."

The two unhappy souls, still sitting at the empty table, heard his sandalled footsteps pass out behind them.

Then they raised their eyes, and for the first time looked into each other's faces.

XIII

WHEN they began to speak it was in scarcely audible whispers:

"Helena!"

"Gordon!"

"Why are you here, Helena? What have you come for? You disliked and distrusted Ishmael Ameer when you heard about him first. You used to say you hated him. What does it all mean?"

Helena did not answer immediately.

"Tell me, Helena. Don't let me go on thinking these cruel thoughts. Why are you here with Ishmael in Khartoum?"

Still Helena did not answer. She was now sitting with her eyes down, and her hands tightly folded in her lap. There was a moment of silence while he waited for her to speak, and in that silence there came the muffled sound of Ishmael's voice outside, reciting the Fatihah:

"Praise be to God, the Lord of all creatures——"

When the whole body of the people had repeated the solemn words there was silence in the guest-room again, and then, in the same hushed whisper as before, but more eagerly, more impetuously, Gordon said:

"He says you put this scheme into his mind, Helena. If so, you must know quite well what it will lead to. It will lead to ruin—inevitable ruin—bloodshed—perhaps great bloodshed."

Helena found her voice at last. A spirit of defiance took possession of her for a moment, and she said firmly:

"No, it will never come to that. It will all end before it goes so far."

"You mean that he will be—will be *taken?*"

"Yes, he will be taken the moment he sets foot in Cairo. Therefore the rest of the plan will never be carried out, and consequently there will be no bloodshed."

"Do you *know* that, Helena?"

Her lips were compressed; she made a silent motion of her head.

"*How* do you know it?"

"I have written to your father."

"You have—written—to my father?"

"Yes," she said, still more firmly. "He will know everything before Ishmael arrives, and act as he thinks best."

"Helena! Hel——"

But he was struck breathless both by what she said and by the relentless strength with which she said it. There was silence again for some moments, and once more in the silence the voice of Ishmael came from without:

"There are three holy books, oh, my brothers—the book of Moses and the Hebrew prophets; the book of the Gospel of the Lord Jesus, and the plain book of the Koran. In the first of these it is written: 'I know that my Redeemer liveth and that he shall stand at the latter day upon the earth.'"

Gordon reached over to where Helena sat at the side of the table, with her eyes fixed steadfastly before her, and, touching her arm, he said in a whisper so low that he seemed to be afraid the very air would hear:

"Then—then—you are sending him *to his death!*"

She shuddered for an instant, as if cut to the quick; then she braced herself up.

"Isn't that so, Helena? Isn't it?"

With her lips still firmly compressed she made the same silent motion of her head.

"Is that what you came here to do?"

"Yes."

"To possess yourself of his secrets, and then——"

"There was no other way," she answered, biting her under lip.

"Helena! Can it be possible that you have deliberately——"

He stopped, as if afraid to utter the word that was trembling on his tongue, and then said, in a softer voice:

"But why, Helena? Why?"

The spirit of defiance took possession of her again, and she said:

"Wasn't it enough that he came between you and me, and that our love——"

"Love! Helena! Helena! Can you talk of our love *here—now?*"

She dropped her head before his flashing eyes, and again he reached over to her and said, in the same breathless whisper:

"Is *this* love—for me—to become the wife of another man— Helena, what are you saying?"

She did not speak; only her hard breathing told how much she suffered.

"Then think of the other man! His wife! When a woman becomes a man's wife they are one. And to marry a man in order to—to— Oh, it is impossible! I cannot believe it of you, Helena!"

Suddenly, without warning, she burst into tears, for something in the tone of his voice, rather than the strength of his words, had made her feel the shame of the position she occupied in his eyes.

After a moment she recovered herself, and, in wild anger at her own weakness, she flamed out at him, saying that if she was Ishmael's wife it was in name only; that if she had married Ishmael it was only as a matter of form, at best a betrothal, in order to meet his own wish and to make it possible for her to go on with her purpose.

"As for love—*our* love—it is not *I* who have been false to it. No, never for one single moment—although—in spite of everything—for even when you were gone—when you had abandoned me—in the hour of my trouble, too—and I had lost all hope of you—I——"

"Then why, Helena? You hated Ishmael and wished to put him down while you thought he was coming between you and me. But why—when all seemed to be over between us——"

Her lips were twitching and her eyes were ablaze.

"You ask me why I wished to punish him?" she said. "Very well, I will tell you. Because—" she paused, hesitated, breathed hard, and then said, "because *he killed my father!*"

Gordon gasped, his face became distorted, his lips grew pale, he tried to speak, but could only stammer out broken exclamations.

"Great God! Hele——"

"Oh, you may not believe it, but I *know*," said Helena. And then, with a rush of emotion, in a torrent of hot words, she told him how Ishmael Ameer had been the last man seen in her father's company; how *she* had seen them together and they were quarrelling; how her father had been found dead a few minutes after Ishmael had left him; how *she* had found him; how other evidence gave proof, abundant proof, that violence, as a contributory means at least, had been the cause of her father's death; and how the authorities knew this perfectly, but were afraid, in the absence of conclusive evidence, to risk a charge against one whom the people in their blindness worshipped.

"So I was left alone—quite alone—for you were gone,

too—and therefore I vowed that if there was no one else.
I would punish him!"

"And that is what you——"

"Yes."

"Oh, God! Oh, God!"

Gordon hid his face in his hands, being made speechless
by the awful strength of the blind force which had governed her life and led her on to the tragic tangle of her
error. But she misunderstood his feeling, and with flashing, almost blazing, eyes, though sobs choked her voice for
a moment, she turned on him and said:

"Why not? Think of what my father had been to me,
and say if I was not justified. Nobody ever loved me as
he did—nobody. He was old, too, and weak, for he was ill,
though nobody knew it. And then this—this barbarian—
this hypocritical— Oh, when I think of it I have such a
feeling of physical repulsion for the man that I can scarcely
sit by his side!"

Saying this she rose to her feet, and, standing before
Gordon, as he sat with his face covered by his hands, she
said with intense bitterness, as if exulting in the righteousness of her vengeance:

"Let him go to Damietta, or to death itself, if need be!
Doesn't he deserve it? Doesn't he? Uncover your face
and tell me. Tell me if—if—tell me if——"

She was approaching Gordon as if to draw away his
hands, when she began to gasp and stammer as though she
had experienced a sudden electric shock. Her eyes had
fallen on the third finger of his left hand, and they fixed
themselves upon it with the fascination of fear. She saw
that it was shorter than the rest, and that, since she had
seen it before, it had been injured and amputated.

Her breath, which had been labouring heavily, seemed to
stop altogether, and there was silence once more in which
the voice of Ishmael came again:

"When the Deliverer comes, will He find peace on the
earth? Will He find war? Will He find corruption and the
worship of false gods? Will He find hatred and vengeance?
Beware of vengeance, oh, my brothers! It corrupts the heart;

it pulls down the pillars of the soul! Vengeance belongs to God, and when men take it out of His hands He writes black marks upon their faces."

The two unhappy people sitting together in the guest-room seemed to hear their very hearts beat. At length Gordon, making a great call on his resolution, began to speak:

" Helena! "

" Well? "

" It is all a mistake—a fearful, frightful mistake."

She listened without drawing breath—a vague foreshadowing of the truth coming over her.

" Ishmael Ameer did not kill your father."

Her lips trembled convulsively; she grew paler and paler every moment.

" I know he did not, Helena, because "—he covered his face again—" because I know who did."

" Then who—who was it? "

" He did not intend to do it, Helena."

" Who was it? "

" It was all in the heat of blood."

" Who was—— "

He hesitated, then stammered out: " Don't you see, Helena?—it was I."

She had known in advance what he was going to say, but not until he had said it did the whole truth fall on her. Then in a moment the world itself seemed to reel. A moral earthquake, upheaving everything, had brought all her aims to ashes. The mighty force which had guided and sustained her soul—the sense of doing a necessary and a righteous thing—had collapsed without an instant's warning. Another force, the powerful, almost brutal force of fate, had broken it to pieces.

" My God! My God! What has become of me? " she thought, and without speaking she gazed blankly at Gordon as he sat with his eyes hidden by his injured hand.

Then in broken words, with gasps of breath, he told her what had happened, beginning with the torture of his separation from her at the door of the General's house.

" You said I had not really loved you—that you had

been mistaken and were punished, and—and that was the end."

Going away with the memory of these words in his mind, his wretched soul had been on the edge of a vortex of madness, in which all its anger, all its hatred, had been directed against the General. In the blind leading of his passion, torn to the heart's core, he had then returned to the Citadel to accuse the General of injustice and tyranny.

" 'Helena was mine,' I said, 'and you have taken her from me, and broken her heart as well as my own. Is that the act of a father?' "

Other words he had also said in the delirium of his rage, mad and insulting words such as no father could bear, and then the General had snatched up the broken sword from the floor and fallen on him, hacking at his hand—see!

"I didn't want to do it, God knows I did not, for he was an old man and I was no coward; but the hot blood was in my head, and I laid hold of him by the throat to hold him off."

He uncovered his face—it was full of humility and pain.

"God forgive me, I didn't know my strength. I flung him away; he fell. I had killed him—my General, my friend!"

Tears filled his eyes. In her eyes also tears were gathering.

"Then you came to the door and knocked. 'Father!' you said. 'Are you alone? May I come in?' Those were your words, and how often I have heard them since! In the middle of the night, in my dreams, oh, God, how many times!"

He dropped his head and stretched a helpless arm along the table.

"I wanted to open the door and say, 'Helena, forgive me, I didn't mean to do it, and that is the truth, as God is my witness!' But I was afraid—I fled away."

She was now sitting with her hands clasped in her lap and her eyelids tightly closed.

"Next day I wanted to go back to you, but I dared not do so. I wanted to comfort you—I could not. I wanted to give myself up to justice—it was impossible. There was nothing for me to do except to fly away."

The tears were rolling down his thin face to his pinched nostrils.

" But I could not fly from myself or from—from my love for you. They told me you had gone to England. 'Where is she to-night?' I thought. If I had never really loved you before, I loved you now. And you were gone! I had lost you for ever!"

Emotion choked his voice; tears were forcing themselves through her closed eyelids. There was another moment of silence, and then nervously, hesitatingly, she put out her hand to where his hand was lying on the table and clasped it.

The two unhappy creatures, like wrecked souls about to be swallowed up in a tempestuous ocean, saw one raft of hope—their love for each other, which had survived all the storms of their fate.

But just as their hands were burning, as if with fever, and quivering in each other's clasp, like the bosom of a captured bird, a voice from without fell on their ears like a trumpet from the skies. It was the voice of the muezzin calling to evening prayers from the minaret of the neighbouring mosque:

AL-LA-HU AK-BAR.　　AL-LA - - HU AK-BAR.
God is Most Great!　　　God is Most Great!

It seemed to be a supernatural voice, the voice of an accusing angel, calling them back to their present position. Ishmael—Helena—the betrothal!

Their hands separated and they rose to their feet. One moment they stood with bowed heads at opposite sides of the table, listening to the voice outside, and then, without a word more, they went their different ways—he to his room, she to hers.

Into the empty guest-room a moment afterward came

22

the rumbling and rolling sound of the voices of the people repeating the Fatihah after Ishmael:

"Praise be to God, the Lord of all creatures! . . . Direct us in the right way, O Lord! . . . not the way of those who go astray."

XIV

THAT day the Sirdar had held his secret meeting of the Ulema, the Sheikhs and Notables of Khartoum. Into a room on the ground floor of the Palace, down a dark, arched corridor, in which British soldiers stood on guard, they had been introduced one by one—a group of six or eight unkempt creatures of varying ages, and of differing degrees of intelligence, nearly all wearing the farageeyah, the loose gray robe as of a Moslem monk.

They sat awkwardly on the chairs which had been ranged for them about a mahogany table, and while they waited they talked in whispers. There was a tense, electrical atmosphere among them, as of internal dissension, the rumbling of a sort of subterranean thunder.

But this subsided instantly, when the voice of the serjeant outside, and the clash of saluting arms, announced the coming of the Sirdar. The Governor-General, who was in uniform and booted and spurred as if returning from a ride, was accompanied by his Inspector-General, his Financial Secretary, the Governor of the town and various minor officers.

He was received by the Sheikhs, all standing, with sweeping salaams from floor to forehead, a circle of smiles and looks of complete accord.

The Sirdar, with his ruddy and cheerful face, took his seat at the head of the table and began by asking, as if casually, who was the stranger that had arrived that day in Khartoum.

"A Bedouin," said the Cadi. "One whom Ishmael Ameer loves and who loves him."

"Yet a *Bedouin*, you say?" asked the Sirdar, in an incredulous tone, and with a certain elevation of the eyebrows.

"A Bedouin, O Excellency!" repeated the Cadi, whereupon the others, without a word of further explanation, bent their turbaned heads in assent.

Then the Sirdar explained the reason for which he had called them together.

"I am given to understand," he said, "that the idea is abroad that the Government has been trying to introduce changes into the immutable law of Islam, which forms an integral part of your Moslem religion and is therefore rightly regarded with a high degree of veneration by all followers of the Prophet. If anybody is telling you this, or if any one is saying that there is any prejudice against you because you are Mohammedans, he is a wicked and mischievous person, and I beg of you to tell me who he is."

Saying this, the Sirdar looked sharply round the table, but met nothing there but blank and expressionless faces. Then turning to the Cadi, who, as Chief Judge of the Mohammedan law-courts, had been constituted spokesman, he asked pointedly what Ishmael Ameer was saying.

"Nothing, O Excellency!" said the Cadi; "nothing that is contrary to the Sharia—the religious law of Islam."

"Is he telling the people to resist the Government?"

The grave company about the table silently shook their heads.

"Do you know if he has anything to do with a conspiracy to resist the payment of taxes?"

The grave company knew nothing.

"Then what is he doing, and why has he come to Khartoum? Pasha, have *you* no explanation to make to me?" asked the Sirdar, singling out a vivacious old gentleman, with a short, white, carefully oiled beard—a person of doubtful repute who had once been a slave-dealer and was now living patriarchally, under the protection of the Government, with his many wives and concubines.

The old black sinner cast his little glittering eyes around the room and then said:

"If you ask me, O Master, I say, Ishmael Ameer is putting down polygamy and divorce and ought himself to be put down."

At that there was some clamour among the Ulema, and the Sirdar thought he saw a rift through which he might discover the truth, but the Pasha was soon silenced, and in a moment there was the same unanimity as before.

"Then *what* is he?" asked the Sirdar. Whereupon a venerable old Sheikh, after the usual Arabic compliments and apologies, said that having seen the new teacher with his own eyes and talked with him, he had now not the slightest doubt that Ishmael was a man sent from God, and therefore that all who resisted him, all who tried to put him down, would perish miserably.

At these words the electrical atmosphere which had been held in subjection seemed to burst into flame. In a moment six tongues were talking together. One Sheikh, with wild eyes, told of Ishmael's intercourse with angels. Another knew a man who had seen him riding with the Prophet in the desert. A third had spoken to somebody who had seen angels, in the form of doves, descending upon him from the skies, and a fourth was ready to swear that one day while Ishmael was preaching in the mosque people heard a voice from heaven crying, "Hear him! He is my messenger!"

"What was he preaching about?" said the Sirdar.

"The last days, the coming of the Deliverer," said the Sheikh with the wild eyes, in an awesome whisper.

"What Deliverer?"

"The Shaidna Isa—the Lord Jesus—the White Christ that is to come."

"Is this to be soon?"

"Soon, O Excellency! very soon."

After this outburst there was a moment of tense and breathless silence, during which the Sirdar sat with his serious eyes fixed on the table, and his officers, standing behind, glanced at each other and smiled.

A moment afterward the Sirdar put an end to the interview.

"Tell your people," he said, "that the Government has no wish to interfere with your religious beliefs and feelings, whatever they may be; but tell them also, that it intends to have its orders obeyed, and that any suspicion of conspiracy, still more rebellion, will be instantly put down."

The group of unkempt creatures went off with sweeping salaams, and then the Sirdar dismissed his officers also, saying:

"Bear in mind that you are the recognized agents of a just and merciful Government, and whatever your personal opinions may be of these Arabs and their superstitions, please understand that you are to give no anti-Islamic colour to your British feelings. At the same time remember that we have worked for the redemption of the Soudan from a state of savagery, and we cannot allow it to be turned back to barbarism in the name of religion."

Both the Ulema and the other British officials being gone, the Sirdar was alone with his Inspector-General.

"Well?" he said.

"Well?" repeated the Inspector-General, biting the ends of his close-cropped mustache. "What more did you expect, sir? Naturally the man's own people were not going to give him away. They nearly did so, though. You heard what old Zewar Pasha said?"

"Tut! I take no account of that," said the Sirdar. "The brothers of Christ Himself would have put Him down, too—locked Him up in an asylum, I dare say."

"That's exactly what I would do with Ishmael Ameer anyway," said the Inspector-General. "Of course he performs no miracles, and is attended by no angels. His removal to Torah, and his inability to free himself from a government jail, would soon dispel the belief in his supernatural agencies."

"But how can we do it? Under what pretext? We can't imprison a man for preaching the second coming of Christ. If we did, our jails would be pretty full at home, I'm thinking."

The Inspector-General laughed. "Your old error, dear

Sirdar. You can't apply the same principles to East and West."

"And your old Parliamentary cant, dear Pasha! I'm sick to death of it."

There was a moment of strained silence and then the Inspector-General said:

"Ah, well, I know these holy men, with their sham inspirations and their so-called heavenly messages. They develop by degrees, sir. This one has begun by proclaiming the advent of the Lord Jesus, and he will end by hoisting a flag and claiming to be the Lord Jesus himself."

"When he does that, Colonel, we'll consider our position afresh. Meantime it may do us no mischief to remember that if the family of Jesus could have dealt with the Founder of our own religion as you would deal with this olive-faced Arab, there would probably be no Christianity in the world to-day."

The Inspector-General shrugged his shoulders and rose to go.

"Good-night, sir."

"Good-night, Colonel," said the Sirdar, and then he sat down to draft a despatch to the Consul-General:

"Nothing to report since the marriage, betrothal, or whatever it was, of the 'Rani' to the man in question. Undoubtedly he is laying a strong hold on the imagination of the natives and acquiring the allegiance of large bodies of workers; but I cannot connect him with any conspiracy to persuade people not to pay taxes or with any organised scheme that is frankly hostile to the continuance of British rule.

"Will continue to watch him, but find myself at fearful odds owing to difference of faith. It is one of the disadvantages of Christian governments among people of alien race and religion that methods of revolt are not always visible to the naked eye, and God knows what is going on in the sealed chambers of the mosque.

"That only shows the danger of curtailing the liberty of the vernacular press, whatever the violence of its spo-

radic and muddled anarchy. Leave the press alone, I say.
Instead of chloroforming it into silence give it a tonic if
need be, or you drive your trouble underground. Such is
the common sense and practical wisdom of how to deal
with sedition in a Mohammedan country, let some of the
logger-headed dunces who write leading articles in England say what they will.

"If this man should develop supernatural pretensions
I shall know what to do. And without that, whether he
claim divine inspiration or not, if his people should come
to regard him as divine, the very name and idea of his
divinity may become a danger and I suppose I shall have
to put him under arrest."

Then remembering that he was addressing not only the
Consul-General, but a friend, the Sirdar wrote:

"'Art Thou a King?' Strange that the question of
Pontius Pilate is precisely what we may find in our own
mouths soon! And stranger still, almost ludicrous, even
farcical and hideously ironical, that though for two thousand years Christendom has been spitting on the pusillan-
imity of the old pagan, the representative of a Christian
Empire will have to do precisely what he did.

"Short of Pilate's situation, though, I see no right to
take this man, so I am not taking him. Sorry to tell you
so, but I cannot help it.

"Our love from both to both. Trust Janet is feeling
better. No news of our poor boy, I suppose?"

"Our boy" had for thirty years been another name for
Gordon.

XV

GRAVE as was the gathering in the Sirdar's Palace at
Khartoum there was a still graver gathering that day in
the British Agency at Cairo—the gathering of the wings
of Death.

Lady Nuneham was nearing her end. Since Gordon's

disgrace and disappearance she had been visibly fading away under a burden too heavy for her to bear.

The Consul-General had been trying hard to shut his eyes to this fact. More than ever before he had immersed himself in his work, being plainly impelled to fresh effort by hatred of the man who had robbed him of his son.

Through the Soudan Intelligence Department in Cairo he had watched Ishmael's movements in Khartoum, expecting him to develop the traits of the Mahdi and thus throw himself into the hands of the Sirdar.

It was a deep disappointment to the Consul-General that this did not occur. The same report came to him again and again. The man was doing nothing to justify his arrest. Although surrounded by fanatical folk whose minds were easily inflamed, he was not trying to upset Governors or giving divine sanction for the removal of officials.

But meantime some mischief was manifestly at work all over the country. From day to day Inspectors had been coming in to say that the people were not paying their taxes. Convinced that this was the result of conspiracy the Consul-General had shown no mercy.

"Sell them up," he had said, and the Inspectors, taking their cue from his own spirit but exceeding his orders, had done his work without remorse.

Week by week the trouble had deepened, and when disturbances had been threatened he had asked the British Army of Occupation, meaning no violence, to go out into the country and show the people England's power.

Then grumblings had come down on him from the representatives of foreign nations. If the people were so discontented with British rule that they were refusing to pay their taxes there would be a deficit in the Egyptian treasury—how then were Egypt's creditors to be paid?

"Time enough to cross the bridge when you come to it, gentlemen," said the Consul-General, in his stinging tone and with a curl of his iron lip.

If the worst came to the worst England would pay, but England should not be asked to do so, because Egypt must meet the cost of her own Government. Hence more distraining and some inevitable violence in suppressing the riots that resulted from evictions.

Finally came a hubbub in Parliament, with the customary "Christian" prattlers prating again. Fools! They did not know what a subtle and secret conspiracy he had to deal with while they were crying out against his means of killing it.

He *must* kill it! This form of passive resistance, this attack on the Treasury, was the deadliest blow that had ever yet been aimed at England's power in Egypt.

But he must not let Europe see it! He must make believe that nothing was happening to occasion the least alarm. Therefore to drown the cries of the people who were suffering, not because they were poor and could not pay, but because they were perverse and would not, he must organise some immense demonstration.

Thus came to the Consul-General the schemes of the great festival of the ——th anniversary of the British occupation of Egypt. It would do good to foreign powers, for it would make them feel that, not for the first time, England had been the torch-bearer of light in a dark country. It would do good to the Egyptians, too, for it would force their youngsters (born since Tel-el-Kebir) to realise the strength of England's arm.

Thus had the Consul-General occupied himself while his wife was fading away. But at length he had been compelled to see that the end was near, and toward the close of every day he had gone to her room and sat almost in silence, with bowed head, in the chair by her side.

The great man who for forty years had been the virtual ruler of countless millions, had no wisdom that told him what to say to a dying woman; but at last, seeing that her pallor had become whiteness, and that she was sinking rapidly and hungering for the consolations of her religion, he asked her if she would like to take the sacrament.

"It is just what I wish, dear," she answered, with the nervous smile of one who had been afraid to ask.

At heart the Consul-General had been an agnostic all

23

his life, looking upon religion as no better than a civilising superstition, but all the same he went downstairs and sent one of his Secretaries for the Chaplain of St. Mary's—the English Church.

The moment he had gone out of the door Fatimah, under the direction of the dying woman, began to prepare the bedroom for the reception of the clergyman by laying a side-table with a fair white cloth, a large prayer-book, and two silver candlesticks containing new candles.

While the Egyptian nurse did this the old lady looked on with her deep, slow, weary eyes, and talked in whispers, as if the wings of the august Presence that was soon to come were already rustling in the room. When all was done she looked very happy.

"Everything is nice and comfortable now," she said, as she lay back to wait for the clergyman.

But even then she could not help thinking the one thought that made a tug at her resignation. It was about Gordon.

"I am quite ready to die, Fatimah," she said, "but I should have loved to see my dear Gordon once more."

This was what she had been waiting for, praying for, eating her heart and her life out for.

"Only to see and kiss my boy! It would have been so easy to go then."

Fatimah, who was snuffling audibly, as she straightened the eiderdown coverlet over the bed, began to hint that if her "sweet eyes" could not see her son she could send him a message.

"Perhaps I know somebody who could see it reaches him, too," said Fatimah, in a husky whisper.

The old lady understood her instantly.

"You mean Hafiz! I always thought as much. Bring me my writing-case, quick!"

The writing-case was brought and laid open before her, and she made some effort to write a letter, but the power of life was low in her, and after a moment the shaking pen dropped from her fingers.

"*Ma'aleysh*, my lady!" said Fatimah soothingly. "Tell me what you wish to say. I will remember everything."

Then the dying mother sent a few touching words as her last message to her beloved son.

"Wait! Let me think. My head is a little—just a little— Yes, this is what I wish to say, Fatimah. Tell my boy that my last thoughts were about him. Though I am sorry he took the side of the false prophet, say I am certain he did what he thought was right. Be sure you tell him I die happy, because I know I shall see him again. If I am never to see him in this world I will do so in the world to come. Say I shall be waiting for him there. And tell him it will not seem long."

"Could you sign your name for him, my heart?" said Fatimah, in her husky voice.

"Yes, oh, yes, easily," said the old lady, and then with an awful effort she wrote:

"Your ever-loving Mother."

At that moment Ibrahim in his green caftan, carrying a small black bag, brought the English Chaplain into the room.

"Peace be to this house," said the clergyman, using the words of his Church ritual, and the Egyptian nurse, thinking it was an Eastern salutation, answered, "Peace!"

The Chaplain went into the "boys' room" to put on his surplice, and when he came out of it robed in white, and began to light the candles and prepare the vessels which he placed on the side-table, the old lady was talking to Fatimah in nervous whispers:

"His lordship?" "Yes!" "Do you think, my lady——"

She wanted the Consul-General to be present and was half afraid to send for him; but just at that instant the door opened again, and her pale, spiritual face lit up with a smile as she saw her husband come into the room.

The clergyman was now ready to begin, and the old lady looked timidly across the bed at the Consul-General, as if there were something she wished to ask and dare not.

"Yes, I will take the sacrament with you, Janet," said

the old man, and then the old lady's face shone like the face of an angel.

The Consul-General took the chair by the side of the bed and the chaplain began the service:

" Almighty, ever-living God, Maker of mankind, Who dost correct those Thou dost love——"

All the time the tremendous words reverberated through the room the dying woman was praying fervently, her lips moving to her unspoken words and her eyes shining as if the Lord of Life she had always loved was with her now and she was giving herself to Him—her soul, her all.

The Consul-General was praying, too—praying for the first time to the God he did not know and had never looked to:

" If Thou art God, let her die in peace. It is all I ask —all I wish."

Thus the two old people took the sacrament together, and when the Communion Service came to a close, the old lady looked again at the Consul-General and asked, with a little confusion, if they might sing a hymn.

The old man bent his head, and a moment later the Chaplain, after a whispered word from the dying woman, began to sing:

> " Sun of my soul, Thou Saviour dear,
> It is not night if Thou be near . . ."

At the second bar the old lady joined him in her breaking, cracking voice, and then the Consul-General, too, albeit his throat was choking him, forced himself to sing with her.

> " When the soft dews of kindly sleep
> My wearied eyelids gently steep . . ."

It was as much as the Consul-General could do to sing of a faith he did not feel, but he felt tenderly to it for his wife's sake now, and with a great effort he went on with her to the end:

> " If some poor wandering child of thine
> Have spurned to-day the voice divine . . ."

The light of another world was in the old lady's eyes when all was over, and she seemed to be already halfway to heaven.

XVI

ALL the same there was a sweet humanity left in her, too, and when the Chaplain was gone and the side-table had been cleared, and she was left alone with her old husband, there came little gleams of the woman who wanted to be loved to the last.

"How are you now?" he asked.

"Better, so much better," she said, smiling upon him, and caressing with her wrinkled hand the other wrinkled hand that lay on the eiderdown quilt.

The great Consul-General, sitting on the chair by the side of the bed, felt as helpless as before, as ignorant as ever of what millions of simple people know—how to talk to those they love when the wings of death are hovering over them; but the sweet old lady, with the wisdom and the courage which God gives to His own on the verge of eternity, began to speak in a lively and natural voice of the end that was coming and what was to follow it.

He was not to allow any of his arrangements to be interfered with, and, above all, the festivities appointed for the King's Birthday were not to be disturbed.

"They must be necessary or you would not have them, especially now," she said, "and I shall not be happy if I know that on my account they are not coming off."

And then, with the sweet childishness which the feebleness of illness brings, she talked of the last King's Birthday, and of the ball they had given in honour of it.

That had been in their own house, and the dancing had been in the drawing-room, and the Consul-General had told Ibrahim to set the big green arm-chair for her in the alcove, and sitting there she had seen everything. What a spectacle! Such gorgeous uniforms! Such glittering orders! Such beautiful toilettes! Ministers Plenipotentiary, Egyptian Ministers, ladies, soldiers!

The old lady's pale face filled with light as she thought of all this, but the Consul-General dropped his head, for he knew well what was coming next.

"And, John, don't you remember? Gordon was there that night, and Helena—dear Helena! How lovely they looked! Among all those lovely people, dear. He was wearing every one of his medals that night, you know. So tall, so brave-looking, a soldier every inch of him, and such a perfect English gentleman! Was there ever anything in the world so beautiful? And Helena, too! She wore a silvery silk, and a kind of coif on her beautiful black hair. Oh, she was the loveliest thing in all the room, I thought! And when they led the cotillon—don't you remember they led the cotillon, dear?—I could have cried, I was so proud of them."

The Consul-General continued to sit with his head down, listening to the old lady and saying nothing, yet seeing the scene as she depicted it and feeling again the tingling pride which he, too, had felt but permitted nobody that night to know.

After a moment the beaming face on the bed became clouded over as if that memory had brought other memories less easy to bear—dreams of happy days to come, of honours, and of children.

"Ah, well, God knows best," she said in a tremulous voice, releasing the Consul-General's hand and ceasing to speak.

The old man felt as if he would have to hurry out of the room without uttering another word, but as well as he could he controlled himself and said:

"You are agitating yourself, Janet. You must lie quiet now."

"Yes, I must lie quiet now, and think of—of other things," she answered.

He was stepping away when she called on him to turn her on her right side, for that was how she always slept, and upon the Egyptian nurse coming hurrying up to help, she said:

"No, no, not you, Fatimah—his lordship."

Then the Consul-General put his arms about her—feeling how thin and wasted she was and how little of her was left to die—and turning her gently round he laid her back on the pillow which Fatimah had in the meantime shaken out.

While he did so her dim eyes brightened again, and stretching her white hands out of her silk nightdress, she clasped them about his neck with the last tender effort of the woman who wanted to be fondled to the last.

The strain of talking had been too much for her, and after a few minutes she sank into a restless doze in which the perspiration broke out on her forehead and her face acquired an expression of pain, for sleep knows no pretences. But at length her features became more composed and her breathing more regular, and then the Consul-General, who had been standing aside, mute with anguish, said in a low tone to Fatimah:

"She is sleeping quietly now," and then he turned to go.

Fatimah followed him to the head of the stairs and said in her husky whisper:

"It will be all over to-night, though—you'll see it will."

For a moment he looked steadfastly into the woman's eyes, and then, without answering her, he walked heavily down the stairs.

Back in the library, he stood for some time with his face to the empty fireplace. Over the mantelpiece there hung a little picture, in a black-and-gilt frame, of a bright-faced boy in an Arab fez. It was more than he could do to look at that portrait now, so he took it off its brass nail and laid it face down on the marble mantel-shelf.

Just at that moment one of his Secretaries brought in a despatch. It was the despatch from the Sirdar, sent in cipher but now written out at length. The Consul-General read it without any apparent emotion and put it aside without a word.

The hours passed slowly; the night was very long; the old man did not go to bed. Not for the first time he was asking himself searching questions about the mystery of life and death, but the great enigma was still baffling him. Could it be possible that while he had occupied himself with the mere shows and semblance of things, calling them by great names, Civilisation and Progress, that simple soul upstairs had been grasping the eternal realities?

There were questions that cut deeper even than that, and now they faced him one by one. Was it true that he had married merely in the hope of having some one to carry on his name and thus fulfil the aspirations of his pride? Had he for nearly forty years locked his heart away from the woman who had been starving for his love, and was it only by the loss of the son who was to have been the crown of his life that they were brought together in the end?

Thus the hoofs of the dark hours beat heavily on the great Proconsul's brain, and in the awful light that came to him from an open grave the triumphs of the life behind him looked poor and small and mean.

But meantime the palpitating air of the room upstairs was full of a different spirit. The old lady had apparently awakened from her restless sleep, for she had opened her eyes and was talking in a bright and happy voice. Her cheeks were tinged with the glow of health and her whole face was filled with light.

"I knew I should see them," she said.

"See whom, my heart?" asked Fatimah; but without answering her, the old lady, with the same rapturous expression, went on talking.

"I knew I should, and I have! I have seen both of them!"

"Whom have you seen, my lady?" asked Fatimah again; but once more the dying woman paid no heed to her.

"I saw them as plainly as I see you now, dear. It was in a place I did not know. The sun was so hot, and the room was so close. There was a rush roof and divans all round the walls. But Gordon and Helena were there together, sitting at opposite sides of a table and holding each other's hands."

"Allah! Allah!" muttered Fatimah, with upraised hands.

The old lady seemed to hear her, for an indulgent smile passed over her radiant face and she said in a tone of tender remonstrance:

"Don't be foolish, Fatimah! *Of course* I saw him. The Lord said I should, and He never breaks His promises. 'Help me, O God! for Christ's sake,' I said. 'Shall I see my dear son again? O God! give me a sign.' And He did! Yes, it was in the middle of the night. 'Janet,' said a voice, and I was not afraid. 'Be patient, Janet. You shall see your dear boy before you die.'"

Her face was full of happy visions. The life of this world seemed to be no longer there. A kind of life from the other world appeared to reanimate the sinking woman. The near approach of eternity illumined her whole being with a supernatural light. She was dying in a flood of joy.

"Oh, how good the Lord is! It is so easy to go now! —John, you must not think I suffer any longer, because I don't. I have no pain now, dear—none whatever."

Then she clasped her wasted hands together in the attitude of prayer and said in a rustling whisper:

"To-night, Lord Jesus! Let it be to-night!"

After that her rapturous voice died down, and her ecstatic eyes gently closed, but an ineffable smile continued to play on her faintly tinted face, as if she were looking on the wings that were waiting to bear her away.

The Doctor came in at that moment and was told what had occurred.

"Delirium, of course," he said. A change had come; the crisis was approaching. If the same thing happened at the supreme moment the patient was not to be contradicted; her delusion was to be indulged.

It did not happen.

In the early hours of the morning the Consul-General was called upstairs. There was a deep silence in the bedroom, as if the air had suddenly become empty and void. The day was breaking, and through the windows that looked over to the Nile the white sails of a line of boats

that were gliding by seemed like the passing of angels'
wings. Sparrows were twittering in the eaves, and through
the windows to the east the first streamers of the sunrise
were rising in the sky.

The Consul-General approached the bed and looked
down at the pallid face on the pillow. He wanted to stoop
and kiss it, but he felt as if it would be a profanation to
do so now. His own face was full of the majesty of suffering, for the sealed chambers of his iron soul had been
broken open at last.

With his hands clasped behind his back he stood for
some minutes quite motionless. Then laying one hand on
the brass head-rail of the bed, he leaned over his dead wife
and spoke to her as if she could hear.

"Forgive me, Janet! Forgive me," he said in a low
voice that was like a sob.

Did she hear him? Who can say she did not? Was it
only a ray from the sunrise that made the Egyptian woman
think that over the dead face of the careworn and weary
one, whose sweet soul was even then winging its way to
heaven, there passed the light of a loving smile?

XVII

WITHIN three days the softening effects on the Consul-
General of Lady Nuneham's death were lost. Out of his
very bereavement and the sense of being left friendless and
alone he became a harder and severer man than before.
His Secretaries were more than ever afraid of him, and his
servants trembled as they entered his room.

It heightened his anger against Gordon to believe that
by his conduct he had hastened his mother's end. In his
absolute self-abasement there were moments when he
would have found it easier to forgive Gordon if he had
been a prodigal, a wastrel, prompted to do what he had
done by the grossest selfishness; but deep down in some obscure depths of the father's heart the worst suffering came

of the certainty that his son had been moved by that tragic earnestness which belongs only to the greatest and noblest souls.

Still more hardening and embittering to the Consul-General than the memory of Gordon was the thought of Ishmael. It intensified his anger against the Egyptian to feel that having first by his "visionary mummery," by his "manœuvring and quackery," robbed him of his son, he had now, by direct consequence, robbed him of his wife also.

All the Consul-General's bull-necked strength, all his force of soul, was roused to fury when he thought of that. He was old and tired and he needed rest, but before he permitted himself to think of retirement, he must crush Ishmael Ameer.

Not that he allowed himself to recognise his vindictiveness. Shutting his eyes to his personal motive, he believed he was thinking of England only. Ishmael was the head-centre of an anarchical conspiracy which was using secret and stealthy weapons that were more deadly than bombs; therefore Ishmael must be put down, he must be trampled into the earth, and his movement must be destroyed.

But how?

Within a few hours after Lady Nuneham's funeral the Grand Cadi came by night, and, with many vague accusations against "the Arab innovator," repeated his former warning:

"I tell you again, O Excellency! if you permit that man to go on it will be death to the rule of England in Egypt."

"Then prove what you say, prove it, prove it!" cried the Consul-General, raising his impatient voice.

But the suave old Moslem judge either could not or would not do so. Indeed, being a Turkish official, accustomed to quite different procedure, he was at a loss to understand why the Consul-General wanted proof.

"Arrest the offender first and you'll find evidence enough afterward," he said.

An English statesman could not act on lines like those, so the Consul-General turned back to the despatches of the

Sirdar. The last of them—the one received during the dark hours preceding his wife's death—contained significant passages:

"If this man should develop supernatural pretensions I shall know what to do."

Ha! There was hope in that! The charlatan element in Ishmael Ameer might carry him far if only the temptation of popular idolatry were strong enough.

Once let a man deceive himself with the idea that he was divine—nay, once let his followers delude themselves with the notion of his divinity—and a civilised government would be bound to make short work of him. Whosoever and whatsoever he might be, that man must die!

A sudden cloud passed over the face of the Consul-General as he glanced again at the Sirdar's despatch and saw its reference to Christ.

"How senseless everybody is becoming in this world!" he thought.

Pontius Pilate! Pshaw! When would religious hypocrisy open its eyes and see that according to all the laws of civilised states, the Roman Governor had done right? Jesus claimed to be divine, His people were ready to recognise Him as King; and whether His Kingdom was of this world or another, what did it matter? If His pretensions had been permitted they would have led to wild, chaotic, shapeless anarchy. Therefore Pilate crucified Jesus, and, scorned though he had been through all the ages, he had done no more than any so-called "Christian" governor would be compelled to do to-day.

"Jesus of Nazareth, the King of the Jews." Why would not people understand that these words were written not in derision but in self-defence? There could have been only one authority in Palestine then, and there could be only one authority in Egypt now.

"If this visionary mummer, with his empty quackeries, should develop the idea that he is divine, or yet the messenger of divinity, I will hang him like a dog!" thought the Consul-General.

XVIII

FIVE days after the death of Lady Nuneham the Consul-General was reading at his breakfast the last copy of the *Times* to arrive in Cairo. It contained an anticipatory announcement of a forthcoming Mansion House Banquet in honour of the King's birthday. The Foreign Minister was expected to speak on the "unrest in the East, with special reference to the affair of El Azhar."

The Consul-General's face frowned darkly, and he began to picture the scene as it would occur: The gilded hall; the crowd of distinguished persons eating in public; the mixed odours of many dishes; the pop of champagne corks; the smoke of cigars; the buzz of chatter like the gobbling of geese on a green; and then the Minister, with his hand on his heart, uttering timorous apologies for his Proconsul's policy, and pouring out pompous platitudes as if he had newly discovered the decalogue!

The Consul-General's gorge rose at the thought. Oh, when would these people who stayed comfortably at home and lived by the votes of the factory-hands of Lancashire and Yorkshire, and hungered for the shouts of the mob, understand the position of men like himself, who, in foreign lands, among alien races, encompassed by secret conspiracies, were spending their strength in holding high the banner of Empire?

"Having chosen a good man, why can't they leave him alone?" thought the Consul-General.

And then, his personal feelings getting the better of his patriotism, he almost wished that the charlatan element in Ishmael Ameer might develop speedily; that he might draw off the allegiance of the native soldiers in the Soudan and break out, like the Mahdi, into open rebellion. That would bring the Secretary of State to his senses, make him realise a real danger and see in the everlasting "affair of El Azhar" if not light, then lightning.

The door of the breakfast room opened and Ibrahim entered.

"Well, what is it?" demanded the Consul-General with a frown.

Ibrahim answered in some confusion that a small boy was in the hall, asking to see the English lord. He said he brought an urgent message, but would not tell what it was or where it came from. Had been there three times before, slept last night on the ground outside the gate and could not be driven away—would his lordship see the lad?

"What is his race? Egyptian?"

"Nubian, my lord."

"Ever seen the boy before?"

"No—yes—that is to say—well, now that your lordship mentions it, I think—yes, I think he came here once with Miss Hel— I mean General Graves's daughter."

"Bring him up immediately," said the Consul-General.

At the next moment a black boy stepped boldly into the room. It was Mosie. His clothes were dirty, and his pudgy face was like a block of dark soap splashed with stale lather, but his eyes were clear and alert and his manner was eager.

"Well, my boy, what do you want?" asked the Consul-General.

Mosie looked fearlessly up into the stern face with its iron jaw, and tipped his black thumb over his shoulder to where Ibrahim, in his gorgeous green caftan, stood timidly behind him.

At a sign from the Consul-General, the Egyptian servant left the room, and then, quick as light, Mosie slipped off his sandal, ripped open its inner sole, and plucked out a letter stained with grease.

It was the letter which Helena had written in Khartoum.

The Consul-General read it rapidly, with an eagerness which even he could not conceal. So great, indeed, was his excitement that he did not see that a second paper (Ishmael's letter to the Chancellor of El Azhar) had fallen to the floor until Mosie picked it up and held it out to him.

"Good boy," said the Consul-General—the cloud had passed and his face bore an expression of joy.

Instantly apprehending the dim purport of Helena's hasty letter, the Consul-General saw that what he had predicted and half hoped for was already coming to pass. It was to be open conspiracy now, not passive conspiracy any longer. The man Ishmael was falling a victim to the most fatal of all mental maladies. The Mahdist delusion was taking possession of him and he was throwing himself into the Government's hands.

Hurriedly ringing his bell, the Consul-General committed Mosie to Ibrahim's care, whereupon the small black boy in his soiled clothes, with his dirty face and hands, strutted out of the room in front of the Egyptian servant, looking as proud as a peacock and feeling like sixteen feet tall. Then the Consul-General called for one of his Secretaries and sent him for the Commandant of Police.

The Commandant came in hot haste. He was a big and rather corpulent Englishman, wearing a blue-braided uniform and a fez—naturally a blusterous person with his own people, but as soft-voiced as a woman and as obsequious as a slave before his chief.

"Draw up your chair, Commandant—closer—now listen," said the Consul-General.

And then in a low tone he repeated what he had already learned from Helena's letter, and added what he had instantly divined from it—that Ishmael Ameer was to return to Cairo; that he was to come back in the disguise of a Bedouin Sheikh; that his object was to draw off the allegiance of the Egyptian Army in order that a vast horde of his followers might take possession of the city; that this was to be done during the period of the forthcoming festivities, while the British Army was still in the provinces, and that the conspiracy was to reach its treacherous climax on the night of the King's birthday.

The Commandant listened with a gloomy face, and, looking timidly into the flashing eyes before him, he asked if his Excellency could rely on the source of his information.

"Absolutely! Infallibly!" said the Consul-General.

"Then," said the Commandant nervously, "I presume the festivities must be postponed?"

"Certainly not, sir."

"Or perhaps your Excellency intends to have the British Army called back to Cairo?"

"Not that, either."

"At least you will arrest the 'Bedouin.'"

"Not yet, at all events."

The policy to be pursued was to be something quite different.

Everything was to go on as usual. Sports, golf, cricket, croquet, tennis-tournaments, polo-matches, race-meetings, automobile-meetings, "all the usual fooleries and frivolities"—with crowds of sight-seers, men in flannels, and ladies in beautiful toilettes—were to be encouraged to proceed. The police-bands were to play in the public gardens, the squares, the streets, everywhere.

"Say nothing to anybody. Give no sign of any kind. Let the conspiracy go on as if we knew nothing about it. But——"

"Yes, my lord? Yes?"

"Keep an eye on the 'Bedouin.' Let every train that arrives at the railway-station and every boat that comes down the river be watched. As soon as you have spotted your man see where he goes. He may be a fanatical fool, miscounting his 'divine' influence with the native soldier, but he cannot be working alone. Therefore find out who visit him, learn all their movements, let their plans come to a head, and, when the proper time arrives, in one hour, at one blow, we will crush their conspiracy and clap our hands upon the whole of them."

"Splendid! An inspiration, my lord!"

"I've always said it would some day be necessary to forge a special weapon to meet special needs, and the time has come to forge it. Meantime undertake nothing hurriedly. Make no mistakes, and see that your men make none."

"Certainly, my lord."

"Investigate every detail for yourself, and, above all, hold your tongue and guard your information with inviolable secrecy."

"Surely, my lord."

"You can go now. I'm busy. Good-morning!"

"Wonderful man!" thought the Commandant, as he went out at the porch. "Seems to have taken a new lease of life! Wonderful!"

The Consul-General spent the whole of that day in thinking out his scheme for a "special weapon," and when night came and he went upstairs—through the great echoing house that was like the bureau of a department of State now, being so empty and so cheerless, and past the dark and silent room whereof the door was always closed—he felt conscious of a firmer and lighter step than he had known for years.

Fatimah was in his bedroom, for she had constituted herself his own nurse since his wife's death. She was nailing up on the wall the picture of the little boy in the Arab fez, and, having her own theory about why he had taken it down in the library, she said:

"There! It will be company for your lordship and nobody will ask questions about it here."

When Fatimah had gone the Consul-General could not but think of Gordon. He always thought of him at that hour of the night, and the picture of his son that rose in his mind's eye was always the same. It was a picture of Gordon's deathly white face and trembling lower lip, as he stood bolt upright while his medals were being torn from his breast, and then said, in that voice which his father could never forget: "General, the time may come when it will be more painful to you to remember all this than it has been for me to bear it."

Oh, that Gordon could be here now and see for himself what a sorry charlatan, what a self-deceived quack and conspirator, was the man in whose defence he had allowed his own valuable life to rush down to a confused welter of wreck and ruin!

As the Consul-General got into bed he was thinking of

Helena. What a glorious, courageous, resourceful woman
she was! It carried his mind back to biblical days to find
anything equal to her daring and her success. But what
was the price she had paid for them? He remembered
something the Sirdar had said of " a marriage, a sort of
betrothal," and then he recalled the words of her first letter: " I know exactly how far I intend to go and I shall go
no farther. I know exactly what I intend to do and I shall
do it without fear or remorse."

What had happened in the Soudan? What was happening there now? In what battle-whirlwind had that
splendid girl's magnificent victory been won?

XIX

MEANTIME Helena in Khartoum was feeling like a miserable traitress.

She had condemned an innocent man to death! Ishmael had *not* killed her father, yet she had taken such steps
that the moment he entered Cairo he would be walking to
his doom!

One after another, sweet and cruel memories crowded
upon her, and in the light of the awful truth, as Gordon
had revealed it, she began to see Ishmael with quite different eyes. All she had hitherto thought evil in his character now looked like good; what she had taken for hypocrisy
was sincerity; what she had supposed to be subtlety was
simplicity. His real nature was a rebuke to every one of
her preconceived ideas. The thought of his tenderness, his
modesty, his devotion, and even the unselfishness which had
led to their betrothal, cut her to the quick. Yet she had
doomed him to destruction. The letter she had written to
the Consul-General was his death-warrant.

That night she could fix her mind on nothing except the
horror of her position, but next morning she set herself to
think out schemes for stopping the consequences of her
own act.

The black boy was gone; it was not possible to over-take him; there was no other train to Egypt for four days, but there was the telegraph; she could make use of that.

"I'll telegraph to the Consul-General to pay no atten-tion to my letter," she thought.

Useless! The Consul-General would ask himself search-ing questions and take his precautions just the same.

"I'll telegraph that my letter is a forgery," she thought.

Madness! The Consul-General would ask himself how, if it was a forgery, she could know anything about it.

"I'll go across to the Sirdar and tell him everything, and leave him to act for both of us as he thinks best!"

Impossible! How could she explain her position to the Sirdar without betraying Gordon's identity and thereby leading to his arrest?

That settled everything. There was no escape from the consequences of her conduct, no way to put an end to the network of dangers by which she had surrounded Ishmael. Mosie was now far on his way to Cairo; he carried to the Consul-General not only her own letter, but also the original of Ishmael's letter to the Chancellor of El Azhar. The hideous work was done.

Two days passed during which her over-excited feelings seemed to paralyse all her powers of thought. Then a new idea took possession of her and she set herself to undo what she had done with Ishmael himself. Little by little, in tremulous tones, and with a still deeper sense of duplicity than before, she began to express halting doubts of the success of their enterprise.

"I have been thinking about it," she said nervously, "and now I fear——"

"What do you fear, O Rani?" asked Ishmael.

"I fear," said Helena, trembling visibly, "that the mo-ment the Government learn from the Sirdar, as they needs must, that the great body of your people have left Khar-toum, and ᴀ̤e travelling north, they will recall the British Army to protect the capital and thus——"

But Ishmael interrupted her with a laugh.

"If the day of the Redeemer has come," he said, "will human armies hinder Him? No!"

It was useless! Ishmael was now more than ever an enthusiast, a fanatic, a visionary. His spiritual ecstasy swept away every obstacle, and made him blind to every danger.

Helena felt like a witch who was trying to undo the effects of her charm. She could not undo them. She could not destroy the potency of the spell she herself had raised, and the effort to do so put her into a fever of excitement.

Two days more passed like this, and still Helena was in the toils of her own actions. From time to time she saw Gordon as he sat at meals or moved about the house. He did not speak to her, and she dropped her head in shame as often as they came close together. But at length she caught a look in his face which seemed to her to say: "Are you really going to let an innocent man walk into the jaws of death?"

That brought her wavering mind to a quick conclusion. Gordon was waiting for her to speak. She must speak! She must confess everything! She must tell Ishmael what she had done, and by what tragic tangle of error she had done it. At any cost, no matter what, she must put an end to the false situation in which she lived, and thus redeem herself in Gordon's eyes and in her own.

At noon that day, being Friday, Ishmael lectured in the mosque, delivering a still more fervent and passionate message. The kingdom of heaven which the Lord Isa had foretold was soon to come! When it came, God would lend them legions of angels, if need be, to protect the oppressed and to uphold the downtrodden! Therefore let the children of God fear nothing from the powers and principalities of the world! Their pilgrimage was safe! No harm could come to them, for however their feet might slip, the arms of the Compassionate would bear them up!

As Ishmael's ecstasy had increased so had the devotion of his people, and when he returned home they followed him in a dense crowd through the streets, shouting the wildest acclamations:

"Out of the way! The Master is coming! The Messenger is here! Allah! El Hamdullillah!"

Helena heard them, but she did not hear Ishmael reprove them, as in earlier days he had been wont to do.

She was standing in the guest-room, and the noise of the approaching crowd had brought Gordon from his bedroom, at the moment when Ishmael, surrounded by a group of his people, stepped into the house.

Ishmael was in a state of excitement amounting to exaltation, and after holding out hands both to Helena and Gordon he turned to his followers to dismiss them.

"Go back now," he said, "and to-night, two hours after sunset, let the Ulema and the Notables come to me that we may decide on the details of our pilgrimage."

"Allah! El Hamdullillah!" cried the people.

More than ever they were like creatures possessed. Hungry and ragged as many of them were, the new magnificence that was to be given to their lives appeared to be already shining in their eyes.

Helena saw this, and her heart was smitten with remorse at thought of the cruel confession she had decided to make. She could not make it in sight of the hopes it must destroy. But neither could she look into Gordon's searching face and remain silent, and as soon as the crowd had gone, she made an effort to speak.

"Ishmael," she said, trembling all over, "there is something I wish to say—if it will not displease you."

"Nothing the Rani can say will displease me," said Ishmael.

He was looking at her with the expression of enthusiastic admiration which she had seen in his eyes before. It was hard to go on.

"Your intentions are now known to everybody," she said. "You have not hidden them from any of your own people. That has been very trustful, very noble, but still——"

"Still—what, my sister?"

"If somebody—should betray your scheme to the Government, and—and the moment you set foot in Cairo——"

Again Ishmael interrupted her with a laugh.

"Impossible!" he said, smiling upon her with his bright and joyous eyes. "Islam has only one heart, one soul, one mind."

And then taking her quivering hand and leading her to the door, he pointed to the camp outside and said:

"Look! Ten thousand of our poor unhappy people are there. They have come to me from the tyrannies of cruel taskmasters and been true to me through the temptations of hunger and thirst. Some of them are from Cairo and are waiting to return home. All are the children of Islam and are looking for the coming of the Expected who brings peace and joy. Is there one of them who will betray me now? Not one! Treachery would injure me, but it would hurt the betrayer more."

Then with the same expression of enthusiastic admiration and in a still tenderer and softer voice, he began to laugh and to rally her, saying he knew well what was going on in his sweet sister's mind—that though her brave spirit had devised the plan they had adopted, yet now that the time was near for carrying it into execution her womanly heart was failing her and affectionate anxiety for his own safety was making her afraid.

"But have no fear at all," he said, standing behind her and smoothing her cheek with a light touch of his tapering fingers. "If this is God's work will God forget me? No!"

With a sense of stifling duplicity Helena made one more effort and said:

"Still, who knows, there may be some one——"

"None, O Rani!"

"But don't you know——"

"I don't want to know anything except one thing—that God guides and directs me."

Again he laughed and asked where was the kufiah (the Bedouin head-dress) which she had promised to make for his disguise.

"Get to work at it quick," he said; "it will be wanted soon, my sister."

And then clapping his hands for the midday meal, he went into his room to prepare for it, leaving Gordon and Helena for some moments alone together.

Gordon had been standing aside in the torment of a hundred mixed emotions, and now he and Helena spoke in whispers.

"He is determined to go into Cairo," she said.

"Quite determined."

"Oh, is there *no* way to prevent him?"

"None now—unless——"

"Unless—what?" she asked eagerly.

"Let us—let us wait and see," said Gordon, and then Abdullah came in to lay the table.

XX

As soon as the midday meal was over Gordon escaped to his own room—the room he shared with Ishmael—and throwing himself down on the angerib with his hands clasped across his face, he tried to think out the situation in which he found himself, to gaze into the depths of his conscience and to see where he was and what he ought to do.

So violent was the state of his soul that he sat there a long time before he could link together his memories of what had happened since he arrived in Khartoum.

"Am I dreaming?" he asked himself again and again, as one by one his thoughts rolled over him like tempestuous waves.

The first thing he saw clearly was that Ishmael was not now the same man that he had seen at Alexandria; that the anxieties, responsibilities, and sufferings he had gone through as a religious leader had dissipated his strong common-sense; and that as a consequence the caution whereby men guard their conduct had gone.

He also saw that Ishmael's spiritual ecstasy had reached a point not far removed from madness; that his faith in divine guidance, divine guardianship, divine intervention had become an absolute obsession.

Therefore it was hopeless to try to move him from his purpose by any appeals on the score of danger to himself or to his people.

"He is determined to go into Cairo," thought Gordon, "and into Cairo he will go."

The next thing Gordon saw, as he examined the situation before him, was that Helena was powerless to undo the work which by the cruel error of fate she had been led to do; that her act was irrevocable; that there was no calling it back, and that it would go from its consequences to the consequences of its consequences.

Helena's face appeared before him, and his heart bled for her as he thought of how she passed before him—she who had always been so bold and gay—with her once proud head bent low. He remembered her former strength and self-reliance; her natural force and grace; her fearless daring and that dash of devilry which had been for him one of her greatest charms, and then he thought of her false position in that house, brought there by her own will, held there by her own act—a tragic figure of a woman in the meshes of her own net.

"She cannot continue to live like this. It is impossible. Yet what can the end be?" he asked himself.

Hours passed like this. His head under his hot hands burned and his temples throbbed, yet no ray of light emerged from the darkness surrounding him.

But at length the man in him, the soldier and the lover, swept down every obstacle, and he told himself that he must save Helena from the consequences of her own conduct, whatever the result might be.

"I must! I must!" he kept on repeating as Helena's face rose before him; and after a while this blind resolution brought him at one stride to a new idea.

Ishmael was determined to go into Cairo, but there was one way to prevent him doing so—that he, Gordon himself, should go instead!

When he first thought of that his temples beat so violently that it seemed as if they would burst, and he felt as if he had been brought to the very brink of despair. Seeing nothing before him but instant arrest the moment he entered the city, it seemed to be a pitiful end to his long journey across the desert, a poor sequel to his fierce struggle with himself, and to the mystic hopes with which he had buoyed up his heart, that immediately after he had reached Khartoum he should turn back to his death.

Work, mission, redemption—all that had so recently had a meaning for him had disappeared. But his heart rose when he remembered that if he did what he had determined to do, the cruel error of fate would be broken whereby Ishmael had been doomed to die for an offence he did not commit.

What was the first fact of this cruel situation? That Helena had believed Ishmael to be guilty of the death of her father. But Ishmael was innocent, whereas he, Gordon, was guilty! Could he allow an innocent man to die for his crime?

That brought him to the crisis of his conscience. It settled everything. Destiny, acting under the blind force of a poor girl's love for her father, was sending Ishmael to his death. But destiny should be defeated! He should pay his own penalty! Ishmael should be snatched from the doom that threatened him, and Helena should be saved from lifelong remorse.

"Yes, yes, I must go into Cairo instead," he told himself.

It had grown late by this time and the bedroom had become dark when Abdullah knocked at the door and said that the Sheikhs were in the guest-room and Ishmael was asking for Omar.

Under its roof thatched with stalks of durah, lit by lamps suspended from its rafters, the Ulema and Notables of Khartoum—the same that visited the Sirdar—had gathered soon after sunset, and squatting on the divans covered by carpets and cushions, had drunk their coffee and talked in their winding, circuitous Eastern way of the business before them and particularly of the White Lady's part in it, while they waited for Ishmael, who was still at the mosque.

24

"Yes," the vivacious old Pasha had said, "no matter how great a man may be, when he undertakes an enterprise like this he should always consult ten of his friends."

"But great ones are not great in friends," said a younger Sheikh. "What if he has not got ten?"

"Then let him consult one friend ten times over."

"Nay, but if he stands so high that he has not got ever one friend?"

"Then," said the old man, with a sly look over his shoulder toward the women's side of the house, "let him consult his wife and whatever she advises let him do the contrary."

When Gordon in his Bedouin dress entered the guest-room, Ishmael was sitting in the midst of his people, and he called to him to take the seat by his right side.

"But where is the Rani?" he asked, looking round, whereupon Abdullah answered that she was still in her room, and the old Pasha hinted that in the emancipation of the Eastern woman perhaps women themselves would be the chief impediment.

"I know! I know!" said Ishmael. "But all the same we must turn our backs on the madness of a bygone age that woman is inferior to man, and her counsel is not to be trusted. Bring her, Abdullah."

A few minutes afterward Helena, wearing her Indian veil but with her face uncovered, entered the guest-room with downcast eyes, followed by the Arab woman and the child.

It cut Gordon to the quick to see her look of shame and of confusion, but Ishmael saw nothing in Helena's manner except maidenly modesty under the eyes of so many men, and making a place for her on his left, he began without further delay on the business that had brought them together.

They were about to win a dear victory for God, but it was to be a white war, a bloodless revolution. The heartless festivities that were to be held in honour of the birthday of the King who lived across the seas while people perished in Egypt, were to reach their climax something more than a month hence. Therefore the great caravan of God's children who were to cross the desert by camel and horse and ass, in order that they might meet the Expected One when he appeared in Cairo, should start within a week. But the messenger of God who had to prepare the path before them must go by train, and he ought to leave Khartoum in four days.

Other preliminaries of the pilgrimage there were to arrange, and after the manner of their kind the Sheikhs talked long and leisurely, agreeing finally that Ishmael should go first into Cairo in the disguise of a Bedouin Sheikh to make sure of the success of their mission, and that Omar (Gordon) should follow him in command of the body of the people.

At length there was silence for a moment and then Ishmael said:

"Is there anything else, my brothers?"

And at that Gordon, who had not spoken before, turned to him and answered, in the style as well as the language of the Arabs.

"Listen, I beg of you, to my words, and forgive me if what I say is not pleasing to you or yours."

"Speak, Omar Benani, speak," said Ishmael, laying his right hand, with an affectionate gesture, on Gordon's left.

There was a moment of silence in which Gordon could distinctly hear the sound of Helena's breathing. Then he said:

"Reverse your order, oh, my brother, and let me go first into Cairo."

A tingling electrical current seemed to pass through the air of the room, and again Gordon heard the sound of Helena's laboured breathing, but no one spoke except Ishmael, who said, in a soft voice:

"But why, Omar, why?"

Gordon braced himself up and answered:

"First, because it best becomes a messenger of God to enter Cairo in the company of his people, not alone and in disguise."

"And next?"

"Next, because I know Cairo better than Ishmael, and all that he can do I can do, and more."

There was another moment of tense silence, and then Ishmael said:

"I listen to your sincere proposal, oh, my brother, but before I answer it I ask for the counsel of my friends."

Then raising his voice, he cried: "Companions, you have heard what Omar Benani has said—which of us is it to be?"

At that the electrical atmosphere in the room broke into eager and impetuous speech. First came, as needs must in an Eastern conclave, some guests of questions, then certain breezes of protest, but finally a strong and unbroken current of assent.

"Master," said one of the Sheikhs, "I have eaten bread and salt with you, therefore I will not deceive you. Let Omar go first. He can do all that Ishmael can do and run no risk."

"Messenger of the Merciful," said another, "neither will I deceive you. Omar knows Cairo best. Therefore let him go first."

After others had answered in the same way Ishmael turned to Mahmud, his uncle, whereupon the old man wiped his rheumy eyes and said:

"Your life is in God's hand, O son of my brother, and man cannot escape his destiny. If it is God's will that you should be the first to go into Cairo, you will go and God will protect you. But speaking for myself, I should think it a shame and a humiliation that the father of his people should not enter the city with his children. If Omar says he can do as much as you, believe him—the white man does not lie."

No sooner had the old man concluded than the whole company with one voice shouted that they were all of the same opinion, whereupon Ishmael cried:

"So be it then! Omar it shall be! And do not think for one moment that I grudge your choice."

"El Hamdullillah!" shouted the company, as from a sense of otherwise inexpressible relief.

Meantime Gordon was conscious only of Helena's violent agitation. Though he dared not look at her he seemed to see her feverish face, and the expression of terror in her lustrous eyes. At length, when the shouts of the Sheikhs had subsided, he heard her tremulous voice saying hurriedly to Ishmael:

"Do not listen to them."

"But why, my Rani?" Ishmael asked in a whisper.

She tried to answer him and could not. "Because—because——"

"Because—what?" asked Ishmael again.

"Oh, I don't know—I can't think—but I beg you, I intreat you, not to let Omar go into Cairo."

Her agitated voice made another moment of silence, and then Ishmael said in a soft, indulgent tone:

"I understand you, oh, my Rani! This may be the task of greatest danger, but it is the place of highest honour, too, and you would fain see no man except your husband assigned to it. But Omar is of me and I am of him, and there can be no pride or jealousy between us."

And then taking Gordon by the right hand, while with his left he was holding Helena, he said:

"Omar, my friend, my brother!"

"El Hamdullillah!" cried the Sheikhs again, and then one by one they rose to go.

Helena arose, too, and with her face aflame and her breath coming in gusts she hurried back to her room. The Arab woman followed her in a moment, and with a mocking smile in her glinting eyes she said:

"How happy you must be, O lady, that some one else than your husband is to go into that place of danger!"

But Helena could bear no more.

"Go out of the room this moment! I cannot endure you! I hate you! Go, woman, go!" she cried.

Zenoba fled before the fury in her lady's face, but at the next moment Helena had dropped to the floor and burst into a flood of tears.

When she gained possession of herself again the child, Ayesha, was embracing her and, without knowing why, was weeping over her wet cheeks.

XXI

Now that Gordon was to take Ishmael's place, Helena found herself deeper than ever in the toils of her own plot. She could see nothing but death before him as the result of his return to Cairo. If his identity were discovered he would die for his own offences as a soldier. If it were not discovered he would be executed for Ishmael's conspiracies as she had made them known.

"Oh, it cannot be! It must not be! It shall not be!" she continued to say to herself, but without seeing a way to prevent it.

Never for a moment in her anxiety to save Gordon from stepping into the pit she had dug for Ishmael did she allow herself to think that being the real cause of her father's death, he deserved the penalty she had prepared for the guilty man. Her mind had altered toward that event since the man concerned in it had changed. The more she thought of it the more sure she became that it was a totally different thing from the thing she had proposed—in the strict sense hardly a crime at all.

In the first place she reminded herself that her father had suffered from an affection of the heart which must have contributed to his death even if it had not been the principal cause of it. How could she have forgotten that fact until now?

Remembering her father's excitement and exhaustion when she saw him last, she could see for the first time, by the light of Gordon's story, what had afterward occurred— the burst of ungovernable passion, the struggle, the fall, the death.

Then she told herself that Gordon had not intended to kill her father, and whatever he did had been done for love of her. "Helena was mine, and you have taken her from me, and broken her heart as well as my own." Yes, love for her and the torment of losing her, had brought Gordon back to the Citadel after he had been ordered to return to his quarters. Love for her and the delirium of a broken heart had rung out of him the insults which had led to the quarrel which resulted in her father's death.

In spite of her lingering tenderness for the memory of her father, she began to see how much he had been to blame for what had happened—to think of the gross indignity, the frightful shame, the unmerciful and even unlawful degradation to which in his towering rage he had subjected Gordon. The scene came back to her with horrible distinctness now—her father crying in a half-stifled voice: "You are a traitor! A traitor who has consorted with the enemies of his country," and then ripping Gordon's sword from its scabbard and breaking it across his knee.

But seeing this, she also saw her own share in what had occurred. At the moment of Gordon's deepest humiliation she had driven him away from her. Her pride had conquered her love, and instead of flinging herself into his arms as she ought to have done, whether he was in the right or in the wrong, when everybody else was trampling upon him, she had insulted him with reproaches and turned her back upon him in his disgrace.

That scene came back to her, too—Gordon at the door of the General's house, with his deathly white face and trembling lips, stammering out: "I couldn't help it, Helena —it was impossible for me to act otherwise," and then, bareheaded as he was and with every badge of rank and honour gone, staggering across the garden to the gate.

When she thought of all this now, it seemed to her that if anybody had been to blame for her father's death it was not Gordon but herself. His had been the hand, the blind hand only, but the heart that had wrought the evil had been hers.

"Oh! it cannot be, it shall not be!" she continued to say to herself, and just as she had tried to undo her work with Ishmael when he was bent on going into Cairo, so she determined to do the same with Gordon, now that he had stepped into Ishmael's place.

Her opportunity came soon.

A little before midday of the day following the meeting of the Sheikhs, she was alone in the guest-room, sitting at the brass table that served her as a desk—Ishmael being in the camp, Zenoba and the child in the town, and old Mahmud still in bed—when Gordon came out of the men's quarter and walked toward the door as if intending to pass out of the house.

He had seen her as he came from his bedroom, with one of her hands pressed to her brow, and a feeling of inexpressible pity and unutterable longing had so taken possession of him, with the thought that he was soon to lose her—the most precious gift life had given him—that he had tried to steal away.

But instinctively she felt his approach, and with a trembling voice she called to him, so he returned and stood by her side.

" Why are you doing this? " she said. " You know what I mean. Why are you doing it? "

" You know quite well why I am doing it, Helena. Ishmael was determined to go to his death. There was only one way to prevent him. I had to take it."

" But you are going to death yourself—isn't that so? "

He did not answer. He was trying not to look at her.

" Or perhaps you see some way of escape—do you? "

Still he did not speak—he was even trying not to hear her.

" If not, why are you going into Cairo instead of Ishmael? "

" Don't ask me that, Helena. I would rather not answer you."

Suddenly the tears came into her eyes, and after a moment's silence she said:

" I know! I understand! But remember your father. He loves you. You may not think it, but he does, I am sure he does. Yet if you go into Cairo you know quite well what he will do."

" My father is a great man, Helena. He will do his duty whatever happens—what he believes to be his duty."

" Certainly he will, but all the same do you think he will not suffer? And do you wish to put him into the position of being compelled to cut off his own son? Is that right? Can anything—anything in the world—make it necessary?"

Gordon did not answer her, but under the strain of his emotion he tightened his lips and his pinched nostrils began to dilate like the nostrils of a horse.

"Then remember your mother, too," said Helena. "She is weak and ill. It breaks my heart to think of her as I saw her last. She believes that you have fled away to some foreign country, but she is living in the hope that time will justify you, and then you will be reconciled to your father, and come back to her again. Is this how you would come back?—Oh, it will kill her! I'm sure it will!"

She saw that Gordon's strong and manly face was now utterly discomposed and she could not help but follow up her advantage.

"Then think a little of me, too, Gordon. This is all my fault, and if anything is done to you in Cairo it will be just the same to me as if I had done it. Do you wish me to die of remorse?"

She saw that he was struggling to restrain himself, and turning her beautiful wet eyes upon him and laying her hand on his arm, she said:

"Don't go back to Cairo, Gordon! For my sake, for your own sake, for our love's sake——"

But Gordon could bear no more, and he cried in a low, hoarse whisper:

"Helena, for Heaven's sake, don't speak so. I knew it wouldn't be easy to do what I intended to do, and it isn't easy. But don't make it harder for me than it is, I beg, I pray."

She tried to speak again, but he would not listen.

"When you sent the message into Cairo that doomed Ishmael to death, you thought he had killed your father. If he had really done so he would have deserved all you did to him. But he hadn't, whereas I had—do you think I can let an innocent man die for my crime?"

"But, Gordon—" she began, and again he stopped her.

"Don't speak about it, Helena. For Heaven's sake, don't! I've fought this battle with myself before and I

25

can't fight it over again. With your eyes upon me, too, your voice in my ears, and your presence by my side."

He was trying to move away and she was still clinging to his arm.

"Don't speak about our love, either. All that is over now. You must know it is. There is a barrier between us that can never——"

His voice was breaking and he was struggling to tear himself away from her, but she leaped to her feet and cried:

"Gordon, you *shall* hear me, you *must!*" and then he stopped short and looked at her.

"You think you were the cause of my father's death, but you were not," she said.

His mouth opened, his lips trembled, he grew deathly pale.

"You think, too, that there is a barrier of blood between us, but there is no such thing."

"Take care of what you are saying, Helena."

"What I am saying is the truth, Gordon—it is God's truth."

He looked blankly at her for a moment in silence; then laid hold of her violently by both arms, gazed closely into her face and said in a low, trembling voice:

"Helena, if you knew what it is to live for months under the shadow of a sin—an awful sin—an unpardonable sin—surely you wouldn't— But why don't you speak? Speak, girl, speak!"

Then Helena looked fearlessly back into his excited face and said:

"Gordon, do you remember that you came to my room in the Citadel before you went into that—that fatal interview?"

"Yes, yes! How can I forget it?"

"Do you also remember what I told you then—that whatever happened that day I could never leave my father?"

"Yes, certainly, yes."

"Do you remember that you asked me why and I said

I couldn't tell you because it was a secret—somebody else's secret?"

"Well?" His pulses were beating violently; she could feel them throbbing on her arms.

"Gordon," she said, "do you know what that secret was? I can tell you now. Do you know what it was?"

"What?"

"That my father was suffering from heart-disease and had already received his death-warrant."

She waited for Gordon to speak, but he was almost afraid to breathe.

"He didn't know his condition until we arrived in Egypt, and then perhaps he ought to have resigned his commission, but he had been out of the service for two years, and the temptation to remain was too much for him, so he asked me to promise to say nothing about it."

Gordon released her arms and she sat down again. He stood over her breathing fast and painfully.

"I thought you ought to have been told at the time when we became engaged, but my father said: 'No! Why put him in a false position and burden him with responsibilities he ought not to bear?'"

Helena's own voice was breaking now, and as Gordon listened to it he was looking down at her flushed face, which was thinner than before but more beautiful than ever in his eyes and a hundredfold more touching than when it first won his heart.

"I tried to tell you that day, too, before you went into the General's office, so that you might see for yourself, dear, that if you separated yourself from my father I—I couldn't possibly follow you, but there was my promise and then—then my pride and—and something you said that pained and wounded me——"

"I know, I know, I know," he said.

"But now," she continued, rising to her feet again, "now," she repeated, in the same trembling voice, but with a look of joy and triumph, "now that you have told me what happened after your return to the Citadel, I see quite clearly—I am sure—perfectly sure—that my dear father died not by your hand at all but by the hand and the will of God."

"Helena! Helena!" cried Gordon, and in the tempest of his love and the overwhelming sense of his boundless relief, he flung his arms about her and covered her face with kisses.

One long moment of immeasurable joy they were permitted to know, and then the hand of fate snatched at them again.

From their intoxicating happiness they were awakened by a voice. It was only the voice of the muezzin calling to midday prayers, but it seemed to be reproaching them, separating them, tearing them asunder, reminding them of where they were now and what they were, and that God was over them.

AL-LA-HU AK-BAR.   AL-LA - - HU AK-BAR.

God is Most Great!   God is Most Great!

Their lips parted; their arms fell away from each other, and, irresistibly, simultaneously, as if by an impulse of the same heart, they dropped to their knees to pray for pardon.

The voice of the muezzin ceased, and in the silence of the following moment they heard a soft footstep coming behind.

It was Ishmael. He did not speak to either of them, but seeing them on their knees, at the hour of midday prayers, he stepped up and knelt between.

XXII

When Gordon had time to examine the new situation in which he found himself he saw that he was now in a worse case than before.

It had been an inexpressible relief to realise that he was

not the first cause of the General's death, and therefore that conscience did not require him to go into Cairo in order to protect Ishmael from the consequences of a crime he did not commit. But no sooner had he passed this great crisis than he was brought up against a great test. What was it to him that he could save his life if he had to lose Helena?

Helena was now Ishmael's wife—betrothed to him by the most sacred pledges of Mohammedan law. If the barrier of blood which had kept him from Helena had been removed, the barrier of marriage which kept Helena from him remained.

"What can we do?" he asked himself, and for a long time he saw no answer.

In the fierce struggle that followed, honour and duty seemed to say that inasmuch as Helena had entered into this union of her own free will—however passively acquiescing in its strange conditions—she must abide by it, and he must leave her where she was and crush down his consuming passion, which was an unholy passion now. But honour and duty are halting and timorous guides in the presence of love, and when Gordon came to think of Helena as the actual wife of Ishmael, he was conscious of nothing but the flame that was burning at his heart's core.

Remembering what Helena had told him, and what he had seen since he came to that house, he reminded himself that after all the marriage was only a marriage *pro formâ*, a promise made under the mysterious compulsion of Fate, a contract of convenience and perhaps generosity on the one side, and on the other side of dark and calculating designs which would not bear to be thought of any longer, being a result of the blind leading of awful passions under circumstances of the most irresistible provocation.

When he came to think of love he was dead to everything else. Ishmael did not love Helena, whereas he, Gordon, loved her with all his heart and soul and strength. She was everything in life to him, and though he might have gone to his death without her it was impossible to live and leave her behind him.

Thinking so, he began to conjure up the picture of a time when Ishmael, under the influence of Helena's beauty and charm, might perhaps forget the bargain between them, and claim his rights as a husband; and then the thought of her beautiful head, with its dark curling locks, as it lay in his arms that day, lying in the arms of the Arab, with Ishmael's swarthy face above her, so tortured him that it swept away every other consideration.

"It must not, shall not, cannot be!" he told himself.

And that brought him to the final thought that since he loved Helena, and since Helena loved him and not her husband, their position in Ishmael's house was utterly false and wrong and could not possibly continue.

"It is not fair even to Ishmael himself," he thought.

And when, struggling with his conscience, he asked himself how he was to put an end to the odious and miserable situation, he concluded at once that he would go boldly to Ishmael and tell him the whole story of Helena's error and temptation, thereby securing his sympathy and extricating all of them from the position in which they were placed.

"Anything will be better than the present state of things," he thought, as he reflected upon the difficult and delicate task he intended to undertake.

But after a moment he saw that while it would be hard to explain Helena's impulse of vengeance to the man who had been the object of it, to tell him of the message she had sent into Cairo would be utterly impossible.

"I cannot say anything to Ishmael about that," he thought, and the only logical sequence of ideas was that he could not say anything to Ishmael at all.

This left him with only one conclusion—that inasmuch as it was impossible that he and Helena could remain any longer in that house, and equally impossible that they could leave it with Ishmael's knowledge and consent, there was nothing for them to do but to fly away.

He found it hard to reconcile himself to the idea of a secret flight. The very thought of it seemed to put them into the position of adulterers, deceiving an unsuspecting husband. But when he remembered the scene in the guest-room that day, the moment of overpowering love, the irresistible kiss, and then the crushing sense of duplicity, as Ishmael entered and without a thought of treachery knelt between them, he told himself that at any cost whatsoever he must put an end to the false position in which they lived.

"We must do it soon—the sooner the better," he thought.

Though he had lived so long with the thought of losing Helena, that kiss had in a moment put his soul and body into a flame. He knew that his love was blinding him to certain serious considerations, and that some of these would rise up later and perhaps accuse him of selfishness or disloyalty or worse. But he could only think of Helena now, and his longing to possess her made him dead to everything else.

In a fever of excitement he began to think out plans for their escape and reflecting that two days had still to pass before the train left Khartoum by which it had been intended that he should travel in his character as Ishmael's messenger, he decided that it was impossible for them to wait for that.

They must get away at once by camel if not by rail. And remembering Osman, his former guide and companion, he concluded to go over to the Gordon College and secure his aid.

Having reached this point he asked himself if he ought not to obtain Helena's consent before going any further, but no, he would not wait even for that. And then, remembering how utterly crushed she was, a victim of storm and tempest, a bird with a broken wing, he assumed the attitude of strength toward her, telling himself she was a woman after all, and it was his duty as a man to think and to act for her.

So he set out in haste to see Osman, and when, on his way through the town, he passed (without being recognised) a former comrade in khaki, a Colonel of Lancers, whose life had been darkened by the loss of his wife through the treachery of a brother officer, he felt no qualms at all at the thought of taking Helena from Ishmael.

"Ours is a different case altogether," he said, and then he told himself that their life would be all the brighter in the future because it had had this terrible event in it.

It was late and dark when he returned from the Gordon College, and then old Mahmud's house was as busy as a fair with people coming and going on errands relating to the impending pilgrimage, but he watched his opportunity to speak to Helena, and as soon as Ishmael, who was more than commonly animated and excited that night, had dismissed his followers and gone to the door to drive them home, he approached her and whispered in her ear:

"Helena!"

"Yes?"

"Can you be ready to leave Khartoum at four o'clock in the morning?"

For a moment she made no reply. It seemed to her an incredible happiness that they were really to go away together. But quickly collecting her wandering thoughts she answered:

"Yes, I can be ready."

"Then go down to the Post Landing. I shall be there with a launch."

"Yes, yes!" Her heart was beating furiously.

"Osman, the guide who brought me here, will be waiting with camels on the other side of the river."

"Yes, yes, yes!"

"We are to ride as far as Atbara, and take train from there to the Red Sea."

"And what then?"

"God knows what then. We must wait for the direction of fate. America, perhaps, as we always hoped and intended."

She looked quickly round, then took his face between her hands and kissed him.

"To-morrow morning at four o'clock," she whispered.

"At four," he repeated.

A thousand thoughts were flashing through her mind but she asked no further questions, and at the next moment she went off to her own quarters.

The door of her room was ajar, and the face of the Arab woman, who was within, doing something with the clothes of the child, seemed to wear the same mocking smile as before; but Helena was neither angry nor alarmed. When she asked herself if the woman had seen or heard what had taken place between Gordon and herself no dangers loomed before her in relation to their flight.

Her confidence in Gordon—his strength, his courage, his power to protect her—was absolute. If he intended to take her away he would do so, and not Ishmael or all the Arabs on earth would stop him.

XXIII

GORDON did not allow himself to sleep that night, lest he should not be awake when the hour came to go. The room he shared with Ishmael was large and it had one window looking to the river and another to Khartoum. Through these windows, which were open, he heard every noise of the desert town by night.

Sometimes there was the dead measured thud of a camel's tread on the unpaved streets; sometimes the light jolt of a donkey's hoofs; at intervals there were the faint and distant cries of the night-watchmen from various parts of the town, intersecting the air like cross currents of wireless telegraphy, and once an hour there was the sharp guttural voice of Black Zogal at the door of their own house, calling the confession of faith.

"There is no god but God—no god but God!"

It had been late when Ishmael came to bed, and even then, being excited and in high spirits, and finding Gordon still awake, he had talked for a long time in the darkness of his preparations for the forthcoming pilgrimage and his hopes of its progress across the desert—three and a half

miles an hour, fourteen hours a day, making a month for
the journey altogether. But finding that Gordon did not
reply, and thinking he must be sleepy, he wished him a good-
night and a blessed morning, and then, with a few more
words that were trustful, affectionate, warm-hearted and
brotherly, he fell asleep.

It was after twelve by this time, and though Gordon intended to rise at three it seemed to him that the few hours
between would never end. He listened to the measured
breathing of the sleeping man and counted the cries outside,
but the time passed as if with feet of lead.

It was never quite dark and through the luminous dark-
blue of the southern night, fretted with stars, nearly everything outside could be dimly seen. Of all lights, that is the
one most conducive to thought, and in spite of himself
Gordon could not help thinking. The obstinate questions
which he had been able to crush down during the day were
now rising to torment him.

"What will happen when this household, which is now
asleep, awakes in the morning?" he asked himself.

He knew quite well what would happen. He would soon
be missed. Helena would be missed, too, and it would be
concluded that they had gone together. But after he had
banished the picture which rose to his mind's eye of the
confusion that would ensue on the discovery of their flight,
he set himself to defend it.

It was true that he was breaking the pledge he had made
to the people when he undertook to go into Cairo, but he
had made his promise under a mistake as to his own position,
and therefore it was not incumbent upon him to keep it now
that he knew the truth.

It was true that Helena was breaking the betrothal which
she had entered into with Ishmael, but she, too, had acted
under an error, and therefore her marriage was not binding
upon her conscience.

But do what he would to justify himself he could not
shake off a sense of deceit and even of treachery. He
thought of Ishmael and how he had heaped kindness and
honour upon him since he came to Khartoum. He thought

of Helena and of the shame with which her flight would
overwhelm the man who considered himself her husband.

"Go on!" something seemed to say in a taunting whisper. "Fly away! Seek your own happiness and think of
nothing else! This is what you came to Khartoum for!
This is what your great hopes and aims amount to! Leave
this good man in the midst of the confusion you have
brought upon him! Let him go into Cairo, innocent though
he is, and die by the cruel error of fate! That's good!
That's brave! That's worthy of a man and a soldier!"

Against thoughts like these he tried to set the memory
of old Mahmud's words at the meeting of the Sheikhs:
"Man cannot resist his destiny. If God wills that you
should go into Cairo you will go and God will protect you!"

But there was really only one way to reconcile himself
to what he intended to do, and that was to think of Helena
and to keep her beautiful face constantly before him. She
was on the other side of the wall, and she would be awake
now—the only other person in the house who was not
asleep—thinking of him and waiting for the hour when they
were to escape.

The luminous dark blue of the air died into the soft
red of early dawn, the "Wahhed" of the night-watchmen
became less frequent, and the call of Black Zogal stopped
altogether. It was now three o'clock and Gordon, who had
not undressed, rose to a sitting position on his bed.

This brought him face to face with Ishmael, whose
angerib was on the opposite side of the room. The Arab
was sleeping peacefully. He, too, had lain down in his
clothes, having to rise early, but he had unrolled his turban,
leaving nothing on his head but his Mecca skull-cap, which
made him look like the picture of a saintly Pope. The dim
light that was filtering through the windows rested on him
as he lay in his white garments under a white sheepskin.
There was a look of serenity, of radiance, almost of divinity in his tranquil face.

Gordon felt as if he were a thief and a murderer—stealing from and stabbing the man who loved and trusted him.
He had an almost irresistible impulse to waken Ishmael

there and then and tell him plainly what he was about to do. But the thought of Helena came back again, and he remembered that that was quite impossible.

At length he rose to go. He was still wearing Hafiz's slippers, but he found himself stepping on his toes to deaden the sound of his tread. When he got to the door he opened it carefully so as to make no noise; but just at that moment the sleeping man stirred and began to speak.

In the toneless voice of sleep but nevertheless with an accent of affection which Gordon had never heard from him before, Ishmael said:

"Rani! *My* Rani!"

Gordon stood and listened, not daring to move. After a moment all was quiet again. There was no sound in the room but Ishmael's measured breathing as before.

How Gordon got out at last he never quite knew. When he recovered his self-possession he was in the guest-room, drawing aside the curtain that covered the open doorway and feeling the cool, fresh, odourless desert air on his hot face and in his nostrils.

He saw Black Zogal stretched out at the bottom of the wooden steps, fast asleep and with his staff beside him. The insurgent dawn was sweeping up, but all was silent both within and without. Save for the Nubian's heavy snoring there was not a sound about the house.

Feeling his throat to be parched, he turned back to the water-niche for a drink, and while he was lifting the can to his lips his eye fell on a letter which had been left for him there, having come by the train which arrived late last night and then been specially delivered after he had gone to bed.

The letter, which was in a black-bordered envelope, was addressed:

"SHEIKH OMAR BENANI *in the care of* ISHMAEL AMEER."

At first sight the handwriting struck him like a familiar face, but before he had time to recognise it, he was conscious of a crushing sense of fatality, a vague but almost heartbreaking impression that while he had been spending the long black hours of the night in building up hopes of flying away with Helena, this little packet of sealed paper had all the time been waiting outside his door to tell him they could not go.

He took it and opened it with trembling fingers and read it at a glance as one reads a picture. It was from Hafiz and it told him that his mother was dead.

Then all the pent-up pain and shame of the night rolled over him like a breaking wave, and he dropped down onto the nearest seat and wept like a child.

XXIV

CONTRARY to Gordon's surmise Helena had slept soundly, with the beautiful calm confidence of one who relied absolutely upon him and thought her troubles were over; but she awoke at half-past three as promptly as if an alarm clock had awakened her.

The arms of Ayesha were then closely encircling her neck and it was with difficulty that she liberated herself without awakening the child also, but as soon as she had done so she could not resist an impulse to kiss the little one, so boundless was her happiness and so entirely at that moment had she conquered the sense that Ishmael's innocent daughter had been a constant torture to her.

Then dressing rapidly in her usual mixed Eastern and Western costume, and throwing a travelling cloak over her shoulders instead of her Indian veil, but giving no thought to the other belongings which she must leave behind, she stepped lightly out of the sleeping-room.

The moment she entered the guest-room she heard a moan, and before realising where it came from, she said:

" Who's there ? "

Then Gordon lifted his tear-stained face to her face, and, without speaking, held out the letter which hung from his helpless hand.

She took it and read it with a sense of overwhelming disaster, while Gordon, with that access of grief which at the first moment of a great sorrow the presence of a loved one brings, heaped reproaches upon himself, as if all that he had done at the hard bidding of his conscience had been a sin and a crime.

"Poor mother! My poor, dear mother! It was I who made her last days unhappy."

Half an hour went by in this way, and the time for going passed. Helena dared not tell him that their opportunity for flight was slipping away—it seemed like an outrage to think of that now—so she stood by his side, feeling powerless to comfort him and dazed by the blow that had shattered their hopes.

Then Black Zogal, being awakened by the sound of Gordon's weeping, came in with his wild eyes, and after him came Abdullah, and then Zenoba, who, gathering an idea of trouble, went off to awaken Ishmael and old Mahmud, so that in a little while the whole of the Arab household were standing round Gordon as he sat doubled up on the edge of a divan.

When Ishmael heard what had happened he was deeply moved, and sitting down by Gordon's side he took one of his hands and smoothed it, while in that throbbing voice which went to the heart of everybody, and with a look of suffering in his swarthy face and luminous black eyes, he spoke some sympathetic words.

"All life ends in death, my brother. This world is a place of going, not of staying. The mystery of pain—who can fathom it? Life would be unbearable but for one thought—that God is over all. He rules everything for the best. Yes, believe me, everything. I have had my hours of sorrow, too, but I have always found it so."

After a while Gordon was able to control his grief, and then Ishmael asked him if he would not read aloud his letter. With some reluctance Gordon did so, but it required all his self-control to repeat his mother's message.

Leaving out the usual Arabic salutations, he began where Hafiz said:

"With a heavy heart I have to tell you, my most dear brother, that your sweet and saintly mother died this morning. She had been sinking ever since you went away, but the end came so quickly that it took us all by surprise."

Gordon's voice thickened and Ishmael said:

"Take your time, brother."

"She had the consolation of her religion and I think she passed in peace. There was only one thing clouded her closing hours. On her death-bed she was constantly expressing an earnest hope that you might all be reunited—you and she and your father and Helena, who are now so far apart."

"Take time, oh, my brother," said Ishmael, and seeing that Helena also was moved, he took her hand too, as if to strengthen her.

Thus he sat between them, comforting both, while Gordon in a husky voice struggled on.

"Not long before she died she wished to send you a message, but the power of life was low in her and she could not write, except to sign her name (as you see below), and then she did not know where you were to be found. But my mother promised her that I should take care that whatever she said should come to your hands, and these were the words she sent: 'Tell my boy that my last thoughts were about him. Though I am sorry he took the side of the false—the false prophet——'"

"Go on, brother, go on," said Ishmael in his soft voice.

"—say I am certain he did what he thought was right. Be sure you tell him I died happy, because—because I know I shall see him again. If I am never to see him in this world I will do so in the world to come. Say—say I shall be waiting for him there. And tell him it will not seem long."

It was with difficulty that Gordon came to the end, for his eyes were full of tears and his throat was parched and tight, and he would have broken down altogether but for the sense of Helena's presence by his side.

Ishmael was now more deeply moved than before.

"How she must have loved you!" he said, and then he began to speak of his own mother and what she had done for him.

"She was only a poor, ignorant woman, perhaps, but she died to save me, and I loved her with all my heart."

At that the two black servants, Abdullah and Zogal, who had been standing before Gordon in silence, tried to utter some homely words of comfort, and old Mahmud, wiping his wet eyes, said:

"May God be merciful to your mother, my son, and forgive her all her sins."

"She was a saint—she never had any," replied Gordon, whereupon the Arab nurse, who alone of all that household had looked on at this scene with dry and evil eyes, said bitterly:

"Nevertheless she died as a Christian and an unbeliever, therefore she cannot look for mercy."

Then Helena's eyes flashed like fire into the woman's face, and Gordon felt the blood rush to his head, but Ishmael was before them both.

"Zenoba, ask pardon of God," he said, and before the thunder of his voice and the majesty of his glance the Arab woman fell back.

"Heed her not, my brother," said Ishmael, turning back to Gordon, and then he added:

"We all serve under the same General, and though some of us wear uniform of red, and some of brown, and some of blue, he who serves best is the best soldier. In the day of victory will our General ask us the colour of our garments? No!"

At that generous word Gordon burst into tears once more, but Ishmael said:

"Don't weep for one who has entered into the ways of Paradise."

When Gordon had regained his composure Ishmael asked him if he would read part of the letter again, but knowing what part it would be—the part about himself—he tried to excuse himself, saying he was not fit to read any more.

"Then the Rani will read," said Ishmael, and far as Helena would have fled from the tragic ordeal she could not escape from it. So in her soft and mellow voice she read on without faltering until she came to her own name, and then she stopped and the tears began to trickle down her cheeks.

"Go on," said Ishmael; "don't be afraid of what follows."

And when Helena came to "false prophet" he turned to Gordon and said:

"Your dear mother didn't know how much I love you— But she knows now," he added, "for the dead know all."

There was no further interruption until Helena had finished, and then Ishmael said:

"She didn't know, either, what work the Merciful had waiting for you in Khartoum. Perhaps you did not know yourself. Something called you to come here. Something drew you on. Which of us has not felt like that? But God guides our hearts—the Merciful makes no mistakes."

Nobody spoke, but Gordon's eyes began to shine with a light which Helena, who was looking at him, had never seen in them before.

"All the same," continued Ishmael, "you hear what your mother says, and it is not for me to keep you against your will. If you wish to go back now none shall reproach you. Speak, Omar, do you wish to leave me?"

There was a moment of tense silence in which Gordon hesitated and Helena waited breathlessly for his reply. Then with a great effort Gordon answered:

"No."

"El Hamdullillah!" cried the two black servants, and then Ishmael sent Zogal into the town and the camp to say that the faithful would bid farewell to Omar in the mosque the following night.

That evening after sunset, instead of preaching his usual sermon to the people squatting on the sand in front of his house, Ishmael read the prayers for the dead, while Gordon and Helena and a number of the Sheikhs sat on the divans in the guest-room.

When the service was over, and the company was breaking up, the old men pressed Gordon's hand as they were passing out and said:

"May God give you compensation!"

As soon as they were gone Gordon approached Helena and whispered hurriedly:

"I must speak to you soon—where can it be?"

"I ought to go to the water-women's well by the Goods Landing to-morrow morning," said Helena.

"At what hour?"

"Ten."

"I shall be there," said Gordon.

His eyes were still full of the strange wild light.

XXV

At ten o'clock next morning Helena was at the well by the Goods Landing where the water-women draw water in their earthern jars to water the gardens and the streets, and while standing among the gross creatures who, with their half-naked bodies and stark-naked souls, were crowding about her for what they could get, she saw Gordon coming down in his Bedouin dress with a firm, strong step.

His flickering steel-blue eyes were as full of light as when she saw them last, but that vague suggestion of his mother which she had hitherto seen in his face was gone, and there was a look of his father which she had never observed before.

"Let us walk this way," he said, indicating a road that went down the empty and unfrequented tongue of land that leads to the point at which the blue Nile and the white Nile meet.

"Helena," he said, stepping closely by her side, and speaking almost in her ear, "there is something I wish to say—to ask—and everything depends on your answer—what we are to do and what is to become of us."

"What is it?" said she, with trembling voice.

"When our escape from Khartoum was stopped by the letter telling me of my mother's death, I thought at first it was only an accident—a sad, strange accident that it should arrive at that moment."

"And don't you think so now?" she asked.

"No, I think it was a divine intervention."

She glanced up at him. "He is going to talk about the betrothal," she thought.

But he did not do so. In his intense and poignant voice he continued:

"When I proposed that we should go away together, I supposed your coming here had been due to a mistake—that my coming here had been due to a mistake—that your sending that letter into Cairo and my promising to take Ishmael's place had been due to a mistake—that it had all been a mistake—a long, miserable line of mistakes."

"And wasn't it?" she asked, walking on with her eyes to the sand.

"So far as we are concerned, yes, but with God—with God Almighty, mistakes do not happen."

They walked some paces in silence, and then in a still more poignant voice he said:

"Don't you believe that, Helena? Wasn't it true—what Ishmael said yesterday? Can you possibly believe that we have been allowed to go on as we have been going—both of us—without anything being meant by it? All a cruel, stupid, merciless, Almighty blunder?"

"Well?"

"Well, think of what would have happened if we had been allowed to carry out our plan. Ishmael would have gone into Cairo as he originally intended, and he would have been seized and executed for conspiracy. What then? The whole country—yes, the whole country from end to end —would have risen in revolt. The sleeping terror of religious hatred would have been awakened. It would have been the affair of El Azhar over again—only worse, a thousandfold worse."

Again a few steps in silence, and then:

"The insurrection would have been suppressed of course, but think of the bloodshed, the carnage! On the other hand——"

She saw what was coming and with difficulty she walked steadily.

"On the other hand if *I* go into Cairo as I have promised to do—as I am expected to do—there can be no such result. The moment I arrive I shall be arrested, and the moment I am arrested, I shall be identified and handed over to the military authorities to be tried for my offences as a soldier.   There will be no religious significance in my punishment, therefore there will be no fanatical frenzy provoked by it and consequently there can be no bloodshed. Don't you see that, Helena?"

She could not answer; she felt sick and faint. After a moment he went on in the same eager, enthusiastic voice:

"But that's not all.   There is something better than that."

"Better—do you say better?"

"Something that comes closer to us at all events—Do you believe in omens, Helena? That some mystic sense tells us things of which we have no proof, no evidence?"

She bent her head without raising her eyes from the sand.

"Well, I have a sense of some treachery going on in Cairo that Ishmael knows nothing about, and I believe it was just this treachery which led to the idea of his going there at all."

She looked up into his face, and thinking he read her thought, he said quickly:

"Oh, I know—I've heard about the letters of the Ulema—that those suggestions of assassination, and so forth, were signed by the simple old Chancellor of El Azhar. But isn't it possible that a subtler spirit inspired them?—Helena?"

"Yes," she faltered.

"Do you remember that one day in the Citadel I said it was not really Judas Iscariot who betrayed Jesus, and that there was somebody in Egypt now who was doing what the High Priest of the Jews did in Palestine two thousand years ago?"

"The Grand Cadi?"

"Yes! Something tells me that that subtle old scoundrel is playing a double-sword game—with the Ulema and with the Government—and that his object is not only to destroy Ishmael, but, by awakening the ancient religious terror, to ruin England as well—tempt her to ruin her prestige at all events."

They had reached the margin of the river and he stopped.

"Well?" she faltered again.

"Well, I am a British soldier still, Helena, even though I am a disgraced one, and I want to—I want to save the good name of my country."

She could not speak—she felt as if she would choke.

"I want to save the good name of the Consul-General also. He is my father, and though he no longer thinks of me as his son, I want to save him from—from himself."

"I can do it, too," he added eagerly. "At this moment I am perhaps the only man who can. I am nobody now— only a runaway and a deserter—but I can cross the line of fire and so give warning."

"But, Gordon, don't you see——"

"Oh, I know what you are going to say, Helena. I must die for it, yes! Nobody wants to do that, if he can help it, but I can't! Listen!"

She raised her eyes to his—they seemed to be ablaze with a kind of frenzy.

"Death was the penalty of what I did in Cairo, and if I did not stay there to be court-martialled and condemned, was it because I wanted to save my life? No, I thought there was nothing left in my life that made it worth saving. It was because I wanted to give it in some better cause. Something told me I should, and when I came to Khartoum I didn't know what fate was before me, or what I had to do, but I know now. *This* is what I have to do, Helena—to go back to Cairo instead of Ishmael and so save England and Egypt and my father and these poor Moslem people and prevent a world of bloodshed."

Then Helena, who in her nervousness had been scraping her feet on the sand, said in a halting, trembling voice:

"Was this what you wanted to say to me, Gordon?"

"Yes, but now I want *you* to say something to *me*."

"What is that?" she asked, trembling.

"*To tell me to go.*"

It was like a blow. She felt as if she would fall.

"I cannot go unless you send me, Helena—not as things stand now—leaving you here—under these conditions—in a place like this—alone. Therefore tell me to go, Helena."

Tears sprang to her eyes. She thought of all the hopes she had so lately cherished, all the dreams of the day before of love and a new life among quite different scenes—sweet scenes full of the smell of new-cut grass, the rustling of trees, the swish of the scythe, the songs of birds and the ringing of church bells instead of this empty and arid wilderness—and then of the ruin, the utter wreck and ruin, that everything was falling to.

"Tell me to go, Helena—tell me," he repeated.

It was crushing. She could not bear it.

"I cannot," she said. "Don't ask me to do such a thing. Just when we were going away, too—expecting to escape from all this miserable tangle and to be happy at last——"

"But should we be happy, Helena? Say we escaped to Europe, America, Australia, anywhere far enough away, and what I speak of were to come to pass, should we be happy—should we?"

"We should be together at all events, and we should be able to love each other——"

"But could we love each other with the memory of all that misery—the misery we might have prevented—left here behind us?"

"At least we should be alive and safe and well."

"Should we be well if our whole life became abominable to us, Helena?— On the other hand——"

"On the other hand you want us to part—never to see each other again?"

"It's hard—I know it's hard—but isn't that better than to become odious in each other's eyes?"

A cruel mixture of anger and sorrow and despair took possession of her, and, choking with emotion, she said:

"I have nobody but you now, yet you want me to tear my heart out—to sacrifice the love that is my only happiness, my only refuge— Oh, I cannot do it! You are asking me to send you into the jaws of death itself—that's it—the very jaws of death itself—and I cannot do it. I tell you I cannot, I cannot! There is no woman in the world who could."

There was silence for a moment after this vehement cry, then in a low tone he said:

"Every soldier's wife does as much when she sends her husband into battle, Helena."

"Ah!"

She caught her breath as if a hand from heaven had smitten her.

"Am I not going into battle now? And aren't you a soldier's daughter?"

There was another moment of silence in which he looked out on the sparkling waters of the Blue Nile and she gazed through clouded eyes on the sluggish waves of the White.

Something had suddenly begun to rise in her throat. *This* was the real Gordon, the hero who had won battles, the soldier who had faced death before, and she had never known him until now!

A whirlwind of sensation and emotions seemed to race through her soul and body. She felt hot, she felt cold, she felt ashamed, and then all at once she felt as if she were being lifted out of herself by the spirit of the man beside her. At length she said, trying to speak calmly:

"You are right, quite right, you are always right, Gordon. If you feel like that about going into Cairo you must go. It is your duty. You have received your orders."

"Helena!" he cried in a burst of joy.

"You mustn't think about me, though. I'm sorry for what I said awhile ago, but I'm better now. I have always thought that if the time ever came to me to see my dearest go into battle, I should not allow myself to be afraid."

"I was sure of you, Helena, quite sure."

"This doesn't look like going into battle, perhaps, but it may be something still better—going to save life, to prevent bloodshed."

"Yes, yes!" he said, and struggling to control herself, she continued:

"You mustn't think about leaving me here, either. Whatever happens in this place I shall always remember that you love me, so—so nothing else will matter."

"Nothing—nothing!"

"And though it may be hard to think that you have gone to your death, and that I—that in a sense I have been the cause of it——"

"But you haven't, Helena! Your hand may have penned that letter, but a higher Power directed it."

She looked at him with shining eyes and answered in a firmer voice, and with a proud lift of her beautiful head:

"I don't know about that, Gordon. I only know that you want to give your life in a great cause. And though they have degraded you and driven you out and hunted you down like a dog, you are going to die like a man and an Englishman."

"And you tell me to do it, Helena?"

"Yes, for I'm a soldier's daughter, and in my heart I'm a soldier's wife as well, and I shouldn't be worthy to be either if I didn't tell you to do your duty, whatever the consequences to me."

"My brave girl!" he cried, clutching at her hand.

Then they began to walk back.

As they walked they encouraged each other.

"We are on the right road now, Helena."

"Yes, we are on the right road now, Gordon."

"We are doing better than running away."

"Yes, we are doing better than running away."

"The train leaves Khartoum this evening and I suppose they want to say farewell to me in the mosque at sunset— You'll be strong to the last and not break down when the time comes for me to go?"

"No, I'll not break down—when the time comes for you to go."

But for all her brave show of courage her eyes were filling fast and the tears were threatening to fall.

"Better leave me now," she whispered. "Let me go back alone."

He was not sorry to let her go ahead, for at sight of her emotion his own was mastering him.

"Will she keep up to the end?" he asked himself.

XXVI

As the hours of the day passed on, Helena became painfully aware that her courage was ebbing away.

Unconsciously Ishmael was adding to her torture. Soon after the midday meal he called on her to write to his dictation a letter which Gordon was to take into Cairo.

"One more letter, O Rani! only one, before our friend and brother leaves us."

It was to the Ulema, telling them of the change in his plans and begging them to be good to Gordon.

"Trust him and love him. Receive him as you would receive me, and believe that all he does and says is according to my wish and word."

Helena had to write this letter. It was like writing Gordon's death-warrant.

Later in the day, seeing her idle, nibbling the top of the reed pen which she held in her trembling fingers, Ishmael called for the kufiah.

"Where is the kufiah, O Rani!—the kufiah that was to disguise the messenger of God from his enemies?"

And when Helena, in an effort to escape from that further torture, protested that in Gordon's case a new kufiah was not essential, because he wore the costume of a Bedouin already, Ishmael replied:

"But the kufiah he wears now is white and every official in Khartoum has seen it. Therefore another is necessary, and let it be of another colour."

At that, with fiendish alacrity, the Arab woman ran off for a strip of red silken wool and Helena had to shape and stitch it.

It was like stitching Gordon's shroud.

The day seemed to fly on the wings of an eagle, the sun

26

began to sink, the shadows to lengthen on the desert sand, and the time to approach for the great ceremony of the leave-taking in the mosque. Helena was for staying at home, but Ishmael would not hear of it.

"Nay, my Rani," he said. "In the court-yard after prayers we must say farewell to Omar, and you must clothe him in the new kufiah that is to hide him from his foes. Did you not promise to do as much for me? And shall it be said that you grudge the same honour to my friend and brother?"

Half an hour afterward, Ishmael having gone off hand in hand with Gordon, and old Mahmud and Zenoba and Ayesha and the two black servants having followed him, Helena put on a veil for the first time since coming to Khartoum, and made her way to the mosque.

The streets of the town as she passed through them seemed to be charged with an atmosphere of excitement that was little short of frenzy, but the court-yard, when she had crossed the threshold, was like the scene of some wild phantasmagoria.

A crowd of men and women, squatting about the walls of the open space, were strumming on native drums, playing on native pipes and uttering the weird, monotonous ululation that is the expression of the Soudanese soul in its hours of joy.

A moment later Helena was in the gallery, the people had made way for her, and she was sitting as before by the Arab woman and the child. Overhead was a brazen, blood-red, southern sky; below were a thousand men on crimson carpets, some in silks, some in rags, all moving and moaning like tumultuous waves in a cavern of the sea.

The Reader in the middle of the mosque was chanting the Koran, the muezzin in the minaret was calling to prayers, the men on the floor were uttering their many-throated responses, and the very walls of the mosque itself seemed to be vibrating with religious fervour.

A moment after Helena had taken her seat Ishmael entered, followed by Gordon, and the people gathered round them to kiss their hands and garments. Helena felt her head reel, she wanted to cry out, and it was with difficulty she controlled herself.

Then the Reader stood up in his desk and recited an invocation and the people repeated it after him:

"God is Most Great!"

"God is Most Great!"

"There is no god but God——!"

"Mohammed is His Prophet——!"

"Listen to the preacher——!"

"Amen!"

"Amen!"

After that Ishmael rose from his knees before the Kibleh, took the wooden sword at the foot of the pulpit, ascended to the topmost step, and, after a preliminary prayer, began to preach.

Never had Helena seen him so eager and excited, and every passage of his sermon seemed to increase both his own ecstasy and the emotion of his hearers.

Helena hardly heard his words, so far away were her thoughts and so steadfastly were her eyes fixed on the other figure in front of the Kibleh, but a general sense of their import was beating on her brain as on a drum.

All religions began in poverty and ended in corruption.

It had been so with Islam, which began with the breaking of idols and went on to the worship of wealth, the quest of power, the lust of conquest—Caliphs seeking to establish their claim not by election and the choice of God, but by theft and murder.

It had been so with Christianity, which began in meekness and humility and went on to pride and persecution— Holy Fathers exchanging their cells for palaces, and their poverty for pomp, forgetting the principle of their great Master, whose only place in their midst was in pictured windows, on vaporous clouds, blessing with outstretched arms a Church which favoured everything he fought against and a world which practised everything he condemned.

"What is the result, oh, my brothers? War, wealth, luxury, sensuality, slavery, robbery, injustice and oppression!

"Listen to the word of the Holy Koran: ' And Pharaoh

made proclamation among his people, saying, Is not this Kingdom of Egypt mine and the rivers thereof?'

"But not in Egypt only, nor alone under the Government of the King who lives across the seas, but all the world over, wheresoever human empires are founded, wheresoever men claim the earth and the fruits of the earth and the treasures that lie in the bowels of the earth—impoverishing the children of men to obtain them or destroying their souls that they may deck and delight their bodies—there the Pharaohs of this world are saying, 'Is not this Kingdom of Egypt mine and the rivers thereof?'

"But the earth and the fruits of the earth and the treasures of the earth are God's, my brothers, and He is coming to reclaim them, and to right the wrongs of the oppressed, to raise up the downtrodden and to comfort the broken-hearted."

The mosque seemed to rock with the shouts which followed these words, and as soon as the cries of the people had subsided, the voice of Ishmael, now louder and more tremulous than before, rang through its vaults again.

"Deep in the heart of man, my brothers, is the expectation of a day when the Almighty will send his Messenger to purify and pacify the world and to banish intolerance and wrong. The Jews look for the Messiah, the Christians for the divine man of Judæa, and we that are Moslems for the Mahdi and the Christ.

"In all climes and ages, amid all sorrows and sufferings, sunk in the depths of ignorance, sold into slavery, the poorest of the poor, the most miserable among the most miserable of the world, humanity has yet cherished that great expectation. Real as life, real as death, real as wells of water in a desert land to man on his earthly pilgrimage, is the hope of a Deliverer from oppression and injustice—and who shall say it is vain and false? It is true, my brothers, true as the sky rolling overhead. Our Deliverer is coming! He is coming soon! He is coming now!"

Ishmael's tremulous voice had by this time broken into hysterical sobs and the responses of his hearers had risen to delirious cries.

More of the same kind followed which Helena did not hear, but suddenly she was awakened to full consciousness of what was going on about her by hearing Ishmael speak of Gordon and the people answering him with rapturous shouts:

"He is not of our race, yet no doubt enters into our hearts of his fidelity."

"El Hamdullillah!"

"He is not of our faith, yet he will be true to God and his people."

"Allah!" "Allah!"

"For us he has left his home, his country, and his kindred."

"Allah!" "Allah!" "Allah!"

"For us he is going into the place of danger."

"Allah!" "Allah!" "Allah!"

"What says the Lord in the Holy Koran?— 'They therefore who had left their country and suffered for my sake, I will surely bring them into gardens watered by rivers —a reward of God.'"

"Allah!" "Allah!" "Allah!"

"The Lord bless the white man to whom the black man is a brother! Bless him in the morning splendour! Bless him in the still of night! Bless him with children—the eye of the heart of man! Bless him with the love of woman— the joy and the crown of life!"

"Allah!" "Allah!" "Allah!"

"And may the Lord of majesty and might, Who has hitherto covered his head in battle, protect and preserve him now!"

At this last word the whole company of men on the floor below—men in silks and men in rags—rose to their feet as if they had been one being animated by one heart, and raising their arms to heaven, cried:

"Allah!" "Allah!" "Allah!" "Allah!"

Helena felt as if some one had taken her by the throat. To see these poor, emotional, Eastern children, with their brown and black faces, streaming with tears and full of the love of Gordon, shouting down God's blessing upon him, was stifling her.

It was like singing his dirge before he was dead.

During the next few minutes Helena was vaguely aware that Ishmael had come down from the pulpit; that the Reader was reciting prayers again; that the men on the crimson carpets were bowing, kneeling, prostrating themselves and putting their foreheads to the floor; and finally that the whole congregation was rising and surging out of the mosque.

When she came to herself once more somebody by her side—it was Zenoba—was touching her shoulder and saying: "The Master is in the court-yard and he is calling for you—come!"

The scene outside was even more tumultuous. Instead of the steady solemnity of the service within the mosque, there was the tum-tumming of the drums, the screeling of the pipes, and the lu-luing of the women.

The great enclosure was densely crowded, but a space had been cleared in the centre of the court-yard, where the Ulema of Khartoum, in their gray farageeyahs, were ranged in a wide half-circle. In the mouth of this half-circle Gordon was standing in his Bedouin dress with Ishmael by his side.

Silence was called and then Ishmael gave Gordon his last instructions and spoke his last words of farewell.

"Tell our brothers, the Ulema of Cairo," he said, "that we are following close behind you, and when the time comes to enter the city we shall be lying somewhere outside their walls. Let them therefore put a light on their topmost height—on the minaret of the mosque of Mohammed Ali—after the call to prayers at midnight—and we shall take that as a sign that the light of the world is with you, that the Expected One has appeared, and that we may enter in peace, injuring no man, being injured by none, without malice toward any and with charity to all."

Then seeing Helena as she came out of the mosque, veiled and with her head down, he called on her to come forward.

"Now do as you have always designed and intended," he said. "Cover our friend and forerunner with the kufiah you have made for him. that until his work is done and the time has come to reveal himself, he may, like the angel of the Lord, be invisible to his foes."

What happened after that Helena never quite knew— only that a way had been made for her through the throng of wild-eyed people and that she was standing by Gordon's side.

Down to that instant she had intended to bear herself bravely for Gordon's sake if not for her own, but now a hundred cruel memories came in a flood to sap away her strength—memories of the beautiful moments of their love, of the little passages of their life together that had been so tender and so sweet. In vain she tried to recover the spirit with which he had inspired her in the morning, to think how much better it was that he should die gloriously than live in disgrace, to feel the justice, the necessity, the inevitableness of what he was going to do.

It was impossible. She could think of nothing but that she was seeing Gordon for the last time, that he was leaving her behind him, among these Allah-intoxicated Arabs, that he was going away, not into battle—with its chance of victory and its hope of life—but to death, certain death, perhaps shameful death, and that—say what he would about Fate and Destiny or the will of God—she herself was sending him to his doom.

She felt that the tears were running down her cheeks under her thin white veil, and that Gordon must see them, but she could not keep them back, and though she had promised not to break down she knew that at that last moment, in the face of the death that was about to separate them, the dauntless heroine of the morning was nothing better now than a poor, weak, heart-broken woman.

Meantime the drums and the pipes and the lu-luing had begun again and she was conscious that under the semi-savage din Gordon was speaking to her and comforting her.

"Keep up! Be brave! Nobody knows what may happen. I'll write. You shall hear from me again."

He had taken off the white kufiah which he had hitherto worn and she could see his face. It was calm—the calmest man's face in all that vast assembly.

The sight of his face strengthened her, and suddenly a new element entered into the half-barbaric scene—an element that was half human and half divine. These poor half-civilised people thought Gordon was going to risk his life for them, that he was going to die—deliberately to die for them—to save them from themselves, from the consequences of their fanaticism, the panic of their rulers, and the fruits of the age-long hatred that had separated the black man from the white.

Helena felt her bosom heave, her nerves twitch, her fingers dig trenches in her palms, and her thoughts fly up to scenes of sacrifice which men talk of with bated breath.

"If he can do it why can't I?" she asked herself, and, taking the red kufiah, which the Arab woman was thrusting into her hands, with a great effort she put it onto Gordon —over his head and under his chin and across his shoulders and about his waist.

It was like clothing him for the grave.

Every eye had been on her and when her work was done, Ishmael, who was now weeping audibly, demanded silence and called on the Ulema to recite the first Surah:

"Praise be to God, the Lord of all creatures——"

When the weird chanting had come to an end the hoarse voices of the people broke afresh into loud shouts of "Allah!" "Allah!" "El Hamdullillah!"

In the midst of the wild maelstrom of religious frenzy which followed—the tum-tumming of the drums, the screeling of the pipes and the ululation of the women—Helena felt her hand grasped, and heard Gordon speaking to her again:

"Don't faint! Don't be afraid! Don't break down at the last moment."

"I'm not afraid," she answered, but whether with her voice or only with her lips she never knew.

Still the drums, the pipes, the zaghareet and the delirious cries of "Allah!" And to show Gordon that she felt no fear, that she was not going to faint or to break down, Helena also, in the fierce tension of the moment, cried:

"Allah! El Hamdullillah!"

"That's right! That's brave! God bless you!" whispered the voice by her side. And again a moment later: "God bless and protect you!"

After that she heard no more. She saw the broad gate of the court-yard thrown open—she saw a long streak of blood-red sand outside—she saw Gordon turn away from her —she saw Ishmael embrace and kiss him—she saw the surging mass of hot and streaming black and brown faces close about him—and then a loud wind seemed to roar in her ears, the earth seemed to give way under her feet, the brazen sky seemed to reel about her head, and again she felt as if she were falling, falling, falling into a bottomless abyss.

When she recovered consciousness the half-barbaric scene was over, and she was being carried into the silence of her own room in the arms of Ishmael, who with many words of tender endearment was laying her gently on her bed.

XXVII

That day, under the two crackling flags, the Crescent and the Union Jack, Lady Mannering had given a party in the garden of the Palace of the Sirdar.

The physiognomy of the garden had changed since "the martyr of the Soudan" walked in it. Where scraggy mimosa bushes and long camel grasses had spurted up through patches of sand and blotches of baking earth there were the pleasant lawns, the sycamores, the date-trees and the blue streams of running water. And where the solitary soldier, with his daily whitening head had paced to and fro his face to the ground, smoking interminable cigarettes, there was a little group of officers of the military administration, with their charming wives and daughters, a Coptic priest, a Greek priest, a genial old Protestant clergyman, and a number of European visitors, chiefly English girls, wearing the lightest of white summer costumes and laughing and chattering like birds.

In pith helmets and straw hats Lady Mannering's guests
27

strolled about in the sunshine or drank tea at tables that were set under the cool shadow of spreading trees, while, at a little distance, the band of a black regiment, the Tenth Soudanese (sons and grandsons of the very men who in the gray dawn of a memorable morning had rushed in a wild horde into those very grounds for their orgy of British blood), played selections from the latest comic operas of London and New York.

The talk was the same all over the gardens—of the new Mahdi and his doings.

"Married to an Indian Princess, you say!"

"Oh, yes! Quite an emancipated person, too! A sort of thirty-second cousin of the Rani of Jhansi. It seems she was educated by an English governess, kicked over the traces, became a sort of semi-religious suffragette and followed her holy man to Egypt and the Soudan."

"How very droll! It is *too* amusing!"

The Sirdar, who had gone indoors some time before, returned to the garden dressed for a journey.

"Going away, your Excellency?"

"Yes, for a few weeks—to the lower Nile."

His ruddy, good-natured face was less bright than usual and his manner was noticeably less buoyant. A few of his principal officials gathered about him and he questioned them one by one.

"Any fresh news, Colonel?" he said, addressing the Governor of the city.

"No, sir. A sort of sing-song to-day in honour of the Bedouin Sheikh—that's all I hear about."

But the Financial Secretary spoke of further difficulties in the gathering of taxes—the land tax, the animal tax and the tax on the date-trees not having yet come in—and then the Inspector-General repeated an opinion he had previously expressed that everything gave evidence of a projected pilgrimage, presumably in a northerly direction and almost certainly to Cairo.

The Governor of the city corroborated this, and added that his Zabit, his police officer, had said that Ishmael Ameer, on passing to the mosque that day, had been saluted in the streets by a screaming multitude as the "Messenger" and the "Anointed One."

"It's just as I say," said the Inspector-General. "These holy men develop by degrees. This one will hoist his flag as soon as he finds himself strong enough—unless we stop him before he goes farther and the Soudan is lost to civilisation."

"Well, we'll see what Nuneham says," said the Sirdar, and at that moment his Secretary came to say that the launch was ready at the boat-landing to take him across the river to the train.

The Sirdar said good-bye to his guests, to his officers and to his wife, and as he left the garden of the palace the Soudanese band, sons of the Mahdi's men, played the number which goes to the words—

"They never proceed to follow that light,
But always follow me."

Half an hour afterward, while the Sirdar's black body-guard were ranged up on the platform of the railway station, and his black servant was packing his luggage into his compartment, the Governor-General was standing by the door of the carriage giving his last instructions to his General Secretary.

"Telegraph to the Consul-General and say—but please make a note of it."

"Yes, sir," said the Secretary, taking out his pocket-book and preparing to write.

"Think it best to go down myself to deal personally with matter of suspected mutiny in native army. Must admit increasing gravity of situation. Man here is undoubtedly acquiring name and influence of Mahdi, so time has come to consider carefully what we ought to do. Signs of intended pilgrimage, probably in northerly direction, enormous numbers of camels, horses and donkeys having been gathered up from various parts of country and immense quantities of food stuffs being bought for desert journey. Am leaving to-night and hope to arrive in four days."

"Four days," repeated the Secretary, as he came to an end.

At that moment a tall man in the costume of a Bedouin walked slowly up the platform. His head and most of his face were closely covered by the loose woollen shawl which the sons of the desert wear, leaving only his eyes, his nose, and part of his mouth visible. As he passed the Sirdar he looked sharply at him; then, pushing forward with long strides until he came to the third-class compartments, he stepped into the first of them, which was full of coloured people, strident with high-pitched voices and pungent with Eastern odours.

"Who was that?" asked the Sirdar.

"I don't know, sir," replied the Secretary. "I thought at first it was their Bedouin Sheikh, but I see I was mistaken."

Then came the whistle of the locomotive and its slow, rhythmic, volcanic throb. The guard saluted and the Sirdar got into his carriage.

"Well, good-bye, Graham! Don't forget the telegram."

"I'll send it at once— In cypher, sir?"

"In cypher, certainly."

At the next moment the Sirdar and Gordon Lord, travelling in the same train, were on their way to Cairo.

FOURTH BOOK

THE COMING DAY

THE Consul-General had taken a firm grasp of affairs. Every morning his Advisers and Under-Secretaries visited him, and it seemed as if they could not come too often or say too much. He who rules the machine of State becomes himself a machine, and it looked as if Lord Nuneham were ceasing to be a man.

Within a week after the day on which he received Helena's letter he was sitting in his bleak library walled with Blue Books, with the Minister of the Interior and the Adviser to the same department. The Minister was the sallow-faced Egyptian Pasha whom he had made Regent on the departure of the Khedive; the Adviser was a tall young Englishman with bright-red hair on which the red tarboosh sat strangely. They were discussing the "special weapon" which had been designed to meet special needs. The Consul-General's part of the discussion was to expound, the Adviser's was to applaud, the Minister's was to acquiesce.

The special weapon was a decree. It was to be known as the Law of Public Security, and it was intended to empower the authorities to establish a Special Tribunal to deal with all crimes, offences and conspiracies committed or conceived by natives against the State. It was to be called at any time and in any place on the request of the Agent and the Consul-General of Great Britain; its sentences, which were to be pronounced forthwith, were not to be subject to appeal; and it was to inflict such penalties as it might consider necessary, including the death penalty, without being bound by the provisions of the penal code.

"Drastic!" said the Pasha, with a sinister smile.

"Necessary," said the Consul-General, with a frown.

The Pasha became silent again while the virtual ruler of Egypt went on to say that the state of the country demanded that the Government should be armed with special powers to meet widespread fanaticism and secret conspiracy.

"No one deplores more than I do," he said, "that the existing law of the land is not sufficient to deal with the new perils by which we are threatened, but it is not, and therefore we must make it stronger."

"Certainly, my lord," said the red-headed figure in the fez, and again the sinister face of the Pasha smiled.

"And now tell me, Pasha," said the Consul-General, "how long a time will it take to pass this law through the Legislative Council and the Council of Ministers?"

The Pasha looked up out of his small shrewd eyes and answered:

"Just as long or as short as your lordship desires."

And then the Consul-General, who was wiping his spectacles, put them deliberately onto his nose, looked deliberately into the Pasha's face, and deliberately replied:

"Then let it be done without a day's delay, your Excellency."

A few minutes afterward, without too much ceremony, the Consul-General had dismissed his visitors and was tearing open a number of English newspapers which Ibrahim had brought into the room.

The first of them, the *Times*, contained a report of the Mansion House Dinner, headed "UNREST IN THE EAST, Important Speech by Foreign Minister."

The Consul-General found the beginning full of platitudes. Egypt had become the great gate between the Eastern and Western hemispheres. It was essential for the industry and enterprise of mankind that that gate should be kept open, and therefore it was necessary that Egypt should be under a peaceful, orderly, and legal Government.

Then, lowering the lights, the Minister had begun to speak to slow music. While it was the duty of Government to preserve order, it was also the duty of a Christian nation in occupation of a foreign country to govern it in the interests of the inhabitants, and, speaking for himself, he thought the executive authority would be strengthened, not weakened, by associating the people with the work of government. However this might be, the public could at least be sure that as long as the present Ministry remained in power it would countenance no policy on the part of its representatives that would outrage the moral, social, and, above all, religious sentiments of a Moslem people.

The Consul-General flung down the paper in disgust.

"Fossils of Whitehall! Dunces of Downing Street!"

For some minutes he tramped about the room, telling himself again that he didn't care a straw what any Government and any Foreign Minister might say, because he had a power stronger than either at his back—the public.

This composed his irritated nerves and presently he took up the other newspapers. Then came a shock. Without an exception the journals accepted the Minister's speech as a remonstrance addressed to him, and reading it so they sympathised with it.

One of them saw that Lord Nuneham, however pure and beneficent his intentions might be, had no right to force his ideals upon an alien race. Another hinted that he was destroying England's prestige in her Mohammedan dominions, and, if permitted to go on, he would not only endanger the peace of Egypt but also the safety of our Indian Empire. And a third, advocating the establishment of representative institutions, said that the recent arbitrary action of the Consul-General showed in glaringly dangerous colours the faults of the One-Man Rule which we granted to the King's representative while we denied it to the King himself.

The great Proconsul was, for some moments, utterly shaken—the sheet-anchor of his public life was gone. But within half an hour he had called for his first Secretary and was dictating a letter to the Premier, who was also the Minister of Foreign Affairs.

"Having read the report of your lordship's speech at the Mansion House," he said, "I find myself compelled to tell you that so great a difference between your lordship's views and mine makes it difficult for me to remain in Egypt.

"I take the view that nine-tenths of these people are still in swaddling clothes and that any attempt to associate them with the work of government would do a grave injustice to the inarticulate masses for whom we rule the country.

"I also take the view that Egypt is honeycombed with agitators, who, masquerading as religious reformers, are sowing sedition against British rule, and that the only way to deal with such extremists is by stern repression.

"Taking these views and finding them at variance with those of your lordship, I respectfully beg to tender my resignation of the post of H. M.'s Agent, Consul-General and Minister Plenipotentiary which I have held through so many long and laborious years, and at the same time to express the hope that my successor may be a man qualified by knowledge and experience of the East to deal with these millions of Orientals who, accustomed for seven thousand years to the dictation of imperial autocrats, are so easily inflamed by fanatics and yield so readily to the wily arts of spies and secret conspirators."

Having finished dictating his letter, the Consul-General asked when the next mail left for England, whereupon the Secretary, whose voice was now as tremulous as his hand had been, replied that there would be no direct post for nearly a week.

"That will do. Copy out the letter and let me have it to sign."

With a frightened look the Secretary turned to go.

"Wait! Of course you will observe absolute secrecy about the contents of it?"

With a tremulous promise to do so the Secretary left the room.

Then the Consul-General took up a calendar that had been standing on his desk and began to count the days.

"Five—ten—fifteen, and five days more before I can receive a reply—it's enough," he thought.

England's eyes would be opened by that time and the public would see how much the Government knew about Egypt. Accept his resignation? They dare not! It would do them good, though—serve as a rebuke, and strengthen his own hands for the work he had now to do.

What was that work? To destroy the man who had robbed him of his son.

II

EARLY the next morning the Consul-General received a letter from the Princess Nazimah, saying she had something to communicate and proposed to come to tea with him. At five o'clock she came, attended by sais, footmen, outriders and even eunuch, but wearing the latest of Paris hats and the lightest of chiffon veils.

Tea was laid on the shady veranda overlooking the fresh verdure of the garden, with its wall of purple bougain-villea, and thinking to set the lady at ease the Consul-General had told Fatimah, instead of Ibrahim, to serve it. But hardly had they sat down when the Princess said in French:

"Send that woman away. I don't trust women. I'm a woman myself and I know too much of them."

A few minutes afterward she said, "Now you can give me a cigarette. Light it. That will do. Thank you!" Then squatting her plump person in a large cane-chair she prepared to speak, while the Consul-General, who was in his most silent mood, composed himself to listen.

"I suppose you were surprised when this woman who blossomed out of a harem wrote to say that she was coming to take tea with you? Here she is, though, and now she has something to say to you."

Then puff, puff, puff from the scarlet lips, while the powdered face grew hard, and the eyes, heavily shaded with kohl, looked steadfastly forward.

"I have always suspected it, but I discovered it for certain only yesterday. And where did I discover it? In my own salon!"

"What did you discover in your own salon, Princess?" asked the Consul-General in his tired voice.

"Conspiracy!"

Trained as was the Consul-General's face to self-command, it betrayed surprise and alarm.

"Yes, conspiracy against you and against England."

"You mean, perhaps, that the man Ishmael Ameer——"

"Rubbish! Ishmael indeed! He is in it certainly. In a country like Egypt the holy man always is. Religion and politics are twins here—Siamese twins you may say, for you couldn't get a slip of paper between them— What's that? The Mahdist movement political? Perhaps it was, but politics on the top of religion—the monkey on the donkey's back, you know. Always so in the East. The only way to move the masses is to make an appeal to their religious passions. *They* know that, and they've not scrupled to use their knowledge, the rascals! Rascals, that's what I call them. Excuse the word. I say what I think, Nuneham."

"*They?* Who are *they*, Princess?"

"The *corps diplomatique*."

Again the stern face expressed surprise.

"Yes, the *corps dip-lo-ma-tique!*" with a dig on every syllable. "Half a dozen of them were at my house yesterday and they were not ashamed to let me know what they are doing."

"And what *are* they doing, Princess?"

"Helping the people to rebel!"

Then throwing away her cigarette the Princess rose to her feet and pacing to and fro on the veranda, with a firm tread that had little of the East and not much of the woman, she repeated the story she had heard in her salon—how Ishmael Ameer was to return to Cairo, with twenty, thirty, forty thousand of his followers and some fantastic dream of establishing a human society that should be greater, nobler, wider and more God-like than any that had yet dwelt on this planet; how the diplomats laughed at the ridiculous hallucination but were nevertheless preparing to support it in order to harass the Government and dishonour England.

"But how?"

"By finding arms for the people to fight with if you attempt to keep their Prophet out! Ask your Inspectors! Ask your police! See if rifles bought with foreign money are not coming into Cairo every day."

By this time it was the Consul-General who was pacing up and down the veranda, while the Princess, who sat to smoke another cigarette, repeated the opinions of the foreign representatives one by one—Count This, who was old and should know better if white hairs brought wisdom; Baron That, who was as long as a palm-tree but without a date, and the Marquis of So-and-So.

"They tell *me* because I'm a Turk, but a Turk need not be a traitor, so I'm telling you."

The iron face of the Consul-General grew white and rigid, but, saying nothing, he continued to pace to and fro.

"Why don't you turn them all out? They are making nothing but mischief. The head of the idle man is the house of the devil and the best way is to pull it down. Why not? Capitulations? Pooh! While the meat hangs above the dogs will quarrel below. Dogs, that's what I call them. Excuse the word. I speak what I think."

"And the Egyptians—what are they doing?"

"What are they always doing? Conspiring with your enemies to turn you out of the country on the ground that you are trampling on their religious liberty."

"Which of them?"

"All of them—pashas, people, effendis, officials, your own Ministers—everybody."

"Everybody?"

"Everybody! The stupids! They can't see farther than the ends of their noses, or realise that they would only be exchanging one master for fourteen. What would Egypt be then? A menagerie with all the gates of the cages open. Oh, I know! I say what I think! I'm their Princess, but they can take my rank to-morrow if they wish to."

The second cigarette was thrown away, and a powder puff and small mirror were taken from a silver bag that hung by the lady's wrist.

"But serve you right, you English! You make the same mistake everywhere. Education! Civilisation! Judicial reform! Rubbish! The Koran tells the Moslem what to believe and what to do, so what does he want with your progress?"

The powder puff made dabs at the white cheeks, but the lady continued to talk.

"Your Western institutions are thrown away on him. It's like a beautiful wife married to a blind husband—a waste!"

The sun began to set behind the wall of purple creeper and the lady rose to go.

"No news of your Gordon yet? No? He was the best of the bunch and I simply lost my heart to him. You should have kept him more in hand, though— You couldn't? You, the greatest man in— Well, there's something to say for the Eastern way of bringing up boys, it seems."

Passing through the drawing-room the Princess came upon the portrait of Helena which used to stand by Lady Nuneham's bed.

"Ah, the moon! The beauty! Bismillah! What did Allah give her such big black eyes for? Back in England, isn't she? My goodness, there was red blood in that girl's veins, Nuneham! God have mercy upon me, yes! You should have heard her talk of your Ishmael!"

The Princess put the portrait to her lips and kissed it, then closed her eyes and said with a voluptuous laugh:

"Ah, *mon Dieu*, if this had only been a Muslemah, you wouldn't have had much trouble with your Mahdi!"

Hardly had the Consul-General returned to his library after the departure of the Princess when his Secretary brought him a telegram from the Sirdar—the same that he had dictated at Khartoum, telling of the intended visit to Cairo, of the preparations for Ishmael's projected pilgrimage, and of the danger that was likely to arise from the growing belief in the Prophet's "divine" inspiration.

"So our friend is beginning to understand the man at last," he said with an expression of bitter joy. "Meet him on his arrival. Tell him I have much to say."

That night when the Consul-General went up to his bedroom—the room in which alone the machine became the man—he was thinking, as usual, of Gordon.

"Such power, such fire, such insight, such resource! My own son, too, and worth all the weaklings put together! Oh, that he could be here now—now when every hand seems to be raised against his father! But where is he? What is he doing? Only God can say."

Then the Consul-General remembered what the Princess had said about Helena. Ah, if those two could have carried on his line—what a race! So pure, so clean, so strong! But that was past praying for now, and woe to the day when they had said to him, "A man-child is born to you."

After that the Consul-General thought of Ishmael and then the bitterness of his soul almost banished sleep. He had known from the first that the man could not be working alone; he had known, too, that some of England's allies were her secret enemies, but a combination of Eastern mummery with Western treachery was more than he had reckoned upon.

"No matter! I'll master both of them!" he thought.

A great historical tragedy should be played before the startled audience of disunited Europe whose international jealousies were conspiring with religious quackeries to make the government of Egypt impossible, and when the curtain fell on that drama, England would be triumphant, he would himself be vindicated and the "fossils of Whitehall" would be ashamed.

Last of all he thought of the Egyptian Ministers. These were the ingrates he had made and worked with, but they were no fools and it was difficult to understand why they were throwing in their lot with a visionary mummer, who was looking for a Millenium.

"I am at a loss to know what to think of a world in which such empty quackery can be supported by sane people," he thought.

There was one sweeter thought left, though, and as the Consul-General dropped off to sleep he told himself that, thanks to Helena, he would soon have Ishmael in his hands, and then he would kill him as he would kill a dangerous and demented dog.

III

DURING the next few days the Consul-General was closely occupied. The Law of Public Security being promulgated, he called upon the Minister of the Interior to call upon the Commandant of Police to issue a warrant for the arrest of Ishmael Ameer.

"But where *is* Ishmael Ameer?" asked the Minister.

When this was reported to the Consul-General his stern face smiled and he said:

"Let him wait and see."

Early one morning his Secretary came to his room to say that the Sirdar had arrived from Khartoum, and had gone on to headquarters, but would give himself the pleasure of calling upon his lordship before long.

"Tell him it must be soon—there is much to do," said the Consul-General.

Later the same day the Commandant of Police came with a knowing smile on his ruddy face to say that the "Bedouin" had reached Cairo, and that he had been followed to the Serai Fum el Khalig, the palace of the Chancellor of El Azhar, where he had already been visited by the Grand Mufti, some of the Ministers, certain of the Diplomatic Corps, and nearly the whole of the Ulema.

"Was he alone?" asked the Consul-General.

"Quite alone, your lordship, and now he is as safely in our hands as if he were already under lock and key."

"Good! What did you say his address was?"

"Serai Fum el Khalig."

"Palace Fum el Khalig," repeated the Consul-General, making a note on a marble tablet which stood on his desk.

Later still—very late—the Grand Cadi came with the same news. The suave old Moslem judge was visibly excited. His pale, lymphatic, pock-marked cheeks, his earth-coloured lips, his base eyes and his nose as sharp as a beak, gave him more than ever the appearance of a fierce and sagacious bird of prey. After exaggerated bows he began to speak in the oily, half-smothered voice of one who lives in constant fear of being overheard.

"Your Excellency will remember that when on former occasions I have had the inestimable privilege of approaching your honourable person in order to warn you that if you did not put down a certain Arab innovator the result would be death to the rule of England in Egypt, your Excellency has demanded proofs."

"Well?"

"I am now in a position to provide them."

"State the case precisely," said the Consul-General.

"Your Excellency will be interested to hear that a person of some consequence has arrived in Cairo."

Trained to self-control, the Consul-General conquered an impulse to say, "I know," and merely said, "Who is he?"

"He calls himself Sheikh Omar Benani, and is understood to be the wise and wealthy head of the great tribe of the Ababdah Bedouins, who inhabit the country that lies east of Assuan to the Red Sea."

"Well?"

"The man who calls himself Omar Benani is—Ishmael Ameer."

At that the base eyes glanced up with a look of triumph, but the Consul-General's face remained immovable.

"Well?"

"No doubt your Excellency is asking yourself why he comes in this disguise, and if your Excellency will deign to give me your attention I will tell you."

"I am listening."

"Ishmael Ameer pretends to be a reformer, intent upon the moral and intellectual regeneration of Islam, and he preaches the coming of a golden age in which unity, peace and brotherhood are to reign throughout the earth."

"Well?"

"With this ridiculous and impracticable propaganda he has appealed to many wild and ardent minds, so that a vast following of half-civilised people, whom he has gathered up in the Soudan, are to start soon—may have started already—

for this city, which they believe to be the Mecca of the new world."

"Well?"

"Ishmael Ameer pretends to have come to Cairo in advance of his followers to prepare for that Millennium."

"And what has he really come for?"

"To establish a political State."

Down to that moment the Consul-General had been leaning back in his chair in the attitude of one who was listening to something he already knew, but now he sat up sharply.

"Is this a fact?"

"It is a fact, your Excellency. And if your Excellency will once more deign to grant me your attention, I will put you in possession of a secret."

"Go on," said the Consul-General.

Instinctively the suave old judge drew his legs up on his chair and fingered his amber beads.

"Your Excellency will perhaps remember that owing to differences of opinion with the Khedive—may Allah bless him!—you were compelled to require that for a while he should leave the country."

"Well?"

"He went to Constantinople with the intention of laying his grievances against England before His Serenity the Sultan—may the Merciful give him long life!"

"Well?"

"The Sultan is a friend of England, your Excellency—the Khedive was turned away."

"And then?"

"Then he went to Paris, as your Excellency is probably aware."

"Well?"

"Perhaps your Excellency supposes that he occupied himself with the frivolities of the gay capital of France—dinner, theatres, dances, races? But no! He had two enemies now, England and Turkey, and he presumed to think he could punish both."

"How? In what way?"

"By founding a secret society for the conquest of Syria,

Palestine, and Arabia, and the establishment of a great Arab Empire with himself as its Caliph and Cairo as its capital."

"Well! What happened?"

"Need I say what happened, your Excellency? By means of his great wealth he was able to send out hundreds of paid emissaries to every part of the Arabic world, and Ishmael Ameer was the first of them."

The Consul-General was at length startled out of all his composure.

"Can you prove this?" he said.

"Your Excellency, if I say anything I can always prove it."

The Consul-General's brow grew more and more severe.

"And his name—his assumed name—what did you say it was?"

"Sheikh Omar Benani."

"Sheikh Omar Benani," repeated the Consul-General, making another note on his marble tablet.

"That is enough for the present," he said. "I have something to do to-night. I must ask your Eminence to excuse me."

After the Grand Cadi had gone, with many sweeping salaams, various oily compliments, and that cruel gleam in his base eyes which proceeds only from base souls, the Consul-General rang sharply for his Secretary.

"We have not yet made out our invitations for the King's Dinner—let us do so now," he said.

He threw a sheet of paper across the table to his Secretary, who prepared to make notes.

"First, the Diplomatic Corps—every one of them."

"Yes, my lord."

"Next, our Egyptian Ministers and the leading members of the Legislative Council."

"Yes, my lord."

"Next, the more prominent Pashas and Notables."

"Yes."

"Of course our own people as usual, and finally——"

"Yes!"

"Finally the Ulema of El Azhar."

The Secretary looked up in astonishment.

"Oh, I know," said the Consul-General. "They have never been invited before, but this is a special occasion."

"Quite so, my lord."

The Consul-General fixed his eyeglass and took up his marble tablet.

"In writing to the Chancellor of El Azhar at the Palace Fum el Khalig," he said, "enclose a card for the Sheikh Omar Benani."

"Sheikh Omar Benani."

"Say that hearing that one so highly esteemed among his own people is at present on a visit to Cairo, I shall be honoured by his company."

"Yes, my lord."

"That will do. Good-night!"

"Good-night, my lord."

It was early morning before the Consul-General went to bed. The Grand Cadi's story, being so exactly what he wanted to believe, had thrown him entirely off his guard. It appeared to illuminate everything that had looked dark and mysterious—the sudden advent of Ishmael, the growth of his influence, the sending out of his emissaries, his projected pilgrimage and the gathering up of camels and horses in such enormous quantities as even the Government could not have commanded in time of war.

It accounted for Ishmael's presence in Cairo, and his mission (as described by Helena) of drawing off the allegiance of the Egyptian Army. It accounted, too, for the treachery of the Ministers, Pashas, and Notables, who were too shrewd and too selfish (whatever the riff-raff of the Soudan might be) to risk their comfortable incomes for a religious chimera.

Yes, the Khedive's money and the substantial prospect of establishing a vast Arab Empire, not the vague hope of a spiritual Millennium, had been the power that worked these wonders.

It vexed him to think that his old enemy whom he had banished had been more powerful in exile than at home, and it tortured him to reflect that Ishmael had developed, with the religious malady of the Mahdi, his political mania as well.

But no matter! He would be more than a match for all these forces, and when his great historical drama came to be played before the eyes of astonished humanity, it would be seen that he had saved, not England only, but Europe and perhaps civilisation itself.

Thus, for three triumphant hours, the Consul-General saw himself as a patriot trampling on the enemies of his country, but hardly had he left the library and begun to climb the stairs of his great, empty, echoing house, switching off the lights as he ascended, and leaving darkness behind him, than the statesman sank back on the man—the broken, bereaved human being—and he recognised his motives for what they were.

A few minutes after he had reached his bedroom, Fatimah entered it with a jug of hot water and found him sitting with his head in his hands, looking fixedly at the portrait in the black and gilt frame of the little lad in an Arab fez.

" Ah, everybody loved that boy," she said, whereupon the old man raised his head and dismissed her brusquely.

" You ought to be in bed by this time—go at once," he said.

" Dear heart, so ought your lordship," said the Egyptian woman.

The Consul-General could dismiss Fatimah, but there was some one he could not get rid of—the manly, magnificent, heart-breaking young figure that always lived in his mind's eye—with its deadly white face, its trembling lower lip and its quivering voice which said, " General, the time may come when it will be even more painful to you to remember all this than it has been to me to bear it."

Where was he now? What was he doing? His son, his only son, all that was left to him!

There was only one way to lay that ghost, and the Consul-General did so by telling himself with a sort of fierce joy that wherever Gordon might be he must soon hear that

Ishmael, in a pitiful and tricky disguise, had been discovered in Cairo, and then he would see for himself what an arrant schemer and unscrupulous charlatan was the person for whom he had sacrificed his life.

With that bitter-sweet thought the lonely old man forced back the tears that had been gathering in his eyes and went to bed.

IV

SERAI FUM EL KHALIG, CAIRO.

MY DEAREST HELENA: Here I am, you see, and I am not arrested, although I travelled in the same train with the Sirdar, met him face to face on the platform at Khartoum, again on the platform at Atbara, again on the landing-place at Shelal, and finally in the station at Cairo, where he was received on his arrival by his officers of the Egyptian Army, by my father's first Secretary, and by the Commandant of Police.

I was asking myself what this could mean, whether your black boy had reached his destination and if your letter had been delivered, when suddenly I became aware that I was being observed, watched and followed to this house, and by that I knew that in this land of mystery my liberty was to be allowed to me a little longer for reasons I have still to fathom.

This is the home of the Chancellor of El Azhar, and I have delivered Ishmael's letter announcing the change of plan whereby I have come into Cairo instead of himself, but I have pledged the good old man to secrecy on that subject, for the present at all events, giving him my confident assurance that in common with the best of the Ulema, he is being wickedly deceived and made an innocent instrument for the destruction of his own cause.

My dear Helena, I was right. My vague suspicions of that damnable intriguer, the Grand Cadi, were justified. Already I realise that after fruitless efforts to inveigle

Ishmael into schemes of anarchical rebellion, it was he who conceived the conspiracy which has taken our friend by storm in the form of a passive mutiny of the Egyptian Army. The accursed scoundrel knows well it cannot be passive, that somewhere and somehow it will break into active resistance, but that is precisely what he desires. As I told you, it is the old trick of Caiaphas over again, and that is the lowest, meanest, dirtiest thing in history.

Query, Is he playing the same game with the Consul-General? I am sure he is, and when I think that England and my father may be in as much danger as Egypt and Ishmael from the man's devilish machinations, I am more than ever certain that Providence had a purpose in bringing me to Cairo, and I feel reconciled to the necessity of living here in this threefold disguise, being one thing to Ishmael, another to the Grand Cadi & Co., and a third to the Government and police. I feel reconciled, too, or almost reconciled, to the necessity of leaving you where you are, for the present at all events, although it rips me like a sword-cut as often as I think of it.

I have sent for Hafiz and expect to hear through him what is happening at the Agency, but I am hoping he will not come until morning, for to-night I can think of nothing but ourselves. When I left you at Khartoum, I felt that higher powers were constraining and controlling me, and that I was only yielding at last to an overwhelming sense of fatality. I thought I had made every possible effort, had exhausted every means and had nothing to reproach myself with, but hardly had I got away into the desert, when a hand seemed to grasp me at the back of my neck and to say, " Why did you leave her behind? "

In Ishmael's house, and in that atmosphere of delirious ecstasy in the mosque, it was easy to think it necessary for you to remain or my purpose in going away must from the first be frustrated, but awakening in the morning in my native compartment, with men and boys lying about on sacks, the sandy daylight filtering through the closed shutters of the carriage and the train full of the fetid atmosphere of exhausted sleep, I could not help but protest to myself that, at any cost whatever, I should have found a way to bring you with me.

Thank God, if I have left you behind in that trying and false position it is with no Caliph, no corrupt and con· cupiscent fanatic, but a man of the finest and purest in· stincts, who is too much occupied with his spiritual mission, praise the Lord! to think of the beautiful woman by his side, so I tell myself it was the will of Providence, and there is nothing to do now but to leave ourselves in the hands of fate.

Good-night, dearest! D. V., I'll write again to-morrow.

II

Have just seen Hafiz. The dear old fellow came racing up here at six o'clock this morning, with his big round face, like the aurora borealis, shining in smiles and tears. Heavens, how he laughed and cried and swore and sweated!

He thought his letter about my mother's death had brought me back, and when I gave him a hint of my real errand he nearly dropped in terror. It seems that among my old colleagues in Cairo, my reputation is now of the lowest, being that of a person who was bribed—God knows by whom—to do what I did. As a consequence it will go ill with me, according to Hafiz, if I should be discovered, but as that is pretty certain to happen in any case, I am not too much troubled, and find more interest in the fact that your boy Mosie is staying at the Agency and that consequently my father must have received your letter.

My dear Helena, my "mystic sense" has been right again. The Grand Cadi continues to pay secret visits to the Consul-General. That much Hafiz could say out of his intercourse with his mother, and it is sufficient to tell me that, by keeping a running sore open with my father, the scoundrel counts on destroying not only Ishmael, but England, by leading her to such resistance as will result in bloodshed and thus dishonour her in the eyes of the civilised world and leave Egypt a cockpit in which half the foreign Powers will fight for themselves, no matter who may suffer.

What should I do? God knows! I have an almost unconquerable impulse to go straight to my father and open his eyes to what is going on. He is enveloped by intrigues and surrounded by enemies in high places—his Egyptian Ministers, the creatures of his own creation; some of the foreign diplomats, the European leeches who suck his blood while they pretend to be his friends, and above all this rascally Cadi, with his sleek face and double-sword game.

But what can I say? What positive fact can I yet point to? Will my father believe me if I tell him that Ishmael's following which is coming up to Cairo is not, as he thinks, an armed force? That the Grand Cadi & Co. are a pack of lying intriguers, each one playing for his own hand?

My father is a great man who probably does not need and would certainly resent my compassion, but, Lord God, how I pity him! Alone, in his old age, after all he has done for Egypt! As for his Secretaries and Advisers, he has not brought them up to help him, and I would enlarge the Biblical warning about not putting one's trust in princes to include parvenues as well.

My dear Helena, where are you now, I wonder? What is happening to you? What occurred after I left Khartoum? These are the questions which during half the day and nearly the whole of the night are hammering, hammering, hammering on my brain. Ishmael was to follow me in a few days, so I suppose you are on the desert by this time. The desert! In the midst of that vast horde! The scourings of a whole continent! Poor old Hafiz had something like a fit when I told him you were not in England but in the Soudan, yet as a fatalist he feels bound to believe that everything will work out for the best and he asks me to send his high regard to you.

It gives one a strange sensation, and is almost like seeing things from another state of existence, to be here in Cairo, walking about unrecognised amid the familiar sights and hearing the gun fired from the Citadel every day; but

28

the sharpest twinge comes of the hacking thought of where *you* are and what circumstances surround you. In fact, memory is always playing some devilish trick with me and raking up thoughts of the condition in which I found you in Khartoum.

Helena, my dear Helena, I have an immense faith in your strength and your courage. You are mine, mine, mine —remember that! *I* do—I have to—all the time. That is what sets me at ease in my dark hours and gives sleep, as the Arabs say, to my eyelids. For the rest, we must resign ourselves and continue to wait for the direction of fate. The fact that I was not arrested in the character of Ishmael immediately on my arrival in Cairo makes me think Hafiz may be right—that, D. V., one way or another, God knows how, everything is working out for the best. It's damned easy to say that, I know, but, upon my soul, dearest, I believe it. So keep up heart, my poor old girl, and God bless you! GORDON.

P. S. I'll hold this letter back until I think you must be nearing Assouan, and then send it, D.V., by safe hands to be delivered to you there.

P. P. S. I open my envelope to tell you of a new development! I am invited with the Chancellor of El Azhar to the Consul-General's dinner in honour of the King's Birthday. This in the character of Sheikh Omar Benani, who is, it seems, the chief of the tribe of the Ababdah, inhabiting the wild country between Assouan and the Red Sea, a person with a great reputation for wealth and wisdom and a man whose word is truth.

What does it mean? One thing certainly—that acting on the information contained in your letter the authorities are mistaking me for Ishmael Ameer, and proposing some scheme to capture me. But why don't they take me without further ado? What unfathomable reason can there be for the delay in doing so? Intrigue on intrigue! I must wait and see.

Meantime I am asking myself where the real Ishmael is

and what he is doing now? Is the belief in his "divine" guidance increasing? Is he acquiring the influence of a Mahdi? If so, God help him! God help his people! God help my father! God help everybody!

But sit tight, my girl! Something good is going to happen to us! I feel it, I know it! All my love to you, Helena! *Maa-es-salamah!*

V

MY DEAR, DEAR GORDON: Gone! You are actually gone! I can hardly believe it. It must be like this to awaken from chloroform after losing one's right hand, only it must be something out of my heart in this instance, for though I have not shed a tear since you went away and do not intend to shed one, I have a wild sense of weeping in the desolate chambers of my soul.

Writing to you? Certainly I am. Gordon, do you know what you have done for me? You have given me faith in your "mystic senses," and by virtue of certain of my own I am now sure that you are not dead, and that you are not going to die, so I am writing to you out of the chaos that envelops me, having no one here to speak to, literally no one, and being at present indifferent to the mystery of what is to become of my letter.

It seems I fainted in the mosque after that wild riot of barbaric sounds, and did not come back to full consciousness until next morning, and then I found the Arab woman and the child attending on me in my room. Naturally I thought I might have been delirious and I was in terror lest I had betrayed myself, so I asked what I had been saying in my sleep, whereupon Zenoba protested that I had said nothing at all, but Ayesha, the sweet little darling, said I had been calling upon the great White Pasha (meaning General Gordon), whose picture (his statue) was by the Palace gates. What an escape!

Of course my first impulse was to run away, but at the

next moment I saw that to do so would be to defeat your own scheme in going, and that as surely as it had been your duty to go into Cairo, it was mine to remain in Khartoum. But all the same I felt myself to be a captive—as surely a captive as any white woman who was ever held in the Mahdi's camp—and it did not sweeten my captivity to remember that I had first become a prisoner of my own free will.

If I am a captive, I am under no cruel tyrant, though, and Ishmael's kindness is killing me. I was certainly wrong about him in Cairo, and his character is precisely the reverse of what I expected. Little Ayesha tells me that during the night I lay unconscious her father did not sleep at all, but kept coming into the guest-room every hour to ask for news of me, and now he knocks at my door a dozen times a day, asking if I am better, and saying, "To-morrow, please God, you will be well." It makes me wretched, and brings me dreadfully near to the edge of tears, remembering what I have done to him and how certainly his hopes will be destroyed.

Naturally his people have taken his cue and last night Black Zogal gathered up a crowd of half-crazy creatures like himself, to say a prayer for me at the Saint's house, which is just outside my window.

"Thou knowest our White Lady, O Father Gabreel, that she is betrothed to our Master, and that his heart is low and his bread is bitter because she is sick. Make her well if it please God, O Father Gabreel!" Thus the simple-hearted children of the desert called down God's spirit to their circle of fire for me, and after loud cries of "Allah!" "Allah!" going on for nearly an hour, they seemed to be content, for Zogal said:

"Abu Gabreel hears, oh, my brothers, and to-morrow, please God, our sister will be well."

I had been reaching up in bed to listen, and when all was over I wanted to lay down my head and howl.

The time has come for the people to start on their pilgrimage, but Ishmael insists upon postponing the journey until I am quite recovered. Meantime Zenoba is trying to make mischief, and to-day when the door of my room was ajar, I heard her hinting to Ishmael that the White Lady was not really ill but only pretending to be—a bit of treachery for which she got no thanks, being as sharply reproved as she was on the morning of your mother's letter.

That woman makes a wild cat of me. I can't help it—I hate her! Of course I see through her, too. She is in love with Ishmael, and though I ought to pity her pangs of jealousy there are moments when I want to curse her religion and the dawn of the day of her birth and her mother and her grandmother.

There! You see I have caught the contagion of the country; but I am really a little weak and out of heart to-night, dear, so perhaps I had better say good-night! Good-night, my dearest!

II

Oh, dear! Oh, dear! I could not bear to play the hypocrite any longer, so I got up to-day and told Ishmael I was well and therefore he must not keep back his pilgrimage any longer. Such joy! Such rejoicing! It would break my heart if I had any here, but having sent all I possess to Cairo, I could do nothing but sit in the guest-room and look on at the last of the people's preparations for the desert journey—tents and beds being packed, and camels and horses and donkeys brought in to a continuous din of braying and grunting and neighing.

We are to start away to-morrow morning, and this afternoon when that fact was announced to me, I was so terrified by the idea of being dragged over the desert like a slave, that I asked Ishmael to leave me behind. His face fell, but —would you believe it?—he agreed, saying I was not strong enough to travel and Zenoba should stay to nurse me. At that I speedily repented of my request and asked him to allow me to go, whereupon his face lightened like a child's, and with joy he agreed again, saying the Arab woman should go to take care of me, for Ayesha was a big girl now and needed a nurse no longer. This was jumping out of

the frying-pan into the fire and I protested that I was quite
able to look after myself, but, out of his anxiety for my
health, Ishmael would not be gainsaid and the Arab woman
said, "I'll watch over you like my eyes, my sister." I am
sure she will, the vixen!

III

We have left Khartoum and are now on the desert. The
day had not yet dawned when we were awakened by a tattoo
of pipes and native drums—surely the weirdest sound in
the darkness that ever fell on mortal ear, creeping into the
pores and getting under the very skin. Then came a din,
a roar, a clamour—the grunting and gurgling and braying
of five thousand animals and as much shouting and bellow-
ing of human tongues as went to the building of the tower
of Babel.

The sun was rising and there was a golden belt of cloud
in the eastern sky by the time we were ready to go. They
had brought a litter on a dromedary for me, and I was almost the last to start. It was hard to part from the child,
for though her sweet innocence had given me many a stab
and I felt sometimes as if she had been created to torture me, I had grown to love her, and I think she loved me.
She stood as we rode away with a big tear ready to drop onto
her golden cheek and looked after me with her gazelle-like
eyes. Sweet little Ayesha, creature of the air and the
desert, I shall see her no more!

Crossing the Mahdi's open-air mosque at Omdurman,
where we said morning prayers, we set our faces northward
over the wild halfa grass and clumps of mimosa scrub, and
as soon as we were out in the open desert, with its vast sky,
I saw how gigantic was our caravan. The great mass of
men and animals seemed to stretch for miles across the yellow sand, and looked like an enormous tortoise creeping
slowly along.

We camped at sunset in the Wadi Bishara, the signal
for the bivouac being the blowing of a great elephant's horn
which had a thrilling effect in that lonesome place. But

more thrilling still was the effect of evening prayers, which began as soon as the camels and horses and donkeys had been unsaddled and their gruntings and brayings and gurglings as well as the various noises of humanity had ceased.

The afterglow was flaming along the flat sand, giving its yellow the look of bronze, when all knelt with their faces to the east—Ishmael in front with sixty or seventy rows of men behind him. It was really very moving and stately to see, and made me understand what was meant by somebody who said he could never look upon Mohammedans at prayers, and I think of the millions of hearts which at the same hour were sending their great chorus of praise to God, without wishing to be a Moslem. I did not wish to be that, but with the odious Arab woman always watching me, I found myself fingering my rosary and pretending to be a good Muslemah, though in reality I was repeating the Lord's prayer.

It is dark night now, the fires at which the people baked their durah and cooked their asida are dying down, and half the camp is already asleep in this huge wild wilderness, under its big white stars.

I must try to sleep, too, so good-night, dearest, and God bless you! I don't know what is to be the end of all this, or where I am to despatch my letter or when you are to receive it, but I am sure you are alive and listening to me—and what should I do if I could not talk to you?

HELENA.

VI

SOUDAN DESERT (SOMEWHERE).

IT is ten days, my dear Gordon, since I wrote my last letter and there has never been an hour between when I dared pretend to this abomination of Egypt (she is now snoring on the angerib by my side, sweetheart) that I must while away an hour by writing in my "Journal."

Such a time! Boil and bubble, toil and trouble! Every

morning before daybreak the wild peal of the elephant's
horn, then the whole camp at prayers, with the rising sun
in our faces, then the striking of tents and the ruckling,
roaring, gurgling and grunting of camels which resembles
nothing so much as a styful of pigs *in extremis;* then twelve
hours of trudging through a forlorn and lifeless solitude
with only a rest for the midday meal; then the elephant's
horn again and evening prayers, with the savage sun behind us, and then settling down to sleep in some blank and
numb and soundless wilderness—such is our daily story.

My goodness, Ishmael is a wonderful person! But all
the same the " divine " atmosphere that is gathering about
him is positively frightening. I suspect Black Zogal of
being the author and " only begetter " of a good deal of
this idolatry. He gallops on a horse in front of us, crying, " There is no god but God," and " The Messenger of
God is coming," with the result that crowds of people are
waiting for Ishmael at every village, with their houses swept,
their straw mats laid down, and their carpets spread on
the divans, all eager to entertain him, to open their secret
granaries to feed his followers or at least to kiss the hem
of his caftan.

Every day our numbers increase and we go off from the
greater towns to the beating of copper war drums, the blowing of antelope horns, and sometimes to the cracking of
rifles. It is all very crude in its half-savage magnificence,
but it is almost terrifying, too, and the sight of this emotional creature, so liable to spasms of religious ecstasy,
riding on his milk-white camel through these fiercely fanatical people like a God, makes one tremble to think of the
time that will surely come when they find out, and *he* finds
out, that after all he is nothing but a man.

What sights, what scenes! The other day there was a
fearful sand-storm, in which a fierce cloud came sweeping
out of the horizon, big with flame and wrath, and it fell on
us like a mountain of hell. As long as it lasted the people
lay flat on the sand or crouched under their kneeling camels,
and when it was over they rose in the dead blankness with
the red sand on their faces and sent up, as with one voice,

a cry of lamentation and despair. But Ishmael only smiled and said, " Let us thank God for this day, oh, my brothers," and when the people asked him why, he answered, " Because we can never know anything so bad again."

That simple word set every face shining, and as soon as we reached the next village—Black Zogal as usual having gone before us—lo, we heard a story of how Ishmael had commanded a sand-storm to pass over our heads without touching us—and it had!

Another day we had stifling heat, in which the glare of the sand made our eyes ache and the air burn like the breath of a furnace. The water in the water-bottles became so hot that we dared not pour it on to the back of our hands, and even some of the camels dropped dead under the blazing eye of the sun.

And when at length the sun sank beneath the horizon and left us in the cool dark night, the people could not sleep for want of water to bathe their swelling eyelids and to moisten their cracking throats, but Ishmael walked through their tents and comforted them, telling them it was never intended that man should always live well and comfortably, yet God, if He willed it, would bring them safely to their journey's end.

After that the people lay down on the scorching sand as if their thirst had suddenly been quenched, and next day on coming to the first village we heard that in the middle of a valley of black and blistered hills, Ishmael smote with his staff a metallic rock that was twisted into the semblance of a knotted snake, and a well of ice-cold water sprang out of it, and everybody drank of it and then " shook his fist at the sun."

Nearly all last week our people were in poor heart by reason of the mirages which mocked and misled them, show-ing an enchanted land on the margin of the sky, with beauti-ful blue lakes and rivers and green islands and shady groves of palm, and sweet, long emerald grasses that quivered beneath a refreshing breeze, but when, from their monoto-nous track on the parched and naked desert, the poor souls would go in search of these phantoms, they would find noth-

29

ing but a great lone land, in the fulness of a still deeper desolation.

Then they would fling themselves down in despair and ask why they had been brought out into the wilderness to die, but Ishmael, with the same calm smile as before, would tell them that the life of this world was all a mirage, a troubled dream, a dream in a sleep, that the life to come was the awakening, and that he whose dream was most disturbed was nearest the gates of Paradise.

Result: At the next town we came to we were told that when we were in the middle of the wilderness Ishmael had made an oasis to spring up around us, with waving trees and rippling water, and the air full of the songs of birds, the humming of bees and the perfume of flowers, and we all fell asleep in it and when we awoke in the morning we believed we had been in heaven!

Good-night, my dear—dear! Oh, to think that all this wilderness divides us! But *ma'aleysh!* In another hour I shall be asleep and then—then I shall be in your arms.

II

Oh, my! Oh, my! Two incidents have happened to-day, dearest, that can hardly fail of great results. Early in the morning we came upon the new convict settlement—a rough-bastioned place built of sun-dried bricks in the middle of the Soudan desert. It contains the hundred and fifty Notables who were imprisoned by the Special Tribunal for assaults on the Army of Occupation when they were defending the house of your friend, the Grand Cadi. How Ishmael discovered this I do not know, but what he did was like another manifestation of the "mystic sense."

Stopping the caravan, with an unexpected blast of the elephant's horn, he caused ten rows of men to be ranged around the prison, and after silence had been proclaimed, he called on them to say the first Surah: " Praise be to God, the Lord of all creatures."

It had a weird effect in that lonesome place, as of a great monotonous wave breaking on a bar far out at sea, but what followed was still more eerie. After a breathless moment in which everybody seemed to listen and hold his breath, there came the deadened and muffled sound of the same words repeated by the prisoners within the walls: "Praise be to God, the Lord of all creatures!"

When this was over Ishmael cried, "Peace, brothers! Patience! The day of your deliverance is near! The Redeemer is coming! All your wrongs will be righted, all your bruises will be healed! Peace!"

And then there came from within the prison walls the muffled answer, "Peace!"

The second of the incidents occurred about midday, when crossing a lifeless waste of gloomy volcanic sand, we came upon a desert graveyard with those rounded hillocks of clay which make one think that the dead beneath must be struggling in their sleep.

At a word from Ishmael all the men of our company who belonged to that country stepped out from the caravan, and, riding round and round the cemetery, shouted the names of their kindred who were buried there: "Ali!" "Abdul!" "Mohammed!" "Mahmud!" "Said!"

After that Ishmael himself rode forward, and addressing the dead as if they could hear, he cried, "Peace to you, oh, people of the graves! Wait! Lie still! The night is passing! The daylight dawns!"

It was thrilling! Strange, simple, primitive, crude in its faith perhaps, but such love and reverence for the dead contrasted only too painfully with the vandalism of our "Christian" vultures (yclept Egyptologists) who rifle the graves of the old Egyptians for their jewels and mummy beads and then leave their bones in tons to bleach on the bare sand—a condition that is sufficient of itself to account for Jacob's prayer, "Bury me not, I pray thee, in the land of Egypt."

And so say all of us! But seriously, my dear Gordon, I quite expect to find at the next stopping place a story of how Ishmael recited the Fatihah and the walls of a prison fell down before him, and how he spoke to the dead and they replied.

III

It has happened! I knew it would! I have seen it coming and it has come—without any help from Black Zogal's crazy imagination, either. There was only one thing wanted to complete the faith of these people in Ishmael's " divinity "—a miracle, and it has been performed!

I suppose it really belongs to the order of things that happen according to natural law—magnetism, suggestion, God knows what—but my pen positively jibs at recording it, so surely will it seem as if I had copied it out of a Book I need not name.

This afternoon our vast human tortoise was trudging along and a halt was being called to enable stragglers to come up, when a funeral procession crossed our track on its way to a graveyard on the stony hillside opposite.

The Sheikh of a neighbouring village had lost his only child, a girl twelve years of age, and behind the blind men chanting the Koran, the hired mourners with their plaintive wail and the body on a bare board, the old father walked in his trouble, rending his garments and tearing off his turban.

It was a pitiful sight, and when the mourners came up to Ishmael and told him the Sheikh was a God-fearing man who had not deserved this sorrow, I could see that he was deeply moved, for he called on the procession to stop, and making his camel kneel, he got down, and tried to comfort the old man, saying: " May the name of God be upon thee! "

Then thinking, as it seemed to me, to show sympathy with the poor father, he stepped up to the bier and took the little brown hand which, with its silver ring and bracelet, hung over the board, and held it for a few moments while he asked when the child had died and what she had died of, and he was told she had died this morning and the sun had killed her.

All at once I saw Ishmael's hand tremble and a strange contraction pass over his face, and at the next moment in a quivering voice he called on the bearers to put down the bier. They did so and at his bidding they uncovered the body and I saw the face. It was the face of the dead! Yes, the dead, as lifeless and as beautiful as a face of bronze.

At the next instant Ishmael was on his knees beside the body of the girl and asking the father for her name. It was Helimah.

"Helimah! Your father is waiting for you! Come," said Ishmael, touching the child's eyes and smoothing her forehead, and speaking in a soft, caressing voice.

Gordon, as I am a truthful woman, I saw it happen. A slight fluttering of the eyelids, a faint heaving of the bosom, and then the eyes were open and at the next moment the girl was standing on her feet!

God, what a scene it was that followed! The Sheikh on his knees kissing the hem of Ishmael's caftan, the men prostrating themselves before him, and the women tearing away the black veils that covered their faces and crying, "Blessed be the woman that bore you!"

It has been what the Arabs call a red day, and at that moment the setting sun, catching the clouds of dust raised by the camels, made the whole world one brilliant fiery red. What wonder if these poor, benighted people thought the Lord of Heaven himself had just come down?

We left the village loaded with blessings (Black Zogal galloping frantically in front), and when we came to the next town—Berber with its miles of roofless mud-huts, telling of dervish destruction—crowds came out to salute Ishmael as the " Guided One," " The True Mahdi," and " The Deliverer," bringing their sick and lame and blind for him to heal them and praying of him to remain.

Oh, my dear Gordon, it is terrifying! Ishmael is no longer the messenger, the forerunner; he is now the Redeemer he foretold! I believe really *he* is beginning to believe it! This is the pillar of fire that is henceforth to guide us on our way. Already our numbers are three times what they were when we left Khartoum. What is to happen when thirty thousand persons, following a leader they believe to be divine, arrive in Cairo and are confronted by five thousand British soldiers?

No! It is not bloodshed I am afraid of—I know *you*

will prevent that. But what of the awful undeceiving, the utter degradation, the crushing collapse?

And I? Don't think me a coward, Gordon—it isn't everybody who was born brave like you—but when I think of what I have done to this man, and how surely it will be found out that I have betrayed him, I tell myself that the moment I touch the skirts of civilisation I must run away.

But meantime our pilgrimage is moving on—to its death, as it seems to me—and I am moving on with it as a slave— the slave of my own actions. If this is Destiny it is wickedly cruel, I will say that for it; and if it is God, I think He might be a jealous God without making the blundering impulse of one poor girl the means of wrecking the hopes of a whole race of helpless people. Of course it acts as a sop to my conscience to remember what you said about God never making mistakes, but I cannot help wishing that in His inscrutable wisdom He could have left me out.

Oh, my dear—dear! Where are you now, I wonder? What are you doing? What is being done *to* you? Have you seen your father, the Princess and the Grand Cadi? I suppose I must not expect news until we reach Assouan. You promised to write to me, and you will—I know you will. Good-night, dearest! My love, my love, my only love! But I must stop. We are to make a night journey. The camp is in movement and my camel is waiting. Adieu!

HELENA.

VII

SERAI FUM EL KHALIG, CAIRO.

Salaam aleykoum! Ten days have passed, my dear Helena, since I wrote my last letter, and during that time I have learned all that is going on here—having, in my assumed character of Ishmael in disguise, interviewed nearly the whole of the Ulema, including that double-dyed dastard, the Grand Cadi.

Under the wing—the rather fluttered one—of the good old Chancellor of El Azhar, I saw the oily reprobate in his own house, and in his honeyed voice he made pretence of receiving me with boundless courtesy. I was his "beloved friend in God," "the reformer of Islam," called to the task of bringing men back to the Holy Koran, to the Prophet, and to eternal happiness. On the other hand, my father was "the slave of power," the "evil doer," the "adventurer," and the "great assassin," who was led away by worldly things and warring against God.

More than once my hands itched to take the hypocrite from behind by the ample folds of his Turkish garments and fling him like vermin down the stairs, but I was there to hear what he was doing, so I smothered a few strong expressions which only the recording angel knows anything about, and was compelled to sit and listen.

My dear Helena, it is even worse than I expected. Some of the double-dealing Egyptian Ministers, backed by certain of the diplomatic corps, but inspired by this Chief Judge in Islam, have armed a considerable part of the native populace, in the hope that the night when England, in the persons of her chief officials, is merrymaking on the island of Ghezirah, and the greater part of the British force is away in the provinces, quelling disturbances and keeping peace, the people may rise, the Egyptian Army may mutiny, and Ishmael's followers may take possession of the city.

All this, and more, with many suave words about the "enlightening help of God" and the certainty of "a bloodless victory," in which the Almighty would make me glorious, and the English would be driven out of Egypt, the crafty scoundrel did not hesitate to propound as a means whereby the true faith might be established all over Europe, Rome, and London."

Since my interview with the Grand Cadi I have learned of a certainty, what I had already surmised, that the Consul-General has been made aware of the whole plot, and is taking his own measures to defeat it. Undoubtedly the first duty of a government is to preserve order and to establish authority, and I know my father well enough to be sure that, at any cost, he will set himself to do both. But what will happen?

Mark my word—the British Army will be ordered back to the Capital—perhaps on the eve of the festival—and as surely as it enters the city on the night of the King's Birthday there will be massacre in the streets, for the Egyptian soldiers will rebel, and the people who have been provided with arms from the secret service money of England's enemies will rise, thinking the object of the Government is to prevent the entrance of Ishmael and his followers.

Result—a holy war, and as that is the only kind of war that was ever yet worth waging, it will put Egypt in the right and England in the wrong.

Does Ishmael expect this? No, he thinks he is to make a peaceful entry into Cairo when he comes to establish his World State, his millennium of universal faith and empire. Do the Ulema expect it? No, they think the Army of Occupation will be far away when their crazy scheme is carried into effect. Does my father expect it? Not for one moment, so sure is he—I know it perfectly, I have heard him say it a score of times—that the Egyptian soldier will not fight alone, and that Egyptian civilians can be scattered by a water hose.

Heaven help him! If ever a man was preparing to draw a sword from its scabbard it is my father at this moment, but it is only because he is played upon and deceived by this son and successor of Caiaphas, the damned. I'll go and open his eyes to the Grand Cadi's duplicity. I'll say, "Bring your oily scoundrel face to face with me and see what I will say. If he denies it you must choose for yourself which of us you will believe—your own son, who has nothing to gain by coming back to warn you, or this reptile, who is fighting for the life of his rotten old class."

The thing is hateful to me, and if there were any other possible way of stopping the wretched slaughter, I should not go, for I know it will end in the Consul-General handing me over to the military authorities to be court-martialled for my former offences, and, as you may say, it is horrible to put a father, with a high sense of duty, into the position of being compelled to cut off his own son.

Meanwhile, I am conscious that the police continue to watch me, and I am just as much a prisoner as if I were already within the walls of jail. For their own purposes they are leaving me at liberty, and I believe they will go on doing so until after the night of the King's Birthday. After that God knows what will happen.

I am writing late and I must turn in soon, so good-night and God bless and preserve you, my own darling—mine, mine, mine, and nobody else's—remember that! Hafiz continues to protest that the Prophet has a love for you, and will bring out everything for the best. I think so, too—I really do, so you must not be frightened about anything I have said in this letter.

There is only one thing frightens, and that is the damnable trick memory plays me when it rakes up all you told me of the terms of your betrothal to Ishmael. I can bear it pretty well during the day, but in that dead gray hour of the early morning when the moonlight slinks into the dawn, before the sparrows begin to chop the air and the Arabs to rend it, I find myself thinking that though Ishmael, when he proposed marriage to you, may have been thinking of nothing but how to protect your good name, being a pure-minded man who had consecrated his life to a spiritual mission, yet the constant presence of a beautiful woman by his side must sooner or later sweep away his pledge.

He wouldn't be a man if it didn't, and, the prophet notwithstanding, Ishmael is that to his finger tips. But heaven help me! I daren't let my mind dwell on this subject or I should have to fly back to you and leave my task here unfulfilled. So as often as I shut my eyes and see you trudging through the desert in Ishmael's camp I tell myself that Providence has something for you to do there—must have —though what the deuce it is I don't yet see.

No matter! D. V. I'll know some day, and meantime I'll nail my colours to the mast of your strength and courage, knowing that the bravest girl in the world belongs to *me*, and wherever she is she is *mine* and always will be.

GORDON.

P. S. I am now despatching my two letters to Assouan by Hamid Ibrahim—the second of the two Sheikhs who went with me to Alexandria—and if you find you can send me an answer—for God's sake do. I am hungering and thirsting and starving and perishing for a letter from you, a line, a word, a syllable, the scratch of your pen on a piece of paper. Send it, for heaven's sake!

I hear that hundreds of native boats are going up to Assouan to bring you down the Nile, so look out for my next letter when you get to Luxor—I may have something to tell you by that time.

VIII

NUBIAN DESERT (ANYWHERE).

OH, MY GORDON: Such startling developments! Ishmael's character has made a new manifestation. It concerns me, and I hardly know whether I ought to speak of it. Yet I must—I cannot help myself.

I find there is something distinctly *masculine* in his interest in me! In Khartoum (in spite of certain evidences to the contrary) I was always fool enough to suppose that it was without sex—what milksops call Platonic—as if any such relation between a man and a woman ever was or ever will be!

Oh, I know what you are saying! "That foolish young woman thinks Ishmael is falling in love with her." But wait, sir, only wait and listen.

We left Berber at night and rode four hours in the moonlight. Goodness! What ghosts the desert is full of—ghosts of pyramids that loom large and then fade away! Such mysterious lights! Such spectral watch-towers standing on spectral heights! It was what the Arabs call "a white night," and besides the moon in its splendour there was a vast star-strewn sky. Sometimes we heard the hyena's cry, sometimes the jackal's ululation, and through the silver shimmering haze we could see the wild creatures scuttling away from us.

Thus on and on went our weary caravan—the camels like great swans with their steady upturned heads, slithering as if in slippers along the noiseless sand, and many of the tired people asleep on them. But I could not sleep, and Ishmael, who was very much awake, rode by my side and talked to me.

It was about love, and included one pretty story of a daughter of the Bedawee who married a Sultan—how she scorned the silken clothes he gave her, and would not live in his palace—saying she was no fellaha to sleep in houses—and made him come out into the desert with her and dwell in a tent. I thought there was a certain self-reference in the story, but that was not all by any means.

At midnight we halted by a group of wells, and while our vast army of animals was being watered, my tent was set up outside the camp so that I might rest without noise. I suppose I had been looking faint and pale, for just as I was listening to the monotonous voice of a boy who, at a fire not far away, was singing both himself and me to sleep, Ishmael came with a dish of medida, saying, "Drink this—it will do you good."

Then he sat down, and, with that paralysing plainness of speech which the Easterns have, began to talk of love again, especially in relation to the duty of renunciation, quoting in that connection "the lord of the Christians," who had said, "There be eunuchs, which have made themselves eunuchs for the kingdom of heaven's sake."

It was more than embarrassing from the beginning, but it became startling and almost shocking when he went on to talk about Jesus in relation to Mary Magdalene (whom he supposed to be the sister of Martha) and of the home at Bethany as the only place in which he found the solace of female society, and how he had to turn his back on the love of woman for his work's sake.

We are so accustomed to think of Jesus' inaccessibility to human affection as if it were a merit in him to be superior to love, that it made my skin creep to hear this person of another faith talk like that. But I shivered a good deal more when he came to closer quarters and said that renunciation was the duty of every one on whom God had laid a great mission *until his task was finished*, and then . . . *then* it was just as much his duty *to live as a man!*

He went away quite calmly, commending me to God, but he left me in a state of terror, and though I was nearly worn to death by the double journey I did not sleep a wink that night, for thinking of that accursed day of the betrothal, and what would happen if he ever broke his promise and came to me to claim the rights of a husband.

The next day or two passed without any serious incident except that Ishmael, who had grown a pair of haunting, imploring eyes, was always riding his camel by its halter and nose-rein at the side of my litter, and talking constantly on the same subject. But then came an event of thrilling interest. Can I—shall I—must I tell you about it? Yes, I can, I shall, I must!

Out here on the desert I always feel as if I were travelling in Bible lands, and if our caravan were to come upon "Abram the Hebrew" and Rachel and Rebecca flying away with some Bedouin Jacob I should not be the least surprised, so it seemed natural enough that yesterday, in the country of the Bisharin Arabs, we lit upon Laban, living as a patriarch among his people.

There were his sons and his sons' sons, big, brawny boys, strong and clean of limb, and with their loins well girt, but hardly anything else covered, and there were "the souls born of his house" in their felt skull caps and blue galabeahs. But what most concerned me were his two splendid daughters. No corsetted women out of Bond Street, sir, but superbly fine and majestic young females, tall and straight, with big bosoms like pomegranates, ringletted black hair, clear oval faces, the olive skin of the purest Arab blood, and large black eyes that shone like gems.

Such a woman, I thought, must Ruth have been when she lay at the feet of Boaz, but lo! it never occurred to me that the people's faith in Ishmael's "divinity" did not forbid their ascribing to him the attributes of a man. Shall I go on? Yes, I will, for already you know that your

Helena, your lady-love, is no mealy-mouthed miss—never was and never can be.

Well, last night, late, while I was looking at the shadowy forms of the camels coming and going in the light of the dying fires, I saw Laban, who had been pouring hospitalities upon us, leading one of his daughters, whose head was low, to Ishmael's tent. It was like something horrible out of the Old Testament, but I had to watch—I simply could not help it—and after a while I saw Laban and Rachel going away together, and then the old man's head as well as the girl's was down.

Act one being fininshed last night, act two began to-day. We are in the middle of the Nubian desert now, and as the heat is great under the red wrath of the fiery mountains on either side, we have to rest for three hours in the middle of every day. Well, at noon to-day Ishmael came to my tent and talked of love again. It was a heavenly passion. Surely God had created it. Yet the Christians had made "mockery," and were thus rebuking the Almighty and claiming to be wiser than He. The union of man and woman without love was sin. That was what made so many Moslem marriages sinful. Marriage was not betrothal, not the joining of hands under a handkerchief, not the repeating of prayers after a Cadi; marriage was the sacrament of love, and love being present and nothing else intervening *renunciation was wrong;* it was against the spirit of Islam, and no matter who he might be, *a man should live as a man.*

I don't know what I said or whether I said anything, but I do know that the blood left my heart and seemed long in making its way back again. My skin was creeping, and I had a feeling which I had never known before—a feeling of repulsion—the feeling of the white woman about the black man. Ishmael is not black by any means, but I felt exactly as if he were, for I could see quite well what was going on in his mind. He was thinking of his journey's end, of the day when his work would be finished, and he was promising himself the realization of his love.

That shall never, never be! No, not under any circumstances! My God, no, not for worlds of worlds! Good-night, Gordon! I may be betrothed to this man, but there is no law of nature that binds me to him. I belong to you, just as Rachel belonged to Jacob, and whatever I may be in my religion I am no trinitarian in my love at all events.

Good-bye, dearest! Don't let what I have said alarm you. Oh, I know what you are saying *now*: "That foolish young woman expects me to hear her when I am in Cairo and she is in the middle of the Nubian desert." But you do, I am sure you do. And I hear you also. I hear your voice at this moment as clearly as I hear it when I awake in the middle of the night and it rings through my miserable tent and makes me wildly hysterical. So don't be alarmed, I can take care of myself, I tell you! My love, my love, my love!

II

Mercy! I don't know who did it, or by whose orders it was done, but last night Ishmael's tent, which has hitherto been set up at a distance, was placed mouth to mouth with mine. More than that, the odious Arab woman, who has always afflicted me with her abominable presence, was nowhere to be seen. I was feeling one of your " mystic senses " that something was going to happen, when late, very late, the last of the fires having died down and the camp being asleep, I heard Ishmael calling to me in a whisper:

" Rani! "

I did not answer—I could not have done so if I had tried, for my heart was thumping like an anvil.

" Rani! " he whispered again, and again I did not reply. I knew *he* knew I was awake, and after a moment of silence that seemed eternal, he said:

" By and by, then! When we come to Cairo and my mission is at an end."

O God! what tears of anger and despair I shed when he was gone and all was quiet. And now I ask myself if I can bear this strain any longer. After all Ishmael is only an Oriental, and perhaps, in spite of himself, and the pledge he gave to me, the natural man is coming to the top. Then I am his *wife*, and he has *rights* in me, according to his own view and the laws of his religion! I am in his camp, too, and we are in the middle of the desert!

How did it happen—that betrothal? Are these things ordained? Gordon, you talk about Destiny, but why don't you see that what took me to Khartoum was not really the desire to avenge my father (though I thought it was) but to revenge myself for the loss of yourself. So *you—you— you* were the real cause of my hideous error, and if you had loved me as I loved you I could never have been put to that compulsion.

. . . . Forgive me, dear! I am feeling wicked, but I shall soon get over it. I have not been sleeping well lately, and there are dark rims under my eyes, and I am a fright in every way. . . . I feel calm already, so good-night, dearest! We cannot be far from civilisation now, therefore there can be no need to run away from here.

III

Hurrah! Hurrah! Hurrah! We camped last night on the top of a stony granite hill, and this morning we can see the silver streak of the Nile with the sweet, green verdure along its banks, and the great dam at Assouan with its cascades of falling water. Such joy! Such a frenzy of gladness! The people are capering about like demented children. Just so must the children of Israel have felt when God brought them out of the wilderness and they saw the promised land before them.

Black Zogal galloped into the town at daybreak and has just galloped back, bringing a great company of Sheikhs and Notables. Egyptians, chiefly, who have come up the Nile to meet us, but many are Bedouins from the wild East country running to the Red Sea. Such fine faces and stately figures! Most of them living in tents, but all dressed like princes. They are saluting Ishmael as the " Deliverer," the " Guided One," the " Redeemer," and even the " Lord Isa," and *he is not reproving them!*

But I cannot think of Ishmael now. I feel as if I were coming out of chaos and entering into the world. If anything has happened to you I shall know it soon. Shall I be able to control myself? I shall! I must!

Oh, how my heart beats and swells! I can scarcely breathe. But you are alive, I am sure you are, and I shall hear from you presently. I shall also escape from this false position and sleep at last, as the Arabs say, with both eyes shut. I must stop. My tent has to be struck. The camp is already in movement.

One word. We were plunging into Assouan, through the cool bazaars with their blazing patches of sunlight and sudden blots of shadow, when I saw your Sheikh sidling up to me. He slipped your letter into my hand and is to come back in a moment for mine. I am staying at a Khan. Oh, God bless and love you! *El Hamdullillah!* My dear, my dear, my dear! HELENA.

IX

THE NILE (BETWEEN ASSOUAN AND LUXOR).

OH, MY DEAR, DEAREST GORDON: Mohammed's rapture when he received from the angel the "holy Koran" was a mild emotion compared to mine when I read your letter. Perhaps I ought to be concerned about the contents of it, but I am not—not a bit of me! Having found out what the Grand Cadi is doing, you will confound his "knavish tricks."

Never mind, my dear old boy, what the officials are saying. They'll soon see whether you have been a bad Englishman, and in any case you cannot compete with the descendants of *all* the creeping things that came out of the Ark.

Don't worry about me, either. Unparalleled as my position is, I am quite capable of taking care of myself, for I find that in the decalogue you delivered to your devoted slave on the day she saw you first, there was one firm and plain commandment, "Thou shalt have no other love but me." I dare say, being a woman, I am faithless to the first instinct of my sex in telling you this, but I have no time for "female" fooleries, however delicious, and be bothered to them, anyway!

As you see, I did not run away from Ishmael's camp on reaching the railway terminus, and the reason was that you said you were writing to me again at Luxor. Hence, I was compelled to come on, for of course I would not have lost that letter, or let it go astray, for all the value of the British Empire.

I was delighted with my day at Assouan, though, with its glimpses of a green, riotous, prodigal, ungovernable Nature, after the white nakedness of the wilderness, with its flash-light peep at civilised frivolities, its hotels for European visitors, its orchestras playing "When we are mar-ried," its Egyptian dragomans with companies of tourists trailing behind them, its dahabeahs and steam launches, and above all its groups of English girls, maddeningly pretty and full of the intoxication of life, yet pretending to be consumed by a fever of self-culture, and devoured by curiosity about mummies and tombs.

It's no use—these pink-white faces after the brown and black are a joy to behold, and when I came upon a bunch of them chattering and laughing like linnets ("Frocks up, children!" as they crossed a puddle made by the watermen) I could hardly help kissing them all round, they looked so sweet and so homelike.

You were right about the boats. A whole fleet was wait-ing for us, which was a mercy, for the animals were utterly done up after the desert journey, and next morning we embarked under the strenuous supervision of a British Bim-bashi, who looked as large as if he had just won the battle of Waterloo.

Of course the people were following Ishmael like a swarm of bees, and, much to my discomfiture, I came in for a share of reflected glory from a crowd of visitors who were evidently wondering whether I was a reincarnation of Lady Hester Stanhope, or the last Circassian slave-wife of the Ameer of Afghanistan. One horrible young woman cocked her camera and snapped me. American, of course, a sort of half countrywoman of yours, sir, shockingly stylish, good-

looking and attractive, with frills and furbelows that gave
a far view of Regent Street and the Rue de la Paix, and
made me feel so dreadfully shabby in my Eastern dress and
veil that I wanted to slap her.

We are now two days down the river, five hundred to a
thousand boat-loads of us, our peaked white sails looking
like a vast flight of seagulls, and our slanting bamboo masts
like an immense field of ripe corn swaying in the wind.
It is a wonderful sight, this flotilla of feluccas going slowly
down the immemorial stream, and when one thinks of it in
relation to its object, it is almost magnificent—a nation
going up to its millennium!

They have rigged up a sort of cabin for me in the
bow of one of the high-prowed boats, with shelter and shade
included, so that I still have some seclusion in which to
write my "Journal," in spite of this pestilent Arab woman
who is always watching me. In the hold outside there must
be a hundred men at least, and at the stern there are a
few women who bake durah cakes on a charcoal stove, making it a marvel to me that they do not set fire to the
boat a dozen times a day.

The wind being fair and the river in full flood—seven
men's height above the usual level, and boiling and bubbling
and tearing down like a torrent—we sail from daylight to
dark, but at night we are hauled up and moored to the bank,
so that the people may go ashore to sleep if they are so
minded.

Oh, these delicious mornings! Oh, these white enchant-
ing nights! The wide, smooth, flowing water, reflecting the
tall palms, the banks, the boats themselves; in the morning
a soft brown, at noon a cool green, at sunset a glowing
rose, at night a pearly gray! Then the broad blue sky with
its blaze of lemon and yellow and burnished gold as the sun
goes down; the rolling back of the darkness as the dawn
appears, and the sweeping up of the crimson wings of day!
If I dare only give myself up to the delight of it! But I
daren't, I daren't, having something to do here, so my
dear one says, though what the deuce and the dickens it is
(except to stay until I receive that letter) I cannot conceive.

II

The people are in great spirits now, all their moaning and murmuring being turned to gladness, and as we glide along they squat in the boats and sing. Strangely enough, in a country where religion counts for so much, there is hardly anything answering to sacred music, but there are war-songs in abundance, full of references to the "filly foal" and of invocations to the God of Victory. These songs the men sing to something like three notes, accompanied by the beat of their tiny drums, and if the natives, who stand on the banks to listen, convey the warlike words to their Moudirs it cannot be a matter for much surprise that the Government thinks an army is coming down the Nile and that your father finds it necessary to prepare to "establish authority."

As for Ishmael, he is in a state of ecstasy that is bordering on frenzy. He passes from boat to boat, teaching and preaching early and late. Of course it is always the same message—the great hope, the Deliverer, the Redeemer, the Christ, the Kingdom or Empire that is to come, but just as he drew his lessons from the desert before so now he draws them from the Nile.

The mighty river, mother of Egypt, numbered among the deities in olden days, born in the heights and flowing down to the ocean, rising and falling and bringing fertility, suckling the land, sustaining it, the great waterway from North to South, the highway for humanity—what is it but a symbol of the golden age so soon to begin, when all men will be gathered together as the children of one Mother, with one God, one Law, one Faith!

It becomes more and more terrifying. I am sure the people are taking their teaching literally, for they are like children in their delirious joy; and when I think how surely their hopes are doomed to be crushed, I ask myself what is to happen to Ishmael when the day of their disappointment comes. They will kill him—I am sure they will!

Gordon, I go through hell at certain moments. It was good of you to tell me I need not charge myself with everything that is happening, but I am hysterical when I think that although this hope may be only a dream, a vain dream, and I had nothing to do with creating it, it is through me that it is to be so ruthlessly destroyed.

Then there is that masculine development in Ishmael's relation to me, and the promise he has made himself that as soon as his task is finished he will live the life of a man!

Thank God, we are close to Luxor now, and when I get that letter I shall be free to escape. Have you seen your father, I wonder? If so, what has happened? Oh, my dear —dear! It is four years—days I mean—since I heard from you—what an age in a time like this! My love—all, all my love!   HELENA.

X

CAIRO.

MY DEAREST HELENA: *El Hamdullillah!* Hamid brought me the letter you gave him at Assouan, and I nearly fell on his neck and kissed him. He also told me you were look-ing "stout and well," and added, with an expression of as-tonishment, that you were "the sweetest and most beau-tiful woman in the world." Of course you are—what the deuce did he expect you to be?

I am not ashamed to say that while I read your letter I was either laughing like a boy or crying like a baby. What wonder? Helena was speaking to me! I could see her very eyes, hear her very voice, feel her very hand. No dream this time, no dear, sweet, murderous make-believe, but Helena herself, actually Helena!

I am not surprised, dearest, at what you tell me of the development of the masculine side of Ishmael's interest in you. It was what I feared and foresaw, yet how I am to stay here, now that I know it has come to pass, heaven alone can say! I suppose I must, or else everything I have come for, lived for, hoped for, and fought for will be wasted and thrown away. Thank God, I have always hitherto been able, even in my blackest hours, to rely on your love

and courage, and I shall continue to do so, and to tell myself that if you are in Ishmael's camp it must be for some
good and useful purpose, although I know that in the dead
waste of every blessed night I shall have some damnable
pricks from the green-eyed monster, not to speak of down-
right fear and honest conscience.

Neither am I at all surprised at what you say of the
growth of the Mahdist element in and around Ishmael,
though that is a pity in itself, and a deadly misfortune
in relation to the Government. Of course it is the old
wretched story over again—the moment a man arises who
has anything of the divine in him, an apostle of the soul
of humanity, a flame-bearer in a realm of darkness, the
world jumps on him, body and soul, and he finds he has
brought not peace but a sword. The Governments of the
world do not want the divine, for the simple reason that the
divine begets divided authority, which begets divided allegiance, which begets riot and insurrection, so down with
the divine, hang it, quarter it, crucify it, which is precisely
what they have been doing with it for two thousand years at
all events.

That, too, is a reason why I cannot carry out my first
intention of going to my father, and another is that I
see only too plainly now that he is playing for a *coup*. Not
that I believe for a moment that like the authorities under
arbitrary governments (Russian for example) my father
would use provocation, even if it were the only means by
which peaceful work and life seemed possible, but I fear
he is becoming a sort of conscientious collaborator of the
accursed Grand Cadi, by acquiescing in conspiracy and permitting it to go on until it has reached a head, in order
to crush it with one blow.

God forgive me if I am judging my own father, but I
cannot help it. There is such a thing as being " drunk with
power," as the Arabs say, and everything points to the
fact that the Consul-General counts on making one sur-
prising and overwhelming effort to suppress this unrest.
That he did not take me (in my character of Ishmael) on
my arrival in Cairo points to it, and that he has invited

me to the dinner in honour of the King's Birthday puts it beyond the shadow of a doubt.

How do I know that? I'll tell you how. Do you remember that when Ishmael's return was first proposed it was suggested that he should enter the city while the Consul-General and his officials were feasting on the Ghezirah, the bridge of their island being drawn and the key of the Pavilion being turned on them? Well, that was the scheme of the Cadi, and I have reason to believe that having obtained Ishmael's consent to it, he straightway revealed it to my father.

What is the result? The Consul-General has invited the conspirators to join him at his festivities, so that while they think they are to hold him prisoner on Ghezirah unti Ishmael's followers have entered Cairo, he will in fact be holding them, the whole boiling of them, including myself, especially myself, thus arresting his enemies in a bunch at the very moment when their rebellion is being put down on the other side of the Nile. There is something tragic in the idea that *if* I go to that dinner my father may find that there has been one gigantic error in his calculations, and I hate the thought of going, but if I go I go, and (D. V.) I shall not shrink.

Good-night, dearest! "Where is she now?" I ask myself for the nine-hundredth time, and for the nine-hundred-and-first time I answer, "Wherever she is she is mine and nobody else's." *In-sha-allah!*

II

Whew! It's comic, and if I were not such a ridiculously tragic person I should like to scream with laughter. The Ulema are at a loss to know what to do about the invitation to the King's dinner, and have been putting their turbaned heads together like frightened chickens in a storm. Never having been invited to such functions before, they suspect treachery, think their conspiracy has got wind, and are for excusing themselves on the ground of a general epidemic among grandmothers, which will require them to be present at funerals in various parts of the country.

On the other hand, Caiaphas, who is giving himself the airs of a hero—a hero, mind you—counsels courage, saying that if there is any suspicion of conspiracy the only way to put it out of countenance is to accept the Consul-General's invitation, which is of the nature of a command, and that this argument applies especially to me (that is to say, Ishmael), who might otherwise expose myself to the inference that I am not the wise and wealthy chief of the Ababdah, but another person who dare not permit himself to be seen. The fox! All the same I may find that it suits my book to go to the King's dinner.

III

The day of the festivities is approaching and already the preparations have begun. Placards on the walls announcing a military tattoo, officials flying about the town, workmen hanging up lanterns for the illumination of the public gardens, and police bands in the squares playing " God Save " and " the Girl I Left," and meantime Ishmael with his vast following coming up the Nile, full of the great Hope, the great Expectation!

Talk about Nero fiddling while Rome burned, that was an act of no particular callousness compared to the infectious merriment of the European population, though many of them know nothing about the tidal wave that is sweeping down, the English press having been forbidden to mention it, and the one strong man in Egypt waiting calmly at the Agency until the moment comes to dam it.

Of course the official classes are aware of what is happening, and their attitude toward the mighty flood that is coming on is a wonderful example of our British pluck and our crass stupidity. Not a man will budge, that much I can say for my countrymen, who are ready to face death any day under a vertical sun, amid deadly swamps and human beings almost as dangerous. But they will not see that while the fanaticism of one hallucinated individual (Ish-

mael, for example) may be a little thing, the soul of a whole
nation is a big thing, and God help the Government that
attempts to crush it!

In order to realise the situation here at this moment
one has to make a daring, audacious, almost impious comparison—to think of the day when Christ entered Jerusalem through a dense, delirious crowd that shouted "Ho-
sanna to the Son of David!" and (forgetting that, soon
afterward, they deserted him when his divinity appeared
to fail) ask oneself what would have happened *then* if the
Roman Consul, prompted by the chief priests, had met that
frenzied multitude with a charge of Roman steel!

God keep us from such consequences in Cairo, but meantime, though the Arabic newspapers are suppressed, the
natives know that Ishmael's host is coming on, and the
effect of the rumour that has gone through the air like a
breath of wind seems to be frantically intoxicating. I confess that the sense of that mighty human wave, sweeping
down the red waters of the high Nile, coming on and on,
as they think to the millennium, but as I know to death, sits
on me, too, like a nightmare. It has the effect of the supernatural, and I ask myself what in the name of God I can
do to prevent the collision that will occur between two forces
that seem bent on destroying each other.

Something I must do, that is certain, and seeing that I
am now the only one who knows what is being done on both
sides, and that it is useless to appeal to either (my father
or Ishmael), what I do must be done by me alone. Alone is
a terrible word, Helena, but what I do I do, and the devil
take the consequences.

I expect to get further information from Hafiz to-morrow, so (D. V.) I'll write my last letter to Bedrasheen,
where, as I hear, you are to encamp. Look out for it there
—I see something I may want you to do for me with Ishmael. Meantime, don't be afraid of him. Remember that
you belong to *me*, to me *only*, and that I'm thinking of you
every hour and minute, and then nothing can go seriously
astray. Good-bye, my beloved, my dear, my darling!

GORDON.

P. S. Is it not extraordinary, my dear Helena, that notwithstanding the torment I suffer at the thought of your position in Ishmael's camp I continue to ask you to remain in it? But wait, only wait! Something good is going to happen! *In-sha-allah!*

XI

THE NILE (BETWEEN LUXOR AND BEDRASHEEN).

MY DEAR, DEAR GORDON: I saw your Hamid Ibrahim the moment I set foot in Luxor, and the way he passed your letter to me and I passed mine to him would have done credit to Charlie Bates and the Artful Dodger in the art of passing "a wipe."

I really think we escaped the eyes of this odious Arab woman, but I am bound to add that almost as soon as I got back to the boat, and began to read your letter and to weep tears of joy over it, I was conscious of a shadow at the mouth of my cabin, and it was she, the daughter of a dog!

No matter! Who the dickens cares! I shall be gone from here before the woman can do me any mischief, and if I am still in Ishmael's camp it is only because you said you were sending your last letter to Bedrasheen, so, you see, I had no choice but to come on.

What you tell me of the course of affairs in Cairo only fills me with hatred of the Grand Cadi ("whom Allah damn"), and I find that I exhaust my Christianity in finding names that seem suitable to "his Serenity"—beginning, of course, with the fourth letter of the English alphabet.

I see already what you are going to do, and when I think of it I feel like a shocking coward. If you cannot work with the Consul-General I suppose you will work without him, perhaps against him, and a conflict between you and your father is the tragedy I always foresaw. It will be the end of one or both of you, and I am trembling at the bare thought.

Oh, I know you are the bravest thing God ever made,
30

and at the same time the most unselfish, but I sometimes wish to Heaven you were not—though I suppose in that event you would fall from your godlike pedestal, and I should not love you so much if I admired you less.

We left Luxor immediately, for although there were still three days to spare before the day of the " festivities," and the river was racing down fast enough to carry a fleet of war, the people were in a fever to reach the end of their journey, so Ishmael consented to go on without a rest.

I find the whole thing more frightening than ever, now that we are so near to the end, for I suppose it is certain that whatever else happens, this vast horde of Ishmael's fanatical followers will never be allowed to enter Cairo, and it will be impossible to convince the Consul-General and the Government that they are not coming as an armed force. Then what will the people do? What will they say to Ishmael? And if Ishmael suspects treachery what will he say? What will he say to *me*? But no matter—I shall be gone before that can occur.

It is now eleven o'clock at night, yet I cannot sleep, so I shall sit up all night and see the rising of the Southern Cross. A silver slip of a moon has just appeared, and by its shimmering light our vast fleet seems to be floating down the river like ships in a dream. Such calm, such silence! Phantoms of houses, of villages, of funereal palms gliding in ghostly muteness past us! Sometimes an obelisk goes like a dark skeleton down the bank—vestige of a vanished civilisation as full, perhaps, of delusive faith as ours. What is God doing with us all, I wonder? Why does He. . . .

II

Another thrilling moment! I *must* tell you—I cannot help myself.

You may have gathered that since the scene in the tent on the desert Ishmael has left *me* alone, but last night he came again.

That grim woman had gone to her crib somewhere outside, and I was writing to you as you see above, when suddenly in the silence, broken by nothing but the snores of the men in the hold, the lapping of the water against the side of the boat and the occasional voice of the Reis at the rudder, I heard a soft step which I have learned to know.

"Rani!" said a voice outside, and in a moment the canvas of my cabin was drawn and Ishmael was sitting by my side.

There was a look in his eyes that told of depths of tenderness, not to speak of consuming emotion, but at first he talked calmly. He began by speaking of you. It seems he had had news of you at Assouan, that you were staying at the Chancellor of El Azhar's house, and that the Old Chancellor had no words warm enough for your wisdom and courage. Neither had Ishmael, who said the whole Mohammedan world was praising you.

I really believe he loves you, and I was beginning to melt toward him, thinking how much more he would worship you if he only knew what you had really done for him, when —heigh-ho!—he began to speak of me and to return to his old subject. Love was a God-given passion, and he was looking forward to the end of his work, when he might give himself up to it. His vow of chastity and consecration would then be annulled and he could live the life of a man!

Very tender, very delicate, but very warm and dreadfully Oriental. My nerves were tingling all over, and I was feeling shockingly weak and womanish while the great powerful man sat beside me, and when he talked about children, saying a woman without them was like a tree without fruit, I found myself for the first time in my life in actual *physical* terror.

At last he rose to go, and before I knew what he was doing he had flung his arms around me and kissed me, and when I recovered myself he was gone.

Then all the physical repulsion I spoke of before arose in me again, and at the same moment, as if by a whirlwind of emotion, I remembered you, and my strength came back.

I have often wondered what sort of horror it must be to the woman who is married to an unfaithful husband or to a drunkard, to have him come in his uncleanness to claim her, and now (though Ishmael is neither of these, but merely a man who has " rights " in me) I think I know.

No matter! , I am not afraid of Ishmael any longer, so *you* need not be afraid for me. It is not for nothing that I have Jewish blood in me, and if Ishmael attempts to *force* me, as surely as I am a daughter of Zion, I will—well, never mind! Dreadful? Perhaps so. Jezebel? I cannot help it. My husband? No, no, no; and if destiny has put me into the position of his wife, I despise and intend to defy it.

III

Of course I did not sleep a wink last night, but I crept out of my hiding-place under the high prow of the boat, when the dawn came up like a bride robed in pearly gray and blushing rosy red. By that time we were nearing Bedrasheen, and now we are moored alongside of it, and the people are beginning to land, for it seems they are to camp at Sakkara, in order to be in a position to see the light which is to shine from the minaret of Mohammed Ali.

Such joy, such rapture! Men with the madra pole sounding the depths of the water: men with sculls pushing the boats ashore; all shouting in strident voices, or singing in guttural tones!

Soon, very soon, their hopes will be blighted. Will they ever know by whom? I wonder if anybody will tell them about that letter? Where is Mosie? I trust the Consul-General may keep him in Cairo. The boy is as true as steel, but with this woman to question him! . . . My God, make her meet a fate as black as her heart, the huzzy!

But why do I trouble about this? It matters nothing to me what becomes of the Arab woman, or of the Egyptians, or of the Soudanese, or even of Ishmael himself—the whole boiling of them, as you say. I know I'm heartless, but I can't help it. The only question of any consequence is what is happening to *you*. After all, it was I who put you where you are, and it is quite enough for me to reproach myself with that.

What is the Government doing to you? What has your

father done? What is going on among the descendants of the creeping things that came out of the Ark?

. . . .

I cannot see Hamid among the crowd on the land, but I hope to find him as soon as I go ashore. If I miss him in the fearful chaos I suppose I shall have to go on to the camp, for, besides my anxiety to receive your letter, I am living under the strongest conviction that there is something for me to do for you, and that it has not been for nothing that I have gone through the bog and slush of this semi-barbaric life.

There! You see what you've done for me! You've given me as strong a belief in the "mystic sense" as you have yourself, and as firm a faith in fatality.

. . . .

No sign of Hamid yet! Never mind! Don't be afraid for me—I am all right.

Gordon, my dear, my dear—dear, good-bye!

HELENA.

XII

FOR more than three weeks the Consul-General had kept his own counsel, and not even to the Sirdar, whom he saw daily, did he reveal the whole meaning of his doings.

When the Sirdar had come to say that through the Soudan Intelligence Department in Cairo he had heard that Ishmael and his vast company had left Khartoum, and that the Inspector-General was of opinion that the pilgrimage must be stopped or it would cause trouble, the Consul-General had said:

"No! Let the man come on. We shall be ready to receive him."

Again, when the Governor at Assouan, hearing of the approach of the ever-increasing horde of Soudanese had telegraphed for troops to keep them out of Egypt, the Consul-General had replied:

"Leave them alone, and mind your own business."

Finally, when the Commandant of Police at Cairo had come with looks of alarm to say that a thousand open boats, all packed with people, were sailing down the river like an invading army, and that if they attempted to enter the city the native police could not be relied upon to resist them, the Consul-General had said:

"Don't be afraid. I have made other arrangements."

Meantime, the great man who seemed to be so calm on the outside was white hot within. Every day, while Ishmael was in the Soudan, and every hour after the Prophet had entered Egypt, he had received telegrams from his Inspectors saying where the pilgrimage was and what was happening to it. So great, indeed, had been the fever of his anxiety that he had caused a telegraphic tape to be fixed up in his bedroom that in the middle of the night, if need be, he might rise and read the long white slips.

A few days before the date fixed for the festivities, one of the Inspectors of the Ministry of the Interior came to tell him that there were whispers of a conspiracy that had been blown upon, with hushed rumours of some bitter punishment which the Consul-General was preparing for those who had participated in it. As a consequence a number of the Notables and certain of the diplomats were rapidly leaving the country, nearly every train containing some of them. A sombre fire shone in the great man's eyes while he listened to this, but he only answered with a sinister smile:

"The air of Egypt doesn't agree with them perhaps. Let them go. They'll be lucky if they live to come back."

As soon as the Inspector was gone the Consul-General sent for his Secretary and asked what acceptances had been received of the invitations to the King's Dinner, whereupon the Secretary's face fell and he replied that there had been many excuses.

Half the diplomats had pleaded calls from their own countries, and half the Pashas had protested with apologetic prayers that influenza or funerals in their families would compel them to decline. The Ministers had accepted, as they needs must, but, with a few exceptions, the Ulema, after endless invocations to God and the Prophet, had, on various grounds, begged to be excused.

"And the exceptions—which are they?" asked the Consul-General.

"The Chancellor of El Azhar, his guest the Sheikh Omar Benani, the Grand Mufti and . . ."

"Good! All goes well," said the Consul-General. "Make a list of the refusals, and let me have it on the day of the dinner."

Before that day there was much to do, and on the day immediately preceding it the British Agency received a stream of visitors. The first to come by appointment was the English Adviser to the Ministry of Justice.

"I wish you," said the Consul-General, "to summon the new Special Tribunal to hold a court in Cairo at ten o'clock to-morrow night."

"Ten o'clock to-morrow night? Did your lordship say *ten?*" asked the Adviser.

"Don't I speak plainly?" replied the Consul-General, whereupon the look of bewilderment on the Adviser's face broke up into an expression of embarrassment and his desire to ask further questions was crushed.

The next visitor to come by appointment was the British Adviser to the Minister of the Interior, the tall young Englishman on whose red hair the red fez sat strangely.

"I wish you," said the Consul-General, "to arrange that the gallows be got out and set up after dark to-morrow night in the square in front of the Governorat."

"The square in front of the Governorat?" repeated the Adviser, in tones of astonishment. "Does your lordship forget that public execution within the city is no longer legal?"

"Damn it, I'll make it legal," replied the Consul-General, whereupon the red head under the red fez bowed itself out of the library without waiting to ask who was to be hanged.

The next visitor to come to the Agency by appointment was the burly Commandant of Police.

"You still hold your warrant for the arrest of Ishmael Ameer?" asked the Consul-General.

"I do, my lord."

"Then come to Ghezirah to-morrow night and be ready to receive my orders."

Then came the Colonel who, since the death of General Graves, had been placed in temporary command of the Army of Occupation.

"Is everything in order?"

"Everything, my lord."

"All your regiments now in the country can arrive at Calioub by the last train to-morrow night?"

"All of them."

"Then wait there yourself until you hear from me. I shall speak to you over the telephone from Ghezirah. On receiving my message you will cause fifty rounds of ammunition to be issued to your men and then march them into the city and line them up in the principal thoroughfares. Let them stay there as long as they may be required to do so—all night if necessary—and if there is unrest or armed resistance on the part of the populace, of the native army, or of people coming into the town, you will promptly put it down. You understand?"

"I understand, my lord."

"But wait for my telephone call. Don't let one man stir out of barracks until you receive it. Mind that. Good-bye!"

The better part of the day was now gone, yet so great had been the Consul-General's impatience that he had not even yet broken his fast, although Fatimah, who alone would have been permitted to do so, had repeatedly entered his room to remind him that his meals were ready.

At sunset he went up to the roof of his house. Every day for nearly a week he had done this, taking a telescope in his hand that he might look down the river for the mighty octopus of demented people who were soon to come. Yesterday he had seen them for the first time—a vast flotilla of innumerable native boats, with white three-cornered sails, stretching far down the Nile, as a flight of birds of passage might stretch along the sky.

Now the people were encamped on the desert between Bedrasheen and Sakkara, a sinuous line of speckled white and black on the golden yellow of the sand, looking like a great serpent encircling the city on the south. As a serpent they fascinated the Consul-General when he looked at them, but not with fear, so sure was he that, by the machinery he had set to work, the vermin would soon be trampled into the earth.

There they were, he thought, an armed force, the scourings of the Soudan, under the hypnotic sway of a fanatic-hypocrite, waiting to fall on the city and to destroy its civilisation. In every saddle-bag a rifle; in every gebah a copy of the Koran; in every heart a spirit of hatred and revenge.

Since the Grand Cadi had told him of the conspiracy to establish an Arab Empire, the Consul-General's mind had evolved developments of the devilish scheme. The practical heart of the matter was Pan-Islamism, a combination of all the Moslem peoples to resist the Christian nations. Therefore, in the great historical drama which he was soon to play, he would be seen to· be the saviour not only of England and of Europe and of civilisation, but even of Christianity itself!

It would be a life and death struggle, in which cruel things could not fail, but the issues were world-great, and therefore he would not shrink. He who wanted the end must not think too much about the means.

Ishmael? The gallows in the square of the Governorat! Why not? The man might have begun as a mere paid emissary of the Khedive, but having developed the Mahdist malady, a belief in his own divinity, he meant to throw off his allegiance to his master and proclaim himself as Caliph. Therefore they must hang him—hang him before the eyes of his followers, and fling his " divine " body into the Nile!

As the Consul-General stepped down from the roof Ibrahim met him with a letter from the Grand Cadi saying he found himself suspected by his own people, and therefore begged to be excused from attendance at the King's Dinner, but sent this secret message to warn his Excellency that by the plotting of his enemies the Kasr el Nil bridge, which connected Ghezirah with Cairo, would be opened immediately after the beginning of the festival.

"The fox!" thought the Consul-General, but interpreting in his own way the dim purpose of the plot—that it was intended to imprison him on the island, while Ishmael's followers entered the city—he merely added to his order for his carriage an order for his steam-launch as well.

Daylight had faded by this time, and as soon as darkness fell the Consul-General received a line of other visitors—strange visitors, such as the British Agency had never seen before. They were women, Egyptian women, the harem, shrouded figures in black satin and the yashmak, the wives of the Ministers who had felt compelled to accept their invitations, but were in fear of the consequences of having done so.

Unexampled, unparalleled event, never before known in an Eastern country, the women, disregarding the seclusion of their sex, had come to plead for their husbands, to make tacit admission of a conspiracy, but to say, each trembling woman in her turn, "My husband is not in it," and to implicate other men who were.

The Consul-General listened with cold, old-fashioned courtesy to everything they had to say, and then bowed them out without many words. Instinctively Ibrahim had darkened the Agency as soon as they began to come, so that veiled they passed in, veiled they passed out, and they were gone before anybody else was aware.

The dinner hour was now near, and leaving the library with the intention of going up to dress, the Consul-General came upon two men who were sitting in an alcove of the hall. They were Reuter's reporters, who, for the past ten years, had been accustomed to come for official information. Rising as the Consul-General approached, they asked him if he had anything to say.

"Be here at ten o'clock to-morrow night, and I shall have something to give you," he said. "It will be something important, so keep the wires open to receive it."

"The wires to London, my lord?"

"To London, Paris, Berlin—everywhere! Good-night!"

Going upstairs with a flat and heavy step, but a light and almost joyous heart, the Consul-General remembered his

letter of resignation, and thought of the hubbub in Downing Street the day after to-morrow when news of the conspiracy, and of how he had scotched it, fell like a thunderbolt on the "fossils of Whitehall."

In the conflagration that would blaze heaven high in
England it would be seen at last how necessary a strong
authority in Egypt was, and then—what then? He would
be asked to use his own discretion, unlimited power be reposed in him, he would hoist the Union Jack over the Citadel, annex the country to the British Crown, cast off all
futile obligations to the Sultan, and so end for ever the
present ridiculous, paradoxical, suicidal situation.

While Ibrahim helped him to dress for dinner, he was
partly conscious that the man was talking about Mosie and
repeating some bewildering story which the black boy had
been telling downstairs of Helena's "marriage to the new
Mahdi."

This turned his thoughts in another direction, and for
a few short moments the firm and stern, but not fundamen-
tally hard and cruel man, became aware that all his fierce
and savage and candid ferocity that day had been no more
than the wild ejaculation of a heart that was broken and
trembling because it was bereaved.

It was Gordon again—always Gordon! Where was "our
boy" now? What was happening to him? Could it be
possible that he was so far away that he would not hear
of the weltering downfall, so soon to come, of the "charlatan mummer" whose evil influence had brought his bright
young life to ruin?

XIII

THAT night the Sirdar dined with the Consul-General,
and as soon as the servants had gone from the dining-room
he said:

"Nuneham, I have something to tell you."

"What is it?" asked the Consul-General.

"Notwithstanding three weeks of the closest observation I have found no trace of insubordination in the Egyptian Army, but nevertheless, in obedience to your warning, I have taken one final precaution. I have given orders that the ammunition with which every soldier is int usted shall be taken from him to-morrow evening, so that if Ishmael Ameer comes into Cairo at night with any hope of——"

"My dear Mannering," interrupted the Consul-General, with his cold smile, "would it surprise you to be told that Ishmael Ameer is already in Cairo?"

"Already? Did you say——"

"That he has been here for three weeks, that he came by the same train as yourself, wearing the costume of a Bedouin Sheikh, and that——"

"But, my dear Nuneham, this is incredible," said the Sirdar, with his buoyant laugh. "It is certainly true that a Bedouin Sheikh travelled in the same train with me from the Soudan, but that he was Ishmael Ameer in disguise is of course utterly unbelievable."

"Why so?"

"Because a week after I left Khartoum I heard that Ishmael was still living there, and because every other day since then has brought us advices from our Governors saying the man was coming across the desert with his people."

"My dear friend," said the Consul-General, "in judging of the East one must use Eastern weights and measures. The race that could for fourteen centuries accept the preposterous tradition that it was not Jesus Christ who was crucified but some one else who took on his likeness and died instead of him, is quite capable of accepting for itself and imposing upon others a substitute for this White Prophet."

"But you bewilder me," said the Sirdar. "Isn't the man Ishmael at this moment lying encamped, with fifty thousand of his demented people, on the desert outside Cairo?"

"No," said the Consul-General.

And then in his slow, deep, firm voice, grown old and husky, he unburdened himself for the first time—telling of Helena's departure for Khartoum on her errand of vengeance; of her letter from there announcing Ishmael's intention of coming into Cairo in advance of his people, in order to draw off the allegiance of the Egyptian Army; of Ishmael's arrival and his residence at the house of the Chancellor of El Azhar; of the visit of the Princess Nazimah, and her report of the conspiracy of the diplomatic corps, and finally of the Grand Cadi's disclosure of the Khedive's plot for the establishment of an Arab Empire.

"So you see," said the Consul-General with an indulgent smile, "that all the bad concomitants of an Oriental revolution are present, and that while you, my dear friend, have been holding your hand in the Soudan for fear of repeating the error of two thousand years ago—troubling yourself about Pontius Pilate and moral forces *versus* physical ones, and giving me the benefit of all the catchwords of your Christian socialism and Western democracy—a conspiracy of gigantic proportions has been gathering about us."

The Sirdar's usually ruddy face whitened, and he listened with a dumb, vague wonder while the Consul-General went on, with bursts of bitter humour, to describe one by one the means he had taken to defeat the enemies by whom they were surrounded.

"So you see, too," he said at last, lifting unconsciously his tired voice, "that by this time to-morrow we shall have defeated the worst conspiracy that has ever been made even in Egypt—meted out sternly retributive justice to the authors of it; put an end to all forms of resistance, whether passive or active, silenced all chatter about Nationalism and all prattle about representative institutions, destroyed the devilish machinery of this accursed Pan-Islamism, crushed the Khedive, and wiped out his fanatic-hypocrite and charlatan-mummer, Ishmael Ameer."

The Consul-General had spoken with such intensity, and the Sirdar had listened so eagerly, that down to that moment neither of them had been aware that another person was in the room. It was Fatimah, who was standing with the deathlike rigidity of a ghost near to the door, in the half-light of the shaded electric lamps.

The Sirdar saw her first, and with a motion of his hand he indicated her presence to the Consul-General, who, with

a face that was pale and stern, turned angrily round and
asked the woman what she wanted; whereupon, Fatimah,
with trembling lips and a quivering voice, as if struggling
with the spirit of falsehood, said she had only come to ask
if the Sirdar intended to sleep there that night, and whether
she was to make up a bed for him.

"No, certainly not! Why should you think so? Go to
bed yourself," said the Consul-General, and with obvious
relief the woman turned to go.

"Wait!" said the Consul-General. "How long have you
been in the room?"

"Only a little moment, oh, my lord," replied Fatimah.

After that the two men went to the library, but some time
passed before the conversation was resumed. The Sirdar
lit a cigar and puffed in silence, while the Consul-General,
who did not smoke, sat in an arm chair with his wrinkled
hands clasped before his breast. At length the Sirdar said:

"And all this came of Helena's letter from Khartoum?"

"Was suggested by it," said the Consul-General.

"You told me she was there, but I could not imagine
what she was doing—what her errand was. Good heavens,
what a revenge! It makes one shiver! Carries one back
to another age!"

"A better age," said the Consul-General. "A more natural and less hypocritical age at all events."

"The age of an eye for an eye, a tooth for a tooth, perhaps—the age of a hot and consuming God."

"Yes, a God of wrath, a God of anger, a God who *did*
something, not the pale, meek, forgiving, anæmic God of our
day—a God who does nothing."

"The God of our day is at least a God of mercy, of pity,
and of love," said the Sirdar.

"He is a lay figure, my friend, who permits wrong without revenging it—in short, no God at all, but an illogical,
inconsequential, useless creature."

The Sirdar made no further resistance, and the Consul-
General went on to defend Helena's impulse of vengeance
by assailing the Christian spirit of forgiveness.

"There was at least something natural and logical as

well as majestic and magnificent in the old ideal of Jehovah, but your new ideal of Jesus is contrary to nature and opposed to the laws of life. 'Love your enemies.' 'Do good to them that hate you.' 'If a man smite thee on the right cheek turn to him the other also.' 'Resist not evil!' 'If any man take away thy coat let him have thy cloak also!' Impossible! Fatal! If this is Christianity I am no Christian. When I am hit I hit back. When I am injured I demand justice. The only way! Any other would lead to the triumph of the worst elements in humanity. And what I do everybody else does—everybody—though the hypocrisy of the modern world will not permit people to admit it."

The Consul-General had risen and was tramping heavily across the room.

"Is there one man alive who will dare to say that he actually orders his life according to the precepts of Christ? If so, he is either a liar or a fool. As for the nations, look at the facts. Christianity has been two thousand years in the world, yet here we are competing against each other in the building of war-ships, the imposition of tariffs, the union of trades. Why not? I say why not?"

The Consul-General drew up and waited, but getting no answer he continued:

"Civilisation requires it. I say requires it. What holds the world together and preserves peace among the nations is not Christianity but cast-iron and gunpowder. Yet what vexes me and stirs my soul is to hear people praying in their churches for 'peace and concord,' while all the time they know that 'peace and concord' is an impossible ideal, that Christianity in its first sense is dead, and that Jesus as a practical guide to life—as a practical guide to life, mind you—has *failed*."

Then the Sirdar lifted his eyes and said:

"Do you know, my dear Nuneham, I once heard somebody else talk like that, though from the opposite standpoint of sympathy, not contempt."

"Who was it?"

"Your own son."

"Humph!"

The Consul-General frowned, and there was silence again for some moments. When the conversation was resumed it concerned the dangers of the Arab Empire, which, according to the Grand Cadi, the Khedive (with the help of Ishmael) expected to found.

"What would it mean?" said the Consul-General. "The utter annihilation of the unbeliever. Does not the word 'Ghazi' signify a hero who slays the infidel? Does not every Mollah, when he recites the Khuttab in the mosque, invoke divine wrath on the non-Moslem? What then? The establishment of an Arab Empire would mean the revolt of the whole Eastern world against the Western world, and a return to all the brutality, all the intolerance of the farrago of moribund nonsense known as the Sacred Law."

The Sirdar made no reply and after a moment the Consul-General said:

"Then think of the spectacle of a conquering Mohammedan army in Cairo! If the Citadel and the Arsenal of the capital could be occupied by that horde outside, it would not be merely England's power in Egypt that would be ended, or the English Empire as a world-force that would be injured—it would be Western civilisation itself that would in the end be destroyed. The Mohammedans in India would think that what their brethren in Cairo had done they might do. The result would be incalculable chaos, unlimited anarchy, the turning back of the clock ten centuries.

The Consul-General returned to his seat, saying:

"No, no, my friend, a catastrophe so appalling as that cannot be left to chance, and if it is necessary to blow these fifty thousand fanatics out of the mouths of guns rather than lay the fate of the world open to irretrievable ruin I —*I will do it.*"

"But all this depends on the truthfulness of the Grand Cadi's story—isn't it so?" asked the Sirdar.

The Consul-General bent his head.

"And the first test of its truthfulness is whether or not these thousands of Ishmael's followers are an armed force?"

Again the Consul-General bent his head.

"Well," said the Sirdar, rising and throwing away his cigar, "I am bound to tell you that I see no reason to think they are. More than that, I will not believe that when our boy took his serious step he would have sided with this White Prophet if he had suspected that the man's aims included an attack upon England's power in Egypt, and I cannot imagine for a moment that he could be fool enough not to know."

Again the Consul-General frowned, but the Sirdar went on firmly:

"I believe he thought and knew that Ishmael Ameer's propaganda was purely spiritual, the establishment of an era of universal peace and brotherhood, and that is a world-question having nothing to do with England or Egypt or Arab Empires, except so far as——"

But the Consul-General, who was cut to the quick by the Sirdar's praise of Gordon, could bear no more.

"Only old women of both sexes look for an era of universal peace," he said testily.

"In that case," replied the Sirdar, "the old women are among the greatest of mankind—the Hebrew prophets, the prophets of Buddhism, of Islam, and of Christianity. And if that is going too far, then Abraham Lincoln and John Bright, and, to come closer home, your own son, as brave a man as ever drew a sword, a soldier, too, the finest young soldier in the King's service, one who might have risen to any height, if he had been properly handled, instead of being——"

But the old man, whose nostrils were swelling and dilating like the nostrils of a broken-winded horse, leaped to his feet and stopped him.

"Why will you continue to talk about my son?" he cried. "Do you wish to torture me? He allowed himself to become a tool in the hands of my enemies, yet you are accusing me of destroying his career and driving him away. You are—you know you are!"

"Ah, well! God grant everything may go right to-morrow," said the Sirdar after a while, and with that he rose to go.

It was now very late, and when Ibrahim in the hall, with two sleepy eyes, hardly able to keep himself from yawning, opened the outer door, the horses of the Sirdar's carriage, which had been waiting for nearly an hour, were heard stamping impatiently on the gravel of the drive.

At the last moment the old man relented.

"Reg," he said, and his voice trembled, "forgive me if I have been rude to you. I have been hard hit and I must make a fight. I need not explain. Good-night!" And he had gone back to the library before the Sirdar could reply.

But after a while the unconquerable spirit and force of the man enabled him to regain his composure, and before going to bed he went up on to the roof to take a last look at the enemy he was about to destroy. There it lay in the distance, more than ever like a great serpent encircling the city on the south, for there was no moon, the night was very dark, and the dying fires of the sinuous camp at Sak-kara made patches of white and black like the markings of a mighty cobra.

Fatimah was at his bedroom door, waiting to bring his hot water and to ask if he wanted anything else.

"Yes, I want you to go to bed," he replied, but the Egyptian woman, still dallying about the room and speaking with difficulty, wished to know if it was true, as the black boy had said, that Miss Helena was in Khartoum and that she had betrothed herself to the White Prophet.

"I don't know and I don't care—go to bed," said the Consul-General.

"Poor Gordon! My poor boy! Wah! Wah! Everything goes wrong with him. Yet he hadn't an evil thought in his heart."

"Go to bed, I tell you!"

It was even longer than usual before the Consul-General slept.

He thought of Helena. Where was she now? He had been telling himself all along that to save appearances she might find it necessary to remain for a while in Ishmael's camp, but surely she might have escaped by this time.

Could it be possible that she was kept as a prisoner? Was there anything he ought to do for her?

Then he thought of the speech he was to make in proposing the King's health to-morrow, and framed some of the stinging ironical sentences with which he meant to lash his enemies to the bone.

Last of all he thought of Gordon, as he always did when he was dropping off to sleep, and the only regret that mingled with his tingling sense of imminent triumph was that his son could not be present at the King's Dinner to see—what he would see!

" Oh, if I could have him there to-morrow night—what I would give for it!" he thought.

At length the Consul-General slept and his big desolate house was silent. If any human eye could have looked upon him as he lay on his bed that night, the old man with his lips sternly set, breathing fitfully, only the tired body overcome, the troubled brain still working, it would have been a pitiful thing to think that he who was the virtual master of millions appeared to be himself the sport of those inscrutable demons of destiny which seem to toss us about like toys.

His power, his pride, his life-success—what had he gained by them? His wife dead, his son in revolt against him—alone, enfeebled, duped, and self-deluded.

God, what a little thing is man! He who for forty years had guided the ship of State, before whose word Ministers and even Khedives had trembled, could not see into the dark glass of the first few hours before him.

Peace to him—until to-morrow!

XIV

SERAI FUM EL KHALIG, CAIRO.

MY DEAREST HELENA: I am going to that dinner! Yes, as Ishmael Ameer in the disguise of the Sheikh Omar Benani, chief of the Ababdah, I am to be one of my father's guests.

This is the morning of the day of the festivities, and from Hafiz, by the instrumentality of one who would live or die or give her immortal soul for me, I have at length learned all the facts of my father's *coup*.

Did you ever hear of the incident of the Opera House? Well, this incident is to be a replica of that, though the parts to be played in the drama are in danger of being differently cast.

As this is the last letter I shall be able to send to you before an event which may decide one way or another the fate of England in Egypt, my father's fate, Ishmael's, and perhaps yours and mine, I must tell you as much as I dare commit to paper.

The British Army, as I foresaw from the first, is being brought back to Cairo. It is to come in to-night as quietly as possible by the last trains arriving at Calioub. The Consul-General is to go to Ghezirah as if nothing were about to happen, but at the last moment when his enemies have been gathered under one roof—Ministers, Diplomats, Notables, Ulema—when the operation of their plot has begun, and the bridge is drawn, and the island is isolated, and Ishmael and his vast following are making ready to enter the city, my father is to speak over the telephone to the officer commanding at Abbassiah, and then the soldiers, with fifty rounds of ammunition, are to march into Cairo and line up in the streets.

Such is my father's *coup*, and to make sure of the complete success of it—that Ishmael's following is on the move, and that no conspirator (myself above all) escapes—he has given orders to the Colonel not to stir one man out of the barracks until he receives his signal. Well, my work to-night is to see that he never receives it.

Already you will guess what I am going to do. I must go to the dinner in order to do it, for both the central office of the telephone and the office of the telegraph are now under the roofs of the Ghezirah Palace and Pavilion.

I hate to do the damnable thing, but it must be done. It must, it must! There is no help for it.

I cannot tell you how hard it is to me to be engaged in

a secret means to frustrate my father's plans—it is like fighting one's own flesh and blood, and is not fair warfare. Neither can I say what a struggle it has been to me, as an English soldier, to make up my mind to intercept an order of the British Army—it is like playing traitor, and I can scarcely bear to think of it.

But all the same I *know* it is necessary. I also know God knows it is necessary, and when I think of that my heart beats wildly.

It is necessary to prevent the massacre which I know (and my father does not) would inevitably ensue; necessary to save my father himself from the execration of the civilised world; necessary to save Ishmael from the tragic consequences of his determined fanaticism; necessary to save England from the possible loss of her Mohammedan dominions, from being faithless to her duty as a Christian nation, and from the divine judgment which will overtake her if she wantonly destroys her great fame as the one Western power that seems designed by Providence to rule and to guide the Eastern peoples; and necessary, above all, to save the white man and the black man from a legacy of hatred that would divide them for another hundred years, and put back the union of races and of faiths for countless centuries.

If I am not a vain fool this is what I (D. V.) have got to do, so why in the name of God need I trouble myself about the means by which I do it? And if I am the only man who can, I must, or I shall be a coward skulking out of his plain responsibility, and a traitor not only to England but to humanity itself.

God does not promise me success, but I believe I shall succeed. Indeed I am so sure of success that I feel as if all the recent events of my life have been leading up to this one. What I felt when I left Cairo for Khartoum, and again when I left Khartoum for Cairo—that everything had been governed by higher powers which could not err—I feel now more than ever.

If I had delivered myself up to the authorities after your father's death my life would have been wasted and thrown away. Nay, if I had obeyed orders over the blun-

der of El Azhar I should not have been where I am now—
between two high-spirited men who are blindly making for
each other's ruin, and the destruction of all they stand for.

This reconciles me to everything that has happened, and
if I have to pay the penalty of playing buffer I am ready
to do so. I have great trust that God will bring me out all
right, but if that is not His plan, then so be it. I am willing to give my life for England, whatever name she may
know me by when she comes to see what I have done, and
I am willing to die for these poor Egyptians, because I was
born and brought up among them, and I cannot help loving
them.

Death has no terrors for me anyway. I think the experiences of the past months have taught me all that death
has to teach. In fact, I feel at this moment exactly as I
have felt at the last charge in battle, when, fighting against
frightful odds, it has not been a case of every man for
himself, but of God for us all.

Besides, I feel that on the day of your father's death I
died to myself—to my selfish hopes of life, I mean—and
if God intends to crush me in order that I may save my
country, and these people whom I love and who love me, I
really wish and long for Him to do so.

But *In-sha-allah!* It will be as God pleases, and I believe
from the bottom of my heart that He is working out His
wonderful embroidery of events to a triumphant issue. So
don't be afraid, my dear Helena, whatever occurs to-night.
I may be taken, but (D. V.) I shall not be taken in disgrace.
In any case I feel that my hour has come—the great hour
that I have been waiting for so long.

This may be the last letter I shall write to you, so I
am sending it by Mosie, lest Hamid should find a difficulty
in getting into your camp. I hope to God you may get it,
for I want you to know that my last thoughts are about
yourself.

Upon my soul, dear, I believe the end will be all right,
but if it is to be otherwise, and we are to be separated, and
our lives in this world are to be wasted, remember that deep
love bridges death.

Remember, too, what you said to me at Khartoum. "I am a soldier's daughter," you said, "and in my heart I am a soldier's wife as well, and I shouldn't be worthy to be either if I didn't tell you to do your duty, whatever the consequences to me."

Good-bye, my dear, my dear! If anything happens you will know what to do. I trust you without fear. I have always trusted you. I can say it now, at this last moment —never, dearest, never for one instant has the shadow of a doubt of you entered into my heart. My brave girl, my love, my life, my Helena!

May the great God of Heaven bless and protect you!

GORDON.

P. S. Oh, how the deuce did I forget? There is something for you to do—something important—and I had almost sent off my letter without saying anything about it.

Do you remember that on the day I left Khartoum it was ordered by Ishmael that after the call of the muezzin to midnight prayers, a light was to be set up in the minaret of the mosque of Mohammed Ali as a sign that he might enter the city in peace?

Well, if I fail and the British Army comes into Cairo, Ishmael must be kept out of it. He may be stubborn—a man who thinks God guides and protects him and makes a special dispensation for him is not easy to dissuade—but if the light does not appear he *must* be restrained.

That is your work with Ishmael—why you are with him still. 1 knew it would be revealed to us some day. Once more, my dear, my dear, God bless and protect you!

XV

UNDER THE PYRAMIDS.

MY DEAR GORDON: Your letter has not yet reached me. What has happened? Has your messenger been caught? Who was it? Was it Hamid?

Not having heard from you, I was of course compelled to

come on with the camp and, therefore, I am with it still. We are under the shadow of the Pyramids, with the mud-built village of Sakkara by our side and Cairo in front of us, beyond the ruins of old Memphis and across a stretch of golden sand.

This is, it seems, the day of " the King's Dinner," and at sunset when the elephant's horn was blown for the last time we gathered for prayers under a sea-blue sky on the blood-red side of the Step pyramid.

It was a splendid, horrible, inspiring, depressing, devilish, divine spectacle. First Ishmael recited from the Koran the chapter about the Prophet's great vision (the Surat er Rassoul, I think) while the people on their knees in the shadow, with the sun slanting over their heads, shouted their responses. Then in rapturous tones he preached, and though I was on the farthest verge of the vast crowd I heard nearly all he said.

They had reached their journey's end and had to thank God who had brought them so far without the loss of a single life. Soon they were to go into Cairo, the Mecca of the new world, but they were to enter it in the spirit of love, not hate, of peace, not war, doing violence to none, and raising no rebellion. What said the Holy Koran? " Whosoever among Moslems, Christians, or Jews believe in God and in another life shall be rewarded."

Therefore let no man think they were come to turn the Christians out of Egypt. They were there on a far higher errand—to turn the devil out of the world! The intolerance and bitterness of past ages had been the product of hatred and darkness. The grinding poverty and misery of the present age was the result of a false faith and civilisation. But they were come to bring universal peace, universal brotherhood, and universal religion to all nations and races and creeds—one State, one Faith, one Law, one God!

Cairo was the gate to the East. It was also the gate to the West. He who held the keys of that gate was master of the world. Who, then, should hold them but God's own, His Guided One, His Expected One, His Christ?

More and yet more of this kind Ishmael said in his thrilling, throbbing voice, and of course the people greeted every sentence with shouts of joy. And then finally, pointing to the minarets of the mosque of Mohammed Ali, far off on the Mokattam hills, he told them that at midnight, after the call to prayers, a light was to shine there, and they were to take it for a sign that they might enter Cairo without injury to any and with goodwill toward all.

"Watch for that light, oh, my brothers! It will come! As surely as the sun will rise on you to-morrow that light will shine on you to-night!"

It is now quite dark and the camp is in a delirious state of excitement. The scene about my tent is simply terrifying. At one side there is an immense Zikr, with fifty frantic creatures crying "Allah!" to a leader, who in wild, guttural tones is reciting the ninety-nine attributes of God. At the other side there is a huge fire at which a group of men, having slaughtered a sheep, are boiling it in a cauldron, with many pungent herbs, that they may feast and rejoice together in honour of the coming day. People are sitting in circles and singing hymns of victory; tambourines, kettle-drums, and one-stringed lutes are being played everywhere, and strolling singers are going about from fire to fire making up songs that describe Ishmael's good looks, and good deeds, and his "divinity"—the wildest ditty being the most applauded.

Where Ishmael himself is I do not know, but he must indeed be carried away by religious ecstasy if he is not trembling at the mere thought of to-morrow morning. What is to happen if these "Allah-intoxicated Arabs" have to meet five-thousand British bayonets? Or, supposing *you* can obviate that, what is to occur when they are compelled to realise that all their high-built hopes are in the dust? O God! O God!

II

El Hamdullillah! Your letter has come at last! Perhaps I wish it hadn't been Mosie who brought it, but the boy was clever in riding into the camp unobserved, and now I have sent him outside to hide in the darkness while I scribble a few lines in reply. He is to come back presently, and meantime, please God, he will keep out of the sight of that she-cat of an Arab woman.

You are doing right, darling—I am sure you are! Naturally you must be troubled with thoughts about England and your father, but both will yet see what motives inspired you, and whatever they do now they will eventually make amends.

Bravo, my boy, bravo! Perhaps we shall all become Quakers some day, but let the peace people croak as they please, it is war that brings out the truly heroic virtues, and though you are trying to prevent bloodshed you are really going into battle. Go, then, and God bless you!

What wretched ink this is—it must have got mixed with water.

Oh, yes, certainly! I will stay here to the end, and if occasion arises I will do what you desire, though I have not the faintest hope of succeeding. The fact is that even if I could persuade Ishmael not to enter Cairo the people would not under any circumstances be restrained.

To tell you the truth I cannot help feeling sorry for him. He really began with the highest aims and the strongest common-sense, but he has become the victim of his people's idolatry, and, being made an idol, he may no longer be a man.

I cannot help feeling sorry for the people also, for I suppose they have only tried in their blind way to realise the dream of humanity in all ages, the dream of all the holy books and all the great prophets—the dream of a millennium.

It seems, too, as if God, who puts beautiful ideals in people's hearts, always calls for a scapegoat to pay the price of them. That is what you are to be, dear, and when I think of what you are going to do to save these poor people I begin to see for the first time what is meant by the sacrificial blood of Christ.

I suppose this is shocking, but I don't care a pin about that. Every heroic man who risks his life for his fellow-man is doing what Christ did. You are doing it, and I don't believe the good God will ask any questions about ways and means.

There! That's something out of my eyes splash on to the very point of my pen. Don't take it as a mark of weakness, though, but as the sign-manual of Helena's heart telling you to go on without thinking about her.

Forget what I said about my Jewish blood and Jezebel and all that nonsense. Ishmael's "work" will not be "finished" until he enters into Cairo, so I run no risk while I am here, you see.

Of course I am in a fever of impatience to know what is happening on Ghezirah to-night, but you must not suppose that I am afraid. In any case I shall stay here, having no longer the faintest thought of running away, and if there is anything to do I'll do it.

This *may* be the last letter I am to write to you, so good-bye, my Gordon, and God bless you again! My dear, my dear, my dear!   HELENA.

P. S. I suppose you are in the thick of it by this time, for I see that the illuminations at Ghezirah have already begun. My dear, my dear, my . . . my . . . .

XVI

AT eight o'clock that night the Pavilion of the Ghezirah Palace was brilliantly lit up for the "King's Dinner." A troop of British cavalry was mounted in front of it under the sparkling lights that swung from the tall palms of the garden, and a crowd of eager spectators were waiting to see the arrival of the guests.

The Consul-General came early, driving in his open carriage with two gorgeously clad sais running before him. When he stepped down at the door, in his cocked hat, laced coat, and gold-braided trousers, he was saluted like a sovereign. The band of a British regiment under the trees played some bars of the national Anthem, and the English onlookers cheered.

In the open court of the Pavilion, which was walled about by Oriental hangings, the Consul-General's own people were waiting to receive him. His old and weakened but still massive and even menacing personality showed out strongly against the shadowy forms of some of the Advisers and Under Secretaries who stood behind him.

It was quickly seen that his manner was less brusque and masterful than usual, but that his tone was cynical and almost bitter. When his first Secretary stepped up to him and whispered that a Reuter's telegram, which had just come, announced that the Khedive had left Paris for Marseilles intending to take steamer for Egypt, he was heard to say:

"I don't care a ―― what the Khedive does or what he intends to do. Let him wait until to-morrow."

The Sirdar was one of the first of the guests to arrive, and after saying in a low tone that he had just taken the necessary steps to withdraw the ammunition from the native troops, he whispered:

"The great thing is to keep calm—not to allow yourself to lose your temper."

"I *am* calm, perfectly calm," said the Consul-General.

Then the other guests came in quick succession: Envoys Extraordinary, Ministers-Plenipotentiary, Chancellors and Counsellors of Legation and Attachés, wearing all their orders; Barons, Counts, and Marquises attired magnificently in a prodigious quantity of pad and tailor work, silk stockings, white, blue, and red coats with frogs and fur collars, stars, ribbons, silver shoe-buckles, tight breeches, and every conceivable kind of uniform and court dress.

Among the diplomatic corps came Egyptian Ministers wearing the tarboosh and many decorations; the Turkish High Commissioner, a gorgeous and expansive person; a Prince of the Khedivial house, a long miscellaneous line of Pashas and Beys, and finally a few of the Ulema in their turbans and flowing Eastern robes.

The Consul-General received them all with smiles, and it was said afterward that never before had he seemed to be so ceremoniously polite.

There was a delay in announcing dinner, and people were beginning to ask who else was expected, when the first Secretary was seen to approach the host and to say something which only he could hear. A moment later the venerable Chancellor of El Azhar entered the hall in his simple gray farageeyah, accompanied by a tall, strong, upright man in the ample folds of a Bedouin Sheikh, and almost immediately afterward the guests went into the dining-hall.

Dinner was served by Arab waiters in white, and while the band in the gardens outside played selections from the latest French operas, some of the European guests consumed a prodigious deal of fermented liquor and buzzed and twittered and fribbled in the manner of their kind. The Egyptian Ministers and Pashas were less at ease, and the Ulema were obviously constrained, but the Consul-General himself, though he continued to smile and to bow, was the most preoccupied person in the room.

He passed dish after dish, eating little and drinking nothing, though his tongue was dry and his throat was parched. From time to time he looked about him with keen eyes as if counting up the number of those among his guests who had conspired against him. There they were, nearly all of them, his secret enemies, his unceasing revilers, his heartless and treacherous foes. But wait! Only wait! He would soon see their confusion!

The Sirdar, who sat on the left of the host, seemed to be conscious of the Consul-General's impatience, and he whispered again:

" The great thing is to be calm—perfectly calm."

" I *am* calm," said the Consul-General, but in a tone of anger which belied his words.

Toward the end of the dinner his Secretary stepped up to the back of his chair and whispered to him that the bridge had been opened, and after that his impatience increased visibly, until the last dish had been served, the waiters had left the room, the band outside had ceased playing, and the toast-master had called silence for the first toast. Then in an instant all impatience, all nervousness, all anxiety disappeared, and the Consul-General rose to propose " The King."

Never had any one heard such a bitter, ironical, biting speech. Every word blistered, every sentence cut to the bone.

He began by telling his guests how happy he was to welcome them in that historic hall "sacred to the memory of the glories of Ishmael Pasha, whose princely prodigality brought Egypt to bankruptcy." Then he assured them that he took their presence there that night as a cordial recognition of what Great Britain had done through forty hard and sleepless years to rescue the Valley of the Nile from financial ruin and moral corruption. Next, he reminded them that England was now reaping the results of the education it had given the country, and among these results were certain immature efforts to found Western institutions on Eastern soil, not to speak of secret conspiracies to embarrass, disturb, and even destroy her rule in Egypt altogether.

"But I am glad to realise," he said in a withering tone, "that all such attempts to carry the country back from civilisation to barbarism have been repelled by the best elements in the community, European and Egyptian alike, and especially by the illustrious leaders by whom I am now surrounded."

Then his eyes flashed like the eyes of an old eagle, while, amid breathless silence, in the husky voice that came from his dry throat, turning from side to side, he thanked his guests, class by class, for the help they had given to the representative of the King in putting down political and religious fanaticism.

"Gentlemen of the diplomatic corps," he said, "you are satisfied with what England has done for Egypt and you do not wish to see her rule disturbed. Between you and ourselves there are no animosities, no selfish interests to serve, no hostile groupings, no rival combinations. Knowing that we are the joint trustees of civilisation in a backward Eastern country, nothing could induce you so to act as if you wanted Egypt for yourselves. Gentlemen, in the name of the King I thank you!"

Turning then to the Egyptian Ministers, he said in tones of blistering irony:

"Your Excellencies, it seems idle to thank you for your loyalty to the nation by whose power you live. You are far too intelligent not to see that a man cannot set fire to his house and yet hope to preserve it from being burned to the ground, far too sensible of your own interests to listen to the revolutionaries who would tear to pieces the country you govern and give it back to bankruptcy and ruin. Gentlemen, in the name of the King, I thank you."

Then facing the Notables he said, with a curl of his firm lip:

"It might perhaps be thought that you, of all others, had least reason to be grateful to the Power that took the *courbash* out of your hands and deprived you of the advantages of forced labour; but you do not want to regain the powers you once held over the great unmoving masses of the people; you are willing to see all false ledgers showing unjust debts burned in the public squares with your whips and instruments of the bastinado. Therefore, gentlemen, in the name of the King I thank you."

Finally, looking down the middle table to where the Chancellor of El Azhar sat with his Bedouin friend beside him, he said:

"And your Eminences of the Ulema, I thank you also. Your enemies sometimes say that you continue to live in the middle ages, but you are much too keenly alive to your interests in the present hour not to realize how necessary it is to you to be assured for the future against the possible recurrence of Mahdist raids and revolutions. You know that the hydra-headed monster called fanaticism would destroy you and your class, and therefore you support with all the loyalty of your eager hearts the Power which in the interests of true religion would crush and quell it. Gentlemen, in the name of the King, I thank you."

The effect of the speech was paralysing. As, one by one, the Consul-General spoke to the classes represented by his guests, there was not a response, not a sound, nothing but silence in the room, with white faces and quivering lips on every side.

At length the Consul-General raised his glass and, in a

last passage of withering sarcasm, called on the company
to drink to the great sovereign of the great nation which,
with the cordial sympathy and united help of the whole
community, as represented by those who were there present,
had done so much for civilisation and progress in the East—
"The King!"

They could not help themselves—they rose, a lame, halting, half-terrified company, getting up irregularly, with
trembling hands and pallid cheeks, and repeated after the
toast-master, in nervous, faltering, broken voices, "The
King!"

After the speaker sat down there was a subdued murmur
which rose by degrees to a sort of muffled growl. The Consul-General heard it, and his keen eyes flashed around the
company. Down to this moment he had done no more than
he intended to do, but now, carried away by the excitement
created within himself by his own speech, he wished to
throw off all disguise and fling out at everybody.

"Better be calm, though," he thought, remembering the
Sirdar's advice, and at the next moment the Sirdar himself,
whom he had missed from his side, returned and said, in a
whisper:

"Afraid I must go. Just heard that some of the Egyptian soldiers have been knocking down the officers who were
sent to remove their ammunition."

At that news, which appeared to confirm predictions, and
to be the beginning of everything he had been led to expect,
the Consul-General lost all control of himself.

"Wait! Wait a little and we'll go together," he whispered back, and then, calling for silence, he rose to his feet
again and faced full upon his guests.

"Your Highnesses, your Eminences, your Excellencies,
and Gentlemen," he said in a loud voice, "I have one more
toast. I have given you the health of the King, and now
I give you 'Confusion to his Enemies.'"

If a bomb had fallen in the dining-hall it could scarcely
have made more commotion. The Consul-General saw this
and smiled.

"Yes, gentlemen, I say his enemies, and when I speak

of the King's enemies I refer to his enemies in Egypt, his enemies in this room."

The sensation produced by these words was compounded of many emotions. To such of the guests as were entirely innocent of conspiracy it seemed plainly evident that a kind of mental vertigo had seized the Consul-General. One of them looked round for a doctor, another rose from his seat with the intention of stepping up to the speaker, while a third took out his gold pencil-case and began to scribble a note to the Sirdar, asking him, as the best friend of their host, to remove the Consul-General from the room.

On the other hand, the persons who were actually participating in conspiracy, had, by operation of that inscrutable instinct which compels guilty men to expose themselves, risen to their feet, and were loudly shouting their protests.

"Untrue!" "Disgraceful!" "False!" "Utterly false!"

"False, is it?" said the Consul-General. "We shall see."

Then glancing over them one by one as they stood about him, his eye fixed itself first upon a foreign representative whose breast was covered with decorations, and he said:

"Baron, did you not say in the salon of a certain Princess that out of your secret service money you were providing arms for the Egyptian populace?"

The baron gave a start of surprise, made some movement of the lips as if trying to reply, and sank back to his seat. Then the Consul-General turned to one of two Egyptian Ministers who, with faces as red as their tarbooshes, were standing side by side, and said:

"Pasha, will you deny that as recently as yesterday you sent somebody to me in secret to say that while *you* were innocent of conspiracy against British rule, your colleague who stands at your right was deeply guilty?"

The Pasha stammered out some confused words and collapsed.

Then the Consul-General faced down to one of the Ulema,

32

the Grand Mufti, who, in his white turban and graceful robes, was trying his best to smile, and said:

"Your Eminence, can it be possible that you were not present at the house of the Chancellor of El Azhar when a letter was sent to a certain visionary mummer then in the Soudan, asking him to return to Cairo in order to draw off the allegiance of the Egyptian Army?"

The smile passed in a flash from the Grand Mufti's face, and he, too, dropped back to his seat. Then one by one the others who had been standing slithered down to their places, as if each of them was in fear that some secret he had whispered in the salon, the harem, or the mosque would in like manner be blurted from the housetops.

The Consul-General swept the whole company with a look of triumph and said:

"You see, gentlemen, I know everything and it is useless to deny. In order to overthrow the authority of England in Egypt you have condescended to the arts of anarchists—you have joined together to provoke rebellion against law and order."

All this time the Sirdar's face had been stamped with an expression of sadness, and now he was seen to be addressing the Consul-General in a few low-toned words, but his warning, if such it was, seemed to be quite unheeded. With increasing excitement and intense bitterness the Consul-General turned hotly upon the foreign representatives and said:

"Gentlemen of the diplomatic corps, joint trustees with me of peace and civilisation in a backward country, you thought you were using the unrest of the Egyptians to serve your own ends, but listen and I will tell you what you were really doing."

Then, more fiercely than ever, his face aflame, his hoarse voice breaking into harsh cries, he disclosed his knowledge of the Egyptian plot as he understood it to be—how the final aim, the vast and luminous fact to which all Moslem energies were directed, was the establishment of an Arab Empire which should have it for its first purpose to resist the Christian nations; how this Empire had originated in the mind of the Khedive, who wished to put himself at the head of it; and how, since it was necessary in an Eastern country to give a religious colour to political intriguing, Ishmael Ameer, the mock Mahdi, the fanatic-hypocrite, had been employed to intimidate the British authorities by bringing up the scourings of the Soudan to their very doors.

This fell on the whole company, innocent and guilty, like a thunderclap.

The great Proconsul, the strong and practical intellect which had governed the State so long, had been deceived on the main issue, had been fooled and was fighting a gigantic phantom!

" Is this news to you, gentlemen of the diplomatic corps? Ask your friends, the Ulema! Is it news to you, too, gentlemen of El Azhar? Ask your Grand Cadi! But that is not all. You have had no scruples, no shame! In hitting at England you have not hesitated to hit at England's servant —myself. You have hit me where I could least bear the blow. By lies, by hypocrisies, by false pretences you have got hold of my son, my only son, my only relative, all that was left to me . . . the one in whom my hopes in life were centred and . . . . "

Here the old man's voice faltered, and it was afterward remembered that at this moment the Bedouin Sheikh rose in obvious agitation, made some steps forward and then stopped.

At the next instant the Consul-General had recovered himself, and, with increasing strength and still greater ferocity, was hurling his last reproaches upon his enemies.

" But you are mistaken, gentlemen. I may be old but I am not yet helpless. In the interests not only of England but of Europe I have made all necessary preparations to defeat your intrigues, and now—now I am about to put them into execution."

Saying this he left his seat and directed his steps toward the door. Nearly the whole of the company rose at the same moment, and all stood aside to let him pass. Nobody spoke, nobody made a gesture. In that room there were now no longer conspirators and non-conspirators. There were only silent spectators of a great tragedy. Everybody felt that an immense figure was passing from the world's stage, and none would have been more surprised if the pyramid of Gheza had crumbled before their eyes.

On reaching the door the Consul-General stopped and spoke again, but with something of his old courageous calm.

"I understand," he said, "that it was part of the plan that to-night at midnight while the British Army were expected to be on the Delta and I and my colleagues were to be held prisoners here at Ghezirah, the horde of armed fanatics now lying outside on the desert were to enter and occupy the city. That was a foolish scheme, gentlemen, such as could only have been conceived in the cobwebbed brains of El Azhar. But whatever it was I must ask you to abide by its consequences. In the interests of peace and of your own safety you will remain on this island until to-morrow, and in the morning you shall see . . . what you shall see!"

Then saying something in a low voice to the Commandant of Police, who was standing near, he passed out of the dining-hall and the door was closed behind him.

XVII

A FEW minutes afterward the military band in the garden was playing again, red and white rockets were shooting into the dark sky from the grounds of the Khedivial Sports Club, and the Consul-General was entering the little insular telephone office of Ghezirah, which was under the same roof as the Pavilion.

"Call me up the colonel commanding at Abbassiah and ask him to hold the line."

"Yes, my lord."

While the attendant put in the plugs of his machine and waited for a reply, the Consul-General walked nervously to and fro between the counter and the door. He was expecting the Commandant of Police to come to him in a moment with news of the arrest of Ishmael Ameer. Without this certainty (though he had never had an instant's doubt of it) he could not allow himself to proceed to the last and most serious extremity.

"Not got him yet?"

"Not yet, my lord."

The Consul-General resumed his restless perambulation. He was by no means at ease about the unpremeditated developments of the scene in the dining-hall, but he had always intended to make sure that his enemies were safely housed on the island and thereby cut off from the power of making further mischief, before he ordered the Army into the city.

"Not got him even yet, boy?"

"Cannot get an answer from the central in Cairo, my lord."

"Try another line. Quick!"

The Consul-General thought the Commandant was long in coming, but no doubt the police staff had removed the supposed "Bedouin" to a private room, so that in making his arrest, and in stripping off his disguise to secure evidence of his identity, there might be no unnecessary commotion, no vulgar sensation.

"Got him at last?"

"No, my lord. Think there must be something wrong with the wires."

"The wires?"

"They seem to have been tampered with."

"You mean—cut?"

"Afraid they are, my lord."

"Then the island—so far as the telephone goes—the island is isolated?"

"Yes, my lord."

The old man's face, which had been flushed, became deadly pale, and his stubborn lower lip began to tremble.

"Who can have done this? Who? Who?"

The attendant, terrified by the fierce eye that looked into his face, was answering with a vacant stare and a shake of the head when the Sirdar entered the office, accompanied by the Commandant of Police, and both were as white as if they had seen a ghost.

"Well, what is it now?" demanded the Consul-General; whereupon the Sirdar answered:

"The Commandant's men have got him, but . . . ."

"But—what?"

"It is not Ishmael Ameer."

"Not Ishma . . . you say it is not Ish . . . "

The Consul-General stopped, and for a long moment he stared in silence into the blanched faces before him. Then he said sharply, "Who is it?"

The Commandant dropped his head, and the Sirdar seemed unwilling to reply.

"Who is it, then?"

"It is . . . it is a British officer."

"A British . . . you say a British . . . "

"A colonel."

The old man's lips moved as if he were repeating the word without uttering it.

"His tunic was torn where his decorations had been. He looked like . . . like a man who might have been degraded."

The Consul-General's face twitched, but in a fierce, almost ferocious voice, he said, "Speak! Who is it?"

There was another moment of silence, which seemed to be eternal, and then the Sirdar replied:

"Nuneham, it is your own son."

XVIII

FROM THE SLAVE OF THE MOST HIGH, ABDUL ALI, CHANCELLOR OF EL AZHAR, TO ISHMAEL AMEER, THE MESSENGER OF GOD, PRAISE BE TO HIM THE EXALTED ONE.

A word in haste to say that he who came here as your missionary and representative has within the hour been arrested by the officials of the Government, having, so far as we can yet learn and surmise, been most treacherously and maliciously betrayed into their hands by means of a letter to the English lord from one who stands near to you in your camp.

In sadness and tears, with faces bowed to the earth and ashes on our heads, we send our sympathy to you and to your stricken followers, entreating you on our knees, in the name of the Compassionate, not to attempt to carry out your design of coming into Cairo, lest further and more fearful calamities should occur.

This by swift and trusty messenger to your hands at Sakkara.

The Slave of your Virtues,   ABDUL ALI.

FIFTH BOOK

THE DAWN

I

THE day that Ishmael had looked for, longed for, prayed for—the day that was to see the fulfilment not only of his spiritual hopes but of his rapturous dream of bliss, the day of his return to Cairo—had come at last.

But the Ishmael Ameer who was returning to Cairo was by no means the same man as the Ishmael who had gone away. In a few short months he had become a totally different person. Two forces had changed him—two forces which in their effect were one.

By the operation of the first of these forces he had become more of a mystic; by the operation of the second he had become more of a man; by the operation of both together he had become a creature who was controlled by his emotions alone.

When he left Cairo he had been a man of elevated spirit but of commanding common-sense. He had looked upon himself as one whose sole work was to call men back to God and to righteousness. But little by little the tyranny of outward events, the pressure of responsibility, and above all the heartfelt and prostrate but dim and perverted adulation of his followers, had led him to believe that he was a being apart, specially directed by the Almighty, and even permitted to be his mouthpiece.

Insensibly Ishmael had come to look upon himself as a "Son of God." When he first saw that the crowds who came to him from East and West were beginning to believe that he was the Redeemer, the Deliverer, the Expected One whom he foretold, he was shocked and he protested. But when he perceived that this belief helped him to comfort and console and direct them he ceased to deny; and when he realised that it was necessary to his people's confidence that they should think that he who guided them was himself guided by God, he permitted himself, by his silence, to acquiesce.

From allowing others to believe in his divinity he had come to believe in it himself. His burning, boundless influence over his people had eemed to his deep heart to be only intelligible as a thing given to him from Heaven, and then the " miracle " in the desert, the raising of the Sheikh's daughter from the dead, had swept down the last of his scruples. God *had* given him supernatural powers and made him the mouthpiece of His will.

And now, at the end of his pilgrimage, if he did not accept the idea that he was in very fact the Redeemer who was to bring in the golden age, the Kingdom of God, he succumbed to a delusion that was nearly akin to it—that just as the Lord of the Christians, being condemned by the Roman Governor, had permitted another to take His form and face and bodily presence and to die on the cross instead of him, so the Messiah, the Mahdi, the Christ who was to come, was now using him as His substitute to lead and control His poor, oppressed, and helpless people until the time came for Him to appear in His own person.

Such was the operation of the force that had made Ishmael more of a mystic, and the force that had made him more of a man had been playing in the same way upon his heart.

It had played upon him through Helena.

When Helena entered into his life and he betrothed himself to her, he honestly believed that he was doing no more than protect her good name. For some time afterward he continued to deceive himself, but the constant presence of a beautiful woman by his side produced its effect, and little by little he came to know that his heart was touched.

As soon as he became conscious of this he remembered the vow he had made when his Coptic slave wife died, that no other woman should take her place, and he also reminded himself of his mission, his consecration to the welfare of humanity. But the more he tried to crush his affection for Helena, the more it grew.

He was like a boy in the first beautiful morning light of love. The moment he was alone, after parting from Helena at the door of her sleeping-room, he would kiss the hand that had touched her hand, and find a tingling joy in stepping afresh over the places on which her feet had trod. A glance from her beaming eyes made his pulses beat rapidly, and when, one day, he saw her combing out her hair, with her round white arm bare to the elbow, his breathing came quick and loud.

His passion was like a flower which had sprung up in the parched place of the desert of his desolate soul, and everything that Helena did seemed to water it. Reading her conduct by the only light he had, he thought she loved him. Had she not followed him from India, breaking from her own people to live by his side? Had she not betrothed herself to him without a thought of any other than spiritual joys?

His pride in him, too, was no less than her affection. Had she not proposed that he should go into Cairo in advance because, that being the place of the greatest danger, was the place of highest honour also? In her womanly jealousy for her husband's rank, had she not resisted and resented the substitution of another when it was decided by the sheikhs that "Omar" should go instead? And, notwithstanding her illness at Khartoum, had she not insisted on following him across the desert, and, weak as she was, enduring the pains of his pilgrimage in order to continue by his side?

Allah bless and cherish her! Was there anything in the world so good as a sweet, unselfish, devoted woman?

During the journey Ishmael's love for Helena grew hour by hour until it filled his whole being, and made his wild heart a globe of infinite radiance and hope. Her beauty, her gifts of mind as well as of body, took complete possession of him. Whenever he saw her everything brightened up. Whenever he turned on his camel, and caught sight of her dromedary at the tail of the caravan, he became excited. Whenever evil things befell he had only to think of the Rani and his troubles died away. All that was good and beautiful in the world seemed to centre in the litter that held her by day and in the tent that covered her by night.

Then, in spite of his mission and the burden of his work he began to remember that all this loveliness, all this sweetness, belonged *to him*. The Rani was *his wife*, and he could not help but think of the possibility of nearer relations between them.

When this thought first came to him he repelled it as a species of treachery. Had he not pledged himself to a spiritual union? Would it not be wrong to break that pledge—wrong to the Rani, wrong to his own higher nature, wrong to God?

But nevertheless the temptation to claim the rights of a husband became stronger day by day, and he struggled to reconcile his faith with his affection. He reminded himself that renunciation was no part of Islam, that it was a Christian error, that " monkery " had been condemned by the Prophet, that it was contrary to the clear law of nature, and that as soon as his task was finished it was his duty to live a human life with woman and with children.

This seemed to solve the sphinx-like problem of existence, but when he tried to talk of it to the Rani, in order to break the ground with her, his tongue would not utter the words that were in his heart, and something made him stop in confusion and go away quickly.

Yet his self-denial only intensified his desire. Keeping away from Helena by day, he was with her in his dreams by night. One rapturous, incredible, almost impossible, and even terrible dream of bliss was always stirring within him. A little longer, only a little longer. The hour in which he would lay down his task as leader, as prophet, would be the hour in which he would take up his new life as a man.

That hour was now near. He was outside the gates of Cairo. Nothing would, nothing could, intervene at this last stage to prevent him from entering the city, and once within his work would be at an end. Oh, God, how good it was to live!

All that day at Sakkara Ishmael had been in the highest

state of religious exaltation, and when night came he walked about the camp as if demented both in heart and brain.

The camp stretched from the banks of the Nile at Berrasheen over the black ruins of Memphis to the broad sands before the Step Pyramid, and everywhere the people sat in groups about their fires, eating, drinking, playing their pipes, tambourines, and drums, and singing to tunes that were like wild dance music their songs of rejoicing.

They were singing about himself, his wise words, his miracles, his miraculous birth (born of a virgin), his good looks, which made all women love him, and his divinity, which would save him from death. Ishmael heard this, yet he had no misgivings, no fear of what the coming day would bring forth. A sort of spiritual lightning blinded him to possible danger, and his heart swelled with love for his people. God bless them! God bless everybody! Bless East and West, white man and black man, sons of one Father, soon to be united in one hope, one love, one faith!

Ishmael felt as if he wanted to take the whole world in his arms. Above all he wanted to take the Rani in his arms. It was not that the lower man, the animal man, was conquering the higher man, the spiritual man, but that both body and soul were aflame, that a sense of fierce joy filled his whole being at the thought of entering into a new life, and that he wished to find physical expression for it.

Before he was aware of what he was doing he was walking in the direction of Helena's tent. Striding along in the darkness which was slashed here and there with shafts of light from the camp fires, he approached the tent from the back, the mouth being toward the city. Close behind it he stumbled upon some one who was crouching there. It was a boy, and he rose hastily and hurried away without speaking, being followed immediately by a woman who seemed to have been watching him.

Ishmael's heart was beating so violently by this time that he had only a confused impression of having seen this, and at the next instant, treading softly on the silent sand, he was in front of the tent looking at Helena, who was within.

She was sitting on her camp bed, her angerib, writing on

a pad that rested upon her lap, by the light of a lamp which hung from the pole which upheld the canvas. Though her face was down, Ishmael could see that it was suffused by a rosy blush, and when at one moment she raised her head, her bright and shining eyes seemed to him to be wet with tears, but full, nevertheless, of joy and love.

Ishmael thought he knew what she was doing. She was thinking of him and writing, as she loved to do, the immortal story of his pilgrimage, happy in the near approach of his great triumph.

Standing in the darkness to look at her he could hardly restrain himself any longer. He wanted to burst in upon her and to be alone with her.

Behind and about him were the lights of the camp and its many sounds of rejoicing, but he did not see or hear them now. His heart was afire. He was intoxicated with love. What had been for so long his almost unconquerable dream of bliss was about to be fulfilled.

"Rani!" he whispered in a quivering voice, and then, plunging into the tent, he caught her up in his arms.

II

HALF blind with tears which belied her brave words, Helena had been writing the letter to Gordon which Mosie was waiting to take away. She had told him not to think of her, for she was quite able to take care of herself whatever happened. Then wiping the tears from her eyes, she had smiled as she told him to forget the nonsense she had written about Jezebel and her Jewish blood and to remember that until Ishmael's work was "finished" and he entered Cairo, she ran no risk by remaining in his camp.

She had got thus far when she thought she heard a step on the sand outside, but raising her eyes to look, and seeing nothing except the red and white stars from the rockets that rained through the air at Ghezirah, she resumed her letter, telling herself as she did so that if the worst came to the worst and matters reached an unexpected crisis with

Ishmael, she could defeat him again, as she had done before, by diplomacy, by finesse, and by woman's wit.

"I suppose you are in the thick of it by this time, for I see that the illuminations at Ghezirah have already begun. My dear, my dear, my——"

Her last word was not yet written when she heard Ishmael's tremulous whisper of the name he knew her by, and, starting up as if she had received an electric shock, she saw the Egyptian coming into her tent with the glittering eyes of one who was about to accomplish some joyous task. At the next moment, before she knew what was happening, she found herself clasped in his arms.

"My life! My heart! My eyes! My own!" he was saying in hot and impetuous whispers, and raising her face to his face he was kissing her on the lips.

She struggled to liberate herself, but felt like a helpless child in his strong, irresistible grasp.

"Leave me! Let me go!" she said with heat and anger, but he did not seem to hear her or to be conscious of her resistance.

"Oh, how glad I am!" he said. "Our journey is at an end! Our new life is about to begin! How happy we shall be!"

All the blood in Helena's body rushed to her cheeks, and putting up her hands between their faces, she demanded angrily:

"What do you mean by this? What are you doing?"

Yet still he did not hear her, for his passion was overpowering him, its intoxicating voice was ringing through his whole being, and he continued to pour into her ears a torrent of endearing words.

"Yes, yes, our new life is about to begin! It is to begin to-night—now!"

Helena was overwhelmed with fear, but suddenly, by the operation of an instinct which she did not comprehend, she smiled up into Ishmael's smiling face—a feeble, frightened, involuntary smile—and pointing to the open mouth of the tent, she said with a sense of mingled cunning and confusion:

"Be careful! Look!"

Ishmael loosened his hold of her and, stepping back to the tent's mouth, he began to close and button it.

While he did so Helena watched him and asked herself what she ought to do next. Cry for help? It would be useless. There were none to hear her except Ishmael's own people, and they worshipped him and looked upon her as his wife, his property, his slave, his chattel. Escape? Impossible! More than ever impossible for what (at her own direction) he was doing now.

"Then what am I do to?" she asked herself, and before she had found an answer Ishmael, having sealed up the tent, was returning with outstretched arms, as if with the intention of embracing and kissing her again.

She read in his great wild eyes the light of a passion which she had never seen in a man's face before, but she put on a bold front in spite of the terror which possessed her, thrust out her right hand to keep him off, looked him full in the face and cried:

"No, no! You shall not! On no account! No!"

At that he dropped his outstretched arms, but, still smiling his joyous smile, he continued to approach her, saying as he did so in a tone of affectionate surprise and remonstrance:

"Why, what is this, O my Rani? Have we not joined hands under the handkerchief? Are you not my wife? Am I not your husband? It is true that I pledged myself to renunciation. But renunciation is wrong. It is against religion, against God."

He came nearer. She could feel his hot breath upon her face. It made her shiver with the race-feeling she had experienced before.

"And then, how can I continue to deny myself?" he said. "I am like one who has been dying of hunger in the sight of food. You are my joy, my flower, my treasure. God has given you to me. You are mine."

With that he threw his irresistible arms about her again, and bringing his glittering eyes close to her eyes he whispered:

"My Rani! My wife!"

Helena knew that the hour she had looked forward to with dread had come at length; she saw that the diplomacy, the finesse, the woman's wit she had counted upon to save her were useless to quell the passion which flashed from Ishmael's eyes and throbbed in his voice, and she made one last and violent effort to escape from his arms.

"Let me go! Let me go!" she cried.

"Am I doing wrong?" he said. "No, no! I would not harm you for all the kingdoms of the world. But every wife must submit to her husband."

"No, no, no!" she cried in tones of repulsion and loathing.

"Yes, yes, yes," he replied, still more tenderly, still more passionately. "But if she is a good woman she has her modesty, her shield of shame. That is only right, only natural. It makes her the more sweet, the more dear, the more charming——"

Helena felt his arms tightening about her; she knew that he was lifting her off her feet, and realised that she was being carried across the tent.

Then she remembered the assurances she had given to Gordon, the promises she had made to herself, and hardly conscious of what she did until it was done, or of what she was saying until it was said, she brought her open hands heavily down upon his face and cried in a fury of wrath and scorn:

"Let me go, I tell you. You shall! You must! Can't you see that you are hateful and odious to me—that you are a black man and I am a white woman?"

At the next moment she felt Ishmael's arms relax and she found herself on her feet. A sense of immense, immeasurable relief came over her. A sense of triumph, too, for what she had said she would do she had done.

When she recovered herself sufficiently to look at Ishmael again he was standing apart from her and his head was down. He could no longer deceive himself. A whirlwind of chaotic darkness had swept over him. The storm of his passion was gone.

Helena saw that he was deeply wounded, and notwithstanding the aversion he had inspired in her a moment before, she pitied him from the bottom of her heart.

"I am sorry for what I said just now," she murmured in a low tone. "It was hateful of me, and I ask your pardon."

She was still panting and she had to pause for breath, but he did not reply, and after a moment she began to excuse herself, saying falteringly:

"But you must see that—that there could never have been anything between you and me because—because——"

Raising his eyes, he looked not into her face, but at the veil that was fixed to her hair, and she found it difficult to go on.

"Did you not say yourself," she said, "that marriage was not joining hands under a handkerchief or repeating words after a Cadi, but a sacrament of love, mutual love, and that everything else was sin? Therefore——"

"Well?"

"Therefore if—if I do not love you——"

"And you do not?"

"No."

"Allah! Allah!" he muttered in a voice that seemed to come up out of the depths of his soul, and at the next moment he sank down onto the angerib, which was close behind him.

But hardly had he done so when he leaped to his feet again and in a voice that rang with wrath he said:

"Then why did you betroth yourself to me? I put no constraint upon you. If you had told me that your heart was far from me I should have gone no further. But I gave you time to consider and you came to me of your own free will. Why was this? Answer me. I have a right to know that, at all events."

It came into her mind to reply that when they were betrothed he did not ask her if she loved him, and she did not understand that she was to belong to him. But what was the use of defending herself? On what ground could she justify her conduct?

"Or if," he said, and his voice shook with the intensity of his emotion, "if it was after our betrothal that your heart left me—if something I said or did lost me your love —why did you follow me from Khartoum? You might have stayed there. I was willing to leave you behind me. Why did you follow me over the desert? Why did you come with my company? Why are you here now?"

She found it impossible to answer him, and feeling how deeply she had wronged him, yet how impossible, how unthinkable, how inconceivable it was that she could have acted otherwise than she had, in the light of her great and undying love for Gordon, she clasped her hands in front of her face and burst into a flood of tears.

Her tears drove away his anger in a moment, for he mistook the cause of them, and deeply and incurably wounded as he was, a wave of sympathy and compassion passed over him. Drawing her hands from her face and holding them in his own, he looked steadfastly into her wet eyes, and said in a softer voice:

"I see how it has been, O my Rani! You followed the teacher, not the man—the message, not the poor soiled volume it was written in—and perhaps you were right—quite right."

Every word he uttered went like iron into Helena's soul.

"I thought a woman lived by her heart alone," he said, "and that when she betrothed herself it must be for love, not from any higher and nobler motive, but it seems I was wrong—quite wrong. I thought, too," he said, "that where love was," and here his voice thickened and almost broke, "there was neither black nor white, neither race nor caste; but it seems I was wrong in that also. Forgive me, forgive me, forgive me!"

He lifted her hands in his own long and delicate ones and put them to his lips, and then gently let them fall.

"But God knows best what is good for us," he said, "and perhaps—perhaps He has sent me this as a warning and a punishment, lest—lest I forget—in the love of home and wife and children, the task—the great task He has laid upon me. *In-sha-allah! In-sha-allah!*"

With that he turned to leave the tent, a shaken and agitated and totally different man from the man who had entered it, and Helena, notwithstanding that she was deeply moved, again felt a sense of immense, immeasurable relief.

But at the next moment a feeling akin to terror seized her, for while Ishmael was unbuttoning the canvas at the tent's mouth, there came, over the dull rumble of many sounds outside, a clear, sharp voice crying:

"Ishmael Ameer! Ishmael Ameer! Urgent news! Where are you?"

Helena's heart stood still. She seemed to know in advance what was coming. The hour of Ishmael's downfall had arrived, and he was to hear that he had been betrayed. She had escaped from her physical danger—what, now, of her moral peril?

III

A MOMENT later Ishmael had torn the mouth of the tent open. An Egyptian was standing there in the turban and farageeyah of an Alim. The man, who was solemnly making his salaams, held a lantern in one hand and a letter in the other. Behind him, against the dark sky, were a number of Ishmael's own people. Their mouths were open and fear was on their faces.

"What words are these, oh, my brother?" asked Ishmael.

Without speaking, the Alim offered him the letter. It was that of the Chancellor of El Azhar, written immediately after the arrest of Gordon.

Ishmael took it, and standing under the lamp that hung from the pole of the tent, he read it. For some moments he did not move or raise his eyes, but little by little his face assumed a death-like rigidity, and at length the paper crinkled in his trembling fingers.

So strong had been his faith in his mission, and so firm his conviction that God would not allow anything to interfere with its fulfilment, that it was almost impossible for him to take in the truth—that his cause was lost that his pilgrimage was wasted, that his people could not enter Cairo, and their hope was at an end.

When at length he raised his eyes he looked with an expression of blank bewilderment into Helena's face.

"See," he said in a tone of piteous helplesssness, and he put the letter into her reluctant hand.

The blood rushed to Helena's head, stars danced before her eyes, and it was with difficulty that she could see to read. But there was little need to do so, for already she knew, as by a sense of doom, what the letter contained.

In a moment the people behind the Alim grew more and more numerous. The mouth of the tent became choked with them, and their faces were blotched with lights and shadows from the lamp within. They were talking eagerly among themselves in low tones, full of dread. At length one of them spoke to Ishmael.

"Is it bad news, O Master?" he asked, but with the expressionless voice of one who knew already what the answer would be.

There was a moment of strained silence, and then Ishmael turned again to Helena and said, in the same tone of piteous helplessness as before:

"Read it to them. Let them know the worst, O Rani!"

Helena could find no escape. With a fearful effort she began to read the letter aloud. But hardly had she finished the first clause of it, telling Ishmael that his messenger and missionary had been betrayed into the hands of the Government by means of a message sent into Cairo from some one who stood near to him in his own camp, than a deep groan came from the people at the mouth of the tent.

Black Zogal was there with his wild eyes, and by his side stood old Zewar Pasha with his suspicious looks.

"Who is the traitor, O Master?" asked the old man in his rasping voice, and it seemed to Helena that while he spoke every eye except Ishmael's was fixed upon her face.

Then a fearful thing befell. Ishmael, the man of peace, whom none had ever seen in any mood but one of tenderness and love, broke into a torrent of fierce passion.

"Allah curse him, whoever he is!" he cried. "Curse

him in his lying down and in his getting up! Curse him in
the morning splendour and in the still of night! Curse him
in the life that now is and in the life that is to come!"

Helena felt as if the tent itself as well as the black and
copper-coloured faces at the mouth of it were reeling around
her. But it was not alone the terror of Ishmael's curse,
with its unrevealed reference to herself, that created her
confusion. She was thinking of Gordon. What did his
arrest imply? Did it mean that he had succeeded in the
perilous task he had undertaken? Or did it mean that he
had failed?

When she recovered consciousness of what was going on
about her she heard, above a wild tumult of voices outside,
the voice of a woman and the voice of a boy. She knew
that the woman was Zenoba and the boy was Mosie. At
the next moment both were coming headlong into the tent,
the one dragging the other through a way that had been
made for them. The boy's shaven black head was bare, his
caftan was torn open at the breast, and his skin was bleeding at the neck as if vindictive fingers had been clutching
him by the throat. The woman's swarthy face was bathed
with sweat, twitching with excitement, and convulsed with
evil passions.

"There!" she cried. "There he is, O Master! and if
you want to know who took the letter to the English lord,
ask him."

"Who is he?" asked Ishmael.

"Your Rani's servant," replied the Arab woman, with
a curl of her cruel lip. "He left Khartoum for Cairo a
month ago, and has not been seen until to-day."

Another deep groan came from the people at the tent's
mouth, and again it seemed to Helena that every eye except
Ishmael's was looking into her face.

Meantime Mosie, thinking the groan of the people was
meant for him, and that his life was in danger from their
anger, had broken away from the woman's grasp and flung
himself at Ishmael's feet, crying:

"Mercy, O Master! I kiss your feet. I take refuge with
God and with you. Save me and I will tell you everything.'

Ishmael, who by this time had regained his self-command, motioned to the Arab woman to stand back. Then he questioned the boy calmly, and the boy answered him in a fever of fear, gasping and sobbing at every word.

" My boy, you have come out of Cairo ? "

" Yes, O Master! yes."

" You went there from Khartoum ? "

" Yes, yes, O Master! yes."

" You took a letter to the English lord ? "

" Yes, Master, a letter to the English lord."

" From some one in Khartoum ? "

" Yes, I will tell my Master everything—from some one in Khartoum."

" What treacherous man sent you with that letter ? "

" No man at all, O Master! You see, I am telling my Master everything."

" Was it a woman ? "

" Yes, Master, a woman. See, I kiss your feet. I keep nothing back from my Master."

Another groan came from the people at the tent's mouth and the black boy clutched at Ishmael's white caftan as if to protect himself from their wrath. Ishmael himself had a confused sense of something terrible that had not yet taken shape in his mind. He looked round at Helena, who was standing by the angerib at the back, but her head was down and her thoughts were far away.

" What woman, then ? " he asked in a sterner voice.

" No, no, I cannot tell you that," said the boy.

" Speak, boy. You shall be safe. I will protect you from all harm. What woman was it ? "

" Master, do not ask me. I dare not tell you."

" Listen," said Ishmael, and his voice grew hard and hoarse. " There is a traitor in my camp, and I must find out who it is. What treacherous woman sent you into Cairo with that letter ? "

The boy struggled hard. His ugly black face under his shaven poll was distorted by his fear. He hesitated, began to speak, then stopped altogether.

At that moment Helena came forward as if she had

suddenly awakened from a dream, and Mosie saw her for the first time since he had been dragged into the tent. In another instant all fear had gone from his face and his eyes were blazing with courage.

"Tell me, I command you," said Ishmael.

"No, no, I will *never* tell you," said the boy.

Again a groan—this time a growl—came from the people at the tent's mouth.

"Torment would make his tongue wag," said one.

"Beat the innocent until the guilty confess—it is a good maxim, O Master!" said Zewar in his rasping tones.

Black Zogal, with his wild eyes, stepped out as if to lay hold of the lad, but Ishmael waved him back.

"Wait!" he said.

He was looking at Helena again, and his face had undergone a fearful change.

"My boy," he said, still keeping his eyes on Helena, "if you do not tell me I must give you back to the people."

At that the boy broke into a paroxysm of hysterical sobs.

"No, no, my Master will not do that. But see," he said, tearing wider his torn caftan so as to expose his breast, "my Master himself shall kill me."

At the next moment Helena's hand was on Ishmael's arm.

"Let the boy go," she said "I can tell you the rest."

A gloomy chill traversed Ishmael's heart. He had a sense of spiritual paralysis—as if everything in the world were crumbling and crashing down to impotent wreck and ruin.

His people at the tent's mouth were muttering among themselves. He dismissed them, sending everybody away, including the boy and the Arab woman. Most of them went off grudgingly, ungraciously, for the first time reluctant to obey his will.

Then he closed up the mouth of the tent, and was once more alone with Helena.

IV

In spite of the dread with which, for more than a month, Helena had looked forward to the hour in which Ishmael should hear of his betrayal, she felt none of the terror from that cause which she had feared and expected.

She could think of nothing but Gordon. Where was he now? What were they doing to him? It seemed to be the only possible explanation of his arrest that his scheme for the salvation of the people had failed. Would he be handed over to the military authorities? Would he be tried by court-martial? And what would be the punishment of his offences as a soldier? Sinking down on the angerib she pressed her hands over her brow and over her eyes that she might think of this and shut out everything else.

Meantime the mind of Ishmael was going through a conflict as strange and no less cruel. Although the plain evidences of his senses had already told him that he had been betrayed by the woman he loved, yet the dread of discovering the traitor in his own tent, in his own wife, filled him with terror, and he tried to escape from it.

Having fastened up the tent he walked to and fro for some moments without speaking, and then sitting down by Helena's side and taking her hand and smoothing it, he said in his throbbing, quivering voice:

"Rani, we have eaten bread and salt together. Be faithful with me—what woman sent that letter?"

Helena hardly heard what he was saying. She was still thinking of Gordon. "They will condemn him to death," she told herself.

"Rani," said Ishmael again, "we have lived under the same roof; you have shared with me the closest secrets of my soul. Tell me—what woman sent that letter?"

Helena looked at him and tried to listen, but Gordon's doom was ringing in her ears, and it drowned all the other sounds of life.

"Rani," said Ishmael once more, "though you denied me the rights of a husband, yet you are my wife. Our lives

have been united not by man but by God, and in the presence
of Him whose name be exalted—of Him who reads all hearts
—I ask you—what woman sent that letter?"

Helena heard him, yet terrible as his question was, and
perilous as she knew her answer must be, she felt no fear.
"I'll tell him," she thought. "Why not? It does not matter now."

"Rani," said Ishmael yet again, "God gives me the right
to command you. I *do* command you. What woman sent
that letter?"

"I did," said Helena, and though the words were spoken
in a faltering whisper they seemed to Ishmael like a deafening roar.

"Allah! Allah!" he cried, leaping to his feet, for
though he had expected that reply he reeled under it as
under a blow.

Helena realised what her answer meant to him, and
again, from the bottom of her heart she pitied him, but
at the next moment her thoughts swung back to her own
trouble.

She remembered that her father had admitted that the
British Army in Egypt was always on active service, and
she asked herself what would happen to Gordon if the military authorities lost their heads in fear of insurrection.
Would they try him by Field General Court-Martial? In
that case would the Court be called instantly? Would the
inquiry last only a few minutes? Would the sentence be
carried into immediate effect?

"O God! can it be possible that it is all over already?"
she asked herself.

Meantime Ishmael, after moments of suffering which
seemed hours of eternity, was again struggling to resist the
only conclusion the facts had left to him. It was true that
the Rani had confessed to sending the letter which had led
to the arrest of his messenger, but all his heart rebelled
against the inference that she had intended to betray his
cause and his people Had she not cast in her own lot with
them? Had she not come from a distant country and a
richer home to live in their poor house in Khartoum? And

had she not endured the hardship of the desert journey in their company?

Like a man who had been shipwrecked in a whirlwind of darkness, he was groping blindly through tempestuous waves for some means of rescue At length a sort of raft of hope came to him, a helpless, impotent thing, but he clung to it, and sitting down by Helena's side again he said in the same piteous voice as before:

"I see how it has been, oh, my Rani. You did not intend to betray my people—my poor people whose sufferings you have seen, whose faith and hopes and dreams you have shared and witnessed. It was Omar you were thinking of. Your heart has never forgiven him for taking the place you meant for your husband. You were jealous of him for my sake, and your jealousy got the better of your judgment. 'I will punish him,' you thought. 'I will make his mission of no effect.' And so you sent that letter. But you did not reflect that in destroying Omar you would be destroying my people also. It was wrong, it was cruel, but it was a woman's fault and you have seen it and suffered for it ever since. Jealousy of Omar, perhaps hatred of Omar—that was it, was it not, oh, my Rani?"

His voice was breaking as he spoke, for the pitiful explanation he had lighted upon was failing to bring conviction to his own mind, yet he fixed his sad eyes eagerly on Helena's face and repeated:

"Jealousy of Omar, perhaps hatred of Omar—that was what caused you to send that letter?"

Helena could not speak. The pathos of his error was choking her. But she replied to him with a look which it required no words to interpret.

"No?" he said. "Not of Omar? Of whom, then?"

Helena could not lie. "He must know some day," she thought.

"Of whom, then?" he repeated in his helpless confusion.

"Yourself," she replied.

"Allah! Allah! Myself! Myself!" he said in a breathless whisper, rising to his feet again and striding across the tent.

At the first moment after Helena's confession it seemed to Ishmael that both sun and moon had suffered eclipse and the world was in total darkness. Why had the Rani betrayed him? From what motive? For what object? He tried to follow her thoughts and found it impossible to do so.

There was a short period of frightful silence, and then, feeling as if he wanted to cry, he drew up before Helena again, and said in a husky voice, his swarthy face trembling and twitching:

"But why, O Rani? I had done you no wrong. From the day you came to me I did all I could for you—all I could to make your nights peaceful and your mornings happy. Why has your heart been so far away from me?"

Helena felt that the time had come to tell him everything. Yet in order to do so she must begin with the death of her father, and she could not speak of that without involving Gordon. "But that is impossible," she thought, "absolutely impossible."

"Speak," said Ishmael. "When you sent your letter to the English lord you must have known that you were dooming me to death—what had I done to deserve it?"

"I cannot tell you—I cannot, I cannot," she answered.

"It is unnecessary," said Ishmael.

In the moment of Helena's silence a terrible explanation of her conduct had come to him, and he thought he saw, as by flashes of lightning, into the dark abyss that was at his feet.

His manner, which had been gentle down to that moment, suddenly became harsh, and his voice, which had been soft, became hard.

"When did you send that letter?" he demanded.

She saw the stern closing of his lips, and for an instant she felt afraid.

"Was it before the meeting of the Sheikhs at which Omar was chosen?"

"Yes," she replied. If Gordon was to be condemned to death it was of no consequence what become of her.

"You told the English lord that Ishmael was coming to Cairo?"

"Yes." His deep, impenetrable eyes seemed to be looking through and through her.

"With what object and in—in what disguise?"

"Yes." She knew she was dashing herself to destruction, but no matter.

"When you sent your letter you said to yourself, 'Ishmael will go into Cairo, but my letter shall go before him.' Yes?"

"Yes." In the lowest depths of her soul she felt that if he killed her now she did not care.

"And when Omar stepped into the place you had meant for me you thought, 'The letter I wrote to destroy Ishmael will destroy Omar instead?'"

"Yes."

"Was that why you tried to prevent Omar from going?"

"Yes." Tears were choking her utterance.

"Why you were unwilling to make the kufiah?"

"Yes."

"Why you fainted in the mosque?"

She bowed her head, being unable to utter another word.

"Then," said Ishmael, and his voice rose to a husky cry, "then it was *love* of Omar, not *hatred* of him, that inspired your letter?"

She made no reply. Filled as she was with shame for what she had done to Ishmael, the image of Gordon was still in her mind. Even at that moment, when terrible consequences threatened her, she could not help thinking of him. If he were tried by Field General Court-Martial tonight he might be executed in the morning!

That thought carried her back to the Citadel. She was on the drilling-ground in the dead gray light of dawn. A regiment of soldiers were drawn up in line. Six of them stood out from the rest with rifles to their shoulders. And before them, standing alone, with his back to the ramparts, was one condemned but dauntless man. "My last thoughts are about you," he was saying to her, and living in that cruel dream she burst into tears.

Again Ishmael misunderstood her weeping, and again a wave of compassion passed over him.

"It is possible I am wrong," he said. "I may be judging you unjustly. In that case tell me so and I will kiss your feet. I will ask your pardon."

She could not speak. "This will end in some was," she thought.

"In the name of Heaven, speak! Tell me you do not love this man. Tell me I am wrong," he cried.

"No, you are not wrong," she said. "I do love him and I am in despair. All you have said is true, but I cannot help it. I am a wicked woman, and my life by your side has been a deception from the first."

With that she burst into another flood of tears, and falling face downward on the angerib she buried her head in the pillow.

"Allah! Allah!" said Ishmael, and all the blood in his body seemed to flush his heart. He was passing through the supreme phase of his agony—perhaps the cruelest that man can suffer—the agony of knowing that the woman he loved. the woman he worshipped, loved and worshipped another man.

In the cloud of maddening thoughts which sprang to his brain he imagined he read the mystery of Helena's conduct from the first. Remembering that she had called him a black man, the wild deep heart in him rose to a fever of jealous wrath.

"I see how it has been," he said. "The white man came to my tent. I welcomed him. I loved him. I trusted him. He was my brother and he slept by my side. I made him free of my harem. I put my honour in his hands. And how did he repay me? By robbing me of the love that was my love, the heart that was my heart."

She tried to speak, to protest, but in a torrent of wrath he bore her down.

"Your white man has overreached himself, though. 'I will outdo Ishmael in her eyes,' he thought. But he has only fallen into the pit that was dug for me. Let him perish there, and the curse of God be on him!"

Again she tried to protest, and again in the blind hurricane of his anger he silenced her.

"And you—it was nothing to you that in betraying me

you were betraying my people also—my poor people who have suffered so much and followed me so faithfully."

His face was terrible—it had the sullen glow of the western sky before a storm.

"You have wrecked my hopes in the hour of their fulfilment. You have made dust and ashes of the expectations of my people. You have uncovered my nakedness and made me a thing to point the finger at and to scorn. You have turned my heart to stone."

Then the wild anguish of the jealous man became united to the fierce wrath of the fanatic, and going nearer to Helena and leaning over her he said:

"Worse than that—a hundredfold worse—you have made the plans and promises of God of no avail. You have allowed the Evil One to enter into your heart and to use your guilty passions to defeat the schemes of the Most High. Therefore," he said, raising his quivering voice until it rang through the tent like a tortured cry, "therefore as the instrument of Satan you have no right to live. I say you have no right to live. And I—I who have loved you—I whose heart has been wrapped about you like the rope about the wheel of the well—I whom you have betrayed and destroyed and—and my people with me—it is I—yes, it is I who must—who must——"

Helena heard him stammering and sobbing over her. At the same time she felt that his strong ferocious hands were laying hold of her. She felt that the long Eastern veil that had hung down her back was being wrapped around her throat. She felt that its folds were growing tighter and yet tighter and that she was being strangled and was losing consciousness.

Then suddenly she became aware that Ishmael's formidable grasp had slackened, that he had stepped back from the angerib on which she lay, and was saying to himself in a tremulous whisper:

"Allah! Allah! What is this I am doing? Allah! Allah! Allah!"

And at the next moment she realised that in horror of his own impulse he had turned and fled out of the tent.

34

V

BEING left alone, Helena's emotions were so strange, so bewildering, so overpowering that she could not immediately make out clearly what she felt The most contradictory thoughts and feelings crowded upon her.

First came a sense of suffocating shame, due to Ishmael's hideous misconception of her relation to Gordon, which put her into the position of an unfaithful wife. But would the truth have been any better—that she was not an Indian Rani, not a Muslemah, that she and Gordon had known and loved each other before Ishmael came into their lives, and that a desire to punish him for coming between them had been the impulse that had taken her to Khartoum?

Next came a sense of her utter degradation during the recent scene, in which her lips had been sealed and she had been compelled to submit to Ishmael's just and natural wrath.

Then came a sense of abject humiliation with the thought that Ishmael had been right from the beginning and she had been wrong, and therefore she had merited all that had come to her. "If he had killed me I could have forgiven him," she told herself.

Finally (perhaps from some deep place in her Jewish blood) came the feeling that after all it was not so much Ishmael who had been shaming her for her treachery as the Almighty who had been punishing her for attempting to take His vengeance out of His hand. "Vengeance is Mine," saith the Lord, and her impious act had deserved the penalty that had overtaken it.

But against all this, opposing it, fighting it, conquering it, triumphing over it, was the memory of her love for Gordon. "I loved him and I could not have acted otherwise," she thought.

More plainly than ever she now saw that her love for Gordon had been the first cause and origin of all she had done. This single-hearted devotion left her nothing else to think about. It wiped out Ishmael and his troubles and all the troubles of his people. "I may be selfish and cruel, but I cannot help it," she told herself again and again, as she continued to lie where Ishmael had left her, face down on the angerib, shaken with sobs.

After a while she heard a step approaching. The Arab woman had entered the tent.

"So you are there, oh, my beauty," said Zenoba with a bitter ring in her voice.

Without raising her head to look, Helena knew that the usual obsequious smiles had gone from the woman's face, and that her eyes were full of undisguised contempt. In another moment all the impulses of hatred which had scoured through her jealous soul for months fell on Helena in bitter reproaches.

"I knew it would come to this. I always told him so, but he would not listen. 'Ask pardon of God, Zenoba,' he said. Now he will have to ask pardon of me."

Helena could hardly control herself, but with an effort she submitted in silence and let the woman have her way.

"Anybody might have seen what was going on from the moment the white Christian came to Khartoum. But no, it was no use talking. When a man looks at a woman he sees her eyes, not her heart, and is blind to those that love and serve him."

Helena's own heart was beating violently and painfully, but she compelled herself to lie still. "It's no more than I deserve," she thought.

And then the Arab woman lashed her to the bone with reports of what the people in the camp were saying. All that had happened might have been foreseen. He who tried to emancipate woman had been the first to suffer for it. Good women did not wish to be emancipated, and the bad women who let their veils fall and meddled with the affairs of men, only wanted to imitate the evil ways of the women of the West. "Our mothers did not do it, and neither shall our wives," said some, while others declared that it was better to have a thousand enemies outside your house than one within.

The camp was utterly disorganised, utterly demoralised.

Instead of the singing and rejoicing of an hour ago, there was now wailing and lamentation; instead of prayer and praise, there was cursing and swearing. Some of the people, in a state of panic, were saying that the soldiers of the Christian government would soon be upon them; that they would be shot dead with bullets; that they would be carried into Cairo as prisoners and crucified in the public streets; that the Christians would eat their flesh and suck their blood; that those who were not slain would be walking skeletons and talking images and made to worship the wooden cross instead of their own God, their Allah. As a consequence, many were packing their baggage hurriedly and turning the heads of their camels to the south. Boats were being unmoored at Bedrasheen and boatloads were preparing to push off.

Desolation was over the whole camp. The hopes of the people were in the dust. Some of the women were kneeling on the ground and throwing the sand over their heads and faces. Some of the men were heaping insults on Ishmael's name—their former love and reverence being already gone. "Where are the promises he made us?" they were asking. "Is it for this that he brought us from our homes?"

Others were calling and searching for the Master. His tent was empty. He was nowhere to be seen. Had he deserted them in their hour of trouble? "Where is he?" they were crying. "What has become of him?" No one knew. Even Black Zogal could not say. And then some were crying, "Ela'an abu, abu, abu!" ("Cursed be his father, and his father's father, and his father's father's father!").

But worse, far worse, because more fierce and terrible than the people's anger against Ishmael, was their wrath against the "White Woman." It was she who had betrayed them. But for her evil influence and secret schemes they might have inherited Egypt and all the rich lands and treasures of the Valley of the Nile. Listen! They were gathering about the tent, and murmuring and shouting excitedly. Hark! That was Zogal's voice—he was persuading them to go away.

"But they'll come back, oh, my beauty," said Zenoba.

"Better get away before they return and tear you to pieces, as a hungry jackal tears a dog."

With that merciless word the bitter-hearted woman took herself off, leaving Helena still lying face down on the angerib in her agony of mingled anger and shame.

Being once more left alone in the tent, Helena continued to see what was going on in the camp. The wailing of the women, who were throwing sand over their heads, seemed as if it would never cease. At length some of them began to sing. They sang songs of sorrow which contrasted strangely with the songs of victory which the men had sung before. The weird and monotonous but moving notes that are peculiar to Arab music sounded like dirges in the depth of night.

The people were in despair. Their consoling and inspiring idea of divine guidance was gone, and the hope that had sustained their souls through the toils of the desert march was dead. The myth of Ishmael's divinity had already disappeared; the Master was no longer the Redeemer, the Mahdi, the Christ. All that had been a hideous illusion, a mirage of the soul, without reason or reality.

It was terrible, it was horrible, it was almost as if the whole people had died an hour ago in "the sure and certain hope," and then suddenly awakened in the other world to find that there was no God, no heaven, no reward for the pains of this life, and all they had looked for and expected had been the shadow of a dream.

Listening to this as she lay on the angerib, and thinking she was partly to blame for it, Helena asked herself if there was anything she could do to save Ishmael and his people.

"O God! is there *nothing* I can do?" she thought.

At first there came no answer to this question. Do what she would to fix her mind on the people's sufferings and Ishmael's downfall, her mind swung back to its old subject and once again she thought of Gordon and his arrest.

Things in that regard were plainer to her now. The idea of a Field General Court-Martial, which had made her chill with fear, had been the figment of an over-excited brain. Whatever had happened to Gordon's efforts in the interests

of peace—whether they had failed or succeeded—his own
trial would take the ordinary course. A military court of
the usual kind would have to be summoned, its sentence
would have to be confirmed and only the King could confirm it.

All this would take time and therefore there was no
need for panic. But meantime what was Gordon's position?
He had been arrested in mistake for Ishmael, and consequently he would, one way or another, be liable to punishment for Ishmael's offence. That was to say, for the offence
she had attributed to Ishmael. Yet Gordon had done no
wrong, he had intended no evil.

"Is there nothing I can do?—nothing at all?" she
asked herself again.

Suddenly a light dawned on her. If the Consul-General
could be made to see what Gordon's motives had really
been—to save England, to save Egypt, to save the good name
of his own father—and if he could be made to realise that
Ishmael's aim was not rebellion and his followers were not
an armed force, but merely a vast concourse of religious
visionaries—what then?

Then as a just man, if a stern and hard one, he would be
compelled to see that his own son was not punished, and perhaps—who could say?—he might even permit Ishmael's
people to enter Cairo.

Vague, undefined and unconsidered as this idea was,
Helena leaped at it as a solution of all their difficulties,
and when she asked herself how she was to bring conviction
to the Consul-General's mind she remembered Gordon's
letters.

Nothing could be better. Being written before the event,
and intended for her eyes only, they must be convincing
to anybody whatever and absolutely irresistible to a father.
Private? No matter! Intimate and affectionate and full
of the closest secrets of the soul? Never mind! She would
share them with one who was flesh of Gordon's flesh, for his
heart must be with her and the issue was life or death.

Yes, she would go into Cairo, see the Consul-General,
show him Gordon's letters, and prove and explain every-

thing. Thus she who had been the first cause of the people's sufferings, of Ishmael's downfall and of Gordon's arrest, would be Gordon's, Ishmael's, and the people's deliverer! Yes, she, she, she!

But wait! Had she not promised Gordon that she would remain in the camp, whatever happened? She had. But that promise was annulled by this time, while this great errand must be precisely what she had been sent there for, and by flying away now she would be fulfilling her destiny in a wider and deeper sense than even Gordon himself could have conceived.

"I'll go at once," she thought, and she sprang up from the angerib to carry out her purpose.

As she did so she saw a little ugly black face, all blubbered over with tears, on the ground beside her. It was Mosie, and he was kissing the hem of her skirt and saying:

"Mosie very sorry. He not know. Will lady ever forgive Mosie?"

Helena's heart leaped up at sight of the boy. She wanted his help immediately, and his unexpected appearance at that moment was like an assurance from heaven that what she intended to do ought to be done.

Comforting the lad and drying his eyes, she asked him in breathless whispers a number of questions. Where was the donkey on which he had ridden into the camp? It was near by, tethered. Did he know the way to the railway station at Bedrasheen? He did. Could he lead her there through the darkness? He could. It was now half-past nine —would there be a train to Cairo soon? Yes, for the Alim had just gone to catch one that was to go to Boulaq Dacrour at ten o'clock.

"The very thing," said Helena. "Bring your donkey to the back of the tent and wait there until I come."

"Yes, yes," said the boy, now ablaze with eagerness, and kissing both her hands alternately, he shot out on his errand.

Then Helena picked up a little locked handbag which contained Gordon's precious letters, added her own letter to them, and after extinguishing the lamp that hung from the pole, stepped out of the tent.

A few minutes later, mounted on a donkey that was led by a boy, a woman, looking like an Egyptian, with her black skirt drawn over the back of her head and closely clipped under her nose, was picking her way through the darkness.

All was quiet by this time. The weeping and wailing had at last come to an end, and from the vast encampment there rose nothing but the deep somnambulant moan that comes up from a great city when it is falling asleep. The fires were smouldering out, and the people, such of them as remained, were lying, some in their tents, others out-stretched on the sand, all weary and heartbroken in the misery of their dead hope, their dead dream, their dead faith.

A kind of soulless silence hung in the air. Even the call of the night-watchman ("God is one!") was no more to be heard. Only the braying of donkeys at intervals, the ruckling of camels and the barking of dogs.

There was no moon, but the stars were thick and one was falling.

VI

Taking his steam-launch which had been moored to the boat-landing of the Ghezirah Palace, the Consul-General returned home immediately after Gordon's arrest. He did not wait to say what was to be done with the prisoner, or to tell his officials what further steps, if any, were to be taken to prevent the expected insurrection. One overwhelm-ing event had wiped everything else out of his mind. His plans had been frustrated; he had been degraded, made a laughing stock of, and by Gordon—his own son.

As his launch skimmed across the river in the darkness he could hear in the back-wash of the screw, the guffaws of the diplomatic corps, and in the throbbing of the engine the choking laughter of the whole world.

His mind was going like a weaver's shuttle, and he was asking himself by what sinister development of fate this devilish surprise had been brought about. He could find no answer. In the baffling mystery of events only one thing seemed clear—that Gordon, when he disappeared from Cairo after the affair of El Azhar, had not gone to America or India or Australia, as everybody had supposed, but straight to the man Ishmael's camp, and that he had allowed himself to be used by that charlatan mummer to further his intrigues. Against his own father, too! His father who had been thinkingof him every day, every night, and nearly all night, and was now, by his instrumentality, made an object of derision and contempt.

"Fool! Fool! Fool!" thought the Consul-General, and his anger against Gordon burned in his heart like a fierce and consuming fire.

On reaching the Agency he went upstairs to his room and rang violently for Fatimah. Somebody within his own household had become aware of his plans and revealed them to his enemies. He had little doubt of the identity of the traitor, for he remembered Fatimah's unexpected appearance in the dining-room the night before, and her confusion and lame excuse when the Sirdar observed her presence.

Fatimah answered her bell cheerfully as one who had nothing to fear, but the moment she saw the Consul-General's face, with the deep folds in his forehead and the hard and implacable lines about his mouth, she dropped on her knees before he had uttered a word.

"What is this you have been doing, woman?" he demanded, in a stern voice, whereupon Fatimah made no attempt at disguise.

"I couldn't help it, O Master!" she said, breaking into tears. "I would have given him my eyes. He was the same as my own son and I had suckled him at my breast. Can a woman deny anything to her own?"

The Consul-General looked down at her for a moment in silence and his drooping lower lip trembled. Then with a gesture of impatience he said:

35

"Get away to your room at once," and opening the door for her he closed and locked it when she was gone.

But the momentary spasm of tenderness toward Gordon which had come to the Consul-General at sight of the foster-mother's love disappeared at the next instant. The only excuse he could find for his son's conduct in duping his ignorant Egyptian nurse was that perhaps he had himself been duped.

After the first plans had been formed in Khartoum and Helena's letter had been despatched, the "fanatic-hypocrite" had probably discovered that his intrigue had become known in Cairo. That he had put Gordon into the gap, and Gordon had been so simple, so innocent, so stupid as to be deceived! There was small comfort in this reading of the riddle and the Consul-General's fury and shame increased tenfold.

"Fool! Fool! Fool!" he thought, and taking from the mantelpiece the portrait of the boy in the Arab fez, he looked at it for a moment and then flung it back impatiently. It fell onto the floor.

Some minutes passed in which the infuriated man was unconscious of his surroundings, for great anger wipes out time and place, and then he became aware that there was a knock at the door of his room.

"Who's there?" he cried.

It was Ibrahim. He had come to tell his Excellency that two reporters from Reuter's Agency were below by appointment and wished to hear what his Excellency had to give them.

"Nothing. Send them away," said the Consul-General.

A moment afterward there was another knock at the door.

"Who's there now?" cried the Consul-General.

It was his First Secretary. The Adviser to the Ministry of Justice had come to say that the Special Tribunal had been summoned and the Judges were waiting for further instructions.

"Tell them there will be no sitting to-night," said the Consul-General.

A little later there was yet another knock at the door. It was the Secretary again. The Adviser to the Ministry of the Interior had called him up on the telephone to say that, according to instructions, the gallows had been set up in the Square in front of the Governorat, and now he wished to know——

" Tell the men to take it down again at once, and don't come up again," said the Consul-General in a voice that was hoarse with wrath and thick with shame.

These interruptions had been like visitations of the spirits of the dead to a murderer who had killed them, and it was some time before the Consul-General could bring his mind back to the mystery before him. When he was able to do so he asked himself how it had come to pass that if Gordon had been in Khartoum, and if he had been duped into taking Ishmael's place, Helena had not informed him of the change? Where had she been? Where was she now? What had become of her? Could it be possible that she, too, by her love for Gordon, had been won over to the side of his enemies?

Thinking of that as a possible explanation of the devilish tangle of circumstance by which he was surrounded, the Consul-General's wrath against Gordon rose to a frenzy of madness. Fierce and wild imprecations broke from his mouth, such as had never passed his lips before, and then, suddenly remembering that they were directed against his own flesh and blood, his own son, he cried, in the midst of his fury and passion:

" No, no! God forgive me! Not that!"

Ibrahim knocked at the door again. The Grand Cadi had come, and begged the inestimable privilege of approaching his Excellency's honorable person.

" Say I can't see him," said the Consul-General, and then, sitting down on a sofa in an alcove of the room, he tried his best to compose himself.

In the silence of the next few minutes he was conscious of the ticking of the telegraph tape that was unrolling itself by his side, and, to relieve his mind of the burden that oppressed it, he stretched out his hand for the long white slip.

It reported a debate on the Address to the Crown, at the opening of a new session of Parliament. Somebody, a rabid, irresponsible Radical, had proposed as an Amendment that " the time had come to associate the people of Egypt in the government of the country," and the Foreign Minister was making his reply.

" This much I am willing to admit," said the Minister, " that there are two cardinal errors in the governing of alien races—to rule them as if they were Englishmen, and to repress their aspirations by blowing them out of the mouth of a gun."

The Consul-General rose to his feet in a new flood of anger. But for Gordon he would have silenced all such babbling. To-morrow morning was to have seen Downing Street in confusion, and in the conflagration that was to have blazed heaven-high on the report of the Egyptian conspiracy and how he had crushed it, he was to have found himself the saviour of civilisation.

But now—what now? Duped by his own son, who had taken sides against him, he was about to become the laughing-stock of all Europe.

" Fool! Fool! Fool! " he cried, and in the cruel riot of anger and love that was going on within him he felt for the first time in his life as if he wanted to burst into tears.

Another knock came to the door. It was Ibrahim again, to say that the Grand Cadi, who sent his humble salaams, had said he would wait, and now the Sirdar had come and he wished to see his Excellency immediately.

" Tell the Sirdar I can see no one to-night," said the Consul-General.

" But his Excellency says his business is urgent, and he must come upstairs if your Excellency will not come down."

The Consul-General reflected for a moment and then replied:

" Tell the Sirdar I will be down presently."

VII

BESIDES the Grand Cadi with his pockmarked cheeks and base eyes, and the Sirdar with his ruddy face (suddenly grown sallow), the plump person of the Commandant of Police was waiting in the library.

The Grand Cadi in his turban and silk robes sat in the extreme corner of the room, opposite to the desk; the Sirdar, in his full-dress uniform, stood squarely on the hearth-rug with his back to the empty fireplace; and the Commandant, in his gold-braided blue, stood near to the door.

No one spoke. There was a tense silence, such as pervades a surgeon's consulting room immediately before a serious operation.

When the Consul-General came in, still wearing his court-dress, it was plainly apparent to those who had seen him as recently as half an hour before that he was a changed man. Although perfectly self-possessed and as firm and implacable as ever, there was an indefinable something about his eyes, his mouth, and his square jaw which seemed to say that he had gone through a great struggle with his own heart and conquered it—perhaps killed it—and that henceforth his affections were to be counted as dead.

The Sirdar saw this at a glance, and thereby realised the measure of what he had come to do. He had come to fight this father for his own son.

Answering the salute of the Commandant, the salutation of the Sirdar and the salaam of the Cadi with the curtest bow, the old man stepped forward to his desk, and seating himself in the revolving chair behind it, said brusquely:

"Well, what is the matter now?"

"Nuneham," said the Sirdar, with an oblique glance in the direction of the Cadi, "the Commandant and I wish to speak to you in private on a personal and urgent subject."

"Does it concern my son?" asked the Consul-General sharply.

"I do not say it concerns your son," said the Sirdar, with

another oblique glance at the Cadi. "I only say it is personal and urgent and therefore ought to be discussed in private."

"Humph! We'll discuss it here. I'll have no secrets on that subject."

"In that case," said the Sirdar, "you must take the consequences."

"Go on, please."

"In the first place the Commandant finds himself in a predicament."

"What is it?"

"The warrant he holds is for the arrest of Ishmael Ameer, but the prisoner he has taken to-night is—another person."

"Well?"

"The Commandant wishes to know what he is to do?"

"What is it his duty to do?"

"That depends on circumstances, and the circumstances in the present case are peculiar."

"State them precisely, please."

The Sirdar hesitated, glanced again at the Cadi, this time with an expression of obvious repugnance, and then said:

"The peculiar circumstances in this case are, my dear Nuneham, that though the prisoner cannot possibly be held under the warrant by which he was arrested, he is wanted by the military courts for other offences."

"Therefore——"

"Therefore the Commandant has come with me to ask you whether the man he has taken to-night is to be handed over to the military authorities or——"

"Or what?"

"Or allowed to go free."

The Consul-General swung his chair round until he came face to face with the Sirdar, and said with withering bitternesss:

"So you have come to me—British Agent and Consul-General—to ask if I will connive at your prisoner's escape! Is that it?"

The Sirdar flinched, bit the ends of his moustache for a moment, and then said, with a faint tremor in his voice:

"Nuneham, if the prisoner is handed over to the authorities he will be court-martialled."

"Let it be so," said the Consul-General.

"As surely as he is court-martialled his sentence will be death."

The old man swung his chair back and answered huskily: "If his offences deserve it, what matter is that to me?"

"His offences," said the Sirdar, "were insubordination, refusal to obey the orders of his general and——"

"Isn't that enough?" asked the Consul-General, whereupon the Sirdar drew himself up and said:

"I plead no excuses for insubordination. I am myself a soldier. I think discipline is the backbone of the army. Without that everything must go to chaos. But the general who exacts stern compliance with military discipline on the part of his officers has it for his sacred duty to see that his commands are just and that he does not provoke disobedience by outrageous and illegal insults."

The old man's face twitched visibly, but still he stood firm.

"Provoked or not provoked, your prisoner disobeyed the orders of his recognised superior—what more is there to say?"

"Only that he acted from a sense of right, and that he *was* right——"

"What?"

"I say he *was* right, as subsequent events proved, and if his conscience——"

"Conscience! What has a soldier to do with conscience? My servant Ibrahim, perhaps, any fellah, may have a right to exercise what he is pleased to call his conscience, but the first and only duty of an English soldier is to obey."

"Then God help England! If an English soldier is only a machine, a human gun-waggon, with no right to think about anything but his rations and his pay, and how to use his rifle, he is a butcher and a hireling—not a hero. No, no, some of the greatest soldiers and sailors have resisted authority when authority has been in the wrong. Nelson did it and General Gordon did it, and if this one——"

But the old man burst out again in a quivering voice:

"Why do you come to tell me this? What has it got to do with me? The case before us is perfectly clear. By some tangle and devilish circumstances the wrong man has been arrested to-night. But your prisoner is wanted by the military authorities for other offences. Very well, let him be handed over to them."

The Sirdar now saw that he had not only to fight the father for his own flesh and blood, but the man for himself. He looked across the room to where the Grand Cadi sat in smug silence, but his clawlike hands clasped before his breast, and then, as if taking a last chance, he said:

"Nuneham, the prisoner is your son."

"All the more reason why I should treat him as I should treat anybody else."

"Your *only* son."

"Humph!"

"If anything happens to him—if he dies before you—your family will come to an end when you are gone."

The old man trembled. The Sirdar was cutting him in the tenderest place—ploughing deep into his lifelong secret.

"Your name will be wiped out. *You* will have wiped it out, Nuneham."

The old man was shaking like a rock which vibrates in an earthquake. To steady his nerves he took a pen and held it firmly in the fingers of both hands.

"If you tell the Commandant to hand him over to the military authorities, it will be the same in the court of your conscience as if *you* had done it. *You will have cut off your own line.*"

The old man fought hard with himself. It was a fearful struggle.

"More than that, it will be the same—it will be the same when you come to think of it—as if with that pen in your hands you had signed your own son's death-warrant."

The pen dropped, as if it had been red hot, from the old man's trembling fingers. Still he struggled.

"If my son is a guilty man, let the law deal with him as it would deal with any other," he said, but his voice shook —it could scarcely sustain itself.

The Sirdar saw that deep under the frozen surface, the heart of the old man was breaking up; he knew that the shot that killed Gordon would kill the Consul-General also, and he felt that he was now pleading for the life of the father as well as of the son.

"It's not as if the boy were a prodigal, a wastrel," he said. "He is a gentleman, every inch of him, and if he has gone wrong, if he has acted improperly, it has only been from the highest impulses. He has sincerity and he has courage, and they are the noblest virtues of the soul."

The old man's head was down, but he was conscious that the Cadi's cruel eyes were upon him.

"He's a soldier, too. In some respects the finest young soldier in the army, whoever the next may be. He saw his first fighting with me, I remember. It was at Omdurman. He had taken the Khalifa's flag. The dervish who carried it had treacherously stabbed his comrade, and when he came up with fire and tears in his eyes together, he said, 'I killed him like a dog, sir.' 'My God,' I said to myself, 'here is a soldier born.'"

The old man was silent, but he was still conscious that the Cadi's cruel eyes were upon him, watching him, interrogating him, saying, "What will you do now, I wonder?"

"God has never given me a son," continued the Sirdar, "but from that day to this I have always felt as if that boy belonged also to myself."

The old man was breaking up rapidly, but still he would not yield.

"His mother loved him, too. Perhaps he was the only human thing that came between her and her God. She is dead, and they say the dead see all. Who knows, Nuneham? —she may be waiting now to find out what you are going to do."

The strain was terrible. The two old friends, one visibly moved and making no effort to conceal his emotion, the other fighting hard with the dark spirits of pride and wrath.

The Sirdar's mind went back to the days when they were young men themselves, at Sandhurst together, and approaching the Consul-General he put one hand on his shoulder and said:

"Nuneham—John Nuneham—John—Jack—give the boy another chance. Let him go."

Then with a cry of agony and with an oath, never heard from his lips before, the Consul-General rose from his seat and said:

"No, no, no! You come here asking me to put my honour into the hands of my enemies—to leave myself at the mercy of any scoundrel who cares to say that the measure I mete out to others is not that which I keep for my own. You come, too, excusing my son's offences against military law, but saying nothing of the other crimes in which you have this very night caught him red-handed."

After that he smote the desk with his clenched fist and cried:

"No, no, I tell you no! My son is a traitor. He has joined himself to his father's and his country's enemies in order to destroy him and to destroy England in Egypt, and if the punishment of a traitor is death, then death it must be to him as to any other, that the same justice may be dealt out to all."

Then to the Commandant, who was still standing by the door, he said:

"Go, sir! Let your prisoner be handed over to the military authorities without one moment's further delay."

It was like the moment of the breaking of an avalanche, and after it there came the same awful stillness. No one spoke. The Commandant bowed and left the room.

The Consul-General returned to his seat at the desk, and, digging his elbows into the blotting-pad, rested his head on his hands. The Sirdar stood sideways with one arm on the chimney-piece. The Cadi sat in his smug silence with his claw-like hands still clasped in front of his breast.

They heard the Commandant's heavy step and the click of his spurs as he walked across the marble floor of the hall.

They heard the front door close with a bang. Still no one spoke and the silence seemed to be everlasting.

Then they heard the outer bell ringing loudly. They heard the front door opened and then closed again, as if after admitting somebody. At the next moment Ibrahim, looking as if he had just seen a ghost, had come, with his slippered feet, into the library, and was stammering:

"If you please, your Excellency—if you please, your Ex——"

"Speak out, you fool—who is it?" said the Consul-General.

"It is—it is Miss—Miss Helena, your Excellency."

The Consul-General's face contracted for an instant, as if he were trying to recover the plain sense of where he was and what was going on. Then he rose and went out of the room, Ibrahim following him.

The Sirdar and the Grand Cadi were left together. They did not speak or exchange a sign. The Sirdar felt that the Cadi's presence had contributed to the late painful scene— that it had been a silent, subtle devilish influence against Gordon—and he was conscious of an almost unconquerable desire to take the man by the throat and wring his neck as he would wring the neck of a bird of prey.

Quarter of an hour passed. Half an hour. Still the two men did not speak. And the Consul-General did not return.

VIII

MEANTIME Helena, in another room, still wearing her mixed Eastern and Western dress, was sitting by a table in an attitude of supplication, with her arms outstretched and her hands clasped across a corner of it, speaking earnestly and rapidly to the Consul-General, who was standing with head down in front of her.

Pale, in spite of the heat of the South and the sun of the desert, very nervous, flurried, and a little ashamed, yet with a sense of urgent necessity, she was telling him all that had happened since she left Cairo—how she had gone to Khar-

toum under an impulse of revenge that was inspired by a
mistaken idea of the cause of her father's death; how, being
there, she had been compelled to accept the position of Ishmael's nominal wife or go back with her errand unfulfilled;
how she had come to know of the base proposals of certain
of the Ulema; and how, at length, when Ishmael had succumbed to the last of them, she had written and despatched
her letter saying he was coming into Cairo in disguise.

Then in her soft voice, with its deep note, she told of
Gordon's arrival in Khartoum, of his own tragic mistake
and awful sufferings, of his confession to her, of her con-
fesssion to him, and of how she realised her error, but found
herself powerless to overtake or undo it.

Finally she told the Consul-General of Gordon's determination to take Ishmael's place, being impelled to do so by
the firmest conviction that his father was being deceived by
some one in Cairo, by the certainty that Ishmael could not
otherwise be moved from his fanatical purpose, and that
while the consequences of his own arrest must be merely
personal to himself, the result of Ishmael's death at the
hands of the authorities might be a holy war, which would
put Egypt in the right and England in the wrong and cover
his father's honoured name with infamy.

The old man listened eagerly, standing as long as he
could on the same spot, then walking to and from with nervous and irregular steps, but stopping at intervals as if
breathless from an overpowering sense of the presence of the
hand of fate.

Having finished her story, Helena produced Gordon's
letters from the little handbag which hung from one of
her arms, and having kissed them, as if the Consul-General
had not been present, she began with panting affection to
read passages from them in proof of what she had said.

Being a woman, she knew by instinct what to read first,
and one by one came the passionate words which told of
Gordon's affection for the father whom he felt bound to
resist.

"My father," she read, "is a great man who probably
does not need and would certainly resent my compassion,

but Lord God, how I pity him! Deceived by false friends, alone in his old age, after all he has done for Egypt!"

The old man stopped her and said:

"But how did he know that—that I was being deceived? What right had he to say so?"

"Listen," said Helena, and she read Gordon's account of his visit to the Grand Cadi, when the "oily scoundrel" had called his father "the slave of power," "the evil-doer," "the adventurer," and "the great assassin."

"Then why didn't he come like a man and tell me himself?" asked the Consul-General.

"Listen again, sir," said Helena, and she read what Gordon had said of his impulse to go to his father, in order to disclose the Grand Cadi's duplicity, and then of the reasons restraining him, being sure that his father was aiming at a *coup* and that acting from a high sense of duty the Consul-General would hand him over to the military authorities before the work he had come to do had been done.

"But didn't he see what he was doing himself—aiding and abetting a conspiracy?"

"Listen once more, please," said Helena, and she read what Gordon had said of Ishmael's pilgrimage—that while his father thought the Prophet was bringing up an armed force, he was merely leading a vast multitude of religious visionaries, who were expecting to establish in Cairo a millennium of universal faith and empire.

"But, even so, was it necessary to do what he did?" demanded the Consul-General.

"Listen for the last time, sir," said Helena, and then in her soft, earnest, pleading voice, she read:

"It is necessary to prevent the massacre which I know (and my father does not) would inevitably ensue; necessary to save my father himself from the execration of the civilised world; necessary to save Ishmael from the tragic consequences of his determined fanaticism; necessary to save England——"

"Give them to me," said the Consul-General, taking—almost snatching—the letters out of Helena's hands in the fierce nervous tension which left him no time to think of courtesies.

Then drawing a chair up to the table, and fixing his eyeglasses over his spectacles, he turned the pages one by one and read passages here and there. Helena watched him while he did so, and in the changing expression of the hitherto hard, immobile, implacable face, she saw the effect that was being produced.

"I cannot say how hard it is to me to be engaged in a secret means to frustrate my father's plans—it is like fighting one's own flesh and blood and is not fair warfare . . .

"Neither can I say what a struggle it has been to me as an English soldier to make up my mind to intercept an order of the British Army—it is like playing traitor and I can scarcely bear to think of it . . .

"But all the same I know it is necessary. I also know God knows it is necessary, and when I think of that my heart beats wildly . . .

"I am willing to give my life for England, whatever name she may know me by . . . and I am willing to die for these poor Egyptians, because . . .

"This may be the last letter I shall write to you . . .

"May the great God of Heaven bless and protect you . . ."

The Consul-General was overwhelmed. The Grand Cadi's duplicity stifled him, Ishmael's innocence of conspiracy humiliated him, but his son's heroism crushed him and made him feel like a little man.

Yet he had just now denounced his son as a traitor, handed him over to the military authorities, and, in effect, condemned him to death!

As the old man read Gordon's letters his iron face seemed to decompose. Helena could not bear to look at him any longer, and she had to turn her own face away. At length she became conscious that he had ceased to read, and that his great, sad, humid eyes were looking at her.

"So you came here to plead with me for the life of my boy?" he said, and, as well as she could for the tears that were choking her she answered:

"Yes."

He hesitated for a moment, as if trying to summon courage to tell her something, and then, in a voice that was quite unlike his own, he said:

"Permit to take these letters away for a few minutes."

And rising unsteadily he left the room.

IX

WHEN the Consul-General returned to the library he looked like a feeble old man of ninety. It was just as if twenty years of his life had been struck out of him in half an hour. The Sirdar stepped up to him in alarm, saying:

"What has happened?"

"Read these," he answered, handing to the Sirdar the letters he carried in his hand.

The Sirdar took the letters aside, and standing by the chimney-piece he looked at them. While he did so his face, which had hitherto been grave and pale, became bright and ruddy, and he uttered little sharp cries of joy.

"I knew it!" he said. "Although I was at a loss to read the riddle of Gordon's presence at Ghezirah I knew there must be some explanation. If he had acted with a sense of conscience in the one case he must have done so in the other. . . . Thank God! Splendid! Bravo! . . . Of course, you will stop the Commandant?"

The Consul-General, who had returned to his seat at the desk, did not reply, and the Sirdar, thinking to anticipate his objection, said eagerly:

"Why not? The Commandant will act as for himself and nobody will know that you have been consulted. . . . That is to say," he added, with another oblique glance in the direction of the Grand Cadi, "nobody outside this room, and if anybody here should ever whisper a word about it I'll —I'll—well, never mind; nobody will, nobody dare."

Then in the fever of his impatience the Sirdar proposed to call up the Commandant of Police on the telephone and tell him to consider his order cancelled.

"Don't stir," he said. "I'll do it. Your Secretary will show me the box."

When, with a light step and a hopeful face, the Sirdar had gone out of the room on this errand the Cadi began for the first time to show signs of life. He coughed, cleared his throat, and made other noises indicative of a desire to speak, but the Consul-General, still sitting at the desk with the look of a shattered man, seemed to be unconscious of his presence. At length he said, in that hushed voice of one who was habitually afraid of being overheard:

"I regret—sincerely regret—that I have been again compelled to approach your Excellency's honourable person —especially at a time like this—but a certain danger—personal danger—made me think that perhaps your Excellency would deign——"

Before he could say any more the Sirdar had returned to the library with a long face and a slow step.

"Too late!" he said. "I called up the Commandant at his office and they said he had gone to the Citadel. Then I called him up there, thinking I might still be in time. But no, the thing was over. Gordon was under arrest."

After that there was silence for some moments while the Sirdar looked again at the letters which he was still holding in his hands. At one moment he raised his eyes, and turning to the Consul-General he said:

"You'll not call down the troops from Abbassiah?"

"No."

"And you'll allow this man Ishmael and his visionary followers to come into Cairo if they've a mind to?"

The Consul-General bent his head.

"Good!" said the Sirdar. "At all events, that will shut the mouths of the fine birds who must be getting ready to crow."

But a look of alarm came into the Grand Cadi's eyes, such as comes into the eyes of a hawk when an eagle is about to pounce upon it.

"Surely," he said, "his Excellency does not intend to allow this horde of fifty thousand fanatics to pour themselves into the Capital?"

Whereupon the Sirdar turned sharply upon the man and answered:

"That is exactly what his Excellency *does* intend to do."

"But what is to become of me?" asked the Cadi. "This is exactly the errand I came upon. Already the people are threatening me, and I came to ask for protection. I am suspected of giving information to his Excellency. Will his Excellency desert me—leave me to the mercy of this man Ishmael, this corrupter and destroyer of the faith?"

Then the Consul-General, who had sat with head down, the picture of despair, rose to his full height and faced the Grand Cadi.

"Listen," he said, with a flash of his old fire. "I give your Eminence twenty-four hours to leave Egypt. If the *people* do not dispose of you after that time, as sure as there is a British Minister in Constantinople, *I will*."

The look of alarm in the Cadi's cunning face was smitten into an expression of terror. Not a word more did he say. One glance he gave at the letters in the Sirdar's hands, and then rising, with a low bow and touching his breast and forehead, he turned to leave the room. Meantime the Sirdar had rung the bell for Ibrahim, and then stepping to the door he had opened it. The ample folds of the Cadi's sleeves swelled as he walked and he passed out like a human bat.

Being alone with the Sirdar the Consul-General's mind went back to Helena.

"Poor child!" he said. "I hadn't the heart to tell her what I had done. Go to her, Reg. She's in the drawing-room. Give her back her letters and tell her what has happened. Then take her to the Princess Nazimah. Poor girl! Poor Gordon!"

The Sirdar made some effort to comfort him, but it was hard to say anything now to the man who in the days of his strength had hated all forms of sentimentality. Yet the shadow of supernatural powers seemed to be over him, for he muttered some simple, almost childlike words about the Almighty permitting him to fall because he had wandered away from Him.

"Janet! My poor Janet!" he murmured, his once proud head hung low.

The Sirdar could bear no more, and he quietly left the library.

As he approached the drawing-room he heard voices within. Fatimah was with Helena. All the mother-heart in the Egyptian woman had warmed to the girl in her trouble, and forgetful of the difference of class, they were clasped in each other's arms.

The Sirdar could see by the tears that were trickling down Helena's cheeks that already she knew everything, but all the same he told her that Gordon had been handed over to the military authorities. She stood the fire of the sad news without flinching, and a few minutes afterward they were in the Sirdar's carriage on their way to the Princess Nazimah's—the black boy on his donkey trotting proudly behind.

"We must not lose heart, though," said the Sirdar. "Now that I come to think of it, to be court-martialled may be the best thing that can happen to him. He'll have a good deal to say for himself. And whatever the sentence may be, there's the Army Council, and there's the Secretary of State, and there's the King himself, you know."

"Then you think there's some hope still," she said faintly but sweetly.

"I'm certain there is," said the Sirdar, and as the carriage passed under the electric arc lamps in the streets he could see that Helena's wet eyes were shining.

After a while she asked where Gordon was imprisoned, and was told that he was at the Citadel, but that he was in officer's quarters and that his Egyptian foster-brother, Hafiz Ahmed, was permitted to be with him.

Then she asked if Ishmael and his people would be permitted to come into Cairo, and was told that they would, and that they might encamp in El Azhar if they cared to— Ishmael being nothing to the Sirdar but an inoffensive dreamer with a disordered brain.

Helena's lovely face looked almost happy. She was thinking of the light that was expected to shine at midnight from the minaret of the mosque of Mohammed Ali, and was telling herself that as soon as she reached the house of the Princess she would call up Hafiz at the Citadel and see what could be done.

Meantime Fatimah, who had gone to the Consul-General's bedroom to see that everything was in order, had found something crunching under her feet, and picking it up she found that it was the portrait of Gordon as a boy in his Arab fez. With many sighs she was putting the pieces aside when the old man entered the room. He did not seem to see her, and though she lingered some little while he did not speak.

Sitting on the sofa he rested his head on his hands and looked fixedly at the carpet between his feet. Half an hour passed—an hour—two hours—but he did not move. At intervals the telegraphic machine which stood in an alcove of the room ticked for a time and then stopped. The debate on the Amendment to the Address was still going on, but that did not matter now. Nothing mattered except one thing—that he, he himself, had sent his own son to his death, thus cutting off his line, ending his family, and destroying the one hope and loadstar of his life.

"Ah, well! It's all over," he thought, and at length, switching off the lights, he went to bed.

While the great Proconsul slept his restless, troubled sleep, the telegraphic machine ticked out in the darkness on the long slip of white paper that rolled onto the floor the future history of Egypt and in some sense of the world.

Far away in London the Foreign Minister was speaking.

"I am one of those who think," he was saying, "that just as religious leaders, Popes as well as Mahdis, may go to wreck under the mental malady which permits them to believe they are the mouthpieces of the Almighty, so statesmen may be destroyed by the seeds of dissolution which power, especially absolute power, carries within itself

"Holding this opinion, I also hold that to place one person in sele charge of millions of people of a different race, creed, and mode of thought, is to put a load on one man's shoulders which no man, whatever his power and influence, his integrity and the nobility of his principles ought to be called upon to bear."

But the heavy-lidded house on the Nile was asleep. The Consul-General did not hear.

X

WHEN Ishmael left Helena's tent he did not return to his own. In the torment of his soul he sought the solitude of the desert. For two hours he walked on the sand without knowing where he was going. The night was dark save for an innumerable army of stars; an Easter night, still and fragrant, but the unhappy man was wandering in it like a creature accursed, a prey to the most terrible upheaval of the soul, the most bitter and sorrowful reflections.

His first thoughts were about Helena—that all the sweetness, all the loveliness which had been his joy by day and his dream by night belonged not to him but to another.

"I am nothing to her," he told himself, and greater grief than he felt at that thought seemed to surpass the bounds of possibility.

But there was worse behind. At the next moment of his anguish he remembered that not only did Helena not love him, but he was repulsive to her. "Don't you see you are hateful and odious to me—that you are a black man and I am a white woman?"

This was more than heartrending—it was physically excruciating, like poison creeping under the skin. But it had its spiritual torture also. He who had built his life on the belief that the sons and daughters of men were all children of one Father, had found out in a moment, in the twinkling of an eye, within his own camp, in his own tent, that Nature gave the lie to his faith, and that he—he himself—was only as a black man to the white woman whom he called his wife.

"I thought that where love was there could be neither race nor colour, but I was wrong, quite wrong," he told himself again, and it seemed as if everything that had built up his soul was crumbling away.

But even worse than all this was the thought that Helena had betrayed him—she who had seemed to sacrifice so much. Pitiful delusion! Cruel snare!

It was maddening to think of the merely human side of his betrayal—that between the guilty wife and her lover he was only the husband who had to be got rid of—but the spiritual aspect was still more terrible. He who had allowed himself to believe that he was specially guided by God, that the Merciful had made him His messenger, had been deceived and duped and was no more than a poor, weak, helpless man who had been led away by his love for a woman.

The shame of his betrayal was stifling, the sense of his downfall was crushing, but still more painful was the consciousness of the penalty which his people would have to pay for the pride and blind love which had misled him. They had followed him across the desert, suffering all the pains of the long and toilsome journey, buoyed up by the hopes with which he had inspired them; they had trusted and loved and looked up to him, hardly distinguishing between his word and the word of God, and now—their leader was deceived, their hopes were dead, the mirage of their dreams had disappeared.

Thinking of this in the agony of his despair, he asked himself why God had permitted it to come to pass that not himself only but the whole body of his people should suffer. "Why, O God! why?" he cried, lifting his arms to the sky.

For some moments a cloud passed between him and the faith which had so long sustained him. He began to regret his lofty mission and to remember with regret his earlier days in Khartoum with the simple girl who loved him and lay on the angerib in his arms. He had been humble then —content to be a man—and recalling one by one the touching memories of his life with Adila, in their prison brightened by rays of love, in their poor desert home, illuminated more than a palace by expectation of the child that was to come, his heart failed him and he wanted to curse the destiny which had led him to a greatness wherein all was vain.

The wild insurrection in his soul had left him no time

to think which course he was taking, but wandering across the Sakkara desert he had by this time come to the foot of the Sphinx.

Calm, immovable, tremendous, the great scarred face was gazing in passionless meditation into the luminous starlight, asking, as it had asked through the long yesterday of the past, as it will continue to ask through the long to-morrow of the future, the everlasting question—the question of humanity, the question of all suffering souls.

" Why ? "

Why should man aim higher than he can reach? Why should he give up the joys of humanity for divine dreams that can never be realised? Why should he be a victim to the devilish powers, within and without, which are always waiting to betray and destroy him? Why should God forsake him just when he is striving to serve him most?

"Allah! Allah! Why? Why?" he cried.

But his higher nature speedily regained its supremacy. It came to him as a flash of light in his darkness that the true explanation of his downfall was that God was punishing him for his presumption in allowing the idolatry of his people to carry him away from his first humility—to forget his proper place as a man and to think of himself as if he were a god.

This led him to thoughts of atonement, and in a moment the image of death came to him—his own death—as a sacrifice. He began to see what he had now to do. He had to take all that had happened upon himself. He had to call his people together and to say: " I lied to you. I was a false prophet! I deceived myself, and in deceiving myself I deceived you also! The wonderful world I promised you—the Redeemer I foretold—all, all is vain! "

And then—what then? What of himself—the betrayed, the betrayer? After he had parted from the people with their broken hearts, he would deliver himself up to the authorities. He had done no wrong to the Government, but he had sinned against his followers and he had sinned against God, and God would accept the one punishment for the other.

Yes, he would go into Cairo and say, "I am here—you want me—take me!"

His regenerated soul saw in his death not only his own salvation but the salvation of his people also. It was not clear to him how this was to come to pass, but death had always been a gain to great causes, and God was over all!

Under this sublime resolution his heart became almost buoyant. He turned to go back to the camp, and as he walked he thought of Helena again. The tender love which had filled his whole being for months could not be banished in an hour, and he began to tell himself that perhaps after all she had not been to blame. Love could not be ruled by a rudder like a boat. The white woman could not help but love the white man. It was a woman's way to risk everything, to sacrifice everybody, to commit sin and even crime for the man she loved—how many good women had done so!

That was the temptation to which the Rani had succumbed, and he—yes, he also—must submit to the pains of it. They were hard, they were cruel, they cut to the core, but with the idea of death before him they could now be borne.

He remembered his unbridled wrath with the Rani, his ferocious violence, and he felt ashamed. It was almost impossible to believe that he had really laid hands upon her and tried to strangle her.

He remembered how he had left her, face down on the angerib, in her misery and remorse. The picture in his mind's eye of the weeping woman in her tent made his heart bleed with pity.

He must go back to her. His people might suspect that she was the author of their trouble and in their fury they might threaten her. He must conceal her fault. He must take her sin upon himself.

"I must cover her with my cloak," he thought.

Thus, thirsting with a desire to drink the cup of his degradation to the dregs, Ishmael got back to camp. It was full of touching sights. Instead of the flare of the lights and the tumult of the excited crowds which he had left behind him, there were now only the ashes of dying fires and the melancholy moanings of the people who were sitting about them.

He made his way first to Helena's tent, and, standing by the mouth of it, he called to her.

"Rani!"

A woman who had been lying on the angerib rose to answer him. It was Zenoba.

"Alas! Your Rani has gone, O Master!" she said, with mock sympathy but ill-concealed tones of triumph.

"Gone?"

"She was afraid the people might kill her, so she fled away."

"Fled away?"

"I did my best to keep her for your sake, but she loves herself more than you, and that's the truth, O Master!"

Ishmael groaned and staggered, but the woman showed no pity.

"Better have contented yourself with a woman of your own people, who would have been true and faithful," she said in a bitter whisper.

Covered with shame, Ishmael turned away. He looked for Zogal.

The black Dervish was at that moment struggling to sustain the people's faith in the Master and his mission by means of a pagan superstition.

"Give me a mutton bone," he had said, and having received one he had looked at it long and steadfastly in order to read the future.

As Ishmael came up to the smouldering fire about which Zogal and his company were squatting, the wild-eyed Dervish was saying:

"It will be well! Allah will preserve his people and the Master will be saved! Did I not tell thee the bone never lies?"

"Zogal," said Ishmael, "sound the horn and let the people be brought together."

The sky was dark. The stars had gone out. It was not yet midnight.

XI

At the next moment the melancholy notes of the great horn rang out over the dark camp and within a few minutes an immense multitude had gathered.

It was a strange spectacle under the blank darkness of the sky. Men carrying lanterns, which cast coarse lights upward into their swarthy faces, were standing in a surging and murmuring mass, while women, like shadows in the gloom, were huddling together on the outskirts of the crowd.

They were Ishmael's faithful people, all of them, broken-hearted believers in his spiritual mission, for at the shadow of disaster those who had followed him for personal gains alone had gone.

Ishmael caused the people to be drawn up in a great square, and then mounting a camel he rode into the midst of them. He was seen to be in a state of great excitement.

"Brothers," he said, "we have passed through many hard days together. You have shared with me your joys and your sorrows. I have shared with you my hopes and my dreams. We are one."

Touched to the heart by his voice as much as his words, the people cried:

"May God preserve thee!"

"Nay," he cried, "may God punish me, for I have permitted myself to be deceived."

The people thought he was going to speak of the woman who was understood to have betrayed him, but he did not do so.

"Look!" he cried, pointing toward the pyramid. "We stand amid the ruins of a pagan world. Where are the Kings and Counsellors who slept in these desolate places? Gone! All gone! Have not strangers from a far country taken away their bodies to wonder at? Where is the king who built this tomb? He thought himself the equal of God, yet what was he? A man, shaped out of a little clay! And I?" he said, "I, too, have been drunk with power. I have been living in the greatness of my own strength. I have

36

permitted myself to believe that I was the messenger of God, and therefore God—God has brought me down. He has laid me in the dust. Blessed be the name of God!"

Only the broken ejaculations of the people answered him, and he went on without pausing:

"In bringing me down he has brought down my people also. Alas for you, my brothers! You cannot go into Cairo. The armed forces of, the Government are waiting there to destroy you. Therefore turn back and go home. Forgive your leader who has led you astray. And God preserve and comfort you!"

"And you, O Master?" cried a voice that rose above the confused voices of the people.

Ishmael paused for a moment and then said:

"In times of great war and pestilence God has accepted an atonement, and perhaps he will do so now. I will go into Cairo and deliver myself to the Government. I will say, 'The man you hold was arrested instead of me. I am your true prisoner. Take me and let him—and let my poor followers—go free.'"

The anguish of the people swelled into sobs and some of them, full of zeal, swore they would never return to their homes without the Master but would follow him to prison and to death.

"If you go into Cairo, so will I!" cried one.

"And I, too!" cried another.

"And I!" "And I!" "And I!" cried others, each holding up his hand and stepping out as he spoke, until the square in which Ishmael sat on his camel was full of excited men.

At that moment of deep emotion, while great tears were rolling down Ishmael's cheeks and the women on the outskirts of the crowd were uttering piercing cries, a loud delirious shout was heard, and a man was seen to be crushing his way through the people.

It was Zogal, and his wild eyes were ablaze with frenzy.

"Wait! Wait!" he cried. "Has the Master forgotten his own message? He says the soldiers of the Franks and Turks are waiting in Cairo to destroy us. But isn't

God greater than armies? We are weak and defenceless, but does He always give His victory to the armed and the strong? What," he cried again, " are you afraid that the Christians will kill us with bullets? That they will eat our flesh and drink our blood? That they will make us worship the wooden cross? If God is with us what can our enemies do? It is not they who throw the javelin—it is God! Therefore," he cried, in a voice that had risen to a scream, " if the Master is to go into Cairo we will *all* go with him."

In vain Ishmael tried to stop the man. His protests were drowned in the rapturous responses of the crowd. People are as easily swayed to as fro, they regain confidence as rapidly as they lose it. In a moment the Master was forgotten and only the wild-eyed Dervish seemed to be heard.

"Did not God promise us, through the mouth of His messenger, that we should go into Cairo—and will He break His word?"

"Allah! Allah!" shouted the crowd.

"Did he not tell us He would send a sign?"

"Allah! Allah!"

"Shall we say it will not come, and call God a liar?"

"Allah! Allah!"

"'At the hour of midnight prayers,' he said, ' the light will shine!'"

"Allah! Allah! Allah!"

"Pray for it, my brothers, pray for it," cried Zogal, and in another moment, with the delirious strength of one possessed, he had cleared a long passage through the people, and begun to lead a wild barbaric zikr, such as he had seen in the depths of the desert.

"The light! The light! Send the light, O Allah!" cried Zogal, striding up and down the long alley of bowing and swaying people, and tossing his sweating and foaming face up to the dark sky.

It has been truly said that everything favours those who have a special destiny—that they may become glorious against their own will and as if by the command of fate. It was so with Ishmael. At the very moment when Zogal, on the desert, was calling for the light which he believed God had promised, Hafiz, at the Citadel, having received the message which Helena had sent over the telephone from the house of the Princess Nazimah, was running with a powerful lantern up the winding stairway of one of the minarets of the mosque of Mohammed Ali.

"The light! The light! Send the light, O Allah!" cried the Dervish, and at the next moment, while the breathless crowd about him were looking through the darkness toward the heights above Cairo, expecting to see the manifestation of God's sign in the sky, the light appeared!

In an instant the whole camp was a scene of frantic rejoicing. Men were shouting, women were lu-luing, camels and asses were being saddled, tents were being struck, and everybody and everything was astir.

Oh, mysterious and divine power of destiny that could make the fate of an entire nation hang on the accident of time and the unreasoning impulses of one poor demented man!

XII

NEXT day Ishmael entered Cairo. News of his coming had been noised abroad and the police at their various stations had been told that beyond the necessary efforts to preserve order they were not in any way to interfere with his procession. Neither Ishmael nor any of his people were to be allowed to pose as martyrs. There was to be no resistance and no bloodshed. If possible, there was to be no scene.

The guests at the King's Dinner had left the Ghezirah long before midnight. Such of them as were innocent of all participation in conspiracy (they were the majority) attributed the Consul-General's strange outbreak to an attack of mental vertigo in an old man whose health had long been failing from the pressure of public work. Nothing was allowed to occur which would give the incident a more serious significance. The bridge which had been opened was closed and the guests had returned to their homes as usual.

In the early hours of morning they were awakened by loud shoutings in the streets. Two hundred men from Ishmael's company had galloped ahead as heralds, and, flying down every thoroughfare to reassure the population of the nature of the vast procession that was coming, they were crying:

"Peace! Peace! It is Peace!"

After that the general body of the native people, who had been on the tiptoe of expectation, were speeding along the streets. They found mounted and foot police stationed at various points, but no military and no guns.

It was a triumphant entry. The procession came in by the Gizeh bridge, and passing down the Kasr el Aini into the place Ismailyah, it turned down the broad boulevard Abul Aziz toward the heart of the city.

The sun was rising, and the scene was a blaze of colour. Banners were swinging from the houses like ship's pennants in stormy seas. The streets seemed to be carpeted with the tarbooshes and turbans of the great, moving, surging masses of humanity, that were slowly passing through them. There were brown faces that were almost white from the fatigue of the long desert march, and white faces that were burned brown by the tropical sun. It was a swarming, shifting, variegated throng, and over all was the dazzling splendour of the Eastern sunrise.

Before the procession had gone far it seemed as if the whole population of Cairo had come out to meet it. Eternal children! There is nothing they love more than to look at a great spectacle, except to take part in it, and they hastened to take part in this one. Every window and balcony was soon full of faces; every house-top was alive with movement and aflame with colour. People were thronging the footpaths on either side as the pilgrims passed between.

The wives and children of the hundred emissaries who left Cairo on Ishmael's errand had come out to look for their husbands and fathers returning home. Eagerly they were scanning the faces of the pilgrims and loud and wild were their cries of joy when they recognised their own.

Many of those who had no personal interest in the procession fell into line with it. A company of Dervishes walked by its side playing pipes and drums. Other musicians joined them with strange-looking wooden and brass instruments. Bursts of wild Arab music broke out from time to time and then stopped, leaving a sort of confused and tumultuous silence.

Carts filled with women and children, who were laughing and lu-luing by turns, jolted along by the pilgrims and shouted to them and cheered them. And then there were the pilgrims themselves, the vast concourse of fully forty thousand from the Soudan, from Assouan, from the long Valley of the Nile, some on horses, some on camels, some on donkeys, some wearing their simple felt skull caps and galabeahs, others in flowing robes and crimson head-dresses. The barbaric splendour and intoxicating arrogance of it all was such as the people of Cairo had never seen before.

To the great body of the Cairenes the entrance of Ishmael Ameer denoted victory. That the Government permitted it indicated defeat. The great English lord, who had closed El Azhar, thereby damming up the chief fountain of the Islamic faith, had been beaten. Either the Powers, or God Himself, had suppressed him and rebuked England. Pharaoh had fallen. The children of Allah were crossing their Red Sea. Even as Mohammed, after being expelled from Mecca as a rebel, had returned to it as a conqueror, so Ishmael, after being cast out of Cairo as the enemy of England, was coming back as England's master and king. So louder and louder became their wild acclamations.

" Victory to Islam! "

" El Hamdullillah! "

" God has willed it! "

When Ishmael himself appeared the shouts of welcome were deafening. He had been long in coming, and the people had been waiting for him all along the line. He came at the end of the procession, and if he could have escaped from it altogether he would have done so.

In spite of all this glory, all this grandeur, a deep melancholy filled the soul of Ishmael. He was not carried away by what had happened. Nothing that had occurred since the night before had touched his pride. When the light appeared on the minaret he had not been deceived. He knew that by some unknown turn of the wheel of chance his people were to be allowed to enter Cairo, but all the same his heart was low.

The only interpretation he put upon the change in events was a mystic one. God had refused his atonement! God had taken the leadership of his people out of his hand! As punishment of his weakness in permitting himself to be betrayed God had made him a mere follower of his own black servant! Therefore his glory was his shame! His hour of triumph was his hour of sorrow and disgrace! He was entering Cairo under the frown of the face of God!

When the camp had been ready to move he had mounted his white camel and ridden last, beset by melancholy preoccupations. But when he came to the Gizeh bridge and saw the crowds that were coming out to greet him, and met Zogal, who had galloped into the city and was galloping back to say that the people of Cairo were preparing a triumph for him, he made his camel kneel and in the deep abasement of his soul he got down to walk.

He walked the whole length of the Kasr el Aini, with head down, like a man who was ashamed, shuddering visibly when the onlookers cheered, trembling when they commended him to God, and almost falling when they saluted him as the Deliverer and Redeemer of Islam and its people.

Although of large frame and strong muscle, he was a man of delicate organisation, and the strain his soul was going through was tearing his body to pieces. At length, as he approached the place Ismailyah, where the crowd was dense, he stumbled and fell on one knee.

Zogal, who was behind, leaped from the ass he was riding and lifted the Master in his arms, but it was seen that he could not stand. There was a moment's hesitation in which the black man seemed to ask himself what he ought to do, and at the next instant he had thrown his white cloak over the donkey's back and lifted Ishmael into the saddle.

Meantime the people in the streets, in the balconies, on

the house-tops, were waiting for the new prophet. They expected to see him coming into Cairo as a conqueror—in a litter perhaps, covered with gold and fringed with jingling coins and cowries—the central figure of a great procession such as would remind them of the grandeur of the Mahmal, the holy carpet, returning from Mecca.

When at length he came, his appearance gave a shock. His face was pale, his head was down, and he was riding on an ass!

But truly everything favours him who has the great destiny. After the spectators had recovered from their first shock at the sight of Ishmael, his humility touched their imagination. Remembering how he had left Cairo and seeing how meekly he was returning to it, their acclamations became deafening.

" Praise be to God!"

" May God preserve you!"

" May God give you long life!"

And then some one who thought he saw in the entrance of Ishmael into Cairo a reproduction of the most triumphant if the most tragic incident in the life of the Lord of the Christians, shouted:

" Seyidna Isa! Seyidna Isa!" ("Our Lord Jesus!")

In a moment the name was taken up on every side and resounded in joyous accents down the streets. The belief of a crowd is created not by slow processes of reason, but by quick flashes of emotion, and instantly the surging mass of Eastern children had accepted the idea that Ishmael Ameer was a reincarnation of that " divine man of Judea" whom he had taught them to reverence, that " son of Mary" whom the Prophet himself had placed first among the children of men.

To make the parallel complete, people rushed out of the houses and spread their coats on the ground in front of him, and some, pushing their adoration to yet greater lengths, climbed the trees that lined the Boulevard, and tearing away branches and boughs flung them before his feet.

The Dervishes ran ahead crying the new name in frantic tones, while a company of grave-looking men walked on

either side of Ishmael, chanting the first Surah: " Praise be
to God the Lord of all creatures," and the muezzin in the
minarets of the mosques (blind men nearly all, who could
see nothing of the boiling, bubbling, gorgeous scene below)
chanted the profession of faith: " There is no god but God!
God is Most Great! God is Most Great!" Men shouted
with delight, women lu-lued with joy, and the thousands of
voices that clashed through the air sounded like bells ringing a joyful peal.

Nothing could have exceeded the savage grandeur of Ishmael's return to Cairo; but Ishmael himself, the white figure
sitting sideways on an ass, continued to move along with a
humbled and chastened soul. He was a sad man with his
own secret sorrow; a bereaved man, a betrayed man, with
a heart that was torn and bleeding.

When he remembered that in spite of his betrayal his
predictions were being fulfilled, he told himself that that was
by God's doing only, not by his in any way. When he heard
the divine name by which the people greeted him he felt as
if he were being burned to the very marrow. He was
crushed by their mistaken worship. He knew himself now
for a poor, weak, blind, deceived and self-deluded man whom
the Almighty had smitten and brought low. Therefore he
made no response to the frantic acclamations. Every step
of the road as he passed along was like a purgatorial procession, and his suffering was written in lines of fire on his
downcast face.

" O Father, spare me, spare me!" he prayed as the people shouted by his side.

Once he made an effort to dismount, but Zogal, thinking the Master's strength was failing, put an arm about him
and held him in his seat.

It took the whole morning for the procession to pass
through the city. Unconsciously, as the blood flows to the
heart, it went up through the Mousky to El Azhar. All the
gates of the University, which had been so long closed, were
standing open. Who had opened them no one seemed to
know. The people crowded into the courtyard and in a little
while the vast place was full. A platform had been raised

37

at the farther side and on this Ishmael was placed with the
chief of the Ulema beside him.

By one of those accidents which always attach themselves to great events it chanced that the day of Ishmael's
return to Cairo was also the first day of the Mouled—the
nine days of rejoicing for the birthday of the Prophet. This
fact was quickly seized upon as a means for uniting to the
beautiful Moslem custom for " attaining the holy satisfaction " the opportunity of celebrating the victory for Islam
which Ishmael was thought to have attained. Therefore, the
Sheikh Seyid el Bakri, descendant of the Prophet and head
of the Moslem confraternities, determined to receive his
congregations in El Azhar, where Ishmael might share in
their homage.

They came in thousands, carrying their gilded banners
which were written over with lines from the Koran, ranged
themselves, company after company, in half-circles before
the dais, salaamed to those who sat on it, chanted words to
the glory of God and His Prophet, and then stepped up to
kiss the hands and sometimes the feet of their chief and
his companions.

Ishmael tried to avoid their homage, but could not do so.
Mechanically he uttered the usual response, " May God repeat upon you this feast in happiness and benediction," and
then fell back upon his own reflections.

Notwithstanding the blaze and blare of the scene about
him, his mind was returning to Helena. Where was she?
What fate had befallen her? At length, unable to bear any
longer the burden of his thoughts, and the purgatory of his
position, he got up and stole away through the corridors at
the back of the mosque.

When darkness fell the native quarters of Cairo were
illuminated. Lamps were hung from the poles which pro-
ject from the minarets of the mosque. Ropes were swung
from minaret to minaret, and from these, also, lamps were
suspended. In the poorer streets people were going about
with open flares in iron grills, and in the better avenues rich
men were walking behind their lantern bearers. Blind beggars in the cafés were reciting the genealogy of the Prophet,

and at the end of every passage other blind beggars were crying, " La Ilaha illa-llah! "

Late at night, when the vast following which Ishmael had brought into the city had to be housed, messengers ran through the streets asking for lodgings for the pilgrims, and people answered from their windows and balconies: " I'll take one "; " I'll take two." Twenty thousand slept in the courtyard and on the roofs of El Azhar; the rest in the houses round about.

The trust in God which had seemed to be slain the night before, awoke to a new life, and when at length the delirious city lay down to sleep, the watchmen walked through the deserted thoroughfares crying, " Wahhed! Wahhed! " (God is One!)

In the dead, hollow, echoing hours of early morning a solitary coach passed through the streets in the direction of the outlying stations of the railway to Port Said. Its blinds were down. It was empty. But on the box seat beside the coachman sat a nervous, watchful person with an evil face, wearing the costume of a footman.

It was the Grand Cadi. He had been the supreme orthodox authority of the Moslem faith, sent from Constantinople as representative and exponent of the spiritual authority vested in the Sultan of Turkey as the Caliph of Islam, but he was stealing out of Cairo like a thief.

XIII

A GENERAL Court-Martial was fixed for the following morning, and Helena was for going to it just as she was, in the mixed Eastern and Western costume which she had worn on the desert, but the Princess would not hear of that. She must wear the finest gown and the smartest Paris hat that could be obtained in Cairo in order that Gordon might see her at her best.

"He may be a hero," said the Princess, "but he is a man, too, God bless him! and he'll want to see the woman he loves look lovely."

So the milliners and dressmakers were set to work immediately and bound by endless pledges.

"Of course they'll promise you the stars at noonday," said the Princess, "but if they don't come up to the scratch they get no money. Keep your cat hungry and she'll catch the rat, you know."

In due time the costume was ready, and when Helena had put it on—a close-fitting silver-gray robe and a a large black hat—the Princess stood off from her and said:

"Well, my moon, my sweet, my beauty, if he doesn't want to live a little longer after he has seen you in *that* he's not fit to be alive!"

But at the last moment Helena called for a thick, dark veil.

"I've no right to sap away his courage," she said, and the Princess, who had heard everything that Helena had to tell and had swung round to Gordon's side entirely, could say no more.

Hafiz came to take the ladies to the Citadel, and as he was leaving them at the gate to go to Gordon in his quarters, Helena gave him the letter she had written at Sakkara.

"Tell him I mean all I say—every word of it," she whispered.

The Court-Martial was held in one of the rooms of the palace of Mohammed Ali—up a wide stone staircase across a bare court, through a grained archway, beyond a great hall which in former days had seen vast assemblies, and past a door labelled "Minister of War," into a gorgeously decorated chamber, overlooking a garden, with its patch of green shut in by high stone walls. It had once been the harem of the great Pasha.

The room was already full when Helena and the Princess arrived, but places were found for them near to the door. This position suited Helena perfectly, but to the Princess it was a deep disappointment, and as a consequence nothing pleased her.

"All English and all soldiers! Not an Egyptian among

them," she said. "After what he has done for them, too! Ingrates! Excuse the word. That's what I call them."

At that moment Hafiz entered, and the Princess, touching him on the arm, said:

"Here, you come and sit on the other side of her and keep up her heart, the sweet one."

Hafiz did as he was told, and as soon as he was seated beside Helena he whispered:

"I've just left him."

"How is he?"

"Firm as a rock. He sent you a message."

"What is it?"

"Tell her," he said, "that great love conquers death."

"Ah!"

At the next moment Helena's hand and Hafiz's found each other in a fervent clasp, and sweetheart and foster-brother sat together so until the end of the inquiry.

Presently the judges of the Court entered and took their places at the table that had been prepared for them—one full colonel and four lieutenant-colonels of mature age, from different British regiments.

"They look all right, but white hairs are no proof of wisdom," muttered the Princess.

Then the accused was called, and amid breathless silence Gordon entered with a firm step, attended by the officer who had him in charge. His manner was calm, and though his face was pale almost to pallor, his expression betrayed neither fear nor bravado. His appearance made a deep impression, and the President told him to sit. At the same moment it was observed that the Sirdar came in by a door at the farther end of the room and took a seat immediately in front of him.

The Court was then sworn and the charge was read. It accused the prisoner of three offences under the Army Act: first, that being a person subject to military law, he had disobeyed the lawful command of a superior in such a way as to show a wilful disregard of authority (A. A., 9, 1); second, that he had been guilty of acts and conduct to the prejudice of good order and military discipline (A. A., 40);

third, that he had deserted his Majesty's service while on
active service (A. A., 12, 1ᵃ).

"He heard it all yesterday morning," whispered Hafiz to
Helena, whose nervous fingers were tightening about his
own.

The charges having been read out to the accused, he
was called upon to plead.

"Are you guilty or not guilty?" asked the President.

There was a moment of breathless silence, and then,
in a measured voice without a break or a tremor, Gordon
said:

"I do not wish to plead at all."

A subdued murmur passed through the room, and Hafiz
whispered again:

"He wanted to plead guilty and the Sirdar had all he
could do to prevent him."

"Enter a plea of 'Not guilty' on the record," said the
President.

Then, addressing Gordon, the President asked if he was
represented by counsel. Gordon shook his head. Did he
desire to conduct his own defence? Again Gordon shook
his head. The President conferred for a moment with other
members of the Court and then said:

"It is within the power of the Court to appoint a
properly-qualified person to act as counsel for the accused,
and in this case the Court desires to do so. Is there any
officer here, subject to military law, who wishes to undertake the task of Defender?"

In a moment it was plainly evident that the sympathies
of Gordon's brother officers were with him. Twenty men
in uniform had leaped to their feet and were holding up
their hands.

"Lord God, how they love him!" whispered Hafiz, and
Helena had to hold down her head lest she should be seen
to cry.

The Defender selected was a young captain of cavalry
who had brought a brilliant reputation from the Staff College, and in a moment he was in the midst of his duties.

"Does the accused desire a short adjournment of the

Court in order to instruct his Defender?" asked the President.

Once more Gordon, who had stood passively during these proceedings, shook his head, and then, without further preliminaries, the trial began. The prosecutor rose to make his opening address. He was an artillery officer of high reputation.

"He'll make it no worse than he can help," whispered Hafiz.

In simple words the prosecutor stated his case, confining himself to the briefest explanation of the facts he was about to prove, and then he called the first of his witnesses. This was the military secretary, Captain Graham, who had been present at the prisoner's interview with the late General Graves.

"Not a bad chap—he'll do no more than he must," whispered Hafiz.

Replying to the prosecutor's questions, the military secretary said that Gordon had refused to obey the order of his superior given personally by that officer in the execution of his office, and that his refusal had been deliberate and distinct and such as showed an intention to defy and resist authority.

"I object," said the young Defender, instantly, whereupon the officer of the Court who filled the post of Judge-Advocate submitted that the witness had drawn an inference which was no evidence and ought therefore to be struck out.

The Defender then rose to cross-examine the first witness, and in a few minutes the military secretary was made to prove, first, that the prisoner had tried to show his superior that the order he was giving him was contrary to humanity and likely to lead to an irreparable result; next that when executed by another officer, it *had* led to an irreparable result, including bloodshed and loss of life; and, finally, that after the order had been disobeyed by the accused the most inexcusable and disgraceful and even illegal and unsoldierly insults had been inflicted upon him by his General.

"That's true! My God, that's true! Illegal and un-soldierly!" whispered Hafiz, forgetting to whom he was talking; and Helena, in the riot of her dual love, for her father and for Gordon, could do nothing but hold down her head.

Then the prosecutor called Colonel Macdonald.

"A brute—he'll do his dam'dest," whispered Hafiz.

Amid scarcely suppressed murmurs Coloned Macdonald, speaking with manifest bitterness, proved the assault upon himself, and then went on to say that it was unprovoked, it was brutal, and it was conduct unbecoming the character of an officer and a gentleman.

"A lie like that has no legs to walk on," whispered Hafiz.

"No, but it has wings to fly with, though," said the Princess.

"Hush!" said Helena.

Again, like a flash of light, the young Defender had leapt up to protest against an inference which the Court alone was entitled to draw, and again the Judge-Advocate had submitted that the inference should be struck out.

Amid obvious excitement among the soldiers in Court, the Defender then rose to cross-exmine the second witness, and in a moment Macdonald's freckled face had become scarlet, as he was compelled to admit that, at the instant when he was assaulted, he had ordered the shooting of a boy (who fell dead from the walls of El Azhar), and was swearing at the boy's mother who was weeping over her son.

"Ah, his rage will be at the end of his nose now," whispered the Princess.

Finally the prosecutor called the officer who was temporarily commanding the Army of Occupation to show that the accused, after disobeying the order of his late General, had disappeared from Cairo and had not been seen since the riot at El Azhar until his capture two days before.

The evidence for the prosecution being now finished, the Court prepared itself for the defence. There was a certain appearance of anxious curiosity on the faces of the judges, and a tingling atmosphere of expectancy among the spectators.

Then came a surprise. The young Defender, who had been holding a whispered conference with Gordon, turned to the President and said:

"I regret to say that the accused has decided not to call any witnesses in defence."

"But perhaps," said the President, turning to Gordon, "you wish to give evidence for yourself. Do you?"

There was another moment of breathless silence, and then Gordon, after looking slowly round the room, in the direction of the place in which Helena sat with her head down, said calmly:

"No."

At that the murmuring among the spectators could hardly be suppressed. It was now plainly evident that Gordon's brother officers were with him to a man. They had been counting on an explanation that would at least palliate his conduct if it could not excuse his offences. The disappointment was deep, but the sympathy was still deeper. Could it be possible that Gordon *meant* to die?

"Lift up your veil, child," whispered the Princess, but Helena shook her head.

After the prosecutor had summed up his evidence, the Defender addressed the Court for the defence. He pleaded extenuating circumstances, first on the ground that the order given to the accused, though not in opposition to the established customs of the army or the laws of the land, was calculated to do irreparable injury and had done such injury, and next on the ground of outrageous provocation.

When the Defender had finished the President announced that his Excellency the Sirdar had volunteered to give evidence in proof of the prisoner's honourable record, and that the Court had decided to hear him.

The Sirdar was then sworn, and in strong, affecting, soldierly words, he said the accused had rendered great services to his country; that he had received many medals and distinctions; that he was as brave a man as ever stood under arms and one of the young officers who made an old soldier proud to belong to the British Army.

There is no company more easily moved to tears than a company of soldiers, and when the Sirdar sat down there was not a dry eye in that assembly of brave men.

After a pause the President announced that the Court would be closed to consider the finding, but in order to assist the judges in doing so it would be desirable that they should know more of the conditions under which the accused was arrested. Therefore the following persons would be asked to remain:

His Excellency the Sirdar,

The Commandant of Police,

Captain Hafiz Ahmed of the Egyptian Army.

Helena, with the other spectators, was passing out of the room when the Sirdar touched her on the shoulder and said, haltingly:

" Have you perhaps got— Can you trust me with those letters for a little while? "

By some impulse, hardly intelligible to herself, Helena had brought Gordon's letters with her, and after a moment's hesitation she took them out of her pocket and gave them to the Sirdar, saying, very faintly but very sweetly:

" Yes, I can trust them to you."

Then, with the Princess, she went out into the great hall and sat there on a window seat while the Court was closed. There was a sad and solemn expression in her face, and seeing this, even through her dark veil, the officers who were pacing to and fro, moved by that delicacy which is the nobler part of an English gentleman's reserve—respect for the intimacies that are sacred to another person—merely bowed to her as they passed.

The strain was great, for she knew what was going on behind the closed door of the Court-room. The judges were trying to find in the circumstances of Gordon's arrest some excuse for his desertion. She could see the Sirdar and Hafiz struggling to show that, however irregular and reprehensible from a disciplinary standpoint, Gordon's had been the higher patriotism that, coming back under those strange conditions and in that strange disguise, he had deliberately returned to die. And she could see the Court powerfully moved by that plea, yet helpless to take account of it.

Half an hour passed; an hour; nearly two hours, and then a young officer came up to tell Helena that the Court was about to reopen.

"I think—I hope they intend to recommend him to mercy," he said, blunderingly, and at the next moment he felt as if he would like to cut his tongue out. But Helena was unhurt. She held up her head for the first time that day, and, to the Princess's surprise, when they re-entered the room, and the officers made way for her, she pushed through to the front and took a seat, back to the wall, immediately before the Sirdar and almost face to face with Gordon.

There was that tense atmosphere in the Court which always precedes a sentence, but there was also a sort of humid air as if the angel of pity had passed through the place and softened it to tears.

Gordon was told to rise, and then the President, obviously affected, proceeded to address him. He might say at once that the judges regretted to find themselves unable to take account of the moral aspects of the case. Nothing but its military aspects came within their cognizance. That being so, the Court, notwithstanding the able and ingenious defence, could find no excuse for insubordination—the first duty of a soldier was to obey. In like manner they could find no excuse for a savage personal attack by an officer in uniform upon another officer in the exercise of his office— it was conduct to the prejudice of good order and military discipline. Finally, the Court could find no excuse for desertion—it was an act of great offence to the flag which a soldier was sworn to serve.

"Under these circumstances," continued the President, "the Court have no alternative but to find you guilty of the crimes with which you have been charged, and though it is within the Court's discretion to mitigate the penalty of your offences, they have decided, after anxious delibera-

tion, remembering the grave fact that the force in Egypt
is on active service, not to exercise that right, but out of
regard to your high record as a soldier and the great provocation which you certainly suffered, to content themselves
with recommending you to mercy, thus leaving the issue
to a higher authority. Therefore, whatever the result of
that recommendation, it is now my duty, my very painful
duty, to pronounce upon you, Charles Gordon Lord, the
full sentence prescribed by military law—death."

There was a solemn silence until the President's last
word was spoken, when all eyes turned toward Gordon.

He bore himself with absolute self-possession. There
was a slight quivering of the eyelids and a quick glint of
the steel-gray eyes in the direction of the opposite side
of the Court—nothing more.

Then a thrilling incident occurred. Helena, whose head
had been down was seen to rise in her seat, and to raise her
thick dark veil. One moment she stood there, back to the
wall, with her magnificent pale face all strength and courage,
looking steadily across at the prisoner as if nobody were
present in the room. Then as quietly as she had risen she
sank back to her place.

Oh, sublime power of love! Oh, pitiful impotence of
words! Everybody felt the thousand inexpressible things
which that simple act was meant to convey.

Gordon was the first to feel them, and when his guard
touched him on the arm he turned and went out with a
step that rang on the marble floor—firm as a rock.

As the Court broke up one of the officers was heard to
whisper hoarsely:

"She's worthy of him—what more is there to say?"

At the last moment the Sirdar turned to her and whispered:

"You must lend me these letters a little longer, my
dear. And remember what I said before—there's still the
Secretary of State, and there's still the King."

XIV

THE strength in Helena's face was not belied by the will behind it. Within an hour she was at work to save Gordon's life. Going to the officer who had acted as Judge-Advocate, she learned that the sentence would not go to headquarters for confirmation until after two days. In those two days she achieved wonders.

First, she approached the President of the Court and made sure that the recommendation to mercy should go to London by the same mail that carried the report of the proceedings.

Next, she visited the lieutenant-colonel of every regiment of the Army of Occupation and secured his signature and the signatures of his fellow-officers to a petition asking for the commutation of the sentence.

Two days and two nights she spent in this work, and everybody at Abbassiah and at the Citadel knew what the daughter of the late General was doing. A woman is irresistible to a soldier; a beautiful woman in distress is overpowering; all the army was in love with Helena; every soldier was her slave.

When, on the evening of the second day when she returned to the house of the Princess, she found three " Tommies," two in khaki and one in Highland plaid, waiting for her in the hall. They produced a thick packet of foolscap, badly disfigured by finger-prints and smelling strongly of tobacco, but containing four thousand signatures to her appeal.

Perhaps her greatest triumph, however, was with Colonel Macdonald.

" I must have his help, too," she said to the Princess, whereupon her Highness put her finger to her nose and answered:

" If you must, my heart, you must, but remember—when you want a dog's service address him as ' Sir.' "

She did. With a blush she told the Colonel (it was a dear divine falsehood) that Gordon had said he had had no personal animosity against him and was sorry if at a moment of undue excitement he had behaved badly.

The curmudgeon took the apology according to his kind, saying that in his opinion an officer who struck a brother officer publicly and before his men deserved to be shot or drummed out of the army, but still, if Colonel Lord was ashamed of what he had done—

Helena's eyes flashed with anger, but she compelled herself to smile and to say:

" He is, I assure you, he is." And before the big Highlander knew what he was doing he had written to headquarters at Helena's dictation, to say that inasmuch as his own quarrel with Colonel Gordon Lord had been composed, that count in the offence might, so far as he was concerned, be wiped out.

The sweet double-face told him how good and noble and even Christlike this was of him, and then, marching off with the letter, she said to herself, " The brute! "

Meantime, Hafiz, acting through his uncle the Chancellor, got the Ulema of El Azhar to send a message to the Foreign Minister saying, with many Eastern flourishes, that what General Graves had ordered Gordon to do, what his subordinate had done, was a deep injury to the religious susceptibilities of the Mohammedan people.

Besides this the Sirdar sent a secretary with Gordon's letters and reams of written explanations of his conduct to the permanent head of the War Office, a friend, a firm disciplinarian, but a man of strong humanity. Why had the prisoner refused to plead? Because he did not wish to accuse his dead General. Why had he made no explanation of his desertion and of his conduct at the time of his arrest? Because he did not wish to impeach his father. Why had he intercepted an order of the army? Because he had been inspired solely by a desire to prevent the tumultous effusion of blood, and he *had* prevented it.

Finally, as a technical point of the highest importance, could it be deemed that the troops in Egypt were on active service when there was no declaration to that effect such as Section 189 (2) of the Army Act required?

Within two days everything was done, and then there was nothing left but to await results. Helena wanted to go up to see Gordon, but she was afraid to do so. When sorrow is shared it is lessened, but suspense that is divided is increased.

After five days the Sirdar began to hear from London and to send his news to Helena over the telephone. The matter was to be submitted to his Majesty personally—had she any objection to the King seeing Gordon's letters? So very intimate? Well, what of that? The King was a good fellow, and there was nothing in the world that touched him so nearly as a beautiful woman, except a woman in love and in trouble.

Then came two days of grim, unbroken silence and then —a burst of great news.

In consideration of Colonel Lord's distinguished record as a soldier and his unblemished character as a man, out of regard to the obvious purity of his intentions and the undoubted fact that the order he disobeyed had led to irreparable results, remembering the great provocation he had received, and not forgetting the valuable services rendered by his father to England and to Egypt, the King had been graciously pleased to grant him a free pardon!

This coming first as a private message from the head of the War Office, threw the Sirdar into an ecstasy of joy. He called up the Consul-General immediately and repeated the glad words over the telephone, but no answer came back to him except the old man's audible breathing as it quivered through the wires.

Then he thought of Helena, but with a soldier's terror of tears in the eyes of a woman, even tears of joy, he decided to let Hafiz carry the news to her.

"Tell her to go up to the Citadel and break the good tidings to Gordon," he said, speaking to Egyptian headquarters.

Nothing loath, Hafiz went bounding along to the house of the Princess and blurted out his big message, expecting that it would be received with shouts of delight, but to his bewilderment Helena heard it with fear and trembling, and, becoming weak and womanish all at once, she seemed to be about to faint.

Hafiz, with proper masculine simplicity, became alarmed at this, but the Princess began to laugh.

"What!" she cried. "You, that have been as brave as a lion with her cub while your man's life has been in danger, to go mooing now—*now*—like a cow with a sick calf!"

Helena recovered herself after a moment, and then Hafiz delivered the Sirdar's mandate that she was to go up to the Citadel and break the good news to Gordon.

"But I daren't, I daren't," she said, still trembling.

"What!" cried the Princess again. "Not go and get the kisses and hugs that— Well, what a dunce I was to have that silver gray of yours made so tight about the waist! For two pins I would put on your black veil and go up myself and take all the young man has to give a woman."

Helena smiled (a watery smile) and declared she would go if Hafiz would go with her. Hafiz was ready, and in less than half an hour they were driving up to the Citadel in the Princess's carriage with the footmen and sais and eunuch which her Highness, for all her emancipation, thought necessary to female propriety in public.

Everything went well until they reached the fortress, and then, going up the stone staircase to Gordon's quarters, Helena began to tremble more than ever.

"Oh! Oh! I daren't! I must go home," she whispered.

"Lord, no, not now," said Hafiz. "Remember, up there is some one who thinks he is going to die, while here are we who know he isn't, and that life will be doubly sweet if it's you that take it back to him. Come, sister, come!"

"Give me your arm, then," said Helena, and, panting with emotion and perilously near to the edge of tears, she went up on shaking limbs to a door at which two soldiers, armed to the teeth, were standing on guard.

At that moment Gordon, in the officer's bright room which had been given to him as a cell, was leaning on the sill of the open window and looking steadfastly down at some object in the white city below. During the past six days he had known what was being done on his behalf, and the desire for life, which he had believed to be dead in him, had quickened to suspense and pain.

To ease both feelings he had smoked innumerable cigarettes and made pretence of reading the illustrated papers which his brother officers had poured in upon him, out of their otherwise dumb and helpless sympathy. But every few minutes of every day he had leaned out of the window to look first, with a certain pang, at the heavy-lidded house which contained his father; next, with a certain sense of tears, at a green spot covered with cypress trees which contained all that was left of his mother, and finally, with a certain yearning, at the trellised Eastern palace of the Princess Nazimah which contained Helena.

This is what he was doing at the moment when Helena and Hafiz were ascending the stairs, and just as he was asking himself for the hundredth time why Helena did not come to see him he heard his guard's gruff tones mingled with a woman's mellow voice.

A deep note among the soft ones sent all the blood in his body galloping to his heart, and turning round he saw the door of his room open and Helena herself on the threshold.

One moment she stood there, with her sweet, careworn face growing red in her passion of joy, and then she rushed at him and fell on his breast, throwing both arms about his neck, and crying:

"Such news, Gordon! Oh, my Gordon, I bring you such good, good news! Such news, dear! Such news, oh, such good, good news!"

Thus trying to tell her tidings at a breath, she told him nothing, but continued to laugh and sob and kiss and say what good news she brought him.

Yet words were needless, and before Hafiz, whose fat, wet face was shining like a round window on an April day, could whisper "the King's Pardon," Gordon, like the true lover he was, had said, and had meant it:

"But you bring me nothing so good as yourself, dearest —nothing!"

XV

Helena was with Gordon the following morning when one of the guard came in hurriedly and announced, amid gusts of breath, that the Consul-General was coming up-stairs.

Not without a certain nervousness Gordon rose to receive his father, but he met him at the door with both hands outstretched. The old man took one of them quietly, with the air of a person who was struggling hard to hold himself in check. He took Helena's hand also, and when she would have left the room he prevented her.

"No, no," he said, "sit down, my child, resume your seat."

It seemed to Gordon that his father looked whiter and feebler, yet even firmer of will than before, like a lion that had been shot and was dying hard. His lips were compressed as he took the chair which Gordon offered him, and when he spoke his voice was hard and a little bitter.

"First, let me give you good news," he said.

"Is it the pardon?" asked Gordon.

"No, something else—perhaps, in a sense, something better," said the old man.

He had received an unofficial message from the War Office to say that the King, taking no half-measures, in-tended to promote Gordon to the rank of Major-General and appoint him to the Command of the British Forces in Egypt.

Helena could hardly contain her joy at this fresh proof of good fortune, but Gordon made no demonstration. He watched the pained expression in the old man's face, and felt sure that something else was coming.

"It's a remarkable, perhaps unparalleled instance of clemency," continued the Consul-General, "and under the circumstances it may be said to open up as momen-tous a mission as was ever confided to a military com-mander."

"And you, father?" asked Gordon, not without an effort.

The old man laughed. A flush overspread his pale face for a moment. Then he said:

"I? Oh, I—I am dismissed."

"Dismissed?"

Gordon had gasped. Helena's lips had parted.

"That's what it comes to—stated in plain words and without diplomatic flourishes. True, I had sent in my resignation, but— The long and the short of it is that after a debate on the Address, and the carrying of an amendment, Downing Street has agreed that the time has come to associate the people of Egypt in the government of the country."

"Well, sir?"

"Well, as that is a policy against which I have always set my face, a policy I have considered premature, perhaps suicidal, the Secretary of State has cabled that, being unable to ask me to carry into effect a change that is repugnant to my principles, he is reluctantly compelled to accept my resignation."

Gordon could not speak, but again the old man tried to laugh.

"Of course the pill is gilded," he continued, clasping his blue-veined hands in front of his breast. "The Foreign Secretary told Parliament that my resignation (on the ground of age and ill health, naturally) was the heaviest blow that had fallen on English public life within living memory. He also said that while other methods might be necessary for the future, none could have been so good as mine in the past. And then the King——"

"Yes, father?"

A hard, half-ironical smile passed over the old man's face.

"The King has been graciously pleased to grant me an Earldom and even make me a Knight of the Garter."

There was a moment's painful silence, and then the Consul-General said:

"So I go home immediately."

"Immediately?"

"By to-night's train to take the P. & O. to-morrow," bowing over his clasped hands.

"To-morrow?"

"Why not? My secretaries can do without me. Why should I linger on a stage on which I am no longer a leading actor, but only a supernumerary? Better make my exit with what grace I can."

Under the semi-cynical tone Gordon could see his father's emotion. He found it impossible to utter a word.

"But I thought I would come up before going away and bring you the good news myself, though it is almost like a father who is deposed congratulating the son who is to take his place."

"Don't say that, sir," said Gordon.

"Why shouldn't I? And why should I gird at my fortune? It's strange, nevertheless, how history repeats itself. I came to Egypt to wipe out the misrule of Ismail Pasha, and now, like Ismail, I must leave my son behind me."

There was a moment of strained silence, and then:

"I have often wondered what took place at that secret meeting between Ismail and Tewfik, when we made the son Khedive and sent the father back to Constantinople. Now I think I know."

The old man's emotion was cutting deep. Gordon could scarcely bear to look at him.

"I wish you well, Gordon, and only hope these people may be more grateful to you than they have been to me. God grant it!"

Gordon could not speak.

"I confess I have no faith in the proposed change. I think all such concessions are so many sops to sedition. I also think that to have raised the masses of a subject race from abject misery to well-being, and then to allow them to fall back to their former condition, as they surely will, and to become the victims of the worst elements among themselves, is not only foolish but utterly wrong and wicked."

The old man rose, and in the intensity of his feelings began to pace to and fro.

"They talk about the despotism of the One-Man rule," he said. "What about the despotism of their Parliaments, their Congresses, their Reichstags—the worst despotisms in the world? Fools! Why can't they see that the difference between the democracy of Europe and America and the government proper to the ancient, slavish, and slow-moving civilisation of the East is fundamental?"

The old man's lips stiffened and then he said:

"But perhaps I am only an antiquated person, behind the new age and the new ideas. If so, I'm satisfied. I belong to the number of those who have always thought it the duty of great nations to carry the light of civilisation into dark continents, and I am not sorry to be left behind by the cranks who would legislate for all men alike. Pshaw! You might as well tailorise for all men alike, and put clothes of the same pattern on all mankind."

Again the old man laughed.

"It's part and parcel of the preposterous American doctrine that all men are born free and equal—the doctrine that made the United States enfranchise as well as emancipate their blacks. May the results be no worse in this case!"

There was another moment of strained silence, and then the Consul-General said:

"I suppose they'll say the man Ishmael has beaten me." He gave a contemptuous but almost inaudible laugh, and then added: "Let them; they're welcome; time will tell. Anyhow, I do not lament. When a man is old his useless life must burn itself out. That's only natural. And after all, I've seen too much of power to regret the loss of it."

Still Gordon could not speak. He was feeling how great his father was in his downfall, how brave, how proud, how splendid.

The old man walked to the window and looked out with fixed eyes. After a moment he turned back and said:

"All the same, Gordon, I am glad of what has happened for your sake—sincerely glad. You've not always been with me, but you've won, and I do not grudge you your victory. Indeed," he added, and here his voice trembled perceptibly, " I am a little proud of it. Yes, proud! An old man cannot be indifferent to the fact that his son has won the hearts of twelve millions of people, even though— even though *he* himself may have lost them."

Gordon's throat was hurting him and Helena's eyes were full of tears. The old man, too, was struggling to control his voice.

" You thought Nunehamism wasn't synonymous with patriotism. Perhaps you were right. You believed yourself to be the better Englishman of the two. I don't say you were not. And it may be that in her present mind England will think that one secret withheld from me has been revealed to you—namely, that an alien race can only be ruled by—by love. Yes, I'm glad for your sake, Gordon, and as for me—I leave myself to Time and Fate."

The old man's pride in his son's success was fighting hard with his own humiliation. After a while Gordon recovered strength enough to ask his father what he meant to do in England.

" Who can say? " answered the Consul-General, lifting one hand with a gesture of helplessness. " I have spent the best years of my life in Egypt. What is England to me now? Home? No, exile."

He had moved to the window again, and following the direction of his eyes Gordon could see that he was looking toward the cypress trees which shaded the English cemetery of Cairo.

A deep and profound silence ensued, and, feeling as if his mother's angel were passing through the room, Gordon dropped his head and tears leaped to his eyes.

It was the first time father and son had been together since the tenderest link that had bound them had been broken, but while both were thinking of this neither of them could trust himself to speak of it.

" Janet, your dream has come true! How happy you would have been! " thought the Consul-General, while Gordon, unable to unravel the intricacies of his emotions, was saying to himself, " Mother! My sweet mother! "

The last moment came and it was a very moving one. Up from some hidden depths of the old man's oceanic soul there came a certain joy. In spite of all that he in his blindness had done to prevent it, by the operation of the inscrutable powers that had controlled his destiny, the great hope of his life was about to be realised. Gordon and Helena had been brought together, and as he looked at them, standing side by side when they rose to bid farewell to him, the man so brave and fearless, the girl so fine and beautiful, he thought, with a thrill of the heart, that, whatever might happen to himself—old, worn-out, fallen perhaps, his life ended—yet would his line go on in the time to come, pure, clean and strong, and the name of Nuneham be written high in the history of his country.

Holding out a hand to each, he looked steadily into their faces for a moment, while he said his silent good-bye. Not a word, not the quiver of an eyelid. It was the English gentleman coming out top in the end, firm, stern, heroic.

Before Gordon and Helena seemed to be aware of it, the old man was gone, and they heard the rumble of the wheels of his carriage as it passed out of the courtyard.

XVI

At nightfall the great Proconsul left Cairo. He knew that all day long the telegraphic agencies had been busy with messages from London about his resignation. He also knew that after the first thunderclap of surprise the Egyptian population had concluded that he had been recalled —recalled in disgrace and at the petition of the Khedive to the King.

It did not take him long to prepare for his departure. In the course of an hour Ibrahim was able to pack up the few personal effects—how few!—which, during the longest residence, gather about the house of a servant of the State.

Perhaps the acutest of his feelings on leaving Egypt came to him as he drove in a closed carriage out of the grounds of the Agency and looked up for the last time at the windows of the room that used to be occupied by his wife. At that moment he felt something of the dumb desolation which rolls over the strongest souls when, after a lifetime of comradeship, the asundering comes and they long for the voice that is still.

Poor Janet! He must leave all that remained of her behind him under the tall cypress trees on the edge of the Nile. Yet no, not all, for he was carrying away the better part of her—her pure soul and saintly memory—within him. None the less, that moment of parting brought the old man nearer than he had ever been to the sense of tears in mortal things.

The Sirdar had accompanied him, but though the fact of his intended departure had become known, having been announced in all the evening papers, there was nobody at the station to bid adieu to him, not a member of the Khedive's *entourage;* not one of the Egyptian Ministers, and even none of the Advisers and Under-Secretaries whom he had himself created.

Never had there lived a more self-centred and self-sufficient man, but this fact cut him to the quick. He had done what he believed to be his duty in Egypt, and feeling that he was neglected and forgotten at the end, the ingratitude of those whom he had served went like poison into his soul.

To escape from the sense of it he began to talk with a bitter raillery which in a weaker man would have expressed itself in tears, and seemed indeed to *have* tears—glittering, frozen tears—behind it.

"Do you know, my dear Reg," he said, "I feel to-night as if I might be another incarnation of your friend Pontius Pilate. Like him, I am being withdrawn, you see, and apparently for the same reason. And—who knows?—perhaps like him, too, I am destined to earn the maledictions of mankind."

The Sirdar found the old man's irony intensely affecting, and therefore he made no protest.

"Well, I'm not ashamed of the comparison, if it means that against all forms of anarchy I have belonged to the party of order, though of course there will be some wise heads that will see the finger of heaven in what has happened."

The strong man, with his fortunes sunk to zero, was defiant to the very edge and last hour of calamity. But standing on the platform by the door of the compartment that had been reserved for him, he looked round at length and said—all his irony, all his raillery suddenly gone:

"Reg, I have given forty years of my life to these people, and there is not one of them to see me off."

The Sirdar tried his best to cheer him, saying:

"England remembers, though, and if—" but the old man looked into his face and his next words died on his lips.

The engine was getting up steam, and its rhythmic throb was shaking the glass roof overhead when Gordon and Hafiz, wearing their military great-coats, came up the platform. They had carefully timed it to arrive at the last moment. A gleam of light came into the father's face at the sight of his son. Gordon stepped up, Hafiz fell back. Lord Nuneham entered the carriage.

"Well, good-bye, old friend," said the old man, shaking hands warmly with the Sirdar. "I may see you again—in my exile in England, you know."

Then he turned to Gordon and took his outstretched hand. Father and son stood face to face for the last time. Not a word was spoken. There was a long, firm, quivering hand-clasp—and that was all. At the next moment the train was gone.

The Sirdar, who had stood watching it until it disappeared, then turned to Gordon, and, thinking of the England the Consul-General had loved, the England he had held high, he said, speaking of him as if he were already dead:

"After all, my boy, your father was one of the great Englishmen."

Gordon could not answer him, and after a while they shook hands and separated. The two young soldiers walked back to the Citadel through the native streets. The "Nights of the Prophet" were nearly over and the illuminations were being put out.

38

Hafiz talked about the Khedive—he had just arrived at Khubbah. Then about Ishmael—the Prophet had shut himself up in the Chancellor's house and was permitting nobody to see him.

"His Highness has asked Ishmael to be Imam to-morrow morning, but it is thought that he is ill—it is even whispered that he is going mad," said Hafiz.

Gordon did not speak until they reached the foot of the hill. Then he said:

"I must go up and lie down. Good-night, old fellow! God bless you!"

XVII

HALF an hour before, Gordon's guard, now transformed into his soldier servant, had been startled by the appearance of an Egyptian, wearing the flowing white robes of a Sheikh and asking in almost faultless English for Colonel Lord.

"The Colonel has gone to the station to see his Lordship off to England, but I'm expecting him back presently," said the orderly.

"I'll wait," said the Sheikh, and the orderly showed him into Gordon's room.

"Looks like a bloomin' death's head! Wonder if he's the bloomin' Prophet they're jawrin' about!"

Since coming into Cairo Ishmael had been a prey to thoughts that were indeed akin to madness. Perhaps he was seized by one of those nervous maladies in which a man no longer belongs to himself. Certainly he suffered the pangs of heart and brain which come only to the purest and most spiritual souls in their darkest hours and seem to make it literally true that their tortured spirits descend into hell.

Now that his anxiety for his followers was relaxed and their hopes had in some measure been realised, his mind swung back to the sorrowful decay and ruin that had fallen upon himself. It was no longer the shame of the prophet but the bereavement of the man that tormented him. His lacerated heart left him no power of thinking or feeling anything but the loss of Helena.

Again he saw her beaming eyes, her long black lashes, and her smiling mouth. Again he heard her voice and again the sweet perfume of her presence seemed to be about him. That all this was lost to him forever, that henceforth he had to put away from him all the sweetness, all the beauty, all the tenderness of a woman's life linked with his, brought him a paroxysm of pain in which it seemed as if his heart would break and die.

He recalled the promises he had made to himself, of taking up the life of a man when his work was done. His work was done now—in some sort ended at all events—but the prize he had promised himself had been snatched away. She was gone, she who had been all his joy. An impassable gulf divided them. The infinite radiance of hope and love that was to have crowned his restless and stormy life had disappeared. Henceforth he must walk through the world alone.

"O God! can it be?" he asked himself, with the startled agony of one who awakes from a single-pillowed sleep and remembers that he is bereaved.

If anything had been necessary to make his position intolerable, it came with the thought that all this was due to the treachery of the man he had loved and trusted, the man he had believed to be his friend and brother, the one being, besides the woman, who had gone to his heart of hearts. The Rani had confessed to him that she loved "Omar," and notwithstanding that all his life he had struggled to liberate himself from the prejudices of his race, yet now, in the melancholy broodings of his Eastern brain, he could not escape from the conclusion that the only love possible between a man and the wife of another was guilty love.

When he thought of that, both body and soul seemed to be afire, and he became conscious of a feeling about "Omar," which he had never experienced before toward any human creature—a feeling of furious and inextinguishable hatred.

He began to be afraid of himself, and just as a dog will shun its kind and hide itself from sight when it feels the poison of madness working in its blood, so Ishmael under the secret trouble which he dared reveal to none, shut himself up in his sleeping room in the old Chancellor's house.

It was a small and silent chamber at the back, overlooking a little paved courtyard containing a well and bounded by a very high wall that shut off sight and sound of the city outside. Once a day an old man in a blue galabeah came into the court to draw water, and twice a day a servant of the Sheikh's came into the room with food. Save for these two, and the old Chancellor himself at intervals, Ishmael saw no one for nine days, and in the solitude and semi-darkness of his self-imposed prison a hundred phantoms were bred in his distempered brain.

On the second day after his retirement the Chancellor came to tell him that his emissary, his missionary, "Omar Benani," had been identified on his arrest, that in his true character as Colonel Lord he was to be tried by his fellow-officers for his supposed offences as a soldier at the time of the assault on El Azhar and that the only sentence that could possibly be passed upon him would be death. At this news, which the Chancellor delivered with a sad face, Ishmael felt a fierce but secret joy.

"God's arm is long," he told himself. "He allowed the man to escape while his aims were good, but now he is going to punish him for his treachery and deceit."

Three days afterward, the old Chancellor came again to say that Colonel Lord had been tried and condemned to death, as everybody had foreseen and expected, but nevertheless the sympathy of all men was with him, because he was seen to have acted from the noblest motives, withstanding his own father for what he believed to be the right, and exposing himself to the charge of being a bad son and a bad patriot in order to prevent bloodshed; that he had indeed prevented bloodshed by preventing a collision of the British and Native armies, that it had been

by his efforts that the pilgrimage had been able to enter
Cairo in peace; and that in recognition of the great sacrifice made by the Christian soldier for the love of humanity, the Ulema were joining with others in petitioning his
King to pardon him.

At this news a chill came over Ishmael. His heart grew
cold as stone, and when the Chancellor was gone, he found
himself praying:

"Forbid it, O God, forbid it! Let not Thy justice be
taken out of Thine awful hands!"

Four days later the old Chancellor came yet again to say
that the King's pardon had been granted; that Colonel Lord
was free; that the people were rejoicing; that everybody attributed the happy issue of the Christian's case mainly to
zealous efforts on his behalf of the woman who loved him,
the daughter of the dead General whose unwise command
had been the cause of all his trouble; and finally that it
was expected that these two would soon heal their family
feud by marriage.

At this news Ishmael's tortured heart was aflame and his
brain was reeling. The thought that "Omar" was not to
be punished, that he was to be honoured, that he was to be
made happy, filled him with passions never felt before. Behind the strongest and most spiritual soul there lurks a
wild beast that seems to be ever waiting to destroy it, and
in the torment of Ishmael's heart the thought came to him
that as his earthly judges were permitting the guilty one to
escape God called on *him* to punish the man.

Irresistible as the thought was it brought a feeling of
indescribable dread. "I must be going mad," he told himself, remembering how he had spent his life in the cause
of peace. All day long he fought against a hatred that was
now so fierce that it seemed as if death alone could satisfy
it. His soul wrestled with it, baffled for life against it,
and at length conquered it, and he rose from his knees
saying to himself:

"No; vengeance belongs to God! When did He ask for
my hand to execute it?"

But the compulsion of great passion was driving him

on, and after dismissing the thought of his own wrongs
he began to think of the Rani's. Where was she now?
What had become of her? He dared not ask. Ashamed,
humiliated, abased, he had become so sensitive to pain on
the subject of the woman whom he had betrothed, the woman who had betrayed him, the woman he still loved in spite
of everything, that he was even afraid that some one might
speak of her.

But in the light of what the Chancellor had said about
the daughter of the General, he pictured the Rani as a rejected and abandoned woman. This thought was at first
so painful that it deprived him of the free use of his
faculties. He could not see anything plainly. His mind
was a battlefield of confused sights, half hidden in clouds
of smoke. That after all the Rani had sacrificed for
"Omar"—her husband, her happiness and her honour
—she should be cast aside for another—this was maddening.

He asked himself what he was to do. Find her and
take her back? Impossible! Her heart was gone from him.
She would continue to love the other man whatever he
might do to her. That was the way of all women—Allah
pity and bless them!

Then a flash of illumination came to him in the long
interval of his darkness. He would liberate the Rani, *and
the man she loved should marry her!* No matter if she belonged to another race—he should marry her! No matter
if she belonged to another faith—he should marry her!
And as for himself—*his sacrifice should be his revenge!*

"Yes, that shall be my revenge," he thought.

This, in the wild fire of his heart and brain, was the
thought with which Ishmael had come to Gordon's door, and
being shown into the soldier's room he sat for some time
without looking about him. Then raising his eyes and
gazing round the bare apartment, with its simple bed, its
table, its shelves of military boots, stirrups and swords and
rifles, he saw on the desk under the lamp a large photograph in a frame.

It was the photograph of a woman in Western costume,

and he told himself in an instant who the woman was—
she was the daughter of the General who was dead.

He remembered that he had heard of her before and that
he had even spoken about her to her father when he came
to warn the General that the order he was giving to Colonel
Lord would lead to the injury of England in Egypt and
the ruin of his own happiness. From that day to this he
had never once thought of the girl, but now, recalling what
the old Chancellor had said of her devotion, her fidelity,
her loyalty to the man she loved, he turned his eyes from
her picture lest the sight of it should touch him with tenderness and make harder the duty he had come to do.

"No, I will not look at it," he told himself, with the
simplicity of a sick child.

Trying to avoid the softening effects of the photograph
under the lamp, he saw another on the table by his side
and yet another on the wall. They were all pictures of
the same woman, and, hastily as he glanced at them, there
was something in the face of each that kindled a light in
his memory. Was it only a part of his haunting torment
that, in spite of the Western costume that obscured the
woman in the photographs, her brilliant, beaming eyes were
the eyes of the Rani?

A wave of indescribable tenderness broke over him for
a moment, an odor of perfume, an atmosphere of sweetness
and delicacy and charm, and then, telling himself that all
this was gone from him for ever and that every woman's
face would henceforth remind him of her whom he had
lost, the hatred in his heart against Gordon gave him the
pain of an open wound.

"O God, let me forget, let me forget!" he prayed.

Then suddenly, while he was in the tempest of these
contrary emotions, which were whirling like hot sand in
a sandstorm about his brain, he heard a footstep on the
stairs, followed by a voice outside the door. It was the
voice of Colonel Lord's soldier-servant, and he was telling
his master who was within—an Arab, a Sheikh, in white
robes and a turban.

"He's coming! He's here," thought Ishmael.

With choking throat and throbbing heart he rose to his feet and stood waiting. At the next moment the door was thrown open and the man he had come to meet was in the room.

XVIII

WITH all his heart occupied by thoughts of his father, Gordon had hardly listened to what Hafiz had been saying about Ishmael, but walking up the hill to the Citadel he began to think of him and of Helena and of the bond of the betrothal which still bound them together.

"Until that is broken there can be nothing between her and me," he told himself, and this was the thought in his mind at the moment when he reached his quarters and his servant told him who was waiting within.

"Ishmael Ameer! Is it you?" he cried as he burst the door open, and stepping eagerly, cheerfully, almost joyfully forward, he stretched out his hand.

But Ishmael drew back, and then Gordon saw that his eyes were swollen as if by sleeplessness, that his lips were white, that his cheeks were terribly pale, and that the expression of his face was shocking.

"Why, what is this? Are you ill?" he asked.

"Omar Benani," said Ishmael, "you and I are alone, and only God is our witness. I have something to say to you. Let us sit."

He spoke in a low, tremulous tone, rather with his breath than with his voice, and Gordon, after looking at him for an instant, and seeing the smouldering fire of madness that was in the man's face, threw off his great-coat and sat down.

There was a moment in which neither spoke, and then Ishmael, still speaking in a scarcely audible voice, said:

"Omar Benani, I am a son of the Beni Azra. Honour is our watchword. When a traveller in the Libyan Desert, tired and weary, seeks the tent of one of my people, the Master takes him in. He makes him free of all that he possesses. Sometimes he sends the stranger into the harem itself that the women may wash his feet. He leaves him there to rest and to sleep. He puts his faith, his honour, the most precious thing God has given him, into his hands. But," said Ishmael, with suppressed fire flashing in his eyes, "if the stranger should ever wrong that harem, if he should ever betray the trust reposed in him, no matter who he is or where he flies to, the Master will follow him and *kill him!*"

Involuntarily, seeing the error that Ishmael had fallen into, Gordon rose to his feet, whereupon Ishmael, mistaking the gesture, held up his hand.

"No," he said, "not that! I have not come to do that. I put *my* honour in *your* hands, Omar Benani, I made you free of my family. Could I have done more? You were my brother, yet you outraged the sacred rights of brotherhood. You tore open the secret chamber of my heart. You deceived me and robbed me and betrayed me and you are a traitor. But I am not here to avenge myself. Sit, sit. I will tell you what I have come for."

Breathless and bewildered, Gordon sat again, and after another moment of silence Ishmael said:

"Omar Benani, there is one who has sacrificed everything for you. She has broken her vows for you, sinned for you, suffered for you. That woman is my wife and by all the rights of a husband I could hold her. But her heart is yours and therefore—therefore *I intend to give her up.*"

Involuntarily Gordon rose to his feet again, and again Ishmael held up his hand.

"But if I liberate her," he said, "if I divorce her, *you* must marry her. *That* is what I have come to say."

Utterly amazed and dumfounded, Gordon could not at first find words to speak, whereupon Ishmael, mistaking his silence, said:

"You need not be afraid of scandal. My people know something about the letter that was sent into Cairo, but neither my people nor yours know anything of the motives that inspired it. Therefore nobody except ourselves will understand the reason for what is done."

He paused as if waiting for a reply, and then said in a voice that quavered with emotion:

"Can it be possible that you hesitate? Do you suppose I am offering to you what I do not wish to keep for myself? I tell you that if that poor girl could say that her feeling for me was the same as before you came between us— But no, that is impossible! God, who is on high, looks down on what I am doing, and He knows that it is right."

Gordon, still speechless with astonishment, twisted about to the desk, which was behind him, and stretched out his hand as if with the intention of taking up the photograph, but at that action Ishmael, once more mistaking his meaning, flashed out on him in a blaze of passion.

"Don't tell me you cannot do it. You must and you shall! No matter what pledges you may have made—you shall marry her. No matter if she is of another race and faith—you shall marry her. She may be an outcast now, but you shall find her and save her. Or else," he cried, in a thundering voice, rising to his feet and lifting both arms above Gordon's head with a terrible dignity, "the justice of God shall overtake you, His hand shall smite you, his wrath shall hurl you down."

Seeing that all the wild blood of the man's race was aflame, Gordon leaped up, and laying hold of Ishmael's upraised arms he brought them, by a swift wrench, down to his sides.

The two men were then face to face, the Arab with his dusky cheeks and flashing black eyes, the Englishman with his glittering gray eyes and lips set firm as steel. There was another moment of silence while they stood together so, and then Gordon, liberating Ishmael's arms, said, in a commanding voice:

"I have listened to you. Now you shall listen to me. Sit down."

More than the strength of Gordon's muscles the unblanched look in his face compelled Ishmael to obey. Then Gordon said:

"You believe you have been deceived and wronged, and

you *have* been deceived and wronged, but not in the way you think. The time has come for you to learn the truth —the whole truth. You shall learn it now. Look at this," he said, snatching up the photograph from the desk and holding it out to Ishmael.

Ishmael tried to push the photograph away.

"Look at it, I say. Do you know who that is?"

At the next moment Ishmael was trembling in every limb, and without voice, almost without breath, he was stammering, as he held the photograph in his hand:

"The Rani?"

"Yes, and no," said Gordon. "That is the daughter of our late General."

It seemed to Ishmael that Gordon had said something, but he tried in vain to realise what it was.

"Tell me," he stammered, "tell me."

Then rapidly but forcibly Gordon told him Helena's story, beginning with the day on which Ishmael came to the Citadel—how she had concluded, not without reason, that he had killed her father, he being the last person to be seen with him alive, and how, finding that the law and the government were powerless to punish him, she had determined to avenge her father's death herself.

Ishmael listened with mouth open, fixing on Gordon a bewildered eye.

"Was that why she came to Khartoum?" he asked.

"Yes."

"Why she prompted me to come into Cairo?"

"Yes."

"Why she wrote that letter?"

"Yes."

Overwhelmed with the terrible enlightenment, Ishmael fumbled his beads and muttered, "Allah! Allah!"

Then Gordon told his own story—how he, too, acting under the impulse of an awful error, had fled to the Soudan, leaving an evil name behind him rather than kill his dear ones by the revelation of what he believed to be the truth; how, finding the pit that had been dug for the innocent man, he had thought it his duty as the guilty one

to step into it himself; and how finally being appeased on
that point, he had determined to come into Cairo in Ishmael's place in order to save both him from the sure consequences of his determined fanaticism and his father from
the certain ruin that must follow upon the work of liars
and intriguers.

By this time Ishmael was no longer pale but pallid.
His lips were trembling, his heart was beating audibly.
Again without voice, almost without breath, he stam-
mered:

"When you offered to take my place you knew that the
Rani—Helena—had sent that letter?"

Gordon bowed without speaking.

"You knew, too, that you might be coming to your
death?"

Once more Gordon bowed his head.

"Coming to your death that I—that I might live?"

Gordon stood silent and motionless.

"Allah! Allah!" mumbled Ishmael, who was now
scarcely able to hear or see.

Last of all Gordon returned to the story of Helena,
showing how she had suffered for the impulse of vengeance
that had taken possession of her; how she had wanted to
fly from Ishmael's camp but had remained there in the hope
of helping to save his people, and how at length she *had*
saved them by going to the Consul-General to prove that
the pilgrims were not an armed force, and by ordering the
light that had led them into the city.

Ishmael was deeply moved. With an effort he said:

"Then—then she was yours from the first! And while
I hated you because I thought you had come between us,
it was really I—I who—Allah! Allah!"

Gordon having finished, a silence ensued, and then Ishmael, looking at the photograph which was still in his
trembling hands, said in a pitiful voice:

"God sees all, and when He tears the scales from our
eyes—what are we? The children of one father fighting
in the dark!"

Then he rose to his feet, a broken man, and approaching

Gordon he tried to kneel to him, but in a moment Gordon had prevented him and was holding out his hand.

Nervously, timidly, reluctantly, he took it and said, in a voice that had almost gone:

"God will reward thee for this, my brother—for kissing the hand of him who came to smite thy face."

With that he turned and staggered toward the door. Gordon opened it and at the same moment called to his servant:

"Orderly, show the Sheikh to the gate, please."

"Yes, Colonel."

"No, I beg of you, no," said Ishmael, and, while Gordon stood watching him, he went heavily down the stairs.

XIX

THAT night at the house of the Chancellor of El Azhar Ishmael was missing. Owing to the state of his health the greatest anxiety was experienced and half the professors and teachers of the University were sent out to search. They scoured the city until morning without finding the slightest trace of him. Then the servant who had attended upon him remembered that shortly before his disappearance he had asked if the English Colonel who had lately been pardoned by his King still lived on the Citadel.

This led to the discovery of his whereabouts, and to some knowledge of his movements. On leaving Gordon's quarters he had crossed the courtyard of the fortress to the mosque of Mohammed Ali. It was then dark and only the Sheikh in charge had seen him when after making his ablutions he entered by the holy door.

It was certain that he had spent the entire night in the mosque. The muezzin going up to the minaret at midnight had seen a white figure kneeling before the Kibleh. Afterward, when traditions began to gather about Ishmael's name, the man declared that he saw a celestial light descending upon the White Prophet as of an angel hovering

over him. There was a new moon that night, and perhaps
its rays came down from the little window that looks
toward Mecca.

The muezzin also said that at sunrise when he went up
to the minaret again the Prophet was still there, and that
an infinite radiance was then around him as of a multitude
of angels in red and blue and gold. There are many stained
glass windows in the mosque of Mohammed Ali and perhaps the rising sun was shining through them.

Certainly Ishmael was kneeling before the Kibleh at
eleven o'clock in the morning when the people began to
gather for prayers. It was Friday and the last of the days
kept in honour of the birthday of the Prophet, therefore
there was a great congregation.

The Khedive was present. He had come early, with
his customary bodyguard, and had taken his usual place
in the front row close under the pulpit. The carpeted floor
of the mosque was densely crowded. Rows on rows of men
wearing tarbooshes and turbans and sitting on their
haunches extended to the great door. The gallery was full
of women, most of them veiled, but some of them with uncovered faces.

The sun, which was hot, shone through the jewelled windows and cast a glory like that of rubies and sapphires on
the alabaster pillars and glistening marble walls. Three
muezzins chanted the call to prayers, two from the minarets facing toward the city, the other from the minaret
overlooking the inner square of the Citadel, where a British
sentinel in khaki paced to and fro.

While the congregation assembled, one of the Readers
of the mosque, seated in a reading desk in the middle, read
prayers from the Koran in a slow, sonorous voice, and was
answered by rather drowsy cries of "Allah! Allah!" But
there was a moment of keen expectancy, and the men on
the floor rose to their feet, when the voice of the muezzin
ceased and the Reader cried:

"God is Most Great! God is Most Great! There is no
god but God. Mohammed is his Prophet. Listen to the
preacher."

Then it was seen that the white figure that had been prostrate before the Kibleh had risen and was approaching the pulpit. People tried to kiss his hand as he passed, and it was noticed that the Khedive put his lips to the fringe of the Imam's caftan.

Taking the wooden sword from the attendant, Ishmael ascended the pulpit steps. When he had reached the top of them he was in the full stream of the sunlight and for the first time his face was clearly seen.

His cheeks were hollow and very pale; his lips were bloodless; his black eyes were heavy and sunken, and his whole appearance was that of a man who had passed through a night of sleepless suffering. Even at sight of him and before he had spoken the congregation were deeply moved.

"Peace be upon you, oh, children of the Compassionate!" he began, and the people answered according to custom:

"On you be peace, oh, servant of Allah!"

Then the people sat and, sitting himself, Ishmael began to preach.

It was said afterward that he had never before spoken with so much emotion or so deeply moved his hearers; that he was like one who was speaking out of the night-long travail of his soul; and that his words, which were often tumultuous and incoherent, were not like sentences spoken to listeners, but like the secrets of a suffering heart uttering themselves aloud.

Beginning in a low, tired voice, that would barely have reached the limits of the mosque but for the breathlessness of the people, he said that God had brought them to a new stage in the progress of humanity. Islam was rising out of the corruption of ages. Egypt was having a new birth of freedom. God had whitened their faces before the world and in His wisdom He had willed it that the oldest of the nations should not perish from the earth.

"Ameen! Ameen!" replied a hundred vehement voices, whereupon Ishmael rose from his seat and raised his arm.

It was an hour of glory, but let them not be vainglorious. Let them not think that with their puny hands they had won these triumphs. Allah alone did all.

"Beware of boasting," he cried; "it is the strong drink of ignorance. Beware of them that would tell you that by any act of yours you have humbled the pride or lowered the strength of the great nation under whose arm we live. Only God has changed its heart. He has given it to see that the true welfare of a people is moral, not material. And now, steadily, calmly, out of the spirit that has always inspired its laws, its traditions and its faith, it shows us mercy and justice."

"Ameen! Ameen!" came again, but less vehemently than before.

Then speaking of Gordon without naming him, Ishmael reminded his people that some of the great nation's own sons had helped them.

"One there is who has been our warmest friend," he cried. "To him, the pure of heart, the high of soul, although he is a soldier and a great one, may Peace herself award the crown of life! Christian he may be, but may God place His benediction upon him to all eternity. May the God of the East bless him! May the God of the West bless him! May his name be inscribed with blessings from the Koran on the walls of every mosque!"

This reference, plainly understood by all, was received with loud and ringing shouts of "Allah! Allah!"

Then Ishmael's sermon took a new direction. For thirteen centuries the children of men, forgetting their prophets, Mohammed and Jesus and Moses, had been given over to idolatry. They had worshipped a god of their own fashioning. That god was gold. Its temples were great cities given up to material pursuits, and under them were the dead souls of millions of human beings. Its altars were vast armies which spilled the rivers of blood which had to be sacrificed to its lust. As men had become rich they had become barbarous, as nations had become great they had become pagan. Islam and Christianity alike had had to fight against some of the powers of darkness which called themselves civilisation and progress. But a new era had begun and the human heart was raising its face to God.

"Once again a voice has gone out from Mecca, from Nazareth, from Jerusalem, saying 'There is no god but God.' Once again a voice has gone out from the desert, crying, 'Thou shalt have no other god but Me!'"

At this the people were carried out of themselves with excitement, and loud shouts again rang through the mosque.

Then Ishmael spoke of the future. The world had been in labour, in the throes of a new birth, but the end was not yet. Had he promised them that the Kingdom of Heaven would come when they entered Cairo? Then let him bend his knee in humility and ask pardon of the Merciful. Had he said the Redeemer would appear? Let him fall on his face before God. Not yet! Not yet!

"But," he cried, leaning out of the pulpit, with a look of inspiration in his upraised eyes, "I see a time coming when the worship of wealth will cease; when the governments of the nations will realise that man does not live by bread alone; when the children of men will see that the things of the spirit are the only true realities, worth more than much gold and many diamonds and not to be bartered away for the shows of life; when the scourge of war will pass away; when divisions of faith will be no more known; when all men, whether black or white, will be brothers; and in the larger destiny of the human race the world will be One."

"That time is near, oh, brothers," cried Ishmael, "and many who are with us to-day will live to witness it."

"You, Master, you!" cried a voice from below, whereupon Ishmael paused for a perceptible moment, and then said in a sadder voice:

"No, with the eyes of the body I shall not see that time."

Loud shouts of affectionate protest came from the people.

"God forbid it!" they cried.

"God *has* forbidden it," said Ishmael. "I pass out of your lives from this day forward. Our paths part. You will see me no more."

39

Again came loud shouts of protest—not unusual in a mosque—with voices calling on Ishmael to remain and lead the people.

"My work here is done," he answered. "The little that God gave me to do is finished. And now he calls me away."

"No, no," cried the people.

"Yes, yes," replied Ishmael, and then in simple, touching words he told them the story of the Prophet Moses—how by reason of his sin he was forbidden to enter the Promised Land.

"Many of us have our promised land which we may never enter," he said. "This is mine, and here I may not stay."

The protests of the people ceased; they listened without breathing.

"Yet Moses was taken up into a high mountain and from there he saw what lay before his people, and from a high mountain of my soul I see the Promised Land which lies before you. But to me a voice has come which says, 'Enter thou not!'"

The people were now deeply moved.

"We are all sinners," Ishmael continued.

"Not thou, O Master!" cried several voices at once.

"Yes, I more than any other, for I have sinned against you and against the Merciful."

Then raising his arms as if in blessing he cried:

"Oh, slaves of God, be brothers one to another! If you think of me when I am gone, think of me as of one who saw the coming of the Kingdom of Heaven on earth as plainly as his eyes behold you now. If I leave you I leave this hope, this comforter, behind me. Think that Azrael, the angel of death, has spread his wings over the desert track that hides me from your eyes. But pray for me—pray for me with the sinner's prayer, the sinner's cry."

Then in deep, tremulous tones which seemed to be the inner voice of the whole of his being, he cried:

"Oh, thou who knowest every heart and hearest every cry, look down and hearken to me now! One sole plea I make—my need of Thee! One only hope I have—to stand at Thy mercy-gate and knock! Penitent, I kneel at Thy feet! Suppliant, I stretch forth my hands! Save me, O God, from every ill!"

The words of the prayer were familiar to everybody in the mosque, but so deep was their effect as Ishmael repeated them, in his trembling, throbbing voice, that it seemed as if nobody present had ever heard them before.

The emotion of the people was now very great. "Allah!" "Allah!" "Allah!" they cried and they prostrated themselves with their faces to the floor.

When the cold, slow, sonorous voice of the Reader began again, and the vast congregation raised their heads, the pulpit was empty and Ishmael was gone.

XX

MEANTIME the General's house on the edge of the ramparts was being made ready for its new tenant. Fatimah, Ibrahim and Mosie, with a small army of Arab servants, had been there since early morning, washing, dusting, and altering the position of furniture.

Toward noon the Princess had arrived in her carriage, which, with her customary retinue of gorgeously appareled black attendants, was now standing by the garden gate. Helena had come with her, but for the first time in her life she was utterly weak and helpless. Just as a nervous collapse may follow upon a nervous strain, so a collapse of character may come after prolonged exercise of will. Something of this kind was happening to Helena, who stood by the window in the General's office, looking down at the city and running her fingers along the hem of her handkerchief, while the Princess, bustling about, laughed at her and rallied her.

"Goodness me, girl, you used to have some blood in your veins, but now—*Mon Dieu!* To think of you who went down *there* and did *that*, and used to drive a motor-car through the traffic as calmly as if it had been a go-cart, trembling and jerking as if you had got the jumps!"

Meantime, the Princess herself, full of energy, was ordering the servants about, and by a hundred little changes was giving to the General's office a look that almost obliterated its former appearance.

"We'll have the desk here and the sofa there—what do you say to the sofa there, my sweet?"

"Hadn't you better ask Gordon himself, Princess?" asked Helena.

"But the man isn't here, and how can I—never mind, leave them where they are, Ibrahim. And now for the pictures—nothing makes a room look so fresh as a lot of pictures."

Ibrahim had brought up from the Agency a number of pictures which had belonged to Gordon's mother, and the Princess, using her lorgnette, proceeded to examine them.

"What's this? 'Charles George Gordon.' I know! The White Pasha. Put him over the General's desk. 'Ecce Homo.' Humph! A man couldn't wish to have a thing like this in his office, and a natural woman can't want it over her bed. Mosie! Take 'Ecce Homo' to a nice dark corner of the servant's hall."

At that moment Fatimah came from the kitchen, which had been shut up since the day after Helena's departure for the Soudan, to say that half the cooking tins had disappeared.

"Just what I expected! Stolen by those rascally Egyptian cooks, no doubt. Rascally Egyptians! That's what I call them. Excuse the word, my dear. I speak my mind. They'd steal the kohl from your eyes—if you had any. And these are the people who are to govern the country! But I say nothing—not I indeed! The virtue of a woman is in holding her tongue— Fatimah, now that you are here, you might make yourself useful. Dust that big picture of the naked babies. What's it called? 'Suffer Little Children.' Goodness! He looks as if he were giving away clothes. Helena, my moon, my beauty, you really must tell me where to put this one."

"But hadn't you better ask Gordon himself, Princess?

It's to be his house, you know," repeated Helena, whereupon the Princess, wheeling round on her, said:

" Gracious me, what's come over you, girl? Here you are to be mistress of the whole place within a month, I suppose, and yet——"

" Hush, Princess."

There were footsteps in the hall, and at the next moment, Gordon, in his frock-coat uniform, looking flushed and excited, and accompanied by Hafiz, whose chubby face was wreathed in smiles, had entered the room.

After he had shaken hands with the Princess, the servants rushed upon him, Mosie, who had come behind, kissing his sword, Ibrahim his hand, and Fatimah struggling with an impulse to throw her arms about his neck.

" So you've come at last, have you?" said the Princess. " Time enough, too, for here's Helena of no use to anybody. Your father has gone back to England, hasn't he? He might have come up to see me, I think. He wrote a little letter to say good-bye, though. It was just like him. I could hear him speaking. 'My goodness,' I said, 'that's Nuneham!' Well, we shall never see his equal. No, never! He might have left Egypt with twenty millions in his pocket and he has gone with nothing but his wages. I suppose they're slandering him all the same. Ingrates! But no matter! The dogs bark, but the camel goes along. And now that I've time, let me take a look at you. What a colour! But what are you trembling about? Goodness me, has *everybody* got the jumps?"

Helena was the only one in the room who had not come forward to greet Gordon, and seeing his sidelong look in her direction, the Princess began to lay plans for leaving them together.

" Ibrahim," she cried, " hang up these naked babies in the bath-room—the only place for them, it seems to me. Fatimah, go back and look if the cooking tins are not in the kitchen cupboard."

" They're not—I've looked already," said Fatimah.

" Then go and look again. Mosie, you want to inspect my horses—I can see you do."

" No, lady I *have* i'spected them."

"Then i'spect them a second time. Off you go!—where's my lorgnette? Oh, dear me. I fancy I must have left it in the boudoir."

"Let me go for it, Princess," said Helena.

"Certainly not! Why should you? Do you think I'm a cripple that I can't go myself? Hafiz Effendi, where are your manners that you don't open this door for me? That's better. Now the inner one."

At the next moment Gordon and Helena were left together. Helena was still standing by the window looking down at the city which seemed to lie dazed under the midday sun. Gordon stepped up and stood by her side. It was hard to realise that they were there again. But in spite of their happiness there was a little cloud over both. They knew what caused it.

While they stood together in silence they could hear the low reverberation of the voices of the people who were praying within the mosque.

"They are chanting the first Surah," said Gordon.

"Yes, the first Surah," said Helena.

Their hands found each other as they stood side by side.

"I saw Ishmael last night. He came to my quarters," said Gordon in a low tone.

"Well?" asked Helena, faintly.

"It was most extraordinary. He came to tell me that —to compel me to——"

"Hush!"

There was a soft footstep behind them. It was the step of some one walking in Oriental slippers. Without turning round they knew who it was.

It was Ishmael. Notwithstanding his dusky complexion, his face was very pale—almost as white as his turban. His eyes looked weary, their light was almost extinct. Perhaps his sermon had exhausted him. It was almost as if there was no life left in him except the life of the soul. But he smiled—it was the smile of a spectre—as he stepped forward and held out his hand.

Gordon's heart shuddered for pity. "Are you well?" he asked.

" Oh, yes."

" But you look tired."

" It's nothing," Ishmael said, and then, with a touching simplicity, he added, " I have been troubled in my heart, but now I am at peace and all is well."

They sat, Ishmael on the sofa, Helena on a chair at his right, Gordon on a chair at his left, the window open before them, the city slumbering below.

Ishmael's face, though full of lines of pain, continued to smile, and his voice, though hoarse and faint, was cheerful. He had come to tell them that he was going away.

" Going away? " said Gordon.

" Yes, my work here is done, and when a man's work is done he stands outside of life. So I am going back."

" Back? You mean back to Khartoum? " asked Helena timidly.

" Perhaps there, too. But back to the desert. I am a son of the desert. Therefore, what other place can be so good for me? "

" Are you going alone? "

" Yes, or rather no! When a man has lived, has laboured, he has always one thing—memory. And he who has memory can never be quite alone."

" Still you will be very——"

Ishmael turned to her with an almost imperceptible smile.

" Perhaps, yes, at first, a little lonely, and all the more so for the sweet glimpse I have had of human company."

" But this is not what you intended to—what you hoped to——"

" No! It's true I nourished other dreams for a while— dreams of living a human life after my work was done. It would have been very sweet, very beautiful. And now to go away, to give it up, never more to have part and lot in— never again to see those who— Yes, it's hard, a little hard."

Helena turned her head aside and looked out at the window.

" But that is all over now," said Ishmael. " Love is

the crown of life, but it is not for all of us. Your great Master knew that as he knew everything. Some men have to be eunuchs for the Kingdom of Heaven's sake. How true! How right!"

His pallid face struggled to smile as he said this.

"And then, what does our Prophet say?—on him be prayer and peace! 'The man who loves and never attains to the joy of his love, but renounces it for another who has more right to it, is as one who dies a martyr.'"

Still looking out at the window, Helena tried to say she would always remember him, and hoped he would be very happy.

"Thank you! That also will be a sweet memory," he said. "But happy moments are rare in the lives of those who are called to a work for humanity."

Then, coming gently to closer quarters, he told them he was there to say good-bye to them. "I had intended to write to you," he said, turning again to Helena, "but it is better so."

Then, facing toward Gordon, he said:

"I must confess that I have not always loved you. But I have been in the wrong and I ask your pardon. It is God who governs the heart. And what does your divine Master say about that, too? 'Whom God hath joined together let no man put asunder.' That is the true word about love and marriage—the first, and the last, and the only one."

Then he rose and both Helena and Gordon rose with him. One moment he stood between them without speaking, and then, stooping over Helena's hand and kissing it, he said, in a scarcely audible whisper:

"I divorce thee! I divorce thee! I divorce thee!"

It was the Mohammedan form of divorce and all that was necessary to set Helena free. When he raised his head his face was still smiling—a pitiful, heart-breaking smile.

Then, still holding Helena's hand, he reached out for Gordon's also, and said:

"I give her back to thee, my brother. And do not think I give what I would not keep. Perhaps—who knows?—perhaps I loved her, too."

Helena was deeply affected. Gordon found it impossible to look into Ishmael's face. They felt his wearied eyes resting upon them; they felt their hands being brought together; they felt Ishmael's hand resting for a moment on their hands; and then they heard him say:

"Maa-es-salamah! Be happy! Keep together as long as you can. And never forget we shall meet again some day."

Then in a voice so low that they could scarcely hear it, he said:

"Peace be with you both! Peace!" and passed out of the room.

They stood where he had left them in the middle of the room, with faces to the ground and their hands quivering in each other's clasp, until the sound of his footsteps had died away. Then Gordon said:

"Shall we go into the garden, Helena?"

"Yes," she replied in a whisper.

They went out hand in hand and walked to the arbour on the edge of the ramparts. There, on that loved spot, the past rolled back on them like billows of the soul. The bushes seemed to have grown, the bougainvillæa was more purple than before, the air was full of the scent of blossom, and everything was turning to love and to song.

They did not speak, but they put their arms about each other, and looked down on the wide panorama below—the city, the Nile, the desert, the pyramids, and that old, old Sphinx whose scarred face had witnessed so many incidents in the story of humanity, and was now witnessing the last incident of one story more.

How long they stood there in their great happiness they never knew, but they were called back to themselves by a shrill, clear voice that came from a minaret behind them:

"God is Most Great! God is Most Great!"

Then, turning in the direction of the voice, they saw a white figure on a white camel ascending the yellow road that leads up to the fort on the top of the Mokattam hills and onward to the desert.

"Look," said Gordon. "Is it——?"

Without speaking, Helena bent her head in assent.

With hands still clasped and quivering, they watched the white figure as it passed away. It stopped at the crest of the hill, and looked back for a moment; then turned again and went on. At the next moment it was gone.

And then once more came the voice from the minaret, like the voice of an angel winging its way through the air:

AL-LA-HU AK-BAR.   AL-LA - - HU AK-BAR.

God is Most Great!   God is Most Great!

EPILOGUE

LORD NUNEHAM lived ten years longer, but never, after the first profound sensation caused by his retirement, was he heard of again. The House of Lords did not see him, he was never found on any public platform, and no publisher could prevail upon him to write the story of his life.

He bought a majestic but rather melancholy place in Berkshire, one of the great historic seats of an extinguished noble family, and there, under the high elms and amid the green and cloudy landscape of his own country, he lived out his last years in unbroken obscurity.

It has been well said that deep tragedy is the school of great men, but there was one ray of sunshine to brighten Lord Nuneham's solitude. On a table, by his bedside, in a room darkened by rustling leaves, stood two photographs in silver frames. They were of two boys, one dark like his mother, the other fair like his father, both bright and strong and clear-eyed. Down to the end the old man never went to bed without taking up these pictures and looking at them, and as often as he did so a faint smile would pass over his seamed and weary face.

After a while the world forgot that he was alive, and when he died the public seemed to be taken by surprise. "I thought he died ten years ago," said somebody.

Gordon held his post as General in command of the British Army in Egypt for four successive terms, his appointment being renewed first by the wish of the War Office and afterward at the request of the Egyptian Government. The civil occupation having become less active since his father's time (the new Consul-General being a pale shadow of his predecessor), the military occupation became more important, and except for his subjection to headquarters,

607

Gordon appeared to stand in the position of a military auto-crat. But in the difficult and delicate task of maintaining order in a foreign country without exasperating the feelings of the native people, he showed great tact and sym-pathy. While allowing the utmost liberty to thought, whether political or religious, he never for a moment per-mitted it to be believed that the Government could be de-fied with impunity in matters affecting peace, order, life, and property.

For this the best elements honoured him, and when the poor and illiterate, who were sometimes the victims of Ex-tremists, whose only aim was to throw flaming torches into pits of inflammable gas, saw that he was just as ready to put down lawlessness among Europeans as among Egyp-tians, they loved as well as trusted him. His life in Egypt lessened the gulf which Easterners always find between Christians and Christianity, and whenever he had to re-turn to England, the streets of Cairo would be red with the tarbooshes of the people who ran to the railway-station to see him off. " Maa-es-salamah, brother!" they would say, with the simplicity of children, and then, " Don't forget we will be waiting for you to come back."

Gordon's love for the Egyptians never failed him, and he was entirely happy in his home, where Helena developed the summer bloom of beautiful womanhood, where the light, merry sound of the voices of her two young boys was al-ways ringing like music through the house.

It must be confessed that for a while Egypt had a hard and almost tragic time. After the Consul-General's depart-ure she went through a period of storm and stress. There were both errors and crimes. These were the inevitable re-sults of progressive stages of self-rule; and even anarchy, the travail of a nation's birth, was not altogether unknown. During the earlier years there were some to regret the ab-sence of the mailed fist of Lord Nuneham and to question the benefit of quasi-Western institutions in an Eastern country. But the atmosphere cleared at last, the sinister anticipations were falsified, a bold and magnanimous policy brought peace, and the destinies of Egypt were firmly united to those of the country that had given her a new lease of life and liberty.

England never regretted what she had done on that day when, true to her high traditions, she decided that a great nation had no longer any right to govern with absolute and undivided authority, another race living under another sky. And her reward seems likely to come in a way that might have been least expected. As "God chooseth His fleshly instruments and with imperfect hearts doeth His perfect work," He seems to have put it into the hearts of the Arab people to sink their tribal differences and to act on the prompting of the gigantic myth with which the Grand Cadi deceived the Consul-General.

Indeed, those who gaze into the future as into a crystal say that the time is near when the long drama of dissension that has been played between Arabs and Turks will end in the establishment of a vast Arabic Empire, extending from the Tigris and the Euphrates Valley to the Mediterranean, and from the Indian Ocean to Jerusalem, with Cairo as its Capital, the Khedive as its Caliph, and England as its lord and protector. No one can foreshadow the future, but this was Napoleon's greatest dream, and the nation that can realise it will hold the peace of the world in the palm of its almighty hand.

And Ishmael?

After he left Cairo he was never seen again by anyone who could positively identify him. Some say he returned to the home of his childhood on the Libyan Desert and that he died there; others that he went back to Khartoum and thence to the heart of the Sahara, and that he is still alive. However this may be, it is certain that his disappearance has had the effect of death, that it has deepened the impression of his life, and that a huge shadow of him remains on those among whom he lived and laboured.

It was said on the day of his departure that Black Zogal, who followed him to the last with the fidelity of a human dog, kept close at his heels until he came to the top of the Mokattam hills, where the Master sent him back after strictly charging him to tell no one which way he was going. Since then, however, Zogal has given it out (with every appearance of believing his own story) that he saw Ishmael ascend to heaven from the Gebel Mokattam in a blinding whirlwind of celestial light, a flight of angels carrying him away.

A Saint's House has been built for Black Zogal on the spot on which he says he saw the ascent; the half-crazy Soudanese inhabits it, and its outer walls are almost covered with the small flags which devotees have brought and fixed to them in their childlike effort to show reverence.

Nothing could exceed the boundless affection which is still felt for Ishmael by those who came into immediate contact with him. He seems to have inspired them with a love which survives absence and could even conquer death. Everybody who ever spoke to him has a story to tell of his wisdom, his power, and his tenderness. The number of his "miracles" has increased tenfold, and though not described as sinless, he is always talked of as if he were divine.

His Mouled (his birthday, a conjectural date) is celebrated by ceremonies which almost outrival the "Nights of the Prophet." About the Saint's House on the Mokattam hills a huge encampment of tents is made, and there, under the blaze of thousands of dazzling lights, the dervishes hold their Zikrs amid scenes of frantic excitement due to exhibitions of hypnotic suggestion which ever include "the effect of tongues," while more serious-minded Sheikhs repeat a long record of Ishmael's genealogy. This is a very circumstantial story with a vague resemblance to something which Christians speak of with bated breath—how, when his mother, who was a virgin, was bearing him, an angel appeared to her in a dream and said, "You carry the Lord of Man," and how, when the child was delivered, three great Sheikhs came from Mecca to pay reverence to him, having seen a star in the sky which told them where he was to be born.

In the course of years a great body of Ishmael's "Sayings" have been gathered up. Some of them are authentic, but most of them are out of the wisdom of the ages, and not a few are directly borrowed from the Christian gospels, which the Moslems, as a whole, do not know. Whatever their sources, they are deeply treasured. Women chant them to the children at their knees, and men lisp them with their last breath and then die with brave faces.

Besides the impression he has produced upon the people, which is strong and likely to be enduring, Ishmael seems to have an almost unaccountable fascination for Arabic scholars and theologians. A number of the professors at El Azhar are already deep in metaphysical disputations about the inner significance of the words attributed to him, and it is whispered that the venerable Chancellor (now nearly a hundred years of age) is compiling a book, half biography and half commentary, that is full of mystical meanings.

More extraordinary still, it seems probable that a large and gorgeous mosque will be built in Ishmael's honour, and that he who loved best to worship in that temple of the open desert whereof the dome is the sky, he who cared so little about dogmatic theology that he never even wrote a line, may, by the wild irony of fate, become the founder of a sect in Islam which will teach everything he fought against and practise everything he condemned.

Chief among the subjects of disputation is Ishmael's expectation of a Kingdom of Heaven upon earth, though the Ulema, less concerned with the spirit than with the letter of the Prophet's hope, are divided as to the source of it. Some say it is plainly indicated in the Koran and the traditions; others, more widely read, say it is borrowed from the Hebrew Bible, while a few refer it to a vague and misty antiquity.

Hardly less interesting to the theologians is the question of Ishmael's identity. Nearly all agree that there was an element of the supernatural about him, so hard is it to attribute to men of ordinary human passions the great movements that affect the world. But while there are those who believe him to have been the Mahdi, sent expressly to earth to destroy Anti-Christ, that is to say, the Consul-General, an influential group hold to the opinion that he was, and is, Seyidna Isa—Our Lord Jesus.

About this latter view there gathers a strange and not unimpressive theory—that Jesus (who, according to the Islamic faith, did not die on the cross) reappears at intervals among different races—now among the Jews, now among the Indians, now among the Arabs—and that he will continue to make these manifestations until the world is ready for the greatest happiness obtainable by man—the establishment of the Kingdom of God.

But not all the disputations of the wise heads of El Azhar can rob the humble of the object of their veneration. Ishmael came from the people, and with the people he will always remain. His blameless life, his touching history, his deep humanity, his simple teaching and, above all, his lofty hopes have made him Sultan of a vast empire of souls —the empire of the poor, the oppressed, the downtrodden, and the broken-hearted. From the central heart of the East his spirit came as a ray of sunlight, inspiring men in the dark places to live nobly, to die bravely, and to keep up their courage to the last.

And what of Ishmael's influence in the West?

Nothing! European historians have written since his time without saying a word about him. One of them who devotes long chapters to accounts of the bombardment of Alexandria, the battle of Tel-el-Kebir, the craven flight of Arabi and his theatrical scene with the Khedive in Abdeen Square, and yet other chapters to the building of the Assouan Dam and the construction of the Cape to Cairo railway, dismisses Ishmael's pilgrimage from Khartoum in five lines of a section dealing with "Mahdism and Sedition in the Soudan."

And indeed, so hard do we find it, in spite of our civilisation and Christianity, to believe that the things of the spirit may be more helpful in sustaining our steps and shaping our destinies than any forces we can weigh, measure, and calculate, that it is difficult to think of any real welcome in the cities of the West for one whose only teaching was that great wealth is an inheritance taken by force from the Almighty, that property beyond the proper needs of civil-

ised human life is pillage; and that God so loves the world that He will come in person to govern it and to save mankind from its suffering and the consequences of its sins.

Certainly the mere thought of anyone holding these opinions, least of all an Arab, the son of a boat-builder, born on the Libyan Desert, brought up in the depths of the Soudan, educated in the stagnant schools of El Azhar, wearing sandals and a turban and probably eating with his fingers— the mere thought of such a one, in the present year of grace, forcing his way into the Cathedrals and Parliament Houses of Westminster, Washington, Rome, Berlin, and Paris, where Archbishops officiate in embroidered copes and Ministers prepare budgets toward the re-paganization of the world, would at least provoke a smile.

Nevertheless, there are some who think that the world is not ruled by its great men, but by its great ideas, that these ideas are few and very old; that when as humanity needs to renew itself it has only to go back to them, and that it is not so often in the " sick hurry " of civilised communities as out of the calm solitude of the desert that we hear the sublime but simple notes of the World's One Voice.

(1)

THE END

40